Reprisal

TOM REILLY

ISBN
978-1-957895-27-7 (Hardcover)
978-1-957895-26-0 (Paperback)
978-1-957895-25-3 (eBook)

*I dedicate this novel to my beautiful Chinese wife, Anne,
who inspired me to continue writing and spent many
late nights as both my critic and editor.*

TABLE OF CONTENTS

PREFACE

Anbar leapt from the Mercedes as it came to a screaming halt in a cloud of dust.

"Park the car out of sight until I return."

Faraj had already spotted the Mercedes. The Leyland 12-cylinder 300 diesel, chug… chug… chugging, ready to cast off, black smoke from the twins exhausts contaminating the air with diesel fumes.

Dahara was in the wheelhouse, his son on deck.

"Anbar, untie the mooring lines from the Bolland then jump aboard." Bakir called, the Armelin straining on its moorings

Anbar hastily jumped the widening gap landing heavily on the deck.

"Not as fit as I used to be." He winced making Bakir laugh.

"My father requests you join him in the wheelhouse."

"And you Bakir?"

"I'll stay on deck and drop the Seiner nets whilst keeping a sharp eye for the Customs and Border Patrol."

TROUBLED WATERS

Los Angeles
Sunday, June 2014

"Wake up sleepy head." Julie gave Bill an overzealous dig to his ribs and after last night's escapade who could blame her. As usual Bill, had made an 'horses ass' of himself with that pilot buddy of his, Chuck Stevens, at the Flying Club in downtown LA, a hangout for 'down and out' aviators from past and present.

Julie didn't hang around and hit the floor hurriedly slipping into her Levi's and white tank top, breakfast high on the agenda. After too many shooters, her lips parched, her dehydrated brain was screaming for sustenance. Bill is a morning man and Julie was taking no chances, sex with this 'booze head loser', on the back burner.

"For Christ sakes Julie go easy." Came Bill's disgruntled cry. "Why so early? Come back to bed. *Awe come on honey*, I don't fly out until tomorrow evening, and it's way too early to parachute the cot."

"Have you looked at the time, you big oaf?" Julie shot back.

Bill gave a 'loser sigh' and inhaled.

"Make my day."

"It's twelve thirty in case you don't know and I'm sure any minute now you'll be getting a call from that 'no hoper' buddy of yours and poor Marge, I don't know how she puts up with that alcoholic womanizer."

"Christ Julie, I don't need this shit on my watch. *Haven't you anything good to say about anyone?*"

Julie just ignored Bill, they had been through this conversation before and she angrily slammed the nonstick on the burner and torched the gas, the noise making Bill cringe and hold his 'eggshell' head. He gave a grunt and rolled over forcing his head below the pillow.

Julie cracked the eggs in silence and placed the bacon rashers into the hot pan, the sizzle filling the air with its tantalizing aroma. The coffee peculator now on the stove, the 'fait ac-com-plie' for the 'all American' breakfast.

The phone rang and Bill made a grab to kill the ear-piercing decibels.

"Don't answer that phone Bill." Julie grabbed the receiver out of his hand and just in time. "I don't want that free loader interrupting our breakfast."

"Julie, for Christ sakes get off my street." Bill snatched the phone back.

"*Ouch!* You clumsy bastard, you almost broke my wrist."

"Go take a hike… eh… err Chuck, no I wasn't talking to you, just a little domestic… Yeah about last night, I don't need you to remind me, I got enough of that shit this morning from Julie… See you when…? Around two at Rod's Bar on the Santa Monica… Yeah, should be okay by then, I'm just about to have breakfast… Remember we have that freighter to Tokyo tomorrow night and I want to pass the breath test… Speak for yourself… Two then."

* * *

Julie Rodgers at 25 was two years younger than Bill, a blonde with all the right credentials. Pretty blue olive shaped eyes, lips to die for, and with her golden shoulder length locks and that smooth unblemished lightly tanned complexion, she could easily have been a 'stand in' for the late Grace Kelly. Air hostesses are selected on brains and looks and July ticked all the boxes having reached Chief Purser with Delta Airways after only four years of service. At five nine she was a dish and when down to the bikini line on the beach, it was 'eat your eyes out guys' But for Bill once the forbidden fruit was bruised, like most guys, they don't appreciate what they really have until it's too late...

* * *

Bill gave an overzealous sigh spontaneously moving his head from side to side cringing at the pain from his self-induced hung-over brain. But Julie was having none of it. If he was looking for sympathy, he was barking up the wrong tree and she ignored the 'drama queen' emptying the sizzling contents of the pan onto the plates before placing them on the breakfast bar accompanied with freshly brewed coffee and squeezed juice.

"You breakfast is ready, I'm going to start without you." Julie was in good form.

"*Yeah…Yeah…* I'm coming." Bill barked accepting he had lost the 'make up' sex initiative.

"*Fucking woman,* oh well I guess breakfast is calling." He muttered below his breath as he kicked off the sheets and threw his feet to the polished timber then stretching his naked lean frame before walking to the open balcony doors.

Julie turned and just shook her head before burying her nose into the 'LA Times'.

"*For Christ sakes go and put something on,* I won't be able to face the neighbors after seeing 'God's answer to woman' standing naked on the balcony flashing the loose change between his legs."

"You didn't always say that."

"Well I've got news for you, I'm saying it now, *and this time I mean it!* Now let me get my fucking breakfast in peace, *that is,* if it's not too much to ask and for the last time put some fucking cloths on or I'll eat my breakfast on the veranda."

"Julie, chill out for Christ sakes, I said I was sorry about last night, I mean what more do you want?"

"*To put your fucking clothes on,* and don't go on, you sound like a long-playing record."

Bill gave a disgruntled sigh and slipped into his jocks and jeans. The Californian climate as normal was a comfortable eighty degrees and the pleasant breeze blowing through the open balcony doors was the 'piece de resistance.'

"Hmmm, this is good." Bill spluttered, his mouth half full, desperately trying to cut to the chase.

Julie just gave a disgusted look, she wasn't buying into it.

"I'm going down for a swim; would it be too much to ask to put the dishes in the washer?"

"Honey listen…"

"*Bill, go fuck yourself…*"

* * *

"Christ Chuck, why did you hang up, I wanted to speak to Julie!"

"So why the big drama, you can call her on your cell, besides we're gonna meet them for lunch around two at Rod's."

"You *do* know Julie and I have an early flight tomorrow?"

"Yeah, you've told me, so what's the big deal?"

"It's just… It's just I thought we could have a quiet day without booze and over indulgence, especially after last night."

"Listen, that blonde was coming on to me… I mean… If that's what this is all about."

"I'm going for a shower." Marge slipped her feet to the floor, her tanned naked silhouette briefly flashing in the morning light from the half open drapes. Chuck was spoiling for a confrontation, it was sensitive territory and Marge wasn't taking the bait.

* * *

Marge Williams and Julie Rodgers were best friends from college years and part of the 'Rat Pack', so to speak, a nick name the Pilots gave to the airhostesses on the LA to London haul. Like Julie she was pretty, slim, tantalizing brown eyes, smooth complexion, narrow face line and full lips and with her five eight-hour glass figure and that shoulder length brown hair she could walk the walk anytime and one could only imagine the male rivalry when these two beauties entered the room.

After flatting together in the big apple and numerous 'go nowhere' jobs the girls decided to jump ship and head to California for fame and fortune and what better place than the 'City of Angles' and when Delta Airlines had openings for stewardesses it was an opportunity too good to miss.

* * *

Standing in the invigorating hot shower, Marge was in another world as the pristine water, like a mini waterfall flushed through her hair and for a fleeting moment nothing seemed important, her memory reflecting as if it was only yesterday…

* * *

"And your name is?" The tall handsome Captain asked, a smile on his face at the young flight attendant's embarrassment.

"Eh, err… Marge… Marge Williams senior flight attendant in business and economy."

"Marge, can you call the chief purser and the cabin crew to the first-class galley for a brief introduction before the flight?"

"Certainly Captain." Marge returned the smile, *this guy is a dish.* "I'll be back in few minutes as the cabin crew are still seating the passengers."

"Julie." Marge tapped her on the shoulder."

"Mr. Stevens this is your seat…1B. My name is Julie Rodgers and I'll be looking after you and the other passengers in first class today. Please make yourself comfortable. We will be serving refreshments in a few minutes." She turned. "Yes, what is it Marge?"

"It appears we have a new Captain and he wants to speak to the cabin crew before takeoff."

Julie gave that look. She was busy and now all she needed is a new Captain throwing his weight around.

"Has it gotta be now?"

"Hey, don't shoot the messenger!"

"I'm sorry Marge, it's just that…."

"Yeah, I know, wrong timing." Marge shrugged.

Tell him that I'll be there in a few minutes after all the seats are occupied."

Marge nodded then disappeared through the galley curtain.

* * *

"Captain, I'm Julie Williams the chief purser."

"Julie." Bill acknowledged. "I'll be brief now that everyone is here as I know that you are all busy. I'm Bill Collins your replacement Captain on the London haul and my First Officer, Chuck Stevens…

* * *

"Marge… Marge… what the hell's keeping you? You know we're meeting Bill and Julie at Rods, don't you?"

"Eh… Err yeah, I hear you." Marge closed the faucet, her memories like the shower water, in an instant disappearing down the drain.

"I suppose." Marge sighed as she flicked her straggled brown hair over her shoulders. She could easily have indulged longer but Chuck was on 'the morning after role' and as usual, a bear with a sore head.

Marge slipped into her bathrobe and began toweling her hair before sitting in front of the vanity mirror. As she vigorously stroked the wide comb for a few moments she widened her eyes and went closer to study the face.

"The lines." She sighed as she gently stretched the skin below her eyes. "Hell, what will I look like when I'm thirty?"

The bathroom door suddenly opened and Chuck streaked past into the shower box.

"Christ Marge, stop sitting there admiring yourself, it's after one."

Marge lifted the hairdryer, how things have changed after only two years. Chuck had asked her to marry him at one point and it was the best thing she ever did when she said no and she dejectedly shook her head at the thought at what might have been.

"I'm gonna give Julie a ring." Marge rose to leave, it was an opportunity to speak to her friend without 'big ears' listening.

She opened the balcony doors and lay on the sun lounger. It was a beautiful day, clear blue skies with a gentle sea breeze, the kinda day you're glad to be alive, if only life could be never ending, like the sunset when the rain sets in.

"*Marge,* I thought you would ring… I'm by the pool relaxing and getting some sun. Yeah, I've made up my mind and there's no turning back. I've found another apartment with two bedrooms and near the beach too, Remember the offer is there should you change your mind… Well don't take too long… Today! I'm going to drop the bombshell at the opportune time at Rod's once I down a couple of shooters to give me Dutch courage. Don't laugh, it's serious… I best get going or Bill will be doing his proverbial… Me too… Ciao."

* * *

Bill was already shaved standing at the vanity mirror, a bath towel wrapped tightly around his waist.

"You took your time, I was almost phoning you, you haven't even showered yet." He complained as Julie brushed past him.

"At least you've shaved that's something." Julie dropped her bikini to her ankles and opened the shower door to turn the faucet, the hot spray steaming up the mirror. She stepped inside and wiped the shower glass in a circular motion with her hand, studying Bill in silence as he finally rinsed his face.

* * *

This tall lean pilot at six one was handsome to say the least. His taught muscled tanned body completely void of fat. At twenty-seven and with those looks, the chiseled jaw line, narrow nose, dimpled chin blue eyes and brown unruly hair and tanned complexion there was no shortage of female cabin crew to fill his cot. Maybe that's why he took Julie for granted and the spark in their relationship now a damp squib. She had her doubts for the last six months, the late nights, all sorts of dubious excuses and the 'I'm too tired I have a flight in the morning'. She had thought when Bill decided to resign from Delta and fly freight with Global things might change being away from commercial airways where the forbidden fruit is always available especially for pilot officers and to marry a Captain, the icing on the cake. When they first met on the London haul and Bill and Chuck asked she and Marge to dinner I was the start of a whirlwind romance and it was only a matter of time before the inevitable and they decided to rent an apartment and move in together. Their joint income in the upper quartile, life was good and renting an apartment in Santa Monica on Ocean Avenue overlooking the beach, just doesn't get any better. As for Marge, her best friend, Chuck was a different kettle of fish, a wild card, a loose cannon and a booze head womanizer. He and Bill were aviators in Desert Storm flying McDonnell Douglas F15 Eagles and became best buddies and after three tours of duty each with commendations they decided not to reenlist and turn their flying skills to commercial jets and hence Global Airways and the rest is history. Chuck was slightly shorter than Bill at five ten with a roundish fresh face, deep blue eyes and swept back blonde hair. His overindulgences gave him a stockier look at ten to fifteen pounds overweight but he was handsome in his own way. What Marge saw in him was her best kept secret but the cracks were now showing and like Julie maybe it was time…!

* * *

The knock on the shower door startled her and she spluttered as the water ran into her mouth.

"Ah… Eh… Ugg." Julie coughed.

"Come on, wake up, for a moment I thought you were asleep in there, we're running late." Bill disappeared into the bedroom.

Julie sighed as she opened the shower door. *So, what's new, another one of these boozy so-called lunches and back to 'Dessert Storm' and all that boring shit she had heard before. When are these guys gonna grow up?* She sighed again… *With Bill and his Chevy Camaro and Chuck's Pontiac Firebird…* She shook her head… *Pilots… Big kids, paid too much and living on the edge'.*

"Julie…" Bill called again emptying his lungs.

"I hear you, keep your fucking shirt on." She stepped out of the shower and began to vigorously towel herself.

Bill was already in jeans white 'T' shirt and deck shoes, patiently waiting in the lounge, his body language adding fuel to the fire and Julie rudely brushed past him, still in her bathrobe on her way to the bedroom.

It was a day for sand and sun and Julie slipped into her white bikini and long colorful loose ankle length low cut beach dress. Julie would look good in anything and today was no exception. She hurriedly grabbed her beach bag and folded two large bath towels, sun tan lotion 'G' string and bra to change. One more glance in the mirror and the comb through her hair, she grabbed the large white sun hat and slipped into her sandals.

"And not before time!" Bill growled as he grabbed the keys for the Camaro. Then he stopped in his tracks having weighed up Julie's beach attire. *"Are you going dressed like that?"*

"So, what's special about Rod's? A bum's bar for losers and sniffers. The drinks are over the top and the food you can get at an 'all you can eat' for half the price of a burger, besides Marge and I want to soak up some sun before cold and smoggy London."

Bill just shrugged, there was no point in blowing it all out of proportion, besides Julie was looking beautiful as always, especially when she's mad and any guy would be proud to have her hang on is arm.

The conversation in the elevator was nonexistent and maybe just as well and when the doors finally opened to the underground car park it was a welcome relief.

The red Camaro was parked next to Julie's yellow VW Bug and Bill wasted no time slipping into the bucket seat and gunning the big four fifty. It was now after two and his patience was shot.

He pressed the pedal and the 55R18 inch wide rims screeched with the smell of burning rubber as the tread bit into the sealed concrete. The boom gate automatically opened, the muscle car swinging a left onto Ocean Avenue and a fifteen-minute drive to Rod's Bar on the beach front.

* * *

Rod's was the 'Beach Bar of Beach Bars' with a location on Ocean Drive to die for. What do they say about location...? *You got that right...!*

The trendy sky-blue glass topped bamboo bar with the hidden LED lighting was complimented by the dozen matching bar stools. It's thatched counterfeit roof stretching out to the open palm lined sidewalk giving the patrons the Waikiki ambience. Sky blue was the theme and the cushioned rattan chairs and glass topped bamboo tables scattered throughout was the 'Mona Lisa' with the smile. The six wooden ceiling fans circulating the spent air could have been a scene from 'Casa Blanca', all that was missing was 'Humphrey' and 'play it again Sam'.

Surfboards and beach bars go together like 'peas in a pod', one compliments the other and these colorful elongated finned platforms from the large old wooden Cruiser boards, to the Malibu mini fiber glass bad boys, with famous surfer autographs, bedecked the walls, the largest of the wave defeaters was spotlighted behind the bar hanging above the huge assortment of colorful bottled spirits. Pictures of giant waves and pipelines crammed a small wall next to the Rest Rooms. Maybe there was a message there... Who knows...?

As for Dan, the barman...? He was part of the furniture having spent over a decade mixing cocktails and performing his shaker juggling acts, but only when he had a full house... *Tom Cruise didn't have patch on this guy!* In his late thirties, the unruly head of unkempt blonde hair, the Hawaiian floral shirt, the board shorts, the stained white Converse decks, was the beach bar uniform. At five ten he was in good shape, tanned complexion, chiseled jaw line, blue eyes and white even teeth but the slight eye bags and 'crow's feet' as the result of too much sun didn't do him any favors, but then again, he kept himself to himself.... Maybe he is in the closet... *Who knows...?* But everyone else's business was his and a good barman is a wealth of information and that's what makes Dan's cocktails special...

* * *

"One Tequila sunrise and a double Vodka on the rocks."

"Coming up Chuck."

"So, what's with the beach bag?"

"Julie and I are gonna chill out while you guys do your 'guy thing'."

"That's as and when they get here." Chuck glanced at his watch and shook his head.

"So, what were you and Julie having a cozy chat about?"

"Nothing that concerns you." Marge shot back, agitation in her voice.

The barman's interjection was timely. "Chuck, when are you flying out again?" Dan asked whilst polishing the glasses.

"Ten thirty tomorrow evening, a freighter to Tokyo."

"You guys, I envy your life style."

"Don't kid yourself Dan, it's not all it's made out to be."

"I'll take my chances..."

"Dan... Coming sir...."

* * *

"There's Chuck's white Firebird parked directly opposite Rod's."

"How do you know?" Julie had that sarcastic tone in her as if she was spoiling for fight.

"The twin dark blue stripes down the hood, now are you happy?"

"Whatever turns you on."

"Julie, for Christ sakes, what's gotten into you today? "Come on, lighten up."

Bill cut the motor and turned to speak to Julie, but the bird had flown already halfway across the road briskly stepping it out toward the famous beach bar.

"Julie honey, you're looking as lovely as ever. Now where's that handsome buddy of mine? Chuck gave Julie a kiss on the cheek.

"Did I hear my name in vane?"

"Bill... I had almost given up on you two, it almost two forty-five in case you don't know."

"Better late than never as the saying goes... *Marge...*" Bill gave her a big hug and a kiss on the cheek.

"So, what'll it be partner?" Chuck asked.

"Just a Michelob and you honey?"

"The same as Julie." Came the somber reply.

Chuck looked toward Bill who just shrugged.

"Grab that stool honey next to Marge... *Dan...*"

"Yeah, coming..."

* * *

The Tequila sunrises downed it was time for the girls to get some sun and escape the boring 'combat sorties' and Julie gave Marge that special look that meant *'let's leave these two bums to enjoy their own company and get some much-needed R&R'.*

"What's the hurry ladies, you've only had one drink?" Bill gave Julie a look, he knew she was the instigator.

"Bill, it's no sweat." Chuck cut in. "Besides, there's something I want to discuss with you."

Bill turned to Julie firing a parting shot. "Don't stay too long, I thought we might hang out at the 'Rainbow Club' tonight and you girls can't go dressed like that."

"Who said we wanna go to that 'over the top' disco joint anyhow?"

"Julie, don't be so fucking difficult, it doesn't become you."

"And don't you speak to me in that tone of voice, I'm not one of your crew! Come on Marge, I'm sure we can find much better company on the beach."

Julie grabbed Marge's arm, she was always the hesitant one.

"Let's go honey, we'll grab a drink from the beach cart."

As the girls disappeared toward the beach Chuck turned to Bill the question begging.

"What is it with Julie?"

Bill shrugged, fire in his eyes.

"Fucking women... *Dan, another Michelob...*"

* * *

"This looks as good a spot as any Marge. Not too many sun worshippers and only about 50 yards from the water."

"Julie, you're not going to break the surf, are you?"

"Are you kidding, we have an early flight tomorrow and with my hair I'm taking no prisoners."

"I thought as much." Marge laughed as she spread the large colorful bath towels on the sand and began to disrobe, the bikini clad beauties drawing immediate attention from the muscle-bound gigolos.

No sooner was the tan spray absorbed when two macho guys, probably in their mid-twenties made their move. Their brightly colored Bermuda's and Hawaiian floral shirts purposely unbuttoned to sport the six packs and the bronzed sculptured pecks.

They were handsome alright and boy did they know it! Both around six plus, workout freaks, sun bleached hair and a tan that 'Amber Solare' would die for.

"Gregg, do you see what I see?"

"Steve, are you talking about these two beautiful lonely ladies in need of protection." 'Superman' flashed his bleached teeth. "Ladies, would it be asking too much for Gregg and me to join you?"

"You got that right ... err Steve." Julie was no slouch.

"Did you hear that Gregg? She knows my name already."

Marge couldn't help but laugh at the would be 'Seinfeld'.

"Don't encourage them Marge, besides guys, we are both spoken for."

"You're not very convincing, eh, err?"

"Julie, if you must know… Now if you don't mind?"

"You can at least let us buy you a drink then if the chemistry doesn't work, we'll walk the walk."

Marge turned to Julie and gave a smile that said it all and maybe it was time to search for new horizons and cut the cord from these two losers.

Steve didn't wait for an answer and waived to the 'Bar Buggy' with the brightly painted sign, "The Beach Oasis', as it was just about to pass.

"Yeah, what'll it be guys?" The young dude pulled up in front.

"Two cold Buds… And ladies?"

Julie thought for a second, still a bit unsure.

"Awe, what the hell… A 'Long Island Tea'."

Marge followed suite "Make that two…"

* * *

"Bill, let me get you another beer."

"Is this the 'lull before the storm'?" Bill had been here before. "Don't beat about the bush, Chuck. Cut the shit and get down to it."

Chuck shrugged his shoulders. "Bill, you gotta believe me this is the last time. I just need five big ones to keep the heavies off my tail."

"Hell Chuck, you're into me for ten already!"

"Bill, you know I'm good for it. We have three long hauls next week that will net me three grand a trip."

"Chuck, there's no winners at the blackjack table, I tell you man, this is the last. Who do I make this check out to…? Let me guess 'Crown Casinos'."

"Christ Bill, don't rub salt in the wounds, I get enough of that shit from Marge."

"Well, whatever partner, you come back again, I don't want to know, and you'll be dog meat after the Casino boys are finished with you. Now on a happier note, how about that beer…?"

* * *

The young dude on the 'Beach Buggy' was doing his 'Cocktail' thing vigorously mixing the lethal 'Long Island Teas' in the ice shaker

"Aruba, Jamaica ooo I want to take ya, to Bermuda, Bahama come on pretty mama…"

Steve had to laugh, I mean who wouldn't. "I hope this kid's cocktails are better than his singing, huh?"

The girls burst into laughter at Steve's comment, the 'beach boys' aren't so bad after all.

"Ladies… Sorry about the plastic glasses but that's the rules." The young barman handed the girls their drinks. "And two Bud's for your boyfriends."

"Boyfriends! That was quick Gregg and we've just met." Steve laughed.

"Don't run away with yourself guys, Marge and I have been around too long to fall for that line."

"That'll be forty straight."

"Here's fifty kid, keep the change."

"And *thaaank* you sir. I'll be coming back this way in around twenty minutes should you want a refill?" The baby-face freshman flashed his teeth, the thought of another ten spot was tempting fate.

"What's the verdict ladies can we join you." Steve asked.

"Oh, I think we can spare a couple of towels Marge, we don't want you standing there like two coconut palms."

Marge smiled and chucked the towels. This was turning out to be an interesting afternoon, after all it had been a long time since two handsome bucks weren't taking no for an answer and it felt good, not to mention the 'Long Island Teas'.

Steve lay next to Julie and Marge suddenly had Gregg by her side. It was like the guys were staking their claims.

"So, can we introduce ourselves… I'm Steve Nelson and my buddy here is Gregg Jonson."

"Steve and Gregg, what do you guys do for a living, except for hitting on two venerable young ladies relaxing on the beach?"

"You make it sound so bad… *eh… err…?"*

"Julie… Julie Simpson…"

"And?" Gregg cut in turning to Marge.

"Marge Williams."

"You still haven't answered my question Steve." Julie wasn't about to let it go."

"It's a long story and for some other time." Steve answered awkwardly.

"Like that huh?"

"Marge, you took the words right out of my mouth."

Gregg burst into laughter. "Were not fugitives from the law or rapists if that's what you're worried about?"

"I you say so." Julie answered unconvincingly. "The jury's out on that one Marge, so I guess it's a rain check."

"And ladies, may we be so polite as to ask?"

"*Well…* If you must know Gregg, we are both airhostesses with Delta Airlines…"

* * *

"What are we hauling tomorrow night?" Chuck asked changing the subject.

"I phoned Brady this morning and it's a full load of microchips and electronic equipment for Matsushita. We depart at 2200hrs from LAX to Narita Tokyo, flying Global F10."

"Tokyo, huh? A nine-hour haul, but that time difference of plus sixteen… *Boy, does that get to me.*" Chuck was shaking his head.

Bill sighed begrudgingly. "Yeah, that means we'll clear Narita around two thirty in the afternoon. And we have a six o'clock return flight on Thursday evening, remember!"

"Not much time to hit the down- town clubs and Karaoke bars, huh?" Check laughed.

"*Maaan*, is that all you think about?"

"Say what's with you today Bill? You seem uptight. I thought after a few beers you'd be back to 'happy hour'."

Bill pondered for a moment before answering Chuck's question, he felt a bit sore about giving him a hard time, but then Chuck is Chuck. You give an inch and he takes a mile.

"If you must know it's Julie."

"*Julie…!* So, what's new? Broads are broads, you can never read em. Do you think *I* don't get shit from Marge?

"Yeah, but this time Chuck, I think it's serious."

"Like she's gonna do a runner?"

Bill gave a big a sigh and shrugged. "I guess it's the hectic life we both lead. I'm flying out one day and Julie the next. It's like, 'You don't bring me flowers anymore'."

"*Get out of it*, you sentimentalist! Julie's crazy about you."

"I wish I had your confidence." Bill made a face. "Yeah, I guess your right dude, maybe I'm reading too much between the lines."

"*That's more like it.* Another one?" Chuck motioned with his eyes at Bill's empty glass.

"I shouldn't, one more, *but that's the last!*" Bill forced a grin.

"That's more like it partner!"

As Bill took a sip from the fresh schooner, there was something still on his mind and it was time to get it off his chest.

"Chuck…"

"Yeah?" Chuck pouted his lips.

"I don't want to make a production out of this but there's something I have to ask. We've been buddies for a long time and in some tight spots, yeah?"

"So?"

"It's like this. I don't like the company you keep at the Casino. Gambling is one thing but drugs is another… Mario Brambilli, need I say more. It's no secret he's peddling ice and coke but he seems for some reason to slip below the police radar. My guess is that some dirty cop is on the payroll."

"Whoa… Whoa…" Chuck cut the slack. "I don't like the tone of this conversation and if I think what you're asking… *I'm fucking disappointed.*"

"Chuck you're a pilot and these heavies are always looking for an opportunity and with your gambling debts." The question was begging.

"Yeah, *well it's no!*"

"Okay… Okay!" Bill raised his hands in surrender. "So maybe I stepped outta line. You've given me your word and I accept it."

But in his mind Bill was not convinced, reflecting on the times when Chuck would hastily disappear to the washroom even when they were flying, to return sort of rejuvenated and hyped up, like he had taken a high dose of anabolic steroids. But for the moment he had to trust his partner and he took another sip of beer…That's for another day……

* * *

Julie glanced at her cellphone. "It's gone six Marge and we have an evening flight tomorrow and I just want to chill out and have a relaxing day before smoggy London, so I think it's about time we make tracks, besides I have a 'jack in the box' that's going to blow you away but that's for later."

Marge was about to throw the question when Steve interrupted.

"So early ladies?" Steve asked disappointed. "I thought we could have at least another one for the road."

Marge turned to Julie, she was enjoying Gregg's company.

"It's tempting but we have to call a cab."

"A cab?" Marge couldn't help herself, what was Julie talking about?

"You mean you girls came by cab?" Even Steve was taken aback.

Julie was quick on her feet. "In our line of work to be charged with a DUI we automatically lose our jobs. So better safe than sorry, *right Marge?"*

"Eh…Err… *Right!"* Marge was still trying to put the pieces together.

"Then can we give you girls a lift? It's the least we can we do… *Gregg?"*

"No sweat it's a pleasure."

"Well if you insist." Julie snuck a sly wink to Marge.

"Here, let me help you Julie." Steve offered his hand.

Within minutes the girls had packed their beach bags and were walking to the car park.

"Here we are ladies. Gregg's Heritage Softail and my Fat Boy."

"Harleys!" Both girls burst into laughter. "This is gonna be something else."

The super bikes burst into life, their unique growl from the exhausts sending shock waves across the beach.

"Where to ladies?" Steve yelled above the rasp.

"Bay View apartment's. Hang a left and it's about seven miles down Santa Monica."

"Nice." Steve commented as the girls took the pillion seats.

"Marge, just put your arm around my waist as tight as you can." Gregg was smiling.

"Yeah, yeah… Come on 'King of the Road', lets burn some rubber……"

* * *

Bill placed his half empty glass on the bar and turned toward the roar of the Harleys.

"Bloody bikies…!" Then he suddenly stopped in the middle of the sentence as the Harleys roared past. "Chuck, I could have sworn that the two broads on the back of these bikes are Julie and Marge."

"Get out of it! I'm getting worried about you partner. You gotta be serious. Julie and Marge picked up by two bikies…! *Maaan…* I ask you? Somehow I don't think that's their style."

Chuck couldn't stop laughing at the thought but little did he know the last laugh would come back to bite them both……

THE BIRDS HAVE FLOWN

"'Ocean View' ladies, here we are, safe and sound." Steve cut the twelve fifty and kicked the stand.

"Here let me help you, Julie."

"The last "Boy Scout" huh?"

"There's hope for me yet." Steve was laughing at Julie's comment.

"Who knows." Julie flashed Steve her special before turning to her friend who was more than preoccupied with Gregg. "Let's go Marge, we got things to do."

"Gregg, I've really enjoyed your company... *Eh... Yeah* Julie, I heard you."

"Marge why don't you try to convince your friend to meet me and Steve this evening over some drinks on the Strip?"

Marge shrugged. "She's a hard head, we have an early flight tomorrow and we need to be at LAX by 0600, so it's a tall order. But *I would* like to see you again. Listen, I'll try my best...Why don't I give you my cell number... 063.... I'll wait for your unexpected call, say around eight?" Marge gave Gregg a sly wink.

"*Marge...*" Julie was becoming impatient.

"*I'm coming... I'm coming...* See you Steve, Thanks again for the lift guys...."

* * *

Marge grabbed Julie's hand pulling her back as the roar of the Harley's disappeared down the Santa Monica.

"If it's not *too* trouble, would you mind telling me what the hell this is all about?"

"I'll tell you in the elevator, time is not on our side."

The elevator chimed as the doors opened and Julie pressed six as she turned to Marge.

"Here's the scoop. I said I was leaving Bill but the game has changed. I'm doing a bunk now, only this time without his knowledge. You may think I'm a coward Marge, but it's a bloodless 'Coup d' etat', and for the better. If I had told him over drinks I can just imagine the shenanigan that would follow. No, I thought it over thoroughly whilst sitting on the beach in the company of Steve and Gregg. I mean these two guys are a breath of fresh of air. Bill and Chuck, if you don't mind me saying, are passed their 'use by dates' and my advice to you Marge, is to drop the ball and pass by your place and pick up your stuff and move in with me before these two losers get wise."

"You're fucking serious!"

"Never been more."

"You've blown me away.!" Marge was in collateral damage, the rules of engagement down the toilet.

"Come on Marge wake up, *get real!* You're in 'go nowhere land." The elevator chimed. "Besides I need your help with my personal effects and wardrobe. Don't worry, I've been secretly sneaking most of it under Bill's nose over to my new apartment during the last couple of weeks."

"Well, *aren't you the one!* I still can't believe it."

Julie was almost dragging Marge by the hand down the hallway in her haste to vamoose the apartment building, *like yesterday.......!*

* * *

Bill covered his empty glass with his hand. "No more Chuck, I've had enough, besides we are supposed to be hitting the Rainbow Club tonight and the girls have to go back and change.

"Whatever you say partner but I'm gonna have one more for the road. *Dan...*" He raised his hand.

"Well you had better make it quick." Bill glanced at his 'Top Gun Miramar' watch. *"Christ,* it's after seven, *what's keeping these two broads?"* He opened his cell and dialed in silence. *"As usual no fucking answer!"* He shook his head.

"Cool it Bill, it's no big deal, I'll try Marge... *Hmmm...* "I'll leave a message... Marge, call back ASAP... Chuck."

"If they don't call back by the time you down that shooter, Chuck, I'm gonna go to the beach and fetch them myself."

"Why the big thing Bill?"

"I just have this uneasy feeling… *Drink up…*"

 "See you guys, have a good flight and watch out for these Geisha's…"

* * *

"I must be crazy but somehow I feel good… Like I've been liberated."

Julie laughed. "The suffragettes, huh? Marge, I tell you, you won't regret it."

"Hell, where's that key of mine?" Marg searched in her bag. *"Ah, here we are."* She nervously slotted the Yale.

"Boy!" Julie commented as she absorbed the disheveled apartment."

"I know what you are thinking Julie, but I've given up on this slob, but enough of that, help me pack. I'm only taking what I need the rest can go to 'The Smith Family'." Marge smiled. "I guess it's a great way to get rid of clothes you never ware, *huh?* I'll select Julie, you fold and stuff those two Samsonite's."

Julie glanced at the wall clock. "Get your ass moving Marge it has just gone seven and we don't want to run into these two jerks in the elevator.

"Should I write a note?"

"Are you serious? It's sayonara baby and good riddance……"

* * *

"I could have sworn I seen the girls sitting around this part of the beach. I'll ask this kid with the Bar Buggy…" Bill was becoming more and more agitated.

"Yeah, a blonde and a brunette… *Man,* they were something else."

"Cut the Mon Lisa's kid. So where did they go?" Bill was rudely impatient. *"So?"*

"Are you cop's, because if you are, I'm clean and I report to my probation officer every week."

"Back off kid, we're not after you, it's the two broads we're interested in."

"I served the four of them drinks and the guy gave me a ten-spot tip."

"What do mean four of them?" Bill eyeballed the kid.

"Hold it mister, I'm just telling it as it is. Two guys, two broads, and they left on the back of Harleys."

Bill fished out a ten. "For your troubles."

"Thanks mister." The smile returned.

"You were right Bill, I wouldn't have read it… *But?*"

"Yeah, you may well ask. Jump into my car Chuck, if my hunch is right……"

* * *

"So how do you feel now that that's over?" Julie asked as Marge energetically squeezed the bulging suitcases into the open hatch of the Dodge.

"Never felt better. But no more talk honey, let's get out of this car park before we get any nasty's… *Hey,* but where to?" Marge stopped in her tracks before opening her car door.

"569 Ocean Avenue, Sea View Apartments, just sit on my tail, its only around thirty minutes from here."

"Nice address… Can't wait." Marge was more than impressed…..

* * *

The red Camaro screeched to a sliding stop, the nauseating smell of rubber choking the air in the underground car park.

"*Hell,* Bill go easy man! No broad's worth getting killed over." But before Chuck could finish, Bill had already reached the elevator and was frantically pressing the red button.

"*Bill,* that won't make it come any faster."

"Who are you, *my mother?*"

Chuck just raised his hand and gave a face. When Bill is in one of his moods…

The door slammed against the stop as Bill barged into the apartment, with Chuck hard on his heels.

"I might have guessed." Bill looked at the empty row of coat hangers in the walk-in robe. "Gone and not even a note. *"Fuck women and fuck the world, I need a drink."*

Bill walked to the cabinet and pored an overzealous measure of Scotch.

"And you Chuck?"

Chuck was oblivious to the question, busy on his cell phone.

"Marge call me, it's urgent."

"You were saying, Bill……?"

* * *

"Boy, is this place something else!" Marge exclaimed standing in the middle of the lounge taking in the scenery.

"You like it Marge?"

"Do I! And that balcony with an unobstructed sea view, it doesn't get any better." Marge walked to the open French doors to take in the view whilst inhaling the fresh sea air.

"Roof top pool, private gymnasium two garage parking, two bed rooms, it ticks all the boxes. Which reminds me there is only one mattress on the floor in my bedroom, so we'll have to rough it tonight. But... On a brighter note." Julie flashed her teeth. "There's plenty of bed linen and pillows which I sneaked from the apartment."

"You never!"

"Don't feel guilty Marge... *Bill*...Well...Let me put it this way. He wouldn't even know how to switch on the laundry machine."

"Ha...Ha... Ha..." Marge laughed holding her sides.

"There's a central bathroom and separate toilet and each room has a view as we are on the corner of the apartment building and more to your liking... Wait for it... *A walk- in robe!"*

"It just keeps getting better. At least you managed to buy a sofa so we don't have to sit on the floor." Marge laughed.

"And no kitchen would be scene dead without a Delonghi." Julie proudly pointed to the coffee maker on the breakfast bar. "Coffee Mademoiselle......?"

* * *

Now it was Chuck's turn to open his apartment only to find it deserted and he shrugged dejectedly turning to face Bill.

"It looks like we both dropped the ball, *big time.*"

"Yeah, shit falls, only we were both too dumb to see it coming."

Bill was still in shock, his mind racing to comprehend how life would be without Julie. *As for Chuck, he almost seemed relieved!*

"So where to now buddy?" Chuck asked as he flopped onto the sofa.

"I say we start with another Scotch and then hit the Strip. Who knows dude?" Bill was back to his old self again a wicked smile crossing his face. "We might just get lucky and get laid tonight."

"I'll drink to that......"

* * *

"That coffee was to die for, *but no TV!*" Marge laughed. "That's something else."

"*Listen.*" Julie cut in. "On a more serious note, we had better start unpacking and get our uniforms aired for that early morning flight. *Remember to…*" But before Julie could finish Marge's cell buzzed. "Marge, if that's Chuck on the line, *don't answer!*"

Marge checked the incoming call. "It's a new number." She paused for a moment unsure. "Hello, who's on the line? … *Steve…* What a surprise…! No, I haven't approached her yet… No, let me handle it…"

Julie had put two and to together when the name Steve came out of the hat she was already flashing daggers.

"I might have known." Julie gave Marge that look. "So, what's the big ask?"

"Awe, come on Julie, besides with no TV and only a coffee machine to admire what's the 'death throws' over a couple of drinks with the 'Harley' boys?"

"Marge." Julie was shaking her head. "I give up on you but I guess when you put it that way I suppose I have no option." Julie finally cracked a smile.

"You heard her…Time and place…Around nine at Bar Stella in Sunset Junction… No, I don't know the place but no sweat… Nine then…"

Julie glanced at her watch. *"Eight fifteen…* 'miss congeniality', we had better start to get ready……."

* * *

"My car?" Chuck asked unsteady on his feet as they entered the car park.

"Something tells me dude, after the booze you have consumed, I had better drive." Bill shook his head.

"Chauffeured tonight, huh. What have I done to deserve this?" Chuck was being humorously sarcastic.

"Cut the shit Chuck." Bill unlocked the Camaro. "More to the point, *where to?*"

"The Rainbow Room, Elton John's old hang out."

"It's pretty up market." Bill was in thought. *"Hell, why not!* I hear the food is homemade, just like your mama's." It was Bill's turn.

Chuck had to laugh. "You haven't tasted my mother's cooking!"

"That bad, huh?"

"You don't want to know."

"Get in and cut the shit." Bill turned the key, the Chevy's big six bursting into life. *"I forgot to ask,* where's this place?"

Chuck was busy studying the screen on his Apple 'I Phone'. "West Sunset Boulevard, CA 90069. Punch it in to your GPS."

"Then let's do it partner, I have a good feeling about tonight......."

* * *

Julie methodically screened the car park on her second round. Saturday night is the big one and 'Bar Stella' it seemed, was a more than popular 'watering hole'.

"Over there Julie!" Marge anxiously pointed to the elusive parking slot and coincidentally just next to two Harley Davidsons.

"Yeah, I see them." Julie cut to the chase.

"Well what do you think of this place?" Marge commented studying the exterior.

"This *is* different. But let's get outa this car, I could do with a drink, it's gonna be one of these humid nights."

"In more ways than one, huh?" Marge laughed.

"Your incorrigible......"

* * *

Bar Stella is a dark and eccentric North African 'watering hole' featuring exposed aged brick complete with dust, surrounding the checkered outdoor patio with its cozy benches, pillows and lanterns. Oil paintings of exotic birds decorated the interior walls complimenting the 'Caribbean' style furniture in the dark sofa seating area. Perfect for the nerve wracking second date.

Romantic music streamed through the jubilant atmosphere, it's 'Old World' charm meeting the 'nouveau chick'. As for the crowd, they were not the usual LA 'T'-shirt clad crew. Stella's unspoken dress code, smart casual, with the occasional 'cool dude' sporting iconic thick rimmed glasses.

'Stella's' resident 'mixologists' dotted the marble topped bar, prominent with their white uniforms and smart black bow ties that could easily fit right into the set of 'Mad Men'. Draft beers were off the radar, but for sure, this was the place to be.

* * *

"Just a sec Julie before we hit the tarmac."

Marge flicked down the sun visor and studied her face close up in the brightly lit mirror, then closed her lips in a pouting motion to equalize her lipstick.

"Okay I'm good." She smiled turning to Julie before opening the door of the bug. "Shall we?"

This was Marge at her best, flamboyant with a touch of wicked humor but a better friend you couldn't find……

* * *

As the girls walked toward the outdoor alfresco heads were already turning and who could blame the guys with these two hot chicks strutting their stuff. Julie, stunning in her stone washed slim line Levi's and flat beige open toed sandals, her white off the shoulder sleeveless blouse and plunging neckline, the perfect blend for the 'Stella' experience... *Marge*... Well Marge is Marge, her micro fitting denim skirt and white Spanish style low cut blouse with laced edging, revealing just enough cleavage to entice the male fraternity into macular degeneration. Her stilettos complimenting her curvaceous figure by at least five inches and with that stunning shoulder length brown hair... *'she had it all, just like Bogie and Bacall.*

* * *

"Marge, over here." Steve's voice rang above the music.

"Yeah, I see them!" Julie cut Marge short, annoyance in her voice, having been outsmarted into a date she didn't want and didn't need.

The guys had staked a nice sofa overlooking the tropical foliage of the romantic lantern lit garden.

"Apologies guys, we are a bit late but we had trouble parking."

"No sweat." Steve rose to his feet moving to one side to pave the way for the girls between himself and Gregg.

"Come, sit here Julie." Gregg patted the cushion with his hand. It was the perfect set up.

"So, what do you think of this place?" Steve asked as the girls settled in.

"It's different that's for sure." Julie answered whilst still taking in the scenery.

"Drinks?" Gregg raised his arm to attract the waiter.

"What are you guys having?" Marge was curious.

"Scotch on the rocks, but this cocktail list is something else." Steve passed the girls the colorful menus.

"Hmmm... I see what you mean." Julie commented as she glanced at the rocket fuel.

"Ladies?" The young waiter with the name tag Harvey, was anxiously waiting to take their orders.

"An Anaconda for me and you Julie?"

"Hmmm... Let me see... This looks intriguing... An Alabama Slammer."

The waiter grinned as he scribbled the orders on his pad. Ladies are suckers for the fancy names of modern cocktail's ranging from 15 to 20 bucks a shot... If they only knew...

"Gimme ten ladies, we're over the top tonight. Shall I keep the tab open sir?"

Gregg nodded in silence. Harvey smiled and disappeared through the 'maddening crowd' toward the cocktail bar.

"Changing the subject guys." Julie had that natural inquisitive streak. "Where do you guys shack up in LA?"

"We don't! We're from outta town." Gregg replied. "We had some leave and we thought what better place to spend it than the City of Angles."

"And where would out of town be?"

"Washington DC."

"Washington DC!" Marge couldn't help herself, the thought of long distance love shattering her anticipation.

"And the Harley's?" Begged the question.

The two friends glanced at one another, a grin crossing their faces.

"You guessed right, *rented*. Sorry to disappoint." Gregg replied with a crease of embarrassment.

"Your drinks Ladies." Harvey's interruption was timely.

"Hmmm... Not bad." Julie took a sip of the Alabama Slammer. Marge grinned, at last something was going for her.

"So, Gregg, when is it goodbye LA?" Marge just had to ask.

"We have a mid-day flight back to Washington on Monday. It's just a pity we didn't meet sooner, I'm sure my buddy here would agree."

Steve turned and looked into Julie's eyes. "I most certainly would."

Julie didn't return the compliment, she had been there and done that and besides they had only just met.

"Would I be crossing the line to ask if you ladies are spoken for?" Steve wasn't about to surrender having been given a polite snub from Julie.

"No." Julie replied. "And if I think what you are asking... Well, let me put it this way. Marge and I are best friends and we flat together. We are not into any relationships and we are not Lesbians."

Julie's last comment brought the house down and Gregg and Steve couldn't stop laughing.

"Another round?" Steve asked his arm already raised to attract Harvey.

"Should we." Marge turned to Julie who just smiled and shrugged her shoulders.

"If I said no, would it matter?"

"Then that settles it, one more......."

* * *

"So, you both became bosom buddies during active service in Iraq and Afghanistan? Julie smiled turning to Marge. "Where have I heard that before?"

"And, *Special forces!* You gotta admit Julie, it's a change from the 'Fly Boys'."

"Are we missing something Steve?" Gregg shrugged, a puzzled look on his face.

"I should apologize." Julie felt a real heal. "Gregg... It's... Well it's just that Marge and I have just gotten over a boring relationship with two Navy pilots from 'Desert Storm' and their precious F15 Eagles."

"Now I get the picture! Gregg cracked a smile. "Don't worry Julie, Steve and I are over it and its way behind us and for your further interest... We share an apartment in DC and we're certainly not in the closet."

Gregg's comment brought another bout of laughter but in today's world there's always an elephant in the room.

"But seriously Steve and I go back a long ways in fact since we were thirteen at our Bar Mitzvah and of course our families are really close. "

"Does it make any difference?" Gregg asked concern in his tone.

"What do *you* think?" Marge laughed. *"In today's world who cares.......!"*

* * *

"And the toilet door jammed in the new Dreamliner with a passenger locked inside and worse still the Flight Engineer had to unscrews the hinges and remove the door. *Get out of it!"*

"I swear to God guys, that's a true story. "Marge was laughing through her words.

"And the 'mile high' club?" Steve asked still laughing.

"That story is for another day and not for 'Virgin Airways'." Julie was in good form.

"One more for the road?"

"Thanks, and no thanks. We have an early one tomorrow. In the words of Nat King Cole… 'The parties over, it's time to call it a day'. Marge…" Julie motioned rising to her feet. "I'm sure Marge will agree that we had a really enjoyable evening. It's a pity you're from DC but I assume Gregg, 'tongue in cheek' you have Marge's cell number and who knows?"

Gregg reluctantly flashed a smile. "We'll take you up on that for sure. It's been a pleasure, ladies."

Little did they know their paths would cross again……..

* * *

Bill tossed and turned before finally stretching over to glance at the bedside clock its brightly lit green numerals on the analog dial reading 08.00.

"With that sunlight streaming through the drapes I thought it might have been much later."

He was talking to himself and for a moment he stared at the empty place next to his, it just wasn't the same without Julie and his loins ached at the thought. It was as if he could sense and smell her feminine odor and the warmth of her naked body locked against his. How foolish could he have been? But now it was too late and knowing Julie the chances of reconciliation would be inconceivable and he turned on his back staring blankly at the ceiling. He had phoned last night, time and time again, but as expected Julie didn't answer his calls. As for Chuck… As usual true to form, too much booze and womanizing and Bill cringed reflecting back on last night's drama…….

* * *

The Rainbow Bar & Grill on Sunset Strip is better known as the Rainbow Room, located directly across from the small parking lot of The Roxy Theatre. Opening in 1972 and christened with a party from Elton John, it is the oldest continually operating restaurant and club on the Strip. Before it became the Rainbow Bar & Grill it was the Vila Nova Restaurant which was owned by film director Vincent Minelli who proposed to Judy Garland at the restaurant in 1945. The venue is often frequented by Hollywood's rich and famous with Marilyn Munroe and Joe DiMaggio enjoying their first date at the diner in 1953.

The 'Rainbow' restaurant downstairs is 'old school' with its famous red vinyl booths and dark wood with every centimeter of its wall crammed with rock star snap shots resembling a setting for a gangster movie.

Then there's the outdoor patio with its tables and plastic chairs to enjoy the constant flow of eccentric humanity passing through its dark interior. The wood planked stairway to the left takes you to the famous 'Over The Rainbow' bar with its live music and dancing. On a Saturday evening on the Strip, this place was to die for.

* * *

As Bill raised his hand to attract the barman, he felt a more than a heavy tap on the shoulder and brusquely turned only to face the oversize ape that was the heavy on the door.

"So, what's *your* problem?" Bill rasped.

"Dude, I don't have a problem, *you do,* if that's your buddy hanging on the end of the bar putting the heavies on that blonde chick, who just so happens to my boss's wife. My advice to you is, ice that drink and drag his ass outta here pronto, before I get the signal to fracture both his eye sockets."

"Just a minute! Who hell do you think *you are?"* Bill futilely retaliated.

"For your information dude, I keep the peace in this part of the world but if you want to try me, *bring it on."*

Bill jumped to his feet but the six-foot three black mountain with the bowling ball head, and no neck made him think twice and he shrugged having second thoughts as he endeavored to move 'Mount Everest' aside like hittin the 'Berlin Wall'.

"That's for another day... So?"

The big guy moved aside. "I'll give you ten and when I return you and that drunken buddy of yours had better be invisible."

Bill shook his head in disgust before killing the remainder if his precious Scotch. The all too familiar scene of his 'booze brained' partner as always coming back to haunt him.

"This I don't need." He crushed through the bar flies and grabbed Chuck by the collar of his Hawaiian shirt.

"What the fuck! Hey man go easy. What's you're the fucking problem?"

"You're the fuckin problem and this lady wants you out of her face."

"Come on honey, tell my buddy to get lost." Chuck was barely able to stand hanging on to 'Wonder Woman's' shoulder for support.

"Get off me you creep!" She yelled giving Chuck one almighty push and luckily Bill just managed to grab him below the arms before he broke the timber.

"Easy buddy... Easy... Now grab onto my arm until I get you to the car......."

* * *

Bill glanced at the wall clock as he walked to the kitchen to grind toasted beans for a fresh brew. It had turned nine thirty and whether Chuck liked it or not it was time to waken 'Sleeping Beauty'.

"There's no point calling him on his cellphone." Bill was conversing with himself as he sat on the bar stool at the breakfast bar and stretched for the wall phone. "He would never hear it anyway after the booze he consumed last night." He sighed then lifted the receiver and dialed.

"For fuck sakes!" Chuck searched for the bedside phone in the dark, the drapes still drawn.

"Fuck it!" He knocked the phone to the floor. *"Maaan...* My fucking head... Where's that fucking light switch? Yeah... Who is it?"

"Who do you think it is?"

"I might have guessed... *Bill, gimme a break, for Christ sakes!"*

"Do you know what time it is mister?"

"No, and I'm not fucking interested!"

"Chuck, we have a twenty-two hundred departure this evening to Tokyo, unless it's slipped your mind?"

"I know... I know... For Christ sakes, I don't need a lecture. Now unless there's something else, call me back in a couple hours I need to get some sleep."

"You listen to me Chuck, *I'm serious.* After that embarrassing episode at 'The Rainbow Club' you're over the line man."

"Awe come on! That broad was coming onto me."

"Chuck, get wise to yourself, that's always your excuse. Do you want a sugarcoat or right between the eyes?"

"Bill, what the hell? I'm gonna hang up."

"You do and I'll call Morgan right now and tell him you're not fit to fly tonight. *Coppice?"*

"You're serious?"

"Never been more. Now you listen to me, booze head. You're into me for fifteen big ones and now when I think of it, you're a big part of the reason why Julie gave me the ass. Here's the deal. You get yourself sobered up to pass the breath test and you had better be ready by seven when I pick you up or this will be our last flight together and you'll be flying a crop duster... *Now,* you can hang up......!"

SHIMARU SHIMA

(Locked Island)

Shimaru Shima is a desolate unhabituated island in the North Pacific Ocean, consisting mostly of volcanic rock and thick tropical vegetation, located approximately 3000km to the east of Japan and at only 350 sq. km (the size of Washington DC) was occupied by the Japanese Imperial Forces during World War II and the best kept secret of the war in the Pacific.

Radar is an object locating system that uses radio waves to determine the range, altitude, location and speed of objects transmitted via a radio dish or antenna which was developed by Marconi and Albert H Taylor in The United Kingdom in the mid-thirties and deployed with considerable success in the 1940's during the historic Battle of Britain. Both Germany and Japan at that time had also entered the Radar race but fortunately for the allies, too late to influence the outcome of the Second World War.

However, Mitsubishi Electric under the cloak of utmost secrecy had established a research and development station on Shimaru Shima for the development of radar but with a difference, namely a Radar blocking system virtually making the island invisible and the perfect supply depot for its submarine fleet and right under the noses of the US Pacific Fleet, hence the island was never discovered to this very day.

With deep water docking facilities and a modest runway for medium size air freight, it was an ideal base for the lucrative drug trade in South East Asia and the Yakuza, better known as the 'Japanese Mafia', were only too keen to exploit this opportunity at the turn of the century.

The Yakuza also known as the Gokudo is a powerful far reaching Japanese criminal enterprise profiting from prostitution money laundering and drugs, like that of the Italian Mafia pyramid with each defined territory having a Godfather. One such leader was the famous Satora Namura, 67, the Godfather of the most violent Yakuza syndicate, the Kudokai, controlling the west coast of Japan. However, Namura was arrested in 1998 over the public shooting of Kinihiro Kajiwari, the head of the local fisherman's co-operative and consequently died in prison. His son Akio, followed in his father's footsteps and true to form controlled the Kudokai's 103,000 members or foot soldiers, with an iron fist, easily recognized by their tattoos and the severed joint of their small finger.

The Japanese reputation for finite detail and organizational skills was abundantly prevalent on the island leaving no stone unturned to ensure their drug empire is never discovered. Miles from the regular shipping lanes and undetectable on the satellite global positioning grid, commercial flights flying at thirty to thirty-five thousand feet would never detect this 'invisible pin head' of an island.

Each month the sixty Yakuza triads, with expertise in electronics, aeronautical engineering and construction are replaced with a new crew, commuting to and fro from the mainland by private jet to Tokushima with its small commercial airport on the South Island of Shikoko the smallest of Japan's big four islands. Needless to say, customs and immigration are on the Yakuza payroll and with no questions asked shipments of uncut cocaine and heroin pass freely to the cartel's underground processing and distribution network and the prized Asian markets.

The island is self-sufficient with its air-conditioned staff quarters strategically camouflaged by dense tropical foliage. Food is shipped by air each month accompanied by the finest Japanese chefs. When it comes to the welfare of the Yakuza no expense is spared right down to a fully equipped infirmary with pharmacy and medical staff. As for H2O? Rain water storage tanks and a small desalination plant ensure an abundant supply.

Two Mitsubishi V16 generators producing 5,000KW were more than sufficient to supply the electricity for the staff quarters and runway lights, a left over from the war, having been painstakingly refurbished as well as heavy construction equipment, such as scrapers, excavators and backhoes. Diesel and aviation fuel tanks were the 'peiz de resistance' and all that's missing is the abundant supply of the raw material, namely cocaine and heroin.

Columbia is the world's cocaine producer and the United States being its largest customer with one in six citizens claiming to have used cocaine during their lifetime. But the war on drugs at the turn of century by North America and Europe in conjunction with the Columbian government, had successfully reduced the demand by 60%. Japan and South-East Asia were now the new markets of opportunity for the illicit narcotics trade and what better partner than the 'North Coast Cartel' based in the Columbian City of Barranquilla headed by Alberto Orlandez-Gamboa a ruthless drug lord with murder and kidnapping and extortion high on his Curriculum Vitae and the perfect partner for Okio Numero and the Yakuza. With the tragedy of 9/11, the United States turned their attention to the capture of Osama bin Laden and the heat was off the Columbian scene and what better time for the Cartel and the Yakuza to broker a deal for the supply of cocaine and heroin to the Kudokai syndicate controlling the west coast of Japan.

When the deal was cut between Okio Numero and Albert Orlando-Gamboa at a secret location in Barranquilla in Colombo in January 2002 for the supply of uncut cocaine, it was a choice of 'honor between thieves' or the 'marshmallow test". The price was the next heat at $25,000 per kilo on the street with Numero demanding $5,000 per kilo based on volume and to cover Japan's costly manufacturing and distribution overheads. A heated disagreement prevailed with Gamboa reluctantly giving the 'Cartel handshake' provided minimum shipments of no less than 2,000 kilos payable in cash and in US Dollars and more to the point, *80% pure!*

RUN SILENT RUN DEEP

It would take a further six months before operation 'Sea Lane' would commence and hence Shimaru Shima's vital role and the key to the success of the Columbian/Japanese drug cartel.

The code name "Run Silent Run Deep" was the purchase by the Yakuza of a decommissioned 'moth- balled'1980 diesel electric Russian Kilo Class submarine, a casualty of the cold war, complete with snorkel and silent running, from the naval graveyard in Pavlovsk Bay in the Black Sea, at the bargain basement price of US$60m plus a further $10m for commissioning and training of the Japanese crew. It just didn't get any better. In Russia with the right connections, be it the Russian Mafia or the Ministry of Defense or both, what's another submarine with over two hundred waiting to be adopted?

At 2350 tons and 70 meters long and with a draft of only 6.5meters the Kilo Class Submarine was the perfect transport for stealth surface operations in the coastal shallow waters around the Island of Gorgona, 35 kilometers from coast of Columbia. It's two 1,000kw diesel generators and 5,100hp propulsion motor producing 12 knots when surfaced and 25 knots when submerged, was the perfect catalyst. The Russian submarine requires a crew of 60 but for non-operational logistics, 16 crewmen plus the first officer is sufficient to man the vessel as a freight runner.

In 1990 Japan commissioned 11 diesel powered attack submarines of its own design, the Oyashio Class, being an integral necessity for its Maritime Defense Force and within 'The Treaty of Mutual Cooperation' signed on June 19, 1960, between the United States and Japan being a constraint of World War II. Many of the Yakuza served in the Japanese Navy as submariners and the perfect solution to crew the Russian craft.

Fully fueled and with enough provision to last six weeks, in June 2002, RU18 slipped silently below the freezing waters of the Black Sea, bound for the Bosporus Straight, the Sea of Marmara, the Dardanelles' Straight, then south through the Aegean Sea and finally the sea of Crete before entering the Mediterranean, on the final leg of its destination, the Straits of Gibraltar. Once into the Atlantic Ocean the 20-day journey to Shimaru Shima would take RU18 round the treacherous Cape Horn then north into the Pacific and finally the illusive 'Locked Island'. From there it was only four days sailing to the island of Gorgona. Once a penal colony it became known as Alcatraz Island. A 2.5k wide, a Volcanic rock formation, with several outlets rising almost vertically from the sea, the largest called El Viudo and with surrounding waters only 25 meters deep it was the perfect 'pickup' rendezvous for RU18 and the sweetheart deal with the Colombian Coast Guard to turn Nelson's eye, creating the most ingenious and largest drug cartel in history…...

THE PALESTINE INCIDENT

*Counterintelligence Agency,
Langley, Virginia
Washington DC
Tuesday, 10 June 2014*

"Hanna," Thomson the director of Counter Intelligence, lifted the secretarial phone. His tone portraying that he wasn't in the best of moods, which was nothing new. This whole middle East Crisis and the so called 'Arab Spring,' was a perpetual headache for the department. "Haul Nelson and Jonson in here, like yesterday, and tell them to drop everything, this is a red alert."

"Will do John." Hanna raised her eyebrows and shrugged… What's new? She had worked for her boss now for over six years and she could read him like a book. As for Nelson and Jonson although only three years with the Agency, had made a name for themselves as two of the best agents 'racking up' an enviable score card. Hanna…? An attractive 26 years old unmarried brunette with olive shaped brown eyes to match, was a head turner at five nine with a figure to die for. She kept her private life to herself and wasn't into the office thing. Office suitors who had crossed the line were still smarting from, 'hell has no fury like a woman's scorn'.

"Steve, Gregg." Hanna called from her desk. Nelson and Jonson's desks were only five meters from the boss's secretary and the whole office looked up momentarily.

"The boss wants you in his office … *Like now!*"

"The 'Mount 'calls, huh?" Steve turned to his buddy raising his shoulders. "What now?"

"Hanna what's the take." Gregg asked as he approached her desk.

"I don't know and even if I did, I wouldn't tell you." She sported her usual cheeky grin. "All I know it's a 'code red'."

"No more donuts and coffee for you." Steve laughed

"Get out of it!" Hanna shot back in good humor. "Guys, if I were you I wouldn't hang around."

"Thanks Hanna for your words of comfort." Steve didn't waist anymore time and knocked on Thomson's door.

"Come in." The blast uninviting.

Thomson looked up, his expression a silent growl to be challenged at your peril.

Take the load off." Thomson pointed to the empty chairs, his nose buried in the document in front of him……

* * *

Thomson had been with the agency since he left university. At 24 his first novice assignment 'The Watergate Crisis' a series of scandals during the presidency of Richard Nixon resulting in the indictment of several of Nixon's advisors and ultimately, he himself resigning on August 9, 1974. They say the first cut's the deepest and a learning curve that Thomson would never forget. Gerald R Ford became the 38th president of the United States and in his own words, 'Under Extraordinary Circumstances'. The war in Vietnam was over and with the fall of Saigon on April 30, 1975 America suffered an embarrassing defeat in a futile war it should never have entered. The lesson… 'you can never beat the people'. A war where 58,000 young Americans died for a cause they would never understand and for a nation who would never appreciate their sacrifice.

Then it was Iraq Freedom and Desert Storm and of course the never-ending Palestine and Israeli problem. But who could forget 'Nine Eleven', the 2001attck on the twin towers of the World Trade Centre and the Pentagon, a terror attack that would remain emblazoned in Thomson's mind forever. The mastermind, Osama bin Laden and the terror group Al Qaeda, would take years of CIA investigations to hunt down the murderers of 2966 people and ten billion US$ in property and infrastructure damage. Thomson, as the Director of Counter Intelligence played a major role in the execution of Americas number one most wanted, who met his bloody end on May 2, 2014 in 'Operation Neptune Spear' in Abbottabad Pakistan, by a secret Navy Seals Team. Of course, 'nine eleven' was the trigger to the Afghan conflict

'Operation Enduring Freedom' to pursue Al Qaeda and the Taliban now fleeing to the mountains and now to top it all, the terrorist group in northern Iraq... *ISIL!*

He had been there and done that. A cool customer with a bright analogical mind and a creative thinker who didn't suffer fools lightly and a low attention span, in short, *don't waste my time!* In 2003, he was promoted to Director of Counter Intelligence and at 53 the youngest CIA agent to hold this post with congratulations from George Bush himself.

At six two, he carried a lean broad muscular frame, careful dieting and gym work keeping him fit. His long narrow face carried premature deep laugh lines and slight eye bags from many sleepless nights. The narrow lips and straight teeth gave him a somber look but he had a sense of humor which occasionally broke through to show he was human after all. His grey blue penetrating eyes sent a message but his seriously thinning grey hair unfortunately made him look slightly older than his fifty-three years but he had gained the one quality that makes a good leader... *respect!*

When one joins the CIA, it's twenty-four seven and a lost social life. His first marriage went down the toilet after only three years, fortunately there were no children. With numerous affairs below his belt (so to speak) he had finally found the right one. Whatever, he had another 'red alert' on his plate and two young agents eagerly waiting their next assignment.

* * *

Thomson sat back in his executive chair thinking for a moment his eyes somewhere else.

"Ah...hmmm." He cleared his throat, a 'wake up' call for the two young agents. He flicked through the pages of the manila folder before extracting three pictures.

"I want you to carefully study these photos." Thomson slipped the pictures across his desk one at a time. "The first is Abud Azis, a naturalized American citizen, 54 years old. Parents came to the US in 1970 from Palestine under refugee status. He is married with two children and lives in Chicago. Graduated from the University of Chicago in Economics and Statistics. This guy is no slouch. Joined the US Treasury at 28 and is now in the department of Controller of Currency and is the senior director of the Chicago District Office. You may well ask, what's the role of this department? *Interesting...* It enforces the law in anti-money laundering and anti-terrorism finance laws and works closely with The Federal Reserve in the printing and the destruction of currency through BEP (Bureau of Engraving & Printing) at Fort Worth Texas and Washington DC."

"So, what's the connection?" Nelson sort of half shrugged and glanced at Jonson as he studied the other two pictures.

"Steve, don't be so bloody impatient! *Now, where was I?*" Thomson gave Nelson that look that only a mother can give. "The other two are Anbar Salibe and Fadil Maalouf. Also, Palestinians. Salibe is 27 and Maalouf 26." Thomson sighed as if to express where do I start? He paused again. "A 'Code Red, is a national security alert of the highest form. As you both know the CIA share intelligence with our counterparts worldwide and this one doesn't get any bigger, vapor trailing all the way down from the Commander in Chief' and of course our director himself, John Brennan. But what's the spook? From what I gather from Brennan's 'ear fill', Netanyahu has been on the blower to Obama and the 'dinosaur' this time has been quick to react. It's the worst kept secret that the terrorist group Hamas will never rest until they destroy Israel and kill every Jew and recover the West Bank and Gaza and the world recognizes Palestine as State.... Taman Pardo... *You may well ask who the hell now is this guy?*"

Nelson and Jonson were desperately trying to follow the 'Snakes and Ladders'.

"Taman Pardo, is the director of Shin Bet, Israel's Counter Intelligence and Internal Security Agency. Their agents, or Mossads in Hebrew, have done some heavy 'gum shoeing' and these three names have been placed on high security alert with intent to commit a terrorist attack on Israel. When where and how we don't know."

Thomson paused again to allow a few moments for the two young field agents to digest the audit trail.

"Coffees?"

"Eh err sure John." Steve replied taken aback. It was not like Thomson to be so benevolent.

"Yeah I could do with one." He lifted the phone. "Hanna, can you do me a favor and bring three coffees from the vendor...? Black...?" He turned to Nelson and Jonson who nodded.

"Yeah Hannah, black all round."

Thomson digressed for a moment to lighten the somber atmosphere with a rare smile.

"I heard on the vine you that you two guys have just returned from some well-deserved R&R. You did well on that last case and it hasn't gone unnoticed." He smiled again.

Getting an appraisement from John was as scarce as hen's teeth but a good feeling when it happens.

"LA, we had a blast." Gregg gave a mischievous grin. "We hired a couple of Harleys and burned the town."

"I hope you didn't tarnish the good name of the CIA?" Thomson laughed. "Reminds of my younger days... Why is youth wasted on the young, huh?"

A timely knock on the door interrupted Thomson's 'runaway', reminiscing is okay in small doses.

"Come in Hanna."

Hanna gave a smile as she placed the polystyrene on Thomson's desk.

"I'm keeping a tab you know."

"Hanna, I promise I'll square with you at the end of the week."

"With interest?"

"Get out of it! Secretaries..." Thomson laughed shaking his head. "Thanks Hanna. *Oh*, and I don't want to be disturbed."

It looked like the boys were in for the long haul.

Thomson took sip of the vendor' brew. It was wet with a slight hint of coffee.

"It doesn't get any worse, huh? Okay let's get down to it. Hamas is Israel's number one enemy and peace negations are a myth that the united nations and specifically Obama continually strive for, with John Kerry the Secretary of State, poor bastard, on the 'Biggest Looser'. At least he doesn't seem to be losing his hair." Thomson grinned, a lead balloon throws away that didn't draw any laughter.

"Ah...hmmm." Thomson composed himself. "Hamas is becoming more and more desperate, their terrorist cult fueled by neighboring extremists and the supply of rockets but let's look at Salibe and Maalouf. Both have been in the US legally for three years on student visas studying at Cornel University graduating with honors in Aeronautics and Rocket Science... Two smart boys... *But get this!* during their stay they also gained commercial pilot licenses for large jets... *Interesting...?* Thomson paused again. "But there's more to come. Their university fees and living expenses were met by none other than Abud Azis."

Thomson fished another document from the folder.

"Now according to Shin Bet these three characters have been on their radar for some time as persons of interest linked to Hamas. It has also been confirmed that although Salibe and Maalouf have different names on their passports they are brothers... But here's the scoop, *Abud Azis is their uncle! Can you believe it!* Changing family names in the Arab world seems to be the flavor of the month but it all adds up because Aziz's brother is none other Abdul Fattah the number one commander of the armed wing of Hamas and on Shin Bet's most wanted list and of course Salibe and Maalouf's father... *The plot thickens...* Israel's Mossad Secret Service and special forces the Sayerat Matakal have been so far unsuccessful in capturing or assonating Fattah as each time they get too close the bird had flown."

Thomson sat back in his chair as if staring for a moment into space his analytic mind at full throttle.

"So, what do we *really* have on these people John, except for the family connections?"

"That's the troubling thing Steve. We've really very little."

"Phone taps... computer hacking... firewalls?" Gregg interrupted.

"The FBI have been active for the past year using all sorts of spy devices... bugs... you name it. Sure, there have been lots of cell calls to Palestine using different numbers and locations with garbage that doesn't make any sense, obviously in code. I have all the information here." Thomson's raised a fistful of A4's.

Steve was brooding his mind searching for a link. *anything... anything!*

"There must be something John, something that we are missing."

"Your right Steve, but there's more to come, I haven't finished yet."

Thomson glanced at his watch then lifted the phone leaving Nelson and Jonson in limbo.

"Hanna, I think it's lunch time......."

THE FRIENDLY SKIES

"Is there anything else I can get you Mr. Jackson?"

* * *

Dinner service in the First-Class cabin was thankfully over and Delta L15 to London Heathrow was two hours into flight. The 2230 departure from LAX was popular with the business fraternity. With the time difference of plus eight hours and one stop at JFK, L15 would touch down in London at 5.30pm the following day with time for R&R and that the so called 'business dinner' and 'my wife doesn't understand me'. Some are born great, some achieve greatness, some get it as a graduation gift. *Whatever* ... In First Class *'you get it all!*

* * *

"That's a tall order... eh... err?"

"Julie... Julie Rodgers, Chief Purser."

"Your face seems familiar, Julie." Jackson gave that look, the line older than "Good Morning Vietnam'.

"Maybe I just have one of those faces, huh? Or you recognize me from a previous flight." Julie forced a smile, there's always one player who thinks he's God's gift to women.

"Can I freshen your Champagne or some caviar, sir" Julie persisted.

"Moet would be fine." Jackson piled it on but Julie was a veteran in the field of phylogeny and she could handle overzealous male passengers in a way that made them feel they had to stay after school.

"I'll take your glass Mr. Jackson, just give me a few minutes." From the corner of her eye she could see the call light flashing in 6B, a timely intervention. "Excuse me sir." Julie motioned.

"Oh. *of course, of course.* Say Julie, why don't you call me, Bill?"

Julie politely ignored the offer and attended to the lady in 6B. The cabin would settle down in around 15 minutes for Siesta time after the gastronomic over indulgence and she was looking forward to catching up with Marge in the First-Class galley for some well-earned refreshment and girly talk, *but first that Moet!*

"Relaxing huh?" Julie commented as she pulled back the galley curtain to find Marge sitting on the edge of the food trolley, coffee in hand, legs crossed, showing more thigh than Christina Aguilera.

"So, what's with you? I thought you would have finished by now?" Marge took another sip of the dark brew.

"A few difficult ones, like this guy Jackson in 1A and 'Norman Bates mother', that old bag in 6B."

"That bad, huh?... *Heh... Heh...*" Marge burst into laughter at Julie's colorful description.

"Worse... I've got a hitter and a psycho... Pass that Moet, Marge."

Julie placed the champagne flute on the tray and slowly poured the bubbly.

"That's 1A and a Remy for 6B... Be back in a jiffy." Julie disappeared through the curtain.

"Mrs. Bates..."

"Thank you... *This is* Remy Martin XO...?" She held the Krosno Vinoteca brandy glass to the light. This witch was either a connoisseur or an alcoholic.

"Most certainly." Julie replied a slight cut in the tone of her voice. "Please excuse me, I have to attend to another passenger.

"Mr. Jackson, your Moet."

"Thanks Julie... Say, which hotel do you girls stay when you are London?"

"I'm sorry Mr. Jackson, that's confidential." Julie forced another smile, the one that Julie would have the most pleasure when driving her knee into his crotch... "Now, should you need anything else sir, just press the call button."

"Can I pour you a coffee Julie?"

"Can yoooou!" Julie pulled the curtain and sat down heavily with an accompanying sigh rubbing her thighs in the process.

"Thanks Marge." She took a sip. *"Boy I needed that!* Let's hope we can get five minutes' peace."

"You know Julie, some people call us First Class waitresses and there are times when I have to agree. Notwithstanding some of the crap we have to put up with, like the front and back brush pasts when we are serving the food, with the 'used by date' excuse, 'excuse me but I have to go to the washroom'... *I tell you."* Marge was shaking her head.

"*Hey*... Come on Marge... We've had some great times, haven't we? But I admit I'm fed up with the London run. When we get back to LAX let's apply for a change of route. What do you think?"

Marge lightened up. "I'm with you."

But by that distant look on her face her thoughts were somewhere else. She interrupted. "I guess Chuck and Bill will be on their way to Tokyo by now."

Marge, *are you fucking serious?* Don't tell me you're still wearing your heart on your sleeve for that looser!"

The attendants light flashed for 1A.

"Christ! Not that creep again?"

Then just before Julie opened the galley curtain she stopped and turned for a moment to face Marge.

"Don't beat up on yourself honey, we did the right thing......."

THE TOKYO RUN

Tuesday, 10 2014

Bill glanced at his watch, he was in relaxation mode laying on the sofa in his white bathrobe, the warm shower still tingling his skin.

"Five thirty." He shrugged as he took in the time on his Breitling Chronomat Evolution wrist watch, it's luminous hands pronounced in the subdued lighting. He pouted his lips and gave an exaggerated sigh' his head turning to the empty space on the sofa where Julie would curl up beside him with a bowl of popcorn as they watched a Bluetooth movie.

"What a jack ass I've been. In hindsight, I should have seen it coming. I feel like a poor version of fucking Stevie Wonder." He mumbled in disgust.

"Fucking Chuck...! Maaan... I don't know why I have put up with that asshole for so long..." He shrugged again. "Well, whatever it takes, I just have to find a way to get Julie back..." Bill quickly threw his feet to the floor.

"There's no point in crying in my beer, I had best get dressed as it will take me a good hour depending on the traffic to get to Chuck's place…....."

* * *

With a last glance in the hallway mirror, Bill straightened the knot in his dark blue tie contrasting against his crisp white epilated double pocketed shirt, the gold-plated captain's wings pronounced above his left pocket. He had just finished packing his airways garment bag containing a change of shirt and slacks and of course his toiletries. With an overnight stop- over before his next flight there was little opportunity for R&R so travelling light was the order of the day. One last look around the apartment to make sure he hadn't forgotten anything. Good to go, he slipped into his jacket then placed his garment bag and briefcase in the hallway, then switched off the lights and turned the Yale. Another flight, another day, in the life of a commercial pilot.......

* * *

The car park as usual, was full, Monday evening in LA is the day after the 'week end' before. Too much partying, sore heads, meth, and *I'm sorry boss I can't make it in today I have that dreadful flue'.* So, what's new? Ocean View apartments is for the executive professionals and at three to four thousand a month rental, kids are not on the agenda.

Bill briskly walked to his baby, the red Camaro. *At least he had one love left!* He pressed the remote to open the trunk and placed the garment bag inside then carefully folded his uniform jacket finally chucking in his cap and slamming the lid before pressing the 'unlock' to open the doors, the bucket seat automatically adjusting to the driver's position, triggered by the electronic ignition key. He made himself comfortable then hooked the safety belt and turned the key. The eight pots stalling for a second in their thirst for the 'fuel of life' before finally bursting into a low growl, almost like that of a young African lion and for a moment Bill was in another world. 'Petrol heads' are all the same.......

* * *

Ocean Avenue was relatively quiet and the ten miles to Montana Avenue, Chuck's apartment, would be a breeze. From there Bill would slip onto the Santa Monica Freeway then it's all the way to LAX and Airport Bulverde. The Camora didn't take kindly to the sixty-mile speed limit and Bill would have to tread easy with the lead foot, the last thing he needed tonight is a speeding infringement.

Chuck, for a change, was patiently standing on the sidewalk outside Montana Towers, a low density up market apartment complex, enjoying the last drag of his cancer stick in the 'free smoking zone. Bill had called him earlier on his cell to be ready at eight as parking on Montana was a challenge in its self.

"For once he's on time." Bill muttered under his breath as he double parked and rolled down the window.

"Chuck, don't hang around, throw your gear onto the back seat." Already a chorus of irate drivers were blasting their horns in annoyance having to maneuver around the parked car into the other congested lane.

"You said eight!" Chuck slammed the door.

"For Christ sakes Chuck, *it's only eight fifteen.*"

Bill signaled and hit the gas. "Do you mind?" Bill was referring to the half-smoked dog still in Chuck's hand.

Chuck gave a disgusted look then shrugged before dispensing the glowing stick out of the window.

"Nice... So much for clean LA... *huh... You smokers..."* Bill was shaking his head.

"What's with you, is it the 'I hate smoker's night'?"

"Cool it Chuck, we have a long flight ahead of us and you look like shit. My advice... Go to the lounge and down a couple of black coffees."

"Thanks for the complement *and I don't think!"* Chuck was a 'bear' with a sore head.

The remainder of the journey was less than cordial which was not unusual after a blast on the town the night before but Chuck always bounced back. Tonight, for some strange reason he was distant, his eyes staring ahead, like a guy on a mission... Maybe it was just the thought of losing Marge... Whatever...? He had better shake it off before the flight.......

* * *

The traffic on the Santa Monica was fast moving and before they knew it there it was the large blue sign on their left... 'Next Exit Airport Bulverde'.

"Not bad!" Bill commented as he glanced at the dash clock. "Eight thirty-five, gives us ample time to check in with Morgan on the flight details and the manifest and finally the infamous alcohol and drug test, *huh?"* A cheap shot at Chuck.

(There are strict Federal Aviation Laws regarding drug and alcohol testing for flight officers and air crew two hours before the flight and must not exceed 0.04 blood alcohol content.)

"Yeah, yeah, I get the message and I don't think that's funny. Anyhow, don't get your knickers in a twist, I'll pass with flying colors."

Bill didn't comment he was too busy weaving his way through the heavy airport traffic. At last... Departures...Terminal 1 Domestic... Terminal 2 International... Terminal 3 International and Domestic Freight........

* * *

Dan Morgan's nose was deep in paperwork, the empty polystyrene coffee cup was his third since six, his tired eyes reflecting the stress of his eight-hour shift and 10pm couldn't come quick enough. Happily married with three young children the job played havoc with his family life but Norma was more than understanding, a rare quality in today's 'marriage go round'.

Morgan sat back for a moment and massaged the back of his neck then stared at the happy picture of the family group on his desk, their smiles said it all and Dan couldn't resist lifting the phone.

"Hi honey... Me too... The kids? That's just like young Sam... Like his father eh... *Ha...Ha...Ha...* When? I should be home by ten thirty I have one last flight to wrap up... A freighter to Tokyo... I promise, not too much coffee... I gotta go honey... Love you......."

* * *

Morgan had been with Global since his graduation in 1995 from the most selective 'Irvine University of California', commencing as a "go for" in head office but ambition isn't a crime and he clawed his way up the ladder to Flight Co-ordination Manager in charge of Global's International Freight Division, a no mean task. In 2014 LAX's ever expanding air cargo system handled more than 2.1 million tons of goods with 'International Freight' accounting for over 50% of this total.

* * *

At 43 his 5-11 frame was muscular and lean, his black unruly thick crop of hair now flashing shades of grey, just enough for that elusive distinguished look. The square jaw line, tucked in ears, high cheek bones and lineless LA tanned complexion gave him a kind of 'Henry Fonda' look and as for those grey blue eyes...? Penetrating or happy...Well...? All in all, he was 'a man for all reasons'.

* * *

There was a distinct knock on the door and for a moment Dan was distracted from his paperwork and looked up. The door half open, Nancy his secretary popped her blonde head around.

"Sorry to disturb you Dan but I have the drug and alcohol test results here for Captain Collins and First Officer Stevens. They are both waiting outside."

Dan smiled, Nancy was a one of a kind.

"Thanks, just put them on my desk. I'll look at them in a few minutes I just need to cross the "I's' and dot the 'T's' for this report to Kennedy regarding the damage to the 'Ajax' shipment.'

"Can I fetch you another coffee Dan, you look bushed?"

"Nancy, you are darling but if I take another dose of caffeine I'll be awake for the next 24."

"Well, I don't want Norma on my back for giving her husband a bout of insomnia." She flashed a smile......

* * *

As she closed the door Dan grinned at Nancy's remark. A more devoted secretary you couldn't find. A divorcee with a teenage daughter, the shift work suited her. In her late thirties, she still had the looks and the figure to match. With her blonde hair swept back in a bun and her blemish-less complexion and those pale blue olive shaped eyes, full lips and straight white teeth and a figure to die for, she was a piece of work alright and needless to say an abundance of suitors knocking on her door. Previously an air hostess with Global for ten years, the stress on the marriage was too much and she and her husband John, decided to go their different ways. After graduating doing part time study for a secretarial diploma, she requested a transfer to administration and the rest as they say is history.

* * *

"I'll get Nancy to type this tomorrow, Kennedy can go and take a hike, another day won't kill the cat." Dan was speaking to himself as he placed the papers in the 'out basket' before lifting the secretarial phone.

"Nancy, inform Collins and Stevens I'll see them now."

There was a light knock on the door.

"Come in." Morgan didn't look up, his eyes still studying the report as he pointed blindly to the empty chairs. "Take the load off." The tone in his voice less than encouraging. Then he finally placed the report on his desk and sat back rubbing his bottom lip with the back of his right forefinger, his penetrating eyes sending a message.

"Steven's." Morgan gave an exaggerated sigh. "As usual you are borderline and I'm warning you for the last time, *you had better get you act together.* You're a loose cannon and I don't need it on my watch *and I don't want it!"*

"Dan, let me expla..."

"Cut it Chuck! I could fill a 'joke book' with your reasons and excuses... One more time and you'll be flying a cargo plane full of rubber dog shit outa Hong Kong... *Do you read me?"*

Chuck gave a half shrug, his face solemn.

"I'm not finished with you yet... *Another thing,* ... If you can't iron a shirt, send it to the laundry... You look like shit with that dog-eared collar and a tie that has more wrinkles than 'Phyllis Diller'. We may be flying freight but that's no excuse to look as if you have just got out of the sack... Now having expressed my displeasure, let's get down to more important business. As usual Bill, you will be flying Global 10 as Captain and Stevens First Officer. You are both well acquainted with the Boing 777 freighter, so there should be no problems. This is the cargo manifest." Morgan passed Bill the paperwork.

Bill flicked through the pages studying each one.

"*Hmmm...* A shipment of semiconductors from Silicon Valley for Matsushita... 80 metric tons. A bit light... 22 tons below our maximum payload. But in saying that ..." He grinned. "With a bit of tail wind, we should be arriving at Narita Tokyo, ahead of schedule." He Turned to Chuck with a smile. "That means we'll clear Narita *before* two thirty tomorrow afternoons, *huh.*"

Morgan cut to the chase. "But remember gentleman you have an eight o'clock return flight on Thursday evening, so my advice is, rest up and get plenty of shut eye *and that means you Stevens!*"

"And the return flight?" Bill asked changing the subject. Morgan was on a roll.

"You'll be flying back to 'Dulles International'."

"*Washington DC!*" Bill was taken aback.

"You heard right Collins, what's the beef?"

"It's just... It's just that it's a bit off our usual flight route returning to LAX."

"Well, look at it this way, you'll get a chance to see the White House." Morgan grinned. At times Dan had a wicked sense of humor.

"The cargo?"

"McGill will provide you with all the details when you get to Narita, that's all I can tell you."

"So why the cloak and dagger?"

Morgan ignored Bill's question glancing at his watch.

"It's after nine and you still have to do your routine safety checks and I want this flight to depart on time. So, if you don't mind?" Morgan made a motion with is eyes toward the door.

Bill stopped in his tracks as Chuck was about to open the door to leave.

"Dan, one more thing"

Morgan gave a disgruntled sigh ad dropped his pen.

"*What* is it now?" He growled.

"I forgot to ask you who's on the tea service tonight."

"Sally Jenkins."

"She's a looker."

Morgan shook his head and made a face at Steven's off the cuff comment.

"You never cease to disappoint me with a that big mouth of yours, Chuck... *Now for the last time, I'm busy.......*"

* * *

"That didn't go too well." Chuck commented as they both walked toward the staff kitchen and rest rooms.

"*For you or for me?*" Bill shot back sarcastically.

Chuck shrugged, it was a lost cause. "Tonight, it looks like I'm 'numero uno' on the shit parade."

"Now what gives you that idea? My advice Chuck, get over it and, put your stuff in your locker and go get a caffeine injection. Do me a favor and take my bag with you while I go check out the aircraft and complete the safety list."

Chuck gave a disgruntled mumble followed by his extensive range of foul language before reluctantly grabbing Bill's garment bag.

"If you say so, Captain."

"*Yeah,* I do say so... *Cappice......?*"

* * *

"Here let me get that."

Chuck had picked up a coffee cup and was about to press the Latte button on the machine.

He turned to face the voice then smiled. "*Sally... Sally Jenkins...*I'll be darned! "Morgan just informed us that you were joining us tonight for the Tokyo run. It's been a long time......"

* * *

Sally Jenkins at 23 was a lush brunette and still single. Maybe she had her head screwed on being her own woman. At 5-8 she was short but what she lost in height she made up for in other places. She had a hypnotic smile which immediately put you at ease returning the compliment. The olive brown eyes complimented her shoulder length brown hair and her pale complexion, obviously not a sun lover. She looked the part in her blue airline jacket and tailored slacks to match, the white open-necked blouse the 'piece de resistance', not to mention the medium high blue regulation heels that made her look special. The petite gold earrings and simple neck chain to match said it all, for sure this babe was too good to be a flight attendant on a lousy freighter!

* * *

"Disappointed?"

"Pleasantly surprised." Chuck smiled, laying it on. "Black, no sugar."

"Watching the waistline huh?" Sally grinned.

"Something like that. *Say*, I thought you had applied for a transfer to commercial flights."

Sally shrugged. "I'm told I'm next in line when a vacancy arises."

"Are you sure you are doing the right thing? Flight attendants work their butts off, not to mention some of the shit you take from rude bastard passengers who think they've nothing else better to do but complain."

"I know what you mean Chuck but being a bloody tea lady on a freighter... It was either that or an underwater basket weaving class."

Chuck couldn't help himself and burst into laughter.

"Well you can fill in the blanks... Listen Chuck, I gotta go and check with catering, I'll catch up with you and Bill on board... *Ciao.*"

As she stepped it out Chuck couldn't help but admire that tight shapely ass... *Well I a guy can look can't he......!*

* * *

Bill was already in the Captain's seat buckled up. The two Rolls Royse Trent engines with 87 thousand pounds of thrust idling in taxi mode, the fierce whine of the jets clearly audible in the cockpit. Chuck and Norma had just arrived. Norma occupying the now redundant flight engineer's chair located behind the first officer.

"Safety harnesses on." Bill gave the order. "And that means you Sally."

"Yes captain." She gave a cheeky salute.

"Chuck, let's run through the check list."

"Doors closed.... Parking brake... Spoilers retracted... Flap position lever 5 degrees...Landing gear... Hydraulics... Transponder on.... Flight data recorder... Cock pit voice recorder............"

Bill nodded. "Everything is good to go. I'll contact the tower, I want this bird to leave on time."

"Global 10 to Tower Captain Collins requesting instructions for takeoff, departure time to Tokyo Narita 2230hrs."

"Tower to Global 10... Understand your anxiety Captain, but there are three aircraft in holding pattern due to landing congestion. You will have to bear with me and wait your turn in the queue. I'll instruct the ground crew for a 'pull push' to position Global 10 onto the taxiway ready to proceed to the takeoff gate."

"Understand tower, will await your instructions."

Bill shrugged turning to Chuck. *"So, what's new?* My guess is we will be delayed for *at least* another thirty minutes."

There was a sudden jolt then a shudder as the ground crew hooked up the 777 to the heavy steel tractor rod before driving into reverse and turning the 636,000 lbs. fully laden aircraft 180 degrees.

"Well at least we're moving." Bill commented as the aircraft finally came to a halt. The tow bar unhooked, the big bird was now positioned ready for its taxi run to the gate.

"The weather is forecast to be clear all the way across the Pacific so we might catch some shut eye tonight." Bill broke the silence.

"That would be a nice change from the last couple of flights we had." Chuck replied smiling at the thought.

"How about you Sally?" Bill asked.

"Me?... I'm just a glorified tea lady, that's always happy when her feet touch the ground."

Sally's comment brought a bout of laughter from both Bill and Chuck.

"You two..." Sally shook her head. *"And I have to put up with you jokers all the way to Japan!"*

Before Bill could reply the controller's, voice came through loud and clear.

"Global 10 proceed at speed 15mph to gate 3B then turn left and position for takeoff behind BA16."

Bill eased the throttle thrust levers gently back, the powerful Rolls Royce Trent's producing a loud whining noise as the 777 accelerated to taxi speed, the large illuminated gate sign, '3B' clearly visible in the distance, the bright taxiway lights flooded the tarmac as Bill nosed the 'lady' onto the florescent centerline.

"At last." Bill commented as he controlled the nose wheel steering slowly turning left as he reached the takeoff position behind BA16.

"Global 10 to tower, now in takeoff position."

Bill sat back twiddling his thumbs so to speak, it was now a waiting game. Takeoffs and landings are the most stressful and tonight was no different.

"I hope these Brits get their asses into gear and don't fuck around... *Oops, excuse my French Sally, I forgot we have a lady on board.*"

Sally smiled. "I've heard worse, but thanks Bill for the 'lady' compliment, I haven't had that for a while."

Chuck interjected, his inquisition laced with his usual motivation. "I'll have to speak to that boyfriend of yours." He smiled.

"With this work...! *Are you serious Chuck?* Two days between flights, who wants 'a part time lover'. It's like 'call up, ring once, then hang up the phone to let me know you made it home'. No, I need my space, at the moment I'm enjoying my own company."

Before the colorful discussion could continue, BA16's four Pratt & Whitney turbo fan jets glowed red as the most reliable passenger jet in the world, the Boeing 747 accelerated down the runway, the huge back draft shaking its smaller sibling the 777 to and fro.

"Boy, isn't that a beautiful sight?" Bill commented. "It never ceases to amaze me to watch this baby take to the sky. *Can you just imagine 147 metric tons?*"

"Global 10, you are now clear for takeoff... Proceed to ten thousand feet and go into holding pattern and wait for further instructions."

"Affirmative Tower. "Chuck, flaps to 30 and throttle lever to 30%."

Chuck eased the levers, the plane shuddering momentarily as the engines kicked in, the 777 thundering down the runway.

"Speed increasing.... 80... 100... 195... Auto throttle engaged... lift off... undercarriage up"

There was a prominent lag then a slight dip as the 777 climbed, its engines at full thrust.

"Set height to ten thousand."

"Affirmative." Chuck replied as the plane leveled out, the engines throttling back.

"Global ten your flight path is now clear you can precede to cruising height of 30 thousand, have a good flight."

'Thank you, Tower, and goodnight"

Chuck eased back the throttle leavers to reach cruising altitude while Bill entered the coordinates for the auto pilot.

"*Now,* we can relax." Bill removed his safety hardness.

"Now, what would you guys like for dinner... I have chicken........"

HONOR AMONG THIEVES

Wednesday, June 14

Okio Namura's eyes narrowed as he studied the Palestinian's mannerisms. The Yakuza had never done business with the Arab nations before but as the say 'there is always a first'.

* * *

The war on drugs by North America and Europe in conjunction with the Columbian government had taken its toll over the last decade and the demand for cocaine had fallen to less than 30%. The new 'drug craze' Ice and Base are methamphetamines and part of the amphetamine family of drugs which also includes Speed. The difference is 'Ice' is more pure and inexpensive and doesn't need 'rocket science' to produce at home. A two-liter soda bottle, several decongestant pseudoephedrine pills purchased over the counter at any Drug Store, crushed with some common household chemicals and shaken, no flame required and *'bingo'*, you have "Ice". The result, the cocaine revenue had fallen considerably to the point that the deal cut between Alberto Orlandez-Gamboa and Okio Namura was in shreds with Gamboa demanding more and more for the uncut coke shipments, forcing the Yakuza and the Kudokai Syndicate to search for new business opportunities.

* * *

Namura was typical Japanese, a Samurai in every aspect proudly following in his father's footsteps. Feared throughout the Yakuza Empire for his ruthless control over Kudokai's 103,000 members foot soldiers, inflicting terminal repercussions for breaking the Samurai code of honor and loyalty.

His narrow beady dark brown eyes with almost invisible lids blended in with his smooth yellowish complexion, void of wrinkles. The straight swept back black hair made his roundish face cold and unfriendly and when coupled with his narrow lips all that was missing was the 'Samurai Yoro Armor' and the 'Katana Sword'. Like most Japanese males at around 5-8, slim and immaculately dressed in a dark blue pin stripped suite, crisp white shirt, cufflinks, dark red tie and solid gold Rolex, looking every bit the successful executive. At fifty years of age he was hard to read and looked much younger, *maybe it's the fish diet... Whatever...* He was sharp and 'don't cross the line'.

* * *

The Palestinian brothers seemed nervous, Namura's uncanny stare was like waiting for 'Hiroshima' or maybe it was just because they had no shoes on. Then Okio suddenly sat back in his plush executive leather chair and rubbing his chin with his right hand as if coming to a conclusion.

* * *

The over indulgent office with the large glass, almost 'space age' desk, was on the 22nd floor of the famous Shin Marunouchi Building in the Shibuya business district of Tokyo opposite the Central Station. At the reception, the gold-plated signage registered 'Nippon Shipping & Logistics'. A legal entity which is a cover up for the Japanese Mafia shipping and freight business.

The office walls were adorned with various expensive block paintings depicting Japanese scenery cherry blossoms and fine rosewood furniture topped with porcelain artefacts. Okio's two mean looking bodyguards prominent in each corner, sporting bulges on the left side of their suite jackets made the Arabs even more uncomfortable.

* * *

Namura finally broke the silence, opening in perfect English.

"I have carefully thought over your plan. But the question is why come to the Yakuza with such a generous offer?"

Salibe gave an impatient sigh, this meeting was not going fast enough for his liking.

"I think we have already explained that in explicate detail without going through it all over again." Maalouf replied, a touch of both nervousness and sarcasm in his voice.

Namura's eyes flashed, this kid was either stupid or just downright rude or both, or he has more balls than a Chinese ping pong tournament!

"Japanese culture does not promote rudeness when discussing business not as the norm in Western societies or now it seems in the Eastern! Now Salibe San maybe you can satisfy my question once more?" The two bodyguards took one step forward, the message loud and clear.

"My apologies Mr. Namura and no offence intended but time is of the essence and I am sure you appreciate the stress that my brother and I are under for the freedom of our country. However, putting that aside and to answer your question… Simply your organization has the logistics that we need and with your connections in customs and the police the success of such an operation, may I stress… *that will shake the world,* can only succeed to our mutual benefit. Palestine appreciates that the 'Diet' is sympathetic to our cause."

Numara raised his hand as if to say *stop,* enough is enough of this crap, let's get down to the real business.

"Let me make this clear Salibe San, there is only one thing the Yakuza is sympathetic to and *that is US Dollars!* Now let's talk the talk……."

THE REAL DEAL

June 10, 2014

Hanna quickly cleared the debris from lunch, it had just turned one thirty and she guessed this could be a long one. She didn't mind working late but tonight she had something on and this guy was special.

"Thanks Hanna, compliments to the Deli. I'm pretty sure contrary to your thoughts, I intend to wrap up this meeting early."

Then a thought occurred to John. "*Listen Hanna,* you have been working late every night this week and if you can confirm the ticketing, I see no reason why you shouldn't take the rest of the day off."

"Thanks Mr. Thomson, *but are you sure?*"

John smiled, loyal secretaries are scarcer than hen's teeth.

"*Surer than I'll ever be.*" He replied smiling. "But I appreciate your concern. *My advice...* Take the opportunity before I change my mind!"

"The plane tickets and traveler's cheques with five hundred in hard currency are on my desk. Would you wish me to fetch them?"

Steve half shrugged raising his eyebrows glancing at Gregg as if to say *'plane tickets'!*

"No Hanna, I'm good." Thomson nodded.

"Thanks again Mr. Thomson." Hanna turned and gave a sly wink to Nelson and Jonson, as if to say 'eat your heart out guys', then one last naughty smile before she closed the door.

"Okay guys now let's cut to the chase to where I left off. Here's the scoop. Three months ago, the FBI reported that both Salibe and Maalouf boarded an Aeroflot Air Bus A310 bound for Sheremetyevo International Airport Moscow." Thomson sat back, pen in his hand, his thought process in overdrive. "And so, the plot thickens, huh?"

"

"So, what's the deal, John? The suspense is killing me." Gregg asked impatiently.

"That's the egg cracker... *Why?...* Our office in Moscow reported that the pair stayed at the five star 'Hotel Savoy' across the street from Red Square and at three hundred and fifty dollars a night! Now they either have good taste and too much money or my guess is someone big is bank rolling them. Our agents bugged their rooms but they are either smart or were tipped off from the inside, whatever... We came up with a blank."

"The inside!" Steve exclaimed referring to Thomson's comment.

"Steve, where money is concerned there are always dirty agents but I'll get to that later. Now here's the real deal. They spilt their time between the Russian Military of Defense and The Department of Aeronautics and Rocket Science."

"And we have nothing...! Phone contacts and so on...?"

"Nothing Gregg... And you may ask where are they now? The answer... *Tokyo!"*

"What!" Steve couldn't help himself.

"You heard right, *Tokyo!* They are staying at the five-star Palace Hotel in central Tokyo not far from the Ginza and the Central Station which they use daily. They are smart alright and cover their trails well but with one slip up... Their meeting with 'Nippon Shipping & Logistics' in the famous Shin Marunouchi Building in the Shibuya business district of Tokyo, a legal entity which is a cover up for the Yakuza dealing in cocaine shipments from Columbia. This we know. The head honcho of the Yakuza is none other than the ruthless Okio Namura which the Government and Police have been trying unsuccessfully to put behind bars for the last decade."

John, may I?" Steve interrupted rising to is feet.

Thomson nodded, he was looking for a break in the clouds and maybe, just maybe, Nelson could come up with something.

"Do you mind if I use the white board.?

"Go ahead."

Steve wrote Abdul Fattah. "Let's start with an audit trail to make sure we haven't missed something. It's the slimmest chance but now what have we really got... *Jack shit!"*

Steve took the marker pen. "Abud Azis." He circled the name. "What do we know about his guy... Palestinian refugee, naturalized US citizen, arrived in the US 1970... Married with two children, graduated from the University of Chicago in Economics and Statistics. Joined the US Treasury at 28 and is the senior director in the Department of controller of Currency. Roll...? Enforces the law in anti-money laundering and anti-terrorism finance laws and works closely with The Federal Reserve in the printing and the destruction of currency through BEP (Bureau of Engraving & Printing) at Fort Worth Texas and Washington DC... Interesting... Salary of $240k per year... My gut feeling is, it all starts here... I mean, can you imagine that this guy is so squeaky clean he doesn't even have a parking ticket...! In fact, he's so clean he could be on the TV ads for OMO! And *so,* upstanding in the community, he sponsors two young Palestinians on student visas and meets all their living expenses... *Can you believe it?"*

Steve circled Abud Aziz name in marker pen then about 24 inches vertically opposite circled Salibe and Maalouf connecting them with a straight line to Aziz.

"Salibe is 27 and Maalouf 26. Both on student passports with different family names. The reason given for Aziz's benevolence... Good Samaritan with humane interest in helping young Palestinians to gain a better life. But get this! Shin Bet has had these two guys on their radar for over three years as persons of interest linked to Hamas. They also confirm that although they have different names on their passports they are actually brothers. *Now why?* And it gets more interesting, Shin Bet has also confirmed that Abud Aziz is in fact *their uncle!* So why the cloak and dagger, I ask you?"

Steve arrowed headed the line at each end empathizing the connection.

"Why go to this extreme...? A cover up for some hidden terrorist plot against Israel...? But what...? But let's draw another name from the hat and circle it down below to from a triangle."

"Abdul Fattah, the number one commander of the armed wing of Hamas and on Shin Bet's most wanted list and none other than Salibe and Maalouf's father...! Israel's Mossad Secret Service and special forces the 'Sayerat Matakal' so far have unfortunately been unsuccessful in capturing or assonating Fattah and he is still on the run."

"The triangle of forces." Steve stood back then connected the circles to form a triangle.

Thomson and Gregg were studying the picture but this was something they already knew.

'*So?"* Thomson interrupted.

"I agree John but what is it they say...? *'A picture paints a thousand words'* Now let's do a listing at the side."

1. Azis ... Department of controller of Currency. "Money!"
2. Salibe and Maalouf graduate from Cornell in Aeronautics and Rocket Science. Not the everyday study stuff.
3. They successfully gained commercial pilot licenses for large jets... Another 9/11...? Doubtful but with every decision we make there is always a motive.
4. "The FBI have been active for the past year using all sorts of spy devices but have drawn a blank.
5. Before leaving the US in March the brother's apartment has a mysterious fire, police suspect arson. The apartment is complexly gutted, leaving no evidence.
6. They leave for Moscow, stay in the best five-star hotel all expenses met by the MOD and a meeting with none other than Sergi Shoigu.
7. They spilt their time between The Department of Aeronautics and Rocket Science supposedly on a training exchange. *Training for what?"*
8. "Hamas is becoming more and more desperate, their terrorist cult fueled by neighboring extremists and the supply of rockets... Rockets... *Ring a bell!*
9. Russia is desperate for foreign currency as the result of the US expanding sanctions in its support of separatists in Ukraine... *Back to money!*
10. They fly to Japan and are in Tokyo right now.
11. Our office in Tokyo confirm the brothers have had a 'so called' business meeting with 'Nippon Shipping & Logistics' a legal entity which is a cover up for the Yakuza (Japanese Mafia) dealing in cocaine shipments from Columbia and a meeting with none other than the 'god father' himself 'Okio Namura'. *Logistics....!* but shipping what? *Back to money!*

"It all ties up John, from Azis in the Department of Controller of Currency, the commercial pilot's licenses then from 'Russia with love' then the Japanese Mafia for illegal logistics... And all about money 'the root of all evil. But where is the money coming from? And that's what we've got to find out. This is bigger than big. The bottom line... There's going to be a major terrorist attack by Hamas on Israel using the latest Russian weaponry. It's well publicized through the UN council that Russia is sympathetic to the Palestine cause but nothing is free. So, we must find the 'source of the Nile'. John, any suggestion as to where we start?"

Thomson smiled, the best was yet to come.

"Steve, you got that right, as you are both flying to Tokyo tomorrow. Hanna has already confirmed your flight reservations and I've informed Daniels at our Tokyo office you will be taking over the case... Nice job Steve but the party's over, I want to go home and for a change have an early diner with my 'desperate housewife'. The travel package is on Hanna's desk accompanied with a clearance letter from the Japanese Embassy to allow you to carry firearms. Now gentleman if you don't mind? *Oh!* And by the way, *good luck......*"

* * *

Namura's penetrating eyes were creepy making the Palestinians decidedly uncomfortable but beggars can't be choosers and the Yakuza had all the cards and for Salibe and Maalouf options were not on the table. The silence deafening, the Japanese 'Kamikaze' business technique was win or die and Namura finally broke the silence.

"Salibe San, let's walk through the deal once more. "Forty percent to the Yakuza, forty percent the Russia and twenty percent to Hamas. Is that correct?"

"Yes, Namura San" Salibe replied, anxiety in his tone. The notoriety of the Yakuza fresh in his mind. "Need I stress that this will be the biggest heist in world history of which the Yakuza will receive an unbelievable forty billion US Dollars in hard currency for services rendered."

Namura was not impressed, or at least he wasn't showing it!

"And the Russians?" Okio asked abruptly.

"They will receive the same but only when they deliver the goods."

"And the serial numbers on the notes?"

"That has been attended to by my uncle who is the senior director in the 'Department of Controller of Currency'. The file will be completely erased and once the money has gone back into circulation throughout the world markets, it will be almost impossible to trace."

"Hmmmm..." Namura was pondering, leaving no stone unturned, his eyes giving nothing away.

"And Hamas's twenty billion?" Okio asked.

"Again, that's where we need your help. Hamas has several bank accounts in various tax havens, of course under different company names and as part of the deal we need your company to TT the funds throughout your various channels."

"Do you trust the Yakuza?" Okio's eyes narrowed.

"Samurais are men of honor."

Okio nodded his approval but time is money and this guy was no dummy.

He pouched his mouth. "Moving billions of US dollars is difficult and the stakes are high and expensive, nothing is free. This *can* be done *but* at a cost!"

Salibe was taken aback by Okio's inference but in hindsight he might have known "money can't buy you love".

"The bottom line, another ten billion." Okio sat back in his chair his cold stare peering directly into Salibe's eyes.

Anbar turned to Fadile searching for a reaction. Then Fadile said something in Arabic.

"Elees dyna anahera." (we have no option) Fadel's expression betraying his anger.

"We accept." Anbar replied offering his hand.

"Domo arigato." Okio finally cracked a smile.

"And the security guards?" Salibe asked.

"Leave that to us..."

THE CARGO

Wednesday, June 11

"Flaps down 30, break flaps up, reduce speed. Global 10 to tower, commencing approach, request clearance to land."

"Tower to Global 10 you have clearance to land on runway 2 check your GPS. Then turn right and taxi to cargo bay 6."

"Global ten to tower will proceed as per your instructions... Chuck, switch to automatic landing."

The big bird touched the runway with a screech as the right undercarriage puffed smoking rubber then leveled out with a shudder as the ABS brakes took control and Bill quickly switched the throttle levers to reverse thrust, the scream of the Rolls Royce Trent's shuddering the big 777, with a deafening roar. Then suddenly quietness as Bill engaged taxi mode.

"Flaps up, break flaps down."

Landings are always dangerous and Bill gave a smile followed by a sigh of relief before glancing at the time on the cockpit dials.

"Fifteen minutes ahead of schedule,

"It's now 1415hrs and we should clear customs in Narita by 1500hrs, if all goes well."

"I'll leave the paperwork and clearance to you Captain." Chuck was still smarting from his previous dressing down and it rang through in the tone of his voice. "I'm heading for the staff lounge for some refreshments... Sally?"

"No Chuck I have to clear catering, I'll be around half an hour. Which hotel are we staying." She turned to Bill.

"The Grand Hayat in the Roppongi district, about 20 minutes from Ginza. That should please *you* Nancy."

She smiled. *"Shopping?* Yeah if I have the time."

Shop till you drop, huh?"

"Something like that."

"You women...! Chuck, a word before you leave... Easy on the booze."

Chuck just shook his head and left for the aerobridge. The less said the better.......

* * *

"Hi Mitsuko, is Jim free?"

"I'll give him a call Bill." The pretty Japanese secretary lifted the secretarial phone speaking in perfect English but with a pronounced accent. "Jim, I have Captain Collins here... *Hmmm*... I'll send him in... He's free Bill." She smiled.

"Thanks Mitsuko." Bilk knocked on McGill's door.

"Come in Bill."

McGill rose to his feet to meet him grasping his hand in a warm crunch.

"Welcome to Tokyo." McGill sat back in his chair. "Take the load off." He pointed to the empty seat in front of his desk. "A good flight?"

Bill grinned. "No dramas Jim, if that's what you mean......?"

* * *

McGill at 54 had done well having bagged the lucrative overseas posting under fierce competition. Vice President Global Freight stationed in Tokyo was no mean task but the perquisites were second to none. House, shofar driven car, servants and overseas salary allowances and free travel, it just doesn't get any better.

A stalky character at only 5,10 somehow, he didn't fit the part but he was better than the best at his job and in Global, that's the bottom line. His shock of black waved hair showing no signs of grey and the olive complexion and dark brown eyes gave him a sort of an Italian look or another Antonio Banderas, the drums spooking that his father was Italian and mother third generation English, a fiery mixture. A 'New Yorker', his accent had a mixture of the Bronx and Brooklyn and sometimes in his adrenaline rush he was difficult to understand. Unmarried and highly sought after by the beautiful Japanese socialites, unfortunately Twas a lost cause. Having come out of the closet years earlier, young muscular males were more to is his taste buds. The world has changed forever.......

* * *

"And Chuck?"

"What's new!" Bill gave that look.

"And Morgan?"

"Dan's still the same, a workaholic."

"I like Dan, he's a really nice guy, but getting down to business and more to the point, your return flight......."

* * *

Julie turned the Yale and opened the apartment door, Marge by her side shouldering the airline garment bags. It had just turned nine in the morning and to say they were bushed after the night flight from London, would be an understatement! Delta L15 didn't have a seat to spare and that spelled trouble for the cabin crew.

As the door closed Julie kicked off her heels trying to balance on one foot to massage her tired extremity before finally giving in and crashing down heavily on the sofa followed by a burst of laughter. Marge joining in, laughter can be contagious and she flopped down happily beside her friend.

"Home sweet home, huh?" Marge commented between inhales.

"Yeah, and no overzealous Casanovas to put up with!" Julie burst into laughter again, Marge was already in her bare feet making herself comfortable in her new abode.

"A sofa, two leather recliners and a 55inch flat screen on the floor, it's not much to look at but it's a start. Look at it this way Marge." Julie turned to face her friend. "Here's the kicker... Two bedrooms with double beds and all to ourselves and *boy* am I looking forward that. We have three days R&R and that means three shopping days, a nice coffee table a TV consul..."

"Whoa...whoa." Marge dropped the anchor. "Your way ahead of me Julie and my AmEx card *is also way ahead of me!"*

"Don't worry Marge, it's only money, remember the song... *Don't worry be happy."* Julie broke into the lyric her 'tin ear' out of kilt making Marge laugh then duet in the Karaoke. "In every life, we have some trouble and when you worry you make it double'... *Ha ... Ha... Ha..."*

Julie had already stepped out of her skirt and blouse standing unashamedly in her 'G' string and half cupped bra.

"Too bad honey I'm first into the shower."

"Rat!" Marge retaliated. "But you forgot on thing ... *the water heater."*

In her overzealousness, Julie disappeared into the bathroom unaware of her pending 'shock wave'.

Marge had that mischievous grin on her face as she picked up her bag and walked down the hallway to her bedroom but not before switching on the water heater as she passed. The highly glazed white ceramic tiles soothing her naked feet in the early morning LA temperature. Julie had made up the beds before they flew out on Monday and Marge slipped out of her Delta jacket before sitting down heavily on the bed and swinging her feet from the floor, the sandman could easily chase her but after that flight the body odor was over the top and the thought of that invigorating shower was adrenalizing. She punched the pillow resting her head in the hollow then gave a relaxing sigh as she stared blankly at the white ceiling, the curtains open, the morning sun blanketing the room as the AC kicked in.

"I gotta admit Julie has something and the split from that loser Chuck, has lots of Merit." She was speaking under her breath. "But there again" Her eyes slightly tearing. The yell from the shower box as Julie took the full force of the icy water, couldn't have come at better time, from depression to laughter, there's no better antidote.

Julie suddenly appeared, her hair wrapped in a turban, a large white bath towel wrapped tightly around her shapely figure tucked in just above those tantalizing breasts.

"I don't know where the hell I put my bathrobe. *And that Alaskan shower...!*"

"I tried to tell you but you didn't listen." Marge just couldn't let it go, the thought creasing a smile.

"Well aren't *you* showering? Julie ignored the cheap shot.

"What do *you* think?" Marge threw her feet to the floor.

"Listen, I managed to stash a couple of bottles of chardonnay in the fridge before I finally did the bunk and they are just waiting for two beautiful ladies to share their pleasure."

"Sounds familiar." Marge laughed. "And on that note, I'm outta here... Say, where are the towels?"

"In the linen cupboard in the hallway. I'll put a couple of glasses in the ice box so get your ass outta here."

"Is this breakfast?'

"Is there any better?" Julie laughed as she disappeared toward the kitchen purposely moving her sexy ass from side to side. She was a card but a better friend you couldn't find.

Marge didn't hang around her clothes now in a bundle around her ankles and for a moment she stared at her naked body in the robe mirror. Her lightly tanned smooth skin gave her 34, 24, 36, hourglass figure the kind a woman dreams of, but there again, women are never happy and Marge placed her hands under each breast cupping them upwards in the process emphasizing her pink nipples.

"A bit saggy... *Bloody gravity!* Nothing a good bra wouldn't fix, huh?"

"Marge, what the hell is keeping you?"

"Gimme ten........"

* * *

McGill paused then seemed to get his faculties together for a big announcement... *but what?*

"*So...?*" Bill asked impatiently, the mystery eating him.

"*Ahhmm.* "McGill cleared his throat. What was this, *the President's speech?*

"Bill, this is a flight like never."

"Are you serious?" Bill raised his eyebrows.

"*As serious as it gets!* You depart on Global 10 from Narita tomorrow evening at 2230 hours bound for Washington DC. The cargo.... 100 billion US dollars in mixed denominations, past their 'use by date' for destruction at The Federal Reserve Washington DC. As far as I'm informed the Diet have already received a promissory note for the replacement of the currency. How they receive it, that's for another day and someone else's headache... The pay lo ad? Maximum 102 metric tons. You'll have no slack, so unless you wanna go back to the simulator you had better fly that bird like the planes going down. Do you get my drift?"

"Couldn't be clearer Jim, but boy is this a springer! *Security...?*"

"Every man and his dog will be there to protect this cargo ... Armored security trucks... Japanese SWAT, you name it, and more to the point, four armed guards will accompany you all the way 'State Side'. *Secrecy...?* You had better make sure you don't speak in your sleep... As for Chuck and the stewardess... What's her name?"

"Sally Jenkins."

"Eh, Sally... They're in the same boat. How you avoid the questions, that's your call... So, if there's nothing else Bill, I suggest you call it a night and rest up and make sure you arrive at the airport no later than 1800 hrs. tomorrow evening. Contact me whenever you and the crew arrive......"

* * *

Julie and Marge were both slouched on the sofa still in bath towel attire.

"I got to hand it to you Julie, you got style." Marge took another sip of the chilled Chardonnay. "If this is breakfast, keep it coming."

Julie's cell suddenly sprung to life.

"Now who the hell can this be?" She placed her glass on the tiled floor searching for the Samsung. *"Where the hell did I put that bloody phone?"*

Marge laughed" In your handbag."

"I know, but more to the point, *where the hell have I put my handbag!*"

"Must be the chardonnay, huh?" Marge was still laughing.

Julie rose to her feet, hands on her hips trying to 'GPS' the sound, so to speak.

"Got it! It's below my garment bag." She hurriedly opened the culprit and searched for the elusive cell. *"Missed it! Damn."* She gave that look.

Samsung's familiar text buzz broke the anxiety and Julie studied it for a moment before turning to her friend.

"Well?"

"It's from head office requesting me to phone Draper urgently."

"So, *what are you waiting for?*"

"Draper here... *Julie* thanks for returning my call... Yeah, something urgent has come up... The chief purser and senior stewardess for Business Class on Delta 14 for Tokyo tomorrow evening have both reported in sick, so I'm in a hole... Yeah, *you got that right...!* I know it's short notice and I appreciate you have just touched down from the London flight... Sure, take a few minutes to think about it..." Draper couldn't help laughing at Julie's remark ... "Yeah, I know I'm generous but listen talking about generous, I'm willing to pay double time... I thought that would awaken the dead...! Done deal...? How about Marge? *She's right beside you...!* Sure... She's given the nod... I'll text you the details.... Thanks ladies, I owe you one......."

* * *

"And the Russians?" Okio asked, with an icy stare

Salibe looked considerably uncomfortable. The question was begging and Anbar sort of paused for a second to compile his best English and more importantly, *his best salesmanship!*

"Ahhmmmm...." He cleared his throat. "The Russians have agreed to deliver the goods by submarine once I contact them that operation 'Fish Tail'

has been successful... You can change the password as you please." It was a throwaway line.

"Small matter, get to the point." Okio didn't mince his words.

"It means that the Yakuza must provide the Russian submarine Captain with the coordinates for the 'drop off', for security purposes, once he is seaborne."

Okio pondered, staring directly into Salibe's eyes. His expression cold and calculating. He was not impressed.

"Yakuza never give location of operations."

Salibe's mouth dropped, he hadn't anticipated Okio's reaction to what he had overlooked as a small point. After all the almighty dollar was like according to Okio, *'Allah'*.

"With respect Okio San, *do you have a better suggestion?*" Salibe half sneered.

Numero's eyes flashed, Salibe had crossed the line with his latest insult and the little yellow man reacted like 'too much Wasabi on his sushi'.

"Do not like tone of voice, English 'say beggars not choosers. Close door when you leave, Dozo."

Salibe's brother had had this guy it up to his gills. *'Like who the hell does this jumped-up midget think he is talking to...?* And he impulsively rose to his feet in a threatening manner, his brother grabbing his jacket to restrain him, the veins on his temple bulging.

The two heavies stepped forward their right hands like lightening inside their jackets, on the pistol grips of their Nambu 8mm semi-automatics.

(Speaking in Arabic)

"Don't be a fool Anbar, your hot temper will get us a ticket to the morgue. Sit down and apologies. We need Nihon-Jin for operation 'Fish Tail' ... *Now sit down...Do you hear me... Sit down!*"

Fadil grabbed his brother's hand tearing it away from his jacket. The look in his eyes could kill. Then mind over matter prevailed and he slowly took to his seat.

Numero raised his hand and the two miniature Sumas bowed and stepped back, the standoff temporarily over.

Okio stared Fadil out then turned to Salibe, who being the older brother had more sense.

"This is not suggestion... Coordinates will be given to Russian Submariner Captain once at sea, but only if operation... Eh, 'Fish Tail' is successful. The transfer of cargos from Nihon submarine and Russian submarine will take place somewhere in Pacific Ocean only known to Yakuza. This is nonnegotiable. *Do I make myself clear?*"

Okio sat back waiting for the reaction which never came. It was a 'fait accompli' by any other name.

"*Good...* Now security... Beards will have to go..."

Fadil turned to his brother taken aback, he hadn't expected this twist.

Anbar shrugged and looked his brother in the eyes. Whatever it takes there was no turning back.

"Can I be so rude to ask why?"

"American security guards, clean shaven..."

Salibe pouted his lips in disinclination but what was the alternative? They were on thin ice as it was.

"Now more importantly let's talk plan. Tomorrow at 4.00 pm sharp, Cliff Arakida." He pointed to one of the heavies. "And Kazuo Tahoka." The other henchman bowed. "Will call you from the front desk of your hotel... Memorize faces... Request late check out but settle bill early. Pay by cash and retrieve and destroy copy of credit card receipt. Discard all personal items such as unnecessary clothing keeping only what you are standing in, then meticulously ensure no fingerprints... *Clear so far?*

Fadil nodded.

"Four security guards will accompany the cargo... My men Arakida and Tahoka will have credentials of that of the Kovan Chousacho, 'The Public Security Intelligence Agency', with license to kill, the equivalent of the MI5 or the American FBI."

"And where do we come in?" Salibe interrupted, this deal was moving too fast and without any impute from the Palestinians.

"*Please.*" Numero raised his hand as if to say, *'don't interrupt!'*

"You will be provided with security uniforms and name tags for Black Hawk Securities, a private security company employed by the US Military both in Iraq and Afghanistan, and may I say not without some controversy. Our computer specialists will hack into the FBI files to enter your backgrounds... Two tours of duty in Afghanistan with the US Marines. When demobilized, you contracted into Black Hawk as security officers. Your parents immigrated from Cicely to the US after the second world war and as brothers you both enlisted in the Marines to proudly serve your adopted country. Why Cicely you may ask...? *Simple...* You have Mediterranean complexions.... Your Black Hawk papers and name tags will show you Salibe, as Jovani Quario and you Fadil, Mario Quario. Suggestion... Memorize your new names and practice American accent... My men will escort you to Narita to change clothes and blend in with the other security personnel to await further instructions... Of course, you will be supplied with firearms...The cargo will arrive in eight armored cars for transfer to the aircraft commencing at 1800hrs. Now I suggest you return to your hotel and contact no one and prepare yourself both mentally and physically for tomorrow. There can be no screw ups. Now gentleman, at the thought of being rude, I have other pending matters."

Numero rose to his feet ignoring Salibe's hand, the proof of the pudding is in the eating and he pointed to the open door, Arakida holding it ajar.

What will tomorrow bring? *Only on the day......*

* * *

Numero had that troubled look on his face, he didn't trust the Arabs and even more so, the *Russians!* There were too many 'chefs in the kitchen' so to speak and when that's the case things go wrong. He was his own man and the 'Taipan' as they say in Mandarin, but the rewards were overpowering and the opportunity for the biggest heist in history, ego breaking. Numero sat back staring blankly for a moment, his mind racing in all directions but he had to pull his thoughts together and his first priority... *Shimaru Shima!*

Okio motioned to his two bodyguards to leave. They bowed obediently then left the room. He had to make an urgent call but first things first, his mouth parched, after too much talk and he lifted the secretarial phone.

(Speaking in Japanese)

"Ayako, can I trouble you for green tea? *Oh...!* And inform Arakida and Tahoka to fetch my car, I will be leaving within the hour, Domo."

"Certainly, Namura San... Please give me a few minutes."

Ten minutes had passed and Okio was becoming more than impatient drumming his fingers on his desk, he always relaxed better over his favorite tea and he was about to lift the phone once more when he was abruptly stopped with a gentle knock on the door.

"Enter."

Ayako raised her eyebrows whilst opening the door with one hand and balancing the tray with the colorful porcelain teapot and cup in the other.

She knew by the tone in her bosses' voice he was not in the best of moods. *Secretaries spend more time with their boss's than their husbands...!*

Okio, a man of few words pointed to the free space on his desk.

Ayako gingerly placed the tray on the 'vacant lot' and poured a cup of the green brew.

"Will that be all, Numero San?"

Okio looked up staring blankly for a moment making Ayako uneasy.

"Ahhh... Hmmm." His thoughts finally unscrambled. "Yes, thank you. Please ensure that I am not disturbed."

Ayako bowed in silence, a mark of respect in the Japanese culture, taking two steps back before turning to leave.

Okio took a sip of his precious tea but what red blooded Japanese man could avoid admiring this shapely beauty as she elegantly departed, her steps restricted by her knee length pencil skirt......

* * *

Ayako had served her boss obediently for the last five years. Efficient secretaries are rare in the Japanese business fraternity and she ticked all the boxes. Around thirty and unmarried, was not unusual for a professional graduate. Most Japanese middle-class women are married in their early twenties and are 'stay at home' mothers while their husbands spend late hours in Karaoke bars or 'Supper Clubs' for 'so called' R&R.

Ayako's hour glass figure pronounced her simple dark blue light weight suite. The waist length three quarter sleeved open jacket, the pencil skirt and modest dark blue heals cocktailed together with her white open necked silk blouse and fine gold neck chain, pushed the envelope. An irresistible Asian beauty to say the least with that highly sought after milky complexion. Asian woman purposely avoids the sun to achieve ageless, blemish less facials, like that of the famous Geisha, *but without the makeup!* Her straight jet-black hair swept tightly back on either side into a rear cox comb gave her an heir of elegance and as for those dark brown olive eyes and narrow face line and pink lips... *Say no more!*

Bosses and secretarial affairs are a recipe for disaster and Okio was no fool, besides the Yakuza owned 80% of the supper clubs in Japan and his recreational bed was never empty......

* * *

Okio took another refill of his precious green tea then sat back for a moment in solace. He had to make an urgent call to Shimaru Shima and his number one-man Kenichi Shendo. Cell phones can be traced and he unlocked the desk drawer to his right to extract the rather cumbersome antique HF Motorola radio phone. Then he checked the frequency numbers from a secret note pasted to the inside of the drawer and began to tune in the dial......

* * *

HF two-way radios are used by airplanes and ships at sea as well as all branches of the military services and in remote locations where there are no cellphone services. Digital messages from computer to computer can also be sent and all without internet or telephone lines, *the perfect communication tool for the Yakuza.......*

* * *

Okio tuned in to the 80m band, when late afternoon atmospheric noises are at their lowest. There was a crackling noise then a temporary whistle before a voice echoed as clear as crystal breaking his impatience.

(Speaking in Japanese)

"Good evening, Namura San."
"Cut the formalities Shendo, *you know why I am phoning.* Time is not on our side and operation 'Fish Tail' takes place at 2200hrs tomorrow evening."
"Fish Tail...?"
"A code name requested by the Palestinians to be used as a password from now on for any further communications. Now, back to business... *The runway!"*
"My men have been working 24/7 but the monsoon season has caused many delays due to flooding."
"Shendo I'll say it for the las time... *Get to the fucking point!"*
"My apologies, Namura San."
"Cut the apologies shit, *time is money.* Now, the good news or the bad news?"
"We have installed monsoon drains at each side of the runway coupled with heavy duty pumps to disperse the rainwater overflow from the camber and they are working satisfactorily. As each section of the extended runway was completed we also used heavy waterproof tarpaulins to keep it dry and

allow the new tarmac to cure. The good news is the weather is forecast to be dry tonight and for the next forty-eight hours..."

"I don't want a fucking weather report... *Just tell me!*"

"The bad news...?"

"It can't get any fucking worse... *I'm waiting...*"

"A Boing 777 requires a landing runway of 8,100ft with a maximum payload of 120 metric tons. This we have no problem with but the takeoff is much more serious requiring 11, 200ft and the bad news is we are short by 300ft. The bottom line.... *We have just run out of land!* The only savior would be that the cargo hold is empty on the return flight reducing the takeoff distance."

"Never mind the takeoff, let's get this fucking plane on the ground first!"
"And plan 2?"

"What the hell are you talking about, *plan 2?* Just make plan 1 work.... Now, is there anything else you haven't told me?"

"Yes... And this is critically important... The pilot must be a veteran with maximum flying hours on commercial jets as he must land the jetliner manually without the aid of the auto pilot. My men have painted a large florescent six-meter line at the start of the runway as a safety precaution and the pilot must touch down exactly on that line to avoid the possibility of an overrun."

"Hmmm..." Numara frowned, he hadn't expected this. "Don't worry leave that problem to me... Just make sure from your side that there are no fuck ups!"

"Namura San, my men are working all through the night...."

Namura cut the call without another word placing the phone back into the locked drawer. The supper club might be a good diversion. Beautiful hostesses and his favorite Scotch, a better combination you can't find. He lifted the secretarial phone.

"Ayako......."

* * *

"Well, that's about it!"

Sally did a last-minute check then signed the manifest for the galley inventory. The remaining untouched food would unfortunately be destroyed as there are strict rules in Japan regarding international inbound flights when it comes to food of any description.

"Thanks Sally, I guess it's the staff lounge now for a well-deserved coffee?"

"Something like that." Sally smiled.

Japanese airport staff are always friendly and polite, something The United States could take leaf from.

"When are you flying out again?" Sakura asked her warm smile intoxicating.

Sally returned the compliment. "Twenty-two hundred tomorrow evening."

"Where to this time?" Sakura asked, her normal conversational piece.

"Would you believe it... 'Dulles International, 'Washington DC!"

"Is that bad?" Sakura gave a puzzled look

"When you live in LA, it is!"

"Now I get it." Sakura smiled again. "Nice to see you again Sally. I'll not be on tomorrow evening but have safe flight..."

Sally flashed the 'plastic' at the security desk then entered the staff lounge, she was looking forward to that coffee. It had been a long boring flight, hopefully her transfer request to passenger aircraft would come sooner rather than later.

"Chuck, *are you still here?'* Sally was surprised, or was she? She poured herself a Latte from the machine then took the seat next to him.

"I've been waiting for Bill to appear but he seems to be stuck in some cloak and dagger meeting with McGill, must be something serious to take this long?"

"Whatever." Sally shrugged then took a sip of her coffee. "But if you want my advice Chuck, *for what it's worth,* go easy on the booze, you're on the line already."

Chuck held up his glass and swallowed the last of his Scotch in childish defiance.

"No, *I don't want your advice, Sally.* It seems everyone wants to be my mother these days."

"There's nothing wrong with a mother's advice." Sally retaliated, with a half-smile.

"Now... If my mother had your looks..."

"Don't get any ideas Chuck, I'm spoken for."

"So, who's the lucky guy?"

Sally shook her head... *I mean this guy...?*

"Chuck I'd tell you to go and take a hike but I'm too much of a lady."

"Heh... heh... heh." Chuck had to laugh. He liked Sally but then what woman didn't he like?

"And how about you and... *What's her name?*"

"Marge... Déjà vu."

"I guess I deserved that."

"Well, I don't know about you Sally, but I'm going to have a refill."

"Chuck I'm bushed so I'll leave you to drink the bar dry, it seems my advice has fallen on deaf ears. Listen, do me favor. When Bill arrives tell him we'll meet up at the Teppanyaki restaurant in the hotel" Sally glanced at her watch then thought for a second. "Say... Around eight."

"Does that include me?'

"Your inconceivable. *What do you think?*"

Chuck sighed then placed his empty glass on the coffee table, he was getting nowhere.

"Say why don't I leave with you, it looks like Bill is still tied up?"

"I'm catching the airport bus to the central station then a taxi from there to the Hyatt."

"I have a better idea." Chuck just wouldn't take no. "We share a taxi, it's much cozier." He had that evil grin.

"Sorry big boy, I'll take a rain check on that one." Sally rose to her feet. "Eight then... Ciao..."

Bill just shrugged, the 'big elbow' was nothing new.

"Oh, what the hell! I might as well have another refill......."

THE ḤEIST.

Thursday, June 12

"That's a turn for the book. Who would have thought we would be flying to Tokyo tomorrow?" Steve was studying his flight itinerary leaning back in his chair, his feet on his desk. he smiled. "I got to hand it to Hanna she does a nice job."

"And I got to a hand it to *you* Steve, you bundled that summary like a pro... Thomson was impressed."

"But Gregg, what do you think?"

"For me, I think you're on the money."

"Well I guess one way or another we'll soon find out. Now let me see... Delta 14, Business Class, departing Dulles international at 0800 hrs. Wednesday June 11, arriving Narita Thursday June 12, 2150hrs. Staying at the Tokyo Sheraton. Boy, that's a long flight considering the time difference."

Gregg shook his head. *"And a Godforsaken early one too!"*

"Life was never meant to be easy, partner." Steve laughed again. "Say," Steve glanced at his watch. 'Would you believe the time! Why don't we get our asses outta here and catch a bar snack at the 'Lord Nelson', on Delaney?"

"That English pub...! Maaan... Warm beer and roast beef, mash and steak pie?"

"Yeah, but it's the 'in' thing, *and as for these office chicks...*"

Gregg burst into laughter. "Say no more. Let's hit the road Jack."

"Now you're talking. We'll need to take two cars so I'll meet you there......"

* * *

The Chardonnay defeated and another bottle well on the way to the graveyard the girls were in a more than happy in a celebrating mood, reminiscing about the good times and the hilarious incidents during their 'down and out' spell in New York.

Julie held the light green bottle to the light.

"Enough for one more and the bar's dry."

"Bring it on honey." Marge raised her empty glass in anticipation. She was on a high.

"And do you remember that...?" Marge was suddenly cut short with the familiar whistle from Julie's Samsung.

"That must be a text message from Draper with our flight itinerary. Gimme a sec Marge. Yeah, it's from Draper alright... *Why that!* This guy has gotta be kiddin me... *That shyster has pulled a fast one on us Marge!*"

"Why the drama Julie, it can't be all that bad!" Marge half grinned, well over the DUI limit.

"*Worse...!* Would you believe that 'con man' avoided telling me that we would be flying out of Dulles International Airport, *Washington DC!*"

"*Your shittin me!* That means we have to take a domestic from Lax to catch the connecting flight to Tokyo."

Julie promptly redialed, her expression like thunder. "Just as I thought the bastard's cut and run and is purposely not answering my call."

Marge shrugged the lost cause. "So, what's the bottom line?"

"We get the 6am shuttle from Lax to catch the connecting flight to Tokyo, departing 0800hrs... *I can't believe this shit.*" Julie was shaking her head still bitching. This was a kicker she hadn't expected.

"Let's face it Julie, we're stuck with it and worse still...*We've just run out of Chardonnay......*"

* * *

Bill walked briskly to the airport exit and taxi stance anxious to get to his hotel. A cab fare was the most time saving rather than the most economical, but for a 55-minute journey at 720yen, was over the top.

"*Awe what the Hell!*" Bill spoke himself." It's on Global's tab."

McGill still fresh in his mind, coming at him like an 'Ian Fleming' thriller.

"I still don't' fucking believe it!" Bill muttered under his breath. "Two hundred billion, McGill's' gotta be shittin me. In fact, if it wasn't so serious it would be fucking hilarious. Awe... *No!*" He quickly stepped back. "Pissing rain... *That's all I fucking need!*"

June in Japan, especially Tokyo, is the start of the six-week rainy season with muggy temperatures from 66 to 86 degrees Fahrenheit and when it rains, *it rains!*

The overzealous taxi attendant in his immaculate white shirt with the yellow arm band, black slacks peaked cap and highly polished shoes rushed toward Bill inflating an oversize umbrella.

"Taxi Captain." He asked in English with a strong accent.

"Yes." Bill replied.

The small man raised his white gloved hand to attract the first cab on the rank.

All Japanese cabs are highly polished black 'Toyota Crowns' with white starched linen seat covers and a peaked capped driver to match complete with white gloves. Homogeneity is the Japanese culture, *maybe that why they lost the war!*

"Where to Captain?"

"The Grand Hyatt Roppongi......"

* * *

Bill slipped into the rear seat of the cab, its white starched seat covers for some reason felt different and the 20 degrees' temperature, a pleasant relief from the muggy humidity of the rainy evening. The driver in his immaculate white shirt, cap and gloves, was silent, being understandable as only 12% of the population can speak fluent English. At last it was time for relaxation and Bill pulled down the center arm rest and settled in for the fifty-five-minute ride to Roppongi. As he stared out the window at the night traffic on the Kanto Highway and the distant lights of Tokyo and its famous tower he couldn't help but admire the astounding progress this small island had made from the ruins of the Second World War. It's infrastructure, bullet trains automobiles and electronics the envy of the world, but unlike most other industrial nations their culture is paramount and Geishas and colorful Kimonos are still a regular sight in most cities.

Tokyo with its eight million population is one of the most popular tourist destinations from western countries, with the magnetic Ginza in central Tokyo featuring major department stores and the famous San Al building on the Ginza 4-Chome Intersection. Ginza in Japanese means 'Silver Mint' historically related to the 'coin mint' in the 1600's and 1700's, but what would Tokyo be without the famous Akihabara district in Chiyoda, nick named 'Akihabara Electric Town' shortly after World War II, being the major shopping center for household and electronic goods.

The constant road drum of the taxi almost made Bill close his eyes but he couldn't help but reminisce over Julie. Should he phone her? He shook his head, maybe it was best he closed his eyes.......

* * *

The Roppongi Grand Hyatt Tokyo, is up there with the top five in the Hyatt Intracontinental Chain. Asian hotels have class when comparing their European or American counterparts. First impressions are the most important to the tourists, especially at the higher end of the continuum and the grandeur of the Roppongi reception was unparalleled, its mirrored marble floor a quarter the size of an NFL football pitch! In the center standing majestically on a single pillared base with a superlative floral display was another marble rectangular stand on a large Indian hand knotted rug in stunning colors of red blue and green. To the right were four large grey concrete pillars about a meter in diameter, stretching all the way to the top of the 40ft ceiling. At the base of each pillar stood four black ceramic highly glazed pots shaped like an inverted cone containing synthetic cherry blossom trees sparkling with red LED lights. The reception desk was spectacular in highly lacquered Cypress wood from the famous Kiso Honokaa district. The six-meter barrel shaped half circled reception desk with its white glass illuminated top and broad stainless-steel edging complimented the backdrop soft lighting, adding to the ambience of the yellow wall was a painting of a beautiful kimono in gold lacquer, a 'Rembrandt' by any other name......

* * *

Bill had finally arrived at the 'check in desk'
"Checking in sir?" The pretty young receptionist enquired, her warm smile encapsulating.
"Captain Collins...! It's alright Akira, I'll take care of the Captain."
It was Derek Bronson the General Manager, an expat from Milwaukee.

* * *

Bronson was typical Americana, 5'9, over weight by twenty pounds which accentuated his short round stature, most likely as the result of over indulgence at the buffet bar. His pinkish fresh face and pale blue eyes put him in his early thirties but the seriously thinning blonde hair was collateral damage. The Hyatt smile was part of the job and he used it well to his advantage. The hotel grapevine ran a number that Bronson joined the chain as a bell hop but in this day and age someone must be in 'clown college'. Never the less he seemed a nice guy with a difficult job. And keeping hotel guests happy... Well... *It's worse than a tour of duty in Afghanistan…....!*

* * *

"It's good to see you again Captain."

"Likewise, Derek."

"How long this time Captain?"

"Eh, Bill."

"Bill." Derek smiled.

"Overnight, and Derek I'll require a late check out."

"A good flight?"

"No dramas just routine." Bill was becoming a bit impatient. The last thing he needed after a long flight was a talkative hotel manager.

"Bill, I'll need a copy of your credit card."

"No sweat." Bill placed the plastic.

"That's... Room 462." Derek handed Bill the security key card then snapped his fingers. "Maître d, Captain Collin's bag."

"There's no need Derek I only have a garment bag. *Oh*... Are there any messages for me?"

"Give me a second. Akira, messages for Captain Collins?"

"Yes, Bronson San... Stevens San and Miss Jenkins will meet you at the hotel's Teppanyaki Restaurant at 8pm."

"Arigato." Bill replied with one of the five Japanese words he knew whilst glancing at his watch. *"Hmmm... It's just turned seven so I had better hit the skids... Thanks Derek."*

"If you need anything Bill, don't hesitate."

"I might just take you up on that." Bill laughed turning to leave.

"My pleasure, Captain... *Eh,* Bill......"

* * *

Steve kerbed down Delaney. Parking in down town Washington is a nightmare waiting to happen and would you believe it, *even on a Thursday!* Horn blasts from the tailgating traffic sending a message to the nonchalant Steve who just shrugged it off, like 'King of the Road'.

"At last." He spoke out loud spotting the reversing lights of a black BMW and quickly double parked to nail the space, his voice drowned by car horns. *"So, what!"* He shrugged finally slipping into the vacated slot. "Christ, I don't envy Gregg's chances." He spoke out loud again. "No sweat, I'll give him a call when I hit the bar…..."

* * *

As he stepped it out, Steve could clearly see the pub about two hundred yards down the street. *I mean,* who could miss the large colorful rectangular neon sign swaying in the evening breeze, dangling on two rings on a black ornamental wrought iron bracket right angled to the facade. The picture of the famous English naval officer in his blue 'Trafalgar' tunic, medals and yellow sash complete with Bicorned hat and silk fanned plume, in a heavy ornate picture frame, a work of art. It's large bold lettering, 'The Lord Nelson' underpinned at the bottom with the words 'Free House'.

The façade was a leaf from Las Vegas, its white Tudor inserts to the black counterfeit beams and what would an English pub be without the heavy oak door? On either side were two stand out colorful leadlight windows depicting a picture of Nelson's flag ship 'HMS Victory' a one hundred and four-gun first rate ship of the line launched in 1765.The oldest commissioned warship in the world now in dry dock in Portsmouth and still manned today by officers of the Royal Navy.

Over the period 1794 to 1805 under Nelson's leadership, the Royal Navy proved its supremacy over the French. His most famous engagement at Cape Trafalgar, saved Britain from the invasion by Napoleon but it would be his last. Before the battle on 21 October 1805, Nelson sent the famous signal to the fleet *'England expects that everyman will do his duty'.* He was killed by a French sniper a few hours later while leading the attack on the combined French and Spanish fleet. His body was preserved in Brandy and transported back to England where he was given a state funeral.

* * *

Steve pulled the heavy door open and walked into a piece of England, the pub near to full capacity. Old English Ale and plowman's lunches were the 'get out of jail' for the office and Investment Banking high fliers with their big bonuses and fancy wheels. The English pub ambience is second to none and 'The Nelson' was true to form. 'Union Jacks' and 'White Ensigns' cluttered the walls with 'squeezed in' framed prints of galleons sea battles and broadsides. In the center stood three mainsails masts a foot in diameter spaced 5 yards apart stretching to the ceiling, each with a stand-up circular bar table at its base. At the top of each one was a yard arm with tied up furled canvas sails and the replica 'Crow's Nest' immediately below gave a touch of genuineness.

The four barmen in their mid-twenties decked in their 'Union Jack' 'T' shirts, two sizes too small, their pecks, biceps and naval haircut's overplayed, was a crowd puller and with their English accents the office chicks just couldn't resist.... *So........?*

* * *

"Room 462 sir." The bell hop in his light grey brass buttoned high collared tunic and black side striped pants slipped the plastic into the slot, the green LED flashed and the 'hop' opened the door.

'It's alright kid, I'll manage from here." Bill slipped him a ten.

In Japan tips were once forbidden, like Singapore, but the good bad and the ugly American culture is the envy of the world and money talks.

Bill placed the card into the utility holder and the lights and air con burst into life, the chilled air immediately circulating the room.

"Now... *that's better!*" He placed his garment bag onto the fold down tray and loosened his tie, it had been a more than long day as he sat down heavily on the 'King-size' bed removing his shoes and jacket before swinging his legs from the floor and hitting the pillow. For a moment, he stared blankly at the ceiling... It was just *so nice* to relax... You *know* the kinda feeling...?"

"I wonder where Julie is now?" He spoke under his breath. "Probably back on the London run, I guess? Well, whatever ..." He sighed. "I have enough on my plate now and they say what goes around comes around." Then he closed his eyes for a fifteen-minute catnap and as always, *cats can't count...!*

The sheep were asleep and so was Bill when the loud ring of the phone detonated his eardrums.

"*What the hell?*" Bill sat bolt upright. "Yes, err... Hello... *Eh...* Room 462..."

"*Bill...* Sally here... *Don't tell me I woke you up...!* Didn't you get my message?"

"I'll take the fifth on that one." Bill turned and glanced at the digital clock. "*Hell*, 8.10... Sorry Sally, I was bushed, so I'm pulling rank ... Gimme say... Twenty, while I shower and change... Is Chuck with you?"

"Where there's alcohol there's Chuck."

"I guessed so... And the restaurant?"

"Keyakizaki, Minato, Teppanyaki restaurant on the mezzanine floor."

"Okay, twenty then..."

The hot shower was relaxing and with a scrape of the Mach 3 and a splash of good old 'Kelvin Cline', his skin felt like a twenty-year-old. He stared into the mirror then ran his fingers through his thick bushy hair, the kind of hair that looks better unkempt.

"I think I'll pass. He grinned keeping the towel around his waist as he unpacked his garment bag.

Within minutes he was dressed in fresh underwire, slacks and crisp white shirt. Tieless would the dress code for the evening.

The lift chimed at the mezzanine and Bill stepped it out. Eight thirty had come and gone and he had to admit he was feeling a bit peckish but Teppanyaki...? Well... *Let's just say it's slimming......*

* * *

The Minato, true to form, was class and no doubt the 'Yen' to go with it. It's long tempered see through glass Teppanyaki bar was most certainly unique, with its accompanying red cushioned leather carver chairs on swivels in front of the barbecue plates with just enough gap to shield the diner from the high temperature cooking. On the facing wall were rows of shadowed down lights revealing the selection of large and small vibrantly labeled green Saki bottles, giving the stepped glass shelves a secondary illumination. Above each of the diner's stations hung soft red shaded lightening providing a sort of private dining experience for the habitué. Almost standing at attention were the Japanese chefs in their traditional whites and double-breasted tunics and Toques, (the tall chef's hat that dates to the 16th century) complete with starched aprons and knife belts with a least six weapons of destruction, this was surely a picture for the album........

* * *

"*Sally... Chuck...*" Bill smiled as he took his seat. "Sorry for being late." He shrugged a throw away. "Now Sally, don't look at me that way. Hell, I feel as if I'm back with Julie!"

"Is that good or bad?" Sally smiled mockingly.

"I'll save that answer for another day."

"Tushay... Now Captain Collins...Getting down to business, I'm starving." Bill turned to Chuck who seemed to be out of it. "And you Chuck?"

"Eh...? What was that?"

"I'm implying are you ready to order?"

"Oh...*Eh*...Sure, sure. I'm not too hungry but don't let me stop you guys." He raised his hand to attract the waiter. "Simusan..."

"San?"

"I'll have another one of these." Chuck pointed his empty whisky glass.

Bill raised is eyebrows and looked at Sally... *Should he?"*

"Chuck, at the thought of ruining a pleasant evening, I think you've had enough. In fact, *I'm telling you*, you've had enough! Tomorrow we have, dare I say, a more than demanding flight and I need you in a fit state of mind and remember if your borderline again on the breath test, it's three strikes and you're history and need I stress, you'll be grounded for three months without pay.... Give us a few more minutes." The waiter bowed and left the menus.

"Bill, for Christ sakes, get off my case..."

But there was something on Chuck's mind and he decided he was going down the road to 'Disaster Ville' and retreated shrugging his shoulders with an apologetic look. *"Okay, Okay...* So, I stepped outta line and I apologize... Simusan, cancel that order."

"Chuck, it's for your own good."

"I know... I know Bill" Then he smiled. "I think I'll order some food after all......"

* * *

Steve crushed his way to the bar.

"What'll it be mate." The blonde-haired barman with the diamond earring asked, his Cockney accent as fake as the diamond.

"Good question..." For a moment, Steve studied the fonts. M&B... Tetley's... Three Tons....Smiths... "I'll try your M&B bitter"

"Good choice mate... A pint?"

Steve gave the nod.

"Move over you mongrel."

"Gregg! And just in time. What'll it be?"

"Oh, I'll suffer the same as you."

Steve signaled to the barman... "Make that two... With the parking problem, I thought you be would arriving much later."

Gregg smiled. "Let's just say I was lucky."

"Maybe this is your night, *huh?*"

"Are you shittin me? Besides we have an early flight in the morning."

"When did a good night's sleep ever stop you?"

"Mates, that'll be a fourteen straight." The barman was becoming impatient.

"Well?" Steve turned to, Gregg, an evil smile in his eyes.

"What? You gotta be kiddin me! You ask me out to this lousy English pub, and *I* pick up the tab! *Maaan...* You must have English blood in your veins or maybe it's the name... *No relation?"*

"Nelson... You never know, maybe a distant uncle."

"Get out of it!"

"Mates, I'm busy."

Gregg fished a ten and five from his bill fold.

"Keep the change."

"Good on yah mate."

"Well at least someone's happy... *Eh... Err... mate."*

Steve had to laugh. This was Gregg's typical dry humor.

"Food?"

"Yeah, if *we can find a place to bloody sit."*

"Gregg, grab your pint, there's a booth over there, a foursome is just leaving... *Shiiit...* Two babes have just pegged our territory."

"So, when's that ever stopped us before?" Gregg grinned... *Remember Nelson...* 'England expects everyman to do his duty'."

"I must admit I like the blonde one." Steve gabbed his pint and began to crash his way through the 'maddening crowd'. Then he turned back "Come on Gregg, don't hang around."

"Excuse me ladies?"

Steve had spilled a quarter of his pint in his haste and the brunette put her hand to her mouth to stifle her laughter. his stained jeans looked as if he had just pissed himself in the toilet.

"What do you think Maggi, shall we let these two undesirables share our booth?"

The blonde smiled. "I think they are inviting us to join them for dinner."

"Then if you put it that way, how can we resist?"

Steve burst into laughter, these two chicks had nailed them good. What's a pub lunch in the company of two lookers? Maybe this would be a late night after all......

* * *

"Sally?"

"I'll have the Miso soup and prawn tempura and a side salad with Wafu dressing."

"Sounds good, *and good for the waistline...* Me?" Bill studied the menu once more. "I'll follow you Sally with Miso soup but I'll have the Kobe Beef medium rare and fried rice.... Chuck?"

"Soup and rice, I'm good."

The waiter jotted the orders...

"Oh, and the drinks guys. I almost forgot... How about warm Saki all round?"

"I'm in Captain." Sally replied jokingly.

"Then that's it." Bill passed the waiter the menus.

"Bill, while we're waiting for the food, what's the big deal on tomorrows flight?" Chuck just couldn't restrain himself. It was a question begging.

"I was hoping you wouldn't ask." Bill raised his eyebrows.

"Bill, I'm curious as well." Sally chimed in.

"Let me put it this way. It's a high security shipment that I can't divulge to anyone. Tomorrow at your briefing with McGill all the cards will be on the table and you will better understand why the secrecy."

"Is it dangerous?" Sally asked.

"Sally at the boring thought of repeating myself..."

"Your Saki San......."

* * *

The Teppanyaki dining experience would have been a pleasant getaway from the friendly or not so friendly skies, except for Chuck's unrelenting pursuance of the fifth amendment, either not understanding plain English or his alcohol soaked brain was in stage one dementia.

"Good night guys, remember 8pm for tomorrow's briefing. I'll be leaving much earlier so you two can arrange your own transport. As for tomorrow, it's a free day, *Me?* It's breakfast in my room and a lazy good for nothing day. Tomorrow evening then... Goodnight...I'll take care of the check."

Bill left the restaurant and headed for the lift, leaving both Chuck and Sally to drain the last of the Saki. After dinner, whatever turns them on is up to themselves. Chaperons are extinct and for sure Bill didn't want a bag of it.

At last he slipped the security card into room 462, opened the door then switching on the soft lighting. Hotel rooms are alike, cold and unfriendly, but when you have had a day like today, it was 'home sweet home'.

Bill crashed on top of the bed sill in his bathrobe. The shower was invigorating, the secret to a good night's sleep.

"I had better call food and beverage while I still remember." He mumbled before picking up the phone.

"Food and beverage."

"Collins San, how can I help you?"

"I need a wakeup call for 9am and I would like my breakfast served in my room at 9:30."

"Paper San?"

"Yes, The New York Times."

"And your order?"

"Black coffee, fresh orange juice, toast and Egg Benedict."

"Thank you, Collins San, I will personally ensure your request."

Bill replaced the phone and thumped his head on the pillow.

"God, I really feel washed out but that Chuck...? There's something bothering me about his arrogant and inquisitive attitude... Like his repetitive questions about this flight... *I just don't know*... Maybe I'm over playing it. But there again I just have a bad feeling about tomorrow."

Bill could feel his eyes heavy and he untied his bathrobe and chucked it to the floor, as always, he slept in the raw but with one exception tonight... *Without Julie......!*

* * *

"You two are not English, are you?" The blonde with the shoulder length hair asked, the twinkle in her pale blue eyes captivating.

She's the one alright. Gregg could see that look in Steve's eyes, the old sucker punch for blondes and he hastily interrupted.

"Heh...heh... heh." Let me set the record straight ladies. The answer is *no*. I'm originally from Chicago and Steve here, is from New York and we're not in the closet."

Gregg's 'tell all' brought another bout of laughter. It seemed their new-found friends had no inhibitions and better still the night was still young!

"Are you feeling a titch thirsty Michelle?" Maggi was the leader of the pack.

"Pardonnez-moi, Mademoiselles, what's your poison?" Steve was piling it on.

"And French too Michelle!"

"Who *are* these guys Maggi?" The laughter was spontaneous.

"Then it's two Heinekens." Michelle replied.

"Ladies, I guess you're not here for the beer."

"That English piss, *are you kiddin me?*"

"Here, here Michelle." Gregg couldn't help himself, he was struggling with the pint of warm ale as it was.

Steve raised his hand to attract the barman.

"Awe Naw, not 'mate' again...!"

"What'll it be mate... For the ladies, is it?" The phony Cockney accent would be enough to make Beckham give up soccer.

"Two Heinekens and can you fetch the pub menu?"

"No sweat mate."

"Menus ladies." The 'Bronx Cockney' was back.

"Before we get to the serious part." The girls were studying the menus. "We haven't introduced ourselves." Steve was making a play for the blonde who sort of raised her eyes and smiled. Was it a 'come on' or just being nice?

"Who goes first?" Maggi smiled.

Steve was first past the post he had to stake his claim.

"Steve Nelson and I'm no relation to the Lord Nelson."

Maggi laughed. "Pity, we might have gotten a 'freebie' tonight Michelle."

"You are!" Gregg chimed in.

"And gentlemen too, Michelle!"

"And?" Maggi turned her attention to Gregg who was taking it all in.

"Gregg Jonson"

"The strong silent one, huh?" Michelle finally entered the Coliseum.

"Michelle, like in French?" Gregg asked.

"Yes... Michelle Laurent. My parents are from Paris. My father came here on a work assignment over thirty years ago, and loved the US so much he decided to stay."

"You speak French?"

"What *do you* think?" Michelle was cool.

"I guess I asked for that one, huh?" Gregg was surmising weather Michelle was taking the 'Michael' or just a throwaway line.

"Don't be so serious Gregg, I'm just teasing."

Gregg cracked a smile. "You had me going there for a moment."

"Your beers ladies... Are you guys ready to order?"

"Maggi?" Michelle turned to her friend.

"I'll go for the bangers and mash with gravy on the side, and...?"

Michelle studied the menu for a second time.

"Steak and kidney pie with chunky cut English chips."

"You girls must be hungry, but good choice." The cockney's accent somewhat losing it.

"And?" He turned his attention to Steve and Gregg.

"Sliced roast beef on crispy dough bread and dunking gravy on the side."

"Make that for two." Gregg followed suite.

"Do you want to pay for the Heineken's now or shall I open a tab?"

"Eh, err, what's your name?" Steve asked the counterfeit cockney.

"Jimmy."

"Creative."

Now Steve *was* being sarcastic and luckily for him the muscle-bound barman chose to ignore it. Maybe it was duty before honor or he just loved his job or more to the point, thick skin...! *Whatever...!*

"Open a tab... *Eh...* Jimmy."

The barman disregarded Steve turning his attention to the fairer sex. "Ladies, your orders will take about fifteen minutes. Enjoy your beers..."

"And Maggi, *eh?"* Steve curiosity was killing him.

"Maggi Benson to my friends." She was being naughty…....

* * *

Steve couldn't help but study this beautiful blonde. Her long shoulder length golden hair in a center style curled like a movie star, and as for those crystal pale blue eyes, the narrow nose and smooth complexion, she had it all, not to mention the plump lips and pearly whites. For sure this babe could be a 'stand in' for 'Cameron Diaz' in 'Charlies Angels'. Most likely in her mid-twenties, Steve could only surmise from the waist up because of the booth bench but what he saw he liked and the white short sleeved tank top didn't lose anything in the bra department either. She was a cool chick with a bubbly personality, the kind you need to break the ice. And as for Michelle... The pretty sedate brunette with the olive brown eyes and the kind of face you have to look at twice before you appreciate her natural beauty, was perceptibly the quiet one, a winning catalyst between two good friends with different personalities. Her blue high collared see through blouse and the fine gold neck chain added to her voluptuousness and one could only imagine what lay below the dining table.......

* * *

"So how did you guys meet?" Steve spoke directly to Maggi, who smiled before answering, turning to Michelle.

"It's a long short story." Maggi laughed. But if you must know, we're both Washingtonians and met during our university studies at the one and only... *'George Washington University'*, graduating in Computer Science. We're unattached and share an apartment downtown and don't even think about it! Jobs...? *Wait for it!* Computer programmers for the IRS."

"Wow! What do you know, Gregg? Now we know who to contact if our Tax Rebates are late."

"I wouldn't bank on it if I were you?" Michelle came in. "We can't even get *our own* on time... And for the book, what line of work are you guys in?"

Steve turned to Gregg." Shall we...?"

"Here we are, Ladies... Your orders... Bangers and mash for the lovely blonde and steak and kidney pie for your friend the brunette. Gents, just bear with me for a few more minutes." And 'Jimmy' true to form was back in a heartbeat.

"Enjoy your dinner." He was just about to leave when suddenly he stopped in his tracks turning to Maggi.

"Did anyone ever tell you, you look the spitting image of..."

Maggi gave as huge sigh like... *Not again!*"

"Let me guess... *'Cameron Diaz'.*" She replied, unmistakable sarcasm in her tone of voice.

"No offence." Jimmy was embarrassed. "But I just had to tell you."

"That's okay... I get it all the time to the extent it becomes really boring."

"Apologies... And again, enjoy your food."

"Come to think of it!"

"Steve, don't *you* start..." Maggi cut to the chase. *"Bon appetite,* I'm starving."

"Now getting back to..." Michelle cleared her throat, drowning the pie pastry with a sip of the famous Belgian Ale. "This pie is delicious... *Eh...* where was I?"

Maggi kicked in... *"Their jobs..."*

"Don't tell me! Unemployed and on social and the bad news, we pay the check." Both girls burst into uncontainable laughter.

"It appears Gregg, we look like a couple of bums, *huh?"*

"Lighten up guys." Maggi was having a problem stifling her laughter. *"Boy,* if only you could see the look on your faces... *Priceless...”*

"Well..." Steve sort of paused like he had no option if he wanted to keep the pot boiling. "For what it's worth ladies, we don't customarily disclose our occupations but as we are certain that you are not 'From Russian with Love'... If you really must know, Gregg and I are both CIA agents."

Maggi almost choked on her mash gabbing a napkin to wipe her mouth.

"You guys are something else. But I gotta hand it to you, that's a new line for me... *Pull the other one... Michelle?"* Maggi was bursting her sides.

Michelle raised her eyebrows, a smile crossing her face but not as boisterous as her friend.

"I don't know Maggi, what say we give them some slack?"

"Or enough rope to hang themselves." Maggi chortled.

Enough was enough and the guys had no option but let the cat out of the bag, so to speak, to save their injured pride and they promptly removed their wallets and flashed the famous CIA gold.

For a moment, there was an embarrassed silence as reality hit home with Maggi running for sanctuary.

"Err... I guess I owe you guys an apology, I feel a real heal."

It was Steve's 'Mr. Nice Guy' opportunity and he wasn't going to let the dog die.

"Maggi, it's no big thing. You're not to blame. There's lots of crazy's out there and let's face it, it's not every day you have the luck to meet two handsome CIA Agents."

Gregg had to laugh to himself, 'Stevie Wonder' had done it again!

Steve's throwback had saved the night and everyone was back on an even keel.

"Gregg." Her laughter now subdued Michele looked into his eyes, her unpretentious warmth sending a message. "I think I've had enough food and 'Horatio Nelson' himself. My suggestion is that 'we go Rollin... Rollin down the river'. Michelle laughed as she sang the chorus of Neil Sadako's 'Proud Mary".

"Michelle, you're not suggesting Karaoke, are you?" Steve had other more interesting thoughts on his mind and Karaoke wasn't one of them.

"Are you serious...*With my vocals...* Something a bit livelier, *Eh Maggi?"*

"Yeah, and I know just the place... The Black Cat on 14th ....!"

* * *

What was that noise in the distance? Bill sank his head into the soft pillow looking for sanctuary.

"What the hell!" He spoke out loud before finally surrendering and opening his eyes to the glare of the early morning sunlight streaming through the partially open drapes.

"The phone... Of course, the bloody phone..." He stretched over to the bedside table falling short, his brain still fuzzed, knocking the receiver to the floor.

"Fucking phone... Now where the hell has that fucking...?" He leaned over the bed, the blood rushing to his head as he blindly searched with his hand. "At last... *Room 426?"*

"Good morning Collins San, your wakeup call. It is now 9 am."

"Eh err... *Eh,* thank you." Bill hitched the phone back into the cradle then crashed his head back onto the pillow.

It had taken ages this morning before he finally dosed over and just when he was enjoying 'sweet dreams' *the phone rings!* Life isn't meant to be easy and today would test a saint.

Nine thirty was the breakfast call and the last thing Bill wanted, was naked as a 'jay bird' when room service arrived and he hurriedly tossed the bedclothes aside and swung his feet to the floor.

"Boy, is this air-con cold!" He gave a slight shiver followed by a *brrrrr, before* retrieving his bathrobe and slipping into the terry toweling and tying the belt.

"Now where the hell is that AC control? *Eighteen degrees C, no wonder...* Twenty-two is *more* like it."

Bill had just finished showering and was relaxing on the sofa still wrapped in his bathrobe, when the door chime echoed.

"Must be breakfast." He spoke to himself rising to his feet whilst glancing at the digital bedside clock. "Nine thirty on the button." He grinned, I gotta hand it to the Japanese." He peered through the security peephole before opening the door.

The immaculate breakfast trolley with its white starched tablecloth *fine* crockery, polished cutlery and heat covered food plates were a picture in itself, almost too good to terminate but the 'hunger game' takes priority and Bill was looking forward to his favorite breakfast, *Egg Benedict!*

"Where to San?" The young man in the crisp hotel uniform asked, trolley at the ready

"In front of the sofa." Bill pointed.

"And your paper San?"

"I'll take it."

The kid maneuvered the breakfast trolley as requested, it's wheels on the deep plush carpet giving subtle resistance.

"Is there anything else San?"

"Yes, just a second kid." Bill took a ten from his billfold.

"Arigato gozaimasu." The kid bowed then left, a lot happier than he came.

The coffee was first off, the rank. Although Bill had gone easy on the Saki the night before the caffeine surge hit the spot.

"Hmmmm… *Is that good!*" He poured the juice then removed the heat container from his favorite calorie destroyer, then sliced a piece of the gooey poached egg… Benedict sauce and English muffin… *"Maaan…! It doesn't get any better."*

Bill opened the New York times and glanced at the pronounced headlines, shaking his head at the doom and gloom.

"What's the world coming too? ISIL CALL TO ARMS RISES THREAT LEVELS … US GENERAL… RUSSIA IS OUR BIGGEST THREAT… Obama's military advisor explains why… US AND EU PARTNERS AGREE FURTHER SANCTUIONS ON RUSSIA… Obama steps up Russia sanctions on Ukraine crises. Putin's defiant speech to Russian Parliament… RUSSIAN ECONOMY IS IN DOWNSPIN SEVERE CRISIS IN FOREING EXCHANGE EFFECTS EXPORTS……

"Enough of that shit I want to enjoy my breakfast." Bill folded the Times and chucked it on the coffee table for later.

"This is the best part of the day. This breakfast…Hmmm…" Bill was mopping up the Benedict sauce with the last of the English muffin.

"What's the time now?" He grabbed the remote and switched on the television pushing the breakfast trolley aside and swinging his feet onto the coffee table.

"This is the eleven am international news bulletin from CNN, Colin McGregor reporting… *Good morning, more bad news from Iraq as ISIL captures the town of Ramadi west of the capital of Bagdad. The militants of the Al-Qaida splinter group ISIS also known as ISIL….*

Bill shook his head in disgust then killed the remote button. *"Christ,* is there no fucking good news in the world these days?"

The heavy breakfast was taking its toll and it was time for an early Siesta and Bill powerlessly closed his eyes the lyrics from the Hollies 1974 hit Julie's favorite ringing in his ears... *'All I need is the air that I breath just to love you'* He had been a real heel jerk and how could he ever make it up to her? There was no need to count the sheep...…

* * *

The sudden chime of the doorbell startled Bill with a jolt and he sat bolt upright... *"What the hell...?"* He rubbed his eyes to clear the haze.

"My God, is it that time already?" He glanced at the digital time piece. *"One thirty?* I don't fucking believe it!"

The doorbell chimed again.

"Yeah... Yeah... Keep your shirt on, I'm coming." Bill opened the door.

"Housekeeping sir, can I take your breakfast trolley and make up your room?" The middle aged Japanese lady dressed in her grey and white collared uniform meekly asked, the heavy stacked trolley with towels and toiletries immediately behind her. She had a pleasant smile but there was no mistaking her conspicuous Japanese features.

"Sure, you can take the trolley but as I'm checking out today why don't you came back in say.... An hours' time?"

"Arigato." She gave a polite bow and proceeded to retrieve the overzealous breakfast cart."

"Just a second." Bill rescued his billfold and parted with a ten. "Thank you..."

"Cannot speak much English san... Arigato, no take." She politely bowed again then struggled with the floppy wheeled vehicle which seemed to have a mind of its own.

"I'll be darned! The most deserving employees have their pride, *now that's a breath of fresh air."* Bill was talking to himself. "Enough of that, I had better get dressed and packed or the day will be running away with itself."

The dark blue captain's uniform with cuffed gold braiding, crisp white shirt and Global's signature tie, painted a thousand words and Bill certainly looked the part. He picked up his garment bag, took one more check of the room then opened the door and walked briskly toward the elevator. It was too early for his meeting with McGill at 1800 but a club sandwich and a cold Asahi at the 'Maduro Bar' would go a long way.

As he stood in the crowded elevator, Bill felt rather embarrassed standing almost two foot taller than the other hotel guests, staring inquisitively at the handsome airways captain.

The elevator chimed and gave a slight bounce as it 'touched down', followed by the heavily accented recorded voice ... *'Ground floor and reception'.* But for Bill there was no escape as three young Japanese beauties blocked his path pointing to their cellphones.

"Simu San... *Eh,* can have picture?"

Bill smiled, how could he refuse 'Miss Japan'.

The photo session over Bill smiled to himself as he took the stool at the 'Maduro Bar, placing his garment bag on the unoccupied seat next to him.

"Japan never ceases to amaze me." A wry grin crossing his face.

"Good afternoon sir." The young Japanese barman was laying it on, after all Americans are renowned for their loose change. "What'll it be sir?"

"A draft Asahi and a club sandwich with fries on the side."

Bill looked around rather surprised that bar was deserted, the Japanese culture most likely prefer action with chopsticks rather than an assortment of toasted bread.

"I'll fetch your beer right away sir, but I'm afraid the sandwich will take around ten to fifteen minutes."

"No sweat, I've got plenty of time." Bill replied removing his cap and placing it on top of the garment bag.

As promised the tall frosted schooner glass appeared containing the famous amber liquid and Bill sank a long one.

"Hmmm... They say, 'the first cut's the deepest'." He placed the frosted glass back on the beer mat and was about to sit back and relax when suddenly his cell vibrated.

"Now who the hell can this be?" He pouted his lips and gave a disgruntled sigh as he fished the Samsung from inside his jacket.

"Collins here... *Jim!* I didn't recognize the number... Just having a light lunch... Last night...? I had dinner with Chuck and Sally... No, I didn't mention anything about the flight, that's what we agreed. *Of course, they were pumping me,* I mean, *can you blame them...?* Chuck... Yeah, he kept the show going and wouldn't take no for an answer I mean he was sucking oxygen to the extent I was glad when it came to pay the check... He worries me... I gotta be honest Jim I have a bad feeling about this flight. Yeah maybe you're right, so why the call? Yeah, I could make that I'm just killing time anyway..." Bill glanced at his watch... "Say four thirty in the staff lounge. Yeah, the others will be there at 1800... *Chuck?* Make no mistake he knows he is on his last strike... *Shit!* Talk of the devil, he has just entered the bar and spotted me, I'll have to hang up Jim... Yeah, Ciao."

"Well fancy finding you here." Chuck took the stool next to Bill. "Aren't you going to shout me one?"

Bill made a 'lost cause' face and raised his hand to attract the barman. "Sir?"

Bill pointed to the Asahi. "One more."

"I was surprised you left early last night, must be something big on the agenda, huh?"

"Chuck, cut the shit, you'll get the 'know all' at the briefing with McGill at six, so cool it, I have enough on my plate as it is."

"Yes Captain." The sarcasm prominent. "Cheers."

"Yeah, and go easy, its only just turned two. Changing the subject what did you two guys get up to last night?"

"Your club sandwich sir."

Bill nodded... "Thanks... Chuck, how about sharing this snack with me, I suddenly feel I've lost my appetite."

"Last night? Sally... Well, she's spoken for and wanted to hit the cot early to do some morning shopping at the Ginza, and me... The night was young and so was I, so I took a cab to Habukicho to spend, shall I say, 'happy hours'."

"What!" The red light and Karaoke district! You gotta be kiddin me."

"Listen Bill there was a time not so long ago when you would be only *too* keen to join me."

"Yeah, well as we get older let's just say we get wiser. So, what happened to Marge? I mean it's only been a matter of days since the breakup, you must still have some feelings for her."

"Bill, I guess it was time for a change and we both knew it, so good riddance, and as they say, 'there's plenty more fish in the sea'."

Bill shook his head. *"Your incorrigible."*

"What's with you and Julie? Don't tell me it's "Tie a yellow ribbon on the old oak tree'?"

"You could say that. You never really appreciate what you've got until you lose it. I would take her back tomorrow if she would have me but then that's for another day."

Bill swallowed the last of the Asahi and raised his hand to attract the barman.

"Sir?"

"Make up my tab, I'll be charging it on my room... 462."

"Aren't you going to have another one for old times?" Chuck asked a bit deflated.

"Nope, I still must check out, I have a meeting with McGill at five and it's 2:30 now. Remember and don't be late for the six o'clock meeting."

Bill signed the tab and slipped the kid a ten spot.

"Thank *you, sir.*"

"At least someone's happy." Bill grinned and glanced at his watch. "Listen Chuck I gotta go..."

Chuck just shrugged, he had been there before.

"*Hmmmm. These fries are good... Barman......*"

* * *

Steve turned to Gregg. What do you think dude? Remember we have an early morning flight to Tokyo."

"*Tokyo!*" Maggi was taken aback. "Are you guys serious? Boy Michelle, this is really CIA stuff." She gave a cheeky smile laying it on to Steve. "Your middle name wouldn't be Bond by any chance?"

Maggi's comment brought the house down and even Steve and Gregg saw the funny side.

"Well if 007 can stay the course so can I." Steve was on roll and Maggi in his imagination was another Bond girl.

Gregg raised his hand to attract 'England's own'. "Jimmy, can we have the check please?"

"Sure, gimme a sec."

"Listen guys I feel a bit embarrassed." Maggi interrupted. "How about going Dutch?"

"*Are you kidding me?* Steve laughed. "007 would never live it down."

"And Maggi, I thought the age of chivalry was extinct." Michelle couldn't resist the cheap shot, she could be a card when she wanted.

"But seriously guys, *thanks.*" Maggi looked into Gregg's eyes.

This foursome was going places and in today's world of promiscuity it could only end in one place...!

"It's our pleasure." Gregg smiled, finally getting a word in edgeways, his eyes locked like lazars onto Michelle's.

"That'll be 156 straight." Jimmy held the tab.

"I'll take it." Steve volunteered extracting the greenbacks from his wallet. "Keep the change Jimmy."

"Thanks mate, I hope you'll come again... *Yeah coming...*"

"Now how do we get to this "Black Cat?" Steve rose from the booth.

"You mean to say that the two CIA agents haven't heard of 'Black Cat!" Maggi held her hand to her mouth almost choking.

"Ladies, it just shows you how innocent we are." Gregg grinned flaunting his innocent guise.

"Yeah, *and I don't think!"* Michelle was quick on the uptake. "But if you're so naïve, it's located on 14th just three blocks from the 'U' Street Roundabout and the Cardoza Metro Station. But I'm sure the CIA have GPS." She was being jokingly sarcastic.

"Hey, not so much of the CIA stuff, there might be KGB agents here."

Maggi burst into laughter *"Get out of it!* Well are we going or what?" She was becoming impatient; the night wasn't getting any younger.

"Gregg, I'll take the ladies in my car and follow you to the apartment, then you can join us."

"I have a better idea, Michelle can come with me then we'll join *you."* Gregg turned to Michelle a wicked smile on his face waiting for her response. *"Eh,* if that's okay by you Michelle?" He had that look...

"Thought you'd never ask." The smile reciprocated.

"Well, what are we waiting for......?"

* * *

As they walked to the cars the question was begging and Maggi as usual was first off, the rank.

"So, where do you guys live?"

"We rent a condo in 'Chancellor Towers' on the Washington Circular in the West End."

"Who *are* these guy Michelle? The CIA must be paying well."

"You might be surprised." Steve laughed as he opened the door of his black BMW 525i."

"And the car...! Are you sure you're not 007.......?"

* * *

The 'Black Cat' is a night club in Washington DC, located on 14th Street, North West in the Shaw 'U' Street neighborhood. The club was founded in

1993 by former 'Grey Matter' drummer Dante Fernando, along with a group of investors including Nirvana, 'Foo Fighters' drummer Dave Grohl. The 'Cat' soon established itself as the venue for independent music as well as their popular DJ/Dance Nights.

The venue's "Mainstage' is on the second floor with a capacity of approximately 700. The first floor of the club also contains a 'no cover' bar/ lounge named the 'Red Room' and the 'Food for Thought' cafe serving primarily vegetarian food along with some meat and vegan dishes and a fully stocked bar featuring beer, Bourbon and Scotch. The bartenders are nice and friendly and the drinks are decently priced with the music befitting the hype, like 'Prince vs Michael Jackson' but the favorites are the 80s and 90s nights.

The bottom line... A place to go for a genuinely fun time with friends and great place to dance the night away.

* * *

"Did you really mean what you said back there, Michelle?" Gregg turned the key of the dark blue Mustang Convertible, the growl from the twin exhausts turning the heads of the passerby's.

Michelle quickly pulled down her knee length skirt to avoid any further exposure of her long smooth thighs as she settled into the low seating of the Mustang,

"That's better." She closed the door... *"Eh err,* what were you saying, Gregg?"

"I said, did you really mean what you said back there when I..."

Michelle cut to the chase, leaning over and gently squeezing his hand.

"What do *you* think?" Giving him the kinda smile that launched a thousand ships.

"You've made my day." Gregg's eyes sort of gleamed as he moved the shift stick.

"Listen big boy, pay attention to the driving and can I please have my hand back." Gregg couldn't help but laugh.

"Ha... Ha... Haaaa.... I don't want to, but you're right, it's difficult driving with one hand, huh?" Gregg was grinning like a 'Cheshire cat'.

"Gregg, can I ask you something?"

"Sure." He shrugged as he accelerated his precious toy.

"You know." Michele paused as if trying to find the right words. *"Eh em..."*

"Go on."

"When two strangers meet for the first time, the body language, although silent, inescapably attracts them to one another and I felt that very feeling tonight… Why?"

"I'm listening." Gregg had that inquisitive smile on his face.

"Well, if you must know. You're the strong silent type, you know 'The Quiet Man' not like your ostentatious friend and more to the point my friend Maggi. *It's like*, I guess, the same body language with them, like two of a kind."

"Michelle, let me assure you that when I first laid eyes on you tonight something clicked… Something that I haven't experienced for a long time. You were like a breath of fresh air. *Sure*, I've had relationships before and at my age, it's inevitable, but sadly to say, they never lasted. Maybe it's my job." Gregg shrugged. "I don't know the answer. Or as you say Michelle, I'm not the most exciting catch but on the other hand the underlying chemistry was never there."

"I never said that!" Michelle was aghast at Gregg's comment and she reached over and squeezed his hand, her warmth and reassurance flowing through. "And I apologies sincerely if I gave you that impression. You are reserved, intelligent and sensitive and I like that quality in a man."

"There's no need for apologies honey, I know you didn't mean it in that way."

"Honey… Hmmm… I like the tone of that."

"Anyhow to put your mind at rest, I'm not in a relationship and I assure you I have only the best intentions tonight."

"Pity!" Michelle burst into laughter.

She had something special and Gregg could only hope that this was the beginning of a budding romance and 'To all the girls I've loved before'.

"Here we are, *eh honey."* Gregg hit the stock switch and hung a left toward the underground car park of 'Chancellor Towers'.

"This place has class Gregg." Michelle commented as the boom gate rose activated by Gregg's windshield tag.

Gregg just smiled at Michelle's remark, the car park guard checking the Mustangs number plate as it screeched down the ramp.

"Not cheap but you get what you pay for nowadays and the security and maintenance is second to none."

"I guess so."

The Mustangs low profile tires screeched on the glazed concrete, eerily breaking the silence in the half-filled car ark.

"I'm on the second floor so one more to go and would you believe it? Steve's here already."

He could clearly see the black BMW as he swung the Mustang into the parking lot next to his partner, the Mustang's headlights catching Steve and Maggi by surprise in the midst of an embarrassing hot and heavy session with Maggi quickly sorting her hair and her disheveled blouse.

"It looks like we disturbed something, huh?" Gregg smiled raising his eyebrows as he cut the engine.

"Will you manage, honey?"

"Yeah, I'm good."

Michelle opened the passenger door keeping her knees together and swinging her feet out onto the concrete. It's no mean feat getting out a sports car with heels and a skin-tight skirt and the flash of creamy thigh didn't go unnoticed.

"I caught you." Michelle embarrassed Gregg.

"Can you blame me?" A bloom on his face.

"I'm not complaining darling, I would be worried if you didn't look."

"Now it's my turn to like the sound of 'darling.'" Gregg smiled as he locked the Mustang.

Steve rolled down the driver's window the engine still running. "What happened to you guys?" A smug look on his face.

"You must have burned the rubber?"

"Well, I keep telling you to trade in that crate and get yourself a decent car."

"*Yeah, yeah...* Just ignore him Michelle, he's like a long-playing record. *Now* can you unlock the door.......?"

* * *

(Speaking in Arabic)

"*Anbar, wake up.* We have a busy day ahead of us." Fadile gave his brother a personal wakeup call.

"*Yeah... Yeah,* I hear you Fadile" Then a smile crossed his face. "How can I disobey my older brother, huh? *Now,* can I put the phone down *please*, as it is just turning six and time for morning prayers..." Then a thought occurred to him. "Listen, big brother, a better idea, why don't you unlock the adjoining door and come and join me?"

Fadile smiled, blood is thicker than water. Their family had been to hell and back in the West Bank and the Gaza Strip. They had lost family members killed by the Israeli Security Forces and their father Abdul Fattah, the Commander of the armed wing of Hamas, hunted relentlessly by Israel's Mossad Secret Service and special forces and the dreaded Sayerat Matakal, and by the grace of Allah have been so far unsuccessful. Now operation 'Fish Tail' was their chance to strike back at the Israelis with a catastrophic blow that could change their people's lives forever.

"Anbar, give me at least ten minutes to shower and wash my feet."

"Don't be too long and bring your prayer mat."

Fadile had to smile. "Little brother, I promised father I would look after you and protect you with my life and here you are looking after me."

"Come on old man, otherwise it will be after six."

"Less of the 'old man." Fadile laughed. "Be patient that's what the Quran teaches..."

Fadile quickly showered and toweled his wet lean frame. Glancing at himself in the vanity mirror it was hostile to see a clean-shaven Muslim and against his religion but sacrifices must be made in the name of Allah and for his beloved Palestine. Unashamedly naked he quickly walked to the mirrored wardrobe and opened the sliding door to gain access to the clothes drawer and his white freshly laundered Thobe. (a long loose robe worn by Muslim men for prayer)

"Ah, here we are." Fadile smiled as he unfolded the crisply starched garment and slipping it over his head. For some reason, the Thobe felt fresh and invigorating, a feeling that only one of the Muslim faith can describe.

"Fadile." He could hear his brother's impatient voice.

"Coming...Coming..." Fadile returned the friendly fire as he searched below the 'King Size' bed for his colorful hand knotted Persian prayer mat, quickly slipping into his open sandals and unlocking the adjoining door.

Anbar was already kneeling on his prayer mat, dressed in the proper attire, his mat placed in the direction of the small green arrow on the hotel ceiling, pointing to Mecca.

"Come brother, join me."

"Allah Ahmad......"

* * *

The prayer session over it was time for breakfast and to discuss the final preparation for their departure and operation 'Fish Tail'.

"I'll lock up and meet you in lobby in say..." Fadile glanced at his Omega. "Thirty minutes."

Anbar nodded, his face solemn, today was the day he had been waiting for but when the clock ticks the final hour the 'reality show' kicks in and the sky is not so clear anymore.

"Little brother, I can see that worried look on your face. Don't worry everything will go as smooth as clockwork. *Scared...* You wouldn't be normal if you weren't."

"Are *you* scared Fadile?" Anbar had always looked up to his older brother.

Fadile smiled. "I would be telling you a lie if I said I wasn't. Now no more of this silly talk. My suggestion is that you start to bundle the clothes you need to dispose of. I'll knock on your door when I'm ready to leave for the elevator."

"Thanks, brother, I feel a lot better now." Anbar touched his heart with the palm of his right hand then hugged his brother giving him a kiss on each cheek......

* * *

As they stood in the elevator their 'Middle Eastern' appearance attracted somewhat unwelcome attention, but even in Japan terrorism is high on the alert list and the brothers were more than relieved when the 'passenger box' finally reached 'ground zero'......

* * *

The Palace Hotel Tokyo, built in 1961, is a beautiful five-star hotel located immediately in front of the Imperial Palace and close to the Tokyo central station in the heart of the business district of Marunouchi. The rooms are exceptionally large and out of the box by traditional Japanese accommodation standards, *but at a price! And at US 450 per night certainly not for the 'back packer' brigade.* With 293 rooms and 23 floors it has all mod- cons including underground parking, a rare commodity in downtown Tokyo. The hotel's famous Ueshima Coffee Shop and breakfast restaurant is located on the ground floor and is part of the famous coffee franchise throughout the Ginza district. Furnished in typical Japanese style although semi modern, it had that special oriental atmosphere. It's long self-service buffet breakfast bar or the al' a' carte menu or the guest's choice of traditional Japanese fare of Okayu, Miso Soup, Natto and the Bento Box, an experience for the adventurous.......

* * *

(Speaking in Arabic)

As the brothers walked toward the Ueshima Coffee Shop, Anbar couldn't help but comment.

"Fadile, although I feel hungry I can't stand that Japanese shit food." He was shaking his head.

"Anbar, for once I have to agree with you, but look on the positive side, in two weeks or less you will be enjoying good Arabic tea, Pita bread, grilled Kibbeh and Jawanah..."

"Don't torture me."

"For two sir?" The Maître D' with the name tag Gingi Iwami asked, snapping his finger to attract the waiter.

Fadil nodded, a man of few words.

"This way sir... My name is Denzo... Would you wish a window table?"

"Whatever." Fadile replied uninterested. Breakfast was all about killing time and the matter of satisfying an empty stomach.

The waiter polity escorted the Palestinians to their table.

"Al' e' carte or buffet sirs?"

"Menu please." Fadile replied gruffly.

"Coffee...?"

"Tea please."

"Certainly sir. Any specific blend?"

"Earl Grey."

"Just give me a few minutes and I'll return for your orders." The young Japanese waiter gave a polite smile then went about his business.

"What'll it be Anbar?" Fadile asked as he scrutinized the menu.

"I'll have the Bento box, and you?"

"I'll have the Okayu rice soup. I must admit I'm with you Salibe, I can't stomach this shit." His comment making them both laugh......

* * *

"Well at least the tea was good!"

Before Fadile could reply, suddenly his cell buzzed in silent mode and he hastily took the phone from his inside pocket. He had been waiting for this call from Chicago but the time difference had thrown him. There was a pause then a whistling sound of that from a public phone box.

"Anbar, quickly take this down."

"On what?"

"The napkin will do..."
 62826173 31325332813231 23636171 2153532142 2142612132
The phone went dead.
"Did you get it all?"
"Yeah, I did." Anbar gave a sigh of relief as he passed his brother the scribbled napkin.

Fadile hastily opened a small notepad and quickly flicked through the pages.

"Quick, give me you pen Anbar while I decipher these numbers. Let me see...

628..."
"NUMS DELETED COMP CRASH ALLAH AHMAD"
"This is good news from uncle. Our Japanese partners will be pleased. I will inform Numero when we meet."
"But can we trust the Yakuza?" Anbar asked.
"As much as they trust us......."

* * *

"Nola, its Ginzo here, I need to speak to Geoff, like it's more than urgent."
Nola smiled. "I thought I preconized that accent. Just a second Ginzo, I'll check to see if Mr. Daniels is free."

"Nola, I don't have the luxury of time, I need to speak to Geoff, like *now!*"

"And I can expect agents Nelson and Jonson in my office first thing in the morning...? Yes, I'll have one of my men meet them at the airport... Thanks John for the call, sure I understand... Sorry but I'll have to cut you short my red call button is flashing like crazy... I'll pass Betty your regards... Take care... "Yes Nola?"

"Geoff, I've got Ginzo on the line and it's like the planes going down."
"Put him through..."

"Geoff, the Palestinians have just left the restaurant in more than a hurry.... Don't worry I'll not blow my cover, I'm phoning from a closet in the men's washroom. Yeah, I told the Maître D', I needed ten for a toilet break... Here's the scoop... Salibe and Fadil received a call on their cell phone and hastily scribbled a message on the only thing availed... A table napkin and guess what? *You got that right!* They left it behind and yours's truly cleared the table... I have it right in front of me... Some kind of code, I'll read it to you over the phone... 62826173...... "Did you get all that...? Good... Just a sec I hear footsteps......."

* * *

"Anbar, *the napkin!*" It had just donned on him and Fadile grabbed his brother's arm as they walked to the check-out desk, stopping him dead in his tracks, the look on Salibe's face painting the picture.

"Don't tell me!"

Anbar went a pale shade of brown.

"Brother, what can I say, how stupid and careless of me."

"It's too late for apologies, *somehow we gotta get that napkin!* Come, with a bit of luck our table may not be cleared."

The brothers quickly about turned and almost sprinted to the restaurant only to be confronted by the Maître D.

"Can I help you gentleman?"

"We left something on our table can we go and check?"

"Yes, I remember you now, table by the window, but I'm afraid it has been taken. Can you perhaps tell me what it was and I'll check with Ginzo, your waiter?"

"Oh, ah...err, it was nothing important, just a scrap of paper." Fadile was caught by surprise and mumbled the first thing that came to out of his mouth.

"Would it be possible to speak to the waiter?" Fadile asked.

"Not at all, but I'm afraid he is on his toilet break now."

"The washroom?" Fadile asked.

"Straight ahead then turn to your left."

"Arigato........"

* * *

Fadil made a signal to Anbar, motioning with his head to proceed to the men's room.

As they stealthily approached the washroom door Fadile gently pushed it ajar putting his finger to his lips signaling to Salibe for absolute silence whilst at the same time popping his head around to see if the coast was clear. Satisfied, he motioned to proceed as he took the Glock 45 semi-automatic from his shoulder holster carefully threading the deadly silencer onto the muzzle then sliding the heavy caliber 'copper nose' into the chamber.

"Ginzo are you alright?"

"Shhhhh." Ginzo whispered. "Geoff, don't say another word." Iwami switched his cell to silent mode whilst keeping the line open.

Fadile spotted a closet immediately in front of the entrance with a stenciled mop and bucket painted on the door and pointed to Anbar to check it out. Nocking gently, he waited for a response.

Nothing...!

Satisfied he opened the door and switched on the light, the room was full of buckets, mops, toilet rolls, paper towels and cleaning detergents. Then something caught his eye... The bright yellow plastic sign... NO ENTRY CLEANING IN PROGRESS... One side in English the other in Japanese... *Perfect!* Signaling to his brother pointing to the sign, to stand it outside in the passageway... *What luck!* He was back in a flash locking the men's room door, his brother now in the process of checking each closet by looking below the doors then gently opening each one to make sure it was unoccupied.

Ginzo could clearly see the assailants' feet coming his way and didn't waste any time in pulling up the right leg of his trousers and removing the 32-double action Smith and Wesson from his ankle holster, releasing the safety catch and cocking the hammer.

Fadile attracted his brother's attention pointing to the tips of Ginzos shoes now clearly visible below the next closet and he didn't waste any time, it was no questions asked. Holding the semiautomatic in both hands he squeezed off two rounds.

Zap... Zap... The Glock kicked twice sending two shells clean through the wooden door, splinters flying like snowflakes. The first bullet passing clean through Ginzo's left shoulder as he pulled the trigger twice of his Smith Wesson, his first round piercing the door, the small hole blowing it apart on the other side, the second shot wildly sinking into the plaster ceiling, with a shower of dust as Fadile's lethal second round found its mark, ripping through Ginzo's left ventricle.

For Ginzo, his tomorrow would never come, his cell phone clattering to the tiled floor, the noise from the discharge of his Smith and Wesson clearly audible as he slumped sideways, jamming his body between the toilet seat and the closet wall. Warm blood pumping from the organ of life, like a red blanket saturating his waiter's uniform.

Fadile kicked the door open and grinned at the sight that met his eyes. *Mission accomplished...* Taking a life was an everyday occasion in the West Bank and this one was no different and he picked up the blood-soaked napkin and back kicked the 32 into the wash area, then stomped on the flashing Samsung.

"Ginzo do you read me...? Ginzo did I hear gunfire?" Daniel's turned a pale shade of grey at the unbearable thought of 'agent down'. Then there was nothing...

"Nola... Nola..." Geoff screamed down the phone.......

* * *

(Speaking in Arabic)

"Anbar, pick up the gun then help me drag this useless piece of CIA shit into the cleaner's closet. We gotta move fast in case someone heard these shots... *Anbar...*"

"Uggg...Ahhh...keh em keh...."

The sound of choking, almost like a death croak, made Fadile turn and he couldn't believe his eyes what he saw.

"What the hell...! Anbar, my little brother... *No... No... No...* Please Allah, not him." Tears swelling in his eyes as he rushed to his brother's side.

Ginzo's first shot had hit its target slicing through Salibe's jugular, blood spurting from the wound like the 'Trevi Fountain'. A large crimson pool gathering by his side, like Lake Victoria with its tributaries trickling down the tile grouting, as if from the falls itself.

Anbar raised his hand to grab his brothers in a vice like grip, his voice now barely audible, almost a gurgle, bleeding profusely from his mouth and nose.

"I'm... I'm, sorry Fadile... *I... I...* Really screwed up... I feel so cold... Am I going to die?"

"No little brother, you're just going to sleep in another bed... You are a martyr and Allah will be waiting to greet you... *Fadile no...!"* Anbar screamed.

Fadile's hand slowly went limp dropping to the floor, his blue eyes wide open, the sparkle gone staring at the ceiling, tears now flowing down his brother's cheeks.

"I love you little brother." Anbar gently closed each of his eyes. "May Allah be with you."

Suddenly there was a loud bang on the door.

"What's going on in there?"

Whoever it was must have heard the gunshots, worse still it could be the hotel security.

"Open this door or I'll call security."

The banging now even louder and Anbar had no option, it was now or never and he quickly placed his body against the wall behind the door, his Glock fully cocked in his right hand, pointing at the ceiling.

"One moment." He yelled in English as he unlocked the door, the Maître D' venturing where only fools would fear to tread.

Fadile was out of sight behind the open door but the Maître D, was in the wrong place at the wrong time as the two copper nosed shells from the smoking silencer found their mark in the back of the Maître D's head, blowing it apart like a ripe water melon, blood spatter bone fragments and brain matter drenching Anbar's face as 'Nihon-Jin' crashed to the tiled floor, face down, giving a couple of 'nerve kicks' before permanently leaving this world.

With three corpses in the washroom there was no time to plan and 'Survival Tokyo" was a reality show that Anbar didn't need. He grabbed a paper towel from the dispenser, revoltingly wiping the blood from his face. Time was of the essences and he holstered the Glock then tucked Ginzo's Smith and Wesson blow his waist belt. If he was cornered he would have plenty of fire power, as for the 'check out' and the plan to meet with Okio's men, now history, and as he crushed through the gathering crowd he had only one thing on his mind... The hotel exit and a taxi to the Shin Marunouchi Building and Nippon Shipping & Logistics......

* * *

"Are you guys good in the back?" Steve glanced in the back mirror of the BMW as he slipped the shift stick to drive.

Gregg smiled and squeezed Michelle's hand as he looked into her eyes.

"Yeah, were good, just concentrate on your driving, dude."

"I get the message." Steve turned to Maggi and gave her a cheeky wink as he gunned the Beamer up the ramp, the security guard touching his cap in recognition as the boom gate rose automatically.

"Hmmm, security is good here. Not like our place, huh, Michelle?" Maggi commented, more than impressed.

"And so, it should, *considering the management fees!"* Steve shot back changing the subject. "Now Maggi that address again.?"

Maggi sighed. *"You CIA guys...!* 14th Street, North West in the Shaw neighborhood on the 'U' Street Roundabout and the Cardozza Metro Station."

"Whoa... Whoa... That's some mouthful, I had better pull over and enter it into the GPS." Steve dropped a gear, slowly pulling into the kerb. "Now let's see.... *Hmmm...* Twenty minutes to arrival, distance 15 miles... Technology, *what we do without it?"*

Maggi couldn't miss a cheap shot when it came begging.

"I could have directed you there in five." She burst into laughter.

"What do you make of this gal, Gregg?"

"She's her own woman and more o the point, she can handle you and *that's something!"*

"Get out of it! I might have guessed it coming from you... Twenty minutes huh? Now what's so special about 'Cats' tonight?" Steve asked as he pulled away from the kerb.

"It's the 80s and 90s night... Prince and Michael Jackson hits... The music and atmosphere is great... I hope you guys can dance?" Maggi was on a roll.

"You gotta be kiddin me! Nobody dances nowadays. The African Americans musta brought that stuff with them, it's easy, you just stand in one spot and shake your body."

"Your something else Steve. What about you Gregg?

"I'll take the fifth Maggi. I just roll with the crowd."

"Here we are the 'U' Street roundabout. Yeah, I can see Cats from here." Steve hung a left searching for a parking spot.

"And there's a bit of a que." Gregg turned to Michelle. "This joint must be really popular considering Wednesday night is a dead night in town."

"Normally Gregg, believe it or not, you need to buy a ticket but don't be concerned Maggi and I are regulars and Norm on the door, with a bit of 'palm greasing' will turn a blind eye."

"It's like that is it...? Steve, I hope you are taking note, we have here a clear self-confessed case of bribery and corruption."

"I hear you, Gregg, but then that means we would have to implicate both Maggi and Michelle."

There was deadly silence, the girls falling for Steve's 'leg pull'.

"Are you guys shittin us?" Maggi couldn't control herself.

Steve and Gregg burst into simultaneous laughter.

"Had you going there, huh?"

"Why you...."

"Ladies, you should have seen the look on your faces, just like that TV program 'Just for Laughs'."

'Oh, is that so! I think we should dump these two jokers Michelle, what do you think?"

"I think probation and a good behavior bond is more appropriate."

Steve couldn't help laughing at Michelle's comment. This was going to be a fun night......

* * *

Steve finally parked the car, the foursome crossing the road to the famous 'Cats'.

"Hi Norm."

The black mountain on the door smiled. "Excuse me, please step aside, this way ladies." His grin larger than life.

"What did I tell you?" Maggi proudly turned to Steve. "I hope you have a spare twenty?"

"And if I don't?"

"*You* can face Norman... Not a pretty thought."

Steve was fishing for his wallet.

"No sweat partner, I got it here." Gregg brushed against the 250 pounds' bouncer clasping his hand, the twenty disappearing faster than the Italian pickpockets at the Coliseum.

"Good to see you again ladies. Have a nice evening." Norm opened the door to Michael Jackson's 'Billy Jean' the loud music spilling onto the sidewalk.

The no smoking ban hadn't hit Cats yet and the haze was worse than Indonesia's sugar cane burns.

"Where shall we take these two jokers Michelle?" Maggi was rubbing it in.

"The Red Room on the second floor, that's where it's all happening and there's no cover charge on the drinks."

"Lead the way ladies......"

* * *

"The Red Room was jumping and true to its name, the walls and ceiling a light red, maybe that's why so many patrons were wearing 'Ray Bans. To the left, the longest bar one can imagine, at least sixty feet in length. The red leather bar stools to match the elbow rests and the teak topped highly polished bar, bearing the battle scars of glass versus wood. Its full glass mirrored wall stacked from end to end with every alcoholic drink imaginable, the brightly colored bottles sparkling from the rays of the concealed low voltage lighting, the ambience a draw card for the female cocktail habitual's and their sucker partners. On the opposite wall was a row of eating booths, with white topped aluminum edged tables and red leather bench seats. The high tech back ground wall impersonating a large printed circuit board with is memory tracks in red neon lighting not to mention the red green and blue lasers crisscrossing the ceiling, synchronized to the beat of the music, Michael Jacksons 'Back or White" filling the Red room. The local band the "Three Waves" drums base and acoustic guitar spilling out the lyrics "But if you're thinking about my baby it don't matter if your black or white'........

* * *

The girls seemed well at home in the club atmosphere and ready for the light fantastic. As for the guys...? They were still taking in this awesome club scene, the dance floor filled with at least 100 gyrating bodies.

"What do you think Gregg?" Michele asked ... *"Cool huh?"*

"I'm virtually blown away. But more important, lets hit the bar scene. We're in luck, I've spotted a couple of vacant stools on our left. *Steve, Maggi...* over here."

"Nice one Gregg, grab the stools ladies, what'll it be?"

"They serve a mean Margareta here." Maggi replied turning to her friend. Michelle nodded. "Make that for two."

At least half a dozen young athletic looking barman in one size too small red 'T' shirts had their work cut out but when Steve raised his hand for attention there was no waiting time.

"Two Margareta's and two light Michelob's."

"Gimme five...Tab or cash?"

"Cash." Steve replied.

"So, what's with the light beers, guys?" Maggi asked intrigued.

"Maggi, in our job breaking, the law of any description, such as a DUI, we'd be queuing up at the labor exchange."

"As strict as that!"

"You better believe it." Gregg interjected. "Anyhow let's forget about the CIA and enjoy ourselves...."

"Your drinks guys... That'll be a straight twenty."

Gregg went for his wallet but Steve stopped him in his tracks.

"It's my shout Gregg." Steve passed the waiter two tens and a five. "Keep the change."

"Thanks dude." The young guy smiled then stuffed the five into the tip jar.

"Hmmm... Cheers ladies, here's to a great night."

"I'll drink to that." Michelle looked into Gregg's eyes, a look that said it all. "Dance?"

"If that's what it's called." Gregg smiled and took Michelle's hand."

"Question, when have you guys gotta be in bed tonight?" Steve asked Maggi as Gregg and Michelle disappeared onto the crowed floor.

"So, are you my chaperon?" She gave a cheeky smile. "If you must know, we don't start work until two tomorrow, it's a lay in day."

"Nice... Dance?"

"Thought you would never ask......"

* * *

"This is a really nice apartment." Michelle commented as she sat comfortably on the leather sofa, her tight denim skirt well above her knees, the Margareta's doing their thing. As for Maggi, she was at the breakfast bar chatting to Steve whilst enjoying her second Chardonnay.

Gregg sat down heavily beside Michelle. "How are you feeling honey?" He asked with a smile.

"I'm feeling great but I think I'll skip the wine. It's not that I am intoxicated." She smiled unconvincedly. "It's just that if I drink too much I tend to get a bit sleepy. *Listen*, I have a better idea, why don't we dance?"

Gregg had to laugh. "But there's no music, honey"

"We don't need music darling, *do we?*"

Michele kicked off her shoes then rose to her feet grabbing Greggs hand and yanking his arm.

"Come on lazy bones, I just want you to hold me and whisper sweet nothings."

"Half a sec honey, we *gotta* have some kind of music!"

As Gregg walked to the music center, Michelle was standing there, her hands on both hips demonstrating what women are best at.

The music burst into life and what better song than Bruce Springsteen's 'I wanna know what love is'.

"This is no coincidence darling." Michelle snuggled into Greggs chest, the dance shuffle all about body contact half singing and half whispering the lyrics in Gregg's ear.... *"I wanna know what love is... I want you to show me... I wanna feel what love is... I know you can show me..."*

Then suddenly out of the blue she whispered. "Take me to bed darling."

"Michelle, do you know what you're saying?"

"Every word darling." She looked up into his eyes.

"But Michelle I've only me you to..."

She cut him short. "Oh, don't be so pious darling."

Then without another word she took Gregg by surprise pulling her tight denim skirt up to her waist exposing her floral panties and sort of leapt from the floor her legs in a scissor grip around his waist, her arms locked around his neck.

"Now are you or are you not.......?"

* * *

"Out of the way... out of the way..." Anbar screamed as he violently pushed guests aside in the reception area sprinting toward the hotel exit in the process knocking baggage and shocked hotel staff screaming and sprawling to the ground. The security guards hearing the commotion rushed to the front exit but on seeing Anbar wildly brandishing the Glock they dived for cover. Dead heroes are not in fashion since world War II.......

* * *

"Ginza... Ginza... Simusan..."

The cab driver froze in his shoes, his yellow skin suddenly looking like a white boy's but staring down the muzzle of a Glock was the best incentive to get behind the wheel and hit the gas.

Fadil jumped into the front seat of the Toyota Crown pressing the cold steel of the automatic into the driver's neck.

"Drive... Drive... Drive." Anbar screamed. *"You understand?"*

The driver nervously nodded and promptly did a 'burn out' turning the car 360, the stench of rubber and smoke filling the air, before screaming into the Tokyo traffic, horns blaring, in the distance the wail of speeding police cruisers.

Within minutes the famous Ginza appeared.

"Pull in here... Do you hear me? Pull in here..."

The cab driver didn't need a second prompt and stomped the brakes, Fadil already had the door open hitting the sidewalk running, disappearing into the milling shoppers.

Still panting he stopped outside the Dimora Mall and the taxi stance. He had to appear cool calm and collective as he approached the first cab on the rank.

The driver bowed and opened the rear door, just another tourist.

"Shin Marunouchi Building."

The driver bowed again closing the rear door. So far so good, but the next challenge was the Yakuza and worse still, Okio Numero and he had to think out of the box, and fast……!

* * *

Anbar searched out his security tag then paid the cabby, Numero had given he and his brother Fadile the tags to gain easy access to 'Nippon Shipping & Logistics' thus avoiding the stressful and lengthy security checks.

The immaculately uniformed guard checked Anbar's credentials, nodded, then swiped his card to open the elevator pressing 20. As the doors closed with the usual chime, Anbar breathed a huge sigh, by the grace of Allah the guard had not requested that he pass through the metal detector frame, what with the Smith and Wesson tucked under his belt and the Glock in his shoulder holster, it would have been Sayonara for sure.

His adrenalin still pumping, the elevator seemed to take forever.

"*What a mess!*" Anbar spoke under his breath, his last words to Fadile echoing in his ears... *'Even the best plans can go astray'* and now he was all alone and even more determined to settle the score with the Israelis'.

Fadile's death was not in vain and Allah will grant him holy martyrdom, the greatest honor in the Muslim world…...

* * *

The large, almost bullet proof look alike plate glass doors in bold gold leaf with chrome plated tubular handles, were intimidating to say the least and Anbar soon found out they were security locked and he pressed the buzzer to attract the receptionist's attention.

Myakka looked up from her laptop and stared for a moment, after all Middle Eastern visitors were not an everyday occurrence. Anbar pressed his

120

security tag against the glass hoping to gain entry with no further ado but Myakka wasn't going to have a bag of it and picked up the phone.

(Speaking in Japanese)

"Ayako, I have a middle eastern nihon requesting to see Numero San. I'm sure it's the same gentleman that was here yesterday, accompanied by another colleague... Yes, I understand, I'll wait for security."

She dropped the phone her face showing no emotion. Whatever was on the cards was not her problem.

The phone rang, Okio sighed and stopped what he was doing.

"What now?" He was in a foul mood.

"Ayako didn't I instruct you that I was not to be disturbed?"

"My apologies Numero San." She raised her eyebrows like what's new? "But Myakka at reception, informs me that one of the Palestinian men that you saw yesterday wants to see you, urgently."

"What...!" Numero couldn't believe his ears. "Instruct Tahoka to go and check it out, there must be some mistake..."

"Dozo, Numero San."

Ayako placed back the secretarial phone, the disgusted look on her face summing up her reaction. When her boss is in one of these foul moods as they say, 'better say nothing at all'.

"Tahoka." The modern-day Samurai bowed.

"Hai."

"Boss wants you to check out the visitor."

"Hai."

The small size Suma opened the secretarial door and upon recognizing Fadil instructed Myakka to immediately release the security lock. There was a loud click and Tahoka signaled Anbar to enter.

Once inside, Tahoka motioned the Palestinian to raise both arms to shoulder level to complete a body search.

The Glock was first from the shoulder holster. Tahoka squeezed the magazine release button then checked the loading before placing the empty weapon on the reception desk. The dark brown grip of the Smith and Wesson was clearly visible above Anbar's belt and the 'Samurai' gingerly removed the loaded weapon and checked the safety. Familiar with firearms he cocked the hammer then flicked the barrel magazine to one side to check the chambers. Two shells were missing and he pushed the ejection rod to remove the four

38's catching the unspent ordinance in the palm of his hand. The smell of cordite attracted his nostrils and he sniffed the empty breach, screwing up his eyes concluding the revolver had recently been discharged.

"Hmmm...." He gave Anbar a hostile look. There was no love lost between these two.

Myakka the young reception continued with her typing as if oblivious to the evolving drama. Working for the Yakuza was an honor in itself, the conditions and remuneration above average and it was just a case of 'hear no evil, speak no evil, see no evil......

* * *

Gregg half walked and half staggered under Michelle's weight as he made his way to the bedroom. As for Steve...? He's a big boy and when it comes to the opposite sex he can look after himself.

Michelle was pressing her moist lips against Gregg's neck, the sensation tantalizing and alluring to uncharted waters.

With his elbow, Gregg struggled to switch the beside lights, then gently laid Michelle upon the bed with a sigh of relief, not unnoticed.

"Was I that heavy?" Michelle teased.

Gregg had to smile. "You *are* funny but gorgeous with it."

Michelle placed one of her fingers to his lips. *"Shussss...* Just kiss me darling... *Just kiss me..."* Gregg's adrenaline off the scale, the bulge in his Levi's desperate to do what comes naturally.

'Darling ...*Oh darling...* Don't disappoint me, unbutton my blouse."

All fingers and thumbs, Gregg clumsily tried to undo the small pearl buttons.

"Here, darling let me help you." She gently pushed his hand aside. "My bra unclips from the front."

If it wasn't so serious it would be funny but the prize was well worth waiting for as her creamy white breasts burst from their captivity. The silky soft skin, the large pink nipples standing proud as if waiting to be caressed and Gregg didn't disappoint her, his tongue aggressively massaging and gently biting the opulent peaks, making Michelle moan and groan in unadulterated ecstasy.

Sexual intercourse is the ultimate act of love between a man and a woman but for once patience is not a virtue and time waits for no man.

"Are you going to make love to me fully clothed?" Michelle whispered impatiently, although she was in heaven she could feel the aches in her loins and more so the rock-hard bulge pressing into her abdomen.

"Undress me darling." Michelle almost pleaded.

"Do you wish to keep the lights on?" Gregg asked embarrassingly, like a guy about to lose his virginity.

"Not unless your Stevie Wonder? Now big boy, I'm waiting... Start at the top."

Michelle raised her arms above her head to allow Gregg easy access to remove her blouse and bra and he pause for a moment to take in the scenery.

"Do you like what you see, darling?"

"Love it!"

"Well there's plenty more where that comes from."

Michele unzipped her denim skirt

"Darling sit on the side of the bed and pull it down from the bottom."

She had either done this before or she was one cool babe...

Within seconds the skirt was on the floor and as for her floral panties...

"Just a sec, 'Romeo', I'll make it easy for you."

Michelle pulled her panties down to her knees and bent both legs, then looped them with one foot and kicked the scanty garment into the air, the mesmerized Gregg now on his feet, captivated by 'Lady Godiva's antics. the hour glass figure, the beautiful full breasts and the mysterious dark patch between her legs, begging to be explored.

Within seconds the Levi's were at his ankles, the shirt gone, the six pack and sculpture pecks, a woman's dream. His red briefs unable to cover his erection dropped to the floor and kicked aside like a pro soccer player taking a penalty. Michelle in anticipation had spread her legs waiting for the final curtain. They say the 'first cut's the deepest' and for a brief second Michelle winced her eyes as Gregg entered the forbidden territory. She had underestimated the size of Gregg's erection but with each thrust, deeper and deeper, their bodies moving in perfect harmony, with insuperable pleasure and 'will you still love me tomorrow'........?

* * *

Michelle was lying on her side fast asleep, her head-on Gregg's shoulder, one arm across his naked chest, when the buzz from his cell phone told him it was 5am. He felt like shit having had only three hours sleep and worse still he hadn't packed yet and it was now a case of getting his ass outta bed and scrambling to the shower, but not before he made sure his partner Steve, was in the land of the living and he gently unfolded Michelle's arm. She gave a sort of moan then turned over on her other side and Gregg took the opportunity to silently slip his feet to the floor and into his jocks. To avoid switching on the beside lamps he sort of staggered in the dark toward the door and finally tthe hallway but not before stubbing his toe on the end of the bed.

"Fuck it!" He tried to balance on one leg while holding his other foot, the outburst waking Michelle.

"Darling, are you alright?"

"I'm good honey, just a little mishap. Try and get some beauty sleep, it's just after five. Remember, I have to catch an early flight to Tokyo."

'Shall I rise and brew some coffee?"

"No honey, you close your eyes, I'll see you before I go."

"Are you sure it's just that I feel so..."

Gregg about turned and smothered her lips with a kiss.

"Close your eyes sugar, I appreciate the kind thought but I gotta get moving. I'll catch a coffee in the airport lounge, but firstly I have to make sure that partner of mine is awake."

"I understand darling, I'll be waiting for you..."

Gregg gently knocked on Steve's bedroom door, the last thing he wanted was to disturb 'morning golf'.

"Steve, are you awake?"

"Yeah...Yeah... You hit the shower fist then I'll be right behind you."

"Okay, but don't hang around, we have to check in by 6.30 and it's a thirty-minute drive to the airport. As soon as I shower I'll call a cab. *Do you hear me?"*

"Of course, I fucking hear you... Gimme a break, my heads bad enough without you shouting down my ear."

Gregg just shrugged and got on with it, a warm shower would be invigorating and just what the doctor ordered, as for Steve...? He'll get over it....

A couple of shirts, ties, underwear, toiletry bag, socks, shoes, dark blue suite. The garment bag almost full Gregg stood back and sort of scratched his head...

"Yeah, I guess that's it... Let me see... *Yep."* He convinced himself, already in his jeans and deck shoes, white open necked short sleeved shirt, his dark blue single-breasted blazer draped over the lounge chair. All that was left was his service weapon and clips.

Suddenly Steve streaked past him clad only in a bath towel.

"Don't even think about it, just call that cab I'll be with you in fifteen,"

"Yeah, going to the airport, International Terminal, in about twenty minutes...? That's cutting it fine... Okay, we'll be waiting on the sidewalk ... You have my cell number and the address is...... "

"Are you awake honey?"

"Of course, how could I ever sleep?"

Gregg smiled and lay beside her for a moment staring into her eyes then gently brushed her lips.

"Thanks for the lovely evening, my only wish is that I could stay longer."

"When will I see you again?" Michelle threw her arms around his neck then smothered him with a long and sensuous kiss to the point he was gasping for air.

"Honey... Honey... Please... Don't make it any more difficult." Gregg struggled to unlock her strangle hold.

"Darling, don't leave me."

"Gregg, *what the hell's keeping you?"*

Gregg shook his head. *"Listen to this guy!* I gotta go honey. Just turn the lock and help yourself to anything for breakfast. You have my cell and I have yours. I'll phone you from Tokyo whenever I get the chance."

"Gregg, for Christs sakes!"

"Keep your fucking shirt on... *Bye honey......."*

* * *

Tahoka pointed to the floor sending a message to Anbar to anchor his feet until told otherwise. He picked up the guns and ammo from the reception desk then disappeared through the secretarial door, as to how his boss would take it was anyone's guess. Okio addresses stupidity with an iron fist and a never-ending headache for the 'missing person's bureau' of the Tokyo Police.

Arakida nodded and opened the door to the 'inner sanctuary'. Okio looked up and stared as Tahoka entered, his steely brown penetrating eyes could send shivers down the spine of the largest Sumo and Tahoka stopped about two meters from his boss's desk and mechanically bowed.

A pot of his favorite green tea had just been refreshed and he slowly and deliberately replenished the small cup before taking another sip.

(Speaking in Japanese)

"Tahoka, don't just stand there, place these guns on my desk."

"Hai." Tahoka bowed again and obeyed his master.

"So?" Okio studied the weapons and ammunition.

"The Palestinian was armed." Tahoka san.

"The Palestinian was armed!" Okio screamed. *"Go fetch this idiot."*

"Hai." Tahoka bowed and took a few steps backwards then turned and left. Within minutes he returned, Anbar walking meekly in front.

(Speaking in English)

To say Anbar was nervous would be an understatement and he just had to let go.

"Okio San, *if you would just let me explain...*"

Okio raised his hand. "I tell you when to speak... Do you understand by coming here to my office, if you are under surveillance by the CIA you could jeopardize not only operation 'Fish Tail'?" Okio sneered. *"Stupid name,* but 'Nippon Shipping & Logistics' cover. The Americans and the Japanese Kempeitai have been trying for years to pin anything they can on the Yakuza and now through your utter stupidity you may have answered their prayers."

Anbar was frustrated not being allowed to state his case but it was worth another shot.

"Okio San, *if you would only let me...*"

"Did I tell you to speak?" Okio picked up the Glock and loaded the magazine sending one cartridge to the chamber then suddenly pointing the loaded weapon directly at Anbar's forehead. "I should blow your fucking brains out, the only thing that's saving your lousy Arab hide is my new teak flooring."

Okio locked the safety catch, Anbar's face regaining its color.

"Speak, *and it had better be good........!*"

* * *

".... And I had no alternative but to kill the CIA agent, *it was either him or me!*"

"This is such a fucking mess..." Okio sighed shaking his head. 'And your brother a corpse, not to mention the Maître D .... *What more do I need?* And when a CIA agent is murdered, everyman and his dog will be looking for you and the world will come down on us like a ton of bricks... That's the bad news and the good news is ... Your uncle in Chicago, the one with the 'Department of Controller of Currency' sends you *this* coded message by public telephone that triggered this whole mess... *I ask you...?*"

Okio lifted the blood-soaked napkin with his pen and spread it on his desk.
NUMS DELETED COMP CRASH ALLAH AHMAD
62826173-31325332813231-23636171-2153532142-2142612132
"I gather from this message that he has induced a computer crash and the serial numbers of the bank notes for destruction, to use the phrase, have disappeared into thin air... *Is that correct?*"

Anbar silently acknowledged, his mind still clouded with sadness mourning the loss of his beloved younger brother and Okio sensed the situation, a powder keg awaiting and he quickly changed the subject.

"And do you think the agent was able to send the coded message to CIA headquarters before you expired him?"

"I have to assume he did as he was on his cell phone at the time when I shot him but even if he did the CIA will have great difficulty breaking the code."

"*You fucking hope!*" Okio sneered.

That was it! Anbar had had enough of this little yellow man with his arrogance and abuse.

"*Have you no fucking compassion,* you *bastard?*" He suddenly screamed. "*I've just lost my brother!*"

Okio's eyes narrowed, he wasn't used to being ridiculed, *especially from an Arab!*

"Compassion costs money, your problem not mine. More important the airport plan is now screwed and we must rethink. And more to the point, if the police paste your face on the TV from the hotel security cameras, *we are really fucked.*"

"*Why you jumped up fucking...*" Anbar stopped abruptly, the cold steel from the muzzle of the Beretta digging painfully into the back of his neck, a mind stopper.

"If you want to join your brother, be my guest..."

Tahoka already had the Berretta cocked, a nod from his boss and Anbar is 'yesterday's man'.

(Speaking Japanese)

Okio raised his hand. "Tahoka, no problem, the Arab is not so stupid to try something silly that will help him escort his brother to the promised land."

The miniature Suma flicked the safety catch then gently uncocked the hammer before placing the '007' special back into his shoulder holster.

(Speaking in English)

Okio pointed to the empty chair.

"*Sit*, and don't be so stupid, I have enough problems, I need another corpse like a hole in the head. Now more importantly the airport plan."

Anbar reluctantly took the seat, if looks could kill. He wouldn't forget this day in a hurry.

Okio rubbed his chin, his mind searching for a solution to the fucked-up plan. Maybe another sip of his special brew would help.

"*Hmmmm...* Better." He refilled the empty cup. "Now let's take a step back... The 4pm departure to the airport is unchanged. By the time the Police Forensic Department finish finger printing your hotel rooms we will have departed from Narita and on our way to Shimaru Shima. As far as the security guards are concerned, now there will be three instead of four. Yakuza security contacts will inform the airline of the changes and a plausible excuse to cover the missing guard. Only one further change... A mustache and small goatee disguise, I'll instruct Ayako to phone a makeup artist immediately." He glanced at his watch. "Now two thirty, we don't have much time. Tahoka will escort you to our restroom and Ayako will provide you with coffee. Departure will now be from here. American passport..."

Okio searched the drawer then placed the forged document in front of Salibe before lifting the phone... "Ayako........"

* * *

"Do you have everything... Passport, electronic ticket, letter from the Japanese Embassy...?

"For Christ sakes Gregg, *gimme some space!*"

The elevator chimed and not too soon the way Steve was feeling.

"What's *your* problem this morning?" Gregg could return fire when the occasion arose.

Steve's expression was somewhere else as he dropped his garment bag on the sidewalk whilst waiting for the cab.

"That fucking Maggi... *Wasted...* Unconscious the whole night."

"For once you backed the wrong horse, huh?" Gregg burst into laughter.

"*Don't fucking rub it in...* Here's the cab and not before time I can't wait to hit that airport lounge."

"I thought you had had enough last night."

"I don't know what you're talking about, booze or sex?"

"Then I guess it's booze."

"How did you guess?"

The cab driver rolled down the window."

"Jonson?"

"Yeah, that's me... Dulles International, Delta Airlines."

"You got it." The cab driver pulled the lever to open the rear door and then the trunk.

Gregg and Steve placed their baggage in the trunk slamming it closed with Steve shaking his head as they entered the rear of the cab.

"Even the fucking taxis are self-service, *can you believe it?*"

"The world has changed buddy, and it's just the beginning......."

* * *

The drive to the airport seemed forever so much so you could cut the atmosphere with a knife.

"Come on man, *lighten up.*" Gregg broke the ice.

"Sorry buddy, I'm still feeling a bit sore... *Fucking blondes! So?*"

"So, where are you coming from...? Like, are you asking about me and Michelle?"

"Not unless there was three of you."

Gregg had to laugh. "That's more like it, dude... *Michelle...*" Gregg paused... "She's something else... Not to mention below the sheets. She's just adorable and although we only met for one night... *'Oh what a night'*... Steve, I tell you, I really want to see her again. I haven't felt like this since Rose and I broke up."

"Yeah, *and wasn't that a disaster*, and don't say I didn't try to warn you, dude!"

"But Michelle, she's different, she's like..."

"Man, gimme some slack or I'll be slashing my wrists."

"Listen Gregg..."

The cab had already pulled into the kerb at 'Delta International Departures', unbeknown to the two Casanovas.

"That'll be thirty-five straight." The driver opened the heavy Perspex security slide to take the fare whilst pointing to the meter.

"It's okay Steve, I'll get this, you go fetch the bags."

Gregg passed the driver two twenties. "Keep the change."

"Thanks guys, have a good flight." The black cabbie smiled, his pearly whites requiring some serious dentistry!

The driver had made good time, arriving at six forty-five, ample time for some welcome R&R in the Business Class lounge to recover 'after the night before'.

"Here we are." Steve pointed to the Delta gate with the flashing red LED sign, Delta 14, Tokyo Check in. Departure 0800 hrs.

"Business Class check in is here, Gregg." Steve pointed to the red carpet with the gold inscription.

"This *is really* class." Steve commented. "And express check in."

"Yeah," Gregg laughed. "It just shows you how the other half live."

"And get a load of the blonde at the desk."

"*You* gotta be kiddin me!"

"Well a guy can look, can't he?"

"Good morning Gentlemen. Tokyo today, is it?"

"I hope so, or we are checking in at the wrong desk."

The pretty young blonde in the smart Delta uniform didn't think the 'wise guy' comment was funny, like 'some mothers *do* have them'.

Steve just shrugged, the 'big elbow' was nothing new.

"Check in luggage?"

"No, were good." Gregg replied with a smile, it pays to be nice when you're on the other side of the desk.

"And your 'E' tickets and passports." She smiled.

"*Eh?*" Gregg glanced at her name tag. "Sandra, we have a letter of clearance from the Japanese Embassy allowing us to carry firearms.

She glanced at the document. "I'm impressed. First time on my watch to take care of the CIA." Back on stream again, she gave a warm smile. "I'll have to check with my supervisor to get clearance to carry firearms on board the aircraft. Can you please step aside for a few minutes while I contact him?" She lifted the phone, "Be with you in a minute sir." She calmed the irritated passenger waiting in line.

True to form a tall Latino looking gentleman in a smart blue uniform with gold braded cuffs, appeared at the check in, and passed a few words with Sandra then perused the letter.

"Good morning, my name is Aldo, I'm the shift supervisor. It's a privilege to have two CIA agents on our flight." He smiled. "And I'm sure if the passengers knew they would feel more than secure. But I'm afraid gentlemen although your documents will clear you in Japan to legally carry firearms in the performance of your duty, unfortunately for safety reasons we cannot allow dangerous materials on board that would compromise the safety of the aircraft and the passengers."

"We didn't anticipate there would be a problem." Steve asked concerned. "So, what's the bottom line?"

"A small formality... Take your firearms and munition to the Hazardous Cargo desk for check in and placement in special explosion proof containers. You'll be given a receipt to clear them at Narita. The desk is just down there to your left." Aldo pointed. "You can't miss it and have a nice flight."

"Mr. Nelson and Mr. Jonson, here are your tickets and your departure forms for completion before custom clearance. On the back of your tickets there are directions to our Business Class Lounge...And again have a nice flight... *Next Please......*"

* * *

Julie was in the Galley putting the final touches to her make up. She closed her lips then sort of pouted them to ensure her lipstick was even.

"I'm bushed I don't know about you Marge, I feel as if I have been up half the night, that Draper did a number on us flying from Lax to catch this flight at Dulles Washington."

"My problem was the Chardonnay." Marge shook her head. *"Ouch,* what's good for a hang over?"

"They say the 'hair of the dog'." Julie replied half smiling, she had been there before.

"Not on your life, looking at the manifest we don't have a vacant seat in Business and Coach so I'm gonna be run off my feet."

"Look on the bright side... Double time... Shopping till we drop in the Ginza and two days R&R."

She gave that sort of unconvinced look "The extra money would help with furnishing our new apartment, *but then...*" Marge grinned. "I guess the Ginza wins by a short nose."

"Listen Julie, in half an hour the plane will be boarding so I had better get going and check the galley inventory against the computer listing."

"Any VIPs on the list this morning in First Class?" Marge asked as she was reading the listing.

"Nah, and you in Business?"

"Let me see... Two CIA agents.... That's different... Messer's Nelson and Jonson."

"Eh?... Marge do these names ring a bell? Let me check my cell... Here we are... Remember the crazy Harley ride to our apartment down the Santana Monica.?"

"You're shittin me?"

"None other........"

* * *

"This is the last boarding call for passengers on Delta 14 bound for Tokyo, please proceeded to Gate 26, departing from Concord one."

"Steve waken up." Gregg shook him by the shoulder.

"God, I must have dosed off."

"Michelob's for breakfast, what do you expect. Move it and lets go pick up our bags at the front desk."

Steve was still half asleep. "If you say so." He rose unsteadily to his feet.

The 'walk on' conveyers made life easier and before they knew it they had arrived at the gate.

"Here we are Gate 26, and just in time, they are about to board."

"Hell, this must be the last gate in the airport." Steve gripped.

"First Class and Business Class only." The Stewardess announced at the ticket gate. "Please have your boarding passes and passports ready."

"I'm beginning to like this, Gregg."

"You've finally woken up."

"Get out of it!"

As they walked down the Aero Bridge to First and Business Class they could see in the distance the two Stewardess greeting the passengers and checking their boarding passes to direct them to their seats.

"Blondes must be in demand today." Steve unknowingly had spotted Julie.

Gregg didn't comment, it was a lost cause, but as they got closer to the cabin door he suddenly grabbed Steve by the arm.

"It can't be!"

"What can't be?"

"The two stewardesses."

Steve stopped and stared for a moment, then it came to him.

"The two broads we met on the beach. *Man,* someone up their likes us."

"Mr. Nelson and Mr. Johnson, both in Business Class, seats 16A and B." Julie was having great difficulty stifling her laughter.

"To your left Gentleman." Marge pointed. "We'll be serving refreshments before take-off."

"You're privileged tonight Marge." Julie gave that naughty look. In the Business Class Cabin with two of the 'President's Men." She placed her hand to her mouth.

"I should be so lucky, but don't they look familiar, Julie?" The girls were having a ball taking the 'Michael'.

"So, did you park your rented Harley's in the long stay carpark?" Marge had to get her fifty cents.

At that comment, they all burst into spontaneous laughter.

"You gals..." Steve was almost choking. "But seriously what a coincidence."

"I'm sorry guys it's great to see you again but I'll have to ask you to take your seats as the passengers are banking up. We'll catch up later."

"Can't wait." Steve was back on form.......

* * *

"These are like beds." Steve slouched back in the over indulgent Business Class seat.

"*Yeah,* and get a load of this." Gregg pressed the button on the arm rest operating a clear Perspex division window about 24 four inches in height between the seats, similar to that of an electric window in an automobile. "Now I won't have to suffer your BO and other body gasses when you hit the sack."

"*Get out of it, you moron! Man...*" Steve was fiddling with the different controls on the arm rest. "This is something else. You need to be a test pilot or have an engineering degree to operate this lot, I hope one is not for an ejector seat?"

Gregg laughed and retracted the partition. Steve could be at bit of a comedian when he is in the mood.

"Are you settled in guys?" It was Marge." I'm in charge of the Business Class cabin, so guys I'm afraid you're stuck with me for the remainder of the flight."

"I can suffer that anytime." Gregg was all smiles. Memories of their beach encounter and clubbing streaming back. He had a thing for her then but being in Washington and Marge in LA, it was highly unlikely that their paths would cross again.

"And Julie?" Steve couldn't wait.

"She's Chief Purser and responsible for the First-Class cabin... Too bad Steve." She laughed.

"But if my memory serves me right you mentioned you were both on the LA to London route, how come...?"

"It's a long story and for another a day. I'm sure Julie will come and see you when she has a break. Sorry guys, great to see you both but unfortunately, I have other passengers... But before I go an aperitif... Champagne and Caviar?"

"I've never tasted caviar before but there is always a first time."

Marge laughed. "Well at least your honest, Steve. I'll be back in five......."

* * *

"Jenny, can you get that?" Thomson was enjoying the last of his breakfast coffee and the New York Times, the ring of the phone echoing annoyingly from the hallway.

"Lazy Bones..." Jenny retaliated. "Yes, Thomson residence?"

"So, formal Jenny, its Ken Daniels here, phoning from Tokyo, sorry to disturb you but I need to speak with John, urgently."

"Hang a sec Ken... It's Ken Daniels from Tokyo, he stresses it's urgent." Not knowing what to expect, Jenny gingerly passed her husband the phone.

"Hmmm..." Thomson made a face. "Ken, what's the take?"

"John, I hope it's not a bad time."

"No, I'm just relaxing after breakfast... But why the...

"It's bad news."

"It's not Stella? No, she's in good health but thanks for the thought... No, it's Ginzo Iwami, he was shot and killed today in the line of duty."

"But how, Ken?"

"He was on an undercover assignment posing as a restaurant waiter at the Palace Hotel where Anbar Salibe and Fadil Maalouf were staying. Ginzo had been tracking their every move when in the breakfast restaurant they received a telephone call which we tracked from a public phone box in Chicago......"

"And he phoned in the coded message before the fire fight?"

"Yeah, but he wasn't going down easily and wasted Salibe's brother, Fadil Maalouf."

"Shit!"

"But that wasn't the final curtain, the restaurant Maître De, the poor bastard, was dropped when he came to search for Iwami in the Male Restroom, taking two 45's in the back of his head, execution style."

"These fucking people!"

"Is everything alright darling?" Jenny was taken aback at her husband's decibel breaking reply.

John raised his hand and nodded motioning her to keep her voice down.

"Ken, *don't tell me that snake Anbar Salibe escaped!*"

"I'm afraid that's the bottom line... A clean pair of heels by taxi of all things. We managed to track down the cab driver who was briefly kidnaped, a semi-automatic pressed against his temple. He dropped Fadil in the Ginza who then disappeared into the crowded shopping precinct without a trace."

"Three homicides, *I don't fucking believe it*, and more so I don't envy you conveying the bad news to Iwami's wife."

Ken gave a mammoth sigh. "Not to mention his two children. But we'll get that bastard if it's the last thing we do, *so help me!*"

"And the coded message?"

"We're still working on it but this one is different, like, it's just a bunch of meaningless numbers in code. Anyhow, I'm also calling to inform you that two of my men will meet Nelson and Jonson at Narita to bring them up to speed and escort them to the Palace Hotel where we have made reservations. I have also informed the Tokyo Homicide Division that two CIA agents will be assisting them in their investigation having been given clearance from the Japanese Embassy."

"What can I say Ken? Thanks for your call. I'll get Hanna to send Stevens an SMS. They will be arriving in Narita on Delta 14 at 21.50 pm your time."

"Thanks John and give my best to Jenny. If anything breaks, I'll call you immediately."

"Is it bad darling?" Jenny asked concerned, her face regaining its color.

"It doesn't get any worse......"

* * *

"Julie, you must be very busy, by the look of it it's a full house."

Steve was spraying the oxygen feeling a bit uneasy, which was most unusual when it comes to blondes. Was Julie still interested? The feeling she gave when reflecting to their evening at Bar Stella was more than positive but when it comes to relationships, here today gone tomorrow.

"Steve, I would have loved to spend more time with you guys but I've been under the gun with the flight bursting at the seams but I'm sure Marge has been looking after you."

"She's been exceptional." Gregg interposed, the body language between them fresh in his mind that day when they first met on the beach.

Julie smiled apologetically. "I'm sorry but I've gotta go. I have some real difficult 'baby boomers' in First today, besides the dinner service will commence in..." She glanced at her wrist. "Fifteen minutes... You have an excellent gastronomic experience ahead with a selection of fine wines and the best French Champagne. I'll catch up with you both later during the fight when most of the passengers are 'working off' their over indulgence." She turned to Marge as she was about to leave. "Can I see you for a moment in the First-Class galley when you are free.?"

"Sure, be with you in a moment... These are the menus, I'll return later for your selection. In the meantime, is there anything I can fetch you?" Marge gave that smile.

Gregg turned to look at Steve who shook his head as a no, no.

"No, we're good Marge......."

* * *

"Can you believe it?" Julie was relaxing on the stainless-steel bench top, her long sexy legs doing a Marilyn.

"They say 'what goes around comes around', huh? I never thought for one moment..."

"Yeah, I know what you mean, it's uncanny. I mean the guys live in Washington and us in LA, but..." Julie gave a wicked smile.

"Let me guess what you're thinking. Steve is cute, Huh? And after all we are back in the market and two nicer guys we couldn't meet."

Julie had to laugh, she was on the same page alright.

"So, what's the scoop?"

"Company rules dictate it's a termination offence for cabin crew to fraternize with the passengers. But there again..." Marge gave that cheeky smile. "Rules are meant to be broken."

"You're incorrigible, besides what's two days R&R in Tokyo without chaperones and I'm sure the way the guys were ogling at us, it's a done deal."

The buzzer sounded. "I Gotta go Marge, I'll discus it later once the dinner service is over."

"You got it..." Looks like Draper done us a favor after all." Marge laughed........."

THE HEIST

It would take a good hour's drive by cab to Narita and 2:30 had come and gone and Bill hastily proceeded to the checkout desk. It was a smart move to fetch his garment bag to the bar to save time and just as well with Chucks unexpected intrusion.

"Checking out Captain?"

"Afraid so Derek... *Eh*, room 462." Bill placed the plastic key card on the marble counter. Akira smiled then preceded to enter Bill's details into the computer.

"How has your stay been?" Derek was either genuinely interested or suffering from boredom, either way Bill wasn't in the mood for small talk, the forthcoming meeting with McGill choking his thought process.

"As always, excellent Ken."

"Here is a copy of your credit card Captain, which I will destroy and take another." Saved by the bell.

Bill passed the Amex as the printer spat out the computer paper.

"Domo Captain." Akira politely bowed. "Please check your account."

Bill briefly scanned the printout then nodded in agreement scribbling his signature.

"Will we see you again Captain?" Akira asked, her smile encapsulating. Sometimes you never see the beauty in a person until you really look again.

In her early twenties, those hypnotic olive shaped brown eyes, the smooth blemish less complexion, the fine nose line and narrow red lips were a cocktail of beauty. And with her black hair swept back into a Japanese style bun, she could be easily model for a 'block painting'. As for what could be seen of her figure above the reception desk, the imagination does wonders.

"*Eh*, I'm sorry Akira, I missed that." Bill replied awkwardly.

Akira smiled unperturbed, taking no prisoners.

"Will we see you again?" She repeated, her voice uncannily seductive.

For a moment, Bill was having a problem navigating his plane but Ken's timely interjection brought him back to the runway.

"Shall I get the Concierge to call you a cab, Captain?"

"Eh...Err... Yes Ken, thanks."

Ken snapped his fingers to attract the Concierge who immediately instructed a bell hop to collect Bill's luggage before proceeding to the hotel entrance.

"Ken, thanks again." Bill offered his hand. "It's always a pleasure to stay at the Grand Hyatt Roppongi... And..." He turned to Akira." I'm sure we will meet again."

She gave him that smile and bowed. "Arigato."

The cab driver was waiting, the rear door of the Toyota Crown ajar.

Bill nodded and took his seat. "Narita International, Global Airways."

"Hai."

As the car sped off Bill turned and stared through the back window, the hotel disappearing in the distance, the image of Akira still fresh in his memory, whatever it was about this beautiful creature, he most certainly will do a 'Douglas Macarthur'......

* * *

"Hmmmm..." Okio sat back in his plush executive chair then leaned forward to indulge in his refreshed green tea.

"Hmmmm..." He grunted again in thought, the tea reducing his 'off the scale' blood pressure... The meeting with Anbar questioning his judgement as to why he didn't send him to join his beloved Profit Mohamed but then Samurai are men of honor and once a contract is made there is no turning back. Tonight, would be the litmus test and the first stage of operation 'Fish Tail' but already cracks were showing with the loss of one of the Palestinians and the corpses of a CIA agent and a senior staff member of the Palace Hotel. Okio shook his head, the thought sending the wrong jibes but now he had to pull himself together and more importantly contact 'Shimura Shima'.

Midafternoon was not the best for atmospheric interference and Okio checked his watch then grunted again as he tuned his HF Motorola to the 80m band. Time was of the essence as the break in the monsoon weather provided only a 12-hour window of opportunity.

(Speaking in Japanese)

Okio drummed his fingers on his desk, his impatience getting the better of him. The crackling and whistling irritating his ear drums and making him wince.

"Come on, come on, the fuck..."

Shendo's voice suddenly echoed loud and clear.

"What fucking took you so long?"

"Eh...Err..." Shendo was taken aback; the messenger was shot before he could defend himself.

"Password?"

"Password...?" Shendo raised his voice, *like what?*

"Do we have a fucking hearing problem, as well now?"

"Fish Tail." Shendo finally uttered.

"At last! Now, you listen to me and listen good! It could have been anyone on this phone, like the CIA, *do you read me?"*

"It won't happen again, Namura San."

"For your sake, *I hope so.* Now getting down to business, the runway?"

"As previously reported the monsoon drains at each side have dispersed the water build up and the Mitsubishi heavy duty pumps are running round the clock. The extended runway is completely dry and we will retain the waterproof tarpaulins in place until the last moment when I receive conformation of the ETA from the pilot. The weather is forecast to remain dry this evening but the monsoon season has no guarantees."

"For your sake Shendo, you had better hope it has... And the six-meter florescent landing line and lights?" Okio was like a runaway train.

"Namura San, you have my word everything is perfect but the success of the landing lies in the hands of the pilot."

Namura ignored Shendo's comment, like don't tell me something a three years old kid would know.

"Now here's the deal...Global 10 will depart Narita on schedule at 2210hrs, and weather prevailing will land on Shimaru Shima at 2410 covering the approximate 2,000 Kilometers. Now is there anything else I may have missed?"

"Yes, Numara San, the lockup for the prisoners and the camouflage for the airliner."

"Speak to me." Numara barked. How could he have forgotten?

"I have secured an unused maintenance shed with barred windows and a steel framed door. It has water and basic toilet amenities and two bamboo cots. We have ample camouflage netting to hide the jet liner in the unlikely event of air detection and besides the end of the runway lye's deep in thick jungle vegetation."

"Well at least that's some good news. Call me when 'Fish Tail' has landed."

"Arigat..." The call went dead.......

* * *

Sally was cursing as she stuffed the last of her shopping into her airway 'carry-on' bag. Fortunately, cabin crew are allowed 30kilos baggage and maybe just as well. It was a 'shop till you drop' morning in the Ginza and operation 'demolish credit card', then a light lunch at the 'Sushi Train' and back to the hotel and the last miracle, *to close that zipper!*

"Wow! Wasn't that something?" She spoke aloud as she chucked her jacket onto the desk chair before crashing to the soft leather sofa and kicking off her shoes, swinging her feet from the floor.

"Boy, am I bushed!" She placed a cushion behind her head then glanced at her Omega.

"One thirty, I still have plenty of time before our meeting and a bit of shut eye wouldn't go stray but I had better call the front desk just in case I over indulge." She had that smile.

The Saki and the late dinner last night, not to mention fighting off the over amorous Chuck, was a fete and with this morning's hectic shopping, she could easily sleep for a week and as Sally leaned over to pick up the room phone she suddenly noticed the red message button flashing crazily.

"Now what can this be?"

: Message at 1pm... "Hi Sally, Chuck here, I wondered if we could meet for lunch, I'll be in the 'Maduro Bar' on the ground floor, then we could share a cab to the airport. I'm in room 377, call me."

Sally shook he head. "Yeah, *that'll be right.* Get a load of this guy... It's a 'rain check' Chuck buddy, and share a cab! *not on your life,* what with those octopus' hands, *you gotta be kiddin me!"* Sally was talking out loud but it was the 'real deal'.

She pressed the button for the front desk.

"This is room 244, Miss Jenkins here."

"Ohio Gozaimasu, how can I help you?"

"Can you please instruct the Concierge to arrange to collect my bags by 2.45 as I will be checking out at three and I also require a cab to Narita International."

"Certainly, Miss Jenkins. Arigato."

"Ah, now I can close my eyes in confidence......."

* * *

The irritating sound of the doorbell made Sally stir. It sounded so far away and yet so near and she rolled over on her side and snuggled her head deeper into the cushion.

"Hmmmm..."

"Ding Dong...Ding Dong..."

"Go away... Go away." She bawled through her deep sleep.

"Miss Jenkins, is there anything wrong?" The Bell Hop rattled his knuckles on the heavy wooden door as a last resort.

"Holy crap!" Sally swung her feet to the floor. *"Coming...Coming."* She rushed to the door. "I'm sorry, my bags are over there." She pointed embarrassingly, looking like the aftermath of "The Big Sleep'.

"Please take them to the lobby, I'll be down shortly after I tidy up."

"Arigato." The young man politely bowed and placed the bags on the oversize brass luggage trolley.

Sally glanced into the full-length mirror. "Hell, *I look like shit.!* And my hair..." She quickly grabbed a brush from her handbag and began stroking her shoulder length brown hair bringing it back to life. "Now where's that lipstick...?"

Within minutes she was legging it to the elevator looking as smart as ever in her dark blue Global stewardess uniform and modest heels to match.

The elevator chimed... "Ground Floor and Reception."

Sally glanced at her watch again. "I'm still good." She opened her steps as she walked toward the checkout desk in the process inevitably passing the 'Maduro Bar' and who the hell was sitting there? The one and only Chuck Stevens, and Sally walked even faster praying by the grace of God she would not be spotted.

"This must be my lucky day," She gave an exaggerated sigh as the cab slowly drove away from the hotel.

"And just maybe, it's time for another nap." She smiled and closed her eyes once more.......

* * *

"Hell, is it that time already! Well, I guess Sally gave me the 'bum's rush." Chuck shrugged. "So, what's the big deal?" He raised his arm to catch the barman's attention.

"Sir?"

"I want two double espresso coffees."

"Both for you sir?" The barman was confused.

"You heard right! Now I'm in a bit of hurry, so if you don't mind?"

"Certainly sir, give me ten minutes."

"I hope these coffees do the trick." He took a gulp of the dark liquid emptying the miniature cup.

"Now wouldn't it be a fucking disaster if I didn't pass the 'breath test'........"

* * *

"Hmmmm... Not bad timing." Bill commented as he glanced at his watch. "It's just turned four fifteen and by the time I check through immigration it couldn't be better timed if I planned it."

He paid the cab driver the meter and threw in a tip, collected his garment bag and stepped it out to 'International Departures'.

"Ah, there it is straight in front."

'Cabin Crew Departures' in bright red computerized signage.

Bill knew the drill and with his passport and credentials ready it was just a formality before he entered the concourse and headed for the 'Staff Lounge'.

"Have a safe flight Captain." The departing comment from the pretty immigration officer always a hype.

"I'll skip the coffee and go straight to McGill's office." Bill spoke aloud.

"Captain Collins! You're early." Mitsuko smiled and promptly applied the brakes to the computer key pad.

"As they say, 'better late than never'." Bill smiled.

The punned comment seemed to confuse Mitsuko... *"Eh, Err...* I'm sorry Captain?" Her eyes reflecting her embarrassment.

"Some other time Mitsuko." Bill changed the subject.

English is hard enough for the English to understand, *never mind the Japanese!*

Mitsuko, was now even more confused but then why push the envelope?

"I'll inform Jim that you're here." She lifted the phone. "I have Captain Collins here... Yes, I'll tell him." She placed the receiver back in its cradle and smiled. "You can go straight in Captain......"

* * *

"Bill...! Grab a seat." Jim offered his hand in a warm gesture. "You look refreshed, you must have had an early night."

"I suppose you could say that..." Then Bill paused, a troubled look on his face... "Sally... I can take, but Chuck...? After all these years, we have been best buddies, I suppose I never really knew the guy. He's changed so much and for the worse, getting into bed with the wrong crowd at the casino, not to mention his overzealous drinking and womanizing... *Jim...*" Bill sighed. "I'm really beginning to think he's a lost cause."

"So, you might have to cut the umbilical, huh?" Jim half laughed.

"Get out of it! Do you think we're joined at the hip?" Bill burst into laughter.

"Changing the subject, what did you guys get up to last night?"

"Teppanyaki and Saki at the Minato Restaurant in the hotel... Exciting, huh?"

"So?"

"Ah, I don't know..." Bill shook his head. "This Chuck was using all the oxygen in the room, even getting Sally involved about tonight's cargo so much so I had to call it a night. *Jim, I mean, it's not as if we are carrying radioactive isotopes or some shit like that!"*

Jim just grinned he had been there and done that. *"Ah..."* Jim laughed. *"The challenges of power...* Being the boss is never easy but then neither's life. Say, how about a coffee to relax?"

"I wouldn't say no..."

"Mitsuko......."

* * *

"So, Julie and you are going through a cooling off period?"

"If you could call it that." Bill sort of shrugged it off.

"You *do* have a few problems, Bill." Jim laughed. "But then don't we all?"

"Jim, getting back to security, you did mention that there will be armed guards accompanying us all the way to Washington?"

"No, I'm sure I didn't but while we are on the subject. Yes, there were originally four but I just received an Email from Head Office with a change of plan reducing it to three. Some sort of emergency or another job where they are short of a man. No big thing."

"Jim, I have to ask the question with three pistol packing ambries on board..."

"Hold it there Bill! I know where you are coming from and I can understand your trepidations but Global and the local Japanese equivalent to the FBI, 'The National Police Agency' have given their blessing and security clearance."

McGill turned his computer screen to face Bill.

"Here they are, the first two are Japanese."

Their pictures and background information flashed up onto the screen.

"Kazuo Tahoka and Akimas Arakida." Jim pointed with his pen to the two mean looking dudes. Both operatives of the 'Kovan Chousacho' the 'Public Security Intelligence Agency', with license to kill, the equivalent of MI5 or the American FBI. You mess with these two at your peril. Now this other guy, he's a different kettle of fish, Jovani Quario with Black Hawk Securities. Yeah, I know what you're thinking, Black Hawk were employed by the US Military both in Iraq and Afghanistan, and not without some major controversy over the murder of Afghan civilians. But this guy is a vet and served with distinction with two tours of duty in Afghanistan with the US Marines. When demobilized, he contracted into Black Hawk as a security officer. His parents immigrated from Cicely to the US after the second world war... He's clean as whistle."

Bill studied Jovani's picture a little closer. "I gotta say this Jim, he doesn't look Mediterranean, more like Middle Eastern."

"Bill, your becoming another 'Sherlock Holmes'. Listen, they have a clean bill of health from the FBI and that's all that matters, *case closed.*"

McGill tapped the face of his watch. "It has just turned six and the three things I hate most are... cold coffee, wet toilet paper and people that waste my fucking time........!"

* * *

(Speaking in English/ Japanese)

Numero lifted the phone.

"Yes, Ayako?"

"Numero San, my apologies but you asked me to call you at four. The police cruiser to the airport has already arrived and is parked in the underground basement car park."

"That time already!" Okio glanced at his watch. "Thank you, Ayako, I've been so engrossed in the 'Beijing Contract' I completely over looked the time. Don't worry, I'll walk through it with you later. Inform the airport contingent that I want to see them in my office before they depart."

"Certainly, Numero San, I will call them now."

There was a loud knock on the heavy teak door and Okio stopped punching the keyboard and saved the work on his desktop.

"Enter." Numero's commanding voice echoed, challenge at your peril.

As the three 'flight security guards' lined up standing to attention, Arakida and Tahoka bowed instantly leaving Fadil totally confused as to what to do and Numero recognized his confusion 'to bow or not to bow', so to speak.

"No need!" He barked in English and waved his arm in a nonchalant gesture. Then he sort of coughed to clear his throat to draw attention, before slowly and deliberately rising from his desk and walking toward 'the valiant three', his beady eyes absorbing every detail of both the Black Hawk Security uniform and that of the 'Kovan Chousacho'.

Numero cast his eyes over the two heavies and the Palestinian, who now looked more than uncomfortable. Maybe it was the Black Hawk uniform but most likely the clean-shaven face sporting a goatee and moustache, verging on the ridiculousness. For sure the 'get up' didn't do him any favors.

"Hmmm." Okio pouted his lips and stroked his chin as he inspected the three 'statuettes' in regimental fashion, like a Sargent Major inspecting his platoon.

"Good!" A man of few words... *"Ayako... Passport for Anbar San."*

Ayako instantly obeyed gingerly passing the forged document.

Okio flicked through the pages to check the various country entries and visa stamps, authenticating 'Jovani's' tours of duty with Black Hawk.

"Security tags and identity cards...?" Okio barked almost making Anbar jump out of his skin. This 'over the top' inspection drama was becoming too much.

Okio stood for a moment in silence as he studied the credentials, his eyes darting two and fro like an electronic print head, capturing every detail.

"Everything is in order." He nodded in satisfaction, a rare compliment from the Samurai and not a glimmer of a smile and he glanced at his watch once more.

"You must leave now, with the office traffic you will need all your time to arrive by six to clear security and immigration and to check in with Global. Our men at the airport will ensure there are no glitches. Police Commissioner Gingi

Iwami, has provided a cruiser at our disposal. He is the senior commandant of the Yakuza's Northern Tokyo Division... *OH...!* I almost forgot. When you arrive at Immigration, you must go to check in desk three which is manned by 'Yakuza'. Any questions?... *Good...!* One other small point, you must leave by the basement carpark using the fire exit stairs to avoid contact with the building populous and prevaricate raising suspicion... Arigato........"

* * *

"Well fancy meeting you here!"

Sally recognized the voice as she handed her passport to the immigration officer before turning to face the joker.

"Chuck, you're such a giant A H." Sally shook her head as she cleared the check point. She was running late for the meeting with McGill and Stevens and all she needed was Chuck cramping her style.

"You know we could have saved a taxi fare if you had joined me for lunch."

"Yeah, and all the rest." Sally returned fire.

"Something tells me that you have a bad opinion of me." Chuck laughed aloud much to Sally's annoyance.

"Chuck, get off my street! Sally retaliated. "Changing the subject, I thought you had a live in?"

"That's one way of putting it. You mean Marge?" Chuck laughed again.

"Whoever..." Sally was panting slightly, opening her legs as she wheeled her carryon bag toward the Admin Office at full speed.

"If that's her name."

"Naw, we decided to go our different ways."

"Wise decision by... Err... Maggie, was it?"

"You're a card Sally but I like your style, straight for the jugular, huh?"

"If you say so... Chuck, this conversation is getting to the point where it's boring... *At last!"* Sally finally opened the door marked 'Global Staff Only'.

"Thanks Sally I almost got the door in my face." Chuck grabbed it just time before almost jamming his bag.

"Mitsuko, my apologies, I'm running a bit late."

McGill's secretary put the brakes on the keyboard and looked up.

"Don't apologies to me Sally, it's my boss that's waiting and may I say he is not in the best frame of mind."

"That bad?"

"It doesn't get any worse." Mitsuko lifted the phone shaking her head at Chuck, sporting that silly grin, like, this guy will never learn.

"Jim, I have Sally Jenkins and Chuck Stevens here.... *Hmmm...* I'll send them in." Mitsuko pointed to the door marked 'J. McGill Vice President Global Freight, in bold gold leaf. *"It's all yours.* You can leave your bags here."

"Here let me." Chuck knocked on the wood.

McGill gave Bill that look.

"Well don't just stand there, *come in... come in!"* A deaf man could sense McGill wasn't happy.

McGill pointed. "Take the load off... Question... Are you people on US time or Tokyo time? Or is it that you both just don't give a shit?" McGill tapped his watch. "Twenty-five minutes late! The flight has gone... *Do you get my drift?"*

"My advice Sally... *Don't...*" Now if it's not too much to ask let's get down to business. I suggest you do the needful Bill. In my state of mind, I might end up firing some people."

"Thanks Jim." A touch of sarcasm ringing through. "Okay, let's start at the beginning... Your flight details... Global 10 departs from Narita this evening at 2230 hours bound for Washington DC. The cargo.... 200 billion US dollars in mixed denominations, past their 'use by date' for destruction at The Federal Reserve Washington DC."

A pin dropping would have felt like thunder and Sally gave a gasp whereas Chuck's silence was deafening.

"There's nothing to be concerned about as we will be accompanied by three-armed security guards throughout the flight. Two Japanese from the 'Kovan Chousacho', the equivalent to our FBI, the other from Black Hawk Securities."

"Bill, are we expecting trouble?" Chuck finally cut the chase.

"No, not at all but it's better to be safe than sorry. In fact, armored security trucks accompanied by Japanese SWAT are loading the cargo this very minute. Which brings me to the point. *The pay load...* We'll need every ounce of thrust from the Trent's to lift the rubber with a maxim cargo weight of 102 metric tons."

Chuck shook his head. "That's a tall order Bill, and with full tanks there's no room for error."

"There's always a first-time Chuck, but that's my problem. Any questions... *Sally...?"*

"No, I'm good Captain."

"Then I suggest Sally, you attend to the catering and keep in mind our two Japanese friends and one Italian."

"So, it's Sushi and Spaghetti huh?" Sally laughed. "I'll check out the kitchen but as normal it's microwave with the exception of course of the sashimi. Can I leave now?" Sally was anxious.

"Of course, if that's alright Jim?" Bill turned.

"Sure, I think you have covered all the salient points."

"Thanks Mr. McGill." Sally rose to leave with Chuck about to follow suite.

"Not you Chuck." McGill interposed. "Thanks Sally, have a good flight ... Chuck." McGill put on his stern look. "I'm reminding you that you must take the mandatory breath test at the Medical Centre, like ASAP, I want to see the results."

"Does that include Bill?" Chuck was being a smart ass.

"Chuck, don't get stroppy with me, you're on the red line already so you had better hope that you pass with flying colors. *Do I have to explain?*"

Chuck just shrugged, this was nothing new, another 'I hate Chuck day'.

"Yeah, I get the drift, so I guess I'm excused?"

"I'll be waiting." McGill wasn't beating about the bush.

"Don't worry Jim, you'll be pleasantly surprised."

"I hope so for your sake." McGill's eyes blazed.

Without another word, Chuck turned tail and left.

"That guy!" Jim shook his head. "I see what you mean Bill."

"Yeah." Bill grimaced. "Say, I had better go and check the ship and meet up with our security guards."

McGill nodded. "Bill, come and see me before you lift off......."

* * *

"This is your third double expresso, what's the take?"

Chuck had doubled back to the staff lounge to hit the caffeine before the breath test.

"It's a long story Jacky and for another day."

"Are *you* still here Chuck?" It was Sally standing behind him waiting in line for her capuchino.

Chuck grinned. *"Well fancy meeting you here!"*

"Chuck, that one's 'past its use by'."

"If you must know, I thought it's better to use a belt and brace option, just to make sure the powerful caffeine kills the alcohol I had at lunch time. At least that's the theory."

"You had better make sure Einstein was right." Jacky burst into laughter.

"Yeah... Yeah, there's always one."

"Now I get it." Jacky was quick on the uptake.

"Yeah and keep it to yourself which being a woman behind the counter, I imagine would be impossible."

"Get out of it, you misogynist."

"Thanks Jacky." Sally carefully balanced the full cup as she searched for a table.

"Can I join you?"

"It's a free country, Chuck." Sally took her seat.

"But shouldn't you be packing it to the medical Centre, it's almost twenty-one hundred, you know."

"McGill can wait."

Sally shook her head; *will this guy ever learn?*

Holding the cup in both hands, Sally cautiously took a sip of the hot coffee.

"Hmmmm... I needed this."

"So?"

"So... So, what Chuck?"

"I mean the cargo?"

"Listen, I'm only interested in the catering, I've got Japanese and Italian cuisine to think about, happily no booze."

"Now isn't that a pity!" Chuck couldn't help himself.

Sally finished the last dregs, wiped her mouth with her napkin then rose to her feet.

"Listen I gotta go, I have to check the galley and sign the manifest."

"Leaving already huh, and Just when I was getting to know you."

Sally shrugged treating the remark with the contempt it deserved, but then this was Chuck.

"Chuck, if you want my advice, which I am sure you don't... If I were you I would be high tailing it to the Medical Centre..." She began to leave. "Best of luck."

"Well isn't that something, I knew it, you like me after all."

"I wouldn't lose any sleep over it." Sally could still hear Chuck's laughter as she left the staff cafeteria........

* * *

As Bill walked the tarmac to Global 10 he almost choked from the diesel fumes spewing from the exhausts of the numerous fork lift trucks busily unloading and loading the aluminum boxes from the armored security cars into the specially designed cargo containers, that fit the contour of the loading bay in the 777 freighters.

"Ah heh...Ceh...Ceh" Bill coughed placing his hand to his mouth as he cleared his airway. The Japanese SWAT and Police Security personnel wearing body armor, were no dummies, covering their noses and mouths with white linen face masks.

In the distance standing below the port engine Bill could make out the silhouette of three uniformed security guards, their attire different from the others.

"I wonder?" Bill spoke under his breath. *"Well*, there's only one way to find out."

As he drew closer in the floodlit darkness, dodging the overzealous fork lift drivers, although the three figures were also wearing face masks he could distinguish the two larger of the three were Japanese and the much slimmer, third man, Caucasian.

"Hmmmm, let's see what we got... Good evening gentlemen I'm assuming from your uniforms that you are the security guards accompanying Global 10 to Washington DC?"

There was no answer.

"Im Captain Collins, your pilot."

Immediately the two mini 'Sumas' bowed. Either they *could* speak English or they recognized the prominent three gold bands on Bill's cuffs.

"Is there anyone here who speaks English?"

"I apologies Captain for my Japanese colleges their understanding of the English language is limited."

"No sweat, and you are?" Bill glanced using his inspection torch at the clipboard he was carrying. "Giovani Quario and..." Bill checked his board again. "Aikido Arakida... and... Kazuo Tahoka?"

The Japanese bowed once more at the mention of their names.

"Hmmmm... Quario, that's Italian?"

Quario nodded.

"Yes, my parents immigrated from Cicely when I was only two years old. I am a naturalized American citizen having served four years in the Marines and now an employee of 'Black Hawk Securities'."

"Strange, you have a bit of an accent."

"Do I! You're the first one to mention."

"Buona sera, come stai." Bill exhausted the few Italian words he knew.

"Eh...Eh... Si." Giovani was conspicuously uncomfortable.

"Living in America almost all my life I've been too lazy to learn my native tongue."

"Hmmmm. I see." Bill changed the subject reluctantly accepting Giovani's feeble excuse, Italians never lose their culture.

"Boarding is 2200hrs, make sure you are on board and on time and have your relevant documentation, passports etc. as it will be thoroughly checked by the US Border Security when we arrive in Dulles International."

"Don't worry captain." Quario replied. "Everything is on order."

"Then 2200hrs, please excuse me, I have to check the aircraft."

Bill continued to inspect the under carriage, tires, flaps, rear rudder... Ticking off each one on his clip board.

Then just as he was about to leave he suddenly stopped in his tracks.

"Hell, I almost forgot the Pitot Tubes!"

Bill flashed his torch onto the two slender eight-inch-long Pitot tubes protruding just below the cockpit to make sure the front and side holes were clear. These tubes are critical in calculating air speed. Satisfied Bill about turned and briskly walked toward the Admin Office to complete his 'sign off' meeting with McGill......

* * *

"Mitsuko, is he free?"

"Yes Bill, you can go right in, he's waiting for you."

Mitsuko's English was impeccable apart from a slight accent, a rare find in Japan and pretty too. *Not that McGill would notice!*

Bill knocked on McGill's door as a matter of respect.

"Come in." McGill's voice echoed. "Take the load off." Jim pointed. .

"Everything is in order." Bill passed McGill the Pilot's check list.

"And the cargo?" McGill asked.

"Yeah it's all battened down and secure. I gotta admit Jim there's not enough room left to swing a cat."

McGill laughed at Bill's comment.

"You'll have to press the gas on this one."

"That's for sure." Bill replied an orny grin crossing his face.

"I'm sure you checked out the security guards bearing in mind your overzealous anxieties."

"I did Jim, and that's a concern I want to pass by you."

"Okay Sherlock Holmes', *let's have it!*"

"Seriously Jim, hear me out."

"So, put me out of my misery." McGill was still not taking it seriously.

"It's the American Italian, Giovani Quario. Like, Italians never lose their language even though, as Quario puts it, he came to the US when he was only two years old."

"Get to the point Bill." McGill glanced at his watch.

"Okay, here's the gripe. I spoke to him in Italian and he didn't understand a word that I said. His excuse... Too lazy to learn. This guy's gotta be kidding me *and wait for it!* The Japanese guards had their left small finger partly amputated."

"Bill, I can see where you're coming from but what do you want me to do? I mean, if you're wrong, what's the deal? Why would we have a bent guard on board and then there's the two Japanese? Sorry Bill, if I throw a spanner in the works at the last minute based on a hunch, we'll end up with egg on our faces, never mind cancelling the flight. Sorry Bill, it's out of the question."

Hmmm, I guess you're right Jim, maybe *I am* being over cautious. Listen I gotta go it's almost 2200."

"Have a safe flight Bill, and oh, I almost forgot. Chuck passed he breath test with flying colors."

"Now isn't *that* something.........!"

* * *

Bill spoke over the intercom.

"Please take the jump seats and ensure your safety belts are tightened to the fullest. Sally, do me a favor and check out our guests to make sure they understand."

Sally picked up the phone. "No sweat Captain, they're buttoned up to the teeth."

"And that goes for you Sally."

"I'm onto it."

"So, are we expecting some drama?" Chuck tossed the throwaway line with a stupid grin.

"Chuck, do yourself a favor and cut the wise cracks, you *know* it's standard safety procedure for passenger and crew. Now as first officer do I need to spell it out?"

"Yes Captain." Chuck's sarcasm unmistakable.

Chuck methodically went through the safety check over dephasing the procedure, his voice a contender for 'American Idol'.

"Doors closed.... Parking brake... Spoilers retracted... Flap position lever 5 degrees... Landing gear... Hydraulics... Transponder on.... Flight data recorder on... Cockpit voice recorder............"

Bill nodded. "Good, I'll contact the tower, I want this bad boy in the air as soon as possible."

"Global 10 to Tower, Captain Collins requesting instructions for takeoff, departure time to Washington DC, Dulles International is 2230hrs

"Tower to Global 10, I will instruct the ground crew for a 'pull push' to position the aircraft onto the taxiway to proceed to the takeoff gate. Captain Collins there may be a short delay due to landing congestion. Please wait for further instructions."

There was a sudden jolt then a shudder as the ground crew hooked up the 777 to the heavy steel tractor rod reversing the fully laden aircraft 180 degrees to position it on the taxiway. From there on it was up to Bill to steer this giant to the departure runway and await instructions.

"Tower to Global 10, proceed to gate 3B on your left. There is a British Airways 747 next in line for takeoff. Ensure one-kilometer distance apart to avoided jet turbulence from the larger aircraft."

"Instructions understood, will taxi to runway 3B and await your instructions." Bill throttled the engines, then sighed and shaking his head before turning to Chuck.

"I don't fucking believe it! *Deja vue*, behind another limy flight and I suppose as usual it'll take forever."

"You seem a bit nervous Captain?" Chuck as always couldn't keep his big mouth shut.

"Cut the 'Captain' shit, you've made your point. With this payload, we'll *all* be happy when the rubber leaves the tarmac......."

* * *

"What kept you?" Julie was already enjoying a sneaked coffee break as Marge entered the galley and pulled the curtains closed.

"*Full house.*" Marge shrugged. "These so-called business men, I wouldn't wish to be their secretaries, *pampered brats.*"

"Wow, you *are* on a roll! *Here,* let me pour you a coffee to calm your nerves."

"A 'Dom Perignon' would be more to my liking."

"*You wish...!* The trouble with you Marge is you don't delegate enough, *make the younger ones do the work.* After all *we* had to go through it!"

"Don't remind me, you're making me feel old just talking about it... *Oh my poor feet.*" Marge kicked off her shoes one at a time then balanced on one foot to massage her toes before pressing both hands behind her back onto the stainless-steel galley to lever her butt from the floor into a sitting position, her legs dangling.

"Marge, your problem is, you always buy shoes a half size too small."

"Who wants a stewardess with military feet...? Julie, the way I'm feeling, I don't need the mother talk, I have enough on my plate in Business Class."

"Im sorry Marge for being so insensitive, let's lighten up and change the subject, like, how are our heroes doing?"

"By that I gather you mean Steve and Gregg?"

"*Hmmmm...* On first names terms, are we?"

"*Get out of it!* You know where I'm coming from, but if you must know, they have been real gentleman keeping a low key. Now if you're asking what I think you're asking...? The body language is heavy."

"That's encouraging." Julie replied a glint in her eye. "Do you think they'll try and contact us in Tokyo?"

"*Julie,* the way Steve was ogling you, it's a done deal. But the next question is, how are they going to get in touch with us?"

"Marge, if my memory serves me right, turn the clock back and, remember you gave Gregg your cell number in LA."

"*Of course, Of course!*" Marge's face brightened, suddenly Business Class was on the back burner.

"That brought a smile to your face, *huh?*" Julie laughed aloud.

"*Shit,* I almost forgot! Yeah, now I remember, problem solved."

The cockpit red light flashed interrupting their hot conversation.

"Julie, that's yours... *The captain is calling.*" Marge teased.

"Cut the comedy, besides wouldn't you agree, Captain Taylor is a dish."

"Yeah, and for your information, he's married."

"And when did that make a difference?"
"Get out of it! Speak for yourself."
"Listen, I gotta go or I'll be placed in solitary confinement."
Marge had to laugh at Julie's wisecrack.
"He probably only want's a second cup of coffee."
"Go on say it."
They both burst into laughter.
"Spoiled brats......."

* * *

Julie returned in a flash.
"So why the call?" Marg asked.
"Awe, nothing much, but a job for you."
"Take me out of my misery."
"It appears our two CIA agents have had a change of hotel."
"Must be important to receive a ground call."
"Yes, and guess what? You're the messenger. Looking at my watch we will be landing in around forty minutes so I suggest you carry out the 'Chief Purser's' orders."
Pulling rank huh? Well, at least now we know where they are staying." Mage laughed.
"Now you're talking......."

* * *

Marge quickly walked the walk through the business Class Cabin only to find two sleeping beauties.
"Excuse me, can I have..."
"Just press the call button on your left sir and a stewardess will attend to you, I'm busy at the moment." Marge finally taking a leaf from Julie's book.
Marge gently pressed Gregg's shoulder.
"Ah... Hmmmm." Gregg stirred rubbing his eyes with both hands before sitting upright... *"Marge!"* He gave a sleepy smile.
"Eh...Err." Mr. Johnson." Marge placed her finger to her lips.
"Mr. Johnson, I have a message here from the Captain, hot off the press from your Tokyo office regarding a change to your hotel reservations." Marge passed Gregg the slip of paper.
Gregg read it in silence then smiled trying to muzzle his laughter.

'Reservations changed, now Palace Hotel, FBI agents Brown and Daily will meet you at Arrival hall'. (Julie and I have two days R&R you have my cell number)

"Is everything alright Mr. Jonson?" Marge half winked.

"It doesn't get any better."

"And Mr. Nelson?"

"Let sleeping dogs lie."

Before Gregg could continue further an announcement come over the communication system.

'This I Captain Taylor speaking to inform you that our estimated time of arrival to Narita International will be delayed by approximately 30 minutes as the result of a security problem. There is no need for alarm as it is just routine. I will keep you informed should there be any further delay. On behalf of Delta Airways, thank you for your patience and understanding.'

The intercom system had awakened Steve and he sat up turning to Gregg.

"Yeah, I heard it...! Marge." Steve was in deep thought. "Would it be possible to speak to the Captain? It's really urgent."

"Just give me five."

Marge recognized Gregg's body language and from the tone in his voice, she knew something was up and accelerated through the First-Class cabin.......

* * *

"It's highly irregular but the Captain has agreed to see you. Please accompany me." Marge was playing the role as she knocked on the security door to the cockpit.

"Yes?" The voice boomed.

"Captain Taylor, I have the two CIA agents here."

There was a slight delay as the first officer entered the numbers to open the bullet proof door.

"Come in... I'm Captain Taylor the middle aged distinguished gentleman turned in his seat. "Now how can I help you?" The first officer closed the door behind them, Marge left out in the cold.

"I appreciate your time Captain... Agents Steve Nelson and Gregg Johnston." Steve passed Taylor their cards

The Captain gave a nod, not really interested in pulp fiction and without looking placed them in his shirt pocket, he had bigger things on his mind, *like landing this albatross!*

"What's so important and more to the point, how can *I* help you?"

"Captain, I'm sure you appreciate our assignment is confidential but you can help by giving us any information you can about the security problem at Narita that's causing the delay."

"I see." Taylor sort of shrugged scrambling his thoughts. "Not much I'm afraid, only that there is a large quantity of aging US currency I gather from Japan's foreign exchange reserves, being repatriated to Washington. I assume to the Federal Reserve for its destruction. That's all I know with the exception that the cargo is being transported on a Global Airway's 777 freighter.

Gregg turned to Steve... *"Money...!"*

"Captain, is there any way you can delay the 777 freighter?"

"Are you serious...? Where the 'Diet' is involved, *not a chance!* Now gentlemen, if you don't mind, I have a full house and I'm running late..."

"Thanks captain, we understand."

As Steve and Gregg were returning to their seats Greg turned to his partner.

"I hope your assumptions are wrong."

"Where there's money Gregg the door is always open........"

* * *

"Global 10 to Tower, positioned on runway 3B, awaiting further instructions."

"Bear with me Captain... Incoming traffic congestion."

"Understand, over and out."

Bill shrugged and turned to Chuck. *"Now the long wait."*

When tensions are high, minutes seem like hours and to pass the time away, Bill couldn't help but focus on the stationary Boeing 747/400 awaiting take off......

* * *

This dynamic streamlined aeronautic wide-bodied airliner with its seating capacity of six hundred passengers and crew, and a three-class cabin configuration, had to be admired as one of the worlds aviation wonders. With a takeoff weight of 447 metric tons, it required all the thrust from the four Rolls Royce RB211 turbo fan engines, each generating 66,500lbs mounted and on a wing span of 244 ft., easily achieving the cruising height of 32,000ft at 570mph and with a range of approximately 15,000 km, the 747/400 is recognized as one of the safest passenger aircraft in service.

* * *

There was a slight shudder as the larger aircraft began to power up bringing Bill back from the 'big sleep'.

"I don't know what came over me there, I guess I was just dreaming."

"Yeah, I gotta admit Bill, it would be a nice thought flying one of these birds, not to mention the salary."

"Hell Chuck, is money all you can think of? It's not what's in your pocket, its what's I your brain that counts."

"Yeah... Yeah... But in case someone hasn't told you, that's what makes the world go around."

Bill shrugged making a face in the process. "Yeah, I guess you're right."

"Bill, think on the positive side. Remember when we were risking our asses flying FA/18 Hornets over Bagdad on night missions taking ground fire from all angles."

"Do I! But I gotta admit Chuck your one helluva navigator. I can't take that away from you."

"But Bill remember after each mission returning in the dead of night landing on that flight deck in seas that would scare the shit out of 'Jaws'?"

Bill smiled at Chuck's colorful comment recollecting as a young Naval Aviator, stationed on the nuclear-powered aircraft carrier 'The USS Dwight D Eisenhower' in the sixth fleet, during the Iraq and Afghan theater of war, he was going to change the world. But the glamour of going to war is short lived when reality kicks in and there is no such thing as immortality.......

* * *

"Do I! I never told you, that each time I landed on that floating postage stamp in the dead of night, I was scared shirtless, my stomach in my mouth."

"Now you tell me! Da Ja vue, your one helluva pilot."

"For sure, we had some close shaves and now were sitting in these comfortable seats flying commercial jets, a long way from 'NAS Pensacola Florida' and the day we both received our 'Naval Aviator Insignias" ....
"Oops...."

Suddenly the lesser 777 shuddered as its big brother started its flight assent, the powerful four RB211's flaming a deep blue then changing to a bright orange as the pilot increased speed, a puff of black smoke coming from the four under carriage bogies as its eighteen tires bit into the tarmac searching for traction to move the 447 metrics tons' giant.

Like a professional golfer striking a ball from the tee, the big bird gracefully climbed into the darkness, the first leg of its journey and the most dangerous, safe and sound.

"Global 10 to Tower, runway now clear do I have permission for takeoff?"

"Global 10, permission given. Climb to 15 thousand feet and await further instructions."

"Understood loud and clear... Chuck let's get this bad boy airborne... Flaps to thirty and throttle lever to 30%."

"Affirmative Captain." The plane shuddering momentarily as the engines throttled picking up speed as the fully laden 777 thundered down the runway, the ear-piercing whine of the 'Trent's' clearly audible in the cockpit.

"Chuck continue to throttle up, we'll need every ounce of power to lift the rubber."

"Auto throttle engaged Captain... Speed increasing... 80... 100... 195... Takeoff speed reached Captain... Full throttle.... Flaps up... under carriage clear."

The 777 seemed to struggle as it wheels departed the runway, its maximum cargo and 181,000 liters of jet fuel was taking its toll, then suddenly all went quiet as the aircraft was airborne climbing at an angle of 30 degrees soaring into the darkness. 'The eagle has flown'.

Chuck turned to Bill. "Altitude Captain?"

"Proceed to fifteen thousand then throttle back."

"Affirmative." Bill replied more than relieved, but little did he know the real drama was about to begin.......

* * *

"Good evening... This is Captain Taylor but this time with some good news. The security problem at Narita has now been cleared and you will be pleased to know that we have been given clearance to land and I will be commencing our decent in approximately ten minutes. Please make sure your seats are upright and your trays are securely folded and your seat belts fastened. The audio system will now be switched off and for those passengers who wish to set their watches to Tokyo time, it has just turned 2300 hrs. or eleven pm in the evening. We should be on the ground by 2330 hrs. The ground temperature is 26 degrees Celsius and 24 percent humidity. A taxi to the city will cost approximately seventy-four US dollars' but there is also an excellent airport bus service which is much cheaper. Once again thank you for your patience."

"Well at least that's something." Steve buckled up.

"What do you think?" Gregg asked, this whole conundrum too much of a coincidence, *or was it?"*

"Yeah." Steve shook his head. "The scoop, a huge shipment of US currency for the recycle bin departing from Tokyo tonight for Washington DC... *Coincidence?* Not to mention Anbar Salibe and Fadil Maalouf our favorite Palestinians in cahoots with the Yakuza... They're up to something alright, *but what?"*

"Maybe the FBI have cottoned onto something and that's why they changed our accommodation, remember Salibe and Maalouf are guests in the same hotel."

"I know where you are coming from Gregg but if the Feds are sleeping with the enemy 24/7, why check us into the same hotel? It's too conspicuous, they may be Arabs but they're no fucking dummies."

Gregg gave an overzealous sigh.

"I know how you feel partner, it's another 'Rubik's Cube'."

Gregg laughed. "For what it's worth I never did solve that one."

"Touché........"

* * *

Steve was staring out the window into the darkness, the beacon lights flashing hypnotically on the oversize wing of the 747/400 with its Eagle tipped turn-ups, the high pitch of its powerful jets drowning his troubled thoughts, a timely diversion both mentally and sociologically.

As the wide-bodied airliner lost altitude its brake flaps continually opened and shut to reduce speed, its giant wings flexing and stretching as the jetliner gradually reduced altitude in its final stages of decent, the colorful lights of downtown Ginza and Akihabara now definitive lighting up the skyline like Christmas in Times Square.

Tokyo, with a populous density per capita of six thousand per square mile reaching thirteen million daily at peak times, the price of property is one of the most expensive in the developed nations.

As the runway became closer and closer, the brake flaps were now fully open to create maximum drag, the engines suddenly becoming almost silent as the undercarriage with its sixteen wheels left a trail of smoking rubber on the tarmac, the cabin shuddering violently, the overhead luggage compartments rattling and flexing as the pilot switched the four Prat & Whitney's into reverse, with a deafening roar, then suddenly silence as Delta 14 throttled down into taxi mode.

The next challenge, deplaning, immigration, then luggage collection, and finally custom clearance. Muslim fanatics have changed air travel forever with airport security adding further delays and stress to the ever-weary traveler. The world will never be the same again... *And all because of religion.......!*

* * *

Marge lifted the intercom phone.

"Will all passengers please remain in your seats until the plane has come to a complete standstill and the Captain switches off the seatbelt sign. During the flight baggage in the overhead bins may have moved so please be careful to avoid injury when opening. We should arrive at the aerobridge for deplaining in around ten minutes. On behalf of Captain Taylor and First Officer McNeil for those passengers whom are returning home or on vacation, we wish to thank you for flying 'Delta, the worlds most trusted airline' and hope to see you again in the not too distant future... Thank you."

Marge placed back the phone relieved, another flight another day, when Suddenly the jetliner came to stop with a slight bounce jolting the passengers to and fro as the shock absorbers took the load.

"Cabin crew please release the door locks for the ground staff to connect the aero bridges. Thank you."

"Well, we're here dude." Steve smiled turning to Gregg.

"And what lies ahead is anyone's guess. Say, what were the names of these two FBI agents again?"

"You worry me, Gregg. *You don't have a family history of Alzheimer's, do you?"*

"Get out of it! Wise guy."

"Brown and Daily, for your information."

"Yeah, yeah... 'The Brains of America'."

Steve laughed aloud. "Well, at least you still have your sense of humor... *Look."* He pointed. "The seatbelt sign is off, so let's get our asses outta here."

"If you can just stay in your seats for a few more minutes' gentleman." It was Marge with the Delta smile. "I'll go fetch you garment bags from the clothing locker."

Gregg smiled turning to Steve. "What did we do to deserve this, huh?"

"In this world, as they say, you never get something for nothing."

"Well, we'll soon find out when we catch up with Brown and Daily........"

* * *

Julie and Marge were standing at the First and Business Cabin door, greeting the departing passengers with the well-rehearsed smile and departing cliché... 'Thank you for flying Delta'.

"Goodbye gentleman, it has been a pleasure having the CIA on board." Julie gave Steve that smile.

"The pleasure is ours." Steve gave Julie a sneaky wink. "I'm sure we will meet again……"

* * *

For certain they would meet again, but with an unbelievable twist...!

* * *

"Well, that was reasonably fast." Steve commentated as they passed through the green light at customs.

"Yeah." Gregg replied. "Carryon bags save time avoiding the crazy crowd at the 'never say die' luggage carousel."

Steve had to laugh at Gregg' comment, being almost run down by a luggage trolley in the Arrival 'Grand Prix'. *"Man,* can you believe these crazies fighting for Taxis like there's no tomorrow?"

Gregg didn't reply he was too engaged scanning the Arrival Hall for the 'Men in Black."

"There they are Steve, *over there!"* Gregg pointed "That guy carrying the small placard with our names."

"I see them. *So, inconspicuous,* six feet plus, black suites with a serious bulge on the left side of their jackets."

"Heh...heh..." Gregg waved to catch their attention.

"Jake Brown and Ben Daily. We thought you would never arrive with all this security at Departures."

"The feeling's mutual Jake and thanks again for your patience, but I'm afraid there's one more chore before we go and that is to collect our firearms at the 'Dangerous Luggage Counter'."

"No sweat, Ben here is fluent in Japanese."

"Must be difficult to learn a second language?" Steve commented in a 'throw away' as they stepped it out to the baggage counter.

"Not really, it's called 'pillow talk'." Ben replied sporting a canny grin.

Jake could see the puzzled look on Steve's face. "Ben is a bit of a joker, what he isn't telling you Steve, is that his wife is Japanese."

Now I get it! 'Pillow talk' huh? I gotta store that one in the 'rabbit hat'."

The firearms collected the two CIA agents feeling more relaxed almost like recovering from a 'transplant'.

"We have a car waiting outside the 'Arrival Hall'. I know it's been a long one but our instructions are to take you directly to our field office in Akihabara. So, guys." Ben shrugged. "I'm afraid it might be a long one. The drive alone will take at least one hour depending on the traffic."

Steve shrugged. "Oh well, in for a penny in for a pound... The old English saying."

"I don't suppose you can enlighten us why our hotel accommodation was changed?" Gregg enquired.

"Daniels, our boss will explain everything when we get there."

A polite way of saying 'stay inside the box'........

* * *

"Global 10 to Tower, have now reached recommended altitude of 15,000, await further instructions."

"I hear you Captain. The air paths are now clear and the good news is you can now proceed to your cruising altitude of 32,000, Bon Voyage Global 10, have a safe flight."

"Thank you, Tower, signing out and goodnight."

"Chuck, increase speed to 280 knots and proceed to cruising altitude 32,000, retract flaps and speed brake lever. Enter GPS coordinates to destination then engage the Auto Pilot. I'll leave you to it, while I complete the logbook and other shit paperwork. *I should have taken a bloody secretarial course rather than a commercial pilots!"*

"Aye, aye, Captain." Chuck grinned, a strange look on his face.

Bill just shook his head, *this guy!* He placed the clipboard on his lap then got down and nasty in the paperwork oblivious that the security door to the cockpit was slowly opening. Then something caught the corner of his eye. *It was Chuck!* He had stretched forward and switched off the Transponder, Flight Data Recorder then the Cockpit Voice Recorder.

A Transponder is an electronic device vitally important to identify aircraft on 'Air Traffic Control Radar'.

"What the fuck! Are you off your fucking brain?"

Bill almost leapt from his seat, but the unmistakable feel of cold steel on the back of his neck stopped him in his tracks. The Muzzle of the Glock .45 pressing against his vertebrae.

"Easy... Easy... Salibe, or whatever you fucking name is? We need the Captain to land this crate on that crazy Island, Shuma...*eh* Shimaru... *eh* Shima...*The first thing these people should do is give themselves some better fucking names!* So, go lightly on that trigger if you want to live another day."

"Why you fucking 'douche bag', I should have cottoned on to you when you kept asking all these fucking questions."

"Control your emotions Captain... If you know what's good for you and that lovely lady stewardess, *you'll do as I say."* Salibe pressed the muzzle harder.

"And if I don't?"

The pain was agonizing as the grip of the Glock smashed down herd on Bill's head. For a moment, there was complete darkness then flashing colors as he endeavored to open his eye lids to a sea of blur as warm blood drowned his vision like a crimson sunset.

"What the fuck Salibe! Are you outta your fucking mind?"

"Captain, that's just a sample of what's to come. Now reduce altitude to 12,000 to avoid being spotted on radar, *and Stevens,* enter the new GPS coordinates and remember as a last resort I have a commercial pilot's license."

"You're a fucking joke." Chuck sneered. "You couldn't drive a fucking taxi in peak hour on Fifth Avenue."

"Watch your mouth Stevens, or I'll be taking *your* seat, Anyhow what's so special about Collins?"

"I'll tell you what! If push came to shove, he could land this bird on 'Noah's Arc'. He was a Naval Aviator flying FA/18 Hornets over Bagdad on night missions from the nuclear aircraft carrier Eisenhower'... *Now does that answer your fucking question?... Bill,* are you okay?"

"Do I look as if I'm fucking okay?"

"Bill, make it easy on yourself. Cooperate with me and there's 20 mill in it for you, half my take."

"I might have fucking known!"

"Why don't you listen for a moment before you take the high road. I already have 20 million in a Swiss account and another twenty to follow once this gig is over."

"Chuck... Get your head outta your ass... You can run but you can't hide, and as long as I have a breath in my body, I'm coming after you and I'll bury you in a mountain of shit so high, even 'Hillary' couldn't climb it!"

"Captain, life is cheap, and before you make a rash decision, it would be in your vested interest to turn your head."

Steve endeavored to wipe the now congealing blood with the back of his hand from his eyes, with little success.

"Why you fucking low life!" Steve screamed at the sight that met his eyes.

Sally was strapped to the jump seat, duct tape everywhere including her mouth, her face turning a blueish hue for lack of oxygen, Tahoka had that evil grin, a pillow pressed against the side of her head, the Berretta's hammer cocked. He spoke to Salibe in broken English.

"Palestinian, tell me when."

"Okay...Okay..." Bill could see the terrified look on Sally's face. "I'll do as you say, *on one condition!*"

"And that is?" Salibe took a step back, the Glock still threatening Bill's cranium.

"You release Sally immediately without harm...You have my word."

Chuck made a gesture to Salibe as if to say, *'I trust him'.*

"Tahoka, release the woman."

The 'Japanese Suma' seemed disappointed and unlocked the trigger of the Berretta a big change from the Kitana Sword. It was not his day but then there's always another.

Sally gasped for breath oblivious to the pain as the insensitive Tahoka ripped the duct tape from her mouth.

"You bastard... You... You...." She was almost in tears but pride got the better.

"Play it cool Sally." Bill yelled from the cockpit. "Besides I would love a cup of coffee."

That brought a smile to Sally's face, she knew where Bill was coming from. Staying alive is one thing and beating these bastards at their own game is another.

The duct tape off, Sally rose unsteadily to here feet, the loss of blood to the arteries in her legs, taking its toll.

"Outta my way you fucking poor excuse for a man."

Without hesitation with both hands, Sally pushed 'Mount Fujiyama' aside rushing to the galley to fetch the first aid kit, the look on Tahoka's face worse than 'Silence of the Lambs'... *American women!* Sally had watched the drama from her imprisoned seat and stopping the bleeding man was her priority.

"My God Bill, that's a real nasty, it needs some needlework, I'll do my best with this kiddy first aid kit... Place your head back while I wash the wound with antiseptic. *It's gonna sting.*"

Bill had to laugh, just like a woman, that was the last thing he had on his mind.

"*Ouch...*"

"*What did I tell you!* I'll improvise with some butterflies... There that should at least stop the bleeding... Now I'll go get you that coffee." She grinned keeping up the charade.

"Thanks Sally, you're a darling..."

Bill suddenly turned his attention to Chuck who was in 'la la' land engrossed with the thought of his 40 million windfall.

"Mr. Millionaire, if it's not too much trouble, can I get your attention?"

"Cut the shit Bill, *so...?*"

"At this altitude, you gotta maintain this bad boy at 250 knots, or we'll all end up in the drink and you can kiss goodbye to your millionaire status"

"You and your smart-ass remarks, *I've got it under control.*"

"You heard him Stevens, *get to it.*"

"When did you get promoted to Captain?"

"Stevens, I've had a bellyful of you, so don't push the envelope."

"And this Palestinian shit...?" Bill interjected. "*Giovani my ass...!* I knew this guy was no Italian... Salibe, huh? I don't know what your fucking game is... Maybe I'm just too dumb..."

"For what it's worth." Salibe retaliated. "This is the Palestine people's chance to strike a blow so devastating against the infidel Israeli's, we will bring them to their knees to surrender."

"*You guys, you never give up!*" Bill shook his head. "Chuck, for the life of me, I don't know what the deal is and the way this crazy is talking, this is bigger than big and a lot of innocent people could lose their lives. *Do you really know what you're getting yourself into?* Remember, to them you're disposable, just like the paper towels in the men's room. *Get wise to yourself.*"

"*Bill,* don't you get it? I'll be 40 mill better off and I'll never have to worry about anything again for the rest of my life."

"*Except facing the death penalty...*Chuck, can't you see it? This guys got his hand so far up your ass he's working your mouth."

"Don't listen to him Stevens, if you know what's good for you. Besides we're now over the North Pacific and touch down at Shimura Shima is approximately two hours."

Salibe turned to Sally, an ugly smile crossing his face. "Honey, how about some coffee for the passengers?"

"You gotta be fucking kiddin me...."

* * *

The black Chevy SUV was in the reserved parking zone, the windows heavily tinted.

"Akihabara?" Gregg quizzed.

Jake smiled he could understand the inquisition, the name alone would draw questions.

"I thought you would ask. "Jake glanced at his watch. *"Hmmm... Best be on our way, I can just picture Danial's twiddling his thumbs. I'll enlighten you both in the car."*

The driver of the SUV was patiently waiting on the sidewalk, there's nothing more boring than collecting passengers at the airport.

"Agent, Denzo Takoma" Who smiled then bowed before politely offering his hand.

In today's carnage, Japanese traditions must be admired when sadly good manners and values unfortunately are history.

"Steve Nelson and Gregg Jonson CIA."

The courtesy's over Denzo opened the rear door of the Chevy. "I think we had better hit the road gentleman, we have a long drive ahead of us......."

* * *

It had started to rain, the beginning of a muggy evening not uncommon in Japan in the month of June. The drizzle on the windshield and the pattern of the wipers moving two and fro displayed strange distortions of red, the reflections from the brake lights of the slow-moving traffic.

"Gentlemen." Denzo smiled looking into the rear mirror of the SUV. "As I believe this is your first visit to my country and for your boring information, we are on the famous Higashikanto Expressway from Narita International approximately 70km from the greater Tokyo area. As for Akihabara, our destination, is a district in the Chiyoda ward of Tokyo. The name comes from Akiba named after a fire controlling deity for a shrine built after the area was destroyed by fire in 1869. Akihabara gained the nick name 'Akihabara Electric Town' shortly after World War ll for being a major shopping center for household electronic goods and the post war black market and what better area to have our field office...! In the electronic district of Japan with WYFY faster than the speed of light... *I hope I haven't put you to sleep?"*

There was burst of laughter from Steve and Gregg in the rear seats.

"Naw, we're still with you."

"I guess that answers your question Gregg." Brown laughed. "Denzo is a wealth of information. Come to think of it, I think that's why we hired him!"

There was another burst of laughter. The supposedly long drive was not so boring after all.

Steve opened. "I keep asking myself, whilst looking out of the window, why are all these women driving? Then it struck me... We're driving on the wrong side of the bloody road."

"Heh... Heh...Heh..." The laughter was spontaneous.

"I'm cracking up Steve."

"Get out of it you moron........!"

* * *

FBI FIELD OFFICE TOKYO

The FBI's heavily fortified field office perimetered by a three-meter-high security wall, is in Chuou Street Tokyo in the main thoroughfare of Akihabara, on two hectares of prime real estate. It's large stainless steel tracked gate operated by a powerful motor bore the famous FBI insignia as its center piece, in brightly colored gold and blue metallic enamel.

'DEPRTMENT OF JUTICE'
'FEDERAL BUREAU OF' 'INVESTIGTION'.

To the left of the gate is a security enclosure manned by a Marine sergeant in 'number two' dress complete with white peaked cap and side arm. The building's grey three level concrete exterior with long narrow dimly lit rectangular windows, was more than drab compared to the colorful neon lit Chuou Street, although its large car park ablaze with security lighting, compensated. The majestic 'Gone with the Wind' pillar-stepped entrance with double red oak timber doors and ornate brass accessories was manned 24/7 by two armed Marine sentries stressing the high level of security. The attack on Benghazi under the then president Bush, with the loss of five American lives, never to be forgotten.......

* * *

The drive was long and tedious but Denzo seemed to enjoy his own rhetoric, so much so, that Steve had dozed off only to be elbowed by Gregg as the SUV came to a stop outside the larger than life stainless steel gate.

"Eh... Err." Steve tried to hide his embarrassment by sitting up straight and widening his eyes.

Denzo smiled looking into the rear mirror as he pressed the electric window switch.

"Don't worry Steve, there's no need to be embarrassed, we've all been there."

Steve smiled, his face flushing momentarily.

The Marine sergeant descended from his sentry box blocking the path of the black Caddy, Denzo knew the procedure, the driver's window fully open.

"Your business?" Sergeant Baker asked, poker faced.

"Meeting with Director Daniels." Denzo replied completing the ritual 'de ja vu'.

Baker glanced at his military issue time piece then entered the information into the tablet.

"Identities please."

Denzo turned to face his passengers and smiled.

"I need your 'ID's gentlemen, it's all in the game."

The Sergeant spent another five minutes examining the photo ID's before laying them in line on the SUV's hood then taking a picture with his Lenovo ten-inch Android Tablet.

"Just a second gentleman I need clearance from the Director."

 The sergeant returned the photo ID's then went to the external security phone incased in thick steel. After a few minutes of indecipherable conversation Baker returned the receiver then spoke into his Motorola shoulder phone.

"Security clearance accepted unlock gates."

The large gates slowly opened with a rattling grinding noise as the heavy gear teeth engaged with the track.

Denzo slowly drove into the large car park steering toward the 'bomb blast shelter' on the far left, rather like a large car port with 'boxed in' concrete reinforced roof and sides but open ended. The theory, an undetected blast would be decimated from the sides and roof exiting through the front and back openings minimizing the gas expansion.

"Okay guys."

Denzo unlocked the doors of the SUV positioning the large vehicle over the hydrolytic inspection lift stops to allow security to scan the floor pan for IED's.

"Let's move it, I can just imagine Daniels, as Burbs so nicely puts it, "Nursing his wrath to keep it warm".

"I didn't know that you study Burns in Japan."

"There's lots of things you don't know about Japanese culture, Steve." Denzo was quick to reply. Maybe Steve had struck a nerve, enemies have long memories.

A marine from the mechanized corps in coverall camouflage fatigues seemed to appear from nowhere.

"Can I have the car keys, sir?"

Denzo obliged and went on his sway, the marine checking the SUV's doors before activating the inspection lift.

"You guys are really thorough." Gregg commented as they walked toward the entrance.

"The world has changed Gregg, with Islamic radical fundamentalists... Jihad suicide bombers, ISIL, Al-Qaida, Hezbollah... Do you want me to continue?" Denzo was shaking his head.

"Yeah." Gregg sighed pouting his lips "I guess you're right, when you put it that way."

"But we're not finished yet." Brown came to life. "We still have to go through the X Ray scanner, just like the airport."

The marine smartly saluted before obligingly opening the heavy oak paneled door.

"Thank you, Sargent." Denzo gave a slight bow, the Japanese protocol of politeness.

"Please place your firearms and clips in each of these blue plastic containers accompanied with your agent's cards, then proceed through the scanner. You can collect your hard ware upon leaving." The young marine gave a forced smile waving them through, it had been a long day.

The office was still a hive of activity as the entourage passed through the various departments, TV monitors and desk top computers reaching saturation point.

Daily could see the look on Steve and Gregg's faces amazed at the populous at this time of night, in their strive for global security.

"It's twenty-four seven here Steve, the city that never sleeps."

"I'm impressed." Steve nodded.

"Ah, here we are." Denzo pointed to the black highly polished wooden door bearing the name in aluminum two-inch lettering, KENETH DANIELS, DIRECTOR.

"Rico, the boss's secretary has left so I'll just get to it and knock on the door." Denzo grinned.

"Come in." The harshness in Daniel's voice reflecting his frustration, the waiting game brings out the worst........

* * *

Daniels, in his late forties, at around 5-11, could lose a few pounds but not to the extent of obesity, whereas unlike his younger staff, becoming a gym freak was not high in his priorities. Never the less he had that 'man of stature' look with his greying side boards and streaks to match flashing through his full head of unruly black hair. His narrow face and jaw line, fell into place with his penetrating blue eyes, Jew like nose, straight lips and dimpled "Michele Douglas" chin. He most certainly looked the part of the Director. The white long-sleeved shirt and the conservative dark blue tie sent a message of 'no nonsense' and a short attention span and 'don't waste my time' but his most important asset was the utmost respect and dedication from his staff. The walls on his modest office were adorned with photos of his inauguration with the FBI and graduation from Michigan University. His prized possession a picture together with Japan's Prime Minister, Abe Shinzo.

Married with two teenage sons their framed picture with Marcy his wife of twenty-five years sat on his desk, the boys both following in their father's footsteps studying at Michigan Uni. Marcy missed them both, only seeing the boys during semester breaks. Having spent three years in Japan she was homesick for the States, but being the wife of an FBI Director, you follow your husband wherever the agency sends him......

* * *

Daniels looked up from his lap top, his slightly bagged reddish eyes reflecting fatigue.

"Denzo, you Brown and Daily can call it a night. Thanks guys, you must be bushed, come and see me first thing tomorrow."

Daniels rose to his feet extending his hand to the CIA agents.

"Grab a seat guys."

"I'm sorry I can't offer you a coffee, Rico my secretary, has gone home but there's always the machine in the passage way?"

"Naw were good Bill." Steve replied speaking for the both of them.

"Before we start, how's my friend John doing? I didn't have much time to speak to him when he phoned."

"John...?" Steve replied with a smile. "He's still the same, a workaholic but a better boss you couldn't find and dam smart with it! They say a man's stature is measured by his enemies and John is not short on stepping on toes."

"Heh... Heh..." Ken laughed. "He's a solid citizen alright and a real nice guy and has my utmost respect." Then he gave wry smile. *"Too bad he never joined the FBI."*

Daniel's comment made both Steve and Gregg laugh.

Then Ken's face changed to somber. "Let's get down to business, you both must be fatigued after that long flight........."

* * *

Suddenly there was a wall of silence, the 'niceties' over, the constant hum of the Rolls Royce Trent's filling the cabin. Bill kept blinking his eyes his vision still blurred from blunt instrument trauma. Flying this baby at 12,000 feet at a constant 250 knots the 777 was prone to engine stall for lack of lift and Shimaru Shima couldn't come soon enough.

"ETA fifteen minutes." Chuck was checking the GPS.

"So, the *'low life'* has come alive!"

"Bill cut the shit, we've all got our problems. Cooperate and you and Sally will live to see another day."

"That makes me feel really good. You must have rocks in your fucking head. Do you think our Muslim friend gives a shit about us or you when it comes to the crunch, Salibe could be another 'Jihadi John' for all we know, sharpening his beheading knife and as far our Japanese friends? *Tell that to the Chinese!"*

Chuck shook his head. "Cut the shit Bill, I'm tired listening to it! You're like the dog on 'His Master's Voice'. Listen, if it's not too much trouble, I can clearly see the runway about twenty kilometers to your right. So, let's bury the hatchet for now and get this bird safely on Terrafirma."

Bill ignored the olive branch. "Climb to 15000, there seems to be some mountainous terrane surrounding the runway. I need to make a sweep to get a clearer picture."

"Affirmative, throttling up now." Chuck slowly pulled back the sticks, the Trent's responding to the call.

"Salibe." Chuck called.

"Yes?"

"We're approaching the runway to get a better picture of the terrain. Get your Jap boys to contact the head honcho to make sure everything is to plan and that runway is lit up like a Christmas tree."

Salibe sort of grunted, he didn't like being ordered around by a 'born again' alcoholic but it was important and he turned to get Tahoka's attention, by raising his hand to his ear to impersonate a phone.

"I need you phone, Kenichi Shendo.... Understand?"

The 'bull' produced his radio phone pointing to the device.

"Yeah... Yeah." Salibe motioned, he had gotten through to his thick cranium. Tahoka new the urgency and didn't waste any time in tuning the frequency......

* * *

(Speaking Japanese)

"Moshi, Moshi." The voice answered. "Password 'Fish Tail'.

"*Good,* Tahoka here. Kenichi, we are about to approach the runway. I think the pilot is making a sweep to judge the difficult terrane before making his final approach. Have you contacted Okio? Over."

"Yes, I have been tracking the flight with our radar and I have assured Okio that everything is to plan. The runway is well lit, powered by our generators. It's now up to your pilot's skills to make sure he touches down exactly on the white two-meter florescent line or he'll over shoot... Over."

"Understood, Arigato." Tahoka closed the phone......

* * *

"*Well?*" Salibe was showing his impatience or was it his nervousness?

Tahoka stared for a moment stony faced, his eyes narrowing.

"*Have you lost your tongue, man?*" Salibe screamed.

Arakida rose to his feet, he didn't like his partner being belittled by a 'rag head' it was a Mexican stand off as the Japanese eyeballed Salibe.

"*Hell,* that's all we need." Bill shook his head. "A war between the Japanese and the Palestinians."

"Makes a change from the Jews, huh?" Steve was notorious for his sick humor.

Salibe was in a hole it was either lose face and back down or it was Tahoka's Beretta, the hammer cocked, the muzzle pointing straight at his forehead.

"Whoa, whoa... whoa....!" Steve screamed. "We're trying to fly this fucking plane and you guys are in the 'OK Corral'. Salibe, you had better cool it and apologies or you won't be seeing Jerusalem any time soon."

Salibe was no dummy, he needed these two apes, so what does a meaningless apology cost? He raised both hands like 'I surrender'.

"I apologies for my rudeness, it's... It's, just the stress... Understand." He bowed.

The bow seemed to do the trick and Tahoka uncocked the semi-automatic placing it back in his holster.

"Runway good... Pilot touch on line." Tahoka replied in broken English, his eyes still reflecting his anger. Salibe would be well advised to watch his back, to a samurai warrior, 'power perceived is power achieved'.

"Yeah, I can clearly see the safety line... Chuck, do a 360 then a 180 at 20 kilometers. Retain the speed until I tell you. Safety belt sign on."

Bill was flying the plane manually utilizing all his experience and concentration.

"Reduce speed to 160 knots and height 1000, I can see the runway now and it's all or nothing. Landing gear down, flaps at three air brakes on."

"Steady... Steady... throttle back, flaps up... Keep that fucking nose up... *Brace yourself... Brace yourself....*"

Bill's knuckles were white as he gripped the steering stick and Chuck's face was the same color as the wheels clipped the drop-dead zone.

"Reverse thrust on now..." Bill yelled as the 18-wheeled giant puffed smoke from its undercarriage. *"Chuck,* hit the reverse thrust. What the fuck's keeping you... *Hit it now........!"*

* * *

"And the funerals this Sunday?" Steve asked.

"I'm afraid so..." Ken shook his head. "Losing one of your own is like losing a son."

"I understand." Steve sighed, turning toward Gregg.

"And worse still, married with two young sons."

One could sense Ken's genuine grief.

"Ken, this is the one time *I don't* envy your job." Gregg meekly interjected.

"Yeah, this is my first *and hopefully my last!"*

"And Maalouf?" Gregg perused.

"Positively identified through DNA and finger prints... But as for that poor guy the Maître De, as they say, *'in the wrong place at the wrong time'*. Listen, let's not waste any more time. I'll make sure you guys get a full written report by tomorrow first thing."

Gregg shrugged in disbelief. "Three corpses in one day, that's something else, and worse still Fadil showed a clean pair of heels!"

"That's the breaker and my recurring nightmare. Dwelling on that point, Tokyo's Homicide Division and agents Brown and Daily will be at your disposal."

"That's good to know, Ken." Steve acknowledged. "We appreciate it."

Then Ken sort of brooded for a moment. "What's really troubling me is that we know Salibe and Maalouf have been having some kind of cloak and dagger meetings at the offices of 'Nippon Shipping & Logistics' whose chairman is none other than Okio Namura, who is the head honcho of the Japanese Mafia, the 'Yakuza'. The company is legit but we know it's 'prima-fascia' and we can't do much about it. I mean the 'Who's Who' and half the police force in Japan are on the payroll. The burning question is, *what are they up to?"* Ken looked dismayed and distant.

"Ken, make no mistake, we at the CIA are in the same boat and have been tracking these two since they travelled to Russia, spending time at the Russian Military of Defense and The Department of Aeronautics and Rocket Science, all expenses paid by the Russian tax payer! It's a real catch '22'." Gregg was baring all.

"Hmmmm..." Ken Leaned forward placing his chin on his hand his elbow on his desk, the same troubled 'going nowhere' look.

"You know Ken, I'm only digressing." Steve just had to get it off his chest.

Ken's eyes focused on Steve maybe the kid had something?

"The floor's yours." Ken gave that 'what's to lose' look.

"When our flight was delayed from landing at Narita because the airport was under 'lock down' for security reasons, which we found out later from the Captain, was because a large shipment of US currency was being returned to the United States. I just have this bad feeling that this is the catalyst to something bigger... *Much bigger!"*

Ken sat back in his chair, disappointment reflecting on his face.

"We did a thorough check in conjunction with the Japanese SIA and everything checked out. For your information, it was a shipment of US currency to be returned to The Federal Reserve in the printing and the destruction of currency at Washington DC. having passed the recommended life span."

"Ken, I hate to say this and at the thought of being a real pain in the butt, I think we should check out that flight."

"Maybe you have something Steve but that's for another day. It's been a long one and I just want to get home to my 'desperate housewife'. He gave a halfhearted smile. "Brown and Daily will drop you at your hotel... *Oh*, by the way, the reason we changed your hotel reservations, so to speak, was that you could be at the crime scene to further your investigations on the spot."

"Ken, just one thing before we go." Steve was like a terrier chasing a rabbit.

"And that is?" Ken's patience was being tried.

"*Eh... Err.*" Steve knew he was on thin ice and 'continue at your peril'. "The coded message?"

"You'll get that in your report tomorrow, we're still working on it... Shall we?"

Ken rose to his feet, there was no mistaking, *it was time to leave.......*

* * *

The 120 metric tons fully laden 777 shuddered, the galley doors bursting open with crockery smashing to the floor in a million pieces as its shocks bottomed out, its huge wings flapping with the weight of its powerful 'Trent's', like a giant bird with its legs outstretched flying in to land.

"*Keep that nose wheels straight... Keep it fucking straight ... do you hear me? Or we'll run off this fucking 'do it yourself' runway.*"

The noise of the reverse thrust was deafening and as for Chuck...? He was hanging on to the steering stick like grim death.

"*I fucking hear you, what do you think I'm fuckin doing?*"

The ABS was finally braking, snatching the wheels on and off as both Bill and Chuck stomped with all their strength on the brake pedals.

"*Come on... Come on... You son of a bitch, slow down.*" Bill yelled at the top of his voice, the end of the makeshift runway looming nearer and nearer.

Then suddenly, as if "Someone up their likes me" the wide-bodied aircraft slowed down to 15k with less than 200meters of runway left.

"*Switch off reverse thrust,*" Bill gave a mammoth inhale. "*Were gonna make it.*"

The 777 was now down to taxiing speed before finally coming to a screeching halt, rocking back and forth, its nosecone two meters inside the jungle foliage.

"Wow!" Bill wiped the sweat from his brow, in disbelief. *"We fucking made it...!* Is everyone one okay?"

"Nice job captain."

Bill could feel the cold steel pressing at the base of his skull.

"Captain my advice... Don't be 'Mr. America'. Lift your hands above your head, wrists together. Whoever invented these plastic zip ties, I take my hat off."

"Easy you bastard." Bill grimaced as Salibe tightened the plastic lock slide.

"My advice, stay in your seat Captain until it's time to disembark." Salibe menacingly waved the Glock. "I think you get the message..." Then he turned to Chuck a sneer on his voice. "I need your help to open the passenger and cargo doors and inflate the emergency chute." There was no love lost between these two.

"Just make sure you press that button to transfer the other twenty mill." Chuck retaliated.

"You'll get your money." Salibe growled, if looks could kill! "When we connect to the Wi-Fi at the office, I'll enter the pin for the transfer, then you can check your account on your cell... *Now I'm waiting... Don't tempt my fucking patience!"*

"Sally are you alright?" Bill yelled concerned at her silence.

"I'm in the same boat as you, Captain."

"Stay cool Sally, we'll soon be on the ground."

Stevens, with no further delay, dollar signs in his retinas, quickly released the large lever on the exit door immediately behind the cockpit entrance, simultaneously pressing the emergency switch, the heavy door opening with a loud 'gun like' explosion inflating the emergency chute like a snake pouncing on its prey.

"Salibe, it's good to go... *Who's first?"* Stevens had that cheeky grin on his face. "It's a long way down for the faint of heart... *Huh?"*

"Yeah, and you can show us just how it's done." Salibe returned the so called 'friendly fire'.

"Heh ... Heh ... Heh." Chuck laughed aloud, full of sarcasm. "The pleasure is all mine."

The bright yellow emergency chute made from heavy thermostable heat resistant material, stood out in the semi darkness, the runway lights flickering, the loud noise of the generators filling the air.

Chuck, quickly rolled onto his feet almost like a 'parachute landing', aircrews practice emergency enactments twice per year and to Stevens this was kiddies stuff but before he could call to Salibe he was immediately surrounded by four Japanese soldiers in World War II light kaki tropical battle dress. Their white open necked shirts worn outside the tunic collar with three quarter length sleeves, their field caps displaying the traditional bronze star, were menacingly pointing their Arisako 99 rifles, complete with 22inch bayonets, almost like a sword, straight at Chuck. As for Shendo... He was dressed immaculately in officer's uniform, his leather chrome buckled belt holstered a Nambu 8mm pistol and military issue Samurai Sword.

"Not move... Understand?" His pigeon English sending a message.

Chuck raised his hands above his head.

"No need." Shendo barked. "More." He pointed to the Emergency Shute.

"Bill, you gotta come and see this, *these guys have gotta to be fucking kiddin me!*"

Suddenly one of the guards pushed his rifle butt hard into Chuck's back, just as a reminder not to insult the 'Imperial Japanese Army'.

"Come on Sally, your next, I'm here to catch you."

Sally turned to Bill as she stood at the top of the emergency chute.

"Does this guy ever give up?" She shook her head.

Collins almost laughed, if it wasn't so serious it would be funny......

* * *

Shendo unlocked the heavy steel door to the maintenance shed and switched on the light from outside, the single bulb dangling on the cable from the galvanized roof, Salibe, acting as the 'go between' to compensate for Shendo's poor English.

"This will be your new home until we decide what do with you, but heed this warning. If, in the unlikely chance you manage to escape... *one,* there is nothing but jungle and mountainous terrain facing you and *two...* The guards have instructions to shoot to kill. As you can see the shed has barred steel windows, fortunately there is water and basic toilet facilities and two bamboo cots. You will have to forgo your modesty but in your western culture, I'm sure that will be not be a problem." Salibe grinned looking toward Sally. "Shendo, get your man to cut the plastic."

Bill rubbed his wrists endeavoring to return the circulation but not before firing a broadside at Chuck.

"You know what they have in mind... *Don't you?* There's no way they can let us go, it's just a matter of when they dig the two six by two's in the Jungle, then a bullet in the back of the head, execution style... *And Chuck...*" Bill grinned. "There just might be a third one, *just for you.*"

"Close the fucking door Salibe, I don't want hear this shit!"

Steven's put on a brave front but deep inside what Bill had said was getting to him.......

* * *

Sally sat on the side of the cot and looked toward Bill who was studying the barred widow and the steel framed door.

"What do you think Bill?"

"This place looks like it's bomb a proof shelter but there's always a way."

"You heard that Arab and do you really think they'll assassinate us?"

"Get that out of your head! I was just trying to scare the shit out of Stevens to make him jump the fence."

"You don't make a good liar Bill."

"Sally, no more of that talk we have to think positive." Before he could continue further, the solitary light bulb was suddenly switched off.

"Bill I'm scared."

"Sally, don't panic. Just stay cool and sit for a few moments until your eyes can focus in the darkness."

"Yeah, I can see a bit clearer now."

Bill cautiously steered himself toward Sally's voice feeling for the cot with his foot. Finally, there, he sat down heavily, the bamboo bed giving a loud crack.

"What was that?" Sally almost jumped out of her skin.

"It's only me sitting on the side of the cot."

"Yeah, your right Bill, I can see you now."

The runway lights suddenly died and now they were in pitch darkness.

"My suggestion Sally is to make a pillow with your jacket and get your head down, tomorrow is another day, I just hope the misquotes don't have a field day. If you need the toilet in this darkness and make a mistake, don't be embarrassed, it's most likely just a hole in the ground to a septic tank."

"I'll try my best. I roughly know in which direction the toilet is. Goodnight Captain."

Collins removed his jacket and tie, the steamy tropical climate would be a sleep challenge and he made a pillow but before laying on his side he edged up the right leg of his trousers just enough to check his ankle holster containing a snug double action .25 Smith & Wesson six chamber revolver. It wouldn't kill a man unless hit a vital organ, but it makes holes, enough to stop a full-grown man in his tracks. He always carried this gun for emergencies such as hijacking and for the love of it, why they never searched him, it's a question for the 'Guinness Book of Records'. Now for sure, the game has changed and the element of surprise was now on their side........

THE GREAT ESCAPE

Steve stirred, groaned, then turned on his side, grabbing for the other pillow to place it over his head and drown that irritating noise. He was in the middle of an enjoyable dream and now he couldn't get it back!

"Go away sound, go away." The phone kept ringing.

"Okay...Okay." He threw the pillow to the floor then stretched for the phone.

"Yes?"

"Christ Steve, don't tell me you are still in bed?"

"Hell! What time is it?"

"For you're in formation it's nine fifteen... Remember breakfast at nine?"

"Where are you now?"

"Where the hell do you think, I am?... Twiddling my bloody thumbs over a cup of tea in the restaurant!"

"Shit Gregg! Gimme thirty and I'll be right with you. Sorry buddy."

"Yeah, yeah, I'll hang on before I order."

"Would you wish to order now sir?" The waiter enquired in perfect English.

"Just freshen up my tea, I'm waiting for a friend. *Say...* Would you happen to have an English paper?"

"Certainly sir, we have todays 'New York Times'."

The waiter quickly returned with the 'ink rag'.

"Thank, you."

Gregg unfolded the oversize paper glancing at the local news but the headlines on the second page unexpectedly caught his eye.

**'TOKYO FLIGHT BOUND FOR WASHINGTON
DC MYSTERIOUSLY DISSAPEARS'**

"What the hell!" Gregg, couldn't believe his eyes, his impulsive outburst turning heads in the restaurant.

"I'll be darned!" He read further.

A 'Global International' 777 freighter bound for Washington DC disappeared from radar approximately one hour after take-off from Narita Airport, Japan... It is feared the plane may have come down somewhere in the North Pacific possibly 800 kilometers from the coast line. Information on its cargo has yet to be released. Air search and rescue....

'Sorry buddy, my fault. I guess...' Steve grabbed a chair whilst raising his hand trying to draw the waiter's attention, coffee high on his priority list.

Gregg cut the conversation, turning the paper toward Steve, who stared at the headline for a moment before eyeballing Gregg.

"Are my eyes seeing, right?" He read on.

"Coffee sir?"

"Yes, black no sugar." Steve placed the paper down. "I had a bad feeling about this flight. It's just too much of a coincidence, Gregg. You know my thoughts. The jigsaw pieces are falling into place... *The Palestinians, none other!"* He paused for a moment deep in thought, then shrugged. *"What the hell...!* Let's enjoy our breakfast before we call Daniels......."

* * *

"What's this bacon and eggs!"

"American breakfast?"

Gregg had returned from the Japanese buffet with a full house Bento Box. Steamed rice... Okay rice porridge... Miso Soup... Natto, fermented Soy Beans and Nori dried seaweed.

Steve stared at the 'Bento Box', its black lacquered wooden sides like a food tray, *but with style.*

"You gotta be shittin me! Are you really gonna eat that stuff?"

"You know what they say, 'When in Rome'?" Gregg laughed.

"Your coffee sir and for the other gentlemen, green tea. Enjoy your breakfast." The waiter smiled, he had seen it all before. "Have a nice day."

"I tell you Gregg, if you get caught short... Let's put it this way. Have you ever tried these Japanese toilets? Because I just hope you can squat with your slacks at your knees?"

"Get out of it!"

But before the friendly barter could continue, the waiter returned, a cordless phone in his hand.

"My apologies gentleman for disturbing your breakfast, but there's an important call for a Mr. Nelson. I took the liberty to check the breakfast names and your table number."

"That's alright, I'll take the call." Steve put the phone to his ear.

"Nelson, here?"

"Good morning Steve... Daniels here... I knew I would catch you both at breakfast."

"What's the scoop, Ken? I'm guessing it's the headlines in the 'New York Times' right in front of me."

"Steve, I gotta hand it to you, it looks like your hunch was right... But on the other hand, let's not jump to conclusions... It could be a 'high jacking' or an 'aircraft disaster'. I'm gonna give your boss a call. I know I'm going to disturb his 'baby sleep' but it's as they say in French 'trtfe taat'. If you can't speak French I'll translate it later. *Oh!* before I hang up I sent the report to the hotel's front desk, take your time with it. No doubt you'll be receiving a call from John in the next hour. Keep me informed of the outcome."

"You can be reassured."

"Enjoy your breakfast......."

* * *

Daylight was now streaming though the singular window of the maintenance shed. The cool early morning bringing a much-needed relief from the muggy tropical temperature they had both suffered during the night. *As for the mosquitos...?*

Ken threw his feet to the floor and ruffled his hair, he felt like shit, his neck and back aching from lying on the unforgiving bamboo mattress. Sally was already awake and in the 'so called' toilet, the door closed.

"Sally, are you alright?" Bill called.

"Yeah, I'm just doing my thing. I won't be long."

Bill smiled. "No sweat, take your time."

Then from the corner of his eye he saw a face peering through the barred window. It was a uniformed guard checking out the prisoners, their voices having attracted his attention and Bill could clearly see the tip of his bayoneted rifle.

"Hmmm... That's interesting, an armed guard." Bill spoke aloud his brain already in escape mode.

"I didn't catch that, Bill?"

"It's okay Sally, I'm just talking out loud."

The steel door from the water closet creaked open, its hinges screaming for grease.

"You're looking fresh!" Bill couldn't help comment.

"Once an air hostess." Sally laughed, she liked her handsome captain and his comment was for another day.

"I gotta warn you Bill that toilet is something else. I hope you have strong knees. There's water in a large tub to wash and a plastic container for drinking."

"Well at least that's something." Bill replied. "It's looks like they had planned this gig well in advance. I heard the head man saying that this is a maintenance shed so they must have cleared all the equipment and spares... Yeah, this was well planned, alright." Bill nodded, his thought process in top gear.

"I guess it's my turn Sally, I'll try and keep the noise down." Bill laughed as he disappeared for his ablutions.......

* * *

Bill glanced at his 'Breitling Chronomat 41', for some reason his captors were not interest in looting their prisoners, I guess with 200 billion US dollars in the safe, *who gives a shit!* The dial showed six thirty and with only a two-hour flight they were still on Tokyo time but before Bill could convey to Sally its importance there was a loud rattling on the steel door as it was being unlocked. Two uniformed guards entered, one carrying a wooden tray of food the other his bayoneted rifle pointed menacingly at both Sally and Bill, the message *'Don't even think about it'...*

The guard placed the tray on the floor then turned to his compatriot saying something in Japanese who nodded before they both turned and left, slamming the 'prison door' behind them.

Sally picked up the tray and set in on the empty cot.

"This is different." She commented sarcastically. "Two bowls of rice and two cups of green tea and no chopsticks!"

'Chopsticks can be dangerous Sally."

"Shall I serve Captain?" Sally laughed.

"Get out of it! At least Sally, you still have your sense of humor." Bill couldn't help laughing.

"Bon appetite........"

* * *

Salibe had risen early, it had been a strenuous and uncomfortable night, the military style dormitory accommodation, hot and humid, the four antiquated ceiling fans, from another era, struggling to circulate the stale air. But more importantly he had to contact the Russian Ministry of Defense once Okio gave his approval that operation 'Fish Tail's was a done deal. After the landing the night before, Shendo had spoken to Okio, but having not understood the language Salibe was not privy to the conversation. The 'run in' he had with Numero still fresh in his mind and he trusted his adversaries like an Indian with a king cobra.

As Salibe walked to the Nissan style the mess hall he noticed the aircraft had been covered with camouflages scrim blending in with the thick jungle foliage, making it almost impossible to spot from the air. The 'so called' Japanese 'Sea Bees' had worked through the night with heavy duty fork lifts to empty the aircraft's cargo bay of its large aluminum reinforced containers and Salibe had to assume that the 'hanger size' building with its corrugated roofing, at the far side of the compound, was where the precious cargo was being stored.

The breakfast was something else, buffet style, porridge, rice, sashimi, miso and green tea. The sixty Yakuza Triads dressed in military style fatigues seemed oblivious to the outside world their chatter drowning the air as they devoured the chop sticked breakfast. When the replacement crew comes at the end of the month they would be back in Tokyo for their much-needed R&R... Karaoke and 'Supper Hostesses', all at the expense of the Yakuza, their pockets well lined.

Salibe joined Shendo, Arakida and Tahoka at the rough wooden table their noses deep in food and conversation. Shendo looked up for a moment as the Palestinian took his seat, a cup of green tea in his hand.

"No eat?" Shendo pointed.

"I'm not hungry." Salibe replied, a polite way of saying the food was anything but enticing.

Salibe had noticed that Tahoka had a better understanding of English although he had hidden it well and he had nothing to lose.

"Kazuo." Salibe began testing his reaction. "I need Shendo to call big boss for me, it's very urgent... *Understand?*"

Tahoka's eyes flashed, he understood alright and immediately turned to Shendo.

(Speaking in Japanese)

"Shendo..."

Kinichi, looked up, his mouth still full of half chewed rice and Sashimi, the wasabi widening his nostrils.

"Hai." Annoyance reflected in his tone.

Tahoka gave a slight bow, respect always high in Japanese protocell.

"Palestine man requests you phone Numero, urgent."

"Did he say why?" Shendo asked sarcastically, another chopstick full of rice in flight.

"No."

"Then tell him to wait till after I finish my breakfast!"

Tahoka bowed again, like 'don't shoot the messenger'......

* * *

"Well?" Salibe barked, the look on Shendo's face sending bad jibes.

"He say, not urgent, can wait till finish breakfast."

"Why you little shit! *Who do you think you are?"* Salibe balled, he had had a 'belly full' of this Japanese superiority.

Shendo put the brakes on the eating process and eyeballed Salibe. Maybe his English wasn't up to scratch but Salibe's outburst and body language didn't need translated and his eyes flashed in anger.

"You dare insult Nihon-jin!" Shendo jumped to his feet and grabbed the grip of his samurai, the blade just showing.

"Well...Well... We can speak some English after all." Salibe scorned.

"Enough!" Shendo retaliated.

But Salibe had to drive his point home. The Russians are intolerant people when they are left in the dark and no one wants conflict with the 'Bratva'.

"Now you listen and listen good... I must contact the Russian Military of Defense to provide the GPS coordinates for the rendezvous point off Shimaru Shima... *Do you understand?* If this deal falls through the Russians can make it very difficult for the Gokudo and you'll not only have the Bratva on your tail but Hamas and Hezbollah... *Am I getting through?"*

Shendo pushed the sword back into the scabbard before slowly and deliberately taking his seat. *If looks could kill!* He sat for a moment in silence deep in thought before opening his tunic pocket to extract the Motorola. It appeared that Salibe had gotten through to him after all.

"Good morning Gentleman." Chuck took the last seat at the table. Sorry I'm late, my back is still recovering from sleeping on that bamboo cot, and as for that fucking shower... Let alone that breakfast... I'll take a rain check on that one."

There was no comment. 'Silence is golden' and Chuck immediately sensed he had interrupted something.

"Sorry guys, have I broken up the party?"

Shendo was now engrossed tuning in to the 80m band.

"So, what's with this radio phone thing?" Chuck just couldn't help himself.

Salibe interrupted. "Now don't go off your fucking brain. I've just discovered there's no Wi-Fi here and we can't use cellular phones for fear of detection."

"Your fucking shittin me! So how about my money?"

Salibe raised his hand to tell Chuck to shut it.

"For your information, Shendo is contacting Okio right now."

"Well when he's at it, you had better remind him to transfer the rest of my loot......."

* * *

The American 'so called' coffee was as bad as the breakfast... Bacon and eggs sunny side up with a slice of over toasted bread, was something else. The eggs had seen better days and as for the bacon... It splintered into a hundred pieces when it was touched with a fork ending with Steve shaking his head as he pushed his almost untouched plate aside.

"I told you, you should have gone Japanese!" Gregg couldn't miss the cheap shot.

"Get out of it you moron!" Steve fired back but he had to laugh.

It was time and Gregg wiped his mouth with his napkin then swallowed the last of the green tea.

"Listen, I say we get out of here partner and get that report from the front desk."

Steve had already risen to his feet in anticipation.

"Yeah, I'm with you."

"Thank you, gentlemen, did you enjoy your breakfast?" The Maître D enquired as they were leaving.

"Yeah, it was good." Steve answered trying to keep a straight face.

"Why you bloody hypocrite!" Gregg couldn't help himself as they left.

"Remember... 'When in Rome'?"

"Get out of it.......!"

* * *

The young Japanese receptionist at the front desk, smartly dressed in her dark blue uniform, her black hair in a tight Geisha bun, smiled warmly as the two Americans approached.

"Can I help you gentleman?"

With a good-looking babe like that, is she kiddin me? Steve thought, he and Gregg returning the smile.

"Rooms 324 and 325, I believe there is a package for us?"

"Just give me a moment sir?" She checked the computer.

"This keeps getting better." Steve spoke under his breath, making Gregg almost burst into laughter.

"That's a Mr. Nelson and a Mr. Jonson?"

"That's correct Chiyoko."

"How did you know her name?" Gregg turned.

"The name tag, Dumbo!" It was Steve's turn to take the shot.

Chiyoko couldn't help smiling, she understood every word.

"Ah here we are." She took the package from the rack.

"Have a nice day gentleman." She smiled again but this time with a distinct naughtiness.

"Nice huh?"

"I thought you were a sucker for blondes?"

"A guy's taste can change, can't it?"

"If you say so." Gregg had to stifle his laughter.......

* * *

"Steve, I suggest we go back to your room and study this report in comfort, besides I'm sure Thomson will be on the phone within the hour."

"Yeah, I guess you're right Gregg, *and we don't want to miss that call!*"

Steve was holding the large manila envelope as they walked to the elevator.

"It looks like there's a bit of reading here." He patted the thick package, the elevator opened and Gregg pressed three.

"Do you think we should take a look at Salibe and Fadile's rooms?"

"It had crossed my mind... But there again, we might be wasting our time. I'm sure Daniel's men in conjunction with the Japanese SIA have gone through them with a fine-tooth comb."

The elevator chimed.......

* * *

"God, this is some reading and disappointingly, what I've read, there's nothing new." Steve was flicking through the pages passing each one to Gregg.

"The report on Ginzo's murder and the finger prints and DNA from Fadile's body, match up. The interesting point is the coded message received by Fadil on that day which he scribbled on the napkin that Ginzo managed to steal. We also know the call came from a public phone in Chicago and my educated guess is it's from the uncle... *Remember... Abud Azis?"*

"Yeah, I remember. You could be right Steve, but let's look at these numbers from the napkin....

62826173-31325332813231- 23636171- 2153532142-2142612132

"There has to be a relationship with these numbers and the letters of the alphabet... But how?" Steve was irritably drumming his fingers on the writing table.

Gregg was silent still staring at the long list of numbers, searching for something to stand out.

"If Daniel's code breakers can't crack it I think we don't have a hope in hell." Gregg commented disgustingly.

"You could be right Gregg, but there's nothing lost in trying."

Suddenly the phone rang before Steve could finish and he quickly lifted the receiver. "I'm sure this will be our boss."

"Rom 324, Mr. Nelson speaking."

"Mr. Nelson this is the hotel operator. You have an international call from the United States, shall I put it through?"

"May I enquire who is on the line?"

"A Mr. Thomson."

"Certainly."

"John?"

"So how are you two guys settling in?"

"A bit jet lagged but other than the crappy food, nothing to write home about."

Steve could hear the laughter.

"Listen, I received a call from Daniels regarding the disappearance of Global 10."

"What's the take, John?"

"Im sure Boeing's 'Air Accident Investigation Branch' are on a plane right now heading for Tokyo in Conjunction with the 'National Transportation Safety Board'. So where am I coming from? I want you to be at these meetings representing the CIA. I'll get Daniels to speak to the 'Japanese Aviation Authorities' to book you a seat at table. The second point is for you to arrange a meeting with a Jim McGill. I want you to dig into every little detail or dirt you can find about the pilot and first officer, their backgrounds and so on, you know the drill. Have you got a pen and paper in front of you?"

"Yeah."

"The number to phone is 81... 673......."

"I've got that John."

"What are you guys doing now?"

"Well, we just received the FBI report covering the murder of Ginzo Iwami and their investigations and the tracking of Anbar Salibe and Fadile Maalouf in Tokyo. I'm sad to say that most of the stuff is 'old hat' but nevertheless something might stand out."

"Okay, I'll leave you two guys with it, I'm off to bed. Call me tomorrow but check the time first, your disturbing my beauty sleep...."

Steve laughed as he placed back the receiver.

Gregg was still into the numbers game oblivious to the phone conversation.

"That was Thomson, he wants us to... *Are you listening Gregg?*"

Gregg had cleared the writing table pushing aside the stack of tourist brochures supplied by the hotel to rip off the unsuspecting guests, he was energetically scribbling down numbers on the phone pad.

"Are you with me?" Steve was getting impatient.

"Sorry Steve, I thought I was onto something."

"Well here's the scoop, Thomson wants us to..."

Gregg was staring at the colorful tourist brochure advertising a Tokyo bus tour with English speaking guides. The bottom line informing how to contact the company for a reservation... Contact 933 Tours.

"Gregg...?"

"Steve... Steve... I think I've cracked it...!"

"Cracked it? What are you talking about?"

"The fucking code!"

"Okay genius, *tell me...!"*

"It's simple... Look at this tour brochure... Contact 933 Tours."

"So."

"Don't you get it? Tours on the phone dialer is 8677, so we work in reverse."

Steve frowned then grinned, maybe Gregg was onto something.

"It's so bloody simple but as you say Gregg, that's the catch. *Well,* there's no harm in trying! Let's get down to business." The Thomson phone call on the back burner. "You call the numbers Gregg and I'll hit the pen." Steve pulled the desk phone in front of him.

"62826173........"

"Got it... NUMS.... Keep going...."

"Okay what have we got... NUMS DELETED COMP CRASH ALLAH AHMAD."

"Gregg, you dumb shit, you've cracked it, *but what the hell does it mean........?"*

* * *

"Wake up sleepy head, this is a 'shop till we drop day' at the Ginza and it's just turned nine. If we want to catch breakfast we had better get our skates on."

Marge groaned and rolled over, her back facing Julie. She had had a couple wines too many after the long flight last night before turning in, or was it three or four? Whatever she was feeling hung over and the last thing she needed was Julie bawling down her ear. Delta, like other carriers, to economize with hotel accommodation, where applicable with same sex staff, slept two to a room.

Julie placed her hands on her hips, still wearing her bathrobe, her hair wrapped with a towel, turban style, ready for war.

"I'm pulling rank, so there's only one thing for it."

She leaned over and with one mighty tug threw the bedclothes to the floor.

Marge was curled up in the fetal position, in her sexy nightdress.

"Last chance lady, the next one *is you on the floor."*

"Okay... Okay... I surrender." Marge turned and gave an unladylike yawn before swinging her feet to the floor then locking both hands above her head with a final stretch.

"Hmmm... That feels better." She glanced at the bedside clock. "Nine ten ... *So early!*"

"Get out of it! Yeah, and you haven't even showered yet."

"I have a better idea, why don't we order room service?"

"I don't think we have much option, by the time *you* get ready breakfast will be over."

"Now you're talking... Julie do me a favor and phone room service while I pop into the shower... Make mine American... You know bacon and eggs and hash browns, toast... *Oh*, and get an English paper."

"Yes, your highness, is there anything else?"

"Oh... I almost forgot... Coffee and orange juice."

"Why you...!"

Julie threw a pillow at Marge as he streaked past on her way to the bathroom.

"Missed... *Ha... Ha... Ha.*"

Julie shook her head, a smile lining her face. Marge will never change.

"Now that breakfast." Julie lifted the phone. "Room Service please... I wish to place a breakfast order for room six twenty-one......."

* * *

Julie had slipped into her Jeans, a hugging white "T' shirt and plain white sneakers. When doing the shopping 'obstacle course' comfort is high on the agenda, besides it was a beautiful summer's day.

"Room service will take a little longer so I might as well blow dry my hair then put on my make-up." Julie was speaking to herself as she sat in front of the vanity mirror and maybe just as well as Marge was drowning out the TV with her 'tin ear' version of 'Some Where Over the Rainbow', a version Judy Garland would never forgive.

"Between Marge and this blow drier, I might as well turn the TV off as I can't hear a dam thing."

'This is CNN with the latest world news.' A 'Global International'.......

"It'll be the same old thing, ISIS or Donald Trump." She pressed the remote.

"Somewhere..."

"Oh no..."

Marge suddenly appeared from the bathroom vigorously toweling her dark chestnut hair, still dressed in her terry towel robe.

"Marge, for Christ sakes, you're not on 'America's got Talent' I'm trying to put on my eye liner and my hand is trembling."

"Get off my street! You don't appreciate a good voice when you hear it!"

"My advice honey, save it for the Karaoke bars."

"Come on... *'Forget your troubles and let's get happy'.*"

"Marge spare me... *please!*"

The doorbell chimed and just in time before the claws came out.

"This'll be room service, I'll get it Julie, I don't want to spoil your facial." The sarcasm showing.

"Are you decent?" Julie turned.

"Don't be a prude... Why not give the poor guy an eyeful?"

"I hope you have something on below?"

"Do *you* shower in your panties and bra?"

Julie just shook her head. I was a lost cause.

"Whose there?" Marge used the peep hole. *"Hmmm,* not bad looking for a Japanese."

"Room Service for six twenty-one."

"Just a sec..."

The young man dressed in his dark blue gold bradded uniform with the high Chines collar smiled as he struggled to push the fully laden breakfast trolley through the doorway, its wheels sinking into the plush carpet giving maximum resistance, the crockery cargo making a loud rattling noise.

Hikaru smiled admiring the scenery, Marge's loosely tied bathrobe showing more cleavage than 'Mariah Carey'.

"Your breakfast madam, shall I serve?" He seemed unperturbed, he had seen it all before but their again, an encore is always interesting.

"No, that will be all... Eh...?" Marge read his name tag.

"Eh... Hikaru... *Oh,* just a sec." Marge went the writing table and opened her purse then passed the kid a ten.

"Oops." Her bathrobe almost opened and she grabbed at the waist tie, pulling it tight.

"Arigato." Hikaru turned to leave, a large smile on his face. The tip was something but then so was the 'burlesque'!

"God, Julie I'm famished." Marge was already removing the food warmers.

"You go ahead I'll be another few minutes Marge, but do me a favor and pour my coffee, I don't like it too hot."

The bacon and eggs looked like yesterday's fry but Marge was taking no prisoners and saddled her toast with two rashers of bacon and an egg sunny side up, a junior 'Dagwood'.

Her mouth full she lifted her coffee cup to chase the food before opening 'The New York Time's'.

'TOKYO FLIGHT BOUND FOR WASHINGTON DC MYSTERIOUSLY DISSAPEARS'

A Global International Boeing 777 freighter disappeared mysteriously from the radar less than one hour after departing from Tokyo Narita International Terminal, bound for Washington DC. William Collins, the Captain and First Officer, Charles Stevens are both experienced pilots with over......

Marge's coffee cup crashed to the floor bouncing on the plush carpet, hot coffee spraying the air.

"What the hell Marge!" Julie yelled.

Tears now flowing from Marge's eyes like mini 'Niagara's'.

"No... No... It can't be!" She was becoming hysterical and Julie dropped everything and rushed to her side.

"Marge... Marge... What is it?"

It was as if she had been stricken dumb as she pointed to the headline.

"My God... Bill..." Julie placed the back of her hand to her mouth in a silent scream........

* * *

"Bill, be honest with me." Sally was sitting on the side of her cot, legs dangling, the breakfast tray at her feet, the 'unenticing' rice barely touched.

"About what Sally?" Bill stared solemnly into her eyes.

"You know where I'm coming from... Like... What do you think is going to happen *to us?*"

"Sally, for once in my life I can't answer that question. But *I can* vouch for Chuck. He may be a villain but he wouldn't stand idly by and see us assonated. The Japanese are remembered for their barbaric atrocities against the Chines people in the Second World War. It is in their genes from the days of the samurais and the Yakuza have been known to be *even more* ruthless to achieve their cause."

"Yakuza?"

"The Japanese Mafia."

"How did you know that Bill?"

"The two Japanese heavies had the tip of their left hand little finger missing, a must to be a member of the Yakuza."

"You *are* observant."

"I only noticed that after we had taken off, If only..." He paused. "If *only I had noticed earlier!*" Bill grimaced, shaking his head.

"What now Bill?"

"Prisoners do what comes naturally..."

"You mean escape!" Sally gasped, placing her hand on her heart, partly through fear and shock.

Bill looked toward the barred window to make sure there was no peeping eyes.

"Sally..." He pointed to his right foot as he slowly lifted his trouser leg just above the ankle but enough to expose the holstered .25 revolver.

Sally's eyes nearly popped out of her head.

Bill put his right finger to his lips to signal Sally to be quiet.

"I haven't worked out an escape plan as yet." Bill whispered, "But I'm working on it."

"Does Chuck know about...?" She pointed to Bill's ankle.

"He does, but for the life of me?" Bill shrugged. "But there's one thing I'm happy about..."

"And that is?" Sally was intrigued.

"Your shoes."

"My shoes!"

"They are flat heeled...! Most stewardess run around in uncomfortable four to five inch heals for vanity and of course they are impractical for distance walking and if *we do* manage to get out of this 'birdcage' and hit that jungle your shoes are your 'ticket to ride'."

"Is that meant to make me feel good?" Sally laughed.

"It makes me feel good because now I know you're up to it. I have some ideas I'm working on."

"Bill, at the thought of being a pain... *I mean...* Would you really shoot to kill?"

"You had better believe it…...!"

* * *

(Speaking in Japanese)

"Password Fish Tail."

There was a distinctive pause as Okio listened cautiously. The missing Boeing Freighter was headlines and although on radio phone the CIA had the latest listening technology.

"Hi."

"Shendo here."

"It had better be!"

Okio was not at his best. The police commissioner, although on the Yakuza payroll had to make a token gesture to investigate the murder of a CIA agent and because of the Palestinians recent meetings with 'Nippon Shipping & Logistics' it was just a formality but upsetting.

"The Palestine needs to speak with you ungently. Can I put him on the phone?"

"Hai."

Salibe placed the radio phone to his ear.

"Okio."

"Speak." A man of few words.

"Now that operation 'Fish Tail' is complete and the money is safely stored on the island I need the co-ordinates for the Russian Submarine to deliver the goods and transfer the cash."

There was a sort of an uncanny silence, Okio was cautious with his words.

"Okio, are you still there?" Salibe was becoming more and more impatient.

"Russians, can you trust?"

"I have no alternative and worse still, I only have a window of 48 hours or the deal is dead in the water."

"The coordinates are ... 39 West......".

"I've got that. I'll immediately contact the Russian Ministry of Defense.... *Hold it!* Before you hang up, I need you to transfer the other 20 million to the account of Charles Stevens in Switzerland."

"Why?"

"That was the deal, Okio."

"American First officer does nothing... There only in case Pilot do stupid thing. He is traitor to his own kind. Twenty million is sufficient for his services."

"What are you saying?"

"Simple, this conversation over......."

* * *

Chuck's problem was secondary. Salibe had to contact the Russians as soon as possible.

"Shendo, I need your radio phone."

Kinichi was cautious and not particularly amorous about passing the Arab the only Motorola.

"Shendo, *gimme the fucking phone.* I cleared it with Okio."

Kinichi read the body language but turned to Tahoka for assurance who nodded his approval.

Salibe removed a small notebook from his pocket and flicked trough pages.

"Ah here it is." He was speaking to himself... "Band frequency 75...." He proceeded to tune the dial.

There was a loud whistling and crackling sound before it cleared, then suddenly something came to him and he switched off the phone. *The time difference!* How could he be so stupid? Moscow time is 5am and no one will be at the Ministry. Salibe glanced at his watch 9.45... He would have to delay his call until at least 3pm.

"Shit!" Salibe cursed, another delay... *What next?"* He turned to Tahoka as he passed the radio phone back to Shendo.

"Tell Shendo I need to call again at around 3 to 3.30 in the afternoon."

Tahoka rattled off a whole bunch of stuff in Japanese which didn't seem to please Kenichi one little bit, besides, he still had the problem of the prisoners on his plate and the first pick-up of the ill-gotten cargo was due today, ETA 6.30pm before dusk. The engineering and construction crew were already packing for the changeover and the camp was abuzz. This month had been particularly arduous extending the runway during the monsoon season and they couldn't wait to set foot on Japanese soil.

Salibe was anything but happy, between his discussion with Okio and the failed call to Russia.

"Now more trouble, I've have to tell Stevens the 'good news'." He was shaking his head.

"I don't like that look, Salibe. I hope it's your bad shit not mine?"

"Well, you had better hope again."

"What the fuck!" Stevens jumped to his feet, murder in his eyes, then he suddenly went quiet. The loaded Glock pointed at his forehead was enough for 'Silence of the Lambs'.

Shendo rose to his feet cool calm and collective, staring Salibe down.

"Point gun away or use, if not sit down and discuss."

"You heard the man... *Plank it.*" Salibe menacingly waved the semi-automatic at Stevens.

Bill breathed a sigh of relief, his face regaining its color and he slowly did what he was told. No sense being a wealthy posthumous hero.

But Salibe couldn't close it. "The next time you open your big mouth, will be your last."

The cold steel digging into Salibe's neck cut the biography short.

"Boss say put gun away."

Salibe knew Tahoka wasn't fooling and flicked the safety catch pushing the Glock back in its holster.

"Now Talk." Shendo barked.

"Let me guess." Suddenly Chuck was back full of confidence, the threat of six feet under, now gone.

"Your other 20mill has evaporated. Okio refuses to pay on the basis you did nothing for it and you're a traitor to your own kind."

"That's fucking rich, coming from him!"

"I would advise you to watch your mouth and be thankful their knowledge of English is poor. Consider yourself lucky with the pay check you received."

"Well fuck you Salibe! Now all I want is to get the fuck off this shit house Island."

"That's up to Shendo. There's a freighter arriving today from the mainland and if I were you... You had better kiss ass. *Now,* let me finish my fucking breakfast......."

* * *

"Control Tower to Captain Katsuro flight NS1...You are now clear for takeoff on runway 1A, have a safe flight captain."

"Thank you tower, will proceed as per your instructions."

(Speaking in Japanese)

"First officer Osumu, have you gone through the safety check list?"
"Hai, Captain."

"Engineer Shiru?"

"All good captain, the safety belt sign is on."

"Affirmative, then let's get this bird in the air... Flaps down 10 degrees...."

The Kawasaki C-1 short range freighter powered up its two Mitsubishi built Prat & Whitney's with 29,000 pounds of thrust began thundering down the runway to achieve the 200k/h for lift off speed........

* * *

The Tokushima Airport is a joint civil military airport owned by the Japan Maritime Self Defiance Force located on the South Island of Shikoko the smallest of Japan's big four islands. It is the busiest airport in Shikoko being the home of the 202 Air Training Squadron equipped with Beechcraft TC-90's and UH-60j's, Search and Rescue helicopters and one squadron of Lockheed Martin F16 Falcons, the backbone of the Japanese Defense Force for the South Islands, under the US government's protection agreement, post-World War II.

* * *

Air transportation to and fro from Shimaru Shima to Tokushima airport was an essential part of the Columbian Japanese drug cartel's distribution channel to the untapped new markets of Asia. Although operation 'Sea Lane' via the decommissioned Russian Kilo Class Submarine, code named 'The Hasashi', successfully ferrying uncut cocaine from the Island of Gorgona, there remained the problem of transporting the illegal cargo to Shikoko, the smallest of the Japanese Islands. The challenge was to find a short-range transporter large enough to carry 70 passengers and crew with at least 40 metric tons of cargo, under the legitimate cloak of 'Nippon Shipping and Logistics', without attracting 'The Japanese Border and Customs Control'.

* * *

In 1966, the 'Japan Air Self Defiance Force' transport fleet was retired mid as the American Curtis C-46's did not fare well in comparison to the newer aircraft such as the Lockheed C-130 Hercules and subsequently the JASDF elected to replace it with a domestically designed and manufactured Japanese transport aircraft.

For this purpose, the government turned to the 'Nihon Aircraft Manufacturing Corporation', a consortium of several major corporations which had begun to commercially produce the YS-11, a twin turbo prop airliner. However, after much deliberation, the NAMC decided that 'Kawasaki Heavy Industries' would be the prime contractor and the newly designed transporter would bear the companies name. Hence the Kawasaki CA-1 which has now been in service since its maiden flight in 1970.

The upgraded Kawasaki CA-2 ticked all the boxes, with the capacity to take sixty soldiers and 45 paratroopers with 40 metric tons of equipment and with a range of range of 1,600kl and a cruising speed of 657k/h at 35,000ft, it was more than ideal for the short run to Shimaru Shima, but the biggest advantage was its short landing distance of 2,300ft and takeoff of 1,200ft, perfect for the 11,200 runway.

Japan Airways had purchased one for domestic short haul freight on a trial basis but found its restrictive in payload uneconomical and placed it in mothballs, an opportunity not to be missed by the Yakuza. Subsequently it was purchased and repainted with the corporate logo of 'Nippon Shipping& Logistics' (NS 1). The retired air crew from the Japanese Defense Force was easy picking and with air traffic control and customs on the payroll, it was a done deal.......

* * *

(Speaking in Japanese, 30 minutes into the flight)

"Osamu, switch off the Transponder, Flight Data Recorder and Cockpit Voice Recorder."

"Hi Captain." Osumu stretched up and did as the Captain ordered.

"Shiru."

"Hai, Captain?"

"Engine check, hydraulic pressure, fuel pumps, generators?"

"All working perfectly, Captain."

"Osamu, descend to 12,00 feet and enter new coordinates then switch to auto pilot and maintain speed at 180nots... ETA?" Katsuro glanced at his watch... 2450hrs, or earlier with this tail wind and its clear skies all the way........"

* * *

The Senior Air Traffic Controller at the Tokushima Airport, 'Toby Norito', smiled as flight NS1 disappeared from the radar, its Transponder having been switched off. It was just another Yakuza routine flight, same day, same time each month, never to be reported. The distinctive tip of Toby's left-hand little finger missing, didn't need an explanation and the monthly envelope containing 10,000 US dollars was enough to put another smile on his face.......

* * *

Steve sat back in his chair, both hands behind his head, the slightest comment from Gregg would send him into uncontrollable laughter.

"I can just see the look on Daniels face when we tell him we've cracked the code." Gregg had a smile on his face like a "Cheshire Cat'.

"For Christ sakes Gregg, don't make me laugh, *or I'll burst my sides!* But there's one thing for sure, were not gonna make many friends with Daniel's 'cryptanalysis' boys!"

Gregg, as usual had that serious look. "Should we phone Thomson first?"

Steve came back to reality rubbing his chin with his right hand then screwing up his eyes.

"Let's kick it around first... NUMS DELETED COMP CRASH ALLAH AHMAD... *Hmmm...* Okay, just say this is a hijack rather than an 'Air Crash Investigation'? Don't forget the two hundred-billion-dollar cargo bound for destruction at 'The Federal Reserve Washington. DC' and knowing the US government I'm sure a promissory note has been given to the Diet for its progressive replacement to secure their foreign currency reserves. So, there is no risk on that side."

"So?"

"If the notes were stolen... Forget the motive at this point rather than just their sheer value... The serial numbers could be traced rendering them useless. Now where would these numbers be stored?"

"Of course!" Gregg chimed in.

"Okay, so now we're on the same page... NUMS DELETED... So... 'Numbers deleted'... Does that make sense?"

Gregg was pondering and didn't answer he was at least two steps ahead.

"'COMP CRASH'... Gregg are you with me?"

'Yeah, but I'm jumping the starter. 'Numbers deleted via a computer crash...' That's the deal... An intentional 'wipe out' by a hacker or someone with direct access to the main frame in 'The Federal Reserve'. So now that the serial numbers are obliterated the bank notes can be dispersed on the open market worldwide as legal tender."

"And the last part...? Steve interjected.

"'ALLAH AHMAD'... Easy... 'God is Great'... Let's jigsaw it all together. 'Numbers deleted, computer crash, God is great'...."

"Now the million-dollar question?" Steve was back in it.

Gregg frowned. "Steve, do you remember the presentation you gave to Thomson?"

"Yeah, but did it go on deaf ears? Remember my statement to Thomson it was all about money 'can't buy me love' and we had to find the source of the Nile?"

"A bit melodramatic and over the top but you certainly made your point but in Thomson's eyes, it was maybe 'The X Files'."

"*Shurrr up...! Gregg,* it all ties up...! Azis... Salibe and Maalouf's uncle, whom it just so happens is the senior director in the 'Department of Controller of Currency' and works closely with the Federal Reserve in the printing and destruction of currency through BEP. Not to mentions his brother and their father, Abdul Fatah, the number one commander of the armed wing of Hamas and on Shin Bet's most wanted list. It's got 'green backs' written all over it. Hamas is desperate for funds to purchase weapons to drive the Israelis out of the Golan Heights and reclaim the Gaza Strip and their 'God given right' to the Palestine State and Jerusalem."

Gregg was still pondering, Steve's summation although palatable was way ahead of its time unless it can be proved that the Global Freighter was hijacked, but why would the Yakuza be a player, they have no interest in the Palestine and Israeli conflict, *in fact to the contrary!*

"Come on Gregg, *out with it.*" Steve was getting impatient.

"Okay, let's just assume the plane went down. You would have to agree Steve, that's one real possibility and we'll have to keep it on the back burner until we meet with the Global's management and Boeing's 'Air Accident Investigation Branch' in conjunction with the 'National Transportation Safety Board'. I mean let's face it, a Boeing 777 is a big bird to hide. It needs infrastructure, like a pretty big runway."

"*Well what do you suggest Sherlock?*" Steve was off the page.

"*Cool it Steve,* I feel just a frustrated as you. You want my suggestion...? We phone Thomson and inform him how we cracked the coded message received by Salibe via the incoming call from a public phone booth in Chicago. Then we get him to check with the FBI for any security images of that phone booth. That's the first step. The second is to check with 'The Bureau of Engraving and Printing' at Fort Worth Texas and Washington DC to see if there has been a major computer crash inflicting the memory loss of the serial numbers of the notes for destruction and does their Chicago office namely, Abud Azis have access to that main frame? If the results are positive haul him in for questioning. Like you Steve, I'm sure he was the guy that made the call but unless we can fill in the blanks I'm afraid it's a 'black hole'."

"*Yeah...*" Steve gave an overzealous sigh. "Your right Gregg, There's no medals for ending up with egg on our face. Let's make that call."

"*Hang on Steve*, let's check the time difference first."

Steve opened his cell phone. "Let me see. Washington is 14 hours behind. I make it 11am now and 9pm in the States. I'll let you do the honors Gregg." Steve passed the phone, a cheeky grin on his face.

"Thanks partner and I don't think!"

The dialing tone seemed to last forever.

"Yes... Jenny Thomson here......."

* * *

Chuck was sitting brooding, breakfast the last thing on his mind and Salibe felt uncomfortable. One can never tell what a rabid dog will do? Sure, it was wrong for Okio to renege on the deal and unusual for the Yakuza, the so called 'men of honor'. But there again why should he worry, the call to Russia clouding is mind.

"When's this supply plane due to arrive with a change of construction crew?" Chuck eyeballed Shendo, straight to the point.

"Mr. Big, I want your assurance that my seat is reserved on the return flight to Tokushima... *Understanday?*"

Shendo turned to Tahoka, he could read Steve's hostile body language but he needed assurance before he pulled the trigger.

Like for two minutes, Tahoka spoke in Japanese, the message reflected on Kinichi's face was less than pleasant and he returned fire to Tahoka.

"I hate to break up your love life but what did your big boss say?"

Tahoka rose to his feet, murder in his eyes. He had had enough of the American's humor, an insult to a Samurai, his hand on the Nambu.

"You're not scaring me, big boy." Chuck retaliated.

As usual Chuck didn't take good advice and was about to learn the hard way.

"American watch mouth... Shendo say plane only take sixty and three crew... No room this trip."

"*Why you...!*"

Tahoka had already drawn his semi-automatic Nambu pistol the hammer cocked, pointed straight at Steven's forehead and it was time for 'mind over matter'.

"Awe, what's the fucking use? Your holding all the cards!" Chuck was now in full retreat reluctantly returning to his seat.

"Okay...Okay." He raised his hands in surrender mode, Tahoka holstering his pistol, the standoff over.

"Salibe, did you get that? Bill couldn't miss the shot. "Chuck was right and if I were you I wouldn't trust these assholes as far as I could throw them. I'm outta here. I might as well go have a kip on my cot."

Chuck rose to leave but not before firing another broadside at Salibe.

"Good luck to you buddy.......!"

* * *

Chuck threw himself on the unforgiving cot then cringed as his back took the full force of the bamboo laced mattress.

"Fuck... Even an Indian Fakir would shy away from this one."

The Nissan hut empty, the base personnel still at breakfast, it was the ideal time to think.

"This Fucking heat!"

Chuck had discarded his pilots jacket, his blue open necked shirt rolled up at the sleeves, sweat stained under the arm pits and chest.

"These fucking fans must be from the Mitsubishi War Museum generated by elastic bands. At least they'll save on Diesel." Chuck grinned, he still had a sense of humor, then seriousness. *"That fucking bastard Numero... I can't get over it!"*

Chuck was moving his head from side to side on the make shift pillow whilst rabbiting on, speaking to himself in denial.

"At least I'm twenty mill to the good but the question is, will I live to spend it?"

Then a thought struck him. "I wonder...? Well, there's only one way to find out and that's to go visit the man himself, but how.......?"

* * *

Julie staggered back in a faint, almost losing her balance before crashing down heavily on the sofa.

"Marge, I need a drink." Her voice almost inaudible, the tears drowning her lips.

"Me to...!" Marge croaked... *"Something strong."* Her mouth quivering.

Having gained her composure Julie rose shakily to her feet but not before grabbing the elbow rest for support, unsteadily making her way to the bar fridge. She grabbed two stubby Scotch glasses, rattled some cubes in each, then opened the door.

"Where the fuck's that Scotch?" She yelled, in her anguish chucking the miniatures all over the place before finally nailing the culprits. The four small bottles with their amber liquid soon found the ice and Julie couldn't wait to taste the 'Water of Life" giving a throat clearing cough as the Chivas hit the spot.

Marge was now sitting on the floor both knees up still sobbing, her head between her hands.

"Here, get this down you." Julie passed the glass.

Marge eagerly grabbed it with both hands, almost swallowing the two fingers in one gulp.

"Hey... Hey... Go easy, getting pissed won't change anything."

"Steve ... Bill... I can't believe their gone."

"Marge, let's not jump to conclusions, it's far too early to write these two characters off. They're probably sitting in a life raft drinking Brandy from the survival kit."

That brought a forced smile and Marge devoured the rest of the Scotch.

"I feel a lot better... A refill?" She pointed to the naked glass.

Julie shook her head. "Not on your life, let's keep our minds clear and decide what to do next. Remember we're flying out again tomorrow, so we really don't have much time."

"Can I ask you something Julie?"

"Of course." Julie calmly replied.

"Is there still a flame burning for Bill?"

"Marge, what we had was special and Bill will always be close to my heart, but that spark has gone and he is now just a very special friend."

Julies words hit Marge hard and she burst into uncontrollable sobs.

"I still love that jerk! I thought it was over until this happened. Julie, what am I to do?" She almost lost her breath.

"Marge, come on, *snap out of it."*

"You're so much stronger than me Julie."

"You only think that. Now wipe these baby blues." Julie passed her a napkin from the breakfast trolley."

"Thanks." Marge sobbed again, she was gradually coming around.

"Let's think about this." Julie sat back, Marge had already joined here on the sofa.

"I think if we tried to phone McGill at Global, we wouldn't have a chance in hell getting past his secretary, with all this shit on his plate, not to mention the media."

"McGill?" Marge was confused.

"Jim McGill, the coordination manager for Global's International Freight Division in Tokyo. *You remember*, we met him once in LA over dinner with Bill and Steve."

"Not really, but whatever."

"I think our best bet is to phone Draper our flight manager."

"That dog!" Marge was still smarting from the dirty trick Tokyo fiasco.

"Awe he's okay. Can you blame the guy, he was in a hole and we fell for the extras and the shopping in the Ginza?"

"Let's give him a call, it's a long shot but he may be able to pull a few strings even though Global is our competitor."

"Let's do it. What's his number?" Marge was in the starter box.

"Whoa...Whoa.... Something tells me *I* had better phone him, I don't trust you, in your state of mind you may say something we'll both regret. Let me see........"

* * *

Draper had just retired with his latest conquest. Still single at 40 he had been there and done that and in his job... *Air hostesses...* Well, it doesn't take much imagination. At 6.1 being a lady's man he kept himself in good shape and the full head of the jet-black hair in a side shade was certainly different, a bit old fashioned but maybe that's what attracted the punters. That tanned complexion and lean face, blue eyes and whitened teeth was a standout and tonight he was doing what comes naturally......

* * *

"I saw you eying that Nora Best in the office today."

"You just imagine things... So, she's attractive, a guy can look, *can't he?*"

"Yeah, but not with your eyes."

"Awe, come on honey, don't spoil the night. Now, where were we?"

"Where you normally are..."

"What the hell! That bloody phone...?"

"Don't answer it!"

"I'm sorry babe but in my job, it's twenty-four seven."

Draper untangled their naked bodies and leaned over the bedside table to answer his cell.

"Draper here..."

"Don, its Julie... Julie Rodgers, phoning from Tokyo."

"Julie Rodgers... Who's Julie Rodgers?"

"For Christ sakes Anne, she's the chief purser on our Tokyo run. You've seen her in the office before... Besides you shouldn't be earing in on this call, *it's private...!"*

"I'm sorry Don what was that?"

"Eh...Err..."

"I beg your pardon, I didn't know you had company." Draper could hear Julie laugh in the background. "Am I disturbing something."

"Do you know what bloody time it is?"

"Don't tell me I'm disturbing your beauty sleep?"

"You're disturbing a lot of things smart ass, now why the call?"

"I was wondering if you can help Marge and I get some information?"

"Information? Information on what?" Draper was becoming more than irate.

"Haven't you heard?"

"For Christ sakes, *heard what?"*

"A Global freighter was lost on a flight from Tokyo to Dulles Washington, last night"

"Sh i i i i t ...! But how can *I* help? Wait a minute don't tell me your partner's, these pilots... What's their names, were on that flight?"

"Bill Collins and Chuck Stevens... You met them once over dinner. ... Don, you have contacts and I'm sure you know Jim McGill, Global's Flight Coordinator in Tokyo."

"Not like a brother if that's what you mean, I'll see what I can find out but it will have to wait until tomorrow... What's your number there?"

"Thanks Don... Tokyo... 81..."

"I'm really sorry Julie, I'll try my best but I'm not promising you anything, don't give up... Good night." Draper closed the phone.

"Now where were we......?"

* * *

Chuck threw his feet to the floor; the Nissan hut was devoid of life as the construction and engineering crews were too busy getting ready to clear the storage areas of used fuel containers and empty gas bottles. Perishable supplies such as food and fresh fruit would be stored in the large refrigerators run on generating power. Over the last two years' solar panels had been gradually installed to take the load off the lighting and save Diesel but it was all hands-on deck today for the six thirty flight and that long awaited R&R.

"*Hmmm...*" Chuck was studying the organized chaos, bodies running everywhere, unlike the Japanese's, but when it comes to Sex in the City...

"The six thirty flight... *Hmmm ...*" Speaking to himself. "The problem is I need to talk this over with Bill and Sally... But will they trust me and then there's that guard..." Steve rubbed his chin. *It was certainly going to be a challenge.*

Then out of the blue something struck him and he gave a wry smile before reaching into his airline duffle and extracting two full packs of Pall Mall. *"Hell, I hope he smokes.......!"*

* * *

The sun was at its highest and Steve donned his airline cap to protect him from the deadly rays. As he left the hut he noticed that one of the giant freezer container doors was open and his sharp eyes caught the sight of a stack of six pack Asahi beers.

"*Hmmm...*" He gave a cunning smile then casually and unobtrusively walked over to the stack and lifted a pack of cold ones as if it was his divine right. Now between the smokes and the beer it was the perfect, contraband bribery the name of the game.

It was around a ten-minute walk to the maintenance hut, Bill and Sally's make- shift prison but more to the point Steve had to look as inconspicuous as possible.

The solitary guard still dressed in his World War II light kaki tropical battle dress was squatting with his back supported against the steel shell of the hut, having a sneak smoko, his Japanese field cap reflecting the humidity, a broad sweat band saturating the crown. Maybe he was on report, *whatever...* this young 'Yakuza' soldier was feeling pretty sorry for himself in the mid-day sun.

Suddenly he saw Chuck approach and jumped to his feet, straightening his field cap and grabbing the cigarette stub from his lips before hastily stomping out the remains with his boot. Then quickly grabbing his bayoneted Arisako rifle and engaged the bolt stepping his right foot forward almost like a boxer in the challenge stance, menacingly pointing the 22-inch bayonet straight at Chuck's chest.

"Ya me te." He yelled. (stop what you are doing) This guy meant business.

Chuck raised his one free hand, the contraband in the other.

"Ohayo Gozaimasu... Konbanwa... Genka Disco."

The guard stopped in his tracks taken aback. *An American speaking Japanese!*

Bill's pigeon Japanese now exhausted, his last ditch the contraband, and he held up the pack of Asahi and the Pall Mall with his other hand. Somehow, he had to gain this guards trust.

"You want beero... smokes?"

The guard was taking no chances and motioned with his rifle for Bill to push the beer and cigarettes with his foot across to him on the ground.

"Yours..." Chuck made a hand motion demonstrating to unstop the beer bottle and drink.

"Me you, we drink." Chuck gave an overzealous smile

Then suddenly the guard's facial expression changed from aggression to 'friendly fire' and he locked the safety on the antique Arisako and stood the rifle against the wall. The thought of a cold beer in this 34-degree heat was more than enticing.

The first cut is the deepest and the look on the guard's face as he swallowed an overindulgent mouthful was a picture within its self. He smiled for a moment and regained his breath then stared his mind indecisive as to the motive of this generous American. And then there was the cigarettes...? Pall Mall hard to get...?

Then a smile crossed his face, like *'Awe what the hell!'* and he bent down and chucked Steve the chilled brown bottle who caught it like a catcher for the 'Yankees'.

"Domo." Steve smiled and opened the top then cautiously leaned forward to clink bottles. The guard smiled and obliged.

"Domo Arigato." He gave a slight bow.

Chuck had cracked it but 'Ground Zero' wasn't over just yet and somehow, he had to speak to Bill and Sally. The guard's total lack of English was a plus but getting the message to him would be another challenge. Sign language was the only solution... If only this guy was deaf...! Steve grinned to himself, the thoughtless joke his specialty.

"*Eh...Ah...*" Steve made a motion with his hand to his lips. "Speak to Americans?"

Bill turned to Sally at the sound of the familiar voice nod threw his feet to the floor.

"That sounds like Chuck. Stay where you are Sally, I'll go stretch up and check it out.

Bill stood on his toes and peered out the barred window. *It was Chuck alright........!*

* * *

"Chuck is that you?" Both the guard and Chuck turned simultaneity toward the voice only to catch the top of Bill's head.

"Yeah, it's me, listen we have to talk..."

Chuck instinctively moved forward but the guard wasn't having any of it and grabbed his rifle.

"*Yamete Kudasi.*" (Go no further)

Bill raised both his hands ... "Dozo... Dozo... I speak only." He made the motion with his hand again to his lips.

The guard drew a line with his boot in the dirt then pointed.

"*Mou Iya Diea.*" (Not past here)

"Arigato." Chuck replied.

The guard seemed satisfied that his new-found friend wouldn't step out of line and placed his rifle once again against the wall then opened a pack of Pall Mall extracting the tobacco stick. Another beer, another smoko... *Break time........*

* * *

"Yeah, it's me. Listen, this guard speaks no English so we can talk but from a distance... How are you and Sally doing?"

"Apart from the shit food, humidity and mosquitoes devouring our bodies... *Yeah...* Everything is dandy."

"*Okay... Okay...* That was a stupid question."

"So why the pleasure?"

"I guess I asked for that... Bill, *come on,* you know I wouldn't allow anything to happen to you and Sally."

"I *had* hoped your conscious, if you had one, would give you a 'wakeup call'. So, again I'm asking the question?"

Steve casually glanced his eyes toward the guard for a sneak peek at his reactions and he seemed more than content enjoying his beer and smokes, his rifle at arm's length standing by his side.

"Bill, I wondered if you still have that 'pop gun' attached to your ankle... You know, the one in case of hijacks?"

"Heh...Heh... Bill couldn't help laughing." I was wondering when you would twig. For the life of me, I don't know why they didn't do a body search. So, what's on your mind?"

"What prisoners normally do?"

"Escape...! What brought this on?"

"Preservation buddy... It seems we're disposable. Yeah, and I don't need a lecture like, *'I told you so'!"*

"It's united we stand divided we fall, huh?" Bill was sinking the boot.

"Are you in or are you out? I don't have a lot of time to discuss this before the guard starts getting suspicious."

"I'm listening........"

"At 6.30 today a relief flight from Tokushima will arrive on the island with a replacement crew and supplies. The camp will be a hive of activity around 5 to 5.30 in preparation for the changeover. I don't know what make of aircraft but I believe it's a freighter that can take a pay load of forty billion dollars, so it can't be that small."

"Go on."

"Here's the deal... I return at say... five, but Bill you need to create a diversion to get the guard to unlock the door and that's when we strike. I'll handle him from this side but if you have to you use that 25, my advice don't hesitate."

The guard's patience was exhausted and he raised his rifle to message Chuck that the conversation was over.

"Remember Bill... Arigato." Steve gave a slight bow to the guard then turned and left, his adrenalin on high. Five o'clock was 'fight time'.......

* * *

Bill turned and slumped back on to the cot turning to face Sally who looked petrified, she had heard it all.

"Christ Bill, I'm scared shitless. Will you have to shoot the guard?"

"Let's skip that part Sally. We have a bigger problem when we hit the Jungle. Survival in the bush is a challenge in itself. So, we must prepare ourselves with supplies such as water, food, and anything else we can get our hands on. Water is the biggest problem as I see that they have installed a desalination plant which means natural water is either scarce or none at all. Which in my opinion is hard to believe with this mountainous volcanic terrane and tropical climate? Anyhow we'll cross that bridge when it comes."

"Steve's no dummy, he'll come equipped."

"I wish I had your confidence, Bill."

The steel door rattled as it was unlocked. It was lunch time and the Guard had the usual menu, green tea and boiled rice. Whatever, it was a start for their survival kit......!

* * *

THE MEETING

"Jenny, its Gregg Johnson phoning from Tokyo, I hope it's not inconvenient but I need to speak to John, it's urgent."

"Just a sec Gregg, I'll go fetch him... *John, it's Gregg Johnson phoning from Tokyo ...*"

"Coming... Thanks Jenny..." Thomson took the phone. "Gregg?"

"Sorry to disturb you John, I hope it's not a bad time."

"In my job Gregg, it's always a bad time." Gregg could hear his boss laugh in the back ground.

"Well, what's the scoop?"

"John, you're not gonna believe this but by a comedy of errors, Steve and I cracked the coded message sent to Salibe."

"Naw, *your shitting me!*"

"It was simple, the numbers used on the dialer of a phone. I'll not go into detail but this is the message..."

'NUMS DELETED COMP CRASH ALLAH AHMAD'

"Well I'll be darned... Great work guys so what's your thoughts....?"

"Someone made that call from a public phone in Chicago, that we already know. Steve and I are back to the shipment of used notes on Global 10 which has mysteriously disappeared without a trace. We feel that there's no doubt its connected to the radical Palestine cause, hence the coded call to Salibe and his brother leading up to the fire fight where we lost one of our own FBI agents Ginzo Iwami and of course Salibe's brother Fadile Maalouf, who are both nephews of Abud Azis......."

"Let's go over this again...." Thomson was pondering.

1. We check with the 'The Bureau of Engraving and Printing' at Fort Worth Texas and Washington DC to see if there has been a major

computer crash inflicting the loss of the serial numbers of the notes for destruction.

2. Does their Chicago office have access to their main frame?
3. Has the FBI any security footage of that phone booth they tracked down?
4. If 2, then we pull Abud Azis in for questioning....

"Yeah, that wraps it up John."

"Hmmmm... We must careful pulling in Azis prematurely as it may blow the FBI's cover and the extremists go to ground... Let me think about that one."

"John, there's one point I forgot..." Steve couldn't finish for laughing.

"Okay, Okay... So, what's the wrap."

"Who's gonna give Daniels the bad news........?"

* * *

Steve glanced at his watch turning to Gregg.

"Time's running away with itself, do you now it's almost 1.30 and we still have to arrange that meeting with McGill at Global! Let's hope he can see us today. Gregg, what was that number John gave us for McGill's direct line.....?"

"McGill here."

"Mr. McGill, Steve Nelson here from the CIA, it's regarding the loss of Global 10."

"Ah yes, your boss phoned me from Washington to arrange that we meet."

"I was wondering how you are placed today?" Steve asked fingers crossed.

"Hmmm... Let me see... I could fit you in say around three if that grabs you? That's the best I can do, I'm sure you can imagine my phone has never been off the hook since this terrible news broke."

"Sure, I understand... Then three it is. My partner and I look forward to our discussions. Thanks again Mr. McGill.... *Oh...*I almost forgot, do we meet at your office in Narita or do you have an office in town?"

"Yes, we are at Nomura Real Estate building 2-4-11 Higashi Shingawa in the business district."

"Got that... Thanks, Ciao........"

* * *

Salibe was putting in the time nervously checking his watch every 15 minutes whilst prancing up and down like a 'cat on a hot tin roof'. The

Russians are intolerant people and keeping a nuclear submarine on 'stand buy' is big bucks. Somehow, he had to phone Sergi Shoigu the Minister of Defense, Putin's right-hand man.

Salibe shook his head, cursing under his breath. "Trust my fucking luck and as for that fucking Shendo and that crazy radio phone he treats like his wife... *I ask you...?*"

The busy 'mess hall' now completely empty, he hadn't noticed the absence of Kenichi who in short, didn't give a rat's ass about Salibe's problems, the arrival of the 6.30 relief flight was 'numero uno' on his agenda.

Salibe sat for a moment in depressive solitaire his chin resting on his hand whilst staring at his half empty cup of green tea. Much water had passed below the bridge in the last three days notwithstanding the loss of his dear brother, still fresh in his mind. Operation 'Fish Tail' is so near and yet so far and even the best plans have a habit of going astray. The sweat stains on his chest and arm pits added to his discomfort, the humid atmosphere parched his lips in dehydration and he leaned forward and swallowed the last of the foul-tasting tea.

"*Hmmm...*" Salibe glanced at his wrist watch again. "*It's...?* Two fifty-five, I had best go and search for that fucking weasel."

Salibe left the confines of the mess hall shading his eyes with the back of his hand from the afternoon sun and begun his search for the elusive Shendo, a task in this environment easier said than done.

The site was a hive of activity, fork lift trucks coming and going busily stacking returnable materials on the loading dock in preparations for the incoming fight.

"That fucking Shendo... *Where the hell? Ah... Tahoka...*" Salibe yelled at the top of his voice to catch the big man's attention.

Kazuo was in deep conversation with his counterpart Aikido Arakida and didn't hear the call, the growling noise of diesel engines clouding the air.

"*Tahoka...*" Salibe yelled again finally catching the attention Aikido who tapped Tahoka on the shoulder and pointed in Salibe's direction.

Tahoka shrugged his shoulders, *what the fuck now?* He gave a slight bow to Aikido as if to say, 'excuse me for being rude but I had better go see what the 'rag head' is complaining about now!

"*Hi?*" Tahoka growled as he approached Salibe.

"I need to find your boss, I have to make that call to Russia and I can't do it without the use of his phone... *Understand?*"

Tahoka made a face like 'go fuck yourself' but then changed his mind, Shendo was one thing but *Namura...* You don't take chances with the 'Godfather'!

* * *

Shendo was busy checking the manifest when the duo approached and from the expression on his face, Salibe was all he needed!

"Tahoka tell Kinichi I need the radio phone to make a call to Russia."

Kazuo like a 'machine gun' rattled off some Japanese with Kinichi showing little reaction.

Enough was enough for Salibe, he knew by the look on Shendo's face he was going to be difficult, like a 'bird in the hand is worth two in the bush' he had the loot and all the cards.

"Shendo, don't fuck me over, I need to make that call, *do you understand?*"

Poker faced Shendo reached into the field pocket of his fatigues then reluctantly passed the phone.

"Fucking arigato..." Salibe scowled, grabbing the Motorola before turning and briskly walking to the Nissan hut, not only to get into the shade but away from that fucking mind crashing noise.

"At last!" Salibe gave a deep breath then wiped his forehead with the back of his hand, he had to calm down and keep his wits, Sergi Shoigu, you don't mess with. He checked his notebook once more, he was only going to get one shot.

"Okay... Got it... Band frequency 85... 81..."

There was the usual whistling and crackling noise as the waveband searched the atmosphere. Then suddenly a voice crackled speaking in Russian.

"Napora aospora ytpa?" (Good morning, password?)

"Mokete bi robpntb ha ahrunnckom rtbike" (Can you speak English?) Salibe had picked up a few phrases during his brief stay in Moscow.

"Jes." Came the reply.

"Password 'Fish Tail'." Salibe replied much relieved.

There was a moment's delay due to the radio signal then a voice with a heavy Russian accent answered.

"General Sergi Shoigu speaking."

"Anbar Salibe here."

"I have been waiting for your call for the last two days, what kept you?" Sergi wasn't holding back.

"It's a long story General, too long for this call."

"So?"

"The bottom line is the aircraft carrying the cargo of 200 billion US dollars was successfully hijacked and the money is now secured here on the island. As agreed 40 billion dollars in four aluminum containers will be transferred to your vessel when I receive the cargo intact with the ordinance as agreed."

After a moments silence Shoigu spoke in a crisp voice somewhat agitated being spoken down to.

"Agreement is agreement, make sure *you* deliver! Now no more talk I need the GPS coordinates for my captain to deliver. The cargo has already been loaded and secured in waterproof containers ... Now, time is money... *The coordinates ..."*

"West 75... Do you want me to repeat?"

"No, I will immediately convey these to the Captain of the unclear powered Lewinsky Komsomol, which will set sail from Pavlovsk Bay at 1200 hrs. Russian time... ETA ten days from now or earlier. You will be contacted by captain Nicolai Chernoff as soon as he reaches the transfer point. It is crucial that you make sure you are ready as the Americans constantly track our undersea movements."

"I understand. Be assured the Yakuza maintenance vessel, complete with a five-ton deck Crain to transfer the four aluminums containers each containing 10 billion dollars, will meet your captain at the rendezvous within 30 minutes of receiving his call."

There was no reply then the phone went dead.

"Hmmm... A man of few words." Salibe killed the phone then gave a big sigh. *"Whatever...* It looks like I'll have to stay another ten days on this shit hole island... *Shendo...* Your phone......."

* * *

The Russian nuclear Boeri Class submarine, the Lewinsky Komsomol, is a fast attack vessel of 19,000 tons with a maximum speed of 48 knots, powered by an OK-650b nuclear reactor and steam turbine and at 175 meters is much lighter than previous vessels of the submarine fleet and with the added capability to launch cruise missiles.

Named in memory of the first Russian nuclear built submarine which on June 17, 1962 was the first to cross the point of the North Pole. Unfortunately, glory turned to tragedy when in June 1967 on exercise in the Mediterranean, when war broke out in the Middle East, while sailing back in the Norwegian

Sea on September 8, the bow torpedo compartment ignited the vapors of flammable hydraulic fluid and tragically caught fire sinking the Lewinsky Komsomol, with the loss of 118 crew.

* * *

(Speaking in Russian)

Shoigu lifted the red phone. "Put me through to Captain Chernoff, *it's urgent.*"

The red phone buzzed in the Captain's quarter's and Chernoff leapt from his bunk, he had just finished morning roll call and was catching some shut eye and when *that* phone rings, *you jump!*

For the last week, the Lewinsky Komsomol had been on standby in port and both the Captain and crew were on edge waiting for the order to set sail to an unknown destination, with a class one security. The large missile chamber now void of ordinance to make use of the space for the special cargo.

Chernoff grabbed the phone almost losing his balance in the process as he hit the floor.

"Chernoff, here." Borya answered nervously, anticipating that the call was from the General himself.

"General Shoigu here."

"Yes General?"

"Make way to sail at dusk, 2200hrs. Your destination is the North Pacific... GPS coordinates... West 75... You already have the instructions regarding the delivery of the cargo at the rendezvous point and the person to call at least one hour before reaching your destination. The return cargo is in four containers with US currency. Make sure that each container is authentic before transferring the cargo... Code name... Fish Tail... Safe voyage Captain......"

* * *

Borya Chernoff was more than relieved. When Shoigu phones one can never tell. He is an extravert, consumed with his own importance and with his closeness to Putin he can walk on water making him untouchable. Officers have been demoted for minor defaults and some even incarcerated with lengthy sentences in military prisons in Siberia and dishonorably discharged.

* * *

(Speaking in Russian)

Borya lifted the intercom microphone, it was time to get the Lewinsky Komsomol underway and he turned and glanced at his cabin clock.

"Hmmm...0900hrs and we set sail at 22, there's not much time." Borya spoke out loud, his mind racing. "I had better call the First Officer immediately."

He grabbed the mike and switched on the speaker button.

"Attention please... Attention please... First Officer Levitsky report to the Captain's cabin immediately."

Borya wasted no time and was already spreading the large sea lane map on his desk, placing paper weights on each corner before studying the GPS coordinates supplied by the General. *"Hmmm..."* He rubbed his chin. "Let me see West 75..."

Suddenly there was a loud knock on the Captain's door.

"Enter." Borya barked, not in the best of moods.

"Yes Capitan." Borya's nose was deep in the map oblivious to Levitsky standing there at attention.

"Capitan?"

"Hmmm...? Chernoff looked up. *"Ah... At ease lieutenant.* I have just received instructions from General Shoigu to make ready the Lewinsky Komsomol for cast off at 2200hrs."

"Destination, Capitan?"

"That's one of the points I want to discuss with you... We are here at Sevastopol and this is our port of call." Chernoff pointed.

He had already tracked the coordinates and pin-pointed the position of the rendezvous in the North Pacific.

Levitsky stared for a few seconds at the cross on the map screwing his eyebrows, *'like what the hell am I looking at'?*

"Forgive me Capitan, *but there's nothing there but sea!"*

Chernoff cut him short. "Operation 'Fish Tail' is a class one security and that's all you need to know. Now more to the point the problem is the *sea route!* Unfortunately, we must sail the long way around as we cannot use the Suez Canal. That means we sail for the Bosporus Straight, then through the Sea of Marmara, entering the Mediterranean, and finally through the Straits of Gibraltar. Then it's round the Cape and all the way to the North Pacific."

Levitsky shook his head, this would be a challenge to avoid NATO radar and spy satellites specifically designed to track Soviet submarines. I would be 'run silent run deep' all the way.

"And the distance Capitan?" Levitsky asked guardedly. To upset Chernoff was at your own risk.

Borya jotted some numbers onto the map then checked the red curved line he had drawn with his dividers.

"Hmmmm... On my calculation, I make it 8,400 kilometers one way If we run at a depth at 500 meters at 40 knots, 8k below our top speed, we can make the round trip in just under 20 days."

"I will ensure the ship is ready Capitan and inform the crew that we will be underway at 2200hrs. Will that be all Capitan?"

"No, give the crew shore leave immediately to allow them to see their families and love ones as this will be a long trip but emphasize roll call is at 2000hrs, late arrivals will be on report. That will be all Lieutenant........"

* * *

"Let's freshen up and get our asses out of here. It has just turned two and we don't want to keep McGill waiting." Steve commented replacing the phone.

"Yeah, I got ya, gimme ten, I'll have to get back to my room to freshen up and pick up my stuff."

"To keep it simple Gregg, why don't I just meet you in the lobby?"

"Makes sense..."

Steve put the final touches to his tie admiring himself in the mirror before flicking back his hair. Who knows, maybe McGill's secretary is a blonde. Highly unlikely in Japan but you never know, he smiled, the thought crossing his mind. The Glock 45 lay on the bedside table. Steve had already slung his shoulder holster and he checked the safety catch before putting it to bed then glanced at his watch once more.

"God, Gregg will be wondering what's keeping me... Now where that's Jacket of mine...?"

As Steve stepped it out to the elevator he was tempted to knock on 325, Gregg's door.

"Nah." He stopped for second in indecision." Knowing Gregg for sure he'll be standing in reception."

With no further delay, Steve pressed the 'down arrow'.

"Steve, hold it there." It was Gregg legging it down the hallway.

"And I thought *I* was running late!" Steve shrugged holding the open elevator door ajar with his hand, the safety switch kicking in.

"Thanks partner." Gregg was breathing heavily, thank goodness the elevator's empty, huh?"

"What kept you?"

Steve's remark drew spontaneous laughter.

"Man, your something else." Gregg was still laughing.

"Ground Floor and Reception." The elevator chimed.

"We'll grab a cab. Gregg, have you get that address handy?"

"Yes mother......"

* * *

The concierge spotted the Americans heading for the hotel entrance and politely intercepted.

"Good afternoon, Gentlemen, can I help you?"

"Yes, we need a cab to..."

Gregg passed Steve the slip of paper, it's much easier than trying to pronounce the truncated address in Japanese.

The taller than usual doorman in his braided peaked cap and over the top uniform was heavily engaged getting the bellhops to unload the luggage of incoming guests and the Concierge snapped his fingers to attract his attention.

Amazingly over the hustle and bustle and road noise, like the jungle drums, the message got through and when the Concierge calls... *Its wake-up time!*

"Hai."

"Taxi for these Gentleman."

"Dozo." The doorman acknowledged, touching the peak of his cap.

"Thank you." Steve replied.

Steve slipped the Concierge a ten and a five to the doorman who blew a short double blast on his whistle to attract the next cab on the rank.

The Toyota Crown with its white starched seat covers pulled up in front of the Americans, the driver as usual in his black peeked cap, white shirt and tie and gloves to match, rolled down the passenger window and spoke to the doorman assumedly enquiring for the address which the doorman obliged showing him the paper.

"Nomura Real Estate building 2-4-11 Higashi Shingawa." The driver acknowledged before returning the note.

"Arigato." The doorman returned the paper to Gregg and touched his cap once more before opening the rear passenger door……

* * *

The taxi trip through the city gave the Americans their first impression of the famous capital of Japan. Unlike the Unite States the traffic although heavy was orderly just like the sidewalks where pedestrians walk in the direction of the arrows marked on the litter free pavements and with the density of the population, it was the appropriate solution, provided it was adhered to where as in the States it would be classed as an infringement of individual liberty. Maybe the Japanese have something that the world could envelope but you can never transpose culture.

* * *

A break in the traffic gave the opportunity for the driver to slowly pull into the kerb in front of the impressive tower block, its granite toned outer shell and sun reflective windows typical of the architecture in the high-density business district of Tokyo's CBD.

The drive was relatively short from the Palace Hotel and the driver pointed to the meter, his English obviously in short supply.

"Nine hundred." Steve commented looking at the red digital read out. "Not bad around 10 US dollars, huh... Gregg..."

"*Man*, your something else."

Gregg fished into his wallet and passed the cabbie a 'one thousand' bill. The driver took the note and began searching in his leather pouch for the change.

Steve waved his hand. "No... No, you keep."

The driver smiled a happy man, in Japan it's rare to get a tip.

"Arigato gozaimasu." He bowed.

"That was generous of you Steve, *considering it was my money!*"

"Well, you said I was like your mother, didn't you?"

"*Touché,* I might have expected. Let's hit the sidewalk before you sucker me for something else."

Steve just laughed and opened the door. "I'll buy you a beer tonight."

"*Gee thanks…….*"

* * *

The large glass rotating door entered a highly-polished marble reception hall. It seemed that by the listing of companies above the reception on a large gilt edge black board, was the 'Airlines Building' with companies such as Delta, JAL, ANA, Global, etc.

"Boy, this is some joint!" Gregg commented as he searched for the appropriate floor.

"Here we are Steve, Global Airlines 4th floor. I suppose we had better check in at reception as security looks tight."

"Yeah, and I don't like the look of these heavies standing at the 'step through' x-ray screens and body search."

"The game has changed through Islamic terrorism and it will never return to normal." Gregg shook his head.

"You can say that again but better safe than sorry. I wonder if you can help us?" Steve approached the young lady at reception. "You *can* speak English?"

"Of course, sir." The pretty Japanese woman most probably in her early thirties greeted the Americans with a warm smile.

"Now how can I be of service......."

* * *

Her black hair swept back in a bun, the typical Japanese blemish less pale complexion, dark brown olive eyes and as for that smile and pearly whites... It doesn't take much painting! Her dark blue tailored suite was made for her slim figure bringing home the difference between the ever-increasing waistlines of miss America. *Whatever,* it was a pleasant change from the obesity trail.

* * *

"We have an appointment with Mr. McGill of Global Airways at 3.pm."
 "And you are?"
"Special agents Nelson and Johnson, CIA. Here are our cards."
The receptionist was taken aback... *CIA*... this was different. She had watched American TV thrillers and now she was face to face with the real deal.
"One moment please." She lifted the phone.

(Speaking in Japanese)

"Security please... This is Akiko from the front desk, I have here......."

* * *

Within minutes two mean looking security guards appeared in their immaculate dark blue uniforms and badged peak caps, their black patent Sam Browns holstering the standard police firearm, the Nambu M60, 8mm semi-automatic. The taller of the two, sporting three silver stars on his epaulets could fortunately speak 'pigeon English'.

"Name, me Toyoku Kamanashi." He pointed to the Bakelite name tag. "You CIA?"

Steve nodded.

Toyoku was no dummy having noticed the distinctive bulge on the left side of the agent's jackets, which could mean only one thing and he was taking no chances.

"Show credentials, please"

As Steve moved his right hand toward his inside jacket pocket to retrieve his gold shield, he was abruptly stopped in his tracks.

"*Stop...* Raise hands." Toyoka yelled.

Toyoka's partner, like lightening, was suddenly pointing his M60 directly at Steve's chest. *This guy meant business!*

"*Whoa... Whoa...* Take it easy guys." Steve yelled.

Steve and Gregg hastily did as they were told raising their hands above their heads. Accidents can happen and there's was no use tempting fate.

"*What the fuck?*" Gregg turned to Steven

"*You got me partner!*"

Toyoku cautiously moved toward Steve, while his partner kept his police issue trained on the two agents.

"Gregg, I hope that fucking gun doesn't have a hair trigger."

"*You can say that again!*"

"*Quiet!*" Toyoka barked, he was taking no shit from the Americans.

Out of the blue another guard suddenly appeared. This was becoming a major security operation.

(Speaking in Japanese)

"*Hoshi,* body search the Americans."

The second guard jumped to it, starting from Steve's ankles frisking upwards.

Within seconds he had opened Steve's jacket exposing the holstered hand gun. He emptied Steve's pockets of his personal effects including his leather tab with the gold shield.

"Remove pistol and place on reception desk with ammunition clips."

"Yes Capitan." Hoshi began repeating the ritual on Gregg. Meanwhile Okiko was sitting dumbfounded taking in the drama.

Toyoku checked the safeties on the Gloks then place each one in separate zipper bags with the spare clips.

"Okay, hands down." Having seen the gold shields Toyoku's tone had slightly changed.

"Thank God!" Steve groaned. "I was getting cramp and for a moment there, it felt like Easter Sunday, *only without the nails!"*

"Apologies." Tayoku bowed. "Americans please understand, security high. No guns allowed, will return before leaving... Your badges." He pointed to the gold shields. "Dozo... Please carry on with business. Arigato."

"Now, where were we?" Steve smiled to Okiko.......

* * *

Steve and Gregg walked through the X Ray frames without a murmur and headed for the elevator, glad that the security drama was over as they were now running late.

The elevator chimed and the doors opened the out coming traffic surprising, air and freight travel is big business.

Steve pressed 4. "Wasn't that something?" He turned to Gregg.

"Boy, that guy with that mean looking handgun pointed at your chest was scary and with the look on his face he was desperate for his first kill."

"Yeah, and thank God it wasn't me!" Steve laughed as the Elevator doors opened.

The plush blue carpeted hallway bore the credentials of money extravagance but that's Airlines for you, always losings money in a cut-throat pricing war but failing to trim their overheads until it's too late.

"Here we are." Steve commented as he opened the large plate glass door toward the curved oak reception desk with the company's logo in front in bold 4-inch gold plated letters. "Global Airways Flying the World'.

"Hell, these receptionists are getting prettier by the minute!" Steve whispered to Gregg.

"Down boy... Down boy." Gregg laughed.

"Can you blame a guy?"

"Do you have an appointment Gentlemen?"

"Eh... Err yes." Steve was taken aback with the young ladies perfect English, his mind scrambling for clarity.

"Yes?" The receptionist asked once again somewhat bewildered and Gregg quickly interjected, he could see his partners mind was on other things.

"Our apologies... *Eh?"* Gregg quickly read the name tag. "Emiko... We are running a bit late, our appointment with Mr. McGill was at 3pm."

"Mr. McGill is our VP Global Freight. Take the passageway to the left and you will come to his office, it's clearly marked."

"Thank you." Gregg tugged at Steve's sleeve. "Let's move it partner, she's for another time."

But Steve as usual had to have the last say.

"If you don't mind me saying so Emiko, you speak perfect English."

"I try." Emiko smiled. "Mr. McGill's office is to your left." A polite *'get lost!*

Steve gave that burned look turning to Gregg who just shrugged.

"Well, I gotta hand it to you for trying." Gregg commented.

"Okay...Okay... Don't rub it in......."

* * *

The glass frosted door bore the name James McGill Vice President Global Freight, in gold letters.

Steve tried the door it was locked.

"I gotta say security is good in this place." Gregg pressed the butting on the right.

"Yes?" Came the voice.

"Mr. Nelson and Mr. Johnson to see Mr. McGill."

There was a loud buzz then a click as the electronic lock disengaged.

Steve shrugged turning to Gregg before pushing open the heavy glass door only to be met with Mitsuko sitting at her desk.

"Good afternoon gentleman." She smiled. "Mr. McGill is expecting you, for security purposes I require some form of identification."

The agents obliged showing their shields.

"Thank you. If you can bear with me for a moment, I'll check to see if Jim is free.' She lifted the phone. "Jim, I have...." Mitsuko smiled once more replacing the receiver. "You can go straight in."

Gregg turned to Steve who had that smile.

"Don't even think about it...!"

"Please take a seat." McGill pointed the empty chairs."

"Coffee?"

"Naw we're good, but thanks." Steve replied warmly.

"Okay, so let's get down to business." McGill leaned back in his exec chair.

"Eh, Mr. McGill." Steve began.

"Jim." McGill smiled.

"Err... Jim... I'm sure you know why the CIA is interested in the loss of Global 10 with its crew and cargo."

"Sure, I can understand why the government is involved, like, to the tune of 200 billion US dollars but *I'm* more interested in the crew. Planes and money, you can replace... *People you can't!"*

"My apologies Jim if I seem callous but you must understand from our prospect should that money get into the wrong hands, like say ISIL, who knows what it can buy, even a dirty bomb?"

McGill nodded in agreement but his mind was on other things.

"Steve, *it is* Steve?"

"Yes, and Gregg."

"Steve, I can see where you are coming from but if what my understanding is, the CIA is already treating this is a hijack? No disrespect but I beg to disagree as in my opinion it's grossly premature. So, let's agree to disagree and take a step back to review the facts... Firstly, the Boeing 777 disappeared from radar approximately 800 kilometers west off the coast of Japan over an hour into its flight from Narita over the North Pacific. Japanese search and rescue have scoured that area in a thousand-kilometer block with no sign yet of wreckage of any description. Bear in mind the depth of the North Pacific can vary by as much as 11,000 meters. Secondly the transponder, an electronic device vitally important to identify aircraft on 'Air Traffic Control Radar' went dead at the same time as Global 10 disappeared from the screen. And thirdly a Boing 777 requires a landing runway of 8,100ft carrying a maximum payload of 120 metric tons. This is a big plane, which in my opinion would be almost impossible to hide. Remember, after two years, Malaysian Airways Boeing 777, MH370, has never been found and under identical circumstances!"

"Jim, with respect, what you are telling me is nothing new." Gregg threw in his card. "The big difference is the cargo."

"So now *you're* telling *me* something that's history!" McGill was getting irate. *"Listen,* what I'm stressing is, it's just *too* dam early to draw that conclusion! *Hell,* we haven't even met with Boeing's 'Air Accident Investigation Branch' and the "National Transportation Safety Board' not to mention the 'Japanese Aviation Authority'. I'm sorry, *CIA or no CIA, your conclusion is just completely premature!"*

"Jim, calm down and let's take it from another angle... *Security?"* Steve entered the arena.

"Like what?" McGill was losing it. "Let's get one thing clear. The local Japanese equivalent to the FBI, 'The National Police Agency' gave their blessing and security clearance."

"How?"

"By computer... What else!"

"Can you download the information for me?" Steve asked delicately, tensions high.

McGill shook his head and went to the keyboard. His face showing confusion as he quickly entered the information for a second time.

"Strange, the file has disappeared!"

"Now isn't *that* a coincidence?" Gregg turned to Steve, a half-smile.

"I don't believe it!" McGill lifted the phone. "Mitsuko, the security information on the guards for Global 10 seems to have mysteriously disappeared... *Do you know anything about it ...!* You haven't erased it buy mistake, have you? I didn't think so. Mitsuko maybe you can just check it out once more."

McGill replaced the phone then raised his left hand and rubbed his chin.

"Beats me!" McGill was not a happy camper.

"Jim, I can't go into the detail why my partner and I have been assigned to Japan for security purposes and why we are working with the FBI. Unfortunately, you are not privy to the bigger picture."

"I see." McGill was now quite subdued.

Gregg interrupted. "Jim, can you refresh your memory and recollect the information on the security guards."

"Hmmm... Let me think... Hell, with all this shit on my plate it's hard to think straight."

*"Anything ... Anything....*That comes to your mind, even the smallest detail may help."

"Let me think...There were two Japanese, I can't remember their names, both operatives of the 'Kovan Chousacho' the 'Public Security Intelligence Agency'... Now the other guy... *Err..."* Jim paused for a moment. "Had an Italian name, was a US citizen from Black Hawk Securities and if my memory serves me right a 'vet' who served with distinction, with two tours of duty in Afghanistan with the US Marines. His parents immigrated from Cicely to the US after the second world war... He's clean as whistle."

"Did you meet with them personally?"

"No, I left that to Captain Collins."

"And did Collins come back to you?"

"Bill's like another Sherlock Holmes, always cautious when it comes to security on his watch after so many hijacks, in fact he carried an ankle holster with a 22 Smith and Weston."

"Interesting Steve." Gregg commented.

"Anything else?" Steve was on a roll, it was getting better by the minute.

"After looking at the Italian's mug shot I specifically remember Bill's comment which was unusual, 'Jim, he doesn't look Mediterranean, more like Middle Eastern'."

Steve searched in his jacket pocket then placed two pictures on McGill's desk.

"The one on the left is Anbar Salibe and on the right his brother Fadile Maalouf who is now deceased. They are both Palestinians. Salbe may have shaved his beard but do you recognize the face?"

"Deceased?"

"It's a long story."

"Brothers? The names are different!"

"That's for another day Jim, just study the face."

Jim sat for a moment.

"Jim?" Steve was anxious.

"Yeah, it's him, I'm pretty sure."

"Now we are getting someplace. At least we have established one thing... The guards were phony."

"So where do we go from here?" McGill asked bewildered. This was turning into a major crime scene.

"Jim, that's *our* problem. Now let's talk about the crew." Gregg asked, it was 'the good cop bad cop' routine.

"Where do you want me to start?"

"The crew, Captain Collins, first officer Stevens and the stewardess... *Eh... Err ...?"*

"Sally Jenkins."

"Okay let's start with the easy one, Jenkins."

Jim opened the screen and punched a few keys.

"Let me see, *ah,* here we are... "Sally Jenkins, 23, single, brunette, 5-8 with Global Freight for three years, on the transfer list for international passenger flights. Good employee with an impeccable service record."

"Nothing much there... Now Collins and Stevens?"

"Both decorated Navy Aviators, flew McDonnell Douglas F15 Eagles from the nuclear aircraft carrier the USS Dwight D Eisenhower during Desert Strom. After demobilization, they decided not to reenlist and turned their flying skills to commercial jets joining Global Airways... Have been with Global now for...? Over three years."

"Anything else about them that we should know?" Gregg was already taking notes.

"Collin's is a solid citizen, has his head screwed on and of course one of, if not, our best pilots. Now Stevens is a different kettle of fish. A womanizer who drinks too much and gambles the same. A loose cannon, Collins and he are best friends and flat mates."

"How about girlfriends, or anything else that comes to your mind." Steve continued.

"*Strange,* you should ask that. I received a call only about an hour ago, from Don Draper, Delta's Flight Manager. I met him once in LA over dinner with Bill and Steve and their partners. He phoned me to find out any information regarding the loss of Global 10. Of course, I told him what I told you."

"*Partners?*"

"Yeah I remember them well and who wouldn't? They were lookers alright. In fact, they are here in Tokyo now having flown in on Delta 14 from Washington DC, both are crew members, I think one is the Chief Purser and I believe they are staying the Hyatt Regency in Nishi Shinjuku, Tokyo Prefecture."

"Jim, you wouldn't happen to remember their names by any chance?"

"Eh... Julie... Julie Rodgers and I think Marge something or other."

"Julie Rodgers and Marge Williams?

"Yeah that's it, hut how...?"

Steve turned to Gregg. *"You gotta be fucking kidding me.......!"*

IT'S TIME!

Chuck wiped his forehead with the back of his hand as he casually strolled back to the Nissan hut dodging a forklift truck in the process.

"Hell, this sun *is* hot. There must be bottled water here somewhere?" Then it came to him. *"That large freezer, of course!* I remember dozens of plastic bottled water stacked up next to the beer. I hope these fucking doors are still open!" Chuck spoke out loud. It was safe to do so as the Japanese haven't a clue when it comes to English.

"Just my fucking luck, the doors are closed." Chuck grimaced turning to check out the landscape.

Shendo was at the loading dock fully occupied directing operations. The afternoon sun was brutal and Chuck couldn't help but wonder what drove these people? On the brighter side, it was perfect timing for the escape plan with no one showing any interests in his movements.

"Fuck it, the doors are closed!" Chuck stood staring for a moment, his mind scrambling for solutions when suddenly the loud horn of another forklift made him jump aside, the driver just missing him by inches whilst screaming above the noise to one of the crew to open the refrigerated box container doors.

Chuck had to smile, if this was the Casino he would be on a roll.

The forklift driver lifted a pallet loaded with large empty ten liter plastic water containers then expertly did a 360 and drove at speed toward the loading dock. He would soon be back for the remainder.

"I gotta move fast." Chuck blurted.

The 'foot soldier' was still standing at the open door waiting for the driver to return and it was now or never.

Chuck approached the 'soldier' a casual smile on his face, who looked suspiciously at the American 'Like what's this guy up to?

"Mizu... Mizu..." Chuck made a motion with his fingers to his slips.

The 'Nihon' was impressed, not many westerners new the Japanese word for water and he nodded his approval whilst making a motion with his hand for Chuck to help himself.

"Katakana." (Okay)

"Domo Arigato." Chuck gave a slight bow then gingerly lifted two six packs of the vacuum wrapped half liter bottles of the precious liquid.

Chuck grinned, he was feeling pretty good with himself and getting smarter by the hour at fooling the Japanese. Maybe that's why they lost the war, huh? He just couldn't wipe that silly grin off his face at the thought.

The dormitory was empty, it couldn't be better and Chuck slid the water 'swag' out of sight below his cot. Someone might wonder why he was so thirsty especially when there was a large water dispenser by the door. He removed his cap then swung his feet from the floor onto the roped mattress of the bamboo torcher bed.

"How these guys can sleep on this shit beats me? Give me good old 'KING COIL' any day. When I get out of the shit, it's Switzerland for me and a chilled magnum of Dom Perignon."

Chuck placed his hands behind his head and stared at the corrugated steel roof, the antiquated ceiling fans struggling to circulate the humid air and the buzz of the mosquitoes searching for their next lunch was not exactly the 'Hilton'!

"The time!" Chuck sat bolt upright and glanced at his watch. *"Hmmmm...4. 15... Time fly's."* He was thinking out of the box.

"These bottles of water are heavy but I can squeeze them with not much room to spare into my duffle bag... *Now food?* Dinner's at five but it's too risky to burgle some rice, especially with Salibe on my tail. *No,* I just hope Bill and Sally have gone hungry at lunch time with the 'a la carte'.......

* * *

It was time, and Chuck had to make his move as the dining area was filling up with hungry workers waiting for their chow and more so, he had to get out of there before the 'head honcho' and his heavies arrived, especially the Palestinian, *whom he wouldn't trust with a camel!*

Chuck stuffed his duffle bag with the water, slung it over his shoulder, donned his cap then entered the yard to begin the ten-minute walk to the maintenance hut. His heart pounding, at the thought of losing the 20mil if it all went wrong. *There's nowhere to spend that money in hell.*

"This fucking water is heavy…...!"

* * *

Bill could sense Sally was more than nervous as she pranced up and down in the narrow passageway between the bamboo cots, continually glancing at her watch.

"Sally, why don't you sit down for a while, we still have around 15 minutes before Chuck arrives. By the way, that rice we had for lunch, did you wrap it in a wet face towel?"

"Bill, the last thing I'm thinking about is food!"

"Sally, your stomach is not interested now but believe me when the going gets tough, that rice will taste like caviar."

"To answer your questing …*Yes…* I've hidden it in my airline vanity bag.' Her voice almost breaking.

Bile grinned. *"Well,* I guess where we're going Sally, you won't be needing make up for a while." It was a corny joke that went down like a lead balloon.

"Now let's see?"

Bill stood on his toes and peered out the barred window to check on the guard. As unusual he was sitting in his boredom, back to the wall, knees up having a late afternoon snooze and who could blame him? In this heat, he must be on report or something.

"Good, the guard seems preoccupied." Bill called to Sally who was staring into space siting on the side of her cot. She had taken Bill's advice but her face was drawn and pale.

"I had better check this little baby." Bill's comment drew Sally's attention as he pulled up his right trouser leg just past his ankle exposing the small 22, caliber. Bill quickly pushed the barrel rod and swung open the six-shot chamber. Satisfied it was fully loaded with copper heads he swung the barrel back into place with a solid click then checked the safety before returning the pistol back in its holster. *The last thing he needed was to shoot himself in the foot!*

"It's just a matter of time now, I'm sure Chuck is on his way." Bill commented, Sally didn't reply but when the time comes self-preservation kicks in and heroes are born.

"Shush… That sounds like Chuck now! Somehow, we must create a diversion to make that guard open the door. Wait until I give the signal Sally, then you open your lungs as hard as you can. You got that Sally…? *Sally you got that?"* Bill yelled.

"Yes...Yes, for Christ sakes... Yes."

Upon seeing his 'drinking partner' again, the guard quickly rose to his feet, a friendly smile on his face anticipating the heavy duffle on Chuck's shoulder was 'bar time', so much so, he didn't even pick up the rifle leaning against the wall.

"I see prisoner Dozo?" Chuck pointed to his eyes with two fingers then motioned to the maintenance hut door, the guard totally confused.

This was the signal and Sally let loose like a soprano, the guard almost jumping out of his skin rushing toward the barred window to check on the commotion. Bill was ready with the 22 to put a hole in the guard's forehead when he showed his face, but for Chuck it was the 'perfect storm' and he grabbed the 'sleeping gun' raising it high above his head and with full force smashed the brass plated butt into the back of the guard's skull. This guy's head was either made of steel or rubber but for sure his blood was real, the warm red sticky liquid oozing from the wound in the back of his neck. The guard stood for a moment in suspended animation swaying like a palm in the breeze but this guy wasn't going down easily and he swung around and made a lunge at Chuck. *Too late!* The 22inch bayonet pierced clean through his chest. His eyes rolled for a moment as he clung onto the rifle stock before falling backwards taking the gun with him, the long knife having gone clean through to his back. He jerked his legs for a couple of seconds and rolling his eyes as life slowly ebbed from his body then he froze staring at the sky, for this Nihonjindansei there was no tomorrow.

"Chuck, are you okay?" Bill yelled the 22 cocked.

"Yeah, the coast is clear, gimme a sec while I get the key."

Chuck placed one foot on the guard's chest and pulled the rifle free with a sickening sort of suction. Then he leaned the rifle against the wall, he was taking this baby with him.

"Now where is that fucking padlock key?" Chuck's hands were trembling as he searched through the guard's tunic. He had never killed a man at close quarters before and it was a feeling that would haunt him for the rest of his life.

"At last!" He fumbled finding the keyhole. *"Fucking lock!"*

Successful Chuck threw the padlock aside and swung the heavy steel door open.

"Chuck?"

"Yeah, I'm good, not a scratch but let's get going as your food will be arriving any minute now."

"Sally, have you got everything." Bill replaced the 22. thankful he didn't have to use it."

"I'm good,"

"Then let's go."

"Sally, take a towel with you to wrap your head like a turban to protect you from the sun."

Chuck had already began stuffing the remaining space in his duffle with the spare ammunition clips from the guard's pouches and he slid back the bolt on the Arisaka rifle.

"The fucking chamber is empty... Can you believe it!" Chuck took a five clip from his bag and pushed it into the breach then closed the bolt sliding a round into the chamber.

"Come on Sally, come on." Bill grabbed her by the arm.

Sally had frozen at seeing the corpse of the dead guard the gaping hole in his chest still oozing a river of blood, rigor mortis on its way.

"I'm gonna be sick." Sally covered her mouth.

Chuck had little sympathy. "Well, get it over with and let's get going or you'll be joining our buddy here."

That brought Sally to her senses.

Bill screamed. "Come on run for cover before we're spotted."

"Just a sec Bill." Chuck bent over and removed the small set of binoculars from around the dead guard's neck. "These will come in handy......."

* * *

The alcohol injection was doing what comes naturally but although more relaxed the reality of losing Bill and Chuck was mind shattering and Julie and Marge were resting on the sofa like two zombies.

"I still can't believe it Marge! Bill... Chuck... They were a pair of assholes but the memories... We had some great times, *didn't we?"*

"For Christ sakes Julie, you sound as if you are about to give a eulogy, now, no more of that shit, remember the old saying 'where there's life there's hope'."

"Do you think Draper will ring us back?"

"That loser, are you serious? He's probably still in the hay with his latest conquest."

"Awe come on, he's not that bad Marge."

"Are you serious? I wouldn't trust him as far as I could throw him."

"Well?" Julie turned to Marge brightening up. "We have to make some choices. We either empty the bar fridge and cry in our beer, *or*, pick ourselves up and go shopping at the Ginza. So, what's it gonna be?"

"Now that's more like the Julie I know. I say let's have one for the road and get cleaned up and outta here... *Eh...* Is that someone knocking on our door?"

Julie broke a smile. "Maybe that's Hikaru from room service hoping for anther cheap show?"

"Get out of it!"

Julie peered through the security peep hole. "Looks like two male Caucasians but I can't make out their faces."

"Bring em on." Marge finally laughed.

Julie opened the door. *"Why...!"*

"Julie Rodgers, Marge Williams, agents Nelson and Johnson, CIA. We would like to ask you a few questions........"

* * *

The girls were absolutely stunned, from brightening up at seeing Steve and Gregg standing in the doorway, they were now possible suspects in a plane hijacking.

"Would you wish to see our identifications?" Steve asked, his expression more than serious.

"No." Julie replied." Still confused. *"Steve,* is this some sort of ...?"

"Before you say it Julie... *No...!* This is an official CIA investigation. I'll explain in a moment... *That's if we can we come in?"*

"Of course, Of course," Julie stepped aside.

Gregg gave Marge a sort of 'someone done me wrong song' smile who was still trying to get her faculties together from the earlier booze session.

"Can we take a seat? I'm sure this won't take too long." Gregg asked.

"Sure." Marge replied pointing to the sofa, a distinctive strain in her voice, the girls taking the chairs opposite in front of the coffee table scattered with spent bar fridge ordinance.

"Some party, huh?" A bit early don't you think?"

"Depends if your celebrating or crying." Julie shot back.

"I'll take your word for it." Steve snubbed her... *"Gregg,* you can take the notes?" Steve commented before once again. turning to Julie. "We may need them to corroborate your statements."

"What statements? Hell Steve, we haven't even begun and we feel like criminals already." Julie was back in it. "You had better tell us what the hell is going on, *mister!"*

"Calm down Julie, the quicker you cooperate, the quicker we can get out of your hair."

"Fuck it! I don't give a shit." Marge rose and walked to the bar fridge extracting a miniature of vodka. "I need this to calm my fucking nerves." Her hand shaking, the neck of the miniature rattling against the crystal glass as she poured it.

"Calm down Marge, there's nothing to worry about, that's, *unless you've got something to hide?"*

"And just what does that mean Gregg?" Marge barked back.

Gregg shrugged and turned to look at Steve for a leg in, *like* we're going nowhere fast, throw me a life line'.

"Okay... Okay, let's just *all* calm down." Steve raised his arms. "Now if it's not *too* much trouble, can we begin?"

He was also losing his cool... *Women!*

The room went quiet for a moment, Julie and Marge temporarily throwing in the towel.

"Can we?" There was a pregnant silence. *"Good,* so let's start at the beginning... How well do you know William Collins and Charles Stevens?

"Are you talking to me or Marge?"

"Julie, don't be so bloody difficult, I'm directing the question to both of you."

"We... Eh... No, you go first, Julie." Marge took a step back.

"Hmmm..." Julie thought for a moment in caution. "Might as well start from the beginning, but why...?"

Steve cut her short. "We'll get to that later... *So?"*

Julie began. "It's like this, Marge and I have been best friends from college and part of the 'Rat Pack', so to speak, a nick name the Pilots gave to the airhostesses on the LA to London haul. After flatting together in the big apple and numerous 'go nowhere' jobs we decided to jump ship and head to California and what better place than the 'City of Angles' and when Delta Airlines had openings for airhostess, well, the rest is history, so to speak."

"Julie, I don't want an autobiography, let's get to Collins and Stevens."

"Then what the fuck *do you* want?" Julie blew her top.

Steve sat back moving his head from side to side, *stupid broads...*

"Julie, do me a favor. Can we keep it in low key?"

Julie paused, her eyes ablaze. "Do I have a choice? *I mean if I don't are you gonna arrest us?*"

"*No,* but the more difficult you become, the more suspicions you place upon yourselves."

Julie gave a half sigh and a half cry her eyes glazing up. It was a lost cause, her confused mind torn between the loss of Bill and now under the microscope by two CIA agents *and for what?*"

Julie sighed. "To get to the point I guess I have no options, a long story. We first met on the Lax to London flight when we had a change of flight officers, namely Captain Collins and first officer Stevens. I'll cut the 'autobiography' short if that pleases you and the bottom line is we have been cohabitating for almost three years since. Of course, not the four of us, we had different apartments, we don't practice polygamy."

"*Boy,* you *are* a piece of work. They say sarcasm is the lowest form of wit. Marge, is she always like this? This is not the same woman I met in LA."

"Steve, you gotta understand we've just had the worst news possible that Bill and Chuck are missing in an air crash. We broke up with these two losers just last week when we met you guys on the beach, having just moved into a new apartment which we share. Our relationships are down the toilet but we have feelings and memories, *can't you get that through your thick skins?*"

Marge's comment went over Steve's head, he wasn't going to get into the heavies, he had bigger problems on his plate than 'somewhere over the rainbow'.

"But you met Collins and Stevens with Delta airlines and now they're with Global, how come?"

"Simple, flying freight has better pay and perc's and no shit from passengers."

"Makes sense." They were back on the same page.

"*Now,* can you open up and tell me a bit more about them?" Steve asked.

"*Like what,* are they hot in bed?" Julie just wouldn't take the heat off and Steve had no alternative, he was down to the wire.

"Okay, here's the kicker. I was trying to save the best till last so let's get down to it. You want the bottom line? *You got it!* Gregg it's yours, I need a break."

Gregg gave a sort of '*oh well*' I was waiting for that.

"Here's the scoop and ladies before I begin I can't stress enough that this is information highly confidential and if leaked could be a breach of National Security."

Julie and Marge looked even more confused. What the hell was coming next, this was becoming another 'spy came from out of the cold'.

"Have I made myself clear?" Gregg went for the jugular waiting for some sort of reaction and you could have heard a pin drop.

"Have I made myself clear?" He repeated.

"As clear as mud." Julie yelled back, she had had enough of this 'go nowhere' shit.

"A last it appears I'm getting through..." Gregg took a breath. *"How serious is this?* As serious as it gets! You see Global 10 per say, flown by your *two ex-partners,* was loaded with 200 billion in US currency from Japan's foreign currency reserves bound for Washington DC. *Now why, you may ask?"* Gregg had finally gotten their attention at last.

"Having been in circulation for over thirty years, *you got it!* Passed its 'used by date' heading for the furnace at the Federal Reserve, the Japanese Diet having already received a promissory note from the US mint for the replacement of the currency. *So... So far so good, huh?"*

"Wait a minute, Don't *gimme that!* So somehow you 'gum shoes' think that Chuck and Bill had something to do with the disappearance of Global 10 and the money?" Marge was really riled, Chuck was Chuck, but a crook, never!

"Marge, now that you brought it up, sure let's talk about Chuck for a moment and I want you to be straight with me."

"I'm waiting."

"To best of your knowledge, did Chuck have a gambling habit?"

"What has that got to with it?"

"Just answer the question and remember withholding information is a criminal offence with a two-year jail term for being an 'accessory after the fact'".

"You're not scaring me with that shit, big boy." Marge retaliated.

"Then just answer the fucking question! Excuse my French but I've just about had it up to here with the both of you."

The 'Mexican standoff' becoming too much Julie just had to let fly.

"Marge, for Christ sakes tell him and let's get this circus over with."

"Thanks for your support." Sarcasm in her voice.

"Well...?"

Marge gave a loser sigh. "Yeah, if you must know he is a compulsive gambler and one of the many reasons why I gave him the big elbow... *Satisfied?"*

"Did he have gambling debts?"

"Don't all gamblers? Now is there anything else?"

"To the best of your knowledge was he involved with undesirables in the Casino business? Gambling and drugs go together just like organized crime."

"Sure, Chuck took a sniff now and again, we've all tried it once but peddling drugs, *no way.*"

"A Mario Brambilli, does that ring a bell?"

The name made Marge's face go a pale shade of white.

"Yeah … Yeah … Okay. Brambilli was putting the heat on Chuck for an outstanding debt threatening a knee cap job if he didn't pay up."

"And?"

"Chuck informed me he approached Bill for a carryover of 15 big ones until he could get a few more pay cheques. I guess Bill came to the party as he has done before because Chuck didn't mention it again before his last flight to Tokyo but if you're asking me to throw him under the bus, that's not gonna happen."

"There's no need, I get the picture." Gregg was taking notes.

"And Bill, Julie?"

'Straight as a die, but full of himself and why he stuck by…" Julie turned to face Marge…" I'm sorry Marge, but it has to be said… His pilot buddy loser, I'll never know."

Steve just shrugged, the personal stuff he didn't want to know and he began. "It's only fair that you understand the significance of the loss of Global 10. In conjunction with our FBI office in Tokyo we know that the Yakuza, the Japanese Mafia, the Russians and the Palestinians are involved in the disappearance of the jet liner and for security reasons that's as much as we can tell. However, *we do know* that the two security guards accompanying the flight were Yakuza Mafia and one Palestinian."

"Steve, I'm sorry to interrupt but I'm more interested in the flight."

"Julie, to answer your question at this stage of the investigation your guess is as good as mine. There will be a meeting at Global's office sometime tomorrow with the Japanese Search and Rescue, and Boeing's 'Air Accident Investigation Branch' and the "National Transportation Safety Board', not to mention Narita's Air Traffic Controllers to piece together all the facts, so it's early days."

"But you must have *some* hunch?"

"Certain information has arisen that points toward a highjack but how the triangle of forces tie together that's for another day and as for hiding a Boeing 777 somewhere in the North Pacific even 'David Copperfield' would have trouble with that one!"

"So, you think there's still hope that Bill and Chuck are alive?"

"When it comes to money, it's anyone's guess. I hate to say this Marge, but we have sound evidence that this is an inside job and Chuck Stevens is high on our radar."

"I... I... Just don't believe it!" Marge was almost in tears.

"So where do we go from here Steve as we are shipping out for Washington tomorrow?" Julie had her head screwed on, there was no weeping for her.

"Listen I hate to lay this on you because I know how stressed you both are but I need you to check in with Ken Daniels the director of FBI at our Tokyo office. Here's his card. Don't worry we'll contact him beforehand but it must be done today. You'll need to provide photographs of your passports your telephone numbers and address in LA."

Steve paused for a moment his eyes meeting Julie's.

"I wish things could have been different as Gregg and I were looking forward to inviting you out to dinner but that's now out of the question as this would be a conflict of interest. I'm sure you understand but who knows?" He gave reluctant smile "Thanks Julie, thanks Marge. On the brighter side, you haven't seen the last of us just yet. It's alright, we can see ourselves out......."

* * *

The trio ran blindly into the thick jungle foliage desperate to escape before the alarm was raised. A dead guard would add fuel to the fire and the hunt would be on to avenge the loss of one of their comrades, Japanese don't take kindly to be made to look like fools.

Chuck quickly removed the bayonet and slung the 7-kilo rifle over his shoulder, it wouldn't be as efficient as a machete but beggars can't be choosers.

"Come on Sally pick it up." Bill was dragging her almost off her feet, the soft muddy earth making heavy weather. "We need at least a half an hour head start before all hell lets lose."

"Easy Bill, my legs are not as long as yours.

"They will be before we're finished."

"Some humor, huh?" Sally gripped.

Chuck was furiously hacking away with the 22-inch bayonet almost in a hate campaign, bits of leaf and plant trunk, flying.

"We need to head for the high ground, Bill." Chuck stopped to catch a second breath wiping his forehead with the cuff of his shirt. "Just in case we get into a shooting war as I need to get a 'bird's eye view' of the comings and goings at the camp."

"Yeah... *I... I* get ya." Physically fit even Bill was panting.

"Bill, do me a favor, between this fucking rifle and this haversack full of water I'll end up a paraplegic. Can you take the load off?"

"Here, gimme it."

"Thanks buddy."

"How much longer Bill I'm running out of steam?" Sally complained struggling to catch her breath.

"Anther fifteen, then we can relax and quench our thirsts......."

* * *

The crew were beginning to fill the mess hall in anticipation of the five o'clock 'cook up'. It wouldn't be Teppanyaki but who cares, soon they would be on that plane to the land of the 'rising sun' and 'wild woman and song'.

Kenichi Shendo seemed pleased as he took his seat at the head table. Japanese work ethics are second to none and the materials for transfer to the mainland via the Kawasaki C2 Freighter, were stacked neatly in rows on the loading dock for a fast turnaround and refuel, departure at 22.00hrs.

"Speaking in Japanese)

"Tahoka, food." Shendo pointed to the servery. Tahoka bowed and went about his business, when Shendo calls, *you jump......*

* * *

Salibe threw his feet to the floor. He had reluctantly forced a nap, his mind exhausted at the thought of spending another ten days in this tropical hell hole with adversaries that would cut his throat in a whiff. He stroked back his unruly black hair and scanned the rows of empty cots in search for the 'rebel without a cause'.

Then he began conversing with himself. "Now where could that American be? I don't trust him, a man with a giant chip on his shoulder spells trouble." He glanced at his watch. *"That time already!* I suppose there's nothing else for it but to go and eat that shit they call food. What I wouldn't do for a Baba Ghanoush with Tahina, sweet Baklava and Cinnamon tea!"

Salibe rose to his feet and stretched his legs then arms. *"Hmmmm,* that feels better."

As he walked toward the mess hall a uniformed guard hurried past unsteadily carrying a tray of food and green tea.

"Must be for the prisoners." Then a grin crossed his face. "We don't have to kill them, that food will do the job for us... *Heh... Heh.*"

Tahoka was already into the food accompanied by his fellow henchman Arakida. Between mouthfuls of rice and the ugly slurping of green tea, they were discussing something in their native tongue which annoyed the Arab, being the height of ignorance and disrespect.

Shendo delayed his loaded chopsticks at the sight of Salibe he would much rather have an all Japanese table than it be contaminated by a Muslim.

Suddenly, from out of nowhere there was a loud commotion. tables and chairs turned over and plates thrashed as the guard that passed Salibe only a few minutes ago, fell to his knees in front of Shendo.

(Speaking in Japanese)

"Shujin wa dasshutsu kimashita." (The prisoners have escaped) He screamed raising a commotion bigger than mount Fujiyama.

Shendo went a shade paler than his rice.

"Gado?" (the guard?)

"Deddo." (dead)

Shendo grabbed the Nambu the from its holster and opened his lungs.

"Tahoka... six Dansei wa ude ware wa immediately sorera o mitsukeru hitsuyaga arimasu." (Tahoka, arm six men, we must find them immediately)

* * *

"What do you see Chuck?"

The 'escapees' had stopped for 'rest camp' and sustenance, namely water, they would reserve the small ration of rice they had until their energy needed replenishing.

Chuck didn't reply his eyes straining through the small binoculars.

"Yeah, they're onto us alright, an armed search party of around six to eight men heading into the jungle and by the looks of their hardware they're not intending to carry any excess baggage back."

"So, what's your take?" Bill asked, as for Sally she was stoked under the shade.

"I say we stay put, we have a 180 view and were on high ground, taking a hill is no push over. Let's see... We have...?" Chuck emptied the ammunition clips from the bullet pouches onto the ground and began counting.

"I make it ten clips of five plus one in the magazine. Not much for a standoff but I didn't get my Navy marksmen pendant for nothing."

"Let's hope we don't get into another Iwi Jima that's all I can say." Bill replied.

"Remember we still have that pop gun your carrying, don't forget!"

Bill laughed. "I almost forgot about that but more importantly Sally would you like a drink?" Bill had unscrewed the plastic top.

"Would I?"

"Just take it easy Sally." Bill had to restrain her. "Remember that's has to last us until we find the 'source of the Nile', *that's if we ever do!"*

"Bill, your humor never ceases to amaze me." Sally was shaking her head......

* * *

Shendo was in an ugly mood, losing the prisoners was one thing but killing the guard was tantamount to Samaria vengeance. No, the Americans had to be executed at all costs or Shendo would have to face the honorable 'Seppuku'.

He checked the magazine in his 9mm Nambu then clipped it back sliding a live round into the chamber. He would be only too happy to blow Steven's skull apart before his boss Numero got wind of this unholy cock up.

"Salibe San you join us? No-good Americans your problem. Now you help correct." Shendo sneered offering Salibe a rifle and pointing the ammunition box.

"No Shendo, I have much bigger responsibilities to my country than chase after expendables to satisfy *your* personal vendetta. It's your problem and you're stuck with it!"

Shendo's eyes said it all, insults were not on his page and he could have easily drawn his sword to end it but 'Operation Fishtail' was still in its infancy and 50 billion dollars was at stake but then, every dog has its day.

(Speaking in Japanese)

"Tahoka, Dansei wa jumbi watashitachi wa ima no mama." (Tahoka get the men ready we leave now)

The search party checked their rifles and water bottles then fanned out in into two groups of four, Shendo controlling one and Tahoka the other, the two-point men wielding their machetes.......

* * *

"They're about four hundred meters to the left of us." Chuck was adjusting the rear site on the rifle. "What we've got going for us is that they haven't a fucking clue in which direction we've gone."

"I suppose *that's* something." Bill answered, a touch of sarcasm.

"Better than nothing, *huh?* My advice is that we stay put for the night where we are. It will be getting dark soon and these guys have more important things on their plate, like getting off 'Alcatraz'."

Sally interrupted. "You mean we sleep out here in the open tonight?"

"Not if you have a better suggestion Sally?" Chuck was taking no quarter.

"Awe, come on lighten up on her Chuck, we've been through worse than this but she hasn't!"

"Sorry Sally, my advice, keep your head down and do as your told and we'll all come out of this alive. Now first things first... Wait a minute, *what's that?*" Chuck looked toward the sky and there it was, the relief flight circling the island to make its final approach.

Chuck grabbed his binoculars. "If my hunch is right, Kenichi will be pissed having to call off the search. "Yeah... *Heh... Heh... Heh...*" Chuck laughed. "The look on this guy's face is priceless. Yeah, he's calling it off alright. I'll start hacking down some of these giant palm leaves to make a mat to lie on and keep out the damp. Tomorrow we can try and build a canopy with bamboo, there's plenty of it around."

"And what do we do to scare off the wild animals?"

"Sally my lovely." Chuck's mood had changed, the heat was off and he cracked a smile. "I'm sure there *are* some animals on this island but the only two wild ones, are me and Bill......."

* * *

Steve and Gregg were standing in the elevator in silence, the look on their faces not exactly happy.

"What goes around comes around, huh?" Gregg broke the silence.

Steve gave a forced smile. "Yeah, and there goes our dates for tonight!"

"Get out of it!" The comment finally made them both laugh.

The elevator chimed and the agents entered the hotel reception both feeling the worse of the wear. Between the jet lag and the meetings with the FBI, Global, and now Julie and Marge, they had had better days.

"What time do you make it Gregg? I forgot to change to Tokyo Time."

Gregg stopped and glanced at his time piece. *"Eh... err...* I make it just after 2.30."

"Hmmm..." Steve pondered for a moment." We have the rest of the day and as a matter of courtesy we should meet up with Daniels to keep him in the loop."

Gregg sighed. *"Yeah,* I guess so but my stomach tells me something else... Like... *We're not on a diet."*

Steve laughed. "Well if you put it that way there's a coffee shop to your right, we can grab a sandwich or whatever?"

"A better idea, I mean we're in Japan so why don't we try what the locals eat?"

"I'm not into sashimi or that... *Err...* What the hell do the Japanese call it? Like puffer fish, or something like that."

You mean the poisonous fish...Fugu?"

"If you say so." Steve shrugged

"No, I was thinking about conveyer belt sushi."

"Conveyor belt sushi, Get out of it!" Steve laughed.

"A true-blue Washingtonian, huh? McDonalds and KFC."

"At least I'm not gonna get poisoned!"

"You *are* really naive!"

"So?"

"I'll ask the concierge. You stay put."

Gregg walked toward the concierge's desk, the guy in the 'over the top' gold breaded dark blue uniform with the seriously thinning hair and 'crows feet' eye sockets smiled as Gregg approached. Americans over tip thinking they like are back in the States and this was his fifteen minutes.

"Excuse me, do you speak English?" Gregg asked.

"Of course, sir. How can I be of assistance?"

"My buddy and I would like to experience 'conveyor belt' sushi, perhaps you can direct us to the nearest restaurant and inform the cab driver?"

The concierge smiled again. These Americans...

"Of course, sir... You mean Kaiten-zushi? Or in English 'sushi go round'."

"That's the ticket." Gregg smiled, he had nailed it.

"If you don't mind me telling you sir, Kaiten-zushi are less expensive sushi restaurants where the sushi dishes are presented to the customers on a conveyer belt. Prices per dish range from 6 to 18 US dollars."

"Sounds good to me. Can you call a cab and give the address of the nearest one?"

"Most certainly sir, that will be in the Ginza district of 'down town' Tokyo."

Gregg palmed the twenty.

"Thank *you*, sir." The concierge gave a huge smile, 2300 yen, not bad for five minutes of 'bull shit'.

"Steve." Gregg called to his wingman. "We're good to go."

The concierge hailed a cab.

* * *

(Speaking in Japanese's)

"Take these two Americans to Kaiten-zushi, Ginza Numerazoka, 8F-803-Kiraritoginza,18-19 Ginza."

The cab driver nodded and pulled the lever to open the rear door.

"Thanks again, err..."

The concierge pointed to his name tag.

"Eh, Daiki......"

* * *

Kaiten- sushi is a sushi restaurant where the plates with the sushi are placed on a rotating conveyor belt that winds through the restaurant and moves past every table and counter seat. Customers may place special orders, but most choose from the steady stream of fresh sushi moving along the conveyor belt. The final bill is calculated on the number and type of colored plates consumed. The most remarkable feature of conveyor belt sushi is the stream of plates winding through the restaurant. Selections are not limited to sushi which may also include beer fruits desserts and customers can place special orders. Plates with different colors and patterns have different prices. The bill is calculated by counting the number of plates of the consumed sushi. *Whatever,* this is an experience not to be missed.

* * *

The cab ride gave Steve and Gregg space to relax, it had been a fruitless day and the mysterious loss of Global 10 wasn't braking any sunshine.

"Listen Gregg." Steve turned to face him. "Something has just crossed my mind."

"Yeah?" That caught Gregg's attention.

"We forgot to change our US currency into Yen."

"Is that all! I thought you were you were gonna tell there was a break in the clouds." Gregg shook his head in disappointment, like what's next?

"I got news for you buddy I changed a thousand bucks at the front desk this morning before we left."

"I never noticed."

"You wouldn't, you were too busy ogling that chick at the 'Check In' desk."

"Gimme a break."

"Deja vue, say no more. Now more importantly we must get in touch with Daniels to keep him in the loop and meet him probably late afternoon, if he's free."

"I agree, say why don't I gave him a call right now?"

"Better you than me." Gregg grinned, the code breaker still fresh in his memory."

Steve opened his cell then checked the number from Daniel's card.

"Rico here, Mr. Daniel's secretary, how can I be of assistance?"

"Rico, unfortunately we didn't have a chance to meet after we arrived from the US when we visited your boss yesterday evening."

Gregg was shaking his head... Like, 'this guy never gives up'.

"And you are?"

"Steve Nelson, CIA and my partner Gregg Jonson. I wondered if we could meet with Ken today, say, late afternoon?"

"If you can bear with me for a moment I'll check to see when he is free."

Gregg nudged Steve. "You had better make it quick as the cab is slowing down and pulling into the kerb."

"Yes, he can see you around 4.00pm."

"Would it be possible to speak to him for a moment?"

Steve could hear Rico sigh then silence.

"Yes Steve?"

"Sorry to bother you Ken I know you must be busy."

"Yes, if you could be brief."

"We interviewed two female acquaintances of the captain and first officer, I think they're clean but when it comes to money you just never know."

"And?"

Steve could sense Daniel's impatience.

"It's like this, they are due to depart from Tokyo tomorrow so I informed them they must present their passports and personal details to your office before they leave. Their names are Julie Rodger and Margery Simpson, both air hostesses."

"I'll alert reception. If that's all then its four o'clock."

The cab pulled into the kerb.

"Well Daniel's was a bunch of joy."

"Maybe he's still smarting from the code breaking 'egg' on his face."

"Heh, Heh, maybe." Steve laughed.

"Kaiten- sushi, domo."

"Let's pay the cabby and get some food, I could do with a cold beer."

"You mean *I* pay the cab?"

"Well, you're the one that changed the money......!"

* * *

"Can you make out the type of plane?" Bill asked.

Chuck was still peering through the tiny binoculars.

"It looks kinda like some sort of military medium range transporter for carrying paratroopers, reminds me of the Boeing G17 Globe Master only much shorter and similarly powered by four turbo fans. A neat little job and does this pilot know how to fly this baby with a text book landing."

"Yeah, I know the one." Bill replied.

"There's one thing for sure." Chuck cut in. "Shendo and his crew will be fully occupied for the next couple of hours and it will be dark by then so we might as well bed down for the night. I'll start hacking down these large palm leaves with this miniature sword... Sally, make yourself useful and lay them cress cross into a thick ground covering to keep the damp out when we bed down for the night."

"Yes sir." Sally gave a cheeky salute, she didn't like being bossed around, especially by Chuck.

"Come on Sally, lighten up, we're all in this together."

"I guess so, it's just... *Oh, what's the point........"*

* * *

"With the look of that sky it will be dark within the hour." Chuck commented staring into the heavens. I think lady luck is on our side with a full moon tonight. So, my suggestion is, while we still have sufficient daylight, let's have our rice and 'Adams wine'."

251

Bill nodded in agreement a slight smile crossing his face before turning to Sally.

"Yeah, I'm with you Chuck... Sally, can you break out the rice?"

Sally's eyes blazed, the last straw was about to break the camel.

"I feel like a fucking servant! It's bad enough serving you guys on the flight but being treated like your polygamous wife, *get off my fucking street!"*

"Sally... Always the lady." Chuck was stirring the pot.

"Listen you two guys, why don't you throw in the towel? We're gonna be in one another faces until I figure out some way to get us off this 'God forsaken' island. *Now Sally,* if it's not *too* much trouble can you fetch the rice from your vanity bag?"

Sally didn't reply, the look on her face said it all.

"Any further movement Chuck?" Bill was busily laying the 'swag' of large palm leaves.

"With the relief crew and the 'island boys', the place is swarming like soldier ants and I recon this freighter will be fueled and fully loaded within the hour."

"Dinner is served."

Sally had laid the damp face towel on the bed of palm leaves apportioning the unappetizing rice three ways accompanied with bottled water.

Bill could see it coming. *"Chuck, save it!"*

The 'fab three' squatted on the bed of palms ready for the gastronomic experience.

"Cheers." Chuck raised his bottled water. "Compliments to the chef."

"Chuck, *give it away."* Bill was showing his colors.

"Okay... Okay... I apologize Sally, for being such a heel."

"Apology accepted." Sally answered coldly.

"Now, can we have our dinner?" Bill asked sarcastically......

* * *

"I was starving, I never thought stale boiled rice would taste so good." Chuck was rinsing his hands with some water.

"Chuck, go easy with that water, it's our most precious commodity, food is one thing bat we can't live without water, *Capisco?"*

Chuck just shrugged. There was no point making a 'Federal' case if it.

"Now that 'café de jungle' is over what about toilet procedures?" Sally just had to raise the ante.

"Toilet procedures?" Bill hadn't thought about it, it wasn't high on his priority survival list but being a woman Sally had a point.

"Sally, it's like this, you do as they do in India. You pick a secluded shade in the bush, take some water with you and use one of these palm leaves and do what comes naturally and pray the mosquitoes don't have a 'field day'."

"It's easy for you guys to say but we women are different."

"Now you tell me!" Chuck couldn't contain his slaughter.

"Chuck, go shove you head up your ass." Sally picked up her half empty bottle of water and the face towel.

"I'll be back in ten minutes and we won't need this anymore." Sally was referring to the 'make shift' table cloth. "Spare me the use of the palm leaf, *please!"* She disappeared into the heavy foliage cursing new swear words on her way.

"Go easy on her Chuck, is not like "Survivor Lost Island" on that crazy TV show."

"Heh...Heh, I like that. And I'm no Jeff Probst, but I gotta tell you some of these chicks..."

"Yeah, yeah, I get the picture. Now how about getting back on these 'four eyes' and paint me the *real* picture......"

*   *   *

The cab settled, Steve and Gregg stared for a moment from the sidewalk at the Kaitan Sushi façade painted in bright red, it's large two-foot neon sign flashing the word 'Sushi'. Directly above the signage was a clever neon tube design in flashing blue of the Bullet Train and to add to the façade, in front of the restaurant on the sidewalk, were six evenly spaced large vintage Saki casks covered in braded straw with rough rope handles and green and black murals in Japanese lettering, portraying the culture of the old and new.

*   *   *

"This is gonna be an experience, I tell you." Steve turned to Gregg still unsure of their decision to go 'raw fish'.

"Well, are we gonna stand here and admire the place or are we gonna eat?"

"My brain tells me different but my stomach wins the battle."

"Well, listen to your stomach!" Gregg fired back impatiently. But the timely opening of the large glass door saved the barter.

"Americans?" The tall Japanese man asked, his head dress could easily be mistaken for an able seaman in the US navy. The white starched three-quarter length double breasted chef's tunic buttoned to the neck in a minister's collar and two vertical rows of five black buttons on either side was unexpectedly French. The black and white small checkered trousers was a 'stand out', maybe hygiene and necessity and US fast food influence is unfortunately changing the world.

"Yes." Steve replied.

"Please." He made a welcome motion.

"Boy this is some joint!" Steve commented at the colorful décor and the snaking narrow conveyor belt pulled by a miniature model of the Bullet Train, laden with different colored plates of sushi, salmon, prawn, tuna, fish eggs and California rolls, but a few.

"You can have a counter seat or a table, sirs?"

Gregg turned to Steve. "The counter seats look the most popular in front of the conveyer."

The 'head honcho' snapped his finger to attract one of many waitresses dressed in dark green chef's tunics, white slacks and the famous Hachimaki red and white head bands.

(Speaking in Japanese)

"Domo kaunta seki ni korera no shinsi o shimesi Simusan."

The young waitress nodded then made a motion with her hand for Steve and Gregg to follow before pointing to the two empty seats in front of the conveyor food train.

"Well I guess the drill is you just help yourself to your plate of choice. The chopsticks are here, soya and wasabi, so it's 'when in Rome do as the Romans'." Gregg laughed.

"My first choice would be a beer but I don't see that on the 'Bullet Train'. I'll ask this waitress." Steve raised his hand. *"Eh,* beero?"

The young waitress understood and pointed to the machine on the far away wall.

"Asahi beero."

"That's a new one on me, *draft beer from a machine!"*

"You get coffee from a machine so why not beer." Gregg replied.

"I'm watching this guy... You put your money in the machine which gives you change then pours the beer into a glass then automatically moves the glass to another station and adds the head. *I gotta hand it to these Japanese."* Steve was more than impressed.

The cold beer was refreshing and the sushi was unexpectedly tasty.

"Well, what do you think partner?" Gregg asked.

"Tomorrow morning will tell the story. You should be thankful we have separate rooms... *Eh,* the check ....?"

* * *

"Steve, do you have Danial's card?"

"Yeah... So?"

"We'll need it for the cab driver." Gregg was already frantically waiving his arm to attract their mode of transportation in the heavy traffic.

"Good, that guy spotted us, we're in luck."

"It's not before time, we could do with some luck. Have you ever had the feeling with this assignment that we're looking up a dead horse's ass?"

"Come on Steve, that's uncharacteristic of you, we broke the coded message, didn't we?"

"You mean, didn't *you?"*

"Changing the subject, let's concentrate on our meeting with Daniels, remember we're only two days into the assignment... *Ah,* here's the cab!"

The cab driver looked uncomfortable at the sight of two suited Americans, most likely as the result of his poor or no English, which is common in Japan and he rolled down the window.

Gregg quickly produced Daniel's card with the Akihabara address.

The driver took a second to digest the words then nodded his understanding.

"Hi, Akihabara, Tori Chuon." He broke a smile before pulling the lever to open the rear door.

"How long to here." Gregg pointed to the card as the driver pulled out."

The driver was more interested in slipping into the three-lane traffic and raised his left hand to wait.

"Hi, isshun..." He slipped into a gap then relaxed. "Feften bun."

"I guess that means fifteen minutes... Arigato." Gregg replied.

"Picking up the lingo, huh?" Steve laughed.

"Get out of it! I've heard that word so many times. Now, while we have some space, let's settle down and talk about our meeting with Daniels."

"Gregg, look at it this way." Steve began. "It's really just a courtesy call to keep Daniels and our boss on good terms. It's the old protocell hype between the FBI and the CIA. We both need one another and after all don't forget we *are* on Daniels patch."

The cab hung a left and pulled up in front of the larger than life stainless steel gates.

"We're here! That was quicker than I expected. We didn't get much space to discuss the points for our meeting with Daniels, *did we?"*

Gregg shrugged. "Well we'll just play it by ear, sometimes that's the best approach rather than a script read... *Yeah... Yeah...*" Gregg changed his tone. "Before you get to it, I'll settle the cab."

The driver pointed to the meter.

"Two thousand Yen, around twenty bucks, that's reasonable Gregg."

"When you not paying, *it is!"* Gregg barked. *"I'm keeping tabs mister."*

The marine sergeant was already out of the sentry box with his hand up blocking the path of the Toyota Crown before knocking on the rear passenger window and Steve promptly hit the window switch.

"Yes sergeant... *eh...* err Sergeant Baker?" Steve read the Bakelite name tag.

"No vehicles are allowed into the compound unless official FBI. Your business gentlemen?" The poker-faced sergeant politely asked ignoring Steve's comment.

"We have a meeting at four with Director Danial's."

"Please step out of the car sirs."

The cab driver seemed relieved at losing his passengers, besides time is money and he quickly reversed before slowly merging into the late afternoon traffic.

"Your ID's gentlemen." The sergeant already had his Android tablet to take pictures.

The agents produced their gold shields. "CIA agents Nelson and Jonson. Sergeant Baker, you *do* remember us from yesterday?" Steve asked trying to avoid the long and tedious security checks.

"Just bear with me Mr. Nelson while I enter your ID's into the system." Baker checked the time and took a picture then started tapping away on his tablet then after a few seconds, he finally cracked a smile and nodded.

"You have security clearance gentleman but I need to phone the Director to confirm your appointment."

Baker walked to the external steel encased security phone and spoke for a few minutes before returning the receiver then immediately switched on his Motorola shoulder phone.

"Security clearance accepted, unlock gates."

Baker turned to the agents. "You will have to wait here gentlemen until a marine arrives to escort you to the main entrance for further security clearance."

Within minutes the armed marine arrived an M14 Carbine slung from his shoulder, muzzle down.

"This way please." The tall marine stepped aside, his face inexpressive, the heavy gates rumbling closed behind them as they stepped it out to the entrance of the FBI's heavily fortified field office.

Another armed marine guarding the entrance gave a smart salute before opening the heavy oak doors.

The X-ray body scanner was straight in front and the sergeant manning the machine approached the agents holding two blue plastic containers.

"Yes sergeant, we know the drill." Steve's humorous sarcasm didn't go down well and Gregg shook his head, *how to make friends!*

"Please place your firearms and clips in each of these blue plastic containers accompanied with your agent's cards and or badges, then proceed through the scanner. You can collect your hardware upon leaving'." The sergeant smiled. "Thank you for your understanding."

"No sweat, sergeant you're only doing your job." Gregg was the peace officer.......

* * *

On the other side of the scanner stood a pretty Japanese lady probably in her late twenties, as if waiting patiently for someone. At around 5-8, slim, dressed in a fitted dark blue knee length skirt, with just enough leg to entice, her white silk opened necked short sleeved blouse with a dainty gold chain and Amethyst pendant adorning her neck... She was a looker alright and with these dark eyebrows and deep brown eyes, narrow nose and with just the right depth of lip shine, to contrast her pale complexion, what man wouldn't be intoxicated? The 'Fait accompli', her jet-black hair tightly swept back into a coxcomb.

* * *

Steve nudged Gregg. *"And who is that?"*

"I thought you preferred blondes?"

"When in Japan..."

"Yeah, Yeah, I've heard that one before. Thanks sergeant, can we go through now?"

"Of course, gentlemen."

The Japanese beauty stepped forward to meet them.

"I assume you are agents Nelson and Jonson?" She spoke in perfect English with an accent to die for.

"And you are Rico, Mr. Daniels secretary, I recognize your voice." There was no holding 'God's answer to women'.

Rico smiled slightly embarrassed.

"If you can come this way gentlemen I will escort you to Ken's office."

As she walked in front Steve he couldn't keep his eyes off her shapely figure.

"Where has she been all my life?"

"For Christ sakes Steve, keep your voice down, besides she is probably married or at least spoken for."

"I'm sorry gentlemen?" Rico Turned.

"It's nothing Rico, we were just talking between ourselves." Gregg replied ill at ease.

"If you can give me a moment, I'll check to see if Ken is free." Rico lifted the secretarial phone.

"Ken, sorry to interrupt... Your free... I'll send them in."

Rico placed back the receiver and a gave a warm smile.

"Just go straight in."

Daniels's nose was deep in papers and he looked up to greet Steve and Gregg.

"Bloody paper work! Grab a seat." Ken pointed.

"I had an interesting call from your boss regarding the deciphering of the coded message that Ginzo Iwami lost his life over and I have to hand it to you guys, our cryptanalysts have egg on their faces."

"Ken, it was just a fluke believe me. Gregg here spotted an advert for overseas holidays with a phone code and you can take it from there."

"I guess it's the old story, sometimes 'you can't see the wood for the tress' whatever, a nice job. Now can you bring me up to speed."

Steve began. "I'll get to the point Ken and not take up too much of your time, I know you're a busy man."

Daniels made a face like 'tell me something new'.

"The message sent to Salibe when decoded read… 'NUMS DELETED COMP CRASH ALLAH AHMAD… So, what does that mean and who sent it?"

"Good question." Daniels sat back in his chair in relax mode his attention full on.

"Here's the scoop… We know that someone made that call to Salibe from a public phone in Chicago. Now as for the shipment of used US currency on Global 10, which has mysteriously disappeared without a trace, both Gregg and I are convinced it's a hijacking somehow linked to Hamas but where the Yakuza come in, the jury is still out. Now to answer your question, 'where do we stand right now'?"

"Before we continue Steve." Daniels glanced at his watch. "It's coffee time for me, how about you guys?"

"After the lunch, we had, *American coffee* … Say no more!"

Ken smiled and lifted the phone.

"Rico… *Heh…Heh.*" Ken laughed. "You were waiting for the call… Make it for three… Just a sec… How do you guys take it?"

"Black straight up…"

"You heard that? Same all round… Thanks Rico."

"I'm intrigued, so what sort of lunch did you have?" Ken placed back the phone.

"Kaitan Zushi."

"*Ha…Ha…Ha.*" Ken burst into laughter again. "*Conveyer sushi*… That must have been an experience. It's very popular and in fact I quite like it. I guess it was the raw fish that got to you guys, huh?"

"*Don't mention it!*" Steve shook his head. "Enough said."

There was a light knock on the door.

"Come in Rico."

Rico opened the door with one hand whilst balancing the tray of coffees on the other.

"Her let me help you." Steve jumped to his feet.

"There's no need Mr. Nelson, I can manage, but thank you."

"Thanks Rico, just place the cups on my desk." Ken moved his paperwork aside to make room. Rico gave a warm smile then left.

Daniels couldn't help noticing Steve's roving eyes and that special smile he tried to connect.

"Yes, Steve she's nice, I don't blame you."

Steve's face flushed.

"Rico has been with me now for, *eh...?* Almost three years and a better secretary one couldn't find. She's 27 and unmarried and comes from a wealthy prominent Japanese family. Her father Misako Moro is a member of the Diet. She keeps herself to herself and I never probe into her personal life. Understandably there has been several office suiters who have abruptly been sent packing. Sorry to disappoint you, Steve."

"Oh, err..." For once Steve was stuck for words.

"Enjoy your coffee break and let's get back to business." Daniels gave a wry grin. He had purposely embarrassed Elson and was enjoying the chase.

"Hmmm... This coffee is good... Now, where were we?" Steve was glad to change the subject. Firstly, Anbar Salibe and Fadile Maalouf are nephews of Abud Aziz who is the brother of Abdul Fatah the number one commander of the armed wing of Hamas and on Shin Bet's most wanted list and of course Salibe and Maalouf's father. So far so good...? I don't have to give you their history, you know their backgrounds Ken, the FBI have had them on their radar for the past three years as a potential terrorist threat."

Danial's nodded with a shrug as if to say, there's nothing new.

"Now, you may ask from the CIA's side where are we...? John is in the process of checking with the 'The Bureau of Engraving and Printing' at Fort Worth Texas and Washington DC to see if there has been a major computer crash inflicting the loss of the serial numbers and does their Chicago office have access to their main frame as Azis is the senior director of the Chicago District Office? Furthermore, John is also waiting for the FBI to check if there is any security footage of that phone booth they tracked down. If there was sufficient tie up I suggested Abud Azis be hauled in for questioning but John wanted more time to think about it, stressing the point that if Azis was pulled in prematurely it may blow the FBI's cover and the Muslim extremists will go to ground. So, I'm afraid Ken it's a waiting game. I'm sure John will keep you in the loop.

"So how did your meeting go with McGill? John informed me when he called, he would set it up."

"Yeah, we met with McGill yesterday at his office and some interesting stuff popped out of the hat. Firstly, McGill is adamant that that the plane went down although Japanese search and rescue have tirelessly searched an area of ten square miles, 800 kilometers from the coast where the control tower radar lost contact and found no sign of debris. It's just like another MH 370. Next, we got a verbal CV of the pilot Bill Collins and the first officer Charles Stevens. Both served as Navy pilots on the air craft carrier the

Dwight D Eisenhower during Desert Storm receiving commendations for bravery. Collins has a clean slate but Stevens is something else, a loose cannon with a reputation for womanizing, alcoholism and gambling, a cocktail for further investigation. Now the only other member of the crew except for the security guards which we will get to later, is the air hostess Sally Jenkins, 23, single, brunette, 5-8 with Global Freight for three years, on the transfer list for international passenger flights. Good employee with an impeccable service record. Now we come to the security guards. We asked McGill if he could remember anything that struck him as unusual, even the smallest detail. At first, he had trouble remembering then there was a break in the clouds. The two Japanese he couldn't remember their names and that is understandable however he could remember that they were both operatives of the 'Kovan Chousacho' the 'Public Security Intelligence Agency'. As for the 'third wheel' he had an Italian name, and a US citizen from Black Hawk Securities and a 'vet' who served with distinction, with two tours of duty in Afghanistan with the US Marines. His parents immigrated from Cicely to the US after the second world war... He's clean as whistle. But get this, when we queried McGill further he said he never met them and he left that to Collins and here's the take on Collins. It seems the Captain was like another Sherlock Holmes, always cautious when it came to security after so many hijacks, in fact he carried an ankle holster with a 22 Smith and Weston."

"Hmmm..." Denials was listening absorbedly.

"But it doesn't end there, McGill remembered Collin's comment that when he studied the Italian's 'mug shot' he looked more Middle Eastern' than Mediterranean. So, we produced the pictures of Salibe and Maalouf stressing that they may have shaved their beards and asked him if he recognized any of the two and guess what? *He pointed to Salibe!* Now here's the kicker, 'The National Police Agency' gave their blessing and security clearance by computer but it doesn't end there, when we asked McGill to down load the security information... No surprises here, because by some mysterious coincidence the file had been completely erased. When he checked with his secretary she was as dumbfounded as her boss. *The bottom line...* The security guards were phonies but McGill still refuses to accept that the disappearance of Global 10 is a hijacking."

"Now, about these two broads that you interviewed this morning?" Daniels moved on.

"They are the ex-girlfriends of Collins and Nelson. We got their names from McGill who had seemingly met them before over dinner for some occasion or other. They are both flight attendants with Delta Airlines and by coincidence they also arrived yesterday on the same flight from Washington DC. They're clean but you never know when it comes down to money and a lot of it! That's the reason we informed them not to leave Tokyo without registering their personal information with your office, and with a photocopy of their passports. As a matter of fact, I would have thought they would have checked in by now."

Daniels sort of ignored the comment and rubbed his chin, like 'let's get on with it'.

"Then what's next on your agenda."

Steve could sense Daniel's impatience and didn't want to lose the page.

"McGill has agreed to allow us to sit in on a meeting planned for tomorrow with Boeing's 'Air Accident Investigation Branch' and the "National Transportation Safety Board' not to mention the 'Japanese Aviation Authority' and most likely on the stand, the air traffic controller."

The phone rang. "Gimme a second while I answer this call... *Hmmm... Hmmm...* Yes, give them security clearance and Rico will attend to them in person." Ken placed back the phone a cheeky crossing his face. "Gentlemen, by another coincidence, a Julie Rodgers and Margery Simpson have just arrived. You guys have been busy I must say, be assured I'll convey my appreciation to your boss for the good work. Thanks for keeping me up to speed and if there's nothing else, as you can see I'm up to my neck. Again, if you need any assistance just call me on my direct line. Rico will see you out........"

* * *

"Well fancy meting you two here!" Julie was rubbing salt into the wound.

"Awe, come on Julie, we're only doing our job." Steve pleaded.

"Huh, where have I heard that before, Marge?"

Rico stood speechless wondering why the barrage, maybe this was the American way of greeting friends.

"Marge, I know what you both are going through but let's not make it any more difficult than it is." *Gregg, still had that thing for that pretty brunette he met on the beach that day in LA. But then there was Michelle and his promise to phone her from Tokyo. Maybe 'a bird in the hand'?*

Rico was becoming impatient, she had other more important work on her plate than chaperoning two airhostesses to the IT section.

"Mr. Nelson, I'm sorry to interrupt but I must escort these two ladies to the security section to input their details into our data bank. I'm stretched at the moment and my boss will be wondering where I've gotten to."

"Rico, just bear with me one more second." Steve laid it on, Rico making a face. "Julie, if you can just take a step back and count to five. We're catching a cab into town and we'll hold it at the front gate until you both are finished and perhaps you can join us over dinner?"

"What happened to the conflict of interest?" Julie eyes blazed, she wasn't letting up.

Steve gave an 'I surrender shrug' "Rules are meant to be broken."

"Well Marge…. If nothing else we can save on the cab fare……"

* * *

The armed marine escorted Gregg and Steve to the front gate. Sergeant Baker had already spotted the two agents and preempted security.

Steve turned to Gregg as the heavy stainless-steel gate opened with a noisy rumble. "Well wasn't that a turn-up for the book?"

"Yeah, talk about coincidences." Gregg couldn't help but smile. "We got our dates after all, huh?"

"Don't run away with yourself partner, that Julie when you get on her wrong side *is one* piece of work…. *Eh… Eh…* Sargent Baker… Sargent, would it be possible you call us a cab?"

"Sorry sir, against the rules. If you make yourself visible on the sidewalk you can easily hail one."

"Thanks, sarg, we understand." Gregg replied having fully anticipated the answer.

"Listen Gregg, the girls shouldn't be too long so why don't we wait until they arrive?"

"Talk of the devil, here they are now *and aren't we two lucky dudes!* These babes can hang on my arm any day." Gregg had that proud smile.

Steve quickly turned to study the form. *"You can say that again!"*

Even the sergeant had to smile and who could blame him in his job?

"Ladies." Steve gave the 'Sir Walter Raleigh' bow crossing his right arm over his waist.

Julie couldn't resist the cheap shot. "Have you two guys been waiting long?"

"Get out of it Julie, but I guess we deserve that." Steve replied offering his hand.

"I'm a big girl, I can manage." Julie retaliated.

"You can take my hand Gregg." Marge still had that thing for Gregg since first they met.

"Hang on Marge, while I see if I can stop this cab… *Good man!*" The black Toyota Crown pulled into the kerb.

"Okay who sits in the front?" Steve winked to Gregg, not unnoticed.

Julie took the shot. "Before you guys toss a coin or whatever I'll accompany the driver and Marge stay away from the middle of the back seat."

The cab driver gave that stare as if to say do you want a cab or not?

"Since you're calling the shots Julie, would it be too much to ask where?"

"We have an early flight tomorrow so it's best we return to our hotel."

"That's okay by us but the least we can do is buy you two girls dinner. Come on Julie crack the ice." Steve laughed but Julie wasn't impressed.

The cab driver shook his head and slipped the 'Crown' into gear.

"Hold it… Hold it." Steve knocked on the passenger window and the driver hit the brakes rolling down the widow once more before pointing to the meter.

"I understand… Hyatt Regency in Nishi Shinjuku."

The driver nodded and pulled the door lever……

* * *

The two 'heroes' crushed together with Marge next to Gregg and the rear door with Julie looking into the rear mirror smiling at the threesome.

"Are you guys comfortable there?"

"I'm okay Julie." Marge gave Gregg that look.

"Changing the subject." Steve wouldn't let go. "So, ladies what sort of food would you like tonight and please don't say *sushi?*"

It was getting a bit boring with Julie's hate campaign and Marge just had to throw in the towel.

"There's an Italian restaurant on the ground floor of the hotel that gets a good write up, *if you guys are agreeable…?*"

"Are we!" Steve butted in. "You couldn't have picked a better choice, Gratsi Marge."

"Prego, molto benne." Marge laughed but Julie… Well… She was still the iceberg waiting for the Titanic.

"That was quicker than I thought!" Steve commented as the cab slowly slipped into the front entrance of the hotel.

"I'll get it." Gregg volunteered. The cab driver pointing once more to the meter with a relieved look… *Americans…….!*

* * *

The Hyatt Regency is a massive luxury five-star hotel in Nishi Shinjuku boasting breath taking views of the city and Mt. Fuji to the west. Like the nearby Keio Plaza Hotel and Tokyo Hilton, it caters to large groups of travelers particularly from China and Asian countries. The hotel is conveniently located about a ten-minute walk west of Shinjuku Station and next to the Tokyo Metropolitan Government Building and Tokyo's City hall. The closest subway line Tochomae, is right by the hotel.

The Hyatt Regency is a vast tower hotel complex with one of the most impressive lobbies in Japan. Three stories tall the cathedral ceiling and enormous chandeliers hung over wall to wall marble. There was a mass of empty space but tastefully decorated with cherry blossom branches. Much to the amazement and pleasure of the guests there is even a humanoid robot-Softbank's Pepper, a household communications robot on hand to greet them.

With 18 suites and 746 rooms with some overlooking the Shinjuku Central Park and on clear days Mt Fuji towering in the distance.

The hotel has all the amenities with 8 eating and drinking establishments. To the right of the lobby is Michelangelo's Restaurant a famous Italian eatery. On the first-floor Gaston Troisgros a French Restaurant with a contemporary twist. Other restaurants in the hotel serve Japanese and Chine's cuisine.

Like all 5-star hotels in Tokyo the room tariffs are not to be sneezed at but for the business traveler on a generous expense account, *spoil yourself.......*

* * *

"The last time Gregg and I came here was on official business and I never really looked at the place. This lobby is stunning and those chandeliers!" The soft touch still wasn't working with Julie who just ignored Steve's comment.

"Listen ladies, it's a touch early for dinner at six thirty so why don't we enjoy an aperitif before going al Italia?"

"Why not!" Julie finally gave that 'certain smile'.

"Can I be of assistance sir?" The concierge in the dark blue uniform with gold braided Mandarin collar and cuffs enquired, having noted Steve's roving eyes.

"The Italian restaurant?" Steve enquired.

"You must mean our famous Michelangelo's sir... It's just to your left, you can't miss it."

"Domo arigato." Steve smiled proud of his total Japanese vocabulary.

"Michelangelo's huh? It's gotta be good." Gregg commented as the entered the restaurant.

"Table for four sirs?" The Maître de was fast on his feet.

"Yes, but we are early and we would like to sit at your lovely bar to enjoy a pre-dinner drink"

"Certainly, sir please…." He pointed to the bar and the row of red leather stools.

"Hmmm… I gotta say this is nice." Julie comment whist taking her seat. Her pleasant smile now a permanent fixture……

* * *

The restaurant was intimate and tastefully decorated in line with the Michelangelo theme, with classic black and white furniture, a glass walled kitchen and an impressive bar to match the color scheme. The long Edison lights strung from the ceiling lit up the bar with a soft tone reflecting on the glass back drop and the stand out array of colored liquor bottles. Cozy and yet modern the ambience had something special and hopefully the menu would follow suite.

* * *

The young barman in the matador style jacket was smiling. Things were slow so early in the evening and it was an opportunity to proudly demonstrate his cocktail skills.

"*Sirs*… I'm at your service and ladies what would you like?"

"*Hmmm*… Marge?"

"*Eh…Err…*I'll have a Long Island Iced Tea… And you Julie?"

"I'll have a Manhattan."

"Gentlemen?"

"Doubly Chivas on the rocks…. *Eh, Gregg?*"

"Make that for two…."

* * *

The drinks had come and gone and the barter was light. Julie had finally turned the corner and was almost back to her old self again.

Almost finishing he second Manhattan she finally turned to Steve.

'It's been a rough couple of days Steve." She began. "And you both deserve an apology. You and Gregg were only doing your jobs."

"*Hey!* Come off it, we understand what your both going through."

"Steve, you will let us know I something comes up."

"Unless it's classified you have my word. Now that the dust has settled and I mean that in the nicest way lets enjoy our dinner after all you will both be gone tomorrow and who knows when well meet again?"

"I'll drink to that. Cheers." Marge after two Long Islands was letting her hair down.

The Maître de had placed the menus on the bar.

"Ladies let's see what we got here." Gregg was studying the Italian fare.

Julie started. "This looks interesting, that's if can pronounce it... Capellini D'Angelo... Get this... A savory aglio olio pasta with a generous portion of mushrooms and cherry tomatoes on angel hair pasta with parmesan and grilled orange slices, rosemary and garlic......"

* * *

"Guys, the food was excellent but we have an early morning flight and 10:30 has come and gone."

"Julie, are you sure you wouldn't like another Latte or a glass of wine?"

"No, but thanks for the lovely dinner. You certainly made our day."

Gregg raised his hand to attract the waiter.

"Sir?"

"Check please."

"Can we see you to the elevator?" Steve sheepishly asked.

"Of course," Marge didn't wait for Julie's reply.

"I would have invited you both up to our room but who knows, maybe next time." Julie seemed sincere.

As they stood waiting for the elevator Marge stood on her toes and suddenly gave Gregg a kiss on the cheek.

"Maybe next time." She smiled.

The elevator chimed......

* * *

The Concierge hailed a cab.

"Where to sir?" He asked.

"Palace Hotel, Marunouchi Chiyodo."

"Certainly sir." Gregg slipped the Concierge a 1000 yen note.

"Arigato." The Concierge bowed. Ten US Dollars is a handsome tip.

"You know Gregg, I think if I had another date with Julie I could melt the ice. She's the full package, looks, intelligence and a temper to match." Steve was grinning as he made himself comfortable for the cab ride.

"And just how do you intend see her again bearing in mind she is domicile in LA and we are in Washington DC.?"

"We could rent two Harley's again!" Steve gave his usual crazy laugh

Gregg shook his head. *"On this case!* We'll be lucky if we get a Sunday off. Which reminds me we have a meeting with Global tomorrow... 'Never on Sunday' *huh?"*

"It's twenty-four seven partner... *Remember?* But changing the subject, that Marge had the hots for you and I wouldn't throw her outta bed in a hurry!"

"Yeah, she's a dish alright but...?" Gregg had that troubled look.

"I don't believe you're still wearing that Michele on your sleeve?"

"So, what if I am? I still haven't phoned her and I promised I would. I don't like promising something and doing the opposite."

"Don't tell me you gave her your virginity!"

"Get out of it! Only you could think up that shit. It's my call, *so if you don't mind...?"*

Steve could sense his buddy was getting agitated and there was no point in breaking up a good partnership over some broad.

"I take it back Gregg."

"Ah... forget it."

The cab pulled in and as usual Gregg settled the fare.

"Do you fancy a nightcap before we turn in its only just turned eleven."

"Na, I'll take a raincheck Steve, but there's nothing to stop you."

"Okay, so breakfast at eight... Ciao."

As Gregg walked to the elevator Michelle was still on his mind, maybe *he should* call her tonight......

* * *

The elevator chimed jolting Gregg from his thoughts on whether to call Michelle or cowardly, take a rain check. But there again he had promised and his conscious was crying out to do the right thing.

"Dozo?" The other gentleman in the lift pointed to the open elevator doors as if to say, *'is this your floor or not'?*

Gregg slightly embarrassed apologized saying "Sorry" and quickly left walking the thick blue carpeted hallway to his hotel room, giving a sort of 'at last sigh' as he slipped the plastic pass key in to the slot. The green LED light shone and the heavy brass security lock unlatched. He switched on the soft lighting with his pass key and flopped on top of the bed. It had been a mixed day of dramas with brick wall progress on the missing jetliner and worse still the disappearance of Anbar Salibe after the murder of a Japanese undercover FBI agent. Then there was Marge, an attractive 25 years old brunette with all the right credentials and the 'come on' body language.

"Hmmmm..." Gregg gave a giant sigh as he tossed his jacket onto the chair, kicked off his shoes and undid his tie.

"Ah... That feels better!"

He placed both hands his behind his head resting on the soft pillows and stared at the ceiling as if waiting for the magic bullet to give him the answers. But life is a perpetual challenge that only the individual can solve, unfortunately often to their detriment and the delusion of never making the same mistake twice.

Gregg glanced at the digital bedside clock.

"Let me see... If it's 11:15 here in Tokyo?" He looked at his Diesel black dial dual time watch to checked Washington DC time.

"10:15 am in DC... *Hmmmm... Darn it she'll be at the office."* Then it struck him. "What the hell am I talking about? *It's Saturday morning!"*

Gregg opened his cell to check the number. "Here we are." He tapped the screen and waited patiently whilst listening to the ringtone at the same time scrambling his thoughts together on just what to say.

Michelle had switched her cell to silent mode. Saturday was a 'lay in' morning having lost count of the Vodka shooters at the Cloak & Dagger cellar bar, a stone's throw from the IRS office and popular with the Friday night crowd. As for Maggi ...? *Well...* As usual she was wasted and as normal wouldn't show her face until midday, searching for the 'hair of the dog'.

The Samsung buzzed vibrating on the highly glazed lacquered bedside table snaking around as if it were alive.

"Hmmmm..." Michelle stirred flicking her shoulder length brown hair from her eyes, her head buried in the pillow.

Brrrrrr...Brrrrrr... Brrrrrr.

"Go away.... Go away." She fumbled in the darkened room, the curtains drawn, trying to get her hands on her cell to strangle it before finally giving up the struggle stretching over to switch on the bedside lamp, quickly covering her eyes to avoid 'snow blindness'. The hangover was bad enough but that light was head splitting.

"Hello, who is this?" Her voice sleepily hoarse.

"Michelle... It's Gregg... Gregg Jonson... Don't tell me you didn't recognize my voice already?"

"Gregg darling, I'm so sorry, *of course I recognize your voice!* Maggie and I well... Friday night is 'detendre nuit' or in English relaxation night."

"I get the picture... Vodka shooters with the office staff, huh?"

"Something like that." Michelle was keeping it close to her chest in case Gregg got the wrong idea. "But darling it's so good to hear your voice again. Every hour since you left I've been waiting for you call."

"I'm sorry Michelle but our assignment is twenty-four seven and tonight I finally had some time to myself when I returned to my hotel room."

"Don't worry darling, I understand. I just knew in my heart you would phone, I've never stopped thinking about you. Gregg, *I really love you."*

Gregg was lost for words. He had real feelings for Michelle but he was momentarily taken aback by her unashamable honesty.

"Gregg, are you there?"

"Yes honey."

Michelle sighed. "I thought I had lost you there for a moment."

"I'll never forget the night we spent together." Gregg continued, his voice shaky.

"Tell me darling!"

Gregg sighed trying to find the right words.

"Honey, we must both be crazy after spending only one night together, but then love is an irrational emotion and when you meet the right partner it's body language that triggers something between two people of the opposite sex, called love. I really love you Michelle, so does that answer your question?"

"With all my heart... Darling, is it too much to ask when I will see you again?"

"I wish I knew honey. For security reasons, can't explain my assignment but it's big and that's all I can say. How long will I be in Japan...? *How long is a piece of string?"*

"I understand darling. Just remember I love you and I'll be waiting for your next call."

"I'll call you as soon as I have some free time... I love you to..."

"Je t'aime. Good night darling."

Gregg closed his cell. Were their feelings moving too fast? Michelle was different but he wasn't foolish enough to think he was her first lover... But as they say, 'love is blind' and tomorrow is another day......

THE BIGGER PICTURE

It had not been a good week for Thomson but then what week *is,* in his job? The morning traffic didn't help either and maybe the solitaire in his 'down town' apartment needed a woman's touch but that's a topic for another day and one that you raise at your peril.

John sat back in in his leather exec chair enjoying the last of the dark brew, his mind actively diagnosing a whole host of outstanding issues relating to the Palestinian investigation. Everything just seemed to be dragging its feet and with the case still open ended if something didn't break soon, he may have to decide to pull Nelson and Jonson back to Washington.

The phone rang...

* * *

"What now? Hell, I can't even get a minute to enjoy my morning coffee break! Yes Hanna?"

"Sorry to disturb you John but I have Mike Stone the Assistant Director of the FBI on the line, I'm sure it's urgent."

"Put him through... *Mike...!* I hope it's good news?"

"It is and it isn't! Comey, our new boss, I'm sure your familiar with the name, has to make his mark by shaking up the 'sleeping giant' as he puts it and at the top of his hit list is the embarrassing loss of one hundred billion dollars for which he has still to release a statement to the press."

"Heh...Heh." John laughed. "So, what's new......?"

* * *

James Comey was the United States Deputy Attorney General serving in President George W Bush's administration. He was subsequently appointed in June 2013 by Barack Obama to be the next Director of The Federal Bureau of Investigation, replacing the outgoing Director, Robert Mueller. Comey was chosen over finalist Lisa Monaco who had overseen national security issues at the Justice Department during the attack on the US Consulate in Bengasi. At 52, a lawyer, Comey is the youngest appointed FBI Director and will serve a ten years' tenure.

* * *

"Well, you know what they say about a new broom? John joked. "I'm sure your boss is competent or he wouldn't have gotten the appointment. Some people climb the tree the easy way others take a lot longer." Thomson sounded a little bitter. "But the bottom line is we're both singing from the same hymn sheet when it comes to National Security. Enough of that Mike, I'm sure you're not calling to check on my health?"

John could hear Stone laughing in the background.

"The good news is we scanned miles of CCTV tapes of that phone box where we tracked the call to Tokyo to Anbar Salibe. You were right John, it *was* none other than the uncle Abud Azis himself. Being a senior director in The Department of Controller of Currency in the Chicago District Office he has access to all sorts of information including The Federal Reserve in the printing and the destruction of currency at Fort Worth Texas and Washington DC."

"Okay, so tell me something new."

"The data bank of US currency serial numbers for different denominations for destruction believe it or not has been hacked before!"

"You're fucking serious!"

"Yeah, I know it doesn't jive in this day and age with the internet security problems we have worldwide."

Thomson shook his head. *"Hell,* after the Julian Assange case, the Editor in Chief of 'WikiLeaks' who hacked into the data banks of none other than the Pentagon, the US Department of Defense, Milnet the US Navy and Nasa, *need I go further?"*

"John, don't rub it in... But it gets even worse... Would you believe we still use firewalls and IBM AS 600 main frames at Fort Worth and in some cases even floppy discs?"

"Your shittin me? That's 1990 tech!"

"Yeah, *or even earlier and get this...* The Treasury Department makes use of 'assembly language code" designed in the 1950's. The recent report from the office of 'Management and Budget' states that they have begun to replace the legacy of 'IT' systems but until this policy is finalized the government runs the risk of maintaining systems that have outlived their effectiveness. Even worse the Pentagon spokeswoman Lt Colonel Valarie Henderson states the current schedule to replace the existing outdated systems with secure digital devises will not be completed until the end of 2017!"

"What a fucking mess!" John shook his head in disbelief. "It's little wonder it was easy to erase the currency numbers, so where do we go from here, or is that a stupid question?"

"It gets even messier John. Abdul Azim and Dabar Bishara, both employed by the Federal Reserve at Fort Worth and naturalized US citizens, Studied at Cornel University graduating with honors in 2006 in computer science then applied for Green Cards, then citizenship. With their credentials, of course they were readily accepted under the skills programme. You may well ask, so what brought them out of the wood work? Well for one thing they are both Palestinians, which is no cause for concern. Both in their early thirties having lived in the United States for almost nine years, married with children and domicile in Washington DC, Azim is a soft wear mogul and Bishara an IT manager. Both close friends with regular family get togethers. They first came 'out of the cold' around 18 month ago when we recorded phone calls to East Jerusalem which were gibberish and in code to numbers that the Israel's Mossad Secret Service confirmed were linked to Hamas."

"Hell Mike, how can they escape our security checks at the Federal Reserve?"

"Don't rub it in John... The bottom line is they both have access to the Reserve's data bank and internal CCTV in the last two weeks has shown abnormal activity entering and leaving the secure computer department and their fingerprint recognition's back up our suspicions that they hacked into the firewall and erased the note numbers. Furthermore, they regularly communicate with Abud Azis, supposedly on business."

"The plot thickens, huh?"

"That's one way of putting it."

"Are we going to haul them in and charge them under the Patriot Act, as engaging in activities that endanger US national security?"

"Charging them is one thing Mike but making it stick is another."

"Yeah, it's a pity we closed Guantanamo Bay."

"Wishful thinking, I wish you luck but what gets me is why the Bank of Japan lost the file and have no back up?"

"Who cares...They have the surety of a promissory note and I'm led to believe the US Treasury is already in the process of transferring the funds. Remember John, this is like the Bermuda Triangle, Hamas, the Russian's and the Yakuza. How they come together and the motive is still with the jury."

"It's such a fucking mess... My boys in Tokyo are sitting in at a meeting tomorrow Sunday, with Global Air and the relevant US and local security air safety and search and rescue operations. I'll keep you in the loop on the outcome. If there's nothing else Mike thanks for the call and good luck and give your new boss my regards."

"Heh... Heh... Heh... Ciao."

"Hmmmm." Thomson was perturbed. The arrest of Abud Azis was always on the cards but that would send shock waves to Hamas and was it premature before setting the mouse trap? He lifted the phone. "Hanna, I need to send a report to McConnell the Director of National Intelligence......"

* * *

Chuck was straining through the miniature binoculars constantly adjusting the lenses.

"They must have used these fucking things for the opera!"

"Stop complaining and tell me what you see." It was Bill's turn.

"I gotta hand it to these guys working in this humidity. *Talk about fast turnaround!* Global could take a leaf outta their book... Japanese work ethics... I tell you, that babes gonna leave on time for sure."

"Anything else other than the Japanese work ethics?" Bill was being both sarcastic and impatient.

"A forklift is placing an airline stainless steel container into the plane's hold... I'm counting one already loaded and two in the que waiting on the tarmac. *I can't believe that miniature transporter! Would you believe it take at least three 'Abram Battle Tanks'!"*

"And the other two." Bill asked.

"Another fork lift is in the process of storing them in the maintenance hangar."

"It looks like it's goodbye to 60 billion of our cargo on its way to somewhere... *But where?"*

"Japan, and the Yakuza?" Chuck ashamedly replied.

"So, you were in on the deal all along, *huh?"* Bill shook his head... *"Maaaan."*

"Don't rub it in Bill, so I made a mistake but a profitable one, 20 mill to be exact and if you and Sally can have a bout of dementia... *That's if we ever escape...?* It's a three-way split."

"*Chuck,* you got some Gaul, considering you got us into this mess in the first place."

"Sally, *come on,* there's six mill in it for you. Now doesn't that tempt you?"

Bill stepped in, enough was enough.

"Since your one of the 'valiant three' s where does the Palestine come into it?"

"I don't know, *this you gotta believe*". Chuck raised both hands in the air. "But get this, Anbar made a call to some high-ranking Russian General."

"About what...?"

Chuck shrugged his shoulders. "Your guess is as good as mine, Bill."

Bill paused for a moment. *"Okay...Okay...* Let's take a step back... What's done is done, now more importantly, how do we get off this fucking island? As I see it there are only three ways, land air and sea."

"That's an 'Einstein' conclusion!" Chuck mocked.

"*Chuck,* cut the shit, unless you have anything better to contribute?"

Sally was just sitting quietly listening to a conversation that was going nowhere.

"Well it goes without saying that we're on an island so the first option is a 'no brainer'. *Air...?* We could attempt to fly that transporter outta here but it will be another six weeks before we can consider that route and with the sheer number of Japs on the ground it would be committing adulterated suicide. *No...* It's gotta be by sea!"

"You mean swim?"

"*Chuck,* you're such a fucking asshole when you wanna be. I can't believe why I suffered your shit for so long... *Now,* if we can get back to 'Good Morning Vietnam'? *No,* the maintenance vessel tied up at the jetty is our only hope."

"And how may I ask your plan to steal that boat?" Chuck just didn't know when.

"I'll come up with something. How about you Sally... Any thoughts?"

"*Me...?* I'm just worried about sleeping tonight in this fucking Jungle......!"

* * *

"What did I tell you? The tractor crew is hooking up the steel pull rod to the nose undercarriage to turn the plane around for takeoff."

Chuck turned to Bill, a cheeky grin on his face.

"I could delay it if you wanted." Rubbing the stock of the Arisaka 99. "This baby is accurate up to 500 yards, it's a copy of the German Mauser, need I say more?"

"Like you Chuck, the thought had crossed my mind but what do we gain? You start pot shooting the crew or even trying to damage the engines, they'll pick up the muzzle flash in this dim light and all hell will be let loose. *Too risky."*

"S0 do we sit back and do nothing?" Chuck was trigger happy.

"Tomorrow's another day and my guess is that Shendo hasn't told his boss yet of the 'Great Escape" and you're going to need every round of that ammunition for a full frontal."

Sally had gone pale at the thought of another "Iwo Jima' and burst into the 'war room' conversation.

"You mean a fire fight, like the stuff you see in the movies?"

"Calm down Sally." Bill cut her short. "That's conjecture. Tomorrow we'll move base camp and keep them guessing, besides Chuck here is an excellent marksman."

Chuck was back on the binoculars.

"You're not gonna believe this! The new crew are all dressed in Japanese World War II jungle fatigues, standing in columns of three with Shendo out in front, his Samurai sword drawn it's like some kind of departing ceremony. There's even a guy raising the Japanese 'rising sun'. Now they are all bowing as the plane begins its ramp up down the runway." Chuck was shaking his head in disbelief. *"It's like the fucking Kami Kasi farewell ceremony!"*

This was Chuck at his best and as for Bill...? *Well...* He just grinned, he could now clearly see the red glow of the four turbo fans as the pilot opened the throttle to gain maximum thrust.

"Well, we won't see that baby again for another six weeks, so let's settle down for the night. Chuck, I'll take first watch...."

SUNDAY MORNING

Shendo tossed and turned in his cot, he had had a restless night, his troubled thoughts keeping him awake and he was more than glad to see the dawn break. It had just turned 7:00am and Kenichi threw his feet to the floor. Breakfast was at eight and he still had to shower and dress. Tahoka would be here shortly with his newly pressed uniform and green tea. Japanese pride themselves to smartly dress as an example to other ranks.

(Speaking in Japanese)

There was a loud knock on the galvanized steel door. Shendo, unlike the rest of the crew, being the 'Suzuki Kacho' or big boss had his own private quarters, a luxury for the special few.

"Hai... Hairu." Okio knew who it was without thinking. Tahoka was one of his most loyal staff.

"Ohayo Gozaimasu... Kacho I have you your uniform freshly pressed." He held up the battle dress on the hanger.

"Arigato... Place uniform in robe." Kenichi pointed. "I'll meet you at breakfast in thirty minutes."

Kazuo bowed. "Yes Kacho." Then quickly turned and left.

Shendo gave a shiver as he stood naked in the cold shower. *"Brrrrr... Cold."* The soap was difficult to lather. It would be another six months before he would be relieved by his opposite number and he could only dream of the comforts of home and his beautiful wife. But he had more important things on his mind than self-indulgence. He had to contact Numero, the "Godfather". Last night it was too late after the transporter departed at 22:00hrs. Although there was no time difference between Shimaru Shima and Tokyo it would be impossible to contact Numero in a Karaoke supper club using the radio phone, besides he would have already been contacted that the transfer of the

US currency had gone without a hitch as the Kawasaki C-2 freighter would have landed safely at Tokushima. His problem now was how he would break the news of the prisoner's escape with as little collateral damage as possible and worse still, the loss of one of his men? He would phone as soon as breakfast was over and once he had designated the work party's schedule for the day.

* * *

Salibe wearily joined Shendo, Tahoka and Arakida at their breakfast table in the mess hall. It had just gone 8:30 with the workday about to begin

The two-henchman looked up momentarily stopping their repulsive slurping noise from the noodle indulgence waiting for their boss to make some sort of unwelcome comment.

Disappointedly Shendo pointed in silence to the empty seat his facial expression would scare the shit out of a zombie. The body guards shrugged then returned to the task of slurping their Natto and Noodle mix, their lips enveloping the bowls whilst Shendo was pre-occupied sipping his miso soup accompanied with boiled rice, Tamagoyaki and green tea.

Salibe didn't need a fortune teller to inform him he was unwelcome, but he had some unfished business with Namura regarding the shipment and he needed Shendo's Motorola to make contact. He poured the green tea then plucked up courage.

"Shendo." Salibe took a sip then paused. "I need to speak to Namura urgently, will you be contacting him this morning?"

Kenichi swallowed the loaded chop sticks of boiled rice and stared into Salibe's eyes his bewildered look conveying his poor understanding of English.

"Tahoka?" Commanding a translation.

"Salibe wa kinkyu Namura suru hanashi o suruhitsuyogaru no o yu wa kesa kara ni remarku o saru u irk?"

"Understand now... Shendo phone shortly after taberu... You understand meaning.... *Breakfast!*"

Salibe nodded, he had no option, he would have to stick to this guy like glue as he couldn't trust Shendo as far as he could throw him. He would have loved to ask Kenichi about the prisoner's escape but first things first.

Kenichi took his time before finally extracting the Motorola from his tunic pocket. Salibe hadn't eaten a thing, hunger the last thing on his mind......

* * *

(Speaking in Japanese)

Numero was running late cursing the traffic as he entered his office brushing past Ayako who rose to greet him. The two replacement bodyguards standing at each side of his office door bowing in respect, completely ignored.

Still cursing Okio opened his Versace leather briefcase, removed a bundle of papers and placed them on his desk before crashing down hard with a satisfied groan in his exec chair. First things first he lifted the secretarial phone but before he could utter a word Ayako answered.

"Your tea is on its way, 'Bosu'."

Okio grinned, secretaries such as Ayako are impossible to find let alone willing to give up their weekend.

Numero would normally never go to the office on a Sunday but having the shipment of money now on Japanese soil, he had a major challenge on his hands to disperse such a huge amount of US currency throughout the Yakuza empire and numerous overseas banking facilities and especially Columbia the heart of the cocaine trade.

"Arigato..." His special brand of green tea would hopefully calm his nerves and make him think straight.

That dainty knock could only be that of Ayaka.

"Hairu." Okio barked as he frustratedly searched below the desk for the secret button that would electronically release the lock to the hidden compartment containing his lap top.

Ayako entered balancing the green jade fired ceramic tea pot and matching cup on the colorful wooden lacquered tray.

Okio was too busy booting his lap top to say, 'thank you' his head down, rudely pointing to the free space on his desk. Ayako bowed then promptly left. When her boss is in this mood, it's prudent to be scarce.

* * *

Numero would firstly have to deposit large sums of hard cash through Japanese banks controlled by senior Yakuza officials then electronically sent overseas. No small task this would take intricate planning to avoid attention from the Public Security Intelligence Agency for possible money laundering and Okio planned to meet tomorrow morning with the Yakuza accountants.

* * *

He entered his pin then opened the file.

"Hmmm... Here we are... Now let's see?"

The sudden vibration coming from the locked drawer on the right-hand side of his desk where he kept the Motorola HF radio phone distracted his attention.

"What the...? Must be Shendo." Okio hastily stopped what he was doing and quickly searched for the key. When Shendo phones it's important and he switched on the phone placing it against his ear.

"Ohayo Gozaimasu, Bosu."

"Shendo if it's about the shipment, *well done!* I was just about to phone you, I have a plan that I need you to address as a matter of urgency."

"When?" Shendo was taken aback, he had been cut short and the thought of reporting the 'prisoner escape' was obstructing his brain.

"Like today!"

"But Bosu?"

"Don't interrupt and just listen... *Wakaru?"*

"Yes, I understand." Shendo nervously replied, not knowing what surprise was in the pipeline.

"At all costs, we must keep the location of Shimaru Shima hidden from the world. It is the life blood of Yakuza's financial survival and the source of income from our worldwide cocaine trade."

"Yes Bosu."

"Shendo, did I ask you to speak?" There was a pregnant pause.

"Good, now listen carefully. A Boeing 777 jet liner is difficult to make disappear and with the latest aerial surveillance technology it could be sayonara unless we do something immediately. Camouflaged is one thing but time is another and we cannot afford to take unnecessary risks. But how do we make a plane of that size vanish? Well, we turn it into a real 'Air Crash Investigation'."

"But..."

"Shendo, for the last time...! Now here's where I'm coming from. Let's start with the relief crew. On the manpower role, you will see two names... Akita Wattori and Hianori Itami, both in their mid-fifties... Retired commercial pilots having flown Boeing 737's and Airbus 320's, for ANA and JAL. They are ex-pilots from the Air Defense Force flying Mitsubishi F15J fighters, so their Curriculum Vitae is unquestionable. So why these two Yakuza soldiers? Firstly, they hate Americans. Both born in Hiroshima, their grandparents survived "Little Boy" detonated on august 6th 1945 but suffered unspeakable burns and eventually died as the result of radiation cancer. Their siblings and

ultimately their wives have all met with the same fate and they feel they now have nothing to live for except for serving our once great country and the Yakuza... Now Kinichi, *you can speak!*"

"So, what has this got to do with making a Boeing 777 vanish?"

"They have both volunteered to be become Yakuza 'Cami Kasi's'."

There was prolonged silence as Kenichi struggled to make sense of Okio's 'bit plan'.

"You mean...?"

"Exactly...! They will fly the 777 under the cover of darkness to the GPS coordinates where the plane disappeared from radar and plunge the plane into the sea within a five-kilometer radius of the official crash site. The wreckage will be discovered some time tomorrow by the air sea and rescue operators."

"But the pilots...? I mean, their bodies and DNA?"

"Don't worry, I've thought of that. Here's the smart part... They will both be wearing suicide vests strapped to their chests using C4 military grade explosives that will blow their bodies and the cockpit into a million pieces and one more terrorist attack against the US."

"And the money?"

"That's for another day and another 'Aircraft Investigation's, unsolved mystery."

"Bosu, forgive me but when do you intend I implement this plan?"

"Tonight! Contact Wattori and Itami after this call and immediately prepare the plane for take-off at midnight. Why midnight? Because that's when there is least air traffic in the Japanese corridor."

Shendo paused for a moment, Okio shoots from the hip with no technical knowledge of the titanic task of flying such a large jet from a mocked up temporary runway.

"Kenichi are you with me?" Okio was becoming agitated, his plan had to succeed at all costs and Shendo's silence was worrying.

"Well?" Numero asked.

"Numero San. Dozo let me speak." Kinichi had that rebellious tone in his voice and to challenge his boss was not for the faint.

"I'm waiting!"

Shendo nervously began. "When the construction crew extended the runway, if I can humbly refresh your memory, a Boeing 777 requires a minimum length of 8,100ft to land and 11,200ft for take-off."

"Get to the fucking point, *Shendo!*"

"The bad news is the runway has only a total length of 10,900ft... 300ft short!"

Now for a change Okio was in silence, he could vaguely remember the discussion but 'apology' was not in the Yakuza's vocabulary.

"Shendo... *Your problem...* Just get the fucking job done, *that's an order. I want that plane to be airborne by 2400:00hrs tonight... Wakaru?"*

"Yes Bosu." Shendo shrugged, there was no point continuing this conversation, besides, he still had to approach Okio on the prisoner's escape and worse still, *the death of a Yakuza!*

"Now, if there's no other bad news..."

"Eh... Okio San..."

"What now... I'm busy so make it brief."

"We lost one of our men... Hachiro Hokama."

"What the hell do you mean we lost one of our men?"

"The American prisoners escaped yesterday evening during dinner, killing the guard."

"Shendo, I hope I am not hearing right for your sake."

"Somehow Steven's, the first officer, managed to confuse and overpower Hokama before stabbing him to death with his own bayonet and retrieving the keys to open the door allowing the captain and the girl to escape into the jungle. When the alarm was raised it was all too late."

Numero leaned forward placing his brow in his hand, his elbow on the desk, this all he needed. *What the fuck now?*

"Don't tell me they're still at large! I told you to get rid of them *after* they landed."

"I had other priorities and besides another day wouldn't matter as we had to call off the search when the relief plane landed to make sure the transporter left on time with the passengers and cargo."

"Are they armed, or is that a stupid question?"

"They have the guard's rifle and ammunition."

"Shendo, you had better find these people and this time do as I tell you. You will call me again tomorrow with the good news or you had better use your Samara short sword and do the honorable... I've had enough for one day so..."

"Bosu... One moment the Arab wants to speak to you."

"Tell him..."

"But Bosu he insists..."

"Okay, okay, but tell him to make it short..."

(Speaking in English)

"Good morning Numero San."

"Cut the formalities Salibe I'm a busy man so get to the point."

"The money... You have 10bilion US that Hamas needs urgently. The deal was, you would electronically transfer the funds to our banks as soon as possible and I need to know when you intend to keep your part of the bargain."

"Just what are you insinuating!" Okio almost blew his top. "When Yakuza makes an agreement, we are men of honor. Your cause is meaningless to me. You want to kill one another that's your problem. You have Yakuza guarantee that the funds will be transferred to the banks of your choice within two weeks as I have more pressing priorities. I will pass you to my secretary Ayako, to give her the details. Now, if you are happy or unhappy I'm not interested just remember you are in no position to make demands. Now I'm busy...?"

(Speaking in Japanese)

Okio lifted the phone. "Ayako please come in and take this call and fetch your notepad......."

* * *

Salibe began. "Ayako the banks are....

Arab Islamic Bank... Account number... AB 760........

Salibe returned the phone to Shendo, both their faces reflecting the stress.

Different horses for different courses, their problems had only just begun.......

* * *

Shendo was in a trance his penetrating Asian eyes staring blankly at Salibe, making the Arab feel more than uncomfortable, the recent phone discussion with Numero clouding his brain.

"Kenichi, is there anything else you want to tell me?" Salibe had to break the trance.

Showing no emotion Shendo rudely waved his hand. *"Ikimasu"*

"You rude bastard! I gather that means get outta of my face?"

Shendo's eyes narrowed, maybe he understood or maybe he didn't, if not, it was just as well.

Salibe jumped to his feet displaying his anger by throwing his cup aside its remains spraying the air. He had had enough of this Japanese arrogance and gave Shendo a contemptible eyeball but Kenichi was unperturbed and just shrugged it off. He had no love for the Arabs or their cause, besides he had more important things on his mind with the latest orders from Numero. The inference from his boss... '*Succeed, or the short sword and Seppuku*'!

As Salibe stormed out of the mess hall Shendo was already giving orders to Tahoka.

(Speaking in Japanese)

"Tahoka, get me Genzo Hattori the replacement chief engineer."

"*Hi,* Shendo San." Tahoka gave a slight bow then hastily exited the mess hall, his first stop the maintenance hangar.

Shendo sat drumming his fingers on the table his impatience showing. His first challenge was how to turn the Boeing 777 around for takeoff would be a formidable task requiring engineering ingenuity but was Hattori up to it? The jetliner's nose almost in the jungle after using the full length of the runway.

Within minutes Hattori was standing facing his boss with the usual protocol bow.

"Ohayogozaimasu, Shendo San... Ogenkidesuka?"

"Domo." Shendo replied his beady eyes narrowing as he sized up the chief engineer, a clean shaven young man in his early thirties. He looked intelligent but then what does looking intelligent really look like?

"Suwarimusu." (sit) Okio pointed to the chair. Hattori nervously pulling out the chair in front of the breakfast table. Shendo had a reputation of bigotry and intolerance and Genzo hesitantly took his seat not knowing what to expect when the big 'Bosu' summons you.

Shendo began. "I have received instructions from Numero that the Boeing 777, you probably noticed sitting at the end of the runway, must fly to a predetermined location departing from Shimaru Shima at midnight tonight. I'll give you one hour to come back and tell me how you are going to achieve this and what recourses and materials you need to meet the deadline.

"*Hai,* I will be back within the hour, sumimasen." He bowed again and left.

"Tahoka... Arakida.... Suwarimusu."

"*Hai,* Shendo, San." They bowed and took their seats.

Shendo sat back and poured a fresh cup of tea then stared for a moment. He was a good officer with a bright mind and his men respected him but now his comfortable position as commander of the island was being challenged and he had a fight on two fronts.

"Tahoka, I'm putting you in charge of operation 'Datsugoku" (prison break) The Americans are somewhere hiding in the heavy volcanic terrain. They are armed and dangerous and could seriously disrupt our operations. My orders from headquarters are to take no prisoners. Wakaru?" (understand)

"Hai."

"I suggest you take six men with supplies fully armed with rifles and ammunition and the 96-light machine gun. Select your best snipers. I want body bag pictures to send to Namura as proof operation 'Datsugoku' is expired."

"Hai."

"Come back and report to me within the hour on your plan on how to proceed."

The two body guards bowed then left. Ascending the mountainous terrain in this humid tropical temperature would be challenge by itself, not to mention that the Americans were on the high ground and had the tactical advantage....

*　*　*

Shendo rose to stretch his legs, sitting drinking green tea was not is past-time. He glanced at his watch. "Where is that bloody chief engineer of mine?"

Okio's office was only five minutes from the mess hall and more to the point it was air-conditioned, a privilege for the higher ranks.

As he walked to his office he turned to study the giant Boeing 777 standing stationary at the end of the runway. *It was big alright*, Okio thought to himself, how to turn that beast around he could only imagine?

"Ah, there he is and not before time!" Kenichi spoke out loud upon seeing Hattori legging it towards his office. He would take another five minutes to reach and Okio opened the door of his 'sanctuary', walked to his desk and took his seat. Now, he could relax in the 20-degree temperature. No sooner had he settled in when there was a loud knock on the door, it could only be Hattori.

"Hairu." (enter)

Genzo's face was flushed, heavy sweat patches showing on the armpits of his fatigues. He removed his cap and wiped his forehead with his handkerchief. Shendo pointed to the empty chair.

"Dozo."

Hattori bowed and took his seat.

"Genzo, I hope you bring good news?" Shendo enquired with a touch of sarcasm.

Hattori glanced at the sheet of paper he had placed on Shendo's desk containing his notes then paused for a moment trying to find the place to start.

"*Well,* have you lost your tongue 'O toko'?" (man)

"No Bosu, I will try and explain to you in non-technical terms how we can turn the jet 180 degrees for takeoff."

"*I'm waiting.*"

"First of all, the runway is only 100 meters wide with little or no margin of error for that jet to land. The American is a good pilot."

"*Okay... Okay...* Tell me something I don't know."

"The wing span is 74 meters and the jungle on either side of the runway has been sufficiently cleared to compensate but the problem is the length of the fuselage."

"So, *get to the point!*"

"If we take the nose wheels as the radius point and the length of the fuselage is 74.5 meters we need a minimum of 150 meters diameter to turn that plane around 180 degrees and the bad news is we only have 100 meters."

"Cut the drama and tell me how you're going to fix it?"

"There's only one way and that's to increase the width of the runway by 25 to 30 meters on either side by an extension of at least 80 meters length for margin of error. That means I'll need two heavy excavators with rock breaking nibblers, two backhoes and a grader and a work crew of at least twenty men."

"*Hmmm...*" Shendo rubbed his chin his mind reflecting on the inventory of the heavy construction equipment they had on base. "Let me think, the existing runway was constructed out of raw jungle and volcanic rock and if my memory serves me right we have all the heavy equipment you require. As for the work crew, check with the site supervisor to provide the manpower you require you have my authority. Now most importantly how long will this take?"

Genzo glanced at his notes. "That's a tough call Bosu, but my best gestimate would be 12 to 14 hours if all goes to plan."

"Then don't waste any more time. Is there anything else?"

"Yes, as a matter of fact there is... The plane will need to be pushed back at least 80 meters for turning taking into account the length of the fuselage also we will need to start up the engines to use the hydraulics to turn the nose wheels and undercarriage."

"Don't worry about that, that's my problem. Join me at lunch and update me on your progress...."

* * *

Seconds after the door closed there was a further knock.

"Hairu." Shendo barked, his mood not the best, to make it worse he still had the funeral to take place for the deceased guard Isamu Gado killed in the line of duty. His rough wooden coffin had been placed in the large refrigeration container and with the plane problem and prisoner escape, just what more could go wrong? He had already written a letter to Gado's wife and dispatched it on yesterday's flight.

Tahoka an Arakida entered then bowed.

"Reporting back Bosu." Tahoka stood waiting for his boss's reaction.

Shendo sat in silence his mind racing. From a controlled and normally unexciting environment now to absolute fucking chaos.

"Bosu?" Tahoka repeated anxiously.

"Eh... Err...Yes...Yes?" Okio was back in business.

"I have selected the men for 'Datsugoku" and we are ready for your instructions, San."

"Hmmmm...." Shendo stared blankly into space. For a moment. he was torn between the devil and the deep blue sea. He needed all the men he could muster to expand the runway to meet the deadline for the midnight flight. Then, there was Gado's funeral and the final thorn in his flesh... *The three Americans!*

"Tahoka, a change of plans. Instructions have come from Tokyo that the 777 must leave the Island by 2400hrs tonight. I'll enlighten you later as to Numero's decision. This requires a major expansion to the runway and Chief Engineer Hattori, will need every man he can muster. So, I have decided to delay operation 'Datsugoku" until first light tomorrow morning."

"Hai."

"Now... Of immediate importance, our funeral customs must respect the death of Isamu Gado killed in the line of duty, a brave samurai and Yakuza soldier. Tahoka, use your men to organize a funeral pile for the cremation at 2pm today. The six men you selected will also be the guard of honor. Our Buddhist priest will perform the ceremony and the traditional bone picking to return the casket to his wife and family on the next flight and oh... Get the Shimaru Shima supervisor."

"Hai."

Tahoka and Arakida bowed, the message was loud and clear as for the plane's departure? *He who dares.......!*

* * *

Things were at last coming together and Shendo felt more comfortable but one mountain is always taller than the other and good noodles depends on the chef. He had the team and now he must show strong leadership for the respect of his men.

The loud knock on the door distracted him for a moment. Today was busier than a doctor's surgery and Kenichi had to stop the bleeding man.

"Hairu."

The tall 'nihon no otoko' in his mid-thirties dressed in jungle fatigues and field cap complete with gold star, bowed.

"Jiro Adachi at your service Bosu."

Kenichi sat back running his fingers through his hair before giving a pronounced sigh. *It had been one of these days and it wasn't over yet!*

"We have been given instructions from Tokyo to make the Boeing 777 disappear."

"Disappear?"

"You heard me!" Kenichi was in a foul mood and explanations were not on his agenda. "To turn the Boeing 180 degrees for takeoff the runway needs both widened and extended."

"For takeoff?" Jiro couldn't help himself begging the question.

"Adachi, hold your tongue and let me finish." Kenichi was losing it. *"Now again..."* Kenichi sighed. "To achieve this miracle before 2200hrs, Hattori our chief engineer, will need every man available from your construction crew including heavy earth moving equipment. When we finish, this meeting contact him immediately to provide him with all the support he needs. Now secondly, Isamu Gado who gave his life in the line of duty will be cremated at two today. That means a funeral pile and a six-man guard of honor. He is a hero and deserves full military honors. Contact our Buddhist mister to perform the ceremony and bone picking. *Now...*" Kenichi sighed again searching for a breathing space. "Adachi, unless you have any questions I suggest you get out of my sight as time is not on your side... *Well?"*

Adachi didn't need a second prompt, bowed, then about turned and left. To fail was not a word in the Yakuza vocabulary and he wasn't going to be the sacrificial lamb........

* * *

"Maaan... Am I stiff! My bones feel as if rigger mortice has set in and *boy,* do I need a drink!"

Bill was sitting on the damp palm leaves rubbing his knees, his eyes bagged from lack of sleep, his mouth parched. Chuck was last on watch and with dawn now here and a clear horizon, he was glued to the 'opera' binoculars.

"What's new Chuck?" Bill asked."

"I don't know. There's something big going on, whatever, we'll just have to wait and see."

Bill turned to check on Sally only to find the bird had flown.

"Chuck, where's Sally gone?"

"Doing what comes naturally... *I guess?"*

"Christ Chuck, I told you to keep an eye on her."

"Come on Bill, do you expect me to do 'toilet watch' as well?"

Bill couldn't help but smile at Chuck's comment, he could just imagine Sally's reaction.

"Did I hear my name mentioned in vain?" It was Sally returning from her ablutions.

Bill was glad to hear her voice but also partly annoyed that she didn't obey his orders to always inform he or Chuck when she ventured into the jungle, for whatever.

"Sally how many times do I have to stress..."

Sally cut him to the bone. "Oh, don't go on like an old woman Bill, I'm, here aren't I?"

"Eeeeh... Women!" Bill just shook his head, it was a lost cause besides he had other more important things on his mind, like food water and an escape plan.

"Sally we've got to work together as a team if we want to get off the godforsaken piece of rock alive."

"Huh!" Sally shrugged nonchalant. "Well captain, what do you suggest?"

"Firstly, the less sarcasm the better and sustenance like food and water."

"Then I'm still in the galley, huh? Like a woman's work is never done!"

"Awe, come on Sally, get that monkey off your back." Bill was becoming more than annoyed.

"Okay so what have we got?" Sally opened the large palm leaf, the temporary refrigerator. "Two spoons of rice each, which if we don't eat now we'll have to feed to the birds and..." She counted the bottles of water. "Eight liters left... So, bon appetite Monsieur's, who wants breakfast first......?"

* * *

"Compliments to the chef." Chuck washed down the stale rice with his miserly water ration

As for Sally, she finally cracked a smile but Chuck's humor would get him no place, she had a long memory and womanizing was not her scene.

"Well, at least there's no dishes to wash." Sally commented back in it.

"Let's take a step back and count to five." Bill interrupted the semi hostile breakfast scene. "We have a lot of brainpower between the three of us, so let's not waste it with petty squabbles. *Now*, most importantly liquid gold...*Water!* Food we can survive without for long periods but water we can't. Dehydration especially in a tropical climate can cause kidney, liver and ultimately brain damage. Remember our bodies contain two thirds water. So, what do we know...? This is a volcanic island with lava soil. Just look around us, there's greenery and thick jungle foliage everywhere. Plants can't live without water although some need less than others and because of the humid climate we assume this island is in the monsoon belt, *so there must be water somewhere?*"

"I agree with you Bill, but it must be in scarce supply and not enough to harness and satisfy a small battalion of over sixty men with their everyday needs, hence the need for a desalination plant." Chuck was with it.

"Yes, that point had crossed my mind but then let's look at it this way... Gravity forces water to the lowest level and we are about 50 meters higher than the runway so let's start by digging around some of these large palms......"

* * *

"Welcome to Shimaru Shima." It was unusual for Shendo to bow, greeting two members of his crew. But then, Akita Wattori and Hianori Itami were special Samurais, willing to give their lives for the honor of their country and the Yakuza......

* * *

Both in their mid-fifties they looked lean and remarkably fit. Wearing their white Hachimaki head bands with the rising sun motifs, a symbol of perseverance and courage, proudly worn by Kamikaze pilots in the last throws of world war II to destroy American moral and inflict maximum damage on the US fleet.

After the fall of Saipan in July 1944 Admiral Takijiro Onishi commander of the 'First Air Fleet' in the Philippines, created a 'Special Attack Group' of suiciding dive bombing pilots known as Kamikazes. Young men inspired to volunteer wishing to die for their country. Pilots were trained in just over one week to fly their modified Mitsubishi A6M Fighters. The first Kamikaze attack on US worships taking place in 1944, from the Philippine's.

During April of that year Kamikaze pilots under Admiral Soema Toyoda launched 1,400 suicide missions as part of operation 'Ten Go' with suicide pitot's sinking 26 US navy ships during the campaign.

More than 2,000 Kamikaze missions were also flown against the US fleet at Okinawa from April to July in 1945.

Kamikazes pilots continued to be active until the dropping of the Atom Bombs on Hiroshima and Nagasaki. Admiral Takijiro Onishi, the commander of the 'Special Attack Group', committed suicide when he heard that Emperor Herohito had surrendered.

* * *

"Domo Arigatou gozaimasu." They replied in tandem.

Shendo began. "I have instructed Jiro Adachi, my site supervisor to provide you with special air-conditioned quarters restricted for high ranking Yakuza Commanders and of course anything else you need within reason to make the remainder of your short stay as comfortable as possible."

"Hai." They both gave a slight bow.

"Now, before you return to your quarters." Kenichi began. "I'm sure Numero San briefed you on the plan to destroy the Jetliner and I just want to make doubly sure you have the GPS coordinates for the fatal crash and of course the crucial 'suicide vests'?"

"Hai... Biggubosu... As for our vests...?" Itami immediately replied. "They are safely stored in a bomb proof 2-inch-thick stainless-steel container stored in the Ordinance hanger. Be assured Bosu the best bomb team in the Yakuza constructed the vests with failsafe detonators that can only be activated by both index fingers at the same time."

"Hmmm..." Shendo although satisfied with the answer, one can never be too cautious when it comes to explosives and he paused for a moment.

"The Yakuza and Japan will always be in your debt and..." Kenichi glanced at his watch. "I suggest you return to your quarters to rest. There will be a funeral ceremony at 2pm today and as a matter of honor I expect you to attend."

"Bosu, would it be dishonorable to enquire who is the deceased?" Wattori asked guardedly."

"Isamu Gado, a brave Samurai who was murdered in cold blood by the American prisoners during their escape."

"Americans!" Wattori was taken aback."

"Yes, and be assured, they will pay the ultimate price."

"Of course, the pilots of the Boeing 777!" The penny had dropped.

"Now I have a very busy day ahead of me, it would be my pleasure that your join me for lunch in the mess hall at 12:30."

"Hai......"

* * *

THE MEETING

Part 1

Gregg had had a restless night, what with the noisy air-conditioning and the late night 'will you still love me tomorrow' phone call to Michelle. Self-inflicted wounds...? Torn between two lovers...? Whatever, when the 7:30 am buzzer released its agony Gregg would have preferred to cock his firearm and blow that fucking electronic clock to pieces and he groaned turning on his side to switch on the bedside lamp and turn off that God-forsaken noise.

"Hmmmm... That's better." He spoke aloud whilst momentarily shielding his eyes from the sudden brightness. No doubt Steve would be on the blower soon asking about breakfast and food was the last thing on his mind.

"Wouldn't it be something this morning to have a lay- in and fuck the world?" The thought made Gregg smile.

"Awe, what the hell another half an hour, huh!" Gregg dug his head into the soft pillow......

* * *

Steve had finished the 'so called' English breakfast and nine o'clock had come and gone.

"Where the hell is that partner of mine?" He impatiently glanced at his watch shaking his head.

"Simusan." Steve called the waiter.

"Sir?"

"Can you fetch me a phone I need to make a call to a guest room?"

"Certainly sir."

Within seconds the young waiter returned with a cordless receiver.

"Thank you... How do I connect to a room?"

"Dial zero sir then the room number."

"Let me see... 0...4..." Steve pushed the buttons.

Gregg was in another world, was it with Michelle or Marge? Maybe he liked twosomes or was it just self-indulgence?

"What the hell!" He sat bolt upright, the phone decibels sounding like thunder.

"Yeah, Jonson here?"

"Where the hell are you...? Do you know the time!"

"I think I'm educated enough to read a clock... So why the drama... I told you last night I wasn't interested in breakfast."

"You haven't forgotten our meeting today with Global even though it's Sunday."

"I'm not that love sick if that's where you're coming from?"

"Give it away Gregg, don't put words into my mouth. Listen, the venue has been changed to Narita but still at the same time 2pm, McGill just phoned."

"We still have plenty of time, what's the big deal?"

"Well, for a starter it will take us well over an hour to get to the airport."

"Okay... Okay, you've made your point. I'm heading for the shower right now."

"I'll be up in around fifteen minutes to raid your minibar once I finish my coffee and sign the check."

"Take your time unless you want to see a streaker cross the room."

"Don't put me off my breakfast the food was bad enough... See you."

Gregg had to smile they had been friends since kids and as for Steve...? *He'll never change......*

* * *

Gregg had just finished showering and still in his bathrobe when the doorbell chimed.

"Shit, that must be Steve and I haven't even shaved yet." Gregg shook his head as he walked to the door.

"That's a long shower, what have *you* been doing?"

"Get out of it! Go grab yourself a drink while I shave and get dressed."

Gregg disappeared into the bathroom his voice echoing behind.

"Why not?"

Steve poured himself a miniature Scotch and bombed a couple of cubes from the ice bucket into the amber liquid.

"I hate these stupid little bottles." Steve commented as he made a basketball throw toward the waste bin.' "Not bad!" The sudden noise startling Gregg.

"*What the hell was that?*" Gregg called.

"Just a little basketball practice, never mind, just you concentrate on getting ready. I'll keep myself occupied watching CNN." Steve grabbed the remote and switched on the "box" …..

* * *

"*This is CNN with the world's latest international and domestic news, Trevor McDonald reporting….*

"*The loss of Global 10 a Boeing 777 freighter enroot from Narita airport Japan to Washington DC on Friday Jane 14 still remains an aircraft investigation mystery. The plane was lost from radar one hour into its flight over the North Pacific. Japanese search and rescue have so far found no debris of any description over a ten-kilometer radius. The mystery remains as to its cargo as the US and Japanese Governments have stressed the information as classified. The plane went down with three crew…. Now on the home front….*"

* * *

Steve just shrugged and switched the TV off. It was depressing enough to be on the case without CNN rubbing it in!

"How's the time going partner?" Gregg was knotting his tie.

"What did you say, 'you are educated enough to read the clock'."

"Get off my street you Moran, it's nearly twelve, I'll fetch my jacket and hardware." Gregg slipped the Glock into his shoulder holster but not before checking the safety.

"So, you're not going to join your bro for one for the road?"

"It's too early for me man, besides I might need a piss on the long drive."

"Thanks partner that reminds me, I'll better go empty my bladder before we leave……"

* * *

"Narita International Airport."

"Hai." The taxi driver replied pressing the meter button before slipping into the midday traffic.

The Toyota Crown was comfortable with freshly starched white seat covers and a pleasant violet deodorant. Steve pulled the rear seat arm rest down and settled in for the 72-kilometer journey.

"We might as well make ourselves comfortable, huh?" Steve commented removing his jacket unintentionally exposing the holstered Glock. The cab driver looking into his rear mirror went a pale shade of grey before signaling and pulling into the kerb breaking hard and raising both his arms.

"Gotos." (robbers) Yelling out loud.

"Shit, the cab driver thinks this is a heist!" Gregg turned to Steve pointing to his exposed Glock.

"Gregg what's the Japanese word for no... *Come on... Come on?*"

"How the hell do I know!"

"I think it's 'le' or something like that... *Le...Le...*" Steve yelled thrusting his CIA card into the petrified driver's face.

The driver studied the card with Steve's picture for a moment before patting his chest with his right hand the color returning to his complexion. He nodded and patted his chest once again as if to say, *'wow,* I *thought I was a goner,* before politely bowing and nervously slipping the cab into drive.

As the cab drove off Steve had to cover his mouth to avoid choking on his laughter.

"That's one for the book bro."

"Yeah." Gregg was also bursting his sides shaking his head at the same time. "That's a party peace......"

* * *

"How do you think this meeting is going to go?" Steve approached Gregg the drama over.

"It's anyone's guess. McGill is still convinced its pilot error or mechanical failure even though we've proved the opposite. He's just protecting his ass for a serious breach of security and Global's reputation. I mean a cargo of 100 billion US dollars destined for the Federal Reserve Washington DC, it doesn't get any worse."

"Yeah, I think it's gonna be another 'bad day at black rock'. The question is *where the hell has that plane gone,* it's not as if it's a Tiger Moth?"

Gregg stretched back to relax, closing his eyes "Well I know what I'm gonna do."

"And what's that?"

"Get my head down, nudge me when we reach the airport......"

* * *

The security check over and as usual the detainment of their firearms it was business as usual with the two the CIA agents legging it to Global's office. They were running thirty minutes early but then there's the old saying...

"How are you feeling now dude?" Steve was being sarcastic.

"I feel refreshed, you should have taken my advice partner. Listen changing the subject we're running a bit early but then maybe we can convince McGill's secretary. What's her name again?"

"Mitsuko."

"I got to hand it to you Steve when I comes to a pretty face you have a photographic memory."

"Are you kidding me?"

Gregg just ignored Steve's return fire, he was more interested in finding McGill's office.

"Now where the hell's is Global's office?" Gregg was becoming more than frustrated whilst squeezing through the passenger pack severely lacking basic good manners.

"Ah, there's the sign at the lift with a whole bunch of other airlines... Global Freight, Level 2."

The elevator chimed and Steve could clearly see the sign in gold leaf on the glass frosted door at the end of the passageway... J. McGill VP Global Freight. Gregg stepped it out and knocked on the door.

"Come in." Came the reply in crisp English.

"Good afternoon gentlemen." Mitsuko gave one of her 'knock out' smiles. "Mr. Nelson and Mr. Jonson, CIA if I'm correct." She smiled again. "You are a bit early and the other participants have yet to arrive. Jim is tied up on the phone and it might be some time before he is free but I'll let him know you are here. I think the best solution would be for you both to wait in the conference room over a cup of coffee."

"Sounds good to me Mitsuko." As usual, Steve was first past the post with Gregg just shaking his head......

* * *

The conference room was spacious bright and modern with a 12-seater glass topped mahogany table, an electronic white board, pads and pens and bottled water at each station and in this humid climate, most importantly, *air conditioning!*

"We might as well make ourselves comfortable huh?" Steve sat down heavily in the soft black leather cushioned chair. *"Hmmm... Comfortable."* But before he could further expand his line of conversation the conference room door opened.

"Your coffee gentleman." Mitsuko placed the small enameled tray on the conference table bearing two cups and a small coffee pot. "I'll leave you to it." She briefly smiled then left.

"A bit strong but good." Gregg commented on the first sip.

"Say, isn't that Mitsuko something! There's something about Japanese woman that fascinates me." Steve commented as he enjoyed the dark brew.

"Yeah, and I know what that something is!" Gregg was quick off the mark.

"Maaan... You always think..."

The conference room door opened. It was McGill with a bunch of other people, Caucasians and Japanese.

Steve and Gregg rose to their feet to greet him

"Jim." They shook hands.

McGill began. "Gentleman let me introduce you...This is Steve Nelson and Gregg Jonson both from the CIA. And... From Boeings Air Accident Investigation Branch, Senior Investigator Ted Anderson. Also in attendance Jack Truman, Senior Aeronautic Engineer from the US National Transportation Safety Board and representing the Japanese Aviation Authority, Hachiro Sakura and Narita Air Traffic Controller, Daichi Matsu, and of course you all know my secretary Mitsuko who will be taking the minutes of the meeting. Gentleman please take your seats."

* * *

"Okay, so what do we have?" McGill opened his notes.

1. Global 10's Boeing 777- 300 freighter disappeared from radar at approximately 0030hrs on July 15 enroot to Dulles Washington DC.
2. After 48 hours of intensive air search by the Japanese Search & Rescue Authority, covering a 10-kilometer radius in the North Pacific based upon the speed, the auto pilot and approximate distance the plane would have travelled, as yet no debris has been found. The JSRA will continue the search for another 48 hrs.
3. For the purpose of National Security, both the Unites States and the Japanese Governments have agreed not release to the media the contents of the cargo and subsequently each person at this meeting

must sign a confidentiality agreement before we adjourn. (Mitsuko passed out the forms)

4. The cargo was 100 billion US dollars destined for destruction at the Federal Reserve, Washington DC.

5. The aircraft was flown by Captain William Collins and First officer Charles Stevens, both experienced pilots and Navy veterans of Desert Storm. The other member of the crew is Sally Jenkins a flight attendant with Global for over two years. All have impeccable records.

6. Maxim security during the loading of the cargo was provided by airport Police with armored security trucks accompanied by Japan's SWAT. A further three security guards were provided as a safety harness to accompany the flight to Dulles International... Two Japanese from the 'Kovan Chousacho' and one US citizen from Black Hawk Securities. I should further stress, Global and the local Japanese equivalent to the FBI, 'The National Police Agency' gave their blessing after maximum security clearance."

7. Finally, there are four scenarios, technical failure, pilot error, a hijack by radical terrorists or a bomb.

McGill looked up from his notes then sat back sort of glad his fifteen was over. The heat was on him as VP, and the elephant was still in the room. He opened the small plastic bottle of so called 'spring water' filling his glass halfway before taking a generous sip. Satisfied, he stared down the table.

"As you have noticed there is a mixture of important agencies round this table from both the United States and Japan not to mention two agents from our own Central Intelligence Agency whom I'm sure will table their investigations. However, I think we should start with Ted Anderson from Boeing and Senior Aeronautic Engineer Jack Truman from the US National Transportation Safety Board... Ted..."

"Thanks Jim.... Whenever any of Boeings planes fall from the sky and may I just stop there for a moment to stress Boeing's impeccable safety record... There is always the possibility of technical failure. The 777 has a safety record second to none when considering freighters especially on long haul routes fly 24 hours around the clock under heavy loads. Please remember Jack and I only arrived from the US yesterday and the information we have so far is sketchy and as much as any of you know. I have already started to check the planes maintenance records and servicing history. Of course, I understand what immediately comes to your minds with the recent loss of Malaysian Airlines MH370 on March 8, 2014 over the Indian Ocean being a Boeing 777-200-ER, and still yet to be recovered... Also, remember Air France Flight 447 from Rio Janeiro was only found after two years of search and took three years to resolve... So only two days into the loss of Global 10 is a 'no brainer'...Ted"

"Thanks Jim... Normally the US National Transportation Safety Board doesn't get in involved in nondomestic air accidents but in this case because of a possible serious breach of National Security the President himself has directed our agency to file a report but like Ted I have little to contribute at this stage. Back to you Jim..."

"Sakura San from the Japanese Aviation Authority."

"Hai." Hachiro gave a slight bow. "Like my other two colleagues from the United States it is too early to make any judgements. Of course, the crash that immediately comes to my mind although it was well before my time was that of JAL 123 on Monday August 12, 1985. Just to refresh your memories it was a scheduled domestic flight from Tokyo Haneda Airport to Osaka international Airport operating a Boeing 747SR. The plane approximately 12 minutes after takeoff and at 24,000ft with an airspeed of 300knots, the aft bulk head ruptured causing decompression separating the vertical fin and the plane crashed resulting in Japan's worst air disaster with the loss of 524 passengers and crew. The 747 had only flown 23500hrs and 18500 landings. In this case, of course the cockpit voice recorder was recovered in tact so getting back to Ted's point it's early days but let's hear from Daichi Matsu, the Air Traffic Controller on duty that evening."

"Hai." The young man in his late twenties looked rather nervous and who wouldn't with this crew of heavies staring down your throat!

"Ah...*Hmmm*." Daichi cleared his throat.

Aviation law dictates English is compulsory for all Air Traffic Controllers, so in this department Matsu should have no problem.

Daichi began again a slight crack in his voice. "On the evening of July 14, I was on duty in the Control Tower at Narita International. Incoming traffic was extremely heavy and I instructed Captain Collins to taxi to runway 3B to await further instructions. Collins is an experienced pilot who knows the drill and the airport extremely well and he proceeded to position Global 10 as instructed. A British Airways 747-400... BA15 bound for Heathrow was parked on the same runway immediately in front of Global 10. Once BA15 had cleared takeoff and airborne, after approximately 15 minutes, I gave instructions to Captain Collins that the runway was now clear and gave permission to proceed for takeoff and climb to 15,000 feet then circle and await further instructions as a number of aircraft were still in holding patterns awaiting permission to land. After a further twenty minutes I gave Captain Collins the good news that their air path was now clear and Global 10 could now increase altitude to 32,000 ft. and continue its flightpath to Washington DC. My exact words were 'Bon Voyage Global 10, have a safe flight' Captain Collins replied… 'Thank you tower, signing out and goodnight'. I tracked the flight on Air Traffic Control Radar as normal with many other flights and of course Global 10 disappeared from the screen an hour into its air corridor. For some reason the transponder, an electronic device vitally important to identify the aircraft on Air Traffic Control Radar', was not responding but fortunately we had the plane's GPS which accurately pinpoints where the aircraft went down. I frantically tried to contact Global 10 with no success then fearing the worst I alerted my superiors and Air Search and Rescue."

Then Matsu stared blankly, emotion showing in his eyes, to lose a flight is a Controller's worst nightmare. Then after a few seconds which seemed like hours, Matsu finally composed himself and broke his silence.

"Unless there are any points you want me to clarify further then that's as much as I can accurately remember."

McGill took the heat off. "Matsu San, on behalf of Global I wish to thank you personally for attending this meeting as I believe you are still on sick leave… Steve… Gregg… Would you wish to continue…?"

Steve turned to Gregg. "I'll take it but anything that comes to your mind feel free."

"No sweat." Gregg replied happy to take a back seat.

Steve began. "Gentleman the CIA is involved in an ongoing investigation and as such there is only so much I can tell you except this is a 'Red Alert' which is a code one national security at the highest level. I'm sure it's no secret that we share intelligence with our counterparts worldwide and this one doesn't get any bigger all the way from the 'Commander in Chief' himself and of course to our director, John Brennan… Netanyahu, the Israeli Prime Minister has been blowing hot air into Obama's ear and our Director of Counter Intelligence John Thomson is working closely with Taman Pardo the Director of Shin Bet, Israel's Counter Intelligence. Their agents, or Mossads in Hebrew, have done some heavy detective work and three names were placed on high security alert with intent to commit a terrorist attack on Israel. When where and how we don't know. Now what has this got to do with Global 10 you may ask? *Money!* It's the worst kept secret that the terrorist group Hamas will never rest until they destroy Israel and kill every last Jew and recover the West Bank and Gaza and the world recognizes Palestine as a State. Three Arab Palestinians whose names for security reasons we cannot divulge are on Israel's most wanted list for terrorist activities. One a US citizen commanding a high position in the Department of Controller of Currency was arrested two days ago, with another two accomplices as part of a terrorist cell to defraud the US government and a threat to national security. They are currently awaiting trial. The other two both studied in the US at Cornell university graduating Aeronautics and Rocket Science. Not the everyday study stuff. Furthermore, they successfully gained commercial pilot licenses for large jets... Another 9/11...? *Doubtful...* We know from the Mossad Secret Service and special forces the 'Sayerat Matakal' that their father is none other than Abdul Fattah the number one commander of the armed wing of Hamas and on Shin Bet's most wanted list. Having expired their student visas, the FBI tracked them to Moscow staying at a five-star hotel all expenses met by the Russian MOD and a meeting with none other than Sergi Shoigu the Minster... During their stay, they split their time between the Russian Military of Defense and The Department of Aeronautics and Rocket Science on a so-called student exchange programme. From there they flew to Tokyo, Japan. They are smart covering their tracks but with one slip... Their meeting with 'Nippon Shipping & Logistics' in the famous Shin Marunouchi Building in the Shibuya business district of Tokyo, a legal entity which is a cover up for the Yakuza dealing in cocaine shipments from Columbia. This we know. The head honcho of the Yakuza is none other than the ruthless Okio Namura which the Government and Police have been trying unsuccessfully to put behind bars for the last decade. So now we have Hamas...The Russians and the Japanese Mafia, but what's the link? That's the 64,000-dollar question!"

McGill rather rudely interrupted. "Steve, this is becoming like a 'B grade' movie, just where the hell are you coming from?"

Steve was riled. *"Jim,* I'm trying to paint a picture with less than a thousand words, if you get my drift? So, I'm asking you and the other members at this meeting to bear with me, after all we're going no place on a 'never on a Sunday', huh?"

Steve's joke went down like a lead balloon and he quickly composed himself disappointed he hadn't drew a smither of laughter.

"Eh err... Now can I...?"

There was a pregnant silence.

"I gather that means affirmative..." Steve replied in sarcasm. "So okay, where was I?"

"The 'Bermuda Triangle'"

Gregg's comment brought the house down. Maybe it was the catalyst they all needed to lighten up.

"Thanks partner." Steve pouted his lips in 'a someone done me wrong song' inferring *'thanks for nothing'*.

"The bottom line...? I'll let you guys draw your own conclusions. So, we have a plane with a cargo of 100 Billion US dollars that has mysteriously disappeared from the sky. As for the Palestinian brothers on our most wanted list we have already established they stayed in The Palace Hotel, downtown Tokyo. One is deceased as the result of an altercation with an undercover FBI agent, unfortunately the agent lost his life as well an employee of the hotel. The remaining brother mysteriously escaped the police cordon and we are almost 100% certain he gained sanctuary with the Yakuza and that he is the US guard under the cloak of Black Hawk Securities. As for the other two Japanese guards of supposedly 'Kovan Chousacho' are members of the Japanese Mafia. Why can't we prove it? Because some person or person's unknown hacked into both McGill's security records and that of the Tokyo Police erasing all the information on these three men. Now it gets even worse... The data bank of US currency serial numbers for different denominations for destruction and printing at 'Fort Worth', believe it or not has been hacked. I can't go into the details of how it was done for obvious reasons and as for The Bank of Japan's foreign currency data bank... Do I need to finish this sentence? The US government fortunately will still honor the agreement to replace the currency. But what's the bottom line? It means 100 billion US dollars can be dispersed throughout the world with no recall. Can you imagine what this means in the wrong hands? Gentlemen whatever way you look at this there is no doubt in the CIA and FBI investigations that this points conclusively to a hijack. As they say in the legal fraternity... *My case rests....*"

Naturally after that marathon there was a few seconds' silence before McGill eventually broke the ice.

*"Eh... Hmmm...*Thanks Steve that's a lot to digest and thinking of digestion." Jim smiled. "My call is, it's time for a break... Mitsuko can you fetch the sandwiches that the cafeteria rustled up and a couple of pots of coffee? Get Emico to help you set up the table in the galley......."

* * *

KAMIKAZE.

"Yeah, your right Bill." Chuck had cut one of the plastic water bottles in half and was using it as a scoop energetically digging up the volcanic black soil.

"I'm the same here Chuck the soil is getting wetter and wetter and a black muddy reservoir of water is beginning to accumulate."

Sally, as usual, standing both hands on her hips a 'hole watcher' like council road workers but most importantly like all women refusing to ruin their precious painted nails.

"Don't tell me you're going to drink *that* black shit!"

"Sally, is that the best you can do? Stop criticizing and make yourself useful."

Woman or no woman, Bill was taking no crap.

"Are you pulling rank Captain?" Her sarcasm slicing the air.

"You bet your sweet ass I am!" Bill couldn't restrain his annoyance. *"Sally!* You are part of a team and although you're a female you need to pull your weight *and stop behaving like a spoiled brat!... Am I getting through?"*

"Yes," She gave that wounded soldier look. *"So...?"*

"Go cut these empty plastic bottles in half with that bayonet, we'll need to fill the bottom half with the soiled water."

"Then what?" Sally rudely asked on a 'bad day' roll.

"Pour the muddy water into the napkin you carried the food in then twist it into a ball and squeeze as hard as you can to filter out the volcanic soil into a clean half bottle. Don't worry Sally lava soil is used in household and commercial water filters, it's very safe. You might have to do it two or three times until the water is clear before carefully pouring it into an empty bottle then sealing it......."

* * *

"Four liters... Not bad Sally."

Bill studied one of the full bottles holding it up against the clear sky.

"Well done, slightly hazy but take it from me it's drinkable. Leave it overnight and any sediment will fall to the bottom."

"Just to prove it." Chuck as usual was adding fuel to the fire unscrewing the plastic top then taking a large swig. "Would be nice if it was chilled, huh?" He smiled.

Bill laughed. "Wishful thinking...Okay, now we know we can find water, our next challenge is *food!*"

"What's your thoughts Bill?" Chuck asked intrigued.

"Look at it this way. We're not gonna be eating protein that's for sure, so it's gotta be fruit."

"And?" Chuck was sitting on the palm leaf mattress his knees up to his chest leaning slightly back his hands supporting his back.

"Yeah, I'm interested Bill." Sally hadn't gotten over it just yet and Bill drew her a look.

"Well, if we take the Hawaiian Islands as an example they are basically big chunks of volcanic rock with the same soil as this hell hole. No rivers, tropical climate and they grow lots of wild fruit."

"Like what?" Sally just couldn't hold it.

"Sally." Bill turned and eyeballed her. "Lighten up for the sake of all of us. Now, where was I?... "Birds and winds carry seeds and water runs to the lowest level and we are relatively low here. So, my guess is we need to stick together and search the heavy tropical foliage around our so called 'base camp' and with a bit of luck well find the same fruits. Now Sally for your education there's a high probability that we'll come across, for example...Rambutan... Jack fruit, Lychees, Papaya and Mangosteens, to name but a few."

"I've never heard some of these." Sally was more subdued.

"Like most American citizens, Sally, that's not unusual, but let's take a break and get out of this midday sun. Chuck, get back on these binoculars and check out what's happening at the camp......"

* * *

Chuck lay stretched out on a bed of soft palm leaves, his elbows supporting the binoculars.

"Hmmm...There's a lot of stuff going on." He mumbled.

Bill and Sally had taken refuge under a large palm to escape the sun.

"Like what?" Bill was quick to ask... As for Sally... Well, she was still studying her nails.

"There's backhoes, excavators and scrapers ripping the shit out of the jungle at the end of the runway in some sort of giant circle around the 777."

"*What the hell!* Gimme these binoculars." Bill planked himself beside Chuck.

"*I'll be darned.*" Bill was adjusting the lenses to get a clearer view. "I wonder?" He pondered rubbing his chin. "And what's going on in the yard in front of the mess hall? Looks like they are building a mound of dried wood... Any suggestions?"

"Could be a funeral pile for that guard. Japanese are Buddhists and they cremate their dead."

"You mean they are cremating that poor guard and we have a ringside seat?"

"No one's asking you to watch Sally, that's if Chucks suggestion is on the money... But the extension of the runway around the plane *that's the kicker!*"

"Would it be a stupid suggestion... *Naw...*" Chuck screwed up his face.

"Chuck, in our predicament there's nothing stupid, so let's have it."

"I suggest that they are clearing the runway for enough space to do a 180 to turn the albatross for takeoff?"

Bill pouted his lips then rubbed his chin again, his brain traveling like the 'bullet train'. Chuck's suggestion was not so stupid but could he be right?

"That's not so stupid Chuck. It could be why the construction crew are excavating the runway in a huge circle around the plane to clear the wing span and the tail plane. But... There again why? And more to the point, who's gonna to fly that bad boy?"

"So how are we going to escape the island of they fly the plane?" Sally had come to life.

Bill rolled his eyes at Chuck as if to say, *'I give up'*.

"Sally, you have obviously not been listening... *Remember by boat! Does that ring a bell?*"

"*Eh...Err...*Now I remember, just too much on my mind." Sally shrugged it off.

But Chuck couldn't resist taking the shot. "Like looking after your nails."

Sally's eyes blazed and she shot back. "Chuck, that's the kinda shit I expect from you, it's no wander Marge gave you the big elbow."

"Guys... Guys... Cool it! The last thing we need is a civil war. Now, my suggestion is, as the 'posse' has been called off for obvious reasons, we join forces on a food expedition........"

* * *

Salibe swung his bared feet to the floor, then glanced at his watch. The body clock is an amazing phenomenon waking you up at the same time each morning. He looked up shaking his head at the antique ceiling fans resembling something salvaged from the Titanic, screaming in pain from worn bearings while uselessly circulating the humid air, in fact it was a tortured relief to get off that uncomfortable rope mattress.

Strange, Salibe thought to himself as he scanned the almost empty dormitory housing a crew of twenty.

"Must be something big today but at least I don't have to que in the communal shower room." Salibe forced a smile mumbling to himself as he stood up stretching his arms above his head, the automatic yawn part of the wakeup call.

The cold shower was invigorating in the humid climate and Salibe vigorously rubbed the poor excuse for a towel against his tingling body then quickly stepped into his jocks, jungle fatigues and open thongs.

As he stepped it out to the mess hall he couldn't help but notice the heavy construction machinery lined up... *but for what?*

"I'll approach Shendo at breakfast to ask what's going on. As usual he'll not be forthcoming but I guess that's nothing new."

Salibe was having his own conversation, being the only non-Japanese, not the most popular guy on the Shimaru Shima Campus' and more so, it seemed the 'Nihon no Otoko' grossly disliked Arabs.

Shendo was sitting at his usual table accompanied by his two henchmen Tahoka and Arakida and Salibe stood patiently in front of Shendo waiting for the invitation to join the 'gang of three', the only positive being Tahoka's grasp of English.

Kenichi rudely pointed to the empty seat unable to speak whilst slurping his noodles.

Suddenly the whole mess hall rose to their feet and bowed keeping their heads down including the Biggubosu. Salibe was taken by surprise *'like what now'?* You can never tell with the Japanese and he turned in the direction of the bowing soldiers. To Salibe's surprise two middle aged men dressed in jungle fatigues wearing white Hachimaki head bands portraying the rising sun entered the main door. They stopped for a moment standing rigid to attention to acknowledge the respect and in protocol gave a slight bow. The ceremony over, Shendo was back on the noodles and the mess hall in loud chatter as the 'special guests' were escorted to their table by the kitchen staff, a selection of food already prepared. But who were these men being treated like royalty... It was time to beg the question but first food.......!

* * *

Without further ado Salibe turned and walked to the servery and picked up his tray.

"If I see another bowl of miso soup, *I'll be fucking sick*... So, what other poison is on the menu today?" Salibe was talking out loud and maybe it was just as well the cook standing at the servery didn't understand English.

"Hmmmm..." Salibe sighed pointing to the selection.

Brown rice... Grilled Saba fish... Egg roll... And Oshinko pickles and of course the repulsive green tea. His tray full he returned to the 'top table' and took his seat. As normal no one took any notice being more interested in finishing their food or was it a hostile gesture toward an Arab, or both?"

"Tahoka, ask Bosu why the ceremony?"

(Speaking in Japanese)

Shendo looked up, unhappy that his breakfast was being disturbed, his steely blue eyes penetrating Salibe's making him feel decidedly uncomfortable. For Anbar to trust the Japanese when he is on the 'low ground' was not only dangerous, but stupid.

"Bosu...Arab ga shiritai naze core hodo juyona Dansei." Tahoka translated the English to Kinichi who threw his chopsticks down on the table displaying his anger then rattled off a string of Japanese whilst almost choking in the process, his temper turning his face a pale shade of red, the veins on his temples protruding.

"So, what did Bosu say?" Salibe asked.

"Bosu say Kamikaze... None of your business, enough said, do not disturb again."

Salibe sort of shrugged moving his head from side to the side, like I expected that, so there's no point asking about that lineup of heavy construction equipment. *"I might as well eat this shit and go back to the dormitory and relax.*

Worse still, he thought the Russian submarine would take twenty days to reach Shimaru Shima and that was even more depressing. Then to make it worse there is the further delay for the Japanese sub to arrive from Columbia with the monthly cocaine shipment and most probably taking another five bloody days. Salibe shook his head again... God, I miss my brother, a least if he was here we could share the shit together."

Then before Salibe could further dwell on his depressing thoughts Shendo and his henchmen abruptly rose from the table and left without saying another word.

"But Kamikaze what the hell is that all about......?"

* * *

As Salibe dejectedly walked back the dormitory he couldn't help but notice that the camp was a hive of activity, the construction crew like 'soldier ants' going about their duties as if tomorrow never comes. But what was with the heavy construction equipment tearing up the ground and clearing the trees around the 777 still hidden in camouflage at the end of the runway? And then there's these old dried trees and wood being piled up in the square? For sure there is something big going on, but what?

Salibe was in deep anaclitic thought his mind grossly troubled at what lay ahead. Things had not gone to plan and the transfer of funds was a giant worry but for now he would just have to stay the course.

Anbar threw himself onto his cot and placed his hands behind his head for anther boring day staring up at the corrugated ceiling but his thought process was still in kinetic.

"Kamikaze... Kamikaze." Anbar kept saying the word again and again. Then it struck him, *of course* during the second world war Kamikaze pilots were young men willing to give their lives for the sake of the Emperor and the 'Land of the Rising Sun' flying suicide missions against the US fleet to destroy as many ships as possible by crashing their bomb laden planes into the enemy vessels. "But what's the significance here?" Anbar was arguing with himself.

"Naw... In this day and age! *Can't be...* But the world has gone crazy and to crash that 777 is not so stupid. Maybe these guys have a grudge against the US or something and it's payback time and that's why they are clearing the runway to turn the plane around. To find the wreckage of the 777 would take the heat off and abort the search... *Clever... But the missing cargo?* I'm sure

the Yakuza have thought their way around that one... *"Well I'll be darned*, it all makes sense now......."

* * *

Salibe rose to stretch his legs after his morning cat nap. He stood for a moment flexing his muscles then walked to the door. It was coming to mid-day with a clear blue sky and the temperature rising. The wood pile was almost finished at about three meters high and four meters' square. One of the workers was taking a breather wiping his forehead with a sweat rag and it was the ideal opportunity for Anbar to approach him to find out what was going on.

"Sumimasen."

The young Japanese 'soldier' turned to face Salibe.

"No English." He signaled touching his mouth with his hand.

But Salibe wasn't going to give up having expired his few words of Japanese.

"Kasai." (fire) Salibe motioned as if striking a match pointing to the wood pile. 'Wakaru?' (understand)

"Hai." He nodded. "Kaso, Isamu Daichi ... Gado." Then he placed both hands together and placed them at the side of head to portray sleep.

Salibe thought for a moment what the hell does he mean! Then the penny dropped.

Of course, a cremation pile for the murdered guard!

"Arigato." Salibe acknowledged with a slight bow. He was becoming more Japanese than the Japanese!

Satisfied, his next challenge was lunch........

* * *

"This fucking bayonet is useless, I need a machete rather than a giant tooth pick." Chuck was hacking a path through the heavy bush.

"Remember we gotta to mark our tracks with palm leaves or stakes to make sure we find our way back, Sally that's your responsibility." Bill was delegating and it was about time Sally took her share of the burden.

"And Just how do I do that may I ask?"

"It's no big deal Sally, pay attention." Bill picked up a branch that Chuck had decimated, pulled off some of the twigs and stuck the main stock into the soft soil. "Savvy?"

"Yeah I get it. How often?"

"Every nine or ten yards but the path that Chuck is clearing will also help."

"What's that up there?" Sally pointed to the stalky thick ringed plant about three meters tall with palm shaped leaves at the top resembling an umbrella. There were four green rugby ball shaped fruits hanging under the shade of the leaves.

"You got good eyes Sally." Bill Grinned. "Popiah's nice work."

"I'm glad I'm good for something."

"Don't temp me." Chuck just couldn't resist.

"Well, we all know what's in *your* deprived mind."

"Come on guys, save it for another day, let's decide how we get that fruit down." Bill was staring up at the tree trying to gauge its height.

"I suggest Chuck you kneel and Sally you put your legs around his neck and I think you can just reach them."

"Yeah, *I like that."* Chuck had a giant grin on his face.

"No way am I going on that pervert's shoulders."

"Hell Sally, don't be so bloody difficult besides your wearing slacks."

"I'll do it Bill but only with you."

Bill gave a big sigh. "Awe, *come on then."* He went down on his knees. "Sally get on my shoulders then grab the tree trunk to steady yourself... *Steady... Steady...* Can you grab the fruit now?"

"Yeah, I got I Bill."

"Good, throw each one down to Chuck."

As Sally climbed down from Bill's shoulders he held her hands to steady her in the process brushing against her breasts and almost touching her face and for a fleeting moment Sally looked into his eyes. It was a look that was something more than a Flight Attendant to her boss and for a milli second their body language sent messages of the third kind.

"Eh... Errr... Sally are you okay?" Sally was still holding Bill's hand and he felt decidedly uncomfortable in front of Chuck.

"Cozy, huh?"

"Give it away Chuck." Bill retaliated his face flushed. "We have four fruits so that's enough let's get back to camp. They are a bit green." Bill was pressing the fruits. "But don't worry tomorrow they will be ready to eat......"

* * *

Shendo was doing his morning rounds to check on 'the work in progress' of both the runway and the preparation for the cremation ceremony. On seeing the Biggubosu, Adachi the site supervisor didn't hang around and almost sprinted to be by Shendo's side. Trouble was Kenichi's middle name and the secret was to beat him at his own game.

(Speaking Japanese)

Adachi bowed. "Everything is going to plan Bosu."

Shendo showed little response, he was a man of few words and even less with the compliments.

"And the funeral ceremony?"

"The coffin was completed by our carpenter and Gado's body is dressed in full military uniform and stored in the refrigerated shipping container. The funeral pile is complete and Tahoka has arranged the guard of honor."

"Hmmm... And the runway?"

Chief engineer Hattori is supervising the construction crew, it will be difficult to finish by midnight but he assures me it can be done. Once the funeral ceremony is over I will place additional men on the job."

"Hmmm... Who is the Buddhist priest on camp?"

"Hiro Araki."

"Tell him I want to see him in my office as so as possible. I'll check with you again at lunch."

"Hai." Adachi bowed and left to go about his business, there was no plan 'B' on Shimaru Shima.......!

* * *

Kenichi sat back in his chair to relax, the air conditioning a much-needed relief from the 33-degree temperature. The cafeteria had placed a tray of fresh green tea on his desk in anticipation for his usual request.

Shendo poured the light green liquid from the braid handled blue ceramic kettle. The matching cups were small and devoid of lugs. The theory being, if you can pick the cup up without burning your fingers it is the correct temperature to drink.

Suddenly there was a knock on the door and Shendo hurriedly swallowed the last dregs.

(Speaking in Japanese)

"Okairikudasai." (come in)

Hiro Araki the camp's Buddhist priest entered. He bowed then waited for Shendo's acknowledgement.

"Suwarimasu." (Sit) Shendo pointed to the empty chair.

"Hai" The priest seemed nervous, when the Biggubosu calls one can never tell.

"Hmmm." Shendo studied the man for a few seconds making him feel even more uncomfortable.

"I just want to double check that the cremation ceremony is sown up and that you will perform the bone picking procedure to fill the urn for Gado's wife and family for burial?"

"Hai, everything is ready Bosu and I will personally perform the bone picking later in the evening once the ashes are cold. Fortunately, I have an urn at our small temple on camp. Gado will be dressed in full military uniform for all to see before the coffin is finally closed. The casket will be draped with the Hiomaru the national flag and a white Kimono has also been placed in the casket as tradition with six coins for the crossing of the Sanzu River and a knife for his protection."

"Good the ceremony starts at two and I want no slip ups.".

"Hai."

"Please leave I'm busy, Arigato........."

* * *

Religious beliefs of most Japanese are a combination of Buddhism and Shintoism. Although Japan has become a more secular society 91% of all funerals are conducted as Buddhist ceremonies.

After death, there is a ceremony called the 'Water of the last moment' or 'Matsugo-no-mizu' where the lips of the deceased are moistened with water.

The cremation bones are not reduced in size as they are in many western cultures so that bones that remain are large and after the cremation (e.g. the thigh bones) require two of the relatives to hold their chopsticks at the same time to pick theses them from the ashes placing the longest bones first in the urn and the smallest bones last to depict the deceased standing up and then to be buried in the 'Haka' or family grave 39 days later.

* * *

As Bill walked behind Sally on their way back to camp he couldn't help thinking he hadn't seen the wood for the trees, so to speak, and her slim trim body was playing havoc with his morality as the Captain of the ship. Her hypnotic smile, olive brown eyes and shoulder length hair, not to mention that tantalizing figure was the real deal. As for her personality, she was her own woman, spunky, fiery, and says what she thinks, a rare commodity in today's environment and if anyone could handle Chuck, *it was Sally!*

When you walk behind a person it's like telepathy kicks in and the person automatically turns. Sally was no different and when she turned to look at Bill it was a look that said it all, *like 'come on baby lite my fire'* and for a moment Bill couldn't help but think of Julie. Their relationship over two years was special in its early days when 'love was in the air' and that was all that mattered. But life is not 'a bowl of cherries' and when the luster wears off and the reality of everyday living and the 'take for granted' attitude becomes a reality and temperaments finally flare, it's time to accept the ultimate and go your different ways, much the wiser from the experience.

But Sally... Could he be just imagining things? Was it the life-threatening predicament they were in, that brings the opposite sexes together in a protectionist way or was it just two people with a natural desirability for one another?

This time he would have to tread carefully as decisions may have to be made that could be compromised because of a sexual relationship.

*   *   *

"Ah, here we are! Nice pegging Sally."

"That's a change getting a compliment from you Chuck!"

"Enjoy it when you can babe."

"I might have guessed! They say you can't change a leopard's spots."

"You two." Bill shook his head. 'Sally wrap these papayas in some palm leaves to keep the ants from devouring them. I think one is ripe enough for our dinner tonight but I'm afraid lunch will have to be a liquid one."

"At least I can keep my figure, huh?" Sally's humor didn't impress her arch rival.

"Women!" Chuck just shook his head but this time 'silence *was* golden'!

"So, who's first on the Adam's Wine?" Sally had retrieved a couple of bottles of the filtered lava sand she had stored half buried in the ground to keep them cool beneath a large bush and she held up one of the ¾ filled bottles to the light. *"Gosh, your right Bill,* I wouldn't believe it if I haven't seen it with my own eyes. The water is crystal clear except for a small layer of sand at the bottom."

"Your first Sally," Bill laughed. "Just be careful you don't disturb the sediment."

"So, I'm the guinea pig huh?" But for a change Sally was in good humor.

"Do you see what you do to her Bill?" Chuck was no dummy and when his comment made Sally blush for a moment and he knew he had struck a nerve.

'Yeah.' Chuck thought to himself. *'She has a thing for Bill that's for sure but the 'Captain's choice' will be interesting'*........

* * *

As Shendo entered the mess hall accompanied by Tahoka and Arakida all dressed in the World War II uniforms of the Imperial Japanese Army the diners rose to their feet and bowed for two minutes as a mark of respect for the Camp Commander and the forth coming cremation of one of their respected comrades.

Shendo certainly looked the part although the war with Japan had ended on September 2, 1945 it was like an episode of 'Back to the Future'. The soft khaki officer's peaked cap, complete with brass star, and buttoned single breasted tunic with four pockets and open neck with a crisp white shirt spread collar. His trousers could easily be mistaken for riding britches with the knee length highly polished brown leather boots, the two red and gold rings on his tunic cuffs identifying the rank of captain. From his highly-polished pistol belt on the opposite side hung the 'Shin Gunto' an army sword similar to the samurai, a weapon and badge of rank used by the Imperial Japanese army between 1935 and ad 1945.......

* * *

By the summer of 1945 the defeat of Japan was a foregone conclusion. The Japanese navy and air forces were destroyed and with the allied naval blockade and intensive bombing the country and its economy was devastated. At the end of June, the Americans had captured Okinawa an island from which the allies could launch an invasion of the mainland and US general Douglas MacArthur was placed in charge of the invasion which was code named 'Operation Olympic' and set for November 1945. However, the invasion of Japan promised to be the bloodiest seaborne attack of all times conceivably with casualties ten times that of Normandy and the mission was aborted and on July 16, a new option became available when the United States secretly detonated the first Atomic Bomb in the New Mexico Desert. Ten days later the Allies issued the Potsdam Declaration demanding the unconditional surrender of the Japanese Imperial Forces.

On July 28, the Japanese Prime minister Kantaro Suzuki responded by telling the press and his government to ignore the US ultimatum. To not comply would mean the inevitable and complete destruction of the Japanese armed forces and the devastation of the Japanese homeland which no one believed.

Consequently, President Harry Truman ordered the devastation to proceed and on August 6 a B29 bomber *Enola Gay* dropped an Atomic bomb on the city of Hiroshima killing 80,000 people.

On August 8 Japan's desperate situation took another turn for the worse with the USSR declaring war against Japan with Soviet forces attacking Manchuria overwhelming the Japanese and a second US Atomic bomb was dropped on Nagasaki and on August 15 at noon Emperor Hirohito went on national radio for the first time to announce Japan's surrender.

On Sunday 1945 more than 250 allied warships lay anchor in Tokyo Bay and on the deck of the USS Missouri Foreign minister Mamoru Shigemitsu signed the Potsdam Declaration with Commander MacArthur on behalf of the United Nations and as the twenty-minute ceremony ended the sun burst through the low hanging clouds and the most devastating war in human history was over.

* * *

Shendo bowed in respect then took his seat at the dining table unhooking his 'Shin Gunto' from his waist belt in its brown leather scabbard leaning it against the wall behind him. That large braded handle pressing into his ribs was not an option during lunch. Tahoka and Arakida followed suite.

Salibe as usual was a late comer and with everyone seated and enjoying lunch Anbar as usual did himself no favors and the normal loud chatter suddenly silenced with obvious hostility at the sight of the Arab accentuating. 'What the hell *is he* doing here?'

"Kon' nichiwa." Anbar gave a slight bow waiting for the 'invitation' really pissing him off having to kowtow to these arrogant bastards.

Shendo nodded without looking up working his jaws on the thinly sliced pork and beans.

"I guess that means to sit!" Salibe retaliated his anger firing a broadside. Strangely there was no reaction, either the food was too good or the hate too hot. *Whatever,* in solitary confinement he would have to go the whole nine.

Salibe's boring lunch almost over Shendo suddenly tapped the face of his watch to draw attention to the time and Tahoka and Arakida acknowledged simultaneously rising from the table. One thirty had come and gone……

* * *

(Speaking in Japanese)

As Shendo rose to his feet every diner followed suite standing to attention as their camp Commander fastened his 'Shin Gunto' and marched in rigid military style to the exit. The funeral ceremony was about to begin and the last thing Kenichi needed was any 'slip ups'. Adachi the camp supervisor didn't need a second prompt and by his bosses' side faster than 'Rodger Bannister' breaking the first 4-minute mile in the 1952 Olympics.

"Get the men to fall in immediately in three rows facing the funeral pile and prepare the coffin bearers to carry the cask once the 'Hinomaru' is raised." Shendo didn't mince his words.

"Hai."

Adachi had plenty on his plate what with the guard of honor the coffin bearers and inspecting the Shimaru Shima 'soldiers' in their authentic khaki world War II jungle fatigues with peak caps and neck flaps and of course Hiro Araki the camp's Buddhist Priest to flame the pile and complete the ceremony.

"Move it, move it." Adachi opened his lungs. "Fall in and form a column of three, tallest on the left shortest on the right. I don't have all day... *Get to it."*

The three columns formed Adachi, like a regimental sergeant major screamed... *"Chui".* (attention) Then immediately stood back to inspect the 'motley crew'.

"Hmmm... Better than I expected." He spoke under his breath.

For sure they really looked the part bringing back nostalgic memories of the once proud 'Imperial Army'.

"Anshin shite sutando." (stand at ease)

Tahoka and Arakida had already lined up the seven-man guard of honor dressed in full dress uniforms to fire the three-volley salute, the polished breaches of their ceremonial Arisaka type 38 bolt action rifles gleaming in the afternoon sun.

Satisfied Tahoka, Arakida and Adachi took their places beside the make shift podium waiting for the 'Commander' to give the eulogy.

* * *

"Today we are honoring our fallen comrade Isamu Gado who died in the line of duty killed by the American Imperialists. A brave Yakuza soldier and an honorable Samurai, who will be given full military honors. Bring the casket and place it on the pile."

At Shendo's command six pole bearers appeared from the rear shouldering the casket, slow marching in perfect time, sweat glistening on their cap less brows as they carried the heavy coffin. The specially constructed planked board platform placed on top of the pile to allow the pole bearers to slide the coffin into place, was a welcome relief.

"Raise the 'Hinomaru'" Shendo's voice echoed across the construction square.

Arakida marched smartly to the flag pole and slowly raised the 'Rising Sun' to half-mast. Araki the Buddhist priest had already torched the jet fuel saturated pile and the flames immediately bust into life with an explosion rising over three meters...

"Guard of honor, port arms and load." Tahoka gave the command.

"On the command... *Arms....* fire your weapons in three volleys."

"*ARMS... Kasai... Fuka... Kasai... Fuka... Kasai....*" (fire... load)

The guard of honor's rifles cracked in perfect timing, the loud gunfire echoing throughout the base......

* * *

"What the hell was that?" Sally nearly jumped out of her skin in the process dropping her half-devoured portion of papaya.

"Gunfire!" Chuck was on the binoculars in a flash peering over the make shift 'fox hole' of branches and palm leaves.

"Come on, come on... What's the take?" Bill yelled.

"Christ Bill, gimme a sec to get this stupid thing focused... Just as I thought, the rifle volley was from the guard of honor. *I knew that had to be a funeral pile!"*

"So."

"It looks like the ceremony is over as everyone is dispersing. *Can you believe these guys all dressed up in world War II uniforms? Hmmmm...*There's some guy dressed like a kinda priest attending to that larger than life bone fire. With the heat from that baby the casket will be toast and I beats me what the hell he's gonna find."

"Well that's a relief... Better than bullets flying over our heads." Bill commented as he scooped the seeds from the papaya. "I've had better for lunch." He screwed up his face at the unappetizing fruit.

Sally was quiet, the thought of being party to murdering that poor guard was still haunting her.

"Sally, are you okay, your very quiet?" Bill asked.

As for Chuck, he just shrugged, it was the start of the 'forbidden fruit'.

"Yeah, I'm okay Bill, I'm still trying to clean my lunch that I dropped."

"I'm really not hungry Sally, you can have mine."

"Naw, I wasn't enjoying it anyhow, but thanks Bill."

"When you two stop the niceties, maybe we can discus if there are pilots on the base that can fly that bird and more to the point, do we want to stop them? Remember they will have to fire up the engines to kick in the hydraulics to turn he nose wheels."

"Less of the sarcasm Chuck, *cool it!*" Bill was showing his annoyance at Stevens cheap shot. "But.... To get back to your point, that thought *had* crossed my mind and more importantly, where the hell are they going to fly that jet? To hide a 777 is no mean fete... Now, back to your grand plan for stopping the flight!"

"Now, *whose being sarcastic, huh?"* Chuck tapped the stock of the Arisaka, an evil grin on his face. *"This baby."* Stevens was just dying to start a war.

Bill shook his head. "Two things, Chuck... Sure, we can delay the flight but that pop gun isn't going to do much damage to the plane. Yeah, you can send them running for cover but secondly, we only have thirty rounds of ammunition which we need to preserve and when you fire that rifle in the dark, the muzzle flash will expose our position and depending on their ordinance, like say heavy machine guns or mortars they can blow us to pieces. No Chuck, I know you have the best intentions but it's just too risky."

"But we just can't sit here and do nothing!" Chuck was getting more and more irate.

"Chuck, *that's exactly what we're going to do.* When the time is right we'll need that rifle but that's for another day. My suggestion is we get some rest from the mid-day sun under a that canopy you made. It's going to be a long afternoon and into the night as we need to continue our vigilance on the camp. My thoughts are Shendo has too much on his plate now but tomorrow...? Well, we'll wait and see......"

* * *

The thought of the unknown and the danger that lay ahead, not to mention the boredom and tropical humidity, would test a saint and Bill's Challenge as Captain at the helm was to keep the team's mind from the real possibly of capture or even death. With only the second day of freedom the cracks were already showing, especially with Sally. Two men and an attractive female is a cocktail for disaster and with tensions already showing between she and Chuck on the 'no love lost scene'... *Well...* No more said......

* * *

Sally gave a gloomy sigh as she took Bill's advice and searched on her knees for a comfortable spot on the bed of palm leaves.

"I guess this is as good as it gets." She complained under her breath before finally lying flat on her back with a pronounced groan, her flight attendant jacket placed below her head rolled up in a make shift pillow.

Chuck was in silent mode deep in thought enjoying a drag from his Marlborough pack.

"I don't think you'll ever give up the habit Chuck." Bill was shaking his head.

"How many times have we been down that road, huh?" Chuck shot back.

"Bill's right Chuck, it's a disgusting habit and besides you should save that lighter fuel in case we need a fire."

"Since when did you become 'miss survival'?"

"Whoa....Whoa... For God's sake, you two, *give it away!* But Sally's right Chuck, you should conserve that lighter fuel."

"I might have known *you two* would agree!"

In defiance Chuck lit another stick and Bill reluctantly restrained his silence, anger prominent in his eyes, but there was no point raising the anti, he had to keep the team together at all costs if they were to survive 'Shimaru Shima'.

Sally for once knew when to be seen and not heard and gave 'a loser' shrug.

"Listen." Bill interrupted. "Since we have plenty of time on or hands I've been thinking about tomorrow and putting myself in Shendo's shoes. This guy wants us and wants us bad and that's when mistakes are made. How many

men he can spare for the 'posse' that's another question? There's a mountain of daily maintenance work required to keep the camp running smoothly, the large refrigeration unit, generators, food you name it..." Bill paused... "My educated guess would be about 6 to 8 men... What do you think Chuck?"

"Including Shendo...? Yeah... You're in the ball park."

"Okay... So, what advantages do *we* have? Well, there are only three of us and we can move fast and use jungle warfare tactics', you know, 'hit and run' like the Communist Terrorists did with the British in Malaya in 48.... Our foxhole is well camouflaged and we are on the high ground with a 180 view of the runway and harbor. I we must make our move the problem is water and food, more to the point if Shendo's men start a shooting war we are heavily out gunned that we know and with only thirty rounds of ammo, Chuck you must make every bullet count. Which brings me to you Sally."

Chuck rolled his eyes as if to say, 'here we go again'.

"Me!" Sally sat bolt upright her eyes wide not knowing what to expect. Having listened in silence to Bill's summation of the crisis *where the hell do I fit in, she thought?*

"Yeah, *you Sally,* but calm down we're not asking you to become a "Navy Seal'!"

"Boy, that's relief *and I don't think!"*

Bill raised his right knee into the bent position then rolled up his trouser leg exposing the holstered 22 Magnum 351 before removing it from the ankle holster.

"Sally, this a perfect ladies gun for self-defense. It has a barrel magazine of seven full metal jackets and is double action, which in laymen's terms means you just keep squeezing the trigger after each round as fast or slow as the situation demands until the magazine is spent. It fits snugly into the palm of your hand with a nice shaped grip and fully loaded weighs around only 11 ounces."

Then Bill pointed to the muzzle of the snub-nosed barrel.

"This is an interesting feature, an orange fiber optic sight which glows in the dark for maximum effectiveness in difficult lighting. The safety catch is this little sort of thumb shaped button just above the left side of the grip which you push down before you fire. There's nothing to it. A 22-caliber shell will not stop a fully-grown man but it makes holes and in the right spot, sure, it could kill. Come and sit beside me Sally and I'll go through it once more."

Sally rose to her feet. "But why are you showing me all this or is that a stupid question?"

"Simple... Because I'm giving you the gun to protect yourself if something unfortunate should happen to Bill or I."

"Your shittin me! You mean...?"

"Precisely..."

Bill unlocked the Velcro holding the miniature holster to his ankle.

"Here let me help you fix this. Roll up your right leg... *You are right handed, aren't you?"*

Sally shrugged and did as she was told her mind still in an enigma. A flight attendant and now a modern day 'Annie Oakley'.

"There how does that feel?"

Sally just shrugged, I mean she was in it for whole nine now.

Bill and Sally were now at close quarters and he placed the Magnum firmly in the palm of her right hand.

"Hold it like you see in the movies."

Sally's hand was shaking she had never held a gun before let alone fire one.

"Now there's the safety catch, and the golden rule is never point a gun at anyone unless you're going to fire it."

"Wow! I'm outta here." Chuck just couldn't resist the wisecrack making *even* Sally laugh.......

* * *

The ceremony over, Shendo wiped the sweat from his brow as he briskly walked to his quarters. Between the heat from the funeral pile and the 33-degree humidity it was as near hell as one can get. He opened the door to his miniature steel box, the AC at 18 felt like heaven, how the other half lived was not his problem. The day had gone well with no hiccups and he felt satisfied as he crashed down heavily on his cot desperate to get into something more comfortable and out of his officer's ceremonial uniform. He unlatched the heavy Shin Gunto and placed it into the small steel military style locker, then his waist belt and pistol before cursing as he struggled to pull off his highly polished knee length brown leather boots.

(Speaking in Japanese)

"Watashi wa korera no kusobutsu o nikumimasu." (I hate these fucking boots)

"Ahhh..." Kenichi heaved and tugged at the heal his hand slipping from the highly-polished leather and paining his hip joint, the mixture of temper

and fatigue taking its toll and he lashed out throwing the boot against the container wall the noise attracting Tahoka as he passed.

Tahoka stood thinking for a moment before knocking on his bosses' door. To disturb Shendo at the wrong moment was never advisable.

"Bosu, is everything alright?"

"Hai..." Shendo yelled. "Now don't bother me I need some rest. Get Chief Engineer Genzo Hattori and site supervisor Jiro Adachi to me at me the runway excavation to check the progress in say...? One hour."

"Hai." Tahoka satisfied was on his way to the dormitory also eager to get into the more comfortable jungle fatigues.

Shendo lay on his cot in his boxers and vest the AC making him feel drowsy, his mind drifting back to his conversation with Biggubosu Numero and his ultimatum to recapture the American's or Seppuku. The thought of using the short sword to terminate his life was not about the pain but the dishonor and he tossed and turned in his forced sleep. Tomorrow he must start the search for the Americans but more importantly tonight's flight must leave on time at midnight. Then there was the Arab another thorn in his flesh. He could easily dispose of him and retain 40 billion for the Yakuza but to cross swords with the Russian MOD and the Bratva was not wise. No, he would just a have to bide his time......

* * *

"What's the use." Shendo spoke aloud as he swung his naked feet to the floor. Japanese work ethics have no room for sleep besides it was almost 5.30pm which meant construction on the runway extension would stop for at least an hour for 'fudo'. Time was not on his side and Kenichi quickly changed into his more comfortable fatigues and slipped on his work boots, finally fastening his holster belt. Then as a precaution he withdrew his Nambo semi-automatic to check the safety catch before sliding it back into the holster then fastening down the leather flap. Satisfied, he donned his soft peaked kaki cap with the neck flap. A final glance in the stainless-steel mirror over the wash basin and he was good to go.

The evening temperature had dropped slightly but the humidity still prevailed and Shendo wasted no time in covering the 9,000-ft. long runway. Tahoka had spotted his boss aggressively striding down the tarmac like a man on a mission and quickly alerted his colleagues to be prepared for the anticipated interrogation.

(Speaking in Japanese)

"Tochu no Biggubosu." (big boss on way)

Lava rock was still being crushed by the surface grader and followed up with the heavy road roller compacting the large circular area for the plane to turn, the noise from of the diesel compressors ear deafening.

As Shendo approached within 20 meters Hattori the chief engineer shouted to Adachi the site supervisor to stop work and kill the noise to speak to the Bosu.

"Jiro, Teishi sagayo." He yelled.

Adachi turned barely hearing Hattori's voice then the penny dropped and he waived both hands in the air shouting to the construction crew to stop work.

"Yameru... Yameru..." The noise immediately ceased and Hattori and Adachi bowed in Shendo's presence.

"Kon' nichiwa." Hattori greeted Shendo.

Kenichi waived his hand to disperse the protocol, progress on the runway extension was more important.

The crushed lava rock looked hostile to the rubber 'nose tires' of the 777 and Kenichi begged the question.

"I worry about the sharpness of the crushed rock puncturing the nose tires of the heavy plane?" Shendo was no dummy.

Hattori immediately responded. "Yes, that is a concern Bosu but Adachi and I have already recognized the potential problem and will place heavy wood planking strips in front of the nose wheels as the plane is turning replacing them say every... Three meters. This will solve the problem. As for the undercarriage wheels, they will act like a fulcrum much like the point if a compass and rotate on the existing tarmac."

"Hmmmm..." Shendo was silent still in thought. The explanation given by both Hattori and Adachi made sense but the proof was in the testing.

"And will the 2400hr dead line be met?" Shendo's voice was sharp and demanding

"Hai." Came the chorus.

Shendo nodded satisfied. "Ima yoshuko no tame ni kowsu yoidesu." (good, now break for dinner)

Shendo bowed then turned tail heading for the mess hall, food now high on his agenda......

* * *

As Salibe left the dormitory he could see Shendo and his entourage heading toward the mess hall for the evening meal break, although necessary he hated not only the food but the racial bigotry of his hosts. Unfortunately, solitaire is the only game in town and he had to play along until the cargo from the Russian nuclear submarine was safely on shore and the transfer of the 20bilion US dollars complete. The burial ceremony and the Military tribute to the deceased guard was certainly educational regarding Japanese culture and so different from the Muslim faith where the belief is that death is a natural part of life and unless extraordinary circumstances prevail the body must be buried within 24 hours of death.

Salibe stopped in his tracks then stood for a moment staring down the runway. From a distance, it appeared that the construction work was going to plan and Shendo would pull off the biggest con in history but then what did *he* care he had his own priorities. Kenichi would most likely call Numero in the morning to report on the 'state of the nation' and the death knell of the 777. More importantly he would have to convince Shendo for an 'ear in' to check on the situation regarding the ten billion dollars to be electronically transferred in manageable deposits into the banks he had detailed to Ayako, Numero's secretary. There was no way he could contact his uncle in East Jerusalem to check it out either by cell or radio phone, it was just too dangerous as Israel's Secret Service the 'Sayerat Matakal' was tracking his uncle Abdul Fattah's every move and it was just a matter of time before someone would betray him for the 10 million US dollar ransom dead or alive. It wasn't going to be a walk in the park to convince Shendo but the success of Operation 'Fish Tail' would establish the State of Palestine and change the Middle East forever........

* * *

Salibe went to the servery and selected his food returning to Kinichi's 'exec' table and taking his seat.

"To hell with Japanese protocol and if Shendo doesn't like it, he can go and take a hike." Salibe spoke out loud in his naïve tongue. Who the heck could understand him anyway?

As Shendo, the site mangers and bodyguards entered the mess hall the diners rose to their feet and bowed standing for a second in silence before resuming the work of eating. As for Salibe he was unperturbed and just ignored the mark of respect, casually taking a sip of the repulsive green tea whilst waiting for the inevitable confrontation.

Kucinich's narrow slanted dark brown Asian eyes were full of hate and contempt as he stood at rigid attention staring down at the Arab.

'Who was this arrogant foreigner, a guest of the Yakuza, flaunting Japanese culture with open disrespect. When the senior officer of the camp arrives at the dining table you stand to attention and bow before you take your seat and wait until you are told to eat'.

Assuming the pending conflict the silence in the mess hall was ear piercing so much so you could hear a pin drop. Their camp commander had been insulted by a Muslim and Kenichi's honor was at stake and the Samurai would never respect him again if he didn't humiliate the foreigner or worse still terminate the perpetrator.

Salibe looked up at Shendo putting on the surprised face look, his nonchalant attitude continuing to drink his tea infuriating Kenichi further.

(Speaking in Japanese)

"Anata wa chumoku ni tatte, watashi wa kayanpu no shirei-kandesu yumi to aneta wa watishi no sonkei hyoji sa remasu... *Wakaru?*" (you will stand to attention and bow, I am the camp commander and you will show me respect... *Understand?*)

Salibe turned to Tahoka. "So, what's all that drama about?"

Shendo had already unfastened the leather flap on his holster clasping the grip of the Nambu pistol. This was the second-time Kenichi had threatened deadly force and Salibe was finally coming to his senses that this was not a good idea after all.

"Never mind explanation. You stand now and bow or you will join Goda the guard... Wakaru?" Tahoka screamed, the more drama the better the show for the camp.

Salibe didn't hesitate and rose to his feet bowing in the process followed with loud clapping from the 'foot soldiers'. It was all over in a flash but Shendo like all Nihonjindansei, honor is honor and as they say, every dog has its day........

* * *

Salibe knew that he had more or less blew it and now to convince Shendo to let him talk to Numero in the morning was an unenviable task. Nevertheless, he had to try and he turned to his faithful translator.

"Tahoka ask Bosu if he is going to phone Numero tomorrow as I need to speak to him urgently?"

The mouthful of noodles disappearing followed with the usual disgusting slurp, Tahoka in annoyance enjoying his food paused to catch his breath.

"Tahoka enjoy food... Not important... Talk later......"

The last of the carbohydrates gone Tahoka gave his usual repulsive burp his cholesterol blocked arteries satisfied, but Salibe just had to approach him once more.

"Tahoka food finished, ask once again if Shendo will allow me to speak with Numero tomorrow.?"

If looks could kill Salibe had a face full. Tahoka stared at Anbar his steely eyes sending bad jibes, like 'does this guy ever give up. Then he rattled a bunch of Japanese turning to Shendo. Whatever he said caused Boso to stop his indulgence and scream at Tahoka. He was obviously in a vile mood after the embarrassing run in with the Arab.

"Watashi ga kimeru imubosuarabu arimasen."

"What's that all about?" Anbar could sense it wasn't good.

"Boso say he decide not you... *Wakaru?*"

Salibe just shrugged shaking his head predicting the answer. Disgusted he threw his chopsticks to the table and rose to his feet to leave. The food was crap anyhow and the company even worse and he needed some air and time to think.

The dormitory at least was empty and Salibe crashed onto the roped cot, a pillow behind his head, staring at the groaning dilapidated fan begging to be put out of its misery. His mind piecing together the events over the last three weeks... Operation 'Fish Tail's was dependent on logistics... In discussions with Numara he knew that the round trip for RU18 from Colombo to Shimaru Shima took 8 days by sailing west to east across the north Pacific. This meant when taking into consideration the time he had spent on the island the Japanese submarine would dock with its shipment of uncut cocaine in 4 to 5 days. Whereas the Russian Nuclear Submarine the Lewinsky Komsomol, a fast attack vessel with a maximum speed of 48 knots, would most probably arrive at the GPS coordinates in 6 to 7 days and the two days' gap could be crucial. As the Japanese say, 'Time means Money' but 40 billion dollars can buy a helluva lot of time! Operation 'Fish Tail' was now in the hands of Allah and Salibe searched below his cot for the prayer mat.......

* * *

(Speaking in Japanese)

The mess hall emptying, the evening meal over, the construction crew had their work cut out to finish the 'rotary' extension to the runway for the midnight flight on time.

As for Shendo, he was deep in thought as he wiped his mouth with his napkin, his appetite satisfied but his mind mentally starved as he struggled to peg his priorities for the remainder of the evening.

"Hmmm..." He rubbed his chin then his lips as he turned to Tahoka, he had to begin somewhere and his first priority depicted that he personally honors the two Kamikaze Pilots in his quarters by performing the traditional 'Tea Ceremony' in recognition of their divine sacrifice for the Empire and the Yakuza......

* * *

The Japanese Tea Ceremony is called Chanoyu, Sado or simply Ocha in Japanese. It is a choreographic ritual of preparing and serving Japanese green tea, called Matcha, together with Japanese sweets to balance the bitter taste of the tea. The whole process is not about drinking tea but is about aesthetics, preparing a bowl of tea from one's heart. The host of the ceremony always considers the guest with every movement and gesture especially for the most honored guest called Shokyaku.

Samurai had once great influence in Japan and much of the Japanese culture of today has its root from the time Samurai ruled the country. These great warriors of elevated status were the army and police of their time and so they searched for ways to entertain themselves. Tea was one and today their customs are still implemented during the Tea Ceremony. The 'Matcha' Tea Ceremony has been an integral part of Japanese culture for centuries. A quiet celebration performed with grace and beauty for the Shokyaku's the most honored guests.

* * *

"Fetch me the chef and Arakida, I need you to report the progress on the runway construction in say...?" Shendo studied his watch for a second. "Two hours." Then he turned to the chief engineer Hattori and site supervisor Adachi. "Make sure you both give maximum cooperation to Arakida, remember we must all work as a team."

"Hai Boso." The group rose to their feet then gave a polite bow before departing for their relative assignments. The message was plain and simple *'succeed or else'!*

Shendo was in no hurry and he sat back and poured another cup of green tea to relax. The plan was falling into place and unless something unforeseeable happened the 777 would depart on time and within minutes Tahoka returned with the senior chef.

"Boso is that all?"

"No Tahoka, stay."

The chef, dressed in his whites and checked blue trousers with 'Crock' footwear bowed.

"Konnichiwa Boso." The tall young man greeted, his black hair swept back in a pigtail, bowed.

"Na?" The steely penetrating eyes of Shendo would make a lesser mortal freeze. (name)

"Aki Hamada." The chef nervously replied wondering why hell he had been summoned by the camp commandant.

Shendo purposely kept his steely stare for a few more seconds with that masochistic look, almost in enjoyment.

"I need you to prepare the utensils and condiments for a tea ceremony to be held in my quarters with in the next hour."

Hamada was taken aback at Shendo's request. *A tea ceremony, he's gotta be kiddin me!* Aki was dumbfounded. A tea ceremony had never been performed on the camp before and he was struck for words.

"Well don't just stand their man say something." Kenichi had no tolerance for losers

"Eh...Hmmm... Boso I have never had this request before, the green powdered tea is no problem and the Chawans I have some bowls that are similar for serving and cooling the tea but the Chasan tea whisk...! We may have to improvise with a shaving brush as with the Chashaku tea scoop by using a piece of shaped bamboo. The Furu I can get maintenance to cut one of my pans to hold the charcoal and I have an unglazed tea pot to contain the water while boiling. As for the Hishaku I have many ladles that would suit the purpose."

Shendo placed both elbows on the table his closed hands supporting his chin. This was a problem that he had not anticipated. But there a again this was a potential 'war footing' and compromises had to be made in the field.

"Hmmm..." The penny had dropped, he was between a rock and a hard place and Shendo dropped his arms and sat back. It was not in his character to admit defeat but... "Hamada." The tone of his voice more relaxed, it was pointless beating up on the chef. "I understand. You seem to be man of resourcefulness and I put my trust in you to do your best... *My quarters in one hour."*

"Hai." Hamada bowed then left, he had a formidable task in front of him and time was of the essence...

"Sumimasen Boso." Tahoka was patiently waiting for his next assignment.

"I need you to fetch Akita Wattori and Hianori Itami, the Kamikaze Pilots to my quarters in one hour."

"Hai...."

* * *

Suddenly the semi darkness was broken by the rows of bright runway lights illuminating the hillside awakening Sally from her afternoon doze.

"Thank God, we have some light at least!" She rubbed her sleepy eyes.

Bill was on watch peering through the binoculars studying every movement in the camp... As for Chuck... Well, he was still in slumber land.

Sally crept over beside Bill and peered over the improvised bunker resting her chin on her elbows.

"Oooops, sorry Captain." She apologized as she purposely brushed her body against his.

"I'm not complaining." Bill grinned.

"I'm such a mess." Sally leaned on one arm and ran her fingers through her hair in a show of vanity.

"I'm not complaining."

"Déjà vu, huh?" Sally laughed.

"Well, if you put it that way."

It was Bill's turn to look into those baby blues, his lips feeling the warmth of Sally's breath and the inevitable. First a light brush as their lips met, *then an explosion!* Their lips locking together in a long breathless kiss with, Sally placing her hands behind Bill's neck in a lip lock, like the plane was going down.

"Ah...Hmmmm." Chuck gave a throat clearer returning to the land of the living.

"Eh...Err, you were saying about the lighting Sally?"

"You two, you crack me up... *You were saying about the lighting Sally?"* Chuck cheekily impersonated Bill. *"Gimme a break!* Anyhow I think it's my watch and time to give you two guys some R&R." Sarcasm biting through his voice.

"Chuck."

"Bill, *don't...* "Just hand me these binoculars......"

* * *

The 'perfect storm' settled, Bill put his finger to his lips, of course out of view behind Chuck's back, to signal to Sally to drop the ball and ignore the fall out. She nodded and sat back resting against the large palm trunk.

"So, what have we got?" Bill asked getting back to the real priority.

"The construction crew is working like there's no tomorrow so I guess that 'bad boy' is gonna disappear into the dark 'blue you yonder' tonight, hence the blaze of runway lights."

"Anything else?"

"Yeah... Just gimme a sec..." Chuck was adjusting the 'opera' eye piece.

"So?"

"Hell Bill, don't be so fucking impatient! Yeah... I got a clear view now and I don't believe my eyes. It's like a scene from a World War II movie."

"A World War II movie? *Your shittin me!"*

"You heard me!" Chuck was becoming more and more irate.

"There's two guys dressed in old style one piece flying suites with fur collars and Hachimaki head bands. In this climate, you gotta be kidding me. All we need now is the aircraft carrier deck and the zeros drumming their propellers with Yamamoto shouting Tora...Tora..."

"Kamikaze." Bill exploded.

"Nothing shocks me on this fucking crazy island." Chuck responded. But Bill's conclusion was not beyond the boundaries of disbelief.

"Don't keep us in suspense, what are they doing?"

"Going around with clip boards checking the tires, undercarriage and engines."

"Then that's it...! Don't you see it Chuck, they are obviously the pilots.

"You could be right. Now they are climbing the improvised stairs to the cockpit... But Kamikaze! *Gimme a break."* Chuck couldn't help laughing. "If it wasn't so serious it would be fucking funny."

"Chuck, *language."*

"Yeah...Yeah... I forgot there's a lady in the camp." A sarcastic tone in his voice.

Sally couldn't help herself and let fly. "Chuck, sarcasm is the lowest form of wit."

"Well darling if the cap fits."

"Chuck, *drop it.*"

"Aye... Aye, Captain." He gave a stupid salute.

"Maaan, you *do* push the envelope." Bill was exasperated. "Now getting back to the plots." Bill paused for a second trying to compose himself.

"Kamikaze... A strike against the US for the atomic bombing of Hiroshima and Nagasaki... Yeah, that would make sense. So, they water ditch the 777 using the GPS coordinates where the flight disappeared from the radar screen. Let's face it, it all makes sense. Two crazies willing to commit suicide for the Empire of Japan. *Perfect...* Pieces of the fuselage are found tomorrow by Japanese search and rescue and the conclusion, the crash was caused due to pilot error, *don't you see?"*

Chuck pouted his lips. "I gotta hand it to you Bill, I think you've nailed it but what do you suggest?"

"Suggest...? Bill was taken aback, it was as clear as crystal. *"We do nothing.* Our first priority is *survival......"*

* * *

(Speaking in Japanese)

Aki Hamada the senior chef on camp was just leaving Shendo's quarters when Kenichi arrived. The deadline of one hour to improvise the utensils, not so much the condiments, for the 'Tea Ceremony' was a task he would wish to forget.

"Kinichi wa, Boso, I have done my best under the circumstances and I hope everything will be suffice considering the unique circumstances and the first occasion in my career to prepare for a 'Tea Ceremony'"

Shendo raised his hand as if to say... *stop...* I don't want excuses or your autobiography.

The charcoal was already glowing below the tea pot and Shendo had to admit under the circumstances Hamada had pulled it off... Although he would never admit it!

"Hmmm..." Shendo almost smiled at the sight of the shaving brush. It would perform the same task as the Chasan to whisk the green tea powder but then not as pretty. The Chawans met the requirements and the improvised bamboo Chashaku tea scoop was a piece of work. The Furu although clumsily cut from a stainless-steel pot was efficiently doing the job of heating the water in the unglazed tea pot. A stainless-steel soup ladle laying on the bench top would be used as a Hishaku, fit for purpose.

"Yoi." (good) Shendo, replied, a man of few words but a welcome relief for Hamada.

"Sore wa, sebute no Boso ni narimasu?" (will that be all Boss?)

"Hai."

"Arigatogozaimashita." Hamada bowed and quickly left, glad the ordeal was over.

Suddenly there was a loud knock on the door.

"Hairu." (enter)

Tahoka entered accompanied by Akita Wattori and Hianori Itami, the pilots.

"Konnichiwa Commandant." Wattori and Hianori bowed in protocell.

"Can I leave Boso." Tahoka interrupted aware that the meeting was of a private nature having spotted the 'Tea Ceremony' utensils and condiments, the tea pot over the glowing charcoal embers making a pronounced burbling sound.

"Hai... Kansha." Shendo nodded his approval and Tahoka left to contact his 'partner in crime' Arakida being fully aware that they would both be at Shendo's beck and call until the departure of the 777 flight at midnight.

"Onegaishimasu." (please) Kenichi pointed to the two empty chairs placed in front of the make shift table covered a in a blue silk cloth displaying the pottery bowels and utensils.

Both men dressed in their World War II flying suits took their seats their expressions reflecting the unknown as to why they were summoned to the camp Commandant's private quarters. Was it to check on the plane's worthiness or the quality of the runway extension, or some other problem... Whatever, they were honored.

Shendo positioned himself behind the silk covered table, he had never performed the tea ceremony before, it was always his wife Arisu's responsibility......

* * *

To give one's life for the honor of the empire and the Yakuza was second to none and must be recognized by the senior rank of the camp. Shendo having been too young to serve his country during the war against the United States, the question now begging was as to why these two men were willing to give their lives especially after the war was over for 70 years. But where could he start and Kinichi pondered for a moment before formally addressing the pilots.

* * *

"Ah...Hmmmm... Misuta Wattori and Misuta Hianori, it would give me great pleasure if you would accept my humble gesture to perform the 'Tea Ceremony' for two of the Empires Bravest Samurais. To give one's life is the greatest sacrifice of all. Life is Shinto's most precious gift and I am honored to be in your presence."

Shendo rose to his feet, standing rigid and for a few seconds silence, then bowed in respect before returning to his seat.

Wattori the slightly taller of the two sporting a grey goatee beard returned the compliment with a slight bow before he replied.

"It is *our* pleasure Commandant and for the honor of our great nation the Imperial Empire of Japan. Although our action may be a small gesture on the world stage, to embarrass the United States, the most powerful nation in the world, would give us both significant gratification bearing in mind their barbaric and inhumane act against the sovereign nation of Japan. Let us never forget that on August 6 and 9 in 1945 the United States with the consent of the United Kingdom agreed to deploy nuclear weapons on the cities of Hiroshima and Nagasaki being fully aware of the destruction and carnage that would follow resulting in the deaths of over 180,000 innocent civilians and children under the feeble cloak of saving the lives of American and British Forces from the invasion of the Japanese mainland, knowing full well that our country would never surrender. On July 16, the 'Allied Manhattan Project' successfully detonated an Atom Bomb in the New Mexico Desert and this was their feeble excuse to test the weapon and Harry S Truman gave the callus order fully aware of the horror and suffering it would inflict on the Japanese people.

Both our wives passed away at the young age of 48 and 50 and childless because of radiation sickness. The destruction of the 777 may be a reprisal of small significance but meaningful to us and for a nation that will bear the scars for generations to come. Arigatogozaimashita......

* * *

"What the hell was that?" Sally was on her feet in a flash rubbing her eyes in the semi darkness. Bill was on watch peering through the binoculars while Chuck was just coming to life after his late afternoon nap. In her scary flurry, Sally threw herself on the palm bed lying next to Bill placing her arm around his neck in a comfort hug, their cheeks touching.

"It's alright Sally calm down, were not being attacked if that's what's spooking you."

It was Chuck's turn to sit bolt upright caught unawares by the scream of jet engines but his expression quickly changed at the sight of the two bodies lying in close proximity and he just shook his head. He would have to get used to these two love birds crowding the picture.

"It sounds like jet engines being fired up." Chuck broke in.

"Your right Chuck, the Trent's are whining up. The make shift stairway to the cockpit is gone and I can just make out these two crazies at the controls."

"It sure looks like the 'albatross' is heading out to sea tonight so I guess Bill your hunch was right. Common sense prevails that there's no place you can hide a 250-metric ton jet, not to mention the 12000 feet runway you need to land this baby. Sadly, I guess she's destined for 'Davy Jones Locker.'"

Bill cut in. "Now they are hooking up the nose wheels to the two heavy duty tractors, I guess that's why they had to fire her up to pump the hydraulics and with plenty of fuel in the tanks there's enough to take her back to Tokyo, *but there's no fear of that!"*

"Bill your convinced they are going to ditch the plane?" Sally was back on line.

"As sure as God made little apples!"

"I can hardly hear you Bill." Sally's voice was at soprano level the whine of the two Trent's ear piercing.

"I'll tell you later." Bill yelled back.

"Can I take over? I can see your occupied." Chuck gave a cheesy grin.

Bill raised his eyebrows making a face to Sally, Chuck's attitude was something they would have to get used to.

"Here." Bill couldn't be any ruder.

Chuck was unperturbed and settled in laying on his stomach his elbows supporting the binoculars.

"Whoever's at the controls are no dummy's and used to flying commercial airlines. Now their throttling up the right engine to turn the plane 180 with the help of the tractors and wooden planking to support the nose wheel tires from shredding on the lava rock. *Yeah, they're doing the miracle...* And there's our mutual friend, Shendo to watch over the finally, for sure there no show without Punch......"

* * *

The 777 was now correctly facing the runway ready for takeoff, the two Rolls Royse Trent's with 87 thousand pounds of thrust idling in taxi mode, the tarmac now clear of construction equipment and bodies.

The whine of the jets growing louder and louder with bright yellow plumes glowing from each engine as the pilots gradually moved the thrust levers to full throttle. The nose wheels and under carriage biting into the runway eager to become airborne. Their safety belts buckled up their suicide vests stacked by their side to avoid any mishaps, Wattori gave the command.

"Hianori furusurottoru." (Full throttle) *"Furappu 15."*

"Hai Capitan."

The noise from the jet engines thrust shook the palms and ground around the make shift fox hole as the 777 thundered down the runway. Requiring 11,300 feet for takeoff, short by 300, the pilots would have to do a 'David Copperfield" to get this elephant in the air. Fortunately, with an empty cargo hold they would at least have a fighting chance but there's nothing like pilot experience.

"Nozuappu.... Nozuappu." Wattori screamed. The end of the runway fast approaching

Suddenly there was a loud scraping noise with sparks flying as the underbelly of the tail plane dragged the runway. Then there was heavenly silence as the 777 became airborne with only a hundred feet to spare before landing in the drink.

"Boy was that a close call." Chuck commented still in focus, the beacon light flashing on the tail fin getting fainter and fainter as it disappeared into the darkness.

"Bill." Chuck put down the binoculars. "You know we flew Global 10 for almost two years and I feel a certain sadness to see the lady heading for the scrap heap in an undignified manner."

"I didn't know you had sentiment."

"There's a lot of things you don't know about me."

"You got that right!" Sally just couldn't miss the temptation.......

* * *

MONDAY MORNING TOKYO

The phone kept ringing and Gregg pulled the bed clothes even further over his head but the ear-piercing decibels just wouldn't surrender.

"What the fuck!" He leaned over and grabbed the bedside receiver.

"Do you know the fucking time?" Steve bellowed making Gregg cringe puling a face moving the phone away from his ear.

"Well I know it now!" You and your one more for the road. My head feels like a beat up fucking melon."

"Nobody was twisting your arm."

"Yeah... Yeah... So, what's the big deal?"

"Breakfast finishes at ten and if you don't get your ass down here in thirty minutes you'll be back on 'Bullet Train Sushi'."

"Maaaan... What did I do to deserve you?" Gregg grumbled, his voice hoarse. "Give me... Say twenty minutes......"

* * *

Steve had just finished the 'so called' American breakfast and was on his third cup of black coffee, he too was feeling fragile but drinks at the cocktail bar were a welcome relief, *that is if you know when to stop!*

His thoughts turning back in boredom. They had made some ground on the Palestinian case with the arrest of Abud Aziz and his two accomplices at the Department of Controller of Currency but although under interrogation no charges have been laid as yet. Maybe 'water boarding' was a better bet and worse still, Anbar Salibe was still on the run, mysteriously disappearing into thin air after the murder of Ginzo Iwami.

"Where the hell is Gregg?" Steve was becoming more and more irritable. "Probably phoning that Michelle, the dumb shit..."

339

"Sumimasen." He called the waiter.

"Sir?"

"You wouldn't happen to have an English paper with the latest news?"

"Today's 'New York Times'?"

"Couldn't be better."

Within seconds the young waiter returned with the folded ink rag.

"Dozo."

"Domo." Steve replied. "Well let's see what's happening in the world!" He unfolded the pulp turning to the front-page news.

Well I'll be... 'DEBRIS OF MISSING PLANE FOUND FIVE MILES FROM CRASH SIGHT' Japanese search and rescue have confirmed.......

Gregg was in the process of toweling down when the phone rang once again.

"What the... *Not Steve again?"* He quickly secured the bath towel round his waist to cover his credentials and half staggered toward the writing desk stubbing his toe in the process.

"Bastard..." He yelled in pain balancing and hopping on one foot. *"I'm coming, I'm coming,* keep your fucking shirt on... *"Yeah?"* He grabbed the receiver.

"You're not gonna believe this!"

"It's not some Japanese chick again?"

"Gimme a break... *No...* They've found debris from what they think is Global 10. Boeing still have to confirm it's from the missing plane, *but can you believe it...?"*

"Fucking hell! Well, isn't that a turn up from the book. I'll be down in a jiff......."

* * *

Steve raised his arm to attract Gregg as he entered the restaurant.

"Over here."

"Yeah, I see you."

"Grab a seat... *There it is...* Front page headlines." Steve patted the paper.

"Shit! We had better make a call to Daniels to find out if he has anything further to go on. What's the time now?"

The young waiter was back again interrupting Gregg.

"What may I get you sir?" He spoke in perfect English.

"American coffee black and fresh orange juice... Now, where was I?"

"Calling Daniels..." Steve answered.

"Hmmm... It's... 10.25... He'll be in the office by now... But what about Thomson?"

"Let's wait to hear what Daniel's has to say first." Gregg answered in thought.

"Yeah, I guess you are right besides it's in the 'New York Times' and I'm sure John's onto it by now."

Gregg drained the last of his coffee then signaled to the waiter for a refill.

"Sir?"

"Keep em coming." Gregg pointed to the empty cup.

"So how are you feeling now?" Steve asked.

"Like shit. You must have a cast iron constitution."

"Let's just put it down to 'The Piano Man'."

"What the hell does that mean?"

"Sharing a drink called loneliness but it's better than being alone." Steve sang a line from Billy Joel's Piano Man.

"I never thought I'd hear you saying you are lonely."

"We all have or moments but let's change the subject and give Daniels a call on your cell. You *do* have the number?"

"Of course, Now maybe I can finish my coffee if it's not too much trouble……?"

* * *

Steve was drumming his fingers on the restaurant table it was like *'this is really important and my partner can only think of finishing his fucking coffee!'*

"Okay...Okay... For Christs sakes, let's get Daniels on the line." Gregg growled slowly and methodically entered the numbers on purpose watching Steve's expression getting even more frustrated.

"Let me see...?" Gregg grinned.

"Get out of it!" Steve retaliated.

"081..." He could hear the ring loud and clear. "Do you want to speak to him or are you gonna leave it to me?" Gregg asked a cheeky tone in his voice.

"Hello." A woman's voice interrupted. "Mr. Daniels secretary here, how can I help you?"

"Rico, its agent Jonson CIA. I wonder if it's convenient to speak to Ken, its rather urgent?"

"Perfect gentleman, huh?" Steve grinned.

Gregg raised his finger to his lips to signal for to Steve to *'shut it'*.

"Give me a minute Gregg while I check. He was on another call but I see the red light on his private line is now clear... Ken, I have Gregg Jonson from CIA on the phone are you free to speak?... Okay I'll put him through."

"Ken, good morning, if there is such a thing in our line of work?"

"You can say that again...! Listen, I'm just off the phone with McGill and I gather your phoning about the same?"

"I had a good idea that's who you were phoning... *So?"*

"It's the same old story Gregg, no one will put their name on the line. McGill's spitting the dummy and Anderson from Boeing tells me its highly probable that the debris is from Global 10 but it could take another week or so before they are sure. They must check the frame numbers and so on. *I mean we don't get 777's falling out of the sky in that crash area every day of the week?* Although the one thing he did say that stuck in my mind, the fuselage fragments were shredded like 'Swiss Cheese' as if an explosion had taken place."

"Hmmm... That *is* interesting."

"And if that *is* the case I don't give much hope recovering the 'black box' and to make things even more interesting the wreckage is in one of the deepest parts of the North Pacific in around 7,000 meters of water. The other point that Anderson made, Global 10 is a freighter so there's not the usual passenger apparel floating to the surface like luggage bags, shoes and so on. Yeah, we got another Mr. Bo jangles on our hands, like when a guy wears loose basketball shorts showing you what he wants you to see but hiding what the girls really want to see."

"That's a new one on me Ken and one for the book."

Ken could hear Gregg laughing in the background.

"It goes without saying Ken, if anything comes ..."

"Don't worry Gregg I'll keep you and John in the loop. Anyhow I'm pretty sure I'll hear from him before the day's done."

"Thanks Ken, appreciate it. Ciao..."

"Well, what's the big joke?" Steve asked feeling out of it.

"I'll tell you later, more importantly, what's next on the agenda?"

"Let's get the check and we're outta here." Steve raised his hand to attract the Maître d.

"Any suggestions?" Gregg was still feeling a bit hung over as they walked toward the lobby, even after the coffees. He was anxiously looking for a place that was quiet and relaxing and where he can think in peace.

"Listen, why don't we go to the business lounge, there's lap tops and all sorts of IT stuff there?"

"That's a good idea... "Let's see." Steve studied the sign outside the elevator." Here we are floor 22."

The elevator gave a spongy jolt as the over emphasized American female's accent conveyed the floor number.

'floor 22... have a nice day'.

At eleven in the morning the plush blue carpeted hallway was demise of guests, a lacquered sign with an arrow pointed to the large double glass doors on the left with highly polished brass door handles, the sign in bold gold leaf read. BUSINESS LOUNGE. (Bijinesu Raunji)

"At least we have the place to ourselves." Steve commented as he heaved open the heavy door.

"Don't speak too soon the Japanese are renowned for their work ethics."

The pretty young woman in a dark blue pin striped business suite complete with slacks and low healed patent leather shoes was displaying a fine gold chain peeping from her open necked white blouse promoting her slim pail neck. Around 5-8 she was tall for her culture and her smooth pale unblemished facial skin gave her that 'Geisha' look. Her hair swept back in a bun, the wet lipstick lips and the dark brown alive eyes gave a typical portrait of how the west imagines Japanese woman. As for Steve... maybe 'Billy Joel' had something the way he was admiring the receptionist.

"Ohayogozaimasu... My name is Aya and I am at your service should you need anything." She gave the usual bow.

Gregg turned to Steve. *"Don't even think about it...!* Arigato."

"Would you like seats by the window or would you prefer a computer desk?"

"By the window is fine, we don't want to be disturbed." Gregg replied with a warm smile.

"There is fresh cut sandwiches and coffee at the servery but I need to see your room key to ensure you are guests." She gave that certain smile.

"Certainly." Gregg showed her the 'plastic fantastic'... *Steve...*"

"That's fine Mr. Jonson, there's no need." She was checking her tablet. "Arigatogozaimashita." She smiled again and returned to the reception desk.

Steve turned to Gregg as he sank into the soft leather lounger. "Boy this *is* class."

"Yeah, and so are the room rates!"

"Ah…Who cares, Uncle Sam's expense account, remember? *Hell,* the hours we work its slave labor."

Steve always had the antidote……

* * *

The servery was stacked with fresh cut sandwiches, sushi and California rolls not to mention the famous pot of Green Tea and a percolator bubbling away with American coffee. There was also white wine and Champagne chilling in pewter ice buckets. Beautiful paintings of cherry blossom trees scattered the walls emphasized with soft lighting. The plush brown leather sofas and matching loungers the large windows overlooking the Palace and flourishing natural light was a true place of tranquility. The walls in pale pastel shades and the lush blue carpet flooring fell together in the perfect setting and couldn't be more relaxing.

* * *

Gregg was now more relaxed as he settled into the quiet atmosphere.

"Coffee?" Steve asked.

"Anymore and I'll be turning into a coffee bean. No, I'll take a rain check but I'm not stopping you." Gregg answered.

"So, what do you think?"

"You mean about the latest developments with Global 10?"

"What else." Steve replied.

"You and I both know that the debris found is from Global 10. The fuselage is shredded because of what seems like an explosion…! But there are larger pieces of wreckage such as the wings, the tail plane and so on which float because of their design and construction and which no one is mentioning. It's the old cloak and dagger stuff. Boeings scared that it's a crash caused by their product and the government is scared to say it's a hijack or a terrorist bomb. There's no body parts found yet and as for the cargo locked in stainless steel like safes, that's for another day. No, it's the old waiting game. *Hell,* they have still to find what happened to MH370 that disappeared on March 2014, even though they found wing parts washed up on Mauritius!"

Steve rubbed his chin then sat in silence for a moment.

"This whole thing stinks and it's like we're in suspended animation. First the Palestinians then the Russians then the Yakuza and the loss of Global 10

with a cargo of 100 billion in US currency and we're still none the wiser...
What the hell Gregg?"

"My guess is we would have been back on a flight by now to DC if the
wreckage hadn't turned up but even if they do find it's that of Global 10,
what about the cargo? It's laying at the bottom of the pacific in 7000 meters of
water and how long will *that* take to recover? We're really in a Conundrum.
We can't sit on our bums here forever but it's John's call."

"Changing the subject...Wouldn't it have been great if the girls had had
a later flight?" Steve grinned.

"Trust you to think of that but maybe your right we need to lighten up.
Crying in our beer isn't going to achieve anything. How about some clubbing
tonight?"

"Now you're talking partner......"

OPERATION FUKUSHU

Shendo woke up early, he was a light sleeper and daylight had yet to break. Yesterday had been a trying day to say the least but it had all gone to plan and he was comfortable in his own skin. He would have to phone Numero after breakfast to report the good news with the exception that the prisoners were still on the loose and today he would have to do something about it. He still had Salibe to pacify regarding the money transfers of 10 billion to the Palestinian banks but that was Numero's call. As the camp commandant, his terms of deployment were different form the rest of the crew in that he would be relieved every four months with his counterpart Aito Fujimoto and with still one month to go he was anxious to see Arisu, his wife and two young daughters. R&R would be heaven after the challenges he had had to face this month, what with the heist of the American plane and its subsequent demise and the murder of Isamu Gado a brave samurai and Yakuza soldier and he glanced at the luminous dial of his Seiko. It had just turned 6.30 and still early. He propped the bolster pillow below is head staring at the ceiling fan in the dimly lit quarters, the blades beating like that of a helicopter in a slow hypnotic motion.

Arisu... He could just picture her now and how beautiful she looked in the colorful silk Kimono she always wore when he arrived home from his tour of duty. At 48 she was younger than Shendo but she was still as beautiful as the day they were married 20 years ago, even after bearing two lovely daughters 14 and 11... Akiko (Beautiful light) and Emiko (smiling child). At 5.6 she was a typical Japanese female with the genetic pale facial futures the West depict... Dark brown olive shaped eyes, narrow face, dainty nose and lips to match. The tucked in ears and her jet-black hair still showing no signs of aging swept back in traditional Japanese styling. Shendo smiled at the painted picture but more so he missed her warm naked body pressing against his.......

* * *

Sally lay crushed against Bill's back her arms locked around his waist. The mosquitos had had a field day, the red blotches on her neck testimony to their over indulgence. Maybe *they* had a taste for western women, *whatever,* Sally was paying the price and she slapped her neck trying to assonate the culprit then snuggled up even closer to Bill.

Chuck, although on watch had dozed off and he too stirred as the mosquitoes launched a second offensive.

"What the hell!" He slapped his unprotected neck.

"There's no use waking these two, huh?" He shrugged at the sight of the entwined bodies. It was a sight he would have to get used to and he stretched over for a mouthful of the tepid bottled water. Dawn was just breaking and the camp was coming to life.

"Let's see?" He focused the binoculars.

"Hell, it seems so naked with the plane gone!" He spoke out loud.

"With the funeral ceremony over I'm guessing what's next." He took another drink of the sieved water and screwed up his face. It was wet, *but that was about all!*

"Yep, an attack on 'Pork Chop Hill'" He exclaimed. "And I hope to hell it doesn't end up the same as the movie!"

Bill stirred at the sound of Chuck having a conversation with himself and sat up peeling Sally's arms from around his waist.

"Wake up honey." The accidental slip of the tongue embarrassing him.

Chuck just raised his eyebrows and went back to surveillance... There was no point...

Sally sat up, groaned, then rubbed her back before stretching her arms above her head accompanied by a large unlady like yawn exposing her extensive dental work, then she gave Bill that seductive look... Like, *if only...?*

"So, what's the take?" Bill asked now fully awake.

"I looks like its mealtime, which reminds me, what's for breakfast? Papaya again, *what a surprise!"* Chuck's macabre humor not going down well.

"Sally?" Bill begged the question.

"I'm going to do my thing first then I'll come back and share out the last of the Papaya, *thank God...!* If I am ever unfortunate enough to ever see one of these again, so help me, *I'll throw up!"* Sally lifted a bottle of water and face towel and headed into the bush.

"Sally, do you want me to accompany you to make you're your safe?" Chuck's foot was in his big mouth again.

"Get out of it, you weed." Sally yelled back as she disappeared enveloped by the large palm leaves.

"Do you know what you're getting yourself into Bill?"

"When I need your advice Chuck, *I'll ask for it."*

"Don't say I didn't warn you. Broads and business don't mix."

"Cut the psychology lesson and let's think about what's ahead of us if Shendo launches a full frontal."

"Do you want something to eat now?" Sally reappeared.

"Might as well finish the fruit and we're running low on water, with only four bottles left, that's our next job and if we retreat deeper onto the jungle, *believe me,* were gonna need it!" Bill was back in the chair again.....

* * *

Breakfast over and the radio call to Numero still hot on the stove... *'Bring the Americans in dead or alive or 'Seppuku'.* Okio's words were still ringing in his ears. Sure, he was happy with the Kamikaze outcome having been reported in the Japanese media but he had a drug empire to run and a problem like this is like a cancer that must be chemo therapized in the bud and compliments were not in Okio's vocabulary.

(Speaking in Japanese)

"Tahoka... Arakida, come to my quarters in ten minutes we need to discuss the capture of the Americans. The Biggubosu is making waves and has given me an ultimatum which I won't repeat."

Tahoka briefly glanced at his wing man. He knew the Samurai rules for failures and what goes around comes around.

"Hai." Tahoka was about to rise.

"Stay." Shendo made a gesture with his hand. Hungry Samurai's are not effectual and he needed all their support.

Kinichi turned and stepped it out to the mess hall entrance the 'soldiers' quickly rising to their feet with the usual bow for the camp Commandant.

As Shendo headed for his table the last person he wanted to bump into was Salibe! He had enough on his mind without being badgered by the Arab.

Salibe had decide to skip the lousy breakfast but he wasn't going to let Shendo off the hook, he still needed confirmation that the electronic transfers were completed and the 'bump in' meeting was no accident.

"Shendo." Salibe blocked his path.

"No time to speak..." Kinichi raised his arm. "Move Dozo."

"Kenichi, I need to get an answer from Numero."

"Numero say money good... *Move.*" Shendo placed his hand on his holster but there was no need for the second amendment. Tahoka and Arakida were only seconds behind their boss and quickly intervened grabbing the Arab under the arm pits almost lifting his 140-pound frame off the ground.

"Boso say go, no more trouble...*Wakaru?*"

Salibe recognized the word and decided posthumous heroes were not his bag and sensibly stepped aside. His continued requests to speak to Numero down the toilet and now it was a waiting game for the Russian sub to arrive then his repatriation to the mainland on the next service plane. Salibe stared one more time into Shendo's eyes then stepped aside while he was still upright.

Kenichi shouldered Salibe like a quarterback brushing him aside signaling his two bodyguards that the standoff was over......

(Speaking in Japanese)

Shendo pointed to the empty seats. *"Take."*

Tahoka and Arakida obeyed. When the boss gives a command, no one questions it.

"Hai."

Shendo was in a less than a good mood after his run in with Salibe and he sat for a moment in silence to gain his composer before laying down the law.

"Biggubosu is very upset at the loss of one of our men and the escape of the Americans is giving me a big headache. Therefore, I'm depending on you Tahoka and you Arakida to get the monkey off my back... *Wakaru?*"

"Hai." Came the reply in tandem.

"On my instructions, you will inform Adachi of my decision that you are both in command and to provide you with whatever men and equipment you request. Operation Fukushu (revenge) is the code name and the deadline is two days. I know it's short notice but we aborted the operation before for the funeral of Gado delaying the capture of the prisoners. You should bear in mind the Captain and First Officer are both decorated veterans of the 'Iraqi

War', or as the Americans colorfully name it 'Operation Desert Storm'." A distinct sneer in Shendo's voice.

Tahoka was first to respond. "Arakida and I have briefly discussed... *eh...?*"

"Operation Fukushu." Shendo interrupted raising his eyebrows.

"Hai..." Tahoka glanced toward Arakida looking for a the 'go ahead' glimpse. With Shendo, you can never can tell which way he'll jump so caution is the name of the game and Kazuo had no alternative but to 'take the bull by the horns'.

"Boso..." He began in caution. "Considering the two-day objective for the success of operation...*Eh... Fukushu...* We feel we..."

"Never mind, *we feel...!* Get to the point, *I don't have all day!*"

"Hai...Bosu... We need ten nihon no otoko who are familiar with the Arisaka 99 rifle and another two that can fire the Nambu gas operated 96 LMG (light machine gun). Also, an adequate supply of standard 7.7 ammunition and water and supplies for two days 'jungle warfare' and the camp medical officer."

"Hmmm." Kinichi gave a sort of half grunt then rubbed his chin. *"Hmmm..."* He started again. "The rifles, ammunition and marksman including the medic and first aid supplies... No problem. *But the LMG...?* That may be a tall order. Check it out with the armory and ordinance store, dekerudake sumiyakani." (as soon as possible) ... *"Now the timing?"*

"We move forward at ten today that gives us time to consolidate and prepare the men before the mid-day sun."

Shendo pouted his lips then cocked his head to one side.

Was it a yes or no? The two bodyguards weren't brave enough to ask the question and quickly rose to their feet then bowed, leaving a vapor trail.....

*　*　*

The Nambu 96 LMG (light machine gun) was the mainstay of the Japanese Imperial Army, manufactured at the Nagoya Arsenal from 1939 to 1945. It is gas operated and uses the 7.7mm brass rimmed standard cartridge. With fire power of 700 rounds per minute and a thirty-cartridge top loading magazine it was classed as the best light machine gun in the second world war.

*　*　*

The 'healthy' breakfast over, washed down with the 'volcanic coffee' it was going to be another challenging day for the so called 'castaways'. Their ablutions over it was water replenishment and food expedition.

"Christ, I feel like I'm the galley Queen again only without the microwave. As they say, 'a woman's work is never done'." Sally gave an exaggerated sigh. She had just finished straining six bottles of water and like all women it wouldn't be the same without some form of bitching.

Bill had just returned with a shirt full of mangosteen, a purple skinned tropical fruit the size of a small apple with snow white sweet pulpy seeds, a delicacy in tropical climates.

"Something different for lunch, huh?" Bill emptied the fruit in a heap next to Sally's 'bottle factory'.

"God, what are these repulsive looking stale apples with that green thing on top? Is this gonna be another 'Guinness Book of Records' challenge?"

"Sally stop fucking griping, they're not gonna poison you!"

"For Christ sakes, you two lighten up." Bill quickly put his shirt back on to retreat from the mosquitoes who were also searching for lunch.

"Chuck, concentrate on what you are meant to be doing and let Sally do *her* thing. It's nearly ten so what's new?"

Chuck returned to his four eyes.

"Let me see... *Hmmm...* Lots of activity... Troops lining up with equipment and supplies... *And...* What looks like a couple of light machine guns... *Boy,* this *is* serious! And there's Shendo with his two henchmen inspecting what looks like a Japanese assault force."

Chuck dropped the binoculars and turned to Sally and Bill.

"We knew this was coming but these guys really mean business. What do you suggest Chuck?" Bill asked the situation seemed intractable and Sally abruptly stopped what she was doing, a pale shade of white enveloping her complexion.

"Looking at the number of men and weaponry, they're not intending to take any prisoners, that's for sure. We would just be another pain for Shendo and his boss. Now let's look at in the light of day?"

"I'm listening."

"They know we armed with a rifle and some ammunition but they don't know we have a second gun."

"You mean my pop gun, are you kid..."

"Hold it Bill, let me finish... Pop gun or no pop gun it's a diversion and 22's *can* kill. No here's where I'm coming from... The Japanese are no dummies when I comes to jungle warfare remembering the Islands in the Pacific like Iwo Jima. So, we must use the element of surprise. They know we escaped from the maintenance hut so we must be in that vicinity of the jungle, say...? Chuck paused... "With a 180 spread."

"So."

"There's about ten or twelve soldiers and in my opinion, they will spread out in probably two platoons of five or six men to start meticulously combing the bush. Now, here's where yon a Sally come in......."

* * *

Shendo inspected the heavily armed 'reconnaissance' party smartly dressed in their jungle fatigues, their bed rolls, food rations and ammunition belts laid out on the runway in a neat line next to their back packs.

"Anshin shite sutando... Portoraifuru." Tahoka gave the command his voice echoing in the still morning silence." (stand at ease... port arms.)

There was a loud clack as the platoon raised their rifles chest high opening the bolt to show the cordite free breach.

Shendo slowly walked down the line inspecting each rifle in turn pressing down the ejector then peering down the barrel.

"Yoi." He turned to Tahoka and Arakida and gave the 'approval nod'. (good) Then he turned and marched to the front of the platoon to address his men like all commanders before a military assault.

Shendo began... "Operation code named 'Fukushu' is a strike against those Americans who not only escaped from custody but savagely and viciously murdered one of our own, Isamu Gado. You have 48hrs to recapture the escapee's dead or alive. Be aware that the prisoners are armed with the stolen Arisaka rifle and ammunition and they will not hesitate to kill for survival. Tahoka assemble the men in full marching order. *Ganbarou."* (good luck)

"Tenno Heika Banzai" Shendo yelled the Samurai war cry at the top of his voice. The men followed suite chanting... *Tenno Heika Banzai... Tenno Heika Banzai....* (long live the Empire)

Shendo stood to attention and gave a rigid bow before turning smartly. It was now up to Tahoka and Arakida to bring home the bacon......

* * *

"So, what's the deal?" Bill asked. Sally was too petrified to utter a word.

"I'm almost certain Tahoka and the other nip, I forget his name, will fan the men out on a broad front roughly guessing that we will be in that vicinity. The bush is relatively clear for about twenty meters deep at the side of the runway so I will have a clear vision to use this baby." Chuck patted the wooden stock of Arisaka.

"You mean you're going to kill people!" Sally blurted out, petrified at the thought

Chuck shrugged pouting his shoulders. "It's like this...You have a simple choice Sally... Either *you* go out feet first or *them!*"

"Chuck's right Sally." Bill interrupted. "We don't have a choice. The odds are heavily stacked against us and remember as far as Shendo is concerned we are dispensable... *So...* getting back... Where do Sally and I come in?"

"Firstly, Sally stays with me as you can run much faster."

"Run much faster! I'm listening."

"Here take the bayonet." Chuck passed Bill the 20-inch killer. "Hack your way through the bush to your right in a straight line if you can, to get a clear run back... *Are you with me?"*

"So far."

"Now here's the scoop. 'Necessity is the mother of invention', so they say and in our case, it's *confusion... Sally...* Bill will need the 3-51 Magnum back. Just hang on to the ankle holster."

Sally gingerly removed the 22 from her ankle holding it as if it was going bite her nervously passing it to Bill.

"Now before these guys start their offensive..." Chuck paused.

"I'm waiting."

"Okay... Okay...Once you roughly think you're at the sweet spot fire one shot from the magnum. With that small pistol and the distance there's not a chance in hell you'll hit anyone."

"I'm still confused."

"Here's the art of confusion...They will not see the muzzle flash but the noise will point them in your direction. Then you fire a second shot and this time they'll see the flash then get your ass outta there like a Jaguar as my guess they'll cut the bush up with that LMG. The only downside is that some smart ass may know the difference between the crack of a pistol and the bark of a rifle, but that's for later. When you get back here, hopefully in one piece, I'll open fire. Thinking that we have more than one firearm throwing them into total disarray."

"Got yah..." Without another word, Bill began to furiously hack a pathway into the heavy foliage then disappeared......

* * *

(Speaking in Japanese)

The men were lined up waiting their instructions and Tahoka turned to Aikido, *it was time!*

"My suggestion is we split the men into two search parties of six, one to the east and the other to the west and use a pincer movement to trap the Americans in the middle as we know they are in the immediate spread of no more than two hundred meters."

"Hai." Aikido replied eager to get started.

Arakida selected his six men giving them instructions to move forward staying ten meters apart and only fire only when they get the command from Tahoka.

"Zennor to anata no kyori o tamochimasu." (forward and keep your distance) Tahoka's voice at maximum pitch echoed in the still morning air.

Bill could hardly catch his breath, his shirt saturated in sweat as he heard Tahoka's command to move forward and he threw himself down and parted the large ferns to get a clearer view.

"I guess this is as good a time and place as any to start a war." He chuckled.

He couldn't understand Tahoka's command in Japanese but he could take an educated guess and he cocked the hammer on the 3-51.

'Crack' the small caliber shell gave a slight kick as the bullet flew in the direction of the search party. Chuck was peering through the binoculars from their makeshift 'fox hole'.

"Heh... Heh... That scattered them!" Chuck laughed out loud. "They're ducking for cover in every direction. *Come on Bill,* give them the second scare."

'Crack'...

But now this time the men could see the muzzle flash and Tahoka gave the command to open fire pointing in the direction where Bill was hiding. That was Bill's cue 'good to go' and do another 'Bolt' and he didn't hang around.

'*Chit... Chit... Chit...*' The distinct sound of the two LMG's barked, the gunners firing from the waist, the lethal stream of lead splintering and savaging every plant in its path.

Bill, head down, was running for dear life as branches and palms shattered around him, bullets zipping everywhere.

"*At last.*" Bill reached 'base camp' crashing down heavily next to Sally. Chuck was right Shendo's men had been fooled into concentrating their fire in the wrong direction.

"Boy *was that* close!" Bill panted rolling flat on his back, staring at the sky.

"*Are you alright honey?*" Sally couldn't help herself laying by his side throwing her arms around his chest, followed by an anxious kiss.

"Yeah, I'm okay." Bill replied somewhat embarrassed.

Chuck didn't even notice he was too engrossed with the turmoil happening below.

Suddenly Tahoka turned and raised his arm.

"Anata no hinan o hikaemasu." (hold your fire)

"Great!" Chuck had that evil grin on his face. "They're gathering their thoughts on their next play. They don't know whether the party's over or we're just waiting for a second drink. *Now,* let me see..."

Chuck carefully adjusted the rear sight on the Arisaka, closing one eye.

"About two hundred... Yeah that's about right" He turned the small knurled circular adjuster to the desired distance marked on the sight, then breathed in, held his breath, then squeezed the trigger, the heavy vintage rifle giving a solid kick.

'*BANG*'. The 7.7mm brass cartridge case ejecting as Chuck slid back the bolt and reloaded.

"*Got im!*" Chuck could see the soldier next to Tahoka stagger back and scream in pain as the copper nose ripped through his shoulder.

"Pity, I was aiming at Tahoka." Chuck grinned.

Now there was real turmoil in the Japanese camp with first blood spilled and more so, rifle fire coming from the opposite direction.

(Speaking in Japanese)

"*Down... Down... Down... Take cover... Medic...*" Tahoka screamed.

"That's spooked them and they know we mean business. Now for another one." Chuck was on a duck shoot.

The Arisaka kicked again the bullet zipping past Aikido's ear making him bite the dust, you never hear the shot that kills you and there's no second chances.

The empty shell case hit the dirt as Chuck opened the breach then locked the bolt for another round. *'BANG'* he third bullet was on its way.

Arakida gave a violent sort of kick, like a sort of full body spasm. The seven mill had going clean through his neck severing his Aorta, blood spurting in a fountain of crimson from the severed artery as his heart relentlessly pumped his life away.

Tahoka ran from his cover keeping his head down to be by his best friends' side, but it was all too late to call the medic and for Arakida would sleep in another bed.

"I nailed Tahoka's mate, now they have a real problem. One captain down and we have the tactical advantage on the high ground and they know they are easy pickings with little or no cover in the semi cleared bush."

"You mean you killed him?" Bill was on his knees beside Chuck.

"Well he's not moving if that's an indication."

"My God!" Sally placed her hand to her mouth. "This is like something out of these crazy movies. *Now we're sure to be on death row!*"

With one man, dead and another seriously wounded Tahoka was in serious trouble. *'BANG'* another soldier staggered back and fell motionless to the ground. The cunningness of the Americans had taken him by surprise and his men were getting cut down in deadly crossfire. He had to do something soon before there were more causalities.

"Enough, let's move it. These guys are no slouches and they'll shred this hill with more lead than the 'South East Missouri Lead Mines', even the monkeys won't be safe. Grab the water and stack the bottles in the backpack... *Come on..."* Chuck screamed. *"Move it... Move it..."*

"Here Sally, put the 22 back in your ankle holster you may need it more than me."

"Come on Bill, don't fuck around." Chuck had already shouldered the rifle and was crashing his way through the heavy ferns down a pathway they had previously partially cleared.

Tahoka gave the command. *"Randamu de kasai."*

All hell was let loose as the hill was cut to pieces with rifle and automatic fire with an ear deafening noise.

"Holy shit." Chuck screamed. *"Hit the dirt... Hit the dirt* and hide behind anything you can find."

Bill grabbed Sally's arm and dragged her down behind a large volcanic rock.

"Now lie still and keep your head down."

"Where's Chuck?" Sally asked as he was nowhere to be seen.

"Never mind him, he can look after himself."

"I can hardly hear you." Sally yelled at top of her voice.

Bill didn't reply he was more interested in mother life, then just as sudden as 'D' day started, the firing stopped. Shendo had called a ceasefire to get the stretcher bearers to recover the wounded and his dead friend with the whole camp to a standstill watching the conflict play out. I was not a pretty sight and Shendo was breaking the 100 on his way to the 'battle' front.

Then there was a deathly silence as the three-lay undercover. Sally wasn't complaining getting as close to Bill as possible.

"*Chuck*, what do you think?" Bill yelled wondering why the onslaught had stopped.

"Chuck, *do you hear me...? Chuck...*"

There was no reply and Bill turned to Sally with the look that mothers and wives have when the postman arrives with a telegram from Uncle Sam.

"*Bill...?*"

"*No Sally,* don't even think about it." But Bill was clearly worried as he tried to calm her and she could sense it......

* * *

(Speaking Japanese)

"*Tahoka*" Shendo screamed not believing his eyes whilst staring at the third stretcher passing him by. *How can a search party of twelve heavily armed men fuck it up so badly?* Shendo was shaking his head in disbelief?

"Boso." Tahoka bowed his voice almost cracking at the sight of Arakida lying motionless on the field stretcher and Shendo could sense his loss as he too had the utmost regards for his bodyguard but now he was in serious trouble and what would he report to Numero?

With two dead and one soldier seriously wounded the horizon was bleak and Kenichi turned to the camp doctor who was attending the wounded man.

"Kare ga dono yo ni ishi?" (Doctor, how is he?)

Akimoto, gave a depressed sigh then gently closed Akari's eyes before covering his face with the blanket.

Araki the camp's Buddhist priest was going to be busy with one officer dead and two 'soldiers'... Samurais of the highest order, it doesn't get any worse.…...!

* * *

Salibe was watching the 'offensive' from the safety of the Nissan hut, a wry grin crossing his face. He had no love for the Japanese and even less for Shendo and he could only imagine the phone call to Numero envious of the fly on the wall. None of his business, Salibe returned to his cot for a nap before lunch, he had more important issues on his mind.

* * *

"Tahoka, Dansei o kaiko." (Dismiss the men)

"Hai... Dokemasu." Kazuo yelled at the top of his lungs. "Clean your weapons and return them to the armory with any unspent ammunition."

The men were clearly unhappy rumbling discontent through the ranks as they picked up their gear and in defiance slowly walking toward the ordinance shed. Samurais never retreat, 'faithful in adversity'. Their chance would come again, only the next time they would hunt the Americans' *till the death!*

As for Shendo, he was even more depressed at the thought of writing three *'I'm sorry to inform you'* letters' to the deceased's families. He had clearly underestimated the combat experience and ingenuity of the decorated veteran's and he turned to Tahoka...

"Come to my quarters once the men have dispersed."

"Hai." Tahoka was clearly shaken. The captured of the Americans was going to be 'a walk in the park' but they had been outmaneuvered and outsmarted much to his humiliation and worse still the loss of three of his men.

Kenichi gave a depressed sigh as he sat down heavily at his desk almost in relief to get a few minutes of solitude to unscramble his muddled thoughts on how to recover 'a worse than bad day'. The heavy knock on the door didn't help and he shook his head in annoyance, the disruption killing his thought process... *It had to be Tahoka...!*

"Hairu." (enter)

The tone in Shendo's voice was not encouraging as Tahoka obeyed and opened the door.

"Suwarimasu." (sit) Shendo pointed.

Tahoka bowed *"Hai Boso."*

Kenichi sat back rubbing his chin in an intimidating manner. His dark penetrating brown eyes threatening repercussion, but the blame game starts at the top and he was as much to blame as anyone.

"Tahoka please explain why 'Datsugoku', a simple search and destroy operation was such a disaster with the subsequent loss of life?" Shendo's voice was more than demanding.

"Eh...Heh." Kazuo was decidedly nervous and he was showing it.

"Yoku?" (well?) Shendo barked.

"Boso, we were outsmarted..." He raised his hands like 'what can I say'? "The Americans began firing on our right flank with two shots and I gave the order to form a 'horse shoe' to encircle them having seen the muzzle flash on the second shot exposing their location. I then ordered Arakida to hold fire until we were in position, but they tricked us, there is no other word for it because the first two shots came from a small caliber firearm... *Em...*". Tahoka paused... "Like a pistol and before I knew it we came under lethal rifle fire on our left flank cutting down Arakida and two of his men before we could regroup."

"Sonogo?" (and then)

"I gave the command to rake the hillside with a lethal rain of lead with rifle and machine gun fire, cutting the hill to pieces. *I tell you Boso,* no human could survive that barrage. Then after ten minutes I gave the command to cease fire as the Americans hadn't retaliated."

"Anata wa karera ga duan shite katto sa reta assumed?" (so, you assumed they were cut down?)

"Dozo Boso." (yes boss)

"If your assumptions are correct then they may be seriously or fatally wounded and if they survived, more so they must be short of water and food so... No, we let sleeping dogs lie and recommence with operation 'Datsugoku' on Wednesday morning two days from now. Tomorrow we will cremate the deceased and I place you in charge as before to make the necessary arrangements. Now I'm tired and I need to make an urgent phone call......"

THE PALACE HOTEL TOKYO

"I think we're done here." Steve glanced at his watch while Gregg finished the last of his coffee.

"Hmmm... Almost one... What time will it be in DC?"

"Are you still thinking of phoning Thomson?" Gregg was puzzled.

"I don't know..." Steve sighed in indecision making a face. "Anyhow, let's check the time difference." he opened his cell and 'Googled'.

"Not good... Five am in the morning... I don't think we should chance the wrath of Jenny." Steve laughed.

"Then why don't we just text John on his secure line? *You have that cell number in case of emergencies."*

Steve shrugged. "Yeah, I guess your right and as you rightly said, he will have read the tabloids and watched CNN by now. Okay you recite the message and I'll enter the text."

"Wreckage of Global 10 found as reported on TV and Tabloids and confirmed by McGill of Global and Daniels of the FBI. Daniels had discussions with Anderson from Boeing who states its highly probable that the debris is from Global 10 but it could take another week or so before they are sure. They must check frame numbers etc. McGill quoted Anderson as saying, 'the fuselage fragments were shredded like 'Swiss Cheese' as if an explosion had taken place and if that's the case not much hope recovering 'black box'… more problems wreckage lies in deepest part of the North Pacific around 7,000 meters. This could be the 'big sleep'. McGill will keep us in the loop but what's your suggestion as our hands are tied? Steve Nelson... One other point, has there been any charges laid against Azis and his two accomplices, Abdul Azim and Dabar Bishara?

"What do you think?" Gregg asked.

"Yeah, that says it all and I'm sure John will get back to us before the day's over."

"You're leaving gentleman?"

"Yes...*Eh*...Aya... You have been an excellent host and we both thank you for your warm hospitality." Steve had that dangerous smile.

"Arigato." Aya bowed. "I will escort you to the lobby and the elevator." She smiled showing the way with her hand.

"Aya, there's really no need, we can see ourselves out."

"Just a second Gregg! Maybe Aya can advise us where to go this evening for clubbing and maybe some Karaoke?"

Aya had a good command of English and didn't need a second prompt.

"My advice gentleman, if that's what you are asking? We have an excellent supper club right here in the hotel on the 19th floor. It's popular with the business fraternity to relax after a hectic day at the office, excellent food and cocktails and pretty female service girls dressed in traditional kimonos to attend to your every need and if you have the vocals, then of course there's Karaoke."

Steve turned to Gregg. "That sounds like a 'made to order' and *right here* in the hotel for convenience."

"Yeah, why not? Thanks, Aya we'll definitely test the water."

"You wouldn't happen to be free tonight?" Steve wasn't slow in coming forward... *Was it a throw away or serious?*

Aya gave one of her smiles, her face slightly flushed. "I am sorry but thank you for the offer, hotel staff are forbidden to fraternize with the guests or customers, besides it's a 'men only' club."

"Well it was worth a try." Steve tried to justify his stupidity speaking in an undertone to Gregg.

"She speaks perfect English and heard every word you said. Now do the right thing."

"*Ah...Hem*...Aya, if I embarrassed you, I sincerely apologize."

For once Steve was the gentleman.

"Not atoll, I'm used to it." Aya smiled again, this time more composed. "Sayonara." She bowed then returned to the reception desk a smile on her face. *'Americans!'*

The elevator chimed and the doors opened. Gregg pressed four then turned to Steve. "*Man,* you embarrass me at times."

"*Awe come on Gregg* it's all in a day's work."

"*Yeah...Yeah!*"

"Listen, it's just coming up to two so we have a lotta time to kill. Do you want to join me in my room and raid the bar fridge?"

"Nah... I'll take a rain check, I'm still recovering from last night... *You and your nightcap!* I'm going back to my room for forty winks... To recap... What time tonight?"

"Say around seven, I'll give you a call."

The elevator chimed.......

* * *

Gregg slipped the plastic key card and opened the door to his hotel room. Housekeeping had just finished making up the room and it had that pleasant aroma of freshness.

"Boy, am I looking forward to getting some peace and quiet, Steve can be heavy weather." Gregg was talking out loud having a one-sided conversation with himself.

He slipped off his jacket and hung it on the back of the chair, then his shoes and finally the stuffy tie before virtually leaping onto the bed like a trampoline then lying on his back.

"Ahhh... But this bloody pillow!" He sat up and punched a hollow with his fist into the poor excuse before turning on his back to rest his head.

"Hmmm, does *that* feel good!"

Between the frustration of the case and yesterday's overzealous booze night, he felt fatigued and washed out and who could blame him......?

* * *

The problem with time on your hands and solitude is one's mind starts to reflect on the good times and bad times and what you could have done better, be it work related or your relationships and Michelle's face flashed onto the 'screen'. Steve had sledged him for getting too serious over a one-night stand as he would rather hook up in LA with the flight attendants, *especially the blonde.* Maybe Steve had something as Marge, in hindsight was sending him 'close encounters of the third kind' and to make it even more difficult she had it all, looks, personality and a figure for the 'cat walk'. To have this babe hanging on your arm would make any dude proud. But there again... *Michelle...* He just couldn't get her out of his mind. For sure she was not a virgin but the love making that night was something special and he was sure she felt the same... Then again there was Marge, an unknown quantity and not to be written off. There was only one thing for it for peace of mind and he stretched over for the bedside phone......

* * *

"I'll most likely catch her before she goes to the office." Gregg glanced at his watch again. *"Hmmm... I make it around seven am in DC... Now that number?"*

He began to dial... 81...1... The delay seemed forever as the annoying dialing tone rang in his ears....

"Come on Come on.... Answer the damn phone...."

*"Hello... Eh...*Who's calling." A sleepy female voice answered.

"Michelle honey...It's me... Gregg."

"Gregg! There was a pause... "Gregg darling for a moment there I thought I was dreaming... *It's really you...* I just knew you would call again... What are you doing now?" .

"Just relaxing on my bed and thinking of you."

"Good thoughts I hope, or good bad thoughts?" She could hear Gregg laughing.

"Did I wake you from your beauty sleep?"

"Yes, but just as well as its nearly eight and I'll have to try and beat Maggi to that shower or *I'll really* be late this morning!"

"Is this a bad time?"

"No darling, I didn't mean it that way, I'm just so happy to hear your voice, you know I love you?"

"I know."

"Your assignment?"

"There's a good chance I may be back in Washington before you know it! I can't explain it to you for security reasons but Steve and I may be called back early, but don't worry you'll be the first to know."

"I can't wait."

"Listen honey I'll let you go. I wanted to phone just to make sure you felt the same way about me as I feel about you."

"So, have I convinced you?"

"You could say that."

"Why you..." Michelle was laughing.

"Goodbye honey, I'll phone you if I have any news."

"Love you."

"Me too." Gregg placed the phone back in the receiver then lay back staring at the ceiling, his hands behind his head. How could he fall head over heels for a woman he slept with for only one night? Love acts in mysterious ways but in the end only time will tell......

* * *

The phone rang... "That'll be Steve he's always on time, no tie tonight, smart casual."

Gregg picked up the phone. "I'm coming, I'll meet you at the elevator."

"How did you know it was me?"

"Asks a silly question." Gregg grinned almost laughing as he put the phone back. He quickly slipped on his jacket, adjusted his open neck shirt and with one last glance in the wall mirror smiled in satisfaction and opened the door. For sure tonight was gonna be interesting.

"So, what did you do today?" Gregg asked as he pressed 'UP' on the elevator's highly polished brass face plate.

Within seconds the doors opened and to their surprise the elevator was congested with around five 'suites' presumably heading for the supper bar.

"This joint must be popular." Gregg commented as the doors closed.

Steve gave a sort of 'well if you must know' shrug.

"Had a cold Asahi at the 'Royal Bar' but there was no action and I got bored and returned to my room and took a leaf from your book and hit the hay."

"And You?"

"Gave Michelle a call then turned in."

"Awe *man*, you're really hung up on that broad, *hell* you only met her for one night!"

"And I suppose you would like us to meet up with these two flight attendants?"

"Could do worse!"

The elevator chimed... 'Floor 19 have a nice evening'.

"Here we are." Steve commented as the doors opened. "Maybe just as well. Say let's call a truce and enjoy ourselves, huh?"

"If you say so..." Gregg replied in sarcasm.

"Welcome to the 'Place Hotel Club Lounge'... The pretty 'Mama-san' gave the hotel's standard smile. "Can I please check your room keys as the supper club is for hotel guests and club members only, I'm sure you understand?"

* * *

Dressed in a stunning sea blue Kimono most probably silk, exquisitely decorated with branched cherry blossoms, the matching ten-inch waist band in cherry pink emphasized the petite waist line of the high collared wide sleeved traditional dress. At around 5-8 her Geta shoes made her slightly taller. Although in her mid-thirties she still had that mystique that Asian women portray with their pale smooth complexions, brown eyes, bright red narrow lips and dark eyebrows. Her flawless black hair was swept up into a sort of circular bun on the top of her crown held in place with two oyster shelled what could only be described as chop sticks protruding from either side. The Bakelite black narrow name plate pinned to her chest on the right side just above her small firm breast bore the name Aki.......

* * *

"Boy this is some joint!" Steve commented trying to take it all in.

"Gentleman would you wish a sofa by the window on the far right with a magnificent view of the lights of 'Akihito' our beloved emperor's palace. It's a beautiful clear evening and you will be able to view the palace grounds and the mote.

"I think that is an excellent suggestion eh...?"

"Aki."

"Aki." Steve was in his element where beautiful women are concerned.

Aki snapped her fingers and from nowhere a much younger version of Aki appeared dressed in the same attire, shuffled toward them in tiny dainty steps in her Geta type clog shoes, her smile overbearing. She was pretty alright not that you would kick Aki out of bed but it was getting better all the time.

"This is Etsuko, whom will be your hostess tonight......

* * *

The "Club Lounge" matched its five-star rating with the plush luxurious black leather sofas and loungers each accompanied with oval shaped coffee tables, their thick clear glass resting on black lacquered wooden rectangular frames. Each table had a short white stubby electronic candle, the flame flickering in the semi darkness undistinguishable from the real thing and for moment one's eyes struggled in the dim light before settling down and absorbing the soft warm ambience. Along one complete wall was tempered plate glass windows, the huge pains separated with almost invisible thin black powder coated aluminum supports giving the impression of a complete glass wall overlooking the magnificent Palace by night. The dark blue patterned lush carpet in a cherry blossom pattern matched the Kimonos of the lookalike 'Geishas' falling together almost in a 'Renaissance Monet'. On the opposite side of the lounge was a magnificent long bar in glass and polished beach, with glass back window panels in the same design of that of the lounge, only this time showing the tall buildings and bright colorful lights of the Ginza. The bar top in black polished marble with slivers of white gave that plush luxurious look to match the prices of the liquor and cocktails. The ten or so high back bar stools in beach and blue leather were demise of patrons whilst the window sofas were fully occupied. Two barmen in red waistcoats and white collared shirts were actively doing the 'cocomo' their stainless-steel shakers sparkling in the dim lighting as they mixed the lethal 'get highs'. On the far left as you entered was a small stage around four meters by four with a microphone and audio equipment for Karaoke, maybe a bit early for the Michael Jacksons or Hanamizuki by 'Yo Hitoto' but then the night is young......

* * *

"Etsuko speaks perfect English, that's why I assigned her to your table."

"Domo." As usual Steve was first past the post when it came to the opposite sex.

"*Ah*, you speak Japanese." Aki was taken aback.

"No, only a few words." Steve replied unabashed.

"Well it's nice to see Caucasians trying... Etsuko will escort you to your table and explain the drinks and food ordering."

"Domo." Steve just couldn't let it go.

Aki smiled then bowed, her smile said it all.

"Dozo... If you can follow me, please." Etsuko executed her dainty steps in quick time. "Here we are gentlemen, I hope you enjoy the view... Please." She motioned with her beautiful manicured hand to take their seats.

"I'm here at your beck and call this evening, just press this button for anything you need. I will join you to pour your drinks. Food can also be ordered but it's more or less snacks, like Club sandwich, Sushi, Sashimi, California Rolls are but a few. Alcohol must be ordered by the bottle except for beer which is on tap. Is everything to your liking

"Yes... Eh... Etsuko." Gregg replied taking a second to read her name tag again. "This view is stunning."

"Thank you." Etsuko bowed a warm smile crossing her face. *These two could be a handful this evening.* "Now what would you wish to start with?"

"Scotch?" Steve turned to Gregg begging the question.

"Sure, Say a single malt?"

"Yeah that fits the bill but I would like to start with a cold beer."

Etsuko acknowledged and passed Steve the beverage menu.

"Hmmmm... Let me see... Glenmorangie 20 years' single malt... *That's the ticket.*"

"Your beer sir?"

"Asahi draught is fine for me to start with."

"And snacks?"

"No, I'm good for the moment... Steve?"

"I'm with you."

"Would you wish ice with your Scotch?"

"Yes, and some water." Steve answered.

"Arigato..." Etsuko smiled and went about her business; the Club Bar was now almost full to capacity.

"*Wow,* that smile almost knocked me out of the park."

"Yeah Steve, for once I gotta admit she's something else."

"So, your human after all!"

"Get out of it! But this bloody sofa is so low I'm almost folding my legs in two!"

"Japanese size *man*, not for six two Americans!"

"For once you got something there. You know, I'm looking forward to this evening it's a break from the shit we contend with every day."

"That's the spirit and on that subject, what do you think of my choice of Scotch?"

"At 250 US, a bottle? *It had better be good!* Anyhow it's going on your expense sheet *and won't Thomson be pleased!*"

"*Hey...* In the heat of the battle we need sustenance, huh?"

"*Heh... Heh... Heh.*" Gregg had to laugh. "*Maaan...* You're a piece a work."

Etsuko kneeled placing the Scotch glasses on the coffee table the bottle of Glenmorangie followed suite as with the pewter ice bucket.

"Would you wish me to pour the drinks now sir?"

"We can manage."

"No sir, that's what I'm here for... Ice?"

"Two cubes." Steve replied. "I'm beginning to like this."

"I'll bring your beer shortly, sir."

Suddenly there was a loud clap as a Japanese man alighted the stage. An attendant on the audio unit had a brief discussion and entered his request into the Karaoke player the song in writing and back ground music appearing on a large colored background screen, before passing the mike to the would be 'Japanese Idol'.

"I'll be darned." Steve nudged Gregg almost spilling his drink. "The famous Karaoke has begun."

'Tegami Haikei jugo no Kimi i' The short man in a smart dark blue business suite and loosened tie announcing the name of the song to a loud round of applause.

"Hiekei kono tegami doko wo shite dare ni mo hansasenai."

"Singing Japanese? That's different but this guy's not bad."

Etsuko was freshening the drinks and couldn't help but overhear he conversation.

"This is a beautiful Japanese song and popular at Karaoke. It was written and performed by Angela Aki. The lyrics are instructions to a 15-year-old on how to appreciate the moment and make the most of life."

"Well we certainly could take a leaf from that book. What say you partner?" Gregg couldn't miss the shot.

"Etsuko, do they have western songs as well?" Steve asked.

"Of course, western songs are very popular as we Japanese just love to practice our English."

"So, if I want to..."

The singer had just left the stage to another round of applause.

"Come, I'll escort you to the stage and assist you with your song."

"This has gotta be good." Gregg couldn't stop laughing.

The applause even louder when an American takes the stage and begins to sing.

> *As my soul heals the shame...*
>
> *I'll grow through the pain...*
>
> *Lord I'm doing all I can...*
>
> *To be a better man......*

THE LEVITSKY KOMSOMOL

(Speaking in Russian)

The Tannoy echoed above the steady whine of the nuclear reactor.

"First officer Levitsky come to the board room immediately." The Kapitan's voice was loud and clear.

Boris was checking the internal guidance system that keeps track of a ships motion from a fixed starting point using gyroscopes to determine the submarine's position.

Levitsky immediately stopped what he was doing and obeyed the captain's command.

The journey to 'Davy Jones Locker' had so far been uneventful and the crew had settled down well after having been laid up in port for three months for the submarine's refit. The long underwater sail without resurfacing was standard in Nuclear fueled submarines as they could stay submerged almost indefinitely, using electrolysis to convert hydrogen and oxygen from sea water to produce an endless supply of air and with a perpetual nuclear reactor to generate steam for the turbines the only problem was *food!*

There was a loud knock on the boardroom door and Chernoff for a moment was distracted from the oceanic charts spread on the table.

"Voyti" He barked not in the best of moods.

The Lewinsky was making good time but running on Passive Sonar to avoid detection requires listening to sounds to identify known ocean floor features, is always fraught with danger.

Nicolai laid down the dividers and turned to his first officer.

"By my estimates, we are approximately twenty kilometers from the Straights. The channel is only 14 kilometers wide and varies from three to nine hundred meters deep in some areas. Are my estimates correct Boris?"

"Kapitan as always you are correct." Boris was taking no chances, in the Russian navy the advice is stay on the right side of your commander or end up in Siberia.

"I'll escort you to the brig and you can take responsibility to sail the Lewinsky through the straights. I need to make sure you are fit for command."

"Da Kapitan Dlya menya bol'shaya chest." (yes, captain I am honored)

The two men walked sprightly through the narrow passageway to the bridge and control room with Boris closely behind Nicolai observing protocell.

When Chernoff entered the crew immediately rose to their feet to attention.

"Neprinuzhdenno vernut'sya k vashey stantsii leytenant Levitsky v Komande." (at ease return to your stations lieutenant Levitsky is in command)

Boris turned to Chernoff slightly unsure of himself but this was his fifteen minutes in the sun and Nicolai gave his nod of approval.

"Tail planes down 30 digress... Front ballast tanks flood to 75... Reduce speed to 15 knots... Submerge to 200 meters and switch to silent mode..."

* * *

The British naval base at Gibraltar would be the challenge as the 'Straights' is only 14 kilometers wide. Fortunately, the refit of the Lewinsky Komsomol incorporated Russia's latest stealth technology making the Nuclear submarines so quiet, so much so, the US military and NATO are unable to detect them. These 'Black Hole' submarines, nick named by the US navy, can freely approach coastlines of the United States without fear of being detected whenever they want. In fact, a Russian nuclear-powered attack submarine armed with long range missiles sailed around the Gulf of Mexico for several weeks in 2012 without being detected. Russia's is now in the process of upgrading and incorporating this 'advanced stealth technology' in all nuclear submarines. The US Navy openly acknowledges that they cannot track these subs when they are submerged....

* * *

As the Lewinsky Komsomol slowly made its way through the straights you could have heard a pin drop in the control room.

"Kapitan." Boris whispered in Chertoff's ear. "Our passive sonar indicates that there are at least three British naval ships at anchor. And with drafts of approximately 8 meters we must be extremely careful when navigating through the narrow channel to avoid any signs of water turbulence."

"Second officer Petrov reduce speed to ten knots." Levitsky gave the command.

Chernoff nodded his approval, caution the name of the game as the next fifteen minutes was crucial to clear the channel without being detected by the British.

Nicolai stood solemn faced, his features divulge of any emotion. The Kapitan, a true Russian from the USSR period and an ardent supporter of Putin to make Russia the greatest military power in the world once more.

The fifteen minutes seemed like from 'Here to Eternity' the crew on edge.

Second officer Petrov broke the silence. "Lieutenant, inform the Kapitan we are now clear of the channel and entering the Pacific Ocean."

"Kapitan?" Levitsky was waiting for a reaction from Chernoff.

"I heard... Lieutenant you are in command, it is your decision."

"Lieutenant Petrov, rear tail planes up four five. Blow bow ballast tanks to five zero... Ascend to one five zero meters and increase speed to forty-five knots. Navigator set course to one eight zero degrees south west for Cape Horn and the Drake Passage to enter the South Pacific Ocean."

"Da leytenant."

"At this speed Kapitan and with a clear run void of major shipping lanes, we will arrive at the rendezvous three to four days ahead of schedule."

Chernoff gave his nod of approval. Well done in the Russian Navy is not in its vocabulary.

"I'm returning to my quarters and I don't want to be disturbed unless for emergencies. I will entertain you and Lieutenant Petrov for dinner at seven this evening in the boardroom. Instruct Petrov to issue the crew with double rations of Vodka......"

THE DILEMMA

Shendo's dilemma was, 'should he phone Numero or leave it until the Americans were either history or captured'? With Okio you can never tell and why take chances? Seppuku or live and then what? The thought either way was not enticing. After all he was the only one with direct contact to Numero by radio phone and he sat back in his chair and for a moment stared blankly into space, his mind fighting 'to tell or not to tell'. Then he nervously wiped his brow with his handkerchief, the air-con struggling in the afternoon humidity.

"Kare no kokoro wa kimaranakatta." He spoke aloud, more relaxed. (no, his mind was made up)

Once the cremation ceremony was over, tomorrow he would discuss the plan with Kazuo Tahoka for a second offensive the day after, only this time it would be 'take no prisoners' and whatever it takes.

His face more relaxed he stretched for the teapot, the chef had preempted his bosses indulgence after a hard day made the warm brew before he arrived.

He glanced at his Seiko. It had just turned five and time for evening mess and as he slowly sipped the second cup of the green tea, his mind was still fuzzed. The atmosphere at dinner would be 'anger management' at the loss of three of their comrades and whatever, he had to show strength and leadership to gain the respect of his men. Easier said than done with their mounting hatred toward the Americans. It was time and he rose to his feet and fastened his holster belt then buckled his 'Shin Gunto' sword. If nothing else, he must look the part of the camp commander.......

* * *

"Stay where you are Sally and keep your head down, you never know. I'll go and check out Chuck."

Sally felt a shiver pass down her spine, thinking the worst, *but it can't be, no it can't be.* She was thinking aloud.

Bill slowly crawled over to Chucks crumpled body hugging mother earth to avoid some cowboy looking for his marksman's crossed rifles.

Chuck was lying motionless on his side and Bill stretched over with one arm shaking him vigorously.

"Chuck, *are you alright?* Chuck, *stop fooling around!*"

Then Bill suddenly went quiet upon seeing the red carpet of blood oozing from Chucks side like a map of California, the reality striking home.

"How is he Bill?" Sally was a train wreck in hypertension.

Two bullets had gone clean through Chuck's side shattering his ribs then passing through his lungs and most likely his spinal column as he ran for cover from the second ferocious volley. Even if he had survived, mercilessly he wouldn't have lasted the day.

Bill turned to face Sally and shook his head in dismay. He had lost his best friend, sure, he had his faults but when the going gets tough...

"He's gone Sally." Sadness streaming through Bill's voice.

Sally covered her mouth with her hand in disbelieve, her eyes filling up. *Chuck dead!* It can't be true! *No... No..."*

Bill pondered for a moment, the game had changed. *Now what?* He crawled over and pushed the thick tropical foliage apart to get a clearer view of the camp and peered through the binoculars.

"It looks like their licking their wounds and called it a day but for sure there will be another tomorrow. Sally, you can stand up now, it's safe."

"Poor Chuck, I can't bear to look." Sally was still in shock, turning her head the other way. After all it's not every day you see a dead body with horrific gunshot wounds, worse still, *someone you know!*

"Bill, what are we going to do?" She sobbed and rushed over throwing her arms around his neck, burying her face into his shoulder. "I'm so scared. Now there's only two of us."

Bill gently held her back, his hands on both her shoulders and stared into her 'Niagara' eyes. Then he searched into his trouser pocket and pulled out a crumpled, less than intriguing handkerchief and began to gently wipe her cheeks.

"There, there, honey. Don't *you* think *I'm* scared?"

"You are?"

"Of course, I wouldn't be human if I wasn't!"

The inevitable, Sally stood on her tip toes and crushed her lips against his. I was a long breathless encounter laced with both love and fear of the unknown.

"Bill, I love you." She looked up into his eyes. The look that launched a thousand ships.

"Sally honey... I... I..."

"Say it Bill."

"I love you too... *But...*" Bill paused again. "This is not the time nor place, we have to bury Chuck before this tropical sun gets to him."

"You mean?"

"Yes Sally, we have to do it and do it now and I need your help."

Bill grabbed the bayonet and looked around for a place that was relatively clear of growth.

"This looks like a good spot. Here, use the bayonet and I'll start clearing the ground......"

* * *

"It's pretty shallow Bill." Sally stood back her hand on her hip the bayonet's blade covered in damp soil. She was staring at the three feet by seven 'trench'.

"Yes, it will have to do. It's getting dark and we don't have much time. I'll cover the base with a thick layer of palm leaves then we're done... *Hmmm...* That looks good." Bill stood back admiring his work.

"Now Sally I need you to help me slide him over. I'll take his arms and you grab his feet... Sally, *are you listening?"*

"Bill, I can't." Sally was standing petrified at the thought of touching a dead person.

"Sally, just close your eyes and when I say pull, *do it...*"

"There... That wasn't so bad. I'll empty Chuck's pockets and remove his watch. I've never met his parents but I know they live in Chicago and he has a brother. If we ever get out of here alive I'll make a point of visiting them and giving them his personal possessions. Here Sally, you hang on to Chuck's cigarette lighter, were gonna need it. I'll cover his face with his airline jacket. I'm not a staunch Christian but I'll say a prayer before we fill the grave."

Bill placed his right hand over his heart.

"The lord is my shepherd, I'll not want, he layeth me down in green pastures... Yay though I walk in the valley of death I fear no ill..."

Sally just couldn't stop sobbing as Bill finally covered Chuck's body with the volcanic soil. The final chapter in his best friend's life, now over.......

* * *

"Please fasten your safety belts and place your seats in the upright position and ensure your hand luggage is safely stored in the overhead bins. We have commenced our decent to Dulles International and Delta 14 will touch down in approximately 14 minutes. It's 7.00.am US time so you can adjust your watches. It's a bright sunny morning with clear blue skies and the temperature is a pleasant 70 degrees. A taxi to the city will cost around 25 US dollars. On behalf of Captain Williams and first Officer Reilly we thank you for flying the friendly skies and look forward to serving you again. For those passengers returning home, a safe journey and for visitors to our beautiful capital city, have an enjoyable stay..."

Julie placed back the microphone. *"I hate singing that bullshit."*

"Hey, keep your voice down!" Marge put the brakes on. "Williams is a grumpy old bastard who won't take kindly to your comments."

"Oh, what the hell! Maybe the London haul has its merits after all.'

"Well, we'll just have to wait and see what Draper has in store for us when we touch down."

"I'm looking forward to that like a hole in the head... *That weasel."*

"Awe, come Julie, lighten up."

There was a sudden jolt as the 777's undercarriage puffed smoke and the ABS brakes locked and unlocked swaying the passengers two and fro in their seats, the reverse thrust almost deafening.

"Please remain in your seats until the aircraft has come to a complete stop."

"Hell, how many times have I said that." June was on a hate campaign. "And they never fucking listen."

"We'll be deplaning in around ten minutes so let's get the paperwork complete on the liquor stocks and duty free."

"Your right Marge, It's just that..."

"I know honey; don't you think I feel the same but no news is good news."

"Come on Marge, do you really believe there's hope for Bill and Chuck?"

"Let's put it this way, I'm hedging my bets until I know otherwise."

"This way please. *No,* please use the other exit this is for First Class passengers only."

"Calm down Julie, what's getting into you today?"

"Are you ladies staying aboard?" It was captain Williams and the first officer about to leave.

"Just clearing up some paper work Captain."

"It was nice having you on board and I hope we can fly together in the not too distant future."

The rather handsome grey-haired Captain with the smooth complexion and the narrow silver mustache gave a warm smile as he took the exit followed by a much younger First Officer with a grin that no flight attendant would trust.......

* * *

"Grab the paperwork Marge and lock up the galley while I fetch our bags from the front wardrobe."

Julie and Marge wearily wheeled their airway bags toward Custom Clearance and Immigration and baggage collection through the ill-mannered passengers who were more interested in purchasing duty free booze, prior to customs, than collecting their luggage.

The young custom's officer scanned their declaration forms, looked up, then smiled.

"You can go through."

Immigration cleared it was now just a matter of meeting up with Draper at his office for further flight instructions and Marge was more than nervous at what Julie might just say in her state of mind.

"*God*, I feel washed out. I don't know about you Julie?" Marge was pushing a diversion.

"I'm with you. What I would do for a fresh bed and hot shower and a good night's sleep." Julie nodded, finally the knock-on Draper's door...

"Grab a seat. I had a feeling it might be you two. Say, would you like a coffee or something?" For some reason, Draper looked uncomfortable.

"No, we're good." Julie answered on behalf of Marge.

"I assume you haven't heard the news?"

"*What news?*" Julie didn't hesitate.

"They found the wreckage of Global 10..."

Both woman's faces drained of color simultaneously.

"I'm afraid there are no survivors. According to the grapevine, although I haven't been privy to an official report but it's from a reliable source, it appears by the state of the wreckage the aircraft was blown out of the sky. The Japanese Aviation Authority search and rescue and Boeings Air Accident Investigation Branch, are still looking for the black box and flight data recorder and it's anyone's guess how long *that* will take. *I*... I'm sorry to have to be the bearer of bad news."

Julie was speechless for a moment but why kill the messenger? Her face now more subdued, returning to its natural color. now more subdued.

"Looking back Don, when Marge and I first the heard the bad news that Bill and Chuck's plane had gone down somewhere in the North Pacific we both knew then that to find the crew alive was highly implausible although we never gave up hope. Now that the reality has come home, I suppose in a sense we are both relieved that the final chapter in the disappearance of Global 10 is closed."

"*Listen,* I've been thinking, between the 'stand in' Flight to Tokyo at short notice and the bad news losing your partners, you two girls need a break. So, I'm sanctioning five days R&R at Delta's expense and Firsts Class tickets back to LA."

"*Don*... What can we...?"

"*Don't!* Just be on your way. The flight to LA leaves at 10.30am. Delta 6...Pick up your tickets from Less…. *Now what's keeping you.......?*"

* * *

Sally wiped the sweat from her brow with the back of her hand then stood back and sighed, a sigh that said it all... A solitary tear trickling down her cheek... "*Why?*" She spoke out loud as she stared at the shallow mound of volcanic soil. Sure, at times Chuck was a pain in the butt with his sarcasms and barter, not to mention sexual harassment but he kept the show on the road with never a dull moment and sadly now he was gone, *and gone forever!* Life is so temporary. Chuck was a one off a guy and for all his short comings Sally had to admit that she would sadly miss him and the 'valiant three' would never be the same again.

"*Sally... Sally...* Are you with me?" Bill could see that empty look on her face and he had to snap her out of it.

"*Eh... Eh...* I'm sorry Bill you were you saying?"

"I'm *saying* we gotta get moving and find a good place tonight before darkness falls to make camp."

"*And Chuck?*"

"Sally, he's gone and we have to move on. Our priority now is to find food and replenish our water supply, we're down to three bottles and four mangosteen." Bill pointed to the open haversack. "As for ammo, we have 26 rifle rounds and four in the camber of the 22 Magnum."

"Christ Bill, when you talk like that you scare the shit crap outta me, like as if we're going to war."

"But that's exactly the situation Sally, so you had better get used to the reality that this is a shooting war and it's 'take no prisoners'. *So...* If you could do me a favor and pick up that haversack, huh? I'll sling the rifle and use this poor excuse for a Parang to clear a pathway through the bush."

Bill shook his head pointing to the bayonet already showing the wear and tear of digging and hacking bamboo and now it couldn't *cut butter!*

Bill shrugged. "Well... We'll, just have to make do... Sally, stay close behind me and watch your step. We need to move further to the west of the island but still remain in view of the runway or I'll be out of range."

"You mean watch out for snakes!"

"Sally, come here honey." Bill laid down the Arisaka and opened his arms. He could sense Sally was scared and he was being rather callous and cold hearted and he gave her a gentle kiss on the lips pressing her body close to his in a reassuring and protective manner.

"I'm so sorry honey... *I... I."*

But before Bill could utter another word Sally threw her arms around his neck and kissed him again, only this time it wasn't a 'throw away' it was the real deal and she wasn't going to let go in a hurry.

"Sally honey." Bill broke the mouth lock, gasping for air. "Sally honey... We really..."

Sally touched his lips with two fingers. "I know what you are about to say, but can't you delay it for another minute or so... Life is so precious, just look what happened to Chuck...! Darling just kiss me once more......."

* * *

"This looks as good a place as any. It's like someone up there likes us. A few bushes to clear and there's plenty of ferns and palms to lay a damp proof bed and more to the point, I have a clear view of the runway and the camp. And if they keep these lights on... It doesn't get any better." Bill smiled pleased with the outcome. "Sally, you look bushed... Here, sit on my jacket and take a drink of water and relax. I'll clear this area and make it comfortable, *if there is such a thing on this godforsaken Island!* Hell, I'm soaked through." Bill pinched his shirt which looked like a wet rag. "What I would do for a cold shower, *huh?*"

Sally rolled Bill's airway jacket into a pillow and planked it, giving a pronounced groan as she slowly bent her knees and sat down.

"Thanks honey, are you sure you don't need my help?" She had already swilled her mouth with the tainted water and spat it out before indulging in a second round, her mouth parched.

Bill grinned. "Just you sit on that pretty behind of yours and take a well-earned rest... *Cappice!*"

"Italian now are we...? *Acqua minerali...?*" Sally smiled offering the half empty bottle.

"*Not bad!* No, I'm good, I'll save the pleasure till I'm finished."

"Are you talking about the water or me?" Sally gave a nervous laugh but at least she was calming down.

"*Heh... Heh... Heh.*" Bill laughed. "Now *that's* the Sally *I* know!"

"You haven't answered my question."

"I'll take the fifth." Bill was still laughing, a cheeky grin on his face.

"*Why you...!*" Sally retaliated by throwing a handful of dirt at him, like a snowball, and Bill ducked just in time.

"*Wow,* I wouldn't like to get on *your* bad side!"

"*Take note mister!*" Sally was grinning all over. *Where has, this big handsome lug been all her life?* She thought... *And to fall in love in these circumstances was something else.* But love doesn't discriminate between reality and dreams when you're thinking from the heart.......

* * *

"Well, what do you think?" Bill stood back, hands on his hips, admiring his work.

"Let me see." Sally rolled over and lay on her back on the soft bed of palm and Pongee ferns. *Five stars...*" She smiled. "*Now,* are you going to lie down beside me...*Or what?*" Sally patted the spot next to her.

"Is that an invitation or what?" Bill smiled taking a drink of the tepid water.

"*Touché...* Maybe *I* should take the fifth?" Sally teased.

"Why you... Now it's my turn." Bill laughed as he crashed down beside her. "I gotta admit this *is* comfortable." He turned on his side and looked into her pale blue eyes, a look that sent a special message.

"I really love you Sally." He blurted.

"You big oaf, are you going to kiss a desperate flight attendant, *or what?"*

"Demanding, now are we?" Bill laughed then didn't hesitate bruising his lips against her soft moist mouth, his adrenaline off the scale. It was a tongue searcher as bodily fluid passed through this most intimate gesture... Then suddenly their Shangri-La was in instant darkness.

Bill turned and looked toward the runway. "They must have switched off the runway lights to conserve generator fuel."

"Darling, who cares..." Sally whispered in his ear as she snuggled closer. "It's a clear night and we always have the stars."

"Honey." Bill hesitated, a "born in America' doing what comes naturally, *but in these surroundings?*

"I lov..."

Bill didn't let her finish smothering her lips again with another crushing kiss.

"Mmmm... Mmmm..." Sally broke loose. "I'm outta breath."

"Do you want me to stop?"

"Did *I* say that? But darling I haven't showered for days!"

"I'm not complaining and believe me, *I'm no better!"*

Sally could feel Bill's rock-hard erection pressing into her abdomen and she wanted him just as much as he wanted her... *But...*

Bill had already stripped to the waist throwing his sweat rag shirt onto hopefully a branch to dry out and deodar. His body was still moist but temperatures drop at night in tropical climates and just as well!

"Bill..." Sally began.

Now it was Bill's turn to 'silence the lambs' closing these soft adoring lips with a long stimulating but gentler kiss, the kind that can't be replicated, whilst at the same time his hands searching clumsily below her tight blouse.

"Honey, let me help you or you'll tear the only blouse I have... *There."*

Bill couldn't wait, his hand adoring her smooth firm breast whilst enjoying the feel of her protruding nipples gently squeezing the surrounding flesh, sending Sally into orbit, the sensation electric through her body.

"Oh...Darling...Oh...Darling, please don't stop." Sally almost shrieked in pleasure as Bill rolled his tongue around and around her nipple, the feeling driving her crazy and she was never more ready as Bill opened the front of

her slacks pulling them down and moving her 'G' string aside, his finger penetrating her wetness to another satisfying groan.

"Darling don't torture me." But Bill was already organized his slacks down below his buttocks.

"Darling... Darling." Sally groaned again as he enveloped her ultimate secret, the prize she kept for only the one she loved and she gave a sort of pained whimper mixed with desire as Bill thrust deeper and deeper in a rhythmic motion, their bodies locked as one, inseparable, until the ultimate climax, a sensation that words can never describe.......

A CHANGE OF PLAN

"I'm surprised how fresh you look this morning after 'American Idol' last night."

Steve pulled his chair into the breakfast table, he had just arrived.

"Get out of it! Someone had to keep the party going. *You and your Michelle."*

"Are you ready to order sir?" The young waiter was standing patiently.

"Yes, I'll have the American breakfast, and you Gregg?"

"Make that for two with black coffee to start."

"Man, I don't know how you can drink that shit Japanese beer all night."

"I could say the same about you and your Scotch!"

"Yeah, but wasn't that Etsuko something... *Man,* these Japanese broad's!"

"Excuse me sirs." The waiter interrupted, a cordless phone in his hand. "I have an International call for a Mr. Nelson, it's urgent."

Steve turned to Gregg... "It can only be... Yes, I'll take it... Nelson here."

"Steve, John here. With the time difference, you guys must be at breakfast?"

"That's no problem, you *did* receive my text?"

"Yes, and that's why I'm phoning...To sum it up, it's going to be a long haul before we reach some conclusions on the crash and I can't afford you two guys away from DC too long. I have other pressing priorities. I'll explain my next move when you arrive at the office."

"Arrive at the office?" Steve was taken back, the news unexpected.

"Yes, I'm pulling you and Gregg back on the next flight you can get to Dulles. I have already contacted McGill so he is aware of my decision. You guys have done a nice job but we still have the problem with the Arabs and Global 10 will just have to wait. Contact me immediately when you touch down no matter the time."

"We'll get on it right away."

"Enjoy your breakfast and have a safe flight."

"Hmmm..." Steve passed the phone back running his fingers through his hair. It was *a* surprise but, then was it?

"Don't tell me, I got the jest of *that* conversation... *So?"*

"First priority. *breakfast!* Then the Business Centre to book seats on the earliest flight back to DC........."

* * *

"So, what do you think?" Gregg asked raising his hand to attract the waiter for a caffeine refill.

"The breakfast?"

"Don't clown around Steve, I'm talking about our recall not the fucking lousy breakfast!"

Steve laughed at Gregg's reaction, maybe he got up on the wrong side this morning, or what?

"Lighten up man, can't you take a joke? Or is this broad getting to you?"

Greg retaliated. "Only you would think of that shit. Get serious for a minute or am I asking too much?... Thanks." Gregg nodded to waiter as he refilled his cup.

"Okay... Okay... I crossed the line, but Gregg I don't want to see you bogged down with this chick that you hardly know... *Man, we gotta a lot of living to do."*

Gregg finally smiled, maybe he was being too sensitive and after all Steve had a point. They had been best buddies for so long even since Bat Mitzvah and he could understand Steve's trepidation.

"Yeah, I guess I'm just frustrated and disappointed that we're going back to the office empty handed."

"Aren't we both!" Steve shook his head. "My thoughts... Our boss thinks it's a lost cause playing the waiting game chasing our ass's in Tokyo when Salibe is still on the loose and the uncle and his accomplices are still not singing. As for the money and the loss of Global 10? I think that's gonna go down as the ninth wonder of the world. The bottom line? It could be the hippo on the roof but we'll soon know. *Now let's get that flight nailed."*

"Yeah, I guess your right Steve, we had better move it....."

* * *

"Ah, here we are!" Gregg pressed floor three, 'Business Centre." The elevator giving a slight jolt as it ascended.

The Business Centre was quiet at this time in the morning and maybe just as well to get priority service.

It was five star alright, the Japanese don't do it in half measures, from the plush dark blue carpet to the highly polished walnut desks manned with three neatly uniformed young receptionists, the quiet air-conditioned ambience setting the scene.

"I could take a lot of this partner." Gregg just shook his head.

"Can I help you sir?" The pretty young lady looked toward Steve her immaculate black hair swept up in a bun whilst emphasizing her narrow lips and dark eyes and displaying that special hotel smile, the plastic name tag pinned to her light grey open necked jacket had the name 'Aya'.

"Ohayogozaimasu." Steve just couldn't resist and Aya gave the 'throw away' smile.

Steve began. "We wish to make reservations on the first available flight to Dulles International Airport Washington DC."

"You are guests at the hotel?" Aya asked.

"Yes rooms 423 and 424."

Aya tapped the key board... "That's a Mr. Sevens and Mr. Jonson... Please take a seat." She pointed the empty chairs in front of her desk. "Can I ask which class?"

"Business." Steve replied.

"Hmmm... Just bear with me for a few minutes while I search the different carriers that fly direct to Dulles."

"That's no problem." Steve was holding the fort.

"There is a JAL flight that departs at 8pm from Narita this evening and arrives in Dulles at 6 am yesterday." Aya smiled. "Remember Japan is 14 hours in front of US time so although this is Friday you will be arriving on Thursday morning."

Steve turned to Gregg and shrugged looking for the 'good to go'.

"Yeah, we save a day." Gregg nodded.

"Then, if you are happy gentleman I will confirm that booking. How do you wish to pay?"

"AMEX......"

* * *

Julie and Marge joined the sparse que at the First Class check in, the 10:30.am flight would arrive in LA at approximately 8.pm yesterday US time and they save a day but as Marge said, *'who cares we have five other days of R&R'.*

"Well I'll be darned! Julie Rodgers and Marge Simpson and traveling First Class. I haven't seen you two ladies since.... I can't remember the last time."

"Jack, don't make a Federal case of it."

"The same old Julie, not to be messed with."

"Who's the Chief Purser on this flight?" Julie asked.

"Just a second till I check your bags through and give you your seat numbers. Can I have your passports...? All good... Seats 1A and 2A right up front with plenty of leg room. The lounge location is marked on the back of your tickets. Departure time is 9.30. Now you were asking?"

"The Chief purser?" Julie gave that face.

"I don't know if you know her... Jenny Jackson."

"We've met before. Thanks Jack, I hope your dog dies."

"Thanks Julie, always the lady... Next sir..."

"That was a bit rough Julie!" Marge commented as they walked to immigration.

"He's a big woman and knows every one's business. He's probably on the blower to that bitch Jackson *right now."*

"Boy, am I gonna enjoy this flight! I hope the Captain is not on your hit list."

"Heh...Heh..." Julie had to laugh at Marge's throw away.

"Marge, let's relax and have a glass of Champagne in the lounge and enjoy some sandwiches, I'm feeling a bit peckish."

"Now you're talking my kinda language and isn't it going to be nice to be served for a change......"

* * *

"This is the last boarding call for Delta 6 to Los Angeles will all passengers on this flight please make their way to gate 12.... Thank you."

"Marge this is your third flute, one more and you will be arriving before the fucking plane."

"Lighten up Julie, after what we've been through can you blame a gall?"

"No, but we don't want to miss this flight so drink up and let's be on our way."

"*Tttttt...* If you say so, anyhow there's plenty more where that came from." Marge proudly held up the empty magnum of Dom Perignon.

"You got taste honey." Julie laughed. "But I don't blame you. *Now,* find your 'sea legs' and let's get going......"

* * *

"Just to your left, second row, welcome to First Class and the friendly skies, I'll be with you as soon as the cabin is settled... Seats 1A and 2A... *Julie!* Well, isn't this a surprise!"

"You remember Marge?"

"How could I forget, you two are like two peas in a pod."

"I've heard more attractive descriptions."

"*Heh...heh....* Still the same Julie." Jenny gave a farcical laugh.

"*Excuse me...* Yes, I'll be with you in a sec... I'll catch up with you guys later I'm sure you know where your seats are... Yes, madam can I see your boarding......"

* * *

"I've always wondered what it would be like to sleep in one of these seats come beds on a long flight." Marge commented as they stacked their airway bags in the overhead bin. "*And pajamas as well!* Get a load of that."

"These new 'Dream Liners' are something else. Who knows maybe we'll be transferred on the long-haul London route on one of theseA380's." Julie commented smiling as she snapped the bin closed.

"You must be a glutton for punishment. Are you serious with 580 passengers on two decks, *you gotta be kidding me?*"

"Window or Isle?" Julie turned to Marge killing the conversation.

"Window."

"*Good,* I like the isle it's easier to go to the restroom without disturbing anyone."

'Smart, huh?" Marge grinned.

"At last now that I'm free, can I get you two ladies an Aperitif?" Jackson was back with that smile.

Marge was first off, the rank... "I'll have a Dom Perignon."

"And you Julie?"

"Make that two."

"Caviar?"

"No, we'll save that for the Vodka." Julie answered in a bitchy tone.

"Just give me a moment, I've a few disgruntled passengers who think I'm a glorified waitress only without the tips."

"No sweat, I know the feeling." Julie grinned.......

* * *

"I heard that Julie Rodgers is on board, we go back a long way."

"Yes Captain, in the First-Class cabin in seat 2A. I'm just about to serve them an Aperitif, I'll accompany you."

"Julie...!"

"Sandy, well look at you! Captain McNeil and all... You deserve it."

"That's for another day. But listen it's great to see you again... I hate to broach the subject but I heard about the loss of Global 10 and of course I knew Bill and Chuck... Pilots are pilots... I'm really sorry I know you were close... I hate to ask but is there any hope?"

"I'm afraid not. They've found the wreckage but no bodies as yet." Julie's voice was breaking slightly and McNeil was feeling more than uncomfortable.

"Listen, I'll leave you to enjoy your drink, I'm sure Jacky will give you First Class service, after all we have to look after our own." He smiled. "If you want to visit the cockpit of our beautiful new plane, Jacky will accommodate you. It's been really nice seeing you again, maybe we can catch up in LA over a cocktail or dinner?"

"I would like that Sandy."

"I would like that too...Now If you can excuse me, I have a plane to fly." He smiled.

As Sandy was about to leave he suddenly turned to face Julie.... *"Oh,* by the way I haven't found the right woman yet."

"Nice to know..." Julie smiled.

"Julie, I'm so sorry... I had heard that a Global Airway's freighter had gone down off the coast of Japan but I didn't know there was a connection... What can I say?"

"Not to worry Jenny, you weren't to know."

"Listen, I'll have to go the buzzer is flashing. Anything you want or need don't hesitate."

"Yes, there *is* one thing... Just a sec."

Julie fished the petite notepad from her bag and scribbled something on the page before tearing it out and folding it.

"Can you pass this to Sandy in case I don't see him before I leave the flight."

"Sure Julie... Now I must go."

"Awe she's not so bad Julie." Marge commented.

"I guess so, but don't judge the book by its cover."

"But that captain, he's a dish. So how do you know him and what's with the secret note?"

"As Sandy said 'that's for another day'." Julie had that glint in her eyes......

* * *

"This airport never ceases to amaze me. *Where the hell are all these people going?*" Julie panted slightly as she and Marge crushed through the crowded Arrival Terminal whilst dragging their wheeled luggage.

"And no bloody manners." Marge was showing her metal.

"Do you have that Uber app on your phone Marge, because that taxi ramp looks like the *'Boston Marathon'!*"

Marge flicked open her Samsung. "Just a sec Julie." She raised the phone to her ear. "Uber...? Yes, we need a pick up at LAX International Arrivals... Going to...? Let me see... Julie what's our new address? Okay... 569 Ocean Avenue, Sea View Apartments... 25 dollars...?" Maggie turned to Julie who nodded her approval. *Deal...* In ten minutes... Your number is?... LA 3768 JB... Got it! We'll be standing in front of the main entrance to the 'Arrival Hall'. You can't miss us dressed in Flight Attendant uniforms.... Ciao."

"Not bad...25... Now I understand why Uber is so popular *and in ten minutes!"* Julie now seamed more relaxed.

It was 8.45 and a slight evening chill in the air as the girls stood patiently on the sidewalk waiting for their low cost 'chariot'.

"What was that number again Julie?"

"LA37...."

"You gotta be kidding me... *A yellow Volkswagen Bug!*"

"That's Uber honey." Julie couldn't contain her laughter. "It's a private car service and I believe the rules are, the vehicle can't be more than three years old. What's the old saying...? You get what you pay for'."

"Don't rub it in... *Sadist.*"

Marge waived her arm to attract the driver who flashed his headlights in reply before pulling over and rolling down his window.

"Ladies going to Ocean Avenue?"

"You got it."

"I'll take your bags."

"I thought the trunk was in the front?"

"Where have you been lady, this is not a Hitler model." The young Indian driver was laughing his ass off and shaking his head... *Women...*

Marge opened the passenger door. "I hate these two door cars, getting in and out is a pain and I suppose I have to sit in the back?"

"You got that right... I'm pulling rank honey."

"Yeah, and I'm pulling my skirt down." Marge cursed moving the front seat forward unlady-like crashing into the back seat.

"Bloody Bug!"

The young Indian, less the rag head was more than jovial as he asked. "So where did you girls fly in from today?" His head on a hinge or maybe he had an elastic neck.

"Tokyo." Marge replied trying to settle into the back seat showing more thigh than 'Kim Kardashian'.

"Nice." He smiled, with the white teeth stand out.

Julie was doubling up glancing in the rear mirror at Marge's predicament.

"It's okay for you Julie you're in First Class."

Marge's comment made them both burst into laughter, the driver joining in even though he hadn't a clue what the hell they were talking about.....!

* * *

"That'll be a straight 25."

"I'll get this Marge since you were in Economy." Julie had that smirk on her face as she grabbed Marge's hand to pull her out of the back seat.

"Just keep the change." Julie had to smile, passing 'Gunged Din' a twenty and a ten the memory of Marge crushed in that back seat exposing her 'credentials' still fresh in her mind.

"Thank you, ladies." The 'teeth' replied an avert for Colgate.

"Your name?" Marge asked still disheveled.

"Balram, anytime time ladies..."

"Yeah, I've got *your* number......"

* * *

"Will *I* be glad to get into that shower." Julie commented as she pressed 6.

The long hallway to the apartment seemed forever as the two weary flight attendants dragged their airline bags to apartment 12. Julie fumbled in her handbag for a few frustrated seconds trying to find the key.

"Here it is, for a moment I was worried there." She gave a sigh of relief as she slipped key into the Yale.

"Switch on the lights Marge, I'll get the luggage... Nice to be home huh...? And the place to ourselves... A bit musty. I'll open the veranda doors to let in some fresh air."

"Sure, we can unpack later, I just want to kick off these shoes and get the Delonghi on."

"I'm with you." Marge slumped onto the sofa flicking her heels off with her toes.

"Julie, we gotta go furniture shopping tomorrow, especially for beds."

"That breeze *is* nice." Julie was standing on the balcony in her bare feet inhaling the sea air. "What was that you were saying?"

'Shopping tomorrow for furniture, *especially beds."* Marge called.

Julie smiled as she returned to the sparsely furnished lounge.

"I don't like that look, that spells, 'sorry Marge you're on the sofa tonight'."

"How did you guess." Julie was laughing.

"I'll get the coffee, I might have guessed. It will have to be black and no sugar the fridge is bare. *Oh,* I almost forgot." Marge toppled her bag on its flat and unzipped the flap. *"DA... DA... DA..."*

"A bottle of Dom... *Why you!"*

"We gotta get this bad boy in the freezer to chill while were showering or it will taste like crap."

"So?"

"So *how* did I get it? Jenny slipped it to me as we were deplaning."
"She did!"

"Come on Julie she's not such a bad egg."

"I guess so... I'll pour the coffee......"

* * *

"Hmmm, this *is* good." Julie joined Marge on the sofa sipping Delongi's best.

"So, who's first in the shower."

"I think since you were in economy be my guest."

"Is this a conscious decision?"

"Make up your mind as I'm just about finishing my coffee. There's plenty of towels and a bathrobe each with compliments from my ex apartment."

Marge was silent for a moment "I know it's hard to mention Bill's name."

"Sure, but Marge time heals everything." Julie paused for a moment in reflection. "But the four of us had some good times didn't we and that's what we should treasure."

"Changing the subject...I hope the waters hot?"

It should be I switched on the heater when I was in the kitchen but don't take all day. Anyhow it will give me a chance to unpack."

Julie trolleyed her bag into her room as Marge stepped out of her skirt and dropped her panties round her feet. Next the blouse and bra followed suite, after all she was sleeping on the sofa tonight and she would hang her clothes up in the morning.

"*Wow,* now it's chilly!" She streaked to the balcony doors and closed them with a bang.

"What was that Marge?"

"No sweat, just closing the balcony doors."

"You're not in the shower yet!"

"No, unless I'm gonna shower fully clothed."

Julie just smiled as she began hanging her clothes in the 'walk in' robe......

* * *

"*Boy,* was that good!" Marge closed the faucet and with both hands threw her shoulder length brown hair over her shoulders before stepping out the shower box and gabbing her bath towel then vigorously toweling her naked body. Women can't help admiring their unadulterated nakedness in the vanity mirror and Marge was no exception.

"*Hmmm...*" She cupped her breasts with both hands, the towel round her head. "*Bloody gravity!* How will these babies look in ten years' time? It scares the crap outta me."

"*Marge,* what's keeping you?"

"*Yeah ...Yeah...* I'm finished. I'm just slipping into my robe." But before she could finish Julie streaked past and disappeared into the 'sauna' box the shower glass steamed up.

"Don't be too long 'Dom' waits for no man." Marge yelled, her voice drowned by the shower.

Still in her robe and turbaned head covering her wet hair Marge curled up on the sofa waiting for her best friend and staring at the apartment void of furniture.

"I love our new pad but with one sofa a coffee machine and refrigerator, not to mention no google box, we gotta do something about this... *Maaan.*" She sighed.

"That's bad talking to yourself you got me worried." Julie suddenly appeared vigorously toweling her hair.

"Can you blame me, *and this is my bed tonight!*"

"Come on Marge think on the positive side. What's the saying... 'Rome wasn't built in a day'!"

"Si, ma io non sono un Italiano."

"Your Italian's getting better, maybe we should put in for a transfer to the Rome route, huh?"

"Be serious, we're losing precious drinking time! Now, *do we do have glasses or what?"*

"Not flutes for the deserved 'Dom', but it's better than drinking that precious liquid from the bottle. I tell you what... I'll fetch the glasses and you get the sparkling......."

* * *

Marge held up the magnum to the light peering through the dark green glass then burst into song.

"I don't pop my cork for every guy I see... Hey big spender... Spend a little time with me... *Ha...Ha...Ha...*" She was on a roll.

"Your incorrigible but it's good to have a laugh after what we've been through."

"Yes, but sadly, I hate to kill the party as this baby is almost half empty and feeling no pain and at the rate we're going we'll end up with 'the pub with no beer'."

Julie was still laughing at Marge's impression of Shirley Bassey.

"Changing the subject... *Listen,* tomorrow..." Julie took a sip of the yellow sparkle... "What say we hit Rodeo Drive, have some comfort food and then go on a shopping spree."

"All I can say is, I hope your credit card isn't maxed out. Here, let me pour you a refill."

"Thanks' Marge and yourself?"

"Don't worry I'm going strong but now that we're more relaxed it's time for 'True Confessions'. So, tell me how you met that handsome captain?"

"*Sandy McNeil?*"

"None other."

Julie laughed. "I was wondering when you would get around to it."

"Can you blame me? *He's a dish... So?*"

"Well if you must know I had a thing for him at college."

"*At college!* You never mentioned him to me."

"Would you have noticed chasing that crazy Jake Duncan?"

"Awe come on, don't bring that up again. He was a loser, we all make mistakes but you gotta admit he had the looks."

"Yeah, *and no brains!*"

"So why then didn't you make out with the handsome McNeil?"

"*I'm surprised you don't remember the Captain of the college football team?*" Julie sort of sighed in reminisce. "I knew he liked me and I was hoping he would ask me to the Prom but I guess he was too busy picking up the panties the "Cheer Girls' were throwing at his feet."

"*Ha... Ha...* Maybe you should have thrown yours in as well."

"Only *you* would think of that." Julie shook her head. "Changing the subject, is there enough for another refill?"

"Of course, *gimme that glass....* Do think he's gonna phone?"

"*Who?*"

"Come on don't play the 'hard to get' card."

Julie crossed a cheeky smile. "Maybe......"

THE PRIDE AND THE PREJUDICE.

"This waiting game is nerve wracking." Sally had just returned from ablutions. "And this water is barely drinkable." She laughed as she held up the slightly murky plastic bottle. "But at least we can wash our credentials."

"I guess that's one way of putting it" A smile crossing Bill's face, his eyes glued to the binoculars.

"*Hmmm*, that feels better." Sally groaned stretching both arms above her head. "Lying on that bed of fern leaves is something else and *what I would do for a cold shower!*"

"*That makes two of us.*"

"Then what have we got?"

"Looks like a big pow wow in Shendo's office with the usual heavies. I have this gut feeling after the cremations yesterday that something big is going to happen today and the 'revenge' mood in the camp."

"*Don't scare me Bill!*"

"I gotta tell ya Sally, it had crossed my mind yesterday to make a brake for it during the rituals and steal that small motor craft tied up at the jetty but Shendo's no dummy and he beefed up the guards on the wharf. *The guy must be a mind reader!*"

"*Whatever darling,* but where do we go from here?"

"Honey, I wish I had the solution, *but I don't,* and as you said, 'it's a waiting game'. Our only hope is for Shendo to decide the loss of more men is not worth it, *after all where can we go?* It's the 'hunger games' by any other name and time will be the deciding factor."

Julie dumped the bottle and lay beside her new-found love.

"Do you think you can drop these 'four eyes' and give this lady a passionate kiss......?

* * *

Another sad day was behind him with the cremation of three of his men and tragically his trusted guard, Aikido Arakida. He had yet to contact Namura and it was playing on his mind not to mention the Arab gloating on the side lines. For Shendo, it was far from good.

Operation 'Datsugoku" had to be rekindled and with breakfast over a meeting with his inner circle was critical.…...

* * *

(Speaking in Japanese)

Shendo unbuckled his 'Shin Gunto' then sat down heavily in his chair, his brow furrowed, face troubled.

"Suwaru." He barked pointing to the empty seats.

Tahoka, Ichiro Akimoto the camp doctor and Jiro Adachi the sight supervisor gingerly took their places. Today was not for the faint of heart and with the vile mood the 'Boso' was in, one wrong word would be at their peril.

"Ah... Hmmm." Shendo cleared his throat then took a hurried sip of the now tepid green tea before sitting back and staring in silence at the 'gang of three'.

"This has been a bloody week on Shimaru Shima with the loss of four of our brave Yakuza's... A week that will be emblazoned in my memory for ever. *Three Americans holding to ransom the pride of the Samurai!* How this could possibly happen?" He was shaking his head.

"Boso." Tahoka fractured the silence.

"Hanasu."

"The Americans tricked us into thinking they were camped on the hill east of the runway drawing our fire in the belief that they had only one operative firearm, the rifle stolen from Isamu Gado, but the two gun shots came from a small caliber pistol, this we now know."

"Jizoku suru." (continue)

"The solution is to somehow trick them to draw their fire and pin point their location, *that is if the Americans are still alive!* Remember, that last barrage on the hill with rifle and machinegun fire was so intense they would be lucky to have survived."

"Watashi wa matteimasu." (I'm waiting)

"This time we take ten men, spread twenty meters apart to make them difficult targets and sweep the hill from the west side of the runway. Ichiro Akimoto the camp doctor of course will accompany us. Adachi your responsibility is to make sure the weaponry, rifles, two LMG's plus a mortar tube and munitions are withdrawn from the armory for the search party by 10.am today. There is no need for you to accompany us."

"Hai." Adachi bowed.

"Now here's the cunning part......"

* * *

"I could lie bedside you like this all day." Sally was snuggling up to Bill, her arm over his chest.

"Even in this I intolerable humidity?" Bill turned and passionately kissed her on the forehead.

"When you love someone facing danger every minute counts... *Now,* how about giving me a proper kiss?" Those eyes would make any full-blooded man surrender

"Where have you been all my life?" Bill didn't hesitate and pressed his lips against hers in a long and sensual lock that seemed to last forever but using up the oxygen was a not an option and Bill had to surface for the precious H20.

"Darling, I *really* love you." Sally gasped panting heavily whilst trying to unbutton Bill's shirt but he grabbed her hand to stop much to her disappointment.

"No honey, as much as I want you, this is not the time nor the place. We must remain vigilant and in a state of 'battle readiness'." Bill glanced at his watch. "It's just turned 10 and I'm surprised that the camp is calm.... They're up to something, *but what?"* He frowned shaking his head. *"And it's getting to me!* You can never trust the 'yellow man'......."

* * *

Shendo had that evil grin on his face.

"Sore wa idesu ne." (I like it)

Tahoka bowed, Boso was pleased, a rare event.

"Arigatogozaimashita." (thank you)

"Purotukoru o wasurete shigoto o awara sete kudasai!" (forget the protocol just get the job done)

"Hai." Tahoka signaled to Akimoto and Adachi to get their asses outta there before Shendo changes his mood......

* * *

"I knew it! Bill blurted. "The 'posse' of 12 to 13 men are lined up on the tarmac armed to the hilt checking their weapons and ammunition and by the looks of it, it's a full-scale assault with machine guns, rifles, and even a mortar tube complete with bombs. *Maaaan,* it looks like we're back in 'Okinawa' in the Sakishima Islands, you couldn't get a bloodier battle... Sally, you know how to us the Magnum and when I say fire just empty these chambers at random in the same direction as my fire."

Sally's face was drained of color, she knew this was the real deal and the chances of survival were slim and she turned to face Bill.

"I just want you to know that whatever happens I'll always love you, I just wish things could have been different..."

"Sally don't." Bill cut her short. "We're gonna come out of this alive and we'll look back in our old age and laugh about it."

"Gimme another kiss darling......"

* * *

(Speaking in Japanese)

"Lock and load your weapons and spread out twenty meters apart. When I give, the command begin to climb the hill and don't fire until I give the order. Do I make myself clear?" Tahoka was in complete command.

"Hai." Came the resounding chorus....

Bill slid the bolt open then squeezed a 7 mill into the breach of the Arisaka then applied the safety carefully adjusting the rear sight to 300 meters by twisting the knurled adjuster.

"That should do it...! They are keeping well apart and using the 'side on' tactic to make a difficult kill shot."

"Bill...?"

"Sally..." Bill raised his hand to suggest, *'don't disturb me I need to concentrate'.*

"Now... what are they up to? *I don't believe it*! Tahoka is raising a white flag tied the barrel of his rifle and placing a megaphone to his lips."

"Christ Bill, what does *that* mean?"

Bill was slow and deliberate with his words. "I don't know... But whatever it is, I don't trust them..."

The megaphone bellowed across the hillside the message in broken English.

"Kenichi Shendo offer safe departure from Island by small boat if surrender... Want no more bloodshed. You have word of Samurai. I give 15 minutes to lay down you weapons."

"Shit, do you believe that Bill?" Sally was panicking.

"I wouldn't trust Tahoka as far as I could throw him and from here I can see these guys loading their rifles. like for a 'duck shoot'." Bill was peering through the binoculars. "But the one thing we have in our favor is they don't know whether we are alive or dead so I'm reluctant to show our hand and expose our position."

"Then what do we do?" Sally was becoming more and more exasperated and Bill could sense by the tone in Sally's voice, the love of his life was petrified, the Magnum shaking precariously in her hand....

* * *

The sniper with the type 97 telescopic rifle was well camouflaged in the thick undergrowth as he pressed home five 6.5 mil rounds into the magazine before locking the bolt. He had a 180 sweep with a 2.5 times mag and open sesame to fire when a kill was in his cross hairs.

"Hmmm." Bill was in a conundrum rubbing his chin then it struck him!

"It's risky Sally but we have no choice. Hand me my jacket, and my Pilot's cap... It's here somewhere?" Bill was searching around.

"Here it is Bill, but..."

"Sally..." Bill raised his hand. "You'll soon find out. It's vital to check if we can trust this Tahoka."

Bill quickly cut a straight branch from the tree behind them then stripped it of its off shoots.

"That's about right." He measured the branch beside him to check the length. "That'll do, now I need a shorter one for the shoulders."

"How's this one darling." Sally held up a piece of a dead wood about 30 inches long.

"Nice one... Now I gotta tie these two pieces together with some vine to form a cross... *There...!"* Bill was admiring is handy work.

"Now I hang my jacket over the cross and place my cap on top to form a decoy."

"Smart." Sally admired the 'scare crow'. "But do you think they'll fall for it?"

"There's only one way to find out."

Before Sally could reply, Bill purposely began to shake the large palm to get the search parties attention and like a fish to water Tahoka took the bait and held his hand up to signal his men to be patient.

"Here goes." Bill slowly raised the fake dummy above the heavy foliage then moved it slowly to one side to create the realism of a person walking.

The sniper adjusted his sight placing the crosshair in the middle of Bill's cap, took a deep breath, held it for a second then squeezed the trigger. The 97 kicked, the heavy caliber copper nose finding its mark tearing Bill's precious cap into shreds.

"The bastards..." I knew I couldn't trust them. Keep your head down Sally there's going to another 5th of July." Bill yanked her by the arm pulling her down beside him. "Don't fire the Magnum till I tell you."

"Ye... Yeah... Yes...!" Sally answered her mind in total confusion.

*"Hmmm...*Tahoka is still unsure if the sniper was successful and the delay just might give me a tactical advantage to get a bead on him for the next candidate on the cremation pile."

Sally just kept quiet.

Bill gently pushed the muzzle of the Arisaka through the ferns to line his sights on Tahoka. If he could kill or seriously wound the man in command it could throw the whole operation into chaos. But before Bill could squeeze the trigger Tahoka pointed his index finger toward the sniper, a special signal that only he would recognize.

Crack... Crack... Crack... The 97-bad boy spewed lethal fire into the location of the decoy until the magazine was spent, bullets zipping into the tropical bush, showering Bill and Sally with shredded palm leaves.

Sally felt a sort of a thud in her left side as if she had been kicked by a horse followed by a burning excruciating pain.

"Phew... Are you alright, honey?"

"Eh...Err, I'm good." Sally was having trouble breathing. Something was wrong and she momentarily panicked. *Was she hit?* She turned slightly on her

side and placed her left hand on the spot cringing in pain, then staring in shock at her crimson soaked palm.

"Just stay there... Stay there..." The Arisaka kicked. *"Got him!"*

Tahoka staggered momentarily as the heavy metal slug ripped his right collar bone apart, bone fragments exiting through his back.

"Ishi." He screamed miraculously still standing. (doctor)

The doctor rushed to Tahoka's side ripping his clothing apart to examine the gaping wound shaking his head at the mutilated carnage. It was worse than bad. But this mountain of a man wasn't going down just yet his anger camouflaging his serious wound.

"Bill... Bill... Give me your hand darling.

Sally stretched over the pain excruciating, blood now oozing from her nose and mouth as her punctured lung began to drown her.

"Christ...!" Bill couldn't believe his eyes as he grabbed her blood soaked hand, her eyes flickering as she was falling in and of consciousness. A sort of a 'don't leave me smile' crossing her face as she desperately crushed her lover's hand.

"Bill darling, always remember *I... I* really loved you." Her voice barely audible

"No Sally... No... Sally no... Don't leave me..."

"Hi...Hi..." Tahoka screamed. (Fire...Fire)

"Sally...*I...*" That was Bill's last word, their hands still locked together in a gesture of never ending love.

A love story and the murder of three Americans that will never be remembered, not even as a 'cold case file'......

BACK TO REALITY

Julie gunned the yellow bug as Marge made herself comfortable in the passenger seat.

"For a moment, I thought this baby wouldn't start!"

The girls were dressed super casual in their fitting white shorts, 'wet' style tank tops and thongs. This was LA and with a pleasant morning temperature of 70 and clear blue skies it was going to be a hot one and as they say, 'the girls were back in town'.

"You should fire up your car Marge when we return or the battery will die on you. Luckily we got two car slots with the apartment."

Julie slipped the 'Bug' into gear and released the hand brake with a slight jolt as Hitler's 'people's car' took to the streets.

"Your right Julie." She glanced out the window at her metallic green Dodge Caliber, SUV. "What with Chuck's fancy Firebird and you with your own wheels I'm neglecting my baby but I'll be using it more now that we are shacking together... More to the point, I need a queen size bed like yesterday or I'm gonna have a permanent chink in my neck."

"*Ha...Ha...Ha...*" Julie laughed at Marge's take. "*Got ya*, so why don't I head straight for Macy's and their 'life style' department. In fact, we can gave breakfast at the cafeteria and kill two birds with one stone."

"You're the chauffeur." Marge laughed....

* * *

"Just give me a moment gentleman and I'll show you to your seats."

The pretty Japanese stewardess in Business Class gave the 'JAL smile'. Her beige colored two piece fitted suite was only meant for her and stretched the imagination as she strutted the isle to attend to another passenger.

"*Maaan*... Am I gonna enjoy this flight!"

Gregg didn't answer he had seen it all before.

"This way gentleman... Seats 6A and 6B. I'll take you garment bags and hang them in the front robe. Please press the call button if you need anything. I'll be returning with refreshments in a few minutes once the cabin is seated." She gave that smile again then went about her business.

"You know Gregg, there's something about these Japanese women..."

"Don't start that again."

"Come on man, lighten up... Say, aren't these seats something else?"

"Champagne beer or juice?" Namika was doing an excellent job balancing a full tray of drinks.

"Champagne for me Namika." Steve had spotted her name tag. "Gregg...?"

"Asahi is fine."

"Please." She offered the tray for Steve and Gregg to take their drinks while precariously balancing it.

"Domo." Steve replied with a smile but Namika wasn't taking the bate she had been there and done that. She nodded politely and then moved to the next row of seats.

"Man, were *you* torpedoed." Gregg had to contain his laughter to avoid choking on his beer.

"She'll come around." Steve had thick skin and maybe just as well. "This champagne is good why do you always stick to beer?"

"Simple, *I prefer it!*"

"I give up on you."

"Can I collect your empty glasses sir?"

"That was quick." Steve commented.

"I apologies sir but we are running slightly behind schedule. Is there anything else I can fetch you?"

"No, we're good." Gregg replied before Steve could get his double six in.

The Tannoy blared... "This is Captain Hikaru Akiyama speaking. We are about to taxi to designated runway for take-off in around ten to fifteen minutes. Please fasten your safety belts and place your seats in an upright position and ensure the overhead bins are securely closed. The skies are clear and I wish you all on behalf of JAL a comfortable and enjoyable flight... Thank you......"

* * *

The take-off was bumpy and noisy as the aging 747's Prat & Whitney's took to the sky, then silence and a quiet drone.

Steve was relaxed in the aisle seat his preference, maybe it was a guise to get a good view of the flight attendants from the waist down, especially Namika, whilst Gregg was quietly sipping his second Asahi.

"Your quiet tonight, a penny for your thoughts."

"Nothing much." Gregg replied. "I guess I'm still smarting from having been recalled to DC with nothing to show for it."

"You heard Thomson stressing we had done a good job but for the road blocks we were experiencing, we would still be in Tokyo next year, besides he hinted there was another assignment waiting in the wings."

"Yeah, maybe your right. But what gets me Steve is that the US National Transportation Safety Board have now confirmed without a doubt that Global 10 was blown out of the sky by a bomb. But get this... The latest is the plane was shredded to pieces and there's little chance of finding any body parts and because of the depth of the ocean, more so the black box and cockpit flight recorder. *I ask you?* It's a cover up by the Japanese Government because the Yakuza is involved and conceal that Global 10 was 'high jacked' for its cargo of the 100 billion in used US currency notes. *If the freight liner was so severely damaged by the explosion why have they never found fragmented bills?* This whole escapade stinks and furthermore we know that Salibe was on that plane!"

"Calm down Gregg and sit back and relax and enjoy the flight the problem will still be there tomorrow... How about another Asahi......?

* * *

"Boy, this place is a jungle!" Steve commented as they crushed through the 'no manner's crowd' in the arrival hall. Having cleared customs and with no baggage the next stop was to collect their side arms.

"A big difference from Narita, *huh?*"

Gregg just shrugged, only half interested.

"Can I see your identification please." The Customs and Border Security Officer was expressionless. Maybe he had a bad day or a 'blue' with his wife or worse still his 'lady' on the side.

The agents wasted no time and flashed the 'gold'.

"Please check the firearm numbers then sign your receipt... Have a nice day gentleman?"

"So, the guy was human after all!"

Gregg gave a 'throw away' grin. "I'll be glad when I'm sitting in that cab."

"Yeah, *that's if we can get one!*" Steve replied as they gloomed at the busy cab rank.

After three attempts standing in the disgruntled que a yellow cab with a Siek driver finally flicked down his meter flag and pulled into the sidewalk.

"I think India wins the cab business in Washington."

"In Washington? Greg laughed. *"You mean in North America!"*

The cab driver was polite and spoke reasonably good English as most Indians do from British Colonial Rule and he opened the trunk to store the garment bags.

"Where to?" He politely asked as he took the driver's seat a slight patter of rain bouncing on the cab's roof.

"Chancellor Towers' on the Washington Circular in the West End." Steve replied settling in for the thirty-minute cab ride.

The driver smiled entering the address into the GPS. It was a reasonable fare around 50 dollars and with two well-dressed passengers that were unlikely to make stupid racial remarks about his turban, things were good.

"A good omen or a bad open... *'I love a rainy night... I love a rainy night'.*" Steve burst into song with the first two lines of the popular jingle.

"Karaoke in a cab, that's a first" Gregg laughed. "What do you think driver?"

The Indian just smiled, when you drive a cab these days there's so many crazies its best you mind your own business.

Washington DC in July can be a bit muggy and wet with average temperatures of 80 to 85 and the light rain tonight would be welcomed.

"We must phone Thomson whenever we arrive at the apartment." Gregg was still uptight.

"Changing the subject, you must have been tired on the flight because you slept the whole way and you never even had dinner! What a waste and in 'Business Class' too". "Don't worry be happy...."

"Enough Karaoke Steve... *Please.*"

"I tell you that Amico or Amiky... Eh...? What the hell was her name?"

"Namika." Gregg shook his head.

"Near enough, whatever... We were getting on like a house on fire and do you know the crew are staying in the Grand Hyatt down town?"

"No, but now you've told me I gather you've cooked up some devious plan."

"And guess what.? They are flying out again Saturday morning!"

"So?"

"So, unless we have nothing on, on Friday night... *You do get the picture?*"

"And what am I, *the third wheel?*"

"She has a friend."

"So now you're a dating agency?"

"Hell Gregg, what's happened to the buddy I used to know. We've has some hoots together."

"I guess I'm just a bit screwed up now, it's not your fault" Gregg seemed more subdued.

"So, it's Michele, is it?"

Gregg remained silent.

"Don't go off your brain, but did you tell her you would be back in Washington this week end?"

"No."

"Then if you haven't licked the envelope man, let it be... Gregg, at 25 it's too early to play the Mr. 'faithful card' I mean let's face it, if you're hoping for a virgin these days then you'll have to catch one in the pram."

"Steve, the one thing I like about you, is your so fucking tactful."

"Maaaan, we've been best friends since 'Bat Mitzvah' when we were only 13 years old then college and special forces in Iraq and Afghanistan? Buddy, *would I give you bad advice?"*

Gregg gave a big sigh and rubbed his chin. Should he do the honorable thing or *'fuck it'* and enjoy life like his best friend who doesn't know what conscience means.

"Listen Ste..."

The cabby interrupted. "We're here sir." He steered the heavy 'brick shit house' Ford Crown Victoria to the kerb in front of Chancellor Towers.

"You were saying, Gregg?"

"I'll take a rain check for the moment, at least until we settle down in the apartment."

"That'll be 55 straight." The Indian 'Grand Prix' driver 'helmet' and all, pointed to the digital meter.

"Keep the change." Steve crushed three twenties in his palm.

"Thank you...Would you like my card if you need the airport run again?"

"No Sahib." Steve grinned trying to cross a smart one.

The Siek smiled. "Wrong way round boss, you are Sahib in Hindi... *Dhanyavaad."* (Thank you)

The 'Char Walla' closed the cab door and slipped the Crown into gear, a cheeky grin on his face. A five-dollar tip was better than nothing, besides for once he was addressed as 'Boss' a term in Hindi reserved for white colonials only.

Steve entered the pin and the security door opened with a distinctive clack.

"Home again buddy."

"As they say there's 'no place like home'." Gregg slid the key into the Yale a sigh of relief before switching on the soft lighting then chucking his garment bag in a heap on the floor.

"Is there any beer in the fridge?" Gregg opened the stainless-steel monster. "Good, you want one?" He unscrewed the metal on a Michelob.

"Not for me, I'm into the coffee." Steve filled the water in the Delonghi and switching it on dropping in his favorite capsule. The machine making a spurting and hissing noise as it extracted the expresso into the small cup.

Steve sipped the dark brew. *"Hmmmm, how good is that?"*

"I'm gonna have a seat on the balcony and enjoy my beer" Gregg chucked his jacket on the chair and removed his tie. "It's raining so don't give me 'Singing in the Rain'."

"Ha...Ha...Ha..." Steve laughed. "I like that, I might just come and join you."

"Bring your cell while you're at it and we can kill two birds with one stone."

"Boy, isn't this heaven?" Steve commented as he placed his cup on the glass table and sank into the cushioned wicker seat, the 23rd floor gave a fantastic view of the city at night. "I just love the sound of the rain and it's nice and cool... Now for Thomson's private number..."

Jenny was watching TV when out of the blue the red phone rang and she knew it must be something to do with John's office.

"Yes...?" She was being cautious.

"Jenny, its Steve Nelson here. Gregg and I have just touched down from Tokyo and John made it clear that we must contact him the moment we arrive in DC."

"I see." She paused. "Unfortunately, Steve, John is not here, he was called to an urgent meeting with the FBI in New York and he won't be returning to the office till Tuesday of next week. I suggest you contact him on his secure cell line, Im sure you have the number."

"Thanks Jenny sorry to disturb you."

"No problem... Goodnight...."

"Well, that didn't sound too encouraging."

"Would you believe it! Thomson is in New York for some kind of high level meeting with the FBI."

"What's the bottom line?"

"He hasn't left any instructions with Jenny so she suggested we call him on his secure cell line."

"Hmmm." Gregg raised his eyebrows. "So?"

"I suppose I had better get to it." Steve punched in the numbers and waited with baited breath.

"Steve, I though you would ring." Thomson recognized the number.

"Yeah, I just phoned your home and Jenny advised me to call you on your cell."

"Listen, I can't talk to you now, I'm having dinner with Comey and the secretary of State. I'll be back in the office on Tuesday so report in at nine. My suggestion is enjoy the break while you can get it. See you both on Tuesday and don't be late...! Ciao."

"I heard it. So, we're on forced vacation?"

"Are you serious! We have three days to recuperate, not that we bust our asses in Tokyo but now we gotta get on the 'happy wagon' and enjoy ourselves and with the way Thomson was putting it, it might be a long time before we pass this way again."

"So, correct me if I'm wrong it's the JAL flight attendants, huh?"

"No, my good buddy, it's rented Harleys and the Santa Monica... *You do still have Marge's number.......?"*

THE PARTY'S OVER

Tahoka raised his good arm.

"Teisen...Teisen" (ceasefire...ceasefire)

Suddenly 'J Day' was over and the silence was deafening.

"Sutetcabira... Sutetcabira" (stretcher-bearer) Ichiro Akimoto the camp doctor screamed as Tahoka was about to keel over like a big red, the doctor struggling to hold him upright. Two burly stretcher bearers grabbed the 'mountain' below the arm pits and laid him on the canvas between the poles.

Tahoka croaked in pain. "Akimoto, instruct the men to search the hillside since there has been no return fire."

"Hai."

Akimoto issued the command and the search party immediately shouldered their rifles and began the long trek up the hill toward where they had seen the decoy.

The doctor injected a high dose of morphine to immune Tahoka's pain, his next major problem was, with the limited surgical recourses on camp, how to fix that shattered shoulder. Without a doubt Tahoka would have to be on the next flight back to the mainland and Shendo would be less than impressed, another headache for another day.

* * *

Shendo looked up from his desk, the barrage had suddenly stopped and he quickly rose from to is feet and buckled his 'Shin Gunto' before opening the door of the 'sardined canned' office. What met his eyes was not a pretty sight, his close friend and bodyguard all bloodied, the orderlies stepping it out with the laden stretcher toward the camp's improvised medical room.

"Nantekotta I?" (what the hell?) Shendo screamed not believing his eyes.

The stretcher bearers stopped momentarily in front of Boso, Tahoka's face pale and paned slipping into unconsciousness, his horrendous wound would shock the most hardened veterans.

Akimoto looked to Shendo and shook his head.

"Orderlies proceed to the medical room." The doctor didn't want the patient to hear his prognosis.

"Kare wa dore kurai waruidesu ka?" Shendo asked. (how bad is he?)

"It's as bad as it gets. Tahoka needs some serious surgery his shoulder is so badly shattered he will never get the full use of his left arm again, in fact, if he doesn't get surgery soon he may lose the arm completely. His life is in danger and he must be on the next relief fight to the mainland."

Shendo stood for a moment in silence the seriousness sinking in. Was 'Datsugoku" worth the three men he lost? He could have easily left the Americans to starve and die but Samurais have a thing called pride, but at what cost?

"Boso, if I can interrupt?"

Shendo nodded his mind not completely cleared.

"Tahoka ordered the men to take the hill and he placed Hiro Takahashi in command. He has a 'walkie talky' and will keep me in touch in real time."

"Yoi." (good) Keep me posted on Tahoka's condition, I might have to consider approaching Biggubosu for a special air lift."

As for Salibe he was gloating on the side lines from his Nissan hut watching the drama play out. It couldn't happen to a better person. He smiled then returned to his cot, dinner would soon be on the menu and who would at Shendo's table this evening? Salibe closed his eyes for his afternoon nap a slight grin crossing his face, 'the end always justifies the means' *or does it......!*

* * *

Akimoto cut through Tahoka's battle dress to get a closer look at the wound. It was bad alright and bleeding like a river. His priority was to cauterize the wound and remove any bullet fragments where possible. Fortunately, Tahoka was going in and out of consciousness, the pain making him cringe at regular intervals and the most painless and humane option was to send him to sleep with the intravenous drug, Pentothal.

Time was critical and Akimoto had to expediently inject the short-term anesthetic piercing the needle through the sealed top of the miniature drug bottle sucking up 210mg. Then he tagged Tahoka's forefinger to the heart and oxygen monitoring machine, the wounded Samurai gently closing his eyes.

Ichiro had stopped the 'bleeding man' using a low temperature cauterizing pen. Now the challenge was to remove the fragments of the soft nosed bullet that had broken into two upon splintering Takoma's collar bone. One piece had taken the easy route exiting through the left shoulder joint taking cartilage and muscle with it. The other, going clean through Tahoka's back blowing a large hole in his shoulder blade but fortunately missing his left lung.

The noise of the two bullet fragments as they rattled into the stainless-steel kidney dish was a welcome relief and Akimoto wiped the beads of sweat from his brow with the back of his hand heaving his chest. Satisfied, he began to close the wound. There was little else he could do now but make Tahoka as comfortable as possible. The shattered collar bone and shoulder joint required specialized orthopedic surgery which could only be carried out in a fully equipped hospital theatre. Satisfied Akimoto turned to the orderly.

"When he wakens give him these pain killers and antibiotics. Start the pain killer with two tablets, then one every two hours and one antibiotic every hour to avoid infection of the wound." He passed the bottles of Endon and Amoxillin. "Call me if anything changes."

"Hai."

His mind still troubled Akimoto was about to leave the medical room when his walkie talky gave a weird whistling sound like something from outer space and the doctor quickly tuned in.

"Takahashi?"

"Hai, good news Ishi. (doctor) We have found the bodies of the Captain and the flight attendant, both deceased from gunshot and shrapnel wounds."

"And the second officer?" Akimoto's voice anxious.

"We found his body buried in a shallow grave about 100 meters from the Captain and the woman, you can inform Boso, operation 'Datsugoku' is over and I await your instructions."

"Arigato, nice job Takahashi. My instruction at this point is to hold, I'm going to see Boso right now to inform him the good news and I will get back to you within the hour."

"Hai."

Was it good news or bad news Akimoto was confused as he walked down the tarmac. Three men lost and another seriously wounded and for *what?* His Hippocratic Oath his priority to save Tahoka and he persuade Shendo to convince Biggubosu to break the rules and send an early relief flight with a changeover crew and medical supplies a soon as possible.

The heavy rattle on the steel door to Shendo's office startled him. He was in deep thought; the deaths of the three Americans would be welcome news and a reprieve from 'seppuku' but he wasn't out of the woods just yet.

"Hairu." He barked. (enter) Shendo was almost at breaking point his face pale and fatigued when Akimoto nervously entered, then bowed.

"Well, don't just stand their man, I haven't all day!"

"Boso, all three Americans are deceased."

"Yoi." (good) Shendo cracked 'a long time coming' smile.

"What do you want done with the bodies?"

"We've had enough cremations and pictures of 'proof of death' can be traced and come back and to bite me... *No."* He rubbed his chin. "Instruct Takahashi to bury them where they fell in unmarked graves."

"Hai, Boso is there anything else?"

"No, except cancel operation 'Datsugoku' and instruct Takahashi to return the men to camp."

The doctor bowed about to leave when suddenly something crossed his mind, he had forgotten to press Shendo for that relief flight.

"Hai, what is it?" Shendo was not in the mood for useless trivia.

"About the relief flight..."

Shendo cut him short. "You made your point already, now I'm busy..." The message *'don't push your luck'!*

Akimoto didn't need a second reminder and turned to leave, his 'tail between his legs'.

"Takahashi." Akimoto spoke into the two way. "Boso, instructs......"

* * *

It was late afternoon in Tokyo at the 'Shin Marunouchi Building' the legal office of 'Nippon Shipping & Logistics', the cloak and dagger entity of the Yakuza and Numara as usual at three in the afternoon was enjoying his break and his favorite indulgence the most expensive green tea in Japan, 'Tien chi flower Tea'. Ayako, Namura's secretary had just returned to her desk glad for the break, her boss would be less demanding for the next hour or so, at least that's what she hoped!

In solitude, the thought crossed Okio's mind that he hadn't heard from Shendo for two days and an update on operation 'Datsugoku' was overdue and he pondered for a few moments on whether to ruin his day and phone Shimaru Shima or continue his self-indulgence.

Uncannily he didn't have to wait too long when hearing the buzz from his HF Motorola and he sat back for a moment as if to say, 'well I'll be darned'. He opened the side drawer in his desk and searched for the secret brass key to the concealed drawer.

"Hai...?"

"Boso, Shendo reporting on operation 'Datsugoku".

"It's not before time." Okio didn't mince his swords. *"Well, I'm waiting!"*

"The three Americans were killed early this morning after a fierce gun battle once they exposed their position and with our fire power it was inevitable they wouldn't survive."

Numara was no fool, he could sense by the nervous tone in Shendo's voice he was leading up to something.

"So, is there anything else you want to tell me?"

"The bad news is Tahoka was seriously wounded and needs urgent surgery to save his arm or worse still his life."

"Tahoka!" Numara sat back in his chair taken aback. He had a soft spot for his previous bodyguard and the news was anything but good.

"And?" Namura bellowed.

"I strongly recommend that he be flown back to the mainland as soon as possible."

"You, strongly recommend...! Watch your mouth Shendo, don't forget you are a Yakuza soldier and because of *your* negligence three prisoners escaped and we lost three good men."

"My apologies Boso."

There was a pregnant pause as Okio's brain searched for a solution. To organize a flight with a relief crew was not as easy as it seemed. The return flight from Shimaru Shima with the changeover crew was only last week, but there again Shendo was right, Samurais never desert their comrades in need.

"Leave it with me." Okio was now in the foulest of moods. "There had better be nothing else to report for *your* sake."

"Le." (no)

"Then get off this phone, I have work to do."

"Hai." Shendo was more than glad the conversation was over and he had survived by the skin of his teeth.

Okio threw the Motorola into the drawer with such ferocity almost smashing the device.

"Ayako..." He screamed at the top of his lungs......

* * *

(speaking in Japanese)

Ayako gave that 'here we go again look' shaking her head as she wearily rose from her desk. Another day another challenge. She had worked for Namura for over a decade and she knew how to handle this bad boy. The 'throw away smile' was first on her agenda as she entered the 'inner sanctum'.

Okio's facial expression said it all as he rudely pointed to the seat in front of his desk. He sat for a moment an angry stare in his eyes, took another sip of his green tea, wiped his mouth, then settled down.

"I need you to contact Katsuro Soto to get his First Officer Haruki Goro and Flight Engineer Shiru Toma to make ready the Kawasaki C-2 for an urgent flight from Tokushima to Shimaru Shima with a full replacement crew and supplies. I know it's not our regular schedule but this is an emergency. I don't want to go into the details but we have lost three of our men and one seriously wounded that needs urgent medical attention on the mainland."

"Seriously wounded?" Ayako was aghast placing the back of her hand against her lips. This was a situation she had never experienced in her ten years of service.

"Yes, I don't want to go into the details but my previous bodyguard Kazuo Tahoka whom you know, is in a serious condition and Akimasa Arakida unfortunately was killed in a fire fight."

"My God!" Ayako was almost in tears recollecting the two men that had become her close friends over the years.

"Ayako, are you, all right?" Numara was human after all.

"Hai, but if you don't mind Boso I'll go to the restroom to freshen up."

Okio nodded, the last thing he needed on is watch was a weeping secretary! His next problem was to contact the replacement site supervisor Aki Hachiro to organize the crew and supplies. The men would not be happy having only had around ten days R&R but that was for another day and he lifted the phone on his private line. "Let me see... The dial code for Tokushima is......."

* * *

"Haroki, something has come up which I don't want to discuss over the phone but I need you to muster your crew for an emergency return flight as soon as possible... *Don't argue with me...! Don't you think I don't know it's going to be difficult...* Just get the job done I want no excuses... That's why you are a site supervisor... To contact them...? That's *your* problem... Return my call when you can confirm with Captain Soto you'll have your men ready on the tarmac with the usual supplies... *Haroki, I'm not going to tell you again, I have other more important things to do than to argue with you!* If you can't hack it... Yes, you had better... Arigato...."

Okio slammed down the phone he had had enough of excuses from Osono, 'when the going gets tough'......

* * *

The last two days on 'Shimaru Shima' had been a mini nightmare for Shendo, what with the cremations and his closest ally in sick bay seriously wounded. The 'good news, *if there is such a thing,* was that Numero had given his blessing for a relief flight to repatriate Tahoka to 'Tokushima' for immediate surgery. However, with the positive there is always the negative being that the earliest ETA was five days from now, a daunting thought for Shendo to say the least.

Salibe had watched the drama with elation at the turmoil the three American escapees had caused, much to their demise, or murder would be a better summation, but once again breakfast was here and what would be the play today?

As he walked in the humidity to the dining hall the sneers and derogative comments were coming fast and furious but not as bad as the hatred from his 'friendly foes' the Israelis. So, *what the hell!* Operation 'Fish Tail' would change the 'Middle East' landscape forever and reunite the Palestinian territories of the West Bank, The Golan Heights including Jerusalem and the Gaza Strip as one nation.

Salibe could just see Shendo entering the mess hall ten meters in front. As usual the Yakuza stood to attention then bowed, the normal protocol and respect for their Commander. *Interesting,* Salibe thought to himself as he entered the dinner to a loud barrage of hissing, the Japanese way to display their hatred, but more to the point who would be at the top table this morning? As normal Shendo scowled at Salibe as he took his seat.

"Hmmmm," Salibe grinned sarcastically. 'A change of faces today, I miss my old friends, *and I don't think,* but I'm sure the new conversation will be interesting'.

The Camp Doctor Ichiro Akimoto and Site supervisor Jiro Adachi had already taken the seats.

Shendo turned to the doctor who had a perfect command of English having graduated in medicine from Edinburgh University.

"Sono bureina basutoraddo wa nan to itta nodesu ka?" (what did that rude bastard say?)

"Not to worry Boso, he is making a disrespectful comment about our fallen heroes."

Shendo's eyes focused on Salibe a penetrating look that said it all.

"Tell rag head we will get rid of him soon as a relief flight is due here in six days and I *will personally make sure he is on it!"*

The doctor conveyed Shendo's message in no mean manner and for a moment the unexpected news threw Salibe. Previously he couldn't wait to get back to Palestine but now he was having second thoughts. The hostile relationship between he and Shendo, not to mention the men, bread an element of doubt. *Would Shendo honor the incoming Russian shipment to be re shipped by the Japanese submarine to the West Bank and the transfer of the 40 billion US dollars?* Six days... *Was that enough time?* And where the hell are these Russians? Probably eating caviar and drinking chilled bloody Vodka!

"The Arab doesn't seem so happy." Shendo had noticed the apprehensive look on Salibe's face.

"Maybe he will miss our Japanese hospitality." The doctor's comment brought the breakfast table to instant laughter.

"And fuck you and fuck your lousy breakfast!" The laughter had stabbed the Arab's pride and he chucked his napkin on the table and abruptly rose only to walk the gauntlet to loud clapping and hissing.

"Fucking Japanese, I can't wait to leave this hell hole and these fucking crazies reenacting the 'The last Samurai'."

The solitude of the dormitory was a welcome relief and Salibe threw himself on the 'fakir' cot, a scene more common by the day. Passing time and the waiting game was getting to him *and that fucking fan!* Salibe leaned over and picked up his boot and with all his strength put the groaning creature out of its misery, the fan blades buckling then grinding in a death knell... *At last peace...!*

"What now?" Suddenly he could hear a commotion coming from the maintenance dock, like clapping and cheering.

"Now where's that fucking boot?" Salibe hopped across the rough timber flooring balancing on one foot and with one boot on before finally retrieving its partner.

"Now what the hell?"

He rushed to the door only to be met with the scene of the Japanese submarine RU18 docking, its crew proudly lining the deck like coming back from Pearl Harbor, 'Mission Impossible'. Its cargo of uncut cocaine from Columbia as normal, to be reshipped on the next relief flight to 'Tokushima' for processing and distribution to the growing market of mainland China.

This was an event that Salibe hadn't predicted and for a moment the sun was shining. How long the RU18 would stay in port was another question or was it planned to coincide with the arrival of the Russian Nuclear submarine the Lewinsky Komsomol. Maybe Numero wasn't so stupid after all. To get this deal put to bed and the Russians off his back would be a 'get out of jail' and back to normal. *The question now is where are the Ruskies and would they arrive before he was frog legged on the next flight to 'Tokushima'.......?*

LOVE IS IN THE AIR

Gregg, as normal was feet on the floor first and the smell of fresh coffee was tantalizing. As for Steve, he was a 'lie in guy' and as always, a last minute 'toast in the mouth' standing in the lift rushing to the office.

It was a normal summer's morning in Washington, a comfortable 75 degrees as Gregg sat on the balcony enjoying the cool breeze and the dark brew. Maybe Steve was right about Michelle and does absence make the heart grow fonder, only time will tell? A few days in LA as 'Kings of the Road' with two gorgeous flight attendants might shatter the 'rose colored' glasses, Gregg grinned as he took another sip of the dark brew. "Yeah, I'm beginning to like the idea...."

"As always up early, *can't you sleep man?*" Steve was standing naked to the waist in his floral jocks. He stretched his arms above his head and a gave an overzealous yawn then went to the coffee machine placed the small cup below, then a capsule and pressed the red button to a hissing and spurting noise.

"What happened to the toast?"

"Get it yourself, you're not in Business Class now! And while you're at it, put a vest on, who wants to stare at these sagging tits!"

"I can sense you're in a good mood this morning, thank God the coffee's good *at least that's something!*"

Steve 'planked it' on the wicker chair next to Gregg and placed his cup on the glass coffee table, a grin crossing his face.

"Back to reality, huh?"

"You could call it that."

"Have you given anymore thought to the LA trip?"

"Yeah, I'm for it but we had better get our asses moving, remember we must be back in the office on Tuesday and we have flights, accommodation and the Harley's to organize."

"Well what's keeping you?"

"What do you mean what's keeping me? Not on your life, I fell for that one with my credit card the last time. *Which reminds me.*"

"*Yeah, yeah,* I still owe you... Next pay check."

"I've heard that one before."

"So?"

"*What do you mean, so?*

"You still have her number, don't you?"

"You mean Marge?"

"Is there any other?" Steve laughed

"So, I do the phoning?"

"*You're the one she's hot on......!*"

* * *

"*Where the hell are these delivery guys from Macy's?* They said they would be here a 10.am!"

"Hey listen." Marge chimed in changing it. "Didn't we do well buying our furniture and accessories from Marcy's floor stock and at great discount prices and immediate delivery?"

Julie half laughed "*Yeah,* but unfortunately our credit cards are not jumping for joy."

"But remember we have the extra pay check from our Japanese trip and in a couple of months if we don't go crazy on the plastic we'll be back in the black."

"Marge, I wish I had your confidence."

Suddenly out of the blue the security phone buzzed. "*Talk of the devil!* This could be them now... Yes?" Julie spoke into the intercom.

"Liquor store, 'on line' delivery."

"Just a sec." Julie studied the camera shot, these days one can never be too sure. "Okay fetch it up." She pressed the security button.

Marge had to laugh. "At least we have the booze, *that's something!*"

The doorbell rang. "*Coming.*"

"Can you get that Marge?"

"Sure." She looked through the security peephole... satisfied, she opened the door.

The young rather good-looking muscle-bound kid in his early twenties in the skin tight white 'T' shirt with bold red lettering 'RAMIREZ LIQUOR' a popular liquor chain in LA, was struggling with the overweight double tier cartons containing enough booze for the '5th of July'.

"Julie Rodgers? Delivery from 'RAMIREZ LIQUOR'?"

"Come in kid before you do yourself an injury."

"Where to lady?" The kid panted trying to control his balance whilst resting the heavy carton on his supportive knee.

"Over there on the island."

"Thanks ma'am... Boy was that something." The kid wiped his brow relieved he wasn't permanently disabled.

"Student?" Marge asked.

"Yes ma'am." He smiled playing the sympathy card.

"Where do I sign?" Julie butted in, Marge was getting a bit too cozy with the young 'Arnold Schwarzenegger'.

"On the dotted line ma'am." He pointed.

"Thanks... Eh?"

"Damien."

Julie slipped him a ten spot.

"Is there anything else I can do for you ma'am?" He had that grin.

"Don't push your luck Damien, there's the door."

The kid smiled, it was worth a try......

* * *

The booze stacked in the refrigerator it was back to the waiting game, *worse still there was no point having a glass of warm Chardonnay to relieve the tension!*

"Say Julie, what are we gonna do with the old sofa?" But before Julie could answer the security phone buzzed once again and her eyes lit up as she turned to Marge. *"Could this finally be?"* Julie nimbly picked up the phone and stared into the camera.

"Macy's furniture delivery for Julie Rodgers apartment 12?"

"You got it! *Bring it on.*"

"Depeche toi." She released the security lock then proceeded to open the apartment door in anticipation, more so, they would have to jam the elevator doors much to the neighbor's annoyance.

"To pick up where you left off Marge, fifty bucks should invisible that piece of shit."

"Hey! Don't be so nasty to the poor thing, it served its purpose when we had nothing else."

"Yeah, but you gotta admit it's past its 'used by'. Now, how about helping me set the place up.

One of the delivery men had already decommissioned an elevator by jamming a wedge in the rail of the open stainless-steel door, making it scream in subtle pain with an irritating bump... bump... bump noise, trying to close.

"Bed.... Where to?" The older of the two men asked......

* * *

"Yeas that's good... A little bit more to the left with the TV console... Yeah that's good... Marge is that your phone?"

"My phone...? Now who the hell can that be, it wouldn't be that weasel Draper phoning me, would it? Yes, Marge Simpson here... *Gregg Jonson...!* Of course, I remember you, I'm too young for Alzheimer's just yet...! So, are you still in Japan and is there anything new on Global 10? I might have guessed *and you and Steve are back in Washington...* You don't know how long for... So the big question is why the phone call? *Ha...Ha...Ha...* I might have guessed and you don't have to return to the office until Tuesday... Fortunately we're in the same boat with 5 days R&R.... *Ha...Ha...Ha....* I get the jest, hang on a sec while I check it out with Julie... That noise in the background? That's the delivery guys from Macy's with our new furniture... Hang on..." Marge covered her phone.

"What's the big deal, I heard some of that conversation?" Julie asked intrigued.

"It's Gregg Jonson from the CIA, remember?"

"How can I forget... Is it about Global 10?"

"Unfortunately, or fortunately no."

"What the hell does that main?" Julie shook her head, Marge is Marge... "Yes, these two lye lows go on the balcony... You were saying Marge?"

"They have leave until Tuesday and their back in DC and want to come down to LA for the weekend... and well... You know what I mean?"

"That might be fun." Julie pouted her lips. *"Hmmm...Why not?"*

"Gregg, are you still there?... Yes, we would love to catch up... Give us a call when you arrive... Oh, I should give you our address... '569 Ocean Avenue, Sea View Apartments'... You got that...? Good... Until then, ciao."

"Hmmm..." Marge sat back on the new sofa a cheeky smile on her face. *"Isn't that a turn for the book!"*

"Hey, stop sitting there dreaming, we have work to do......!"

* * *

"So, what's the scoop?" Steve was standing over Gregg on the phone, coffee cup in his hand, bear chested in his hideous jock attire.

"Can't you put on something decent on?"

"Awe come on, cut the slack and put me out of my misery."

"Yeah, it's on...! LA here we come..." Gregg yelled... *"Sun sand and a drink in my hand..."* As for *Michelle?* Well... That's for another day and another time...!

* * *

"I told you, *maan!"* Steve was ecstatic, he could just picture the look alike Grace Kelly and her hot real estate.

Gregg killed the 'dream thoughts'. "We've got a lot to do buddy if we want to hit the Santa Monica, like tonight!"

"Like?" Steve was playing the field, Gregg was the organizer so why change?

"The airline tickets, the hotel... Do you want me to go on...?"

"Come on Gregg, you're a born organizer and besides you love making yourself useful."

"You're full of shit, just gimme your Amex plastic and I'll be happy, besides your still in hawk to me from the last trip."

"Maaan..." Steve laughed. "You're wasting your time, you could've auditioned for the part of Shylock in 'The Merchant of Venice'."

"Get out of it! I don't know where you get that stuff... Now the card or its sayonara to that gorgeous Julie."

"Still with the Japanese, huh? But then when you put it that way, you got your 'pound of flesh' after all......"

* * *

"I'm for the shower." Steve sipped the last of his coffee with Gregg was already on the phone, Amex fortitude.

"It's about time... Eh...No... No... My apologies I'm talking to someone one else... Trivago...? Yes... *Eh...*Alice... I'm looking for reasonably priced accommodation in LA near the Santa Monica highway and the beach... How many nights...? Checking in late today Friday, departing Monday afternoon... The Comfort Inn on Santa Monica Boulevard 3 miles from the Pier and 5 from Muscle Beach and the tariff for a double room with two single beds, 250

per night with breakfast free parking and Wi-Fi, sounds good... Amex...? The booking will be under a Mr. Steven Nelson... Yes, that's correct..."

"I think I'll grab another coffee."

Steve suddenly appeared still toweling his hair but more respectively in white 'T" shirt and shorts.

"Slacking, are we?"

"What do mean, I've already made reservations for the hotel."

"How about the bikes? I might as well join you." Steve slipped another capsule into the machine and joined Gregg on the balcony.

"Plane tickets first... "Yes, Delta Airlines Reservations...?"

"Now that that's confirmed. The earliest flight we can get seats is the 2.30 and returning twelve noon. A bit late but the night is still young... Now the bikes... Harleys?"

"Is there any other?" Steve laughed.

"Steve, can you remember the company we rented the bikes from the last time?"

"Eh... Something like... Easy, whatever."

"It's okay I'll Google it... Yeah, your right, 'Easy Rider Motor Cycle Rentals LA'. The same?"

"Easy Rider Motor Cycles, Yes I would like to rent...Yes that's correct, two Soft Tails with pillion back supports..." Gregg covered the phone. "Steve they're only 2 miles from the airport shall we pick them up when we arrive or he next morning."

"We're travelling light so the airport sounds good. But what's the fight time?"

"Yeah, I forgot about that... Four and a half hours... Just a sec when do you close? 10 pm... Yes, we'll pick them up around say 7... 7.30 pm......."

* * *

Both girls in their wet look "T's and skin-tight shorts, were putting the finishing touches to their makeup. For sure they would turn a few heads toady on the sand.

"Have you got you beach bag packed?" Julie turned to Marge.

"Yeah, lotion, towels that kinda stuff, it's gonna be a nice day for the beach the forecast is 106. What's the time?"

"Just on eleven." Julie replied glancing at her watch, then looking into the vanity mirror and putting the finishing touches to her lipstick. *"Hmmm...*

That's more like it! Say, come to think of it you never told me what Gregg said to you on last night's phone call?"

"Nothing juicy, if that's where you're coming from?"

"I think you had a little too much chardonnay last night."

"You can speak, you're the one that kept filing my glass!"

"I'm waiting." Julie was more than inquisitive.

"The usual stuff... Can't wait to see me, pick us up tomorrow around eleven for brunch, bring your beach stuff, they would have met us last night but they arrived too late...*blah ...blah... blah.*"

"So where are they staying, *you did ask?*"

"The Comfort Inn on Santa Monica Boulevard."

"That's not far from our apartment, the guys must have done their homework. So where was Gregg phoning from, the hotel, or were the guys out on the town?"

"God, *you are* inquisitive. I think this Steve is getting to you. I could hardly hear above the background noise but I think he said Busby's Bar, you know the one near the pier."

"Yeah, the sport's bar." Julie raised her hand to keep quiet. "And if I'm not mistaken I think I hear the rasp of Harley's from the apartment's open-air car park."

"And on time... *Not bad!*"

Marge's Cell rang. "We'll be down in sec, Gregg......"

* * *

The city as usual woke up to the beautiful LA sunshine. Clear blue skies with temperatures for the 'beach lovers' reaching 106 by 12 noon. As the 'bikers' proudly stood in the car park sporting their 'Soft Tail Harleys' the chrome-work glistening in the sun, the cool morning breeze was perfect for the 'wind in the hair' and the 'throaty' exhaust down the Santa Monica and the guys couldn't wait to get their precious cargoes on board.

* * *

Steve gave Gregg a nudge upon seeing these two class acts crossing the car park.

"Wow... What did I tell you? Now aren't you glad I convinced you to call Marge?"

Gregg was non-committal. "Something like that." He replied, although the look on his face was more than convincing.

"*Well look at you two!* Board shorts, Hawaiian shirts and sneakers, you look like the real deal Angelinos." Marge laughed the smile lighting up her face.

Steve couldn't help himself. "I gotta hand it to you two ladies, you both look absolutely stunning."

"Thanks for the compliment." Julie flashed the look at Steve.

"Where do we...?"

"*Your beach bags?* Stack them in the side poniards, here, let me help you Marge." Gregg the 'ice man' was finally melting.

"I hope you guys are hungry?" Steve asked.

"*Of course*, we purposely skipped breakfast." Marge was also giving Gregg the heavies but then she had a thing for him since they last met on that fateful day on the beach.

"A suggestion?" Steve asked.

"You mean the restaurant?" Julie turned to Marge who just shrugged like 'it's your call'.

"How about Rod's?" *That took Marge aback!*

"*Are you sure?*"

Julie turned to Steve confusion written on his face.

"It was our favorite haunting place with Bill and Chuck just across the from the beach where we first met you guys."

"It's okay, we understand." Steve shrugged. "I'm sure there's plenty of other places, no sweat"

"No, Marge and I have to put that behind us and turned a new page."

"Okay, Rod's it is then ladies! Let's fire up these bad boys. Are we all loaded and ready to go?"

"Yeah, we're good but which is which?" Marge asked looking at the cruisers.

Gregg smiled. "The sky blue is mine and the red is Steve's. Cover your ears." He pressed the starter button and opened the accelerator the Harley exhausts singing their familiar put... put... put, baritone.

"*Wow*, that noise!" Julie exclaimed. "*But it's exciting.*"

"Just before we go..." Gregg yelled above the noise. "Relax and sway with the bike. If you feel uncomfortable place your arms around our waists and oh, make sure your feet are firmly on the rear foot rests and not the exhaust or you'll burn the soles of your sneakers... Okay hop on... *Now Rod's Bar...?*"

Julie yelled above the rasp. "Hang a left onto Ocean Avenue and its fifteen minutes, you can't miss it."

"Comfortable ladies? Gregg, you ride 'shot gun' and watch the speed, we don't want the Highway Patrol on our ass's......"

*   *   *

The fifteen-minute drive to Rod's was white-knuckle and as for the girls, they just loved it, not only the Harleys but the head turning and the attention from the sunning public. *After all it's not every day you see two macho guys on Soft Tails with rear cargos to match!*

"That's Rods coming up on the right you can't miss it." Julie yelled into Steve's ear as he pushed on the handlebars and hung a right toward the kerb and the car park.

"Yes, I can clearly see it, it's the one with the blue sun brollies and the thatched roof sloping onto the beach.

"That's the one!" Julie opened her lungs.

Steve raised his right arm and pointed to let Gregg know they were approaching the famous 'Rod's Beach Bar' in around 200 yards signaling with his indictor then squeezing the clutch leaver before breaking slightly and opening the accelerator dropping a gear. The sudden burst of power turning the heads of the beach freaks to the laughter of the 'bikies mauls'.

"Here we are." Steve cut the engine as Gregg pulled up beside him.

"Ladies, if you could do the needful and dismount while we hold the bikes upright?"

Steve balanced the 703lb machine then flicked the foot stand the bike leaning to one side in all its glory.

"So, ladies, did that whet your appetite?" Gregg laughed at their disheveled hair with Julie and marge hurriedly trying to salvage their dignity.

"That was absolutely exhilarating." Julie was catching her breath turning to Marge. "I think we have to go to the powder room, huh?" She gave her friend a cheeky wink.

"We understand ladies. Take your time, we'll grab some stools at the bar."

Gregg turned to Steve as they entered the restaurant a smile crossing his face. "It always intrigues me why women must to go to the restroom in twos?"

"Most likely to talk about us and of course the war paint."

"*Ha...Ha...Ha...* If you put it that way." Gregg laughed at Steve's description. "So, shall you accompany me to the Gents?"

"*Maaan,* your something else. The next thing you'll be wearing the LBGT lapel badge!"

"So, what'll it be guys?" Dan the barman was fast on his feet ditching the boring glass polishing.

"I you can just hold on... Eh?"

"Dan."

"Dan, we're waiting for two ladies who are indisposed at the moment." Steve smiled.

"Sure, I get the picture. If you're interested in food, I'll go fetch the menus to save time?"

"Yeah, we'd like to start with some cocktails and brunch." Steve answered.

"Then I'm your man... Be back in a jiff."

"*Hmmm.*" Gregg was taking it all in. "I can see why the girls like this joint, the ambience is relaxing with that whole surf thing, boards and all......"

* * *

"*God.* my hair's such a mess!" Julie was looking in the mirror frantically backcombing her golden locks.

"I just loved that ride down Ocean Avenue. You know meeting these two guys couldn't have come at a better time... *And that Gregg...* He's kinda reserved but handsome and nice with it." Marge was down to the 'wet lip' look.

"Yes, it's strange, life is so unpredictable. We meet these guys on the beach after assing Bill and Chuck that day and we've just done a 360, *it's uncanny!* Washington... Japan... and here we are back in LA. I've gotta pinch myself, I'm beginning to believe in fate... Of course, I'll never forget Bill." And for a moment Julie's eyes teared up.

"*Come on honey,* don't you think I don't feel the same?" Listen, changing the subject. What do you think about Steve because by that look in his eyes, I know what he thinks about you!"

Julie was silent for a moment. "He kinda reminds me a bit like Chuck, wild and unpredictable. *Sorry Marge...!*" Julie could have bitten her lip. "I didn't mean to... That was so insensitive of me."

"That's okay, it wasn't intentional... Let's get back to the bar or these two heroes will be thinking we've done a runner......."

* * *

"Marge... Julie, I'll *be* darned!" The girls took the stools between each of their hosts.

"Dan..." Julie acknowledged halfheartedly, still in denial.

"Say, I'm sorry to bring it up but I heard the news on CNN. Listen if it's too sensitive I'll cut the cord."

"Naw, it's okay." Marge stepped in. "We've been friends over the years and I can't blame you, Dan."

"Any news?"

Marge shrugged and sighed at the same time, like a lost cause.

"They've found what's left of the plane and I'm afraid the prognosis is not good."

"Gee, I'm sorry. They broke the mold with these characters. Eh, say what can I get to cheer you up." Dan cracked a false smile.

"My favorite a 'Negroni'." Julie was quick off the mark.

"A 'Negroni'!" Gregg laughed. "You're kidding me, I've never heard of that one."

"Serious? You should try one, is that right Dan?"

"She's right big boy... There's plenty of drama in that baby."

Dan was already placing the concoction on the bar, three of the 'ten green bottles'. Aged Bourbon, Campari and Italian Vermouth the heavy measures splashed over the cubes, the stainless-steel shaker frosting up ready for the gyro.

Steve turned to Julie. "I can't wait for *your* order!"

"Tell em honey." Dan was in his element, a poor 'Tom Cruise'.

"Are you ready?"

Dan had already poured the ruby colored 'lethal weapon' into the wide brimmed cocktail glass with a slice of lemon.

"A Robert De Niro." She laughed.

"Oh man, this is getting better by the minute." Steve was cracking up. *"This I gotta see."*

"Absolute Vodka, Ocean Spray and White Cranberry Juice. There you go Marge. I'm on to yours in a sec Julie."

"Is there such a drink as a Michelob here, I'm embarrassed." Greggs comment brought the house down.

"Can you imagine these guys Dan? Like where have you been on the cocktail scene? And don't tell me Steve *you're* gonna be liven dangerously."

"A Heineken?" Steve almost choked trying to stifle his laughter, this was beginning to have all the makings of a more than interesting 'brunch'."

"The beers are coming up guy's glasses or bottles?"

"Bottles." Steve replied having seen the funny side.

Marge took a sip of her Negroni. "Boy does this blow the cobwebs away! Say we never introduce you... Dan this is Steve and this is Gregg, believe it or not, all the way from Capitol Hill, DC."

"You're not politicians, are you?" Dan laughed.

"No, but we *do* work for the Government... 'CIA'."

"Your shittin me!"

"Please yourself..." Steve was used to the immature comments, and for fleeting moment out of the box, he noticed the sadness in Julie's eyes and unexplainably gently held her hand, a gesture that was unexpected and touching and Julie returned the 'crush'. This guy was different after all and maybe there *was* a spark but only if she put Bill behind and accepted the realty that no matter what, Bill and Chuck will never return.

"Julie, you haven't touched your drink." Marge was on the comeback trail.

"What am I thinking about... *Cheers.*" She gave Steve another crush of the hand, a simple way of saying thanks......

* * *

"Alcoholics need to eat." Steve passed the menus.

Marg laughed. "I was wondering when someone would pop that question... Let me put it this way, I could eat the 'elephant in the room!'"

Gregg laughed. "Reverse phycology, huh?" The smile was back on Julie's face.

"Let me see." She took another sip of the 'Robert'.

"Would you guys like a table in the courtyard under the sun brolly, it's a lovely sea breeze today."

"Yeah, that would be nice Dan... Unless." Julie turned to the 'rat pack' for an endorsement.

The guys sort of shrugged. "Knock yourself out honey, we're good with that." Gregg assured.

"Before you leave the bar it looks like you need some refills?"

"Play it again Sam or should I say Dan?"

"Gregg, I'll keep that one in mind for the next one." Marge laughed.

"There's plenty of free tables so I'll leave it to you guys. Settle down and I'll fetch your drinks in a few minutes."

"Thanks Dan."

"No sweat. Julie, it's really great to see you guys again...."

"We couldn't have picked a better day." Marge commented as they took their seats overlooking the beach.

"Your spoiled in LA with this weather compared to boring Washington and its horrible winters."

"That can easily be fixed Steve, *move to LA.*"

"Easier said than done Julie, in our jobs you never can tell where we'll be assigned tomorrow."

"Your drinks guys." Dan was precariously balancing the tray with the cocktails and the lop-sided beers.

"Now, let me just run through your orders. Julie... Six freshly chucked oysters... Chargrilled Calamari, silvery sardines marinated in chili garlic and lemon on a Lillo of seaweed short crust... And Marge... Your sticking to our Pizza of gently risen thin crust gorgonzola with black kale and San Marzano tomatoes?"

"You got it, but guys you may have to help me with it as it's a bit over the top."

"Gregg?"

"I'm still thinking... Gimme another sec."

"Steve?"

"Yeah I'm good... Let me see... I'll have the salt grass Lamb rack roasted with parsley and mustard crust and mash on the side with sage scented rabbit ragout... *Come on Gregg, make up your mind!*" Steve couldn't wait to get into the heavies.

"*Oh man.*" Gregg scratched his heed... "*Decisions ... Decisions...* Let me see, something simple... Here we are." He was running his finger over the small print. "Potato gnocchi with smoky scamorza cheese and guanciale." Gregg puffed his lips shaking his head.

"That was a mouthful, I don't know how they come up with all that stuff.....?"

* * *

After three hours on the beach the 'Miss LA's' had had enough sun and more so the enjoyment of the suntan applicators whose firm hands were becoming more enjoyable by the hour. It was certainly a giant leap from Bill and Chuck 'who only had eyes' for the bikini clad landscape to the annoyance of both Julie and Marge.

The Beach Buggy cocktail bar had come and gone at least three times and the Tequila Sunrises were a change from the fifteen-dollar hits from Dan the cocktail man. Steve and Gregg had stuck to two beers, when you're riding mean machines with two trusted pillions, sobriety is the name of the game.

"How do you make the time?" Julie asked draining the last of the 'Sunrise' from the disgusting plastic cup.

Gregg glanced at his watch. *"Eh...* I make it just gone five."

"I think it's time we hit the road guys if we want to get ready for the Saturday night blast."

"We, Julie? Does that mean we're getting an invitation?" Steve was being cheeky.

"Not unless you have other pressing appointments?"

Steve put on the acting shrug, turning to is partner in crime. "I suppose we could cancel them..." Steve was playing the joker. "What do you think Gregg?"

"I'm taking the fifth, the jury's still out on that one."

It was Julie's turn with the barter. "What say you Marge? Should we truest these two losers?"

"Ehhh, let me think." Marge put on the 'let me decide face'. But on the other hand?" She grinned. "Come to think of it *we do* need a ride back to the apartment."

"So?"

"I guess we'll let them off the hook." Marge was enjoying the game.

"We got two smart ladies here Gregg. Have you gals ever thought of applying for the CIA?"

As for Gregg, he was now too busy concentrating on his body language with the lovely Marge.

"Getting serious. I think it's getting late Marge and it's about time we got changed. Give us ten guys and we'll meet you out front in the carpark."

"No sweat." Steve acknowledge giving Gregg a nudge and a wink. It was all going to plan.

As Julie and Marge trudged through the soft sand to Rod's, Steve could hear their voices. "So, tonight Marge, where would you recommend we take the guys for 'Saturday night Fever'...? *Heh... Heh....*" They could hear Marge laugh. "How about........?"

* * *

"Julie, are you going to be much longer, it's coming up to six thirty and we're meeting the guys in an hour?" Marge had brutalized her second glass of her favorite 'Yellow Tail' Australian Chardonnay.

"I here you, I'll be out in five." Julie yelled above the noise of the shower spray.

"The next apartment will have bedrooms with ensuites." Marge, grumbled giving herself a hard time but the wine was compensating for the 'big wait'.

"I really like this apartment though." Her private conversation continuing. "And I just love that 55inch Samsung smart TV… Gosh, *Trump again,* when are they gonna let up on this guy?"

"Okay, Marge the showers free."

"Coming… It's not before time. She camouflaged her last words below her breath, after all she was next in the box and there's no point in the pot calling the kettle black.

Julie immerged her face fresh, bare footed, her hair wrapped in a turban towel and wearing loose bathrobe showing more cleavage than the 'Hoover Dam' or 'Climb every Mountain'.

"Well, what's keeping you now?" Julie asked whilst vigorously toweling her entangled blonde hair.

Marge laughed as she drained the last of the yellow liquid.

"The last of my Chardonnay, that's what!" She exclaimed.

"I can see that." Julie held up the half empty bottle. "Marge go easy, we have the whole night ahead of us."

"No more, I promise, cross my heart." She made the sign with her right forefinger.

"Listen, before you disappear what are you wearing tonight?"

Marge sort of shrugged. "Haven't really thought about it… Something cool and casual and of course sexy." Her voice shallowing as she disappeared into the washroom shedding her clothes a garment at a time.

"What was that you said?"

"I can't hear you." Came the muffled reply.

Julie shrugged there was no point in wasting anymore oxygen, she had her hair to dry and the makeup challenge……

* * *

"I like that Marge, the off the shoulder white blouse with the floral neck line and the Levi blues and with these six inch heels your gonna knock Gregg cold."

Marge sucked the oxygen, she loved compliments. The annoying blow dryer drowning the conversation as she busily fluffed up her shoulder length brown hair.

"So, what do you think Marge…? DA… DA… DA." Julie did the 'ballerina 380'.

"Sexy! I didn't read you in leather pants tonight."

"Is it too much?"

"No, but I don't know how you got into them and with a that low cut sleeveless white blouse and those heels… *Sweet…* You look like Olivia Newton John in 'Grease'!"

"Yeah, but Steve aint no John Travolta!" Julie burst into laughter it was a fun start to the night.…...

* * *

"So, what club did you come up with?" Marge asked still full on in the vanity mirror.

"I came across this club as one of the ten best 10 disco night spots in LA… I don't know if you've heard of it?"

"Well, don't keep me in suspense!" Marge had returned to the sofa her six inch heals taking a back seat on her fallen arches.

"Let me see if I got this right." Julie was reading from her cell. "It's called 'Bootie LA'."

"Never heard of it." Marge shot back.

"Don't be so impulsive, let me finish."

Unperturbed, Marge was back in the admiration mode, 'mirror, mirror on the wall'.

"Julie, do you think my hair looks okay?

Julie sighed shaking her head. *"Are you listening…?*

"Yes, your hair looks good… *Now can you pay attention for one moment?"*

"Go on then."

"I googled the ten best disco clubs with a dance floor in LA near the Strip, for driving convenience."

"And?"

"So, I settled with, 'Bootie LA'."

"Bootie LA…*Strange name!"*

'It's on 'Glendale Avenue' just off the Strip and conveniently about 15 to twenty minutes from Steve and Gregg's hotel. There's a fifteen-dollar cover charge that gets you one drink. I paid for four over the net."

"Sixty bucks, huh? Getting generous, are we?"

"Awe come on Julie, these guys weren't locking their bill folds when we hit Rod's and the beach this morning!"

"Yeah, I guess you're right, so what's the scoop on the 'Bootie'?" Marge was finally paying attention.

"It has a five-star rating, which caught my eye. Here's some of the write up… Let me see… I'll just read the meat… 'If you love dancing this is one of the most unique clubs where you can have your own dance space if you hate touching shoulders… Affordable beers and cocktails and no bag checks… dress code… casual… you can dress either up or down… The DJ is unique with lots of old greats from the sixties and seventies and the stage dancers definitely know how to throw a party… Overall the place to be…' "What do you think?" Marge turned to Julie waiting for her reaction.

"It's different that's for sure!"

"On a more serious note, one for the road, huh?"

"Not on your life! Now changing the subject. I was thinking the 'Bug' has two doors and the back is really cramped…"

"Oh, no you don't, I know where you're coming from, use the Dodge, huh? No deal, I'm quite comfortable crushing in the back with Gregg."

"I had a bad feeling you would say that… *Hey, look at the time…!"*

* * *

You could hear the distinct click clack of the girls heals as they walked the deserted car park.

"Everyone must be out on the town tonight." Julie commented a she pressed the remote to unlock the bug the bleep bleep sound echoing rather eerily.

"Now before I hit the gas I need to enter the address of the hotel. Can you read this out to me Marge?" Julie passed her the folded paper.

"Sure… It's…? God, your writing is something else… Eh… The Comfort Inn…"

"Slow down… Okay go onto the Santa Monica Boulevard… Number…."

Julie gunned the 'Bug', the newly incarnated VW 's engine now in the front sounding like a conventional automobile… *Volkswagen, big mistake……!*

* * *

"Two Glenmorangie's, one cube of ice in each." The young barman just smiled, with single malt, *who needs ice!*

Gregg glanced at his watch. "The girls are running a bit late."

"You're always a stickler for time, haven't you heard, it's a woman's privilege?"

"Obviously, *you have!*" Gregg wasn't slow.

"Thanks." The drinks had arrived.

The barman acknowledged. "Do you want to charge these to your room?"

"Yeah… room 22" Steve replied showing the key tag. "Keep the tab open, were expecting friends… *Now…*" Steve turned to Gregg raising his glass. "Cheers."

"All kidding put aside I really enjoyed today and that Marge… She's a dish."

"*What did I tell you!* So 'Michelle ma Belle' sont les mots qui vont tres bien ensemble…" Steve burst into song.

"Your karaoke is worse than your fucking French not to mention the macabre humor." But Gregg was forced to laugh. "Don't spoil my night. Michelle is my problem and I'll deal with it in my own way when I return to DC. *Now… Cheers.*"

"Same again guys?" The barman was at the ready.

"You read it." Steve smiled.

"Looks like your guests have arrived." The kid nodded his head in the direction of the bar entrance. "And if you don't mind me saying so…*Nice.*"

"Yeah, we do mind you saying so." As they say complacency is the mother of contempt.

"*Oops*…Apologies, I'll go fetch you drinks." There's always one.

"*Ladies!*" Steve rose to his feet. "You both look absolutely adorable."

"Thank you."

The French 'kiss cheek' pecks over, the girls took their seats at the bar.

"Sorry we're a bit late." Marge eyed Gregg, who just smiled.

"No sweat." Steve replied. "Say, what can I get you ladies?" He raised his hand.

"I'll have a Vodka Cosmopolitan with lime and Marge?'

"Make mine a Vodka Kamikaze."

"Coming up ladies." Dean gave a cautious smile.

"You girls sure know your cocktails." Gregg shook his head.

"Remember, flight attendants, huh?" Marge was fast on the uptake.

"How could we forget!" Steve had that 'ga ga' smile as he stared into Julie's eyes.

It was Julie's turn with the compliments. "You guys look good tonight, 'The Forever in Blue Jeans' deck shoes and these colorful short sleeved shirts. Your certainly becoming part of the LA scene."

Steve couldn't resist the shot. "As they say 'When in Rome'."

"Ladies your cocktails."

"Thanks... Eh?"

"Dean."

"This Hotel is nice for a four star." Marge commented taking in the bar ambience.

"Yeah." Steve replied. "There's a beautiful pool, gym, you name it. Say, maybe you girls would like to come and join us tomorrow morning around the pool for breakfast. *That's unless you have church?"*

Gregg, just shook his head, typical Steve humor.

"Ha... Ha... Ha..." Julie laughed. "That would be a first. But the breakfast invitation is a nice thought and we might just take you up on that." Julie turned to Marge who gave an 'I like it' smile.

"So, what have you ladies got in store for us tonight?" Steve asked.

"Let's put it this way." Julie smiled. "I hope you like dancing?"

"Whatever, Julie." Steve interjected. "What's the old saying...? It's the company that counts... We're not novices when it comes to disco clubbing, but a word of caution, I hope you know a good Podiatrist!"

"Ha... Ha... Ha..." The girls burst into laughter again and this time even Gregg had to join in.

"Ladies, same again?" Dean was back with the 'Cocomo' smile.

"I'll have to take a 'rain check' I'm the driver tonight, remember?"

"Julie, if LA is anything like Washington parking is a combat sport or you're a Green Beret, so a better suggestion would be to grab a cab then we can all relax?"

"Yeah, why not?" Gregg echoed Steve's suggestion.

"Marge?"

"I'm okay with that Julie."

"Ladies?"

"Play it again Sam... or should I say Dean?" Marge was stoking for her second 'Kamikaze'........

* * *

The black cab driver pressed the meter button. "Where to, tonight guys?" The overdone smile tip orientated.

Gregg had taken the front passenger seat whilst Steve was in the back squeezed between the two beautiful damsels a proud smile on his face.

Gregg turned. "Julie, do you have the address of that club?"

"Yeah it's…" She read from the crumpled piece of paper she had fished from her bag. "It's… *Eh*…The Bootie Club… 1154 Glendale Avenue, off Sunset Boulevard."

"I know the one, it's around a 15-minute drive from here. Are you guys okay in the back?"

"Yeah, we're good… *Eh*?"

"Denver."

Cabbies are a wealth of information and Julie didn't waste any time exploiting.

"Denver, do you know the club well?"

"I've never been inside Ma'am, if that's what you're asking? At 45, married with three kids, I think my disco days are over." Denver laughed. "But to get back to your question, it's jumping on a Saturday, in fact you're my third fare there tonight. I hope you have a prepaid ticket as there's always a long que?"

"Fortunately, we have." Julie replied.

"Then you're all the way."

"You bought the Tickets Julie?" Steve asked.

"Yes, and I'm glad I did!"

"So, what do we owe you?" Gregg asked from the front.

"It's a small thing, not to worry, our cocktails cost more…."

* * *

"Here already?" Gregg exclaimed as the cabbie pulled into the kerb in front of the anticipated long que.

Although almost 50 yards, the crowd seemed jovial, dressed in all sorts of casual attire, the two black heavies on the door having their work cut out.

The large neon sign above the entrance, 'BOOTIE LA' in three feet 'brush script' lit up the whole street in a strange purple hue.

"That'll be 17 straight." Denver pointed to the meter.

Steve was quick to impress and took a twenty from his bill fold.

"That's okay."

"Thanks guys." The dollar smile and the purple neon reflection gave his teeth a florescent whiteness. "Take your time getting out. Have a good one. If you want me to pick you up again when the parties over, here's my card."

Gregg took the card and slipped it in his jeans.

"We just might take you up on that, just a sec Denver… Marge, let me take your hand." Marge was struggling in her skin-tight blues to get out of the back seat and still retain her modesty.

"'Sir Walter Raleigh' I like it."

"Come on you two." Julie and Steve were almost at the entrance, the large glass doors reflecting the flashing crisscross computerized multicolor lasers continually changing to the beat of the DJ's music.

The two heavies on the door in the traditional undersize tuxedoes, to emphasize their ape like physiques, or maybe the rental company just didn't have their size, blocked the entrance, the slightly larger of the two mumbled in garbled LA English, *"Tickets only or the que."*

Julie had predicted in advance opening her cell and showing the downloads.

The miniature 'King Kong' glanced momentarily at the Samsung then nodded to his 'twin' to open the heavy glass door, the blast of 'Johnny O'Keefe's' sixties hit *You know you make me wanna shout… Hold my hands up and shout'* drowning any hope of conversation…...

* * *

The size of the venue stunned the foursome, the warehouse's open ceiling the size of a quarter football pitch, the lasers crisscrossing in blues purples reds and greens. At the extreme far end was a stage with eight female dancers clad in gold bikinis and 'boots were made for walking' gyrating to the beat of the music. In the center on the right wall was the DJ with the ten-gallon Stetson. Around twenty feet high from the dance floor was what looked like a cherry picker, *only without the hydraulic arm* the 'wanna be cow dude' working feverishly on the neon music mixer to distribute the sound clarity and achieve the best acoustics through a multifaceted complex of large speakers hanging from the wall at calculated locations. The warehouse ambience was further tinted with the open steel triangular trusses supporting the galvanized roof, expressly painted in a dark grey to accentuate the maximum effect of the rainbow leasers not to mention the silver jacketed insulated twenty-four-inch air condition ducts snaking their way on cable ties to keep the temperature from turning into a sauna. On the far left was a larger than life polished wooden bar about fifteen yards long, the dangling lights in equal hangs above the drinking fraternity dimming the bar area with Edison bulbs to soften the glare from the colorful back drop and the low voltage spotlights striking the glass shelved rows of liquor bottles reflecting against a full-length wall mirror. Their labels requiring elocution lessons for the pronunciation. The iced-up bar fonts with popular drafts of Heineken, Stella, Michelob, Millar's and Budweiser was the 'Fait Accompli', the barmen working overtime. Scattered around the area in front of the dance floor were an inundation of pole tables minus the stools, in short standing room only… Whatever… 'Bootie La was the place to be……

* * *

"Did I tell you guys, we have free drinks thrown in with the cover charge?" Julie turned.

"Well that's something!" Marge commented. *"Now*, I'm beginning to like this place".

"I knew that would cheer *you* up, Marge". Julie's comment bringing a laugh all round.

"I suggest we get to the bar before it' s the 'pub with no beer'. Steve grabbed Julie's hand.

"So, what do we get for this?" Julie pounced the opportunity of a vacant space at the bar, the over worked barman who seemed rather old for the job, maybe doing a moonlighter, glanced at the screen of the Samsung.

"Vodka shots, or Johnny's." He shrugged, straight to the point.

Marge was first off, the rank. *"I knew it was too good to be true!"*

"What will it be girls?" Steve asked. "Not much choice I'm afraid." The barman patiently waiting.

"Vodka shooters and you guys?" Julie asked.

"Johnny, with plenty of ice to kill the taste."

"Coming up." The barman smiled, whisky drinkers hate 'Johnny Red' and these two guys were no different.

"Julie, you and Marge go and grab that vacant table, Gregg and I will fetch the drinks."

The barmen didn't waste much time, his name being rudely called by the thirsty 'bar flies'.

"We were lucky to snare this table." Marge commented as the drinks arrived.

"Cheers." Marge raised the 'Mexican stand offs' disappearing in one mouthful with the guys slowly sipping the whisky poison.

"I really like this place Julie, good choice."

"Thanks guys, it was a shot in the dark and I'm glad it came off."

Suddenly the music changed to Michele Jackson's 'Billy Jean'

"I love this guy, too bad he made the wrong choices, come on let's hit this dance floor. Leave the glasses on the table to stake our claim."

Marge grabbed Gregg's hand and dragged him onto the space-less floor.

In her element, Marge was soon performing body contacts of the 'third kind' and Gregg wasn't protesting. Julie and Steve were almost Siamese twins joined at the hip. The fun had just begun.......

* * *

"You guys look as if you've had a blast, you just caught me in time as I was about to call it a day… Two, am is my limit or I'll never see my wife…" Denver smiled. "On the other hand, maybe that's a good thing, after three kids, *huh?* Are we good to go?"

"Yeah, we're okay in the back." This time 'Malcolm in the middle' was Gregg. I mean, what guy would complain, crushed between these two beauties?

Denver switched the meter. *"Now,* a better question, where to?"

Before the guys could answer Julie took the 'Q' line. "Comfort Inn on Santa Monica Boulevard."

Denver just smiled and slipped the 'Ford Crown' into gear, *these babes are no dummies.*

"Julie." Steve turned from the front. "Gregg and I are sharing a room, of course single beds…"

"Whoa, whoa…! Let's not runaway with over ourselves! I don't know what's in your mind Steve, but as 'Napoleon' said "It's not tonight Josephine', or should I say, *Steve?"*

Julie's answer brought a moment's silence, the two 'heroes' stuck for words, their self-indulgence down the toilet and Gregg half smiled. Julie had politely put Steve in his place like only a woman could, or maybe it was her flight attendant training?

"Err…Eh…" Steve stuttered, looking for cover.

"Julie, I'm sorry if we gave you the wrong impression."

"What's with the 'we'? Speak for yourself, Steve."

"Who needs a friend, huh?" Steve shook his head.

Marge timely interrupted the 'go nowhere' embarrassing conversation.

"Look on the bright side, guys. Julie and I have decided to meet you tomorrow for breakfast at the hotel and spend the day soaking up the sun and maybe an afternoon on 'kings of the road'."

"Here we are folks." Denver had been quietly enjoying 'The clash of the Titans'.

"I'll get this Steve." The diversion timely, Gregg passed Denver two tens then turned to Marge.

"We had a great night and I'm looking forward to see…" Marge crushed her lips against his, choking his apologies. As for Julie? She was feeling like the 'third wheel' but there was no way she was going to throw herself at Steve!

"Eh…" Gregg had to break the lip crush and catch his breath.

Should he a take another bite of the forbidden fruit or play the gentleman? *What the hell!* He gently placed his hand behind Marge's head and returned the compliment only this time he was calling the shots. The oxygen in scarce supply they finally parted lips.

"Ah…Hmmm… If it's not too much trouble guys I still have to take these two ladies home?"

"Will anther ten cover it?" Steve asked feeling like the Matador who just got gored by the bull.

"That's plenty." Denver smiled, glad to be on his way, maybe he was having second thoughts about his wife Jane, after all.

"By Julie." Steve had the condemned man's look but all was not lost as Julie crushed his hand as the cab moved off, you could say, *making his day….*

* * *

Steve had perked himself up as they walked to their room, feeling all was not lost.

"I almost screwed that one up, didn't I?" He turned to Gregg as he opened the door.

"I'm not buying into that one. I had a great night and I'm really looking forward to seeing Marge tomorrow and a now for a shower and a good night's sleep, *it's after two you know!".*

"Yeah, I guess you're right, Gregg. Do you mind if I shower first?"

"Knock yourself out." Gregg kicked off his deck shoes and threw himself on the bed, his hands behind his head resting on the pillow. He could hear Steve in the shower and the less he knows the better. His cognizance eating into his denial that he preferred Marge over Michelle and there was only one thing to do irrespective of the time, and that was to call her and give himself peace of mind.

He checked the number and dialed, an unsureness of what to say feeling like a cheater. The long ring tones making him even more uncomfortable as she was most likely fast asleep.

"Come on… Come on!" The last thing he needed was Steve to appear from the bathroom. Suddenly a sleepy male's voice answered.

"Yeah, who's this?"

Gregg was silent for a few moments, taken aback. Did he dial the wrong number, or what?

"Tell Michelle it's, Gregg."

"Who is it darling?"

"It's some guy called Gregg."

"Shiiiiit…!"

Gregg placed the receiver back. Steve was right after all… When the cat's away….

* * *

"You were throwing yourself at Gregg last night, another refill?" Julie had the coffee pot at the ready.

"Thanks, my head belongs to someone else."

Julie refilled Marge's empty cup as they sat on the balcony enjoying the early morning breeze.

"I can imagine, you weren't slow on these Tequila shooters!"

"Lighten up Julie, the point is for a change it was good to let my hair down after the trauma of the last three weeks and Gregg… He's a really nice guy."

Julie was quietly sipping her coffee. Marge had something but as for Steve…? It was a bit premature to jump into another relationship although there was something there.

"Why so quite Julie, what are you thinking about?"

"I guess I'm just a little mixed up. My feelings tell me one thing and my brain tells me another." Julie made a face pouting her lips.

"What's the time Julie? We promised the guys we would meet them for breakfast."

"Hell, its 10:30 already, *would you believe it?"* Julie shook her head in disbclicf as she glanced at the wall clock.

"Of course," It suddenly came to Marge. "I'll have to use the Dodge, as your car is still at the hotel, I almost forgot about that."

"Whatever… Who's first in the shower…....?

* * *

The girls as usual looked the part in their shorts 'T's' and sneakers, their shapely figures the main attraction.

Marge gunned the Dodge SUV and hung a left onto Ocean Avenue, it was now 11:30 and the guys must be wondering if they fed them a lemon but there was one consolation, Julie's car…..!

* * *

It was a beautiful 'pool morning' with temperatures forecast to reach a mid-day 80, normal for July in LA.

"It's a bit late for breakfast so I guess it's going to be lunch. I wonder what's keeping them?" Steve was sipping an early morning beer.

"You said it yourself, remember, 'it's a woman's privilege'?"

"Get out of it, *smart ass.*"

"Guys, they are over there at the far end of the pool." The attendant pointed.

The boyd were lying on the cushioned Lillo's under the large sun umbrellas when they heard the familiar voices.

"Talk of the devil!" Steve turned and waved to attract Julie.

"Boy, we should be so lucky. These tight shorts bring out the worst in me."

"For once I agree with you." Gregg laughed swinging his feet to the terracotta. *"Wow, these tiles are hot!"* He grabbed for his deck shoes to Steve's laughter.

"Marge, Julie, hear grab a Lillo under the shade." Gregg gave Marge a kiss on the cheek.

The pool boy didn't need an invitation arriving with two large white bath towels.

"Can I fetch you two lady's refreshments?" The kid was model material, his muscular frame emphasized with the undersize white hotel 'T' and shorts that hugged in all the right places, his dark hair in a shade and the poolside tan was an audition for a male stripper.

"Here, let me help you ladies with these towels."

"Thanks David." Marge read the name tag whilst admiring the body standing patiently waiting for the order.

"Julie?" Steve enquired.

"I feel like having a large cold Margareta."

"Make that for two, but I know what I'm going to do first."

Without another word, Marge pulled her 'I love LA' top over her head before slipping out of her sneakers and shorts then without warning in her white bikini covering the pyramids of Giza, plunged into the cool water, the huge plash showering the sun lovers.

"Wow." Gregg wiped his drenched face.

Marge surfaced full of laughter at the mini tsunami soaking her friends.

"The water is absolutely gorgeous, aren't you going to join me?" She spluttered clearing her eyes and sweeping back her wet hair.

Gregg didn't need a second invitation, already in his Bermuda's he slipped off the Hawaiian shirt and disappeared under the sparkling blue water.

"Julie?" Steve begged the question.

"Nah, I'll stay ashore today." Julie was more interested in her hair than doing the 'Esther Williams'.

As for Marge, she was treading water looking for the elusive Gregg who was deep sea diving admiring her elusive shapely legs and he grabbed her by the waist pulling her below the surface.

Barely filling her lungs, Marge disappeared with Gregg's hungry lips searching for the prize. Their lips finally connecting, air bubbles exploding from their noses as passion prevailed. It was a short but sweet kiss the life-giving oxygen now in big demand as the two undeclared lovers surfaced, gasping for air.

"Why you…" Marge splashed water in Gregg's face. *"You almost drowned me."* Then she burst into laughter. "The next time tell me first so I can prepare myself for 'Water world'."

"Come, I'll race you to the end of the pool." Gregg was in his element.

"These two!" Julie smiled turning to Steve as the Margaretta's arrived, the junior 'Mr. Universe' purposely flexing his biceps as he placed the drinks on the glass topped side table.

"Shall I leave these menus sir?"

"Sure." Steve replied.

"I'm sorry to bother you again sir, but will you be dining in the restaurant, because I have to remind you there is a dress code, or round the pool?"

"We'll be dining round the pool… "Come back in say…?" Steve glanced at his watch. "Half an hour."

Marge and Gregg were enjoying the close contact pool activities and it was an opportune time for Steve to get closer to Julie in private.

"*Hmmm…* This barman can sure make a mean Margareta." Julie sipped the chilled salt lipped green Mexican experience.

Steve just smiled and took another sip of the draft Heineken.

"Julie, about last night." Steve began unsureness in his voice.

"*Steve,* there's no need to apologize, you did nothing wrong in fact I would have been disappointed otherwise. It's just that…Well…" She paused again… "I'm on a guilt trip. Although Bill and I had parted we had been together for over two years. I guess in hindsight we both new our relationship had run its course and it was time to go our different ways. Never the less we had some good times and that's the ones you remember. And after only two weeks…?" Her voice almost braking. "You can fill in the rest."

Steve reached over and held Julie's hand.

"I know how you must feel honey, but unfortunately death is permanent and Bill will never come back and as they say, 'life must go on'."

"Let's change the subject Steve, it's depressing."

"Julie, before Marge comes back I err… Eh… I just want to tell you and I know we have only met twice before and under very different circumstances that I really like you in fact you could say more than like you."

"Steve, I know where you are coming from but save it for later and let nature take its course… Here's Marge and Gregg now." Julie cut the conversation short.

"*Wow…!* You two you don't know what you're missing.' Marge panted, out of breath, in haste grabbing her Margaretta almost spilling its contents in the process. "I needed that."

"Here let me dry you." Gregg was on the towel with Julie turning to Steve and raising her eyebrows.

Gregg raised his arm to attract the pool boy.

"Sir?"

"Two more fresh towels please."

"No problem sir, let me take these wet ones…..."

* * *

"So, what have you guy's been up to?" Marge was making herself comfortable on the fresh towel, her straggled wet shoulder length hair giving her that rugged look, like a contestant in 'Survival'.

"Nothing much." Julie replied. "Just enjoying this lovely summer's day and the Mexican experience." But Marge was no dummy she knew it was a cover up.

"Well?"

"Well what?" Marge turned to Steve with a jovial smile.

"Are you guys hungry?"

"Starved… Steve, just to let you know, Julie and I skipped breakfast just be here… *Well,* slightly late."

Gregg burst into laughter. "My friend Steve has a saying about that."

"Oh, does he now!" Julie made the eyes. "Gimme that menu Mr. before I smack you over the head with it."

"Ha… Ha… Ha…" Steve joined in the laughter. "Now I see the other side."

"Men…! Julie was finally letting her guard down.

"Excuse me sir. Have you decided on your orders as the kitchen closes at three?" David was doing his 'Goliath'.

"That time already!" Gregg glanced at his watch.

As usual Marge, didn't hesitate. "Firstly, the drinks." She held up her empty Margarita glass…..."

* * *

The guys revved up the 'soft tails' as they pulled into the hotel car park, slipping the 1584 V twins into neutral.

Julie and Marge nimbly dismounted avoiding the hot tail pipes while the guys kicked the foot stands balancing the 310kg roadsters.

"Guys, that was absolutely invigorating." Marge was desperately trying to do whatever with her hair.

"So, you're going to miss us, huh?" Steve was being cheeky.

"Yeah, *the bikes!"* Julie couldn't miss the shot.

"We deserve that, Gregg."

"Hey, *speak for yourself!"* Gregg was now openly holding Marge's hand.

"Yeah, I can see *you two* are fully occupied!" Then Steve turned to Julie. "It's almost seven so what do you girls fancy for the rest of the evening?"

Julie looked toward Marge for some reaction.

"We both have our cars parked here, so I suggest we drive back to our apartment and if the guys want to join us we can order some Chines 'take home' and buy some wine and beer at the liquor store on the way."

"I couldn't have said it better myself.' Julie smiled turning to Steve.

"Sounds good to me. We'll ride shot gun on the Harleys… Gregg?"

"*Eh…Err…Yeah…* I'm all for it." Gregg gave Marge the 'telepathy' smile.

"David." Steve raised his arm to attract the 'so-called' pool boy.

"*Sir?*" He was there in a second, dollar signs in his eyes.

"We are just about to leave. I need to sign and this is for you." Steve, slipped him a ten.

"Thank you, sir, it's been a pleasure, I'll only be a minute."

"Ladies, we'll have to leave you for about fifteen minutes while Gregg and I change into something more respectable."

"Not to worry Steve, we haven't finished our drinks. We'll meet you in the car park. *Cheers.*" Marge raised her half empty glass.

"Thanks David." Steve signed the tab. "Fifteen minutes then…..."

* * *

The Bug and the nitro followed by two Harleys looking like an episode from 'Highway Patrol" attracted a few horns and claps from overtaking motorists on the Santa.

As for the girls, they were enjoying the attention, the couple of days with Steve and Gregg was just what the doctor ordered and it was time to get on with their lives. Like the old Chinese saying, 'wherever you go, go with all your heart'…...

* * *

The guys had parked their bikes in the visitor's car park. Everything had gone to plan, four bottles of sparkling Prosecco and a two pack of Heineken had been collected at the liquor store and all that was left was the Chinese cuisine, over the phone.

"What was the apartment security number again?" Steve asked as he stood in front of the keypad staring at the numbers.

"8146."

"Good memory, huh?"

"Yeah, and it's on the twelfth-floor."

Steve entered the numbers followed by a loud click as the glass security door unlocked.

"This is a pretty nice place." Gregg commented as they stood in the elevator. "They got taste."

"Yeah, and their feet on the ground." Steve laughed. "Ah, here we are apartment 6." Steve pressed the bell.

"That must be them now Marge, are you respectable?"

"You can open the door, I'm just slipping into my jeans."

"Come in... Come in... make yourselves comfortable. Marge will be through in a minute. You can help yourselves to beer in the refrigerator. It might not be as cold as you like but at least it's wet, I'll be back in in a minute, I just have to put on some lipstick."

Julie disappeared down the hallway.

"No sweat." Steve replied heading for the ice box. "Nice place." He yelled.

"Yeah, we like it." Came the muffled reply.

When Marge finally appeared, the two guys had already taken the leather sofa and were sipping beer from the dark green bottles.

"I'm glad to see you made yourselves comfortable. What do you think of our new place?" Marge as usual was the 'Bell of the Ball'.

"It's nice, I mean *really* nice. You'll have to come to DC and give us some tips."

"Is that an offer Gregg?" Marge laughed, but underneath her façade there was an element of seriousness.

"What do *you* think?" Gregg threw the line.

Julie cut the conversation short. "Guys, why don't we enjoy the evening breeze and retire to the balcony?"

"That sounds good, but what are you girls drinking?"

"Don't worry Steve, Marge will attend to that."

"I put the Prosecco in the freezer and the temperature should be just right about now. I'll be with you in a sec once I get the glasses......"

* * *

Two bottles of the 'Italian sparkling' and four of the six green bottles later, the Chinese 'buy in' demolished, it was time to relax and enjoy the privacy of the apartment.

"When's your flight tomorrow." Julie asked more relaxed.

Steve gave a big sigh. "Don't remind us, but if you must know. noon."

"Let's change the subject and go through to the lounge and play some music and if you are up to it, 'trip the light fantastic?'"

"Julie, are you sure your feet can take the punishment?"

"I'll take my chances." She laughed grabbing Steve's hand. "Come on big boy don't just sit there when a lady asks you for a dance......"

'Unforgeable that's what you are… Unforgettable though near or far… Like a song......'

The Nat King Cole oldie accompanied by his daughter, melodied throughout the apartment their bodies locked together in a slow 'fox trot' that never was.

Cheek to cheek Marge kept pulling Gregg toward the hallway and the bedrooms.

"Hey, where are you going?"

"Keep your voice down and let me lead."

The penny dropped, Gregg smiled. "If you say so…."

"Have you noticed something?" Julie looked into Steve's eyes.

"Yeah, the dance floor's crowded."

"Ha… Ha…" That made Julie laugh. "Well, now that we are alone why don't we make ourselves comfortable on the sofa and listen to the music?"

"Ah, this is much better." Steve commented as he sank into the Aniline soft leather. Julie had crossed her legs making herself comfortable, her short skirt having crept up much to Steve's pleasure.

"You're sitting so far away, *I'm not gonna bite you!*" The 'ice queen' was melting.

Steve cautiously edged his way closer until their bodies touched. The music had changed to Ann Murrays 'See the pyramids along the Nile'.

"You certainly like the oldies but I must admit it's a change from Michael Jackson and romantic, a bit strange coming from a guy, huh?"

"No, I think men should express more how they feel instead of thinking it's a 'gay' thing."

It was time to test the water and Steve gently placed his arm around Julie's shoulder then snuggled even closer.

"You know Julie, and I know this may sound a bit cheesy, but at my age I've never had a serious relationship. I suppose in hindsight I've been too interested in myself, to the extent of being self-opinionated and selfish. Like my decision to join the military and now a career with the CIA."

"*Steve,* we all go through these stages it's part of growing up but when the right person comes along, you'll know."

"Julie, what would think if I said…"

"Don't! Just press your lips against mine."

Steve didn't need a second prompt. The kiss was long and sensuous, Julie's moist lips sending messages. Then Steve buried his lips into the soft nape of her neck, the floral aroma of her perfume enticing, and he began to gently massage her firm breast and Julie gave a whimper of unadulterated pleasure. Steve could only imagine the pleasure of caressing these firm nipples, desperate to break free from their imprisoned houses and he began nervously fumbling with the pearl buttons on her blouse.

Julie suddenly restrained his hand. "No, not here darling, save it for the bedroom… Come". She rose to her feet pulling Steve by the hand, the conspicuous bulge in his slacks making her smile.

The bedside lamps gave the bedroom a soft warm glow as Julie sat on the bed then swung her feet from the floor and stretching out, her blonde hair glowing in the shadowed light.

"This is heaven… Darling, can you do me favor and slip off my sandals?"

It was a good move as Steve was just standing admiring the beautiful but unpredictable Julie and at a loss just what to do next.

"Your wish is my command." Steve always had a line.

"So, where's your lamp?" Julie laughed.

"The la…? Yeah, now I get it, but let this 'Gini' massage these beautiful feet."

Steve gingerly turned and sat on the bed beside her. The burgundy red nail polish on her manicured toes might be a turn on for some guys but as Steve lifted her foot to perform his magic what he saw at the top of those milky thighs was more important. *Still,* he had to start somewhere!

"Oh, darling that is *so* nice." Julie groaned

Starting from a toe job was something new but if fetishism turns her on, who cares and he slowly walked his hand up her smooth shaved leg waiting for the 'no go zone' to react but still working with his other hand as a foot masseuse.

Julie was just lying there her legs now slightly apart and Steve could now glimpse her tight white panties. Maybe this was a temptation turn on and there was only one way to find out and he gently pulled her panties open and slid his middle finger into the soft moistness of her vagina.

"Steve." She pulled his hand away.

"Yes?"

"Why don't you start where you left off and unbutton my blouse?"

Steve was now feeling like a barrel of gunpowder on a slow fuse and if things didn't move soon, he might embarrass himself.

'These bloody pearl buttons' he thought to himself as he fumbled like a kid trying to open a packet of M&B's and Julie sensed his frustration assisting with the last three.

"Do you need more help?" She teased a naughty smile on her face. *Maybe she was testing him or even worse just a teaser.*

"The clip is in the front."

When it comes to woman's underwear men can be ignorant in their haste.

Steve unhooked the bra and Julie's voluptuous breasts seemed to burst out like two volcanos, her protruding pink nipples ready for consumption and Steve immediately buried his face into the crevasse squeezing her firm breasts with both his hands against the sides of his face. Julie placed her hand on the back of his head in silent ecstasy.

"Darling." She reluctantly pushed his head away. "It's about time we undressed and got between these sheets."

Steve couldn't wait, almost tearing his 'T' shirt off and dropping his jeans at his feet. Then the jocks exposing his large erection. Julie seamed unperturbed as she slowly undressed and neatly hung her clothes over the chair. She was one cool broad, but that body was to die for.

Then she pulled back the top sheet and lay on top of the bed, unashamedly naked in all her glory and patted the bed beside her.

"Darling, don't just stand there like the statue of liberty, this 'desperate stewardes's is patiently waiting."

Within seconds they were locked together in passionate kissing Steve's hand exploring every part of her body but the time had come for the ultimate act of love and Julie accommodated widening her legs for the final curtain.

Steve groaned as he entered the dark passage of her body and the forbidden apple. Their bodies moving in perfect harmony.

"Steve darling, take your time… Take your……."

* * *

Gregg was up early siting on the balcony sipping a cold one when Steve appeared.

"A bit early for that."

"I couldn't work that stupid coffee machine. Do you want to join me?"

"Nah, I'll just have a glass of water. Listen, we had better make tracks as it's just after nine and remember we have to return these bikes."

"Then let's move it. The girls are still asleep but I woke up Marge to say my goodbyes. And you?"

"I didn't want to disturb Julie so I scribbled a note and left it on the bedside table."

"Sweet, so if you're ready…..."

* * *

Julie turned then stretched and moved her arm to touch Steve.

"He's gone!" Shocked she sat bolt upright then noticed the note on the bedside table.

Parting is such sweet sorrow that I shall say goodnight till it be tomorrow…. I love you Steve…..

* * *

THE RENDEZVOUS

The cremations over, the camp was in a hostile mood especially after losing Akimas Arikida a brave officer and respected Samurai and the hate campaign was becoming almost intolerable for Salibe.

It was now Monday, four days since the Japanese Submarine RU18 had docked arriving from Columbia with its cargo of uncut cocaine, for refueling and supplies. The relief flight to take Tahoka back to 'Tokushima' for life saving surgery was due tomorrow and Salibe knew his time was running out and he would be forcibly placed on that flight. If only the Russian submarine would make contact!

The crew of RU18 were enjoying their R&R but for how long? As for Shendo, trying to get information was like drawing blood from a stone. On the bright side, he still had 48 hours and by the grace of Allah all would be well.

Breakfast with the 'gang of four' was the last thing on his mind besides it was the holy month of Ramadan and these ignorant Japanese wouldn't have a clue. Salibe lay on his cot staring at the ceiling. He had come a long way since leaving the US and his plan to strike a catastrophic blow on the Israelis hinged on the arrival of the Russian submarine before he left Shimaru Shima. He had to make sure both sides kept their word. It was going to be the 'big wait' and a lonely 48 hours…...

* * *

Running on passive sonar and the latest stealth technology the Lewinsky Komsomol, was the real deal 'Black Hole Sub', operating without fear of being detected by the US Navy or NATO. Chernoff, a veteran and highly decorated submariner with over twenty years' service was taking no chances with the 2.4 billion state of the art, pride of Russia. One can never tell with the Americans.

Like any undersea mission, the crew, although receiving the best food and conditions in the Russian Navy, sailing blindly in the underwater darkness, depending on guidance technology, is always stressful and to see the sun again is utopia.

(Speaking in Russian)

The Captain drowsily awakened after dinner. The three overzealous vodkas had helped him sleep and he was feeling lazily comfortable. Suddenly he was disturbed by a loud knock on his cabin door and he glanced at his watch, less than pleased. Eastern time showed 7.30pm… *"Hmmm?"* Chernoff made a face raising his eyebrows.

"Voyti." He barked rubbing his eyes. "Chto teper?" (what now) He grumbled throwing his feet to the floor.

Levitsky, the first officer popped his head around the door.

"You've already fucked up my sleep, *don't just stand there, come in."* Chernoff barked.

"Kapitan." Levitsky stood to attention and saluted.

"At ease lieutenant. Forget the protocol, just get to the point!"

"Kapitan, we have made excellent time and we will reach the rendezvous co-ordinates for 'Fish Tail' in less than thirty minutes."

That shook Chernoff. *"Let me dress.* I'll meet you in the Board Room in ten."

"I…I, Kapitan." Levitsky clicked his heels and gave another smart salute. Chernoff just shook his head. A graduate from Kuznetsov Naval Academy in St Petersburg, Levitsky was still wet behind the ears.

When Chernoff reached the board room, his first officer was already engrossed with the navigation sea lane chart spread on the board room table. With a Divider and Parallel Rule, he had been manually checking the coordinates east and west, a lap top computer by his side to further substantiate his conclusions.

"Kapitan." Levitsky stood to attention.

Chernoff raised his hand brushing aside the decorum.

"Ob' yasnyat'." (show me) Chernoff as usual was impatient and not in the best of moods having disturbed the 'sand man'.

Levitsky wasted no time pointing to the red flag pin on the map.

"Here we are and… this is the 'Fish Tail'…74 west…"

"What is our speed lieutenant?" Reality striking home.

"Maximum speed 48 knots Kapitan."

"Meet me in the brig while I go and fetch my cap." The Kapitan when addressing the crew must always wear his cap.

When Chernoff entered the brig the crew immediately rose to their feet.

"Spokoyno vozvrashchaytes' k svoim staonam." (at ease return to your stations)

"Kapitan I await your command." Levitsky stood like a statue.

"Reduce speed to 15 knots."

"Second officer Petrov reduce speed to 15 knots."

"I, I, ser. Starshina Petrov, Snizit skorst do 15 uzlov."

"I, I, ser, 15 uzlov."

The commands were coming fast and furious. Time was not on Chertoff's side. The Lewinsky Komsomol could only surface for a maximum of thirty minutes to avoid being spotted by US Spy satellites or drones and he must contact Shendo, *like now…!*

"Tail planes up 30. Blow rear ballast tanks to 25… Ascend 50 meters."

"I…I Kapitan… 15 uzlov v 50 meters."

"Khorosho." (good) "Levitsky down periscope."

"I…I Kapitan."

Chernoff stood patiently waiting by, the heavy whine of the hydraulics lowering the 15-inch steel barreled periscope.

"Vzoyti na pyat' metrov." (ascend to 5 meters)

"I, I, Kapitan pyat metrov." (captain five meters)

"Levitsky, up periscop."

"I, I, Kapitan."

Chernoff pulled the knurled handle bars down on each side of its high polished steel barrel and peered through the large glass lens before slowly turning the full 360.

"Poberezh'ye yasno." (coast clear) "Up periscop……"

* * *

Time was running out and Chernoff must phone Shendo immediately to make sure the maintenance vessel was on its way with the exchange cargo of 40 Billion US dollars. *But his biggest problem was communications!* Shendo spoke very little English and no Russian and sa for Chernoff…? *He spoke neither!*

(Speaking in Russian)

Chernoff checked the frequency number from his orders to tune into the band on his American HF radio phone. Fortunately, first officer Levitsky had an excellent commanded of English having spent six months on an exchange programme at the world's largest Naval Base in Norfolk Virginia.

"Lieutenant Levitsky."

"I, I, Kapitan."

"I need you to convey a message in English to the camp commandant on the island, a Japanese man by the name of Kenichi Shendo. Give me a moment to tune into his frequency then I will I will inform exactly you what to say."

"I, I, Kapitan."

Chernoff turned the tuning knob to the desired numbers and listened patiently. The ear-piercing whistling and burring made him screw up his eyes and hastily move the phone away from his ear…...

* * *

Shendo had just finished dinner accompanied by the Camp Doctor Akimoto, Chief Engineer Genzo Hattori and Site Supervisor Adachi.

It had just turned 7:30 pm and Salibe had entered the dining hall to collect food from the serverery to break-fast, when Shendo's phone buzzed.

Kenichi shrugged as if to say, *'who can this be?'* hoping it wasn't the Biggubosu, Numero. His ears still burning from their previous encounter.

Salibe was no dummy and from the corner of his eye he caught Shendo hurriedly extracting the Motorola from his tunic pocket. He always carried the HF phone just in case.

"Could this be?" Salibe thought to himself… *'Na,* no such luck! But there again?' He just had to find out and he purposely delayed selecting his food, the chef sending him daggers.

"Can I speak to Kenichi Shendo I'm phoning on behalf of Kapitan Boris Levitsky of the U.S.S.R, Lewinsky Komsomol."

Shendo panicked. "Eh… Shendo-go o hanasu." (Shendo speaking)

"Eh?" Levitsky shrugged, what the hell was he saying?

Shendo quickly passed the phone to Akimoto the camp doctor.

"Kaito." (answer)

"Hai… Yes, Ichiro Akimoto speaking on behalf of our commandant, Kenichi Shendo… Yes, I understand the urgency… Inform your Captain the maintenance vessel with the transfer cargo will leave port in fifteen minutes and should arrive at the GPS coordinates for 'Fish Tail' in another 15… I

understand Lieutenant but please understand at such short notice… Yes, I'll do my best and inform the Commandant immediately."

"Nani wa messejidesu?" (What is the message?) Shendo was impatient.

Akimoto quickly rattled off the message in Japanese making Shendo jump to his feet, the news obviously catastrophic for whatever reason and as for Salibe, he just had to get a piece of the action.

Shendo turned. "Adachi, get the maintenance vessel ready without further delay, the Russian Submarine has arrived. We only have a window of thirty minutes or the submarine will set sail for reasons of Russian National Security.

"Hai, Bosu." The table immediately dispersed striding for the exit.

It was now or never for Salibe and he almost ran across the dining hall into the path of Okido and his henchman.

"Ido." (move) Shendo grabbed the Kosuka of his 'Shin Gunto'.

Salibe immediately backed off, he knew Shendo's vicious temper only too well, but he wasn't going to give up just yet. This was something big and he needed to be part of it.

"Shendo, bear with me. All I'm asking is, if this is the arrival of the Russian submarine I need to be on board the maintenance ship to meet the Captain and ensure the cargo is correct and receive the technical instructions and training manuals."

Shendo turned to Akimoto his facial expression showing his sanger

"Hon'yaku shite kudasai." (please translate)

Akimoto quickly gave Shendo the message in Japanese and Kinichi listened for a moment in silence then abruptly turned to Salibe.

"Hai…For suru." (come follow)

Salibe bowed, being a hypocrite was all part of the game… As for the food? He would continue his fasting until sunrise tomorrow. This was bigger than big and at last the 'big sleep' was over……

* * *

The maintenance ship with the four-customized water tight stainless-steel containers each with ten billion in US currency, its ten-ton crane struggling to lift each of the 20,000 pound pay loads.

Shendo the camp doctor and chief engineer Genzo Hattori were all on board not to mention the Palestinian. The sea was relatively calm as the Akashi, named after the famous Japanese naval repair vessel in World War

II, raised anchor and cast off, Jiro Adachi the site supervisor in full command giving the order… *"Furusupido ahead."*

At a maximum speed of 20 knots to reach the rendezvous with the Russian Submarine in 15 minutes would be pushing the envelope…...

* * *

"Up periscop… reduce speed to 5 knots."

"I, I, Kapitan."

Chernoff peered through the highly-polished lens of the periscope.

"Vessel approaching two kilometers… Blow ballast tanks and surface."

"I, I, Kapitan."

The 'zeppelin' shaped Lewinsky was like an oversize whale as it majestically broke the surface producing waves surfers would die for, its conning tower resembling a mini sky scraper.

"Reduce speed to zero, open hatch."

"I, I, Kapitan… Arm deck party… Lieutenant Levitsky accompany me on deck… Petty Officer Petron open the armory and issue Kalashnikov AK12 rifles and ammunition."

"I, I, Kapitan."

The Kapitan and First Officer clambered up the narrow spiral stairway to the open hatch, followed by Petron and the five-armed able seamen for deck duty, their boots making a loud ringing sound on the steel rungs.

Chernoff switched on the large signal light and flashed the powerful beam three times. To switch on the deck lights too early could give spy satellites an advantageous bead on the nuclear sub.

Chernoff was on the bridge of the Akashi scanning the dark horizon with his night vision binoculars when suddenly he spotted the signal from the Lewinsky.

"Hard to starboard, full speed ahead."

The problem would now be the delicate docking procedure to secure the Akashi of only 10 thousand tons next to the much larger 19, Lewinsky Komsomol.

"Reduce speed… hard to port… Steady… Reverse engines… Steady as she goes…"

The sudden bump shook the Akashi although greatly reduced by the 'shock tires' slung at equal intervals on the portside.

"Throw the rope lines to the submarine." Hattori screamed above the roar of the Mitsubishi 3,600hp V12 engine.

The armed deck crew of the Lewinsky, their Kalashnikovs slung across their chests, grabbed the heavy ropes tying them to the sub's bollards. Chernoff and Lewinsky were already on the deck waiting to meet the Japanese, the lights from the Akashi silhouetting the nuclear sub in the eerie darkness.

The crew of the Akashi quickly opened the bulk head on the port side and slid a gang plank to the deck of the Lewinsky.

Chernoff stood to attention and saluted Shendo who was in full military uniform and Shin Gunto.

Okido bowed in respect as he alighted on the deck of the Russian submarine, accompanied by Akimoto his English translator and of course Anbar Salibe.

"Kapitan, Nicolai Chernoff, dobro pozhalova' na borty. Izvinit'sya ne mogu spak-anglisky."

"I am First Officer Levitsky. The Kapitan welcomes you on board and apologizes that he can't speak English.'

"Arigatogozaimashita." Shendo bowed once more.

Akimoto, smiled breaking the tension. "Lieutenant the Commander also speaks little or no English and I am his translator."

Levitsky turned to Chernoff and quickly translated the conversation bringing a smile to the Kapitan's face.

Akimoto turned to his two compatriots. "Let me introduce you to our Chief Engineer, Genzo Hattori and captain of our vessel, Jiro Adachi."

Levitsky saluted and the Japanese bowed in return.

"Aren't you going to introduce me?" Anbar was livid at being ignored, after all he was the one that brokered the deal with the Russian Ministry of Defense!

Akimoto turned to Shendo to explain the outburst and he clenched his teeth in dumb insolence. Levitsky was no fool he had been fully briefed by the Captain regarding the mission and he could sense the tension between the Japanese and the Muslim and he had to delicately break the deadlock and get on with the real business.

"Dobro pozhalovat'l." Levitsky smiled offering his hand "In Russian tongue means, welcome."

As for Shendo, he would love the opportunity to throw the Arab overboard.

"A…Eh? Excuse please I have difficulty with Japanese name.

"Akimoto."

"Eh, Akimoto, me must hurry as we cannot surface for too long."

"Hai, I understand…...."

* * *

The watertight hatches of the empty Ballistic Missile silos were removed exposing two stainless steel containers. Pitched darkness was proving a hazard to the operation and Chernoff had no alternative but to order the switching on of the submarine's weather deck lighting, a Japanese copy of the McGeoch Naval lighting, the standard in the British Royal Navy.

Each container resembled a miniature submarine minus the Conning Towers and propellers. At five meters, long and two meters in circumference with what could only be described as miniature ballast tanks on either side with 20-centimeter holes, 50 centimeters apart. Two crane lugs had been welded one meter from either end for lifting.

As Chief Engineer Hattori and Supervisor Adachi peered into the hold the question was begging

"Korera no yoki no omo sa?" (How heavy are these containers?)

Akimoto turned to Levitsky who had the 'what now' look. He was desperate to get this transfer over with. The Akashi roped to the Submarine was holding it stable.

"They are asking the weight of the containers Lieutenant?"

"Your ten-ton crane has sufficient lifting capacity, as each container weighs only 500 kilograms. I will instruct the Arab before we depart the procedure to refloat them once they are released at the bottom of the sea."

Akimoto conveyed the message to Adachi. "Karera wa sorezore 500 kiro no omo sadesu." (they weigh 500 kilograms each)

Hattori and Adachi gave the nod then proceeded to order the crane operator to swing the jib over the open silos, the Russian seaman grabbing the twin hooks on the crane's heavy chains to secure the load.

As the chain took the strain Chernoff raised his hand and out of the blue ordered to stop the lift.

"Stop!" He shouted in English then turned to Levitsky to explain his decision.

"The Kapitan instructs me to tell you before we continue further he must see inside your containers to check the content."

This was becoming a cat and mouse game with translations going to and fro and the delay was making Salibe decidedly uncomfortable……

* * *

Chernoff and Salibe, satisfied with 'Operation Fish Tail', the captain was anxious to get the Lewinsky Komsomol underway. The hatches battened down, the sub ship shape 'in Bristol fashion' ready to submerge, the crew looking forward to returning to their beloved Russia and Pavlovsk Bay.

Levitsky was standing on the deck of the Akashi. Chernoff having dealt with protocol was now back in the conning tower of the Lewinsky, anxious to submerge and avoid an international incident as to why his vessel surfaced in the North Pacific if spotted by the US spy satellites.

"I have here two aluminum briefcases, one with technical and operational details, the other training. Here is the combination to the locks which of course is highly secretive for only known to you."

Salibe nodded. Shendo, as usual, was showing his annoyance not being privy to the conversation.

"Now, most importantly." Levitsky held in his hand what looked like two cellphones to the 'T'. "Customs and Border Security will assume it's a normal phone and as you can see they bear the Samsung logo. Let me explain, I will try and be as brief as possible"

Please follow me." Levitsky walked over to the two stainless steel containers resting on heavy wooden blocks. He pointed. "On one side of each container you will notice a steel plate 1 meter long and 30 cm thick riveted to the shell. The numbers 1, 2 and 3 on your phone's dial index are crucial. The plates are magnetic and clamp against the hull of your RU18. The reason they are steel is if course stainless steel is nonmagnetic. These containers are custom designed to resemble miniature submarines right down to the ballast tanks on either side. When the Kapitan reaches his destination, he presses 1 to reverse the magnetic field and the containers will sink to the ocean floor. Then he presses 2 to activate a 'ping' signal just like a plane's black box, the location can then be pinpointed on your phone by pressing the GPS maps. One thing that's crucial, the containers must not be more than 150 meters deep or the signal will be lost."

"How long will the signal last?" Salibe asked.

"Good point… A maxim of four weeks."

"Hmmm… That should be sufficient… And number 3?"

"That activates the compressed air to blow the ballast tanks and raise the containers to the surface, the air sealed inside is sufficient to make them float. "Any questions?"

"No, I'll instruct the captain of RU18. Thank you again lieutenant… Bezopasnoye plavaniye." (safe voyage)

"You can speak Russian!"

"I spent some months in your country and picked up a few words."

"I'm impressed." Levitsky shook Salibe's hand.

'A you can see My Kapitan

"I spent some months in your country and picked up a few words."

"I'm impressed." Levitsky shook Salibe's hand, strange bedfellow

"As you can see my Kapitan is anxious to be underway."

"Of course." Salibe was also anxious to reach shore.

"Spasibo…." (thank you)

"Sbrosit' galstuki" Chernoff was back in command and within minutes the Lewinsky Komsomol submerged just as quick as it had surfaced and 'Operation Fish Tail' was now with 'Davy Jones'……

* * *

The cargo safely ashore, it was time for some shut eye. There was no point in discussing the next step with Shendo but Salibe required his permission to speak with captain of RU18, Eito Takahashi, whom he had discovered was educated in the United States before joining the Japanese Defense Force and could speak perfect English, but he still needed to tread lightly with Shendo.

Having just turned nine in for the evening Salibe had yet to Break Fast and drink fluids. He had some food and bottled water left over from first light and in this tropical climate he desperately was looking forward to satisfying his parched lips.

Salibe crashed on the side of his cot, with both anger and relief. The meager portion of boiled stale rice in the process of being digested followed by the luke warm bottled mineral water was hardly fine dining but then Ramadan was not meant to be walk in the park and once he had finished, it was time for evening prayer. Tonight, he would sleep sound at the thought of being on the relief plane tomorrow evening. The end of the mission had been fraught with danger but he had come a long way and little did he know the worst was still to come……

* * *

Salibe was already showered and dressed ready to make his way to the mess hall as first light was breaking and the ritual of 'Break Fast'. Ramadan would last another three weeks before the Eid Al-Fitr (the festival of breaking of the fast) celebrations, but the Japanese were ignorant to anything related to Muslim customs and the 'Holy Quran'.

It had turned 6:30am and the kitchen had just began preparing the food for the 7:am breakfast. The mess hall would be crowed this morning with the addition of 6 officers and 40 crew of the RU18.

As Salibe walked to the servery, the kitchen staff scowled menacingly as he filled his plastic container with the only food availed, *boiled rice!* The top table empty, at least he could sit in peace to consume his meager breakfast. Once finished he would return to the dormitory for prayer, his next challenge to arrange a meeting with Shendo and the Submarine Captain, Eito Takahashi

Shendo's table had been extended to accommodate the additional officers as recognition of their rank and the importance of the key role they play in the Yakuza cocaine trade. As Kenichi unhooked his 'Shin Gunto' the large table bowed as the 'Biggubosu' took his seat and the table quickly settled down to asa gohan, the only person missing now was Anbar Salibe, the Arab from 'out of the cold'.

The chatter and the clatter of bowls and chopsticks suddenly silenced as Salibe took the remaining vacant seat. Shendo stared irately showing his displeasure. *The faster the Arab was off the island, the better!*

Was this the time for Salibe to make his move and approach Kenichi? It had to be done and is there ever a good time with these 'egotistical' Japanese? Fortunately, with the Camp Doctor and Naval Captain present, both speaking fluent English, would hopefully relieve Shendo's frustration and annoyance over the delayed translation.

"Shendo, I need to discuss with Captain Takahashi the destination for the Russian cargo and the technical details for offloading. The relief flight will arrive this evening and I'm sure you want me on it as much as I do?"

Kenichi looked calm and collective ignoring Salibe indulging in his favorite tea whilst washing down an oversize portion of rice and for a moment the diners went quiet waiting for a reaction from the Biggubosu.

"Akimoto, Hon'yaku shite kudasai." (please translate)

The camp doctor obliged with Kenichi showing little of no response continuing with his breakfast purposely mocking Salibe.

"Akimoto, please tell Shendo I don't have much time and I want an answer *now!*"

"Salibe san." Akimoto sighed. "My advice is, don't mandate and let Bosu finish his breakfast in peace. You can approach him at his office in say…

One hour. I will convey my recommendation and make sure the Captain is available."

"I suppose doctor, I have to be thankful for small mercies?" Salibe's anger blatant.

"I will be there within the hour." He rose to his feet and stormed from the mess hall but not before cursing abuse in Arabic. Shendo just shrugged and half smiled. He had the upper hand and Salibe had better understand 'the shoe is on the other foot'....

* * *

Salibe was still up tight as he knocked on Shendo's door. Kenichi was a difficult creature at the best if times and there was no love lost between them. The order of the day was to keep cool even though he would have to 'kowtow' to this arrogant bastard.

At the loud knock, Shendo looked toward the door of his miniature office. The Doctor and the Captain had already joined him partaking in his favorite pastime. They had had a discussion on the 'wrap up' of "Operation Fish Tail' and the forthcoming delivery of the Russian cargo to Gaza. The Yakuza had agreed to deliver and had given their word, Samurais never renege as a principal of honor.

"Hairu." Kenichi's voice demanding.

Salibe shrugged, *will this guy ever change?* The tone in Shendo's voice sending the usual signal of intimidation. Never the less, hopefully this would be the last meeting before he departed this 'shithole island' and whatever it takes, he was up for it.

The gang of three turned to face the Arab as he entered, Anbar carrying a rolled-up map below his arm, their faces reflecting their dislike for the Muslim was nothing new and Salibe reluctantly bowed.

"Captain."

Anbar had to start somewhere as having not been offered a seat at the 'Knights Templar' to discuss the details of the sea route and 'drop off' was not an option.

He continued. "I need to discuss the handling and the transportation of the cargo and the destination. I'm sure your aware via the 'World Media' that the Israelis' have stringent security patrols in the Mediterranean Sea off the coast of Gaza and we must to discuss how to avoid a serious international incident for both Japan and Palestine."

"I agree." The Captain nodded. "So, what do you suggest?" At least Takahashi was amicable.

"We retire to the mess hall where we have peace and quiet and a table to review the sea routes and GPS coordinate for the 'drop off'."

Shendo had that vacant look on his face turning Akimoto, who quickly gave an abbreviated translation of Salibe's recommendation siting for a moment his expression troubled unable to be a party to the discussions, but he had other more pressing priorities like organizing the changeover of the relief flight and the repatriation of his close friend and bodyguard Tahoka. No doubt the doctor would keep him in the loop.

"Hai, Doi shita." Shendo motioned with a rude wave of his hand to leave, his arrogance and disrespect deplorable...…

* * *

"And number three on the dialer on the phone device?" The Captain asked.

"That's my signals to activate the compressed air to float the containers to the surface. So, whatever, *you do not touch three!"*

"I understand." Eito pouted his slips and nodded.

"Now the sea route Captain?" Salibe had spread the large map on the dining table.

"In anticipation, I have already analyzed the route that I must take, in fact *the only route!"* Takahashi shook his head placing his finger on the map then tracing it from Shimaru Shima to the 'drop off' coordinate in the Mediterranean.

"Unfortunately, I cannot sail via the Suez Canal for obvious reasons and that leaves me no alternative but to take the much longer route via the Philippine Sea, past Indonesia, through the Indian Ocean and round the Cape, finally reaching the Straits of Gibraltar.… Distance.… Approximately 6,000 kilometers."

"Hmmmm..." Anbar rubbed his chin in anticipation of the 'crunch line'.

"With our 15 fuel tanks to the full capacity the RU18 has a range of just over 13,000 kilometers which can be supplemented by switching to electric propulsion providing another 800. In short, we can make the return trip to Shimaru Shima without refueling.… *That's the good news!"*

"Proceed Captain." Salibe was anxious.

"Firstly, our maximum speed submerged is 30 knots or 15 kilometers per hour therefore our ETA would be 17 days from cast off. The problem is our air regeneration is only 260 hours which means we must use the snorkel and or surface, adding at least another two days as our surface speed is only 14knots."

"Hmmmm…" Salibe was pondering…17 to 19 days…? "And food and supplies?"

"Good question… Fully loaded with a crew of 6 officers and forty men we carry enough food and provisions for 45 days. *Oh…* One further technical point, the RU18 has an anechoic coating to deaden the propulsion noise which will give us an advantage when passing through the British Naval base at Gibraltar… What's your summation?" Eito turned to Salibe.

"If that's the best Captain, when can you get your vessel ready to sail?"

"First light tomorrow."

"Well at least I can check the cargo before I depart this evening."

"Is there anything else we may have missed Salibe San?"

"Yes, there is a fishing limit for we Palestinians of 6 miles from the shore and the GPS 'drop off' is one mile within. The patrol boats sweep the six mile limit every four hours, so check your timing. The GPS coordinate has been purposely set to accommodate the maximum depth of 150 meters for the location signal to operate. I can't emphasize enough that you be as accurate as possible before releasing the cargo."

"Don't worry Salibe San, we will use the periscope to check the 'no go zone' before we enter. If there's nothing else, as you can imagine, I have a heavy schedule before fist light tomorrow."

"I understand… Arigato." Salibe bowed.

"I will report our discussions to Biggubosu…..."

* * *

Satisfied, Salibe walked back to the dormitory for mid-day prayer. The quarters deserted, the men busy preparing for the flight back to Tokushima, a welcome diversion from the dramas of the past week.

Prayer over, Salibe's next priority was to pack his personal belongings and decide what to do with the two aluminum briefcases. Only one 'hand carry' baggage is allowed on international and domestic flights and he had to decide which one to unpack and store in his 'check in' luggage. The technical manuals were the heaviest so it was a 'no brainer' they would go into his green Samsonite luggage bag.

"Hmmmm… Good idea." Salibe spoke to himself pleased with his decision as he unpacked the heavy volume of paperwork. According to the 'grape vine' the 'mercy flight' would touch down at around 8:30pm and depart at 9:30 so he still had sufficient time to check out the loading of his precious cargo.

Salibe finished packing his meager clothing and toiletries, locked the cases then placed them on his cot. One job down and one more to go, a short walk to the maintenance dock….

* * *

Approaching mid-day, the sun was almost at its fullest and the temperature was rising. Salibe wiped his brow with the back of his hand and inhaled as he stepped it out to cover the 500 meters or so to the loading dock where RU18 was berthed.

When he finally arrived, the crane had placed the two submarine shaped containers magnetically locked on each side of the submarine above the ballast tanks. Their shape purposely designed to create minimum drag on the hull to avoid using additional fuel and reducing speed.

Captain Takahashi was standing on the pier conducting the operation when Salibe arrived. The dock was stacked with supplies for the long haul, the crane driver busy loading the sub's hold.

"Nice job Captain." Anbar was not only pleased but relieved.

Takahashi nodded in appreciation. "Arigatogozaimashita… Will you be joining us for lunch?"

"No, not today Captain, as I depart this evening for Tokushima on the first leg of my journey back to Ben Gurion International. Once again, I thank you and I wish you safe passage, Arigato……

* * *

The Kawasaki C-1 medium range transporter was on schedule to touch down at 8:30pm and Captain Katsuro Soto was at the controls. He had landed the C2 many times on treacherous Shimaru Shima and the narrow runway was not to be taken for granted.

"What have we got Goro?" Soto ordered his First Officer Haruki Goro to check with the Flight Engineer who was studying the navigation map on the onboard computer.

"Our position?" Toma was busy calculating. "Eh… I make it 50k from the island, Captain. The runway should be visible in approximately 15 minutes."

"Yes, I can see the lights now… Goro prepare to land… Reduce speed to 150 knots and descend to 200 meters, flaps down 30."

"I… I, Captain." Goro lifted the phone. "We have begun our decent and should be on the runway in under 15 minutes. Fasten your safety belts and place your seats in the upright position…"

Jiro Adachi, the camp supervisor had already prepared the runway, the high intensity lighting on each side resembling Christmas candles in the pitch-black darkness, powered by the Mitsubishi V16 diesel generators.

"Steady, reduce speed, brake flaps up…"

The ten-wheeled undercarriage puffed burning rubber as the transporter's tires bit the tarmac.

"Reverse thrust… ABS on."

The plane shuddered a few tines as the brakes opened and shut before finally coming to a halt rocking to and fro on its shocks.

'The eagle has landed……'

* * *

The relief crew settled in and the wounded Kazuo Tahoka stretchered safely on board, the men were lined up with their kits resembling troops ready to board the relief flight. Salibe was given no preference and waited his turn like any other 'soldier'.

As he finally boarded the flight he had hoped Shendo would have at least wished him luck and a begrudged hand shake but Sumerians are men of honor and unforgiving with their enemies.

The doors finally closed ready for takeoff Salibe stared out the port window, the lights silhouetting the ground crew in the darkness. Was he sad…? Not really, but the memories of his time on Shimaru Shima would stay with him forever.

"Fasten safety belts we are ready for takeoff…..."

WASHINGTON DC

Gregg's cell alarm kept buzzing in the distance, the sound although necessary, was a sleep breaker of the worst kind.

"What the fuck!" Gregg fumbled on the bedside table to kill the beast, the phone snaking around with the vibration. *"Got you!"* He pressed the button on the side then swiped the screen. *"At last."* He lay back on the pillow for a few moments in complete seclusion, the comfort of the bed more than relaxing as he stared into the darkness. It was only 6:30am, but with a central bath room and only one shower 'he who dares wins'.

He reached over and switched on the bedside lamp shielding his eyes with the back of his hand from the sudden brightness. Steve, as usual will be dragging his ass in sleepy valley but more to the point, Gregg thought to himself. *'What would today bring?'* He gave a big sigh. The long weekend in LA and the intimate memories of the time he spent with Marge were still fresh in his mind and whatever... *He just had to see her again!*

Mornings in late June in the capital are always a bit chili and today would be no different. As the temperature rises to 79 mid-day, thunder storms are common place and he checked his Samsung for the weather forecast.

"Would you believe it!" He spoke out loud. *"Rain!"*

"Just our fucking luck!" Gregg, threw his feet to the floor and pulled the shade aside. *"I might have guessed!* He shook his head. "The drive to the office will be worse than 'Katrina'. Awe what the hell!" He stretched both arms above his head. "Ah, that's better." Bare footed standing in his stripped 'Tommy John' boxers and white 'T', he gave a shiver.

"Brrrrrr... I had better get showered before that ill-tempered partner of mind wakes up." Gregg was having a conversation with himself and he was winning!

He quickly switched on the apartment lights and walked down the hallway to the central bathroom looking forward to that warm and invigorating shower. As he passed the vanity mirror over the twin sinks he stopped for a moment to stare at his sleep deprived face.

"*God*, I look like shit!" He ground his teeth together and stared at his pearly whites, then ran his finger through his unruly 'Robert Redford' reddish hair. "Time waits for no man, huh…?"

The warm spray on his face and body was almost better than sex. "*Maaan*, I could stay here forever." He grinned.

Time was running away with its self and he closed the faucet and stepped into the steam filled room grabbing the large bath towel from the rail and began vigorously drying his tanned muscular frame before slipping into his bathrobe. A quick shave and a spray of his favorite cologne, he was ready for the coffee pot.

"I might have known you would be up at the crack of dawn." Steve had suddenly appeared in the kitchen; the aroma of freshly brewed coffee must have activated his taste buds. A sight for sore eyes and being sarcastic as usual he walked to the island kitchen and grabbed a stool.

"Aren't you gonna pour me one as well?"

Gregg just shook his head and filled another coffee mug.

"Listen, it's raining cats and dogs so my advice would be to get showered, dressed and hit the road early. You know what the traffic is gonna be like?"

Steve took a sip of the dark brew. "*Hmmm*, I got to hand it to you partner, you make a mean cup of coffee."

"*Yeah… Yeah…* Come on, get your ass into gear its coming up to seven fifteen…..."

* * *

As they entered the car park Steve begged the question. "Two cars or one?"

"The Beamer." Gregg replied instantly.

"*Hmmm*, I thought after work you might be seeing the beautiful Michelle?"

Gregg just ignored the sarcastic remark standing patiently at the passenger door waiting for him to unlock the 525i.

"It's like that, is it?"

"*Get out of it*, mind your own business."

"*Okay…Okay…*" Steve raised his arms in the 'I surrender' pose.

But as Steve turned the key and gunned the engine Gregg abruptly stopped him in his tracks.

"Hold it for a moment. I want to check 'Google Map' for the shortest route to the office while avoiding the worst of the traffic jams in this shit weather."

"Go on then." Steve sighed impatiently.

"Connecticut Avenue, then the Whitehurst Fwy North West and slip off at Virginia Avenue onto the East Street Expressway and you know the way from there. Estimate time, 50 minutes."

"Are you finished?"

"Just drive, huh…..."

* * *

Steve shook the rain from the golf brolly before entering the elevator.

"This shit weather." He commented shaking his head as he pressed 6.

Gregg glanced at his watch. "9:15… Not bad considering. We're a bit late but my guess is John will be in the same boat."

"You hope…"

"Well, look at you two, suites and all."

"We may not be 'The President's Men" Hanna but we sure look like them."

Hanna laughed. "I'm sure John's going to be impressed."

"Which brings me to the question."

"No Steve, he hasn't arrived, he's most probably stuck in the traffic."

Steve slipped off his jacket and draped it over the back of his chair before turning to Gregg. "That gives us a breather, would you like some coffee from the machine?"

"I thought it would be Saki this morning." Hanna just had to take the shot.

"Nice one Hanna, don't give up your day job just yet."

Hanna had to laugh, she deserved that one.

"Na, I've had enough coffee Steve. As for that poison from the machine you must have a cast iron stomach."

Gregg had also disrobed making himself comfortable, placing his jacket on the back of his chair.

Suddenly Hanna's phone rang. "That could be John now... Yes Mr. Thomson... I gathered that... Another half hour... Yes, Nelson and Jonson have just arrived... I'll pass on your message."

"Im sure you got that... John wants to see you in his office when he arrives to update him on your Tokyo assignment."

Steve shrugged and turned to Gregg. "That's going to be interesting…..."

* * *

Thomson stormed into the office, brolly under his arm, laden briefcase in the other, being late was not on his watch.

"Morning Hanna, Steve, Gregg. Don't get up, I have a few calls to make, I'll contact you when I'm free……"

* * *

Thomson pointed to the empty chairs. "Before we start our discussions I just want to say you guys did a fine job. I know you must be disappointed but under the circumstance, we'll leave it at that."

"I guess so." Steve looked dejected."

"Steve, the one thing you guys should be proud of, is you deciphered the coded message that *even* the FBI's code breakers couldn't!"

"Just luck." Gregg answered.

"Don't do yourselves an injustice, but more importantly let's get down to business. The loss of 100 billion US dollars in used notes and no real answers is in the 'hot basket' of the 'Commander in Chief' and the heats coming down like a burning oil rig on Brennan and Comey and as the Director of Counter Intelligence... *Well*... I think you get the picture."

"Loud and clear John, but where do we go from here? Our assignment in Tokyo met road block after road block. *I mean these people*, should I go on?"

"Be my guest." Thomson sat back semi relaxed.

"What gets me John is everyman and his dog had Salibe and his brother Maalouf on their radar as potential terror suspects...The FBI, the CIA and Israel's Sayerat Matakal and what have we got? *The hole in the donut!*"

Thomson gave a big sigh, he knew where Steve was coming from but the truth always hurts.

"John, if I'm stepping out of line, tell me to slam the brakes."

"Carry on, you'll soon know when the rope's taut."

"Where was I? Yeah, the bottom line is the FBI, and I have the greatest respect for the bureau, for the past year having used all sorts of spy devices, wiretapping, bugs and monitoring cell calls to Palestine from these two characters and their uncle, the question begs, why didn't we haul them in for questioning?"

"Steve, *hold it there!* There was a reason for that, in that we didn't want to blow our cover too early because we felt sure there was something bigger in the pipe line."

It was Steve's turn to sigh. Maybe he was beginning to sound like a long-playing record when the needle's stuck and he picked up the pace.

"Three months back, Anbar and Maalouf boarded an Aeroflot Air Bus bound for Sheremetyevo International Airport Moscow and shacked up in the five star 'Hotel Savoy' across the street from Red Square at three hundred and fifty dollars a night, compliments of the Russian Tax Payer. Our agents bugged their rooms but they were either too smart or were tipped off from the inside, whatever, we came up egg faced. Where money is concerned, there are always takers."

"Steve, *don't cross the line!*" Thomson took the shot his anger showing.

"*Okay… Okay*, my apologies, I'm outta line. Do you want to come in here Gregg? I could do with a drink of water…."

"Sure." Gregg paused for a few moments searching for the 'Q' line. "*Hmmm.*" He paused again furrowing his brow. "Okay, let's take up the slack where Steve cut the ambilocal… John, I can clearly remember Steve's summation of the facts you presented at the 'red alert' meeting when he took 'the third rail'. The motive! *Money!* But for what…? A major terrorist attack by Hamas on Israel?" Steve pouted his lips and shrugged.

"I'm listening."

"Before leaving the United States for Russia, Salibe and Maalouf's apartment is mysteriously gutted by fire destroying any hope of gathering any evidence. After Russia, they fly to Tokyo for a 'so called' business meeting at Nippon Shipping & Logistics, a legal entity and a cover for the shipments of Cocaine from Colombia. *And with guess who?* None other than Okio Namura the Godfather of the Yakuza. This we know!"

"Get to the point Gregg." Thomson had heard it all before.

"John, with respect, Steve and I were there and this summation is a big difference from a long-distance phone conversation."

Thomson nodded, no comment.

"Sending Steve and I to Tokyo on assignment made sense to work with the FBI on the ground to hang enough on the Arabs for an arrest. But what happened? Before we arrive Ginzo Iwami, an undercover FBI agent is killed in a fire fight but not before wasting Maalouf and unfortunately an innocent by stander the Maître D'. And as for Salibe? He suddenly becomes the invisible man! The police? No point, their carrying water for the Yakuza. But is Salibe really the invisible man? I'll come back to that later. Do you get the picture now John?

"Are you finished?"

"I'm only halfway there… Fortunately Iwami phoned the coded massage to Daniels before he croaked it. We decipher it and you must be a dummy not to conclude that this is related to the shipment of the expired currency. *And…* Guess what? Suddenly Global 10, the crew and cargo disappear from the radar, 800k into the North Pacific, off the coast of Japan without trace."

"Get to the point Gregg."

"We've been slow walked at every turn, McGill's playing the safety card as his ass is on the line for shit poor security. Collins the Captain, raises his concern about one of the security guards Giovani Quario, supposedly from Black Hawk Securities whose file on McGill's data base suddenly disappears. Then when we show him Salibe and Maalouf's mug shots he has a memory snapback and identifies Salibe. *The invisible man suddenly reappears!* Now coming to the missing 777 and we throw the Hijack scenario at McGill's meeting we get the thumbs down in the 'Coliseum'. Well it isn't over yet… No trace of plane then after days of searching the wreckage mysteriously floats to the surface in pieces that you get in a jigsaw box in a toy store. The black box and voice cockpit recorder has not a hope in hell of being recovered, no body parts have been found and no trace of the 100Bilion US dollars. Reluctantly Boeing's Air Accident Board and the National Transportation Safety Board conclude the plane may have been brought down by a bomb but still avoiding the possibility of a high jack inferring it could be terrorist linked. I ask you? You think we are frustrated John? *That's an understatement!*"

"And how do you think I feel? Mike Stone, whom I'm sure you know as the Assistant Director of the FBI, and as I already informed you, his team arrested Abud Azis as the caller to Salibe and Maalouf in Tokyo, based on the CCTV tapes of the public phone box. As for the decoded message, it was loud and clear that the data bank of US currency serial numbers was hacked. *Why?* The Security in the Treasury Department's is antiquated and outdated so it's relatively easy to erase the numbers. *Again…* Using CCTV, Abdul Azim and Dabar Bishara, both Palestinians employed at the Federal reserve at Fort Worth showed abnormal activity entering and leaving the secure computer department verified by their fingerprint recognitions. The plot thickens, Israel's Mossad Secret Service has confirmed they are both linked to Hamas and are close friends of none other than Abud Aziz! Now why am I in the same boat as you two, good question! All three have been arrested under the Patriot Act as engaging in activities that endanger US notional security. Charging them is one thing but convicting is another. They can only be held for one month without charge and they have employed the best lawyers who are playing the islamophobia card and the way it's going they'll walk the walk and may even receive compensation from the government for wrongful internment and phycological stress to their families. *Am I frustrated,* Déjà vu! Now, after 'true confessions' what I want you to do is return to your desks and start again and go through every point in detail, even the smallest clue… *Anything…* As for me? I'm gonna have a well-deserved coffee and read 'The Washington Times'……."

THE PRODIGAL SON RETURNS

The Kawasaki C1 landed with a heavy thud, the cabin of the short-range transporter shuddering and shaking as Captain Soto switched its four FRJ710 turbo fan jets into reverse with a deafening scream. Then the snatch and grab of the ABS breaking before final taxiing to the special bay allocated to 'Nippon Shipping & Logistics', to disembark and unload. 'Customs and Border Control' a mere formality, 'pay rolled personnel' of the Yakuza.

It had just turned 10 in the evening and a muggy 26c and flights to Osaka or Tokyo International would be Salibe's next hurdle.

The journey to his turmoiled homeland and the old city of East Jerusalem and the West Bank was about to begin. Another challenge for another day but the cause as they say, 'worth the sacrifice'.

An ambulance was on standby with a medical team to transport the badly wounded Kazuo Tahoka to the Trauma Unit of the Tokushima University Hospital, 14 kilometers from the airport.

At this time in the evening, domestic flights were out of the question and an overnight stay would be necessary in Awandori.

The airport had a typical Japanese tourist hotel mostly for local business men with rooms you couldn't swing a cat in and a stand-up toilet and shower straight from the molding machine. Salibe had little or no option, he must enquire as to the availability of domestic flights to either Osaka or Tokyo, departing first thing in the morning, before he checked in to the hotel. Fortunately, he had around 10,000 US dollars in his possession, the remainder of his bank roll from Abud Aziz his uncle which would be sufficient to see him though. Dragging his Samsonite and the heavy Aluminum briefcase was a feat in itself as he wearily walked to the airport enquiry desk and just in time before it closed. The young female receptionist didn't appear none too happy about anticipated delay to the Sushi Bar and maybe her impatient boyfriend.

(Speaking in Japanese)

"Eigo o hanasisemasu ka?" (do you speak English?)
"Yes of course." She replied arrogantly. This was not her night.
"I need to get a domestic flight first thing tomorrow to either Osaka or Tokyo?"
She booted the computer a glum look on her face.
"There is an ANA flight to Tokyo at 0.800hrs. The gate opens at 7. You can purchase a ticket at their check in. I suggest you be there early."
"Can't you do it now for me?"
"No, Im sorry their line is closed. Now if that's all?"
Salibe nodded, a 'fait accompli'…...

* * *

Although the bed was Japanese size it was crispy and clean and at least the miniature room had air-conditioning! Salibe had selectively unpacked his toiletries, besides there was little room left in his Samsonite case with the bulky training manuals and laborious unpacking was not an option. His next obstacle was the Israeli security check on arrival at Ben Gurion Airport. His shaven face was now showing a thick seven o'clock shadow and this could be a problem as his passport showed a heavily bearded Arab. He would have to have a good excuse if questioned…...

* * *

Money always talks irrespective of nationality color or religious beliefs and the Israel's Border Security are no exception. Anbar Fattah, Salibe's father and the Commander of the armed wing of Hamas has the right connections and kickbacks can change any information on the Israeli Immigration data bank regarding Palestinians living overseas for education, especially those holding visas to the United States.

The Government of the Palestinian Territories (Gaza and the West Bank) the Palestinian National Authority since 1995 issued passports which are recognized by practically all countries including Israel. The PA passport is available to any individual who can present a birth certificate showing he/she was born in Palestine and must also hold a Palestine identity card. The

Palestine passport currently reads 'Palestinian Authority' on the cover and not 'Palestine' to avoid confiscation by the 'Israeli Border Authorities'.

Since Jorden annexed part of Palestine in April 1950 (Old City and East Jerusalem and the West Bank) most Palestinians in the West Bank have Jordanian citizenship or a right to it. Although some Palestinians have seen their Jordanian citizenships revoked in recent years. When Egypt controlled Gaza from 1948 to 1967 they never granted citizenship to its residents like Jorden had to the West Bank, and Palestinians living in Egypt have several difficulties regarding status, discrimination, work, etc.

Therefore, Palestinians in the West Bank and Jerusalem most often travel through Queen Alia International Airport in Amman Jorden, because Israel Authorities very rarely grant the documents required to use 'Ben Gurion....

* * *

Anbar stretched over to his waist wallet, his forged passport crossing his mind. He pulled out the blue covered document with the Arab crest and studied the picture. Is this a piece of work, right down to my US visa?

"Hmmm... If the beard becomes a problem I have a good excuse but now I must remember my new name... *"Ahmad Sarraf... Ahmad Sarraf".* Salibe repeated it aloud again and again to lock it in. Then there was the new Identity Card... WB5001978... Satisfied, he set the alarm on his cell then rolled over on his side hopefully to get some sleep and halt the Kinetic energy in his overactive brain......

* * *

As predicted Salibe arrived early at the check in desk of All Nippon Airways. (ANA)

"I sorry sir, you have been given the wrong information. The 0.800 flight is to Tokyo International and you require a connecting flight to Ben Gurion Airport Tel Aviv. All flights to Israel depart from Narita."

Salibe sighed, *what a fuck up!* "Well, can you tell me when your next flight is to Narita?"

"At 10am, would you wish me to reserve a seat?"

"And the connecting flight to Ben Gurion?"

"10 pm this evening."

"Can you reserve a seat on that flight as well?"

"Certainly sir, if you can just give me a second. Oh, I almost forgot, which class?"

"Eh, err, the cost of business class one way?" Salibe enquired.

"Awandori to Narita twelve hundred US Dollars one way, and from Narita to Ben Gurion?" She paused for a moment. "Eh, three thousand two hundred US Dollars."

Salibe nodded his approval, he has sufficient hard cash.

"Then that will be four thousand four hundred dollars. Do you wish to pay by credit card? Oh, firstly, I need to check your passport."

"Cash…" Salibe replied placing his passport in front of the young lady who methodically opened each of the pages then studied the passport picture then looked at Salibe straight in the face.

"For a moment, I didn't recognize you without the beard Mr. Sarraf."

Salibe just smiled, the less said the better.

She quickly checked the cash and printed out the reservations to Narita and Ben Gurion.

"Thank you can I check in now?"

"I'm sorry that gate opens two hours before departure. You can return before eight and check in and use the business class lounge. Is there anything else I can help you with Mr. Sarraf?"

"Can I check my luggage straight though to Ben Gurion?"

"Yes, you can. Make sure at the check in desk you request this service."

"Arigato." Salibe broke a reluctant smile, time on his hands in this boring airport was unenviable…...

* * *

Steve crashed down heavily in his chair with a giant sigh as if it was his last. Gregg had gone to the water dispenser.

"A good meeting, huh?"

"Hanna, sarcasm is my specialty, you're not good at it."

"*Water?*" Gregg had returned with two paper cups.

"*Nah*, I need something stronger, like a double short black."

"Well, your outta luck here buddy with that 'Made in Russia' coffee machine."

Gregg's comment cracked a smile.

"Between you and Hanna's humor… *Maaan!*" Steve was shaking his head.

"By the looks on you faces…"

"Hanna, there is such a thing as rubbing 'salt in the wounds'."

"Okay, no offence taken. I'll leave you guys to cry in your beer."

"Gee, thanks!" Now it was Steve's turn.

Gregg was sitting on the edge of his desk his leg dangling.

"You know Steve, Thomson wants no stone unturned. We know the dragon is blowing fire but we're in the same boat with another 'Arthur Conan Doyle', only without Sherlock and the Doctor."

Steve grinned. "That's one way of putting it."

"What have we got?" Gregg took to his chair.

"You mean from the beginning? *Give me a break!*"

"Then, you call the shots."

"Okay...Okay... Let's start with the plane. A Boeing 777 is not a Lego plane, and at 775,000lbs, where can you hide that baby?"

"I agree, and why was the cockpit voice recorder and the transponder switched off half an hour into the flight?"

Steve sighed again. "More to the point if the plane didn't go down why wasn't it picked up on International radar?"

"Because it was flying at around 800ft to avoid detection."

"Hmmm..." Steve rubbed his chin.

"Gregg, let's just say hypothetically you are right, but there's no Airports in the North Pacific or Islands that we know of could land that bird?"

"Yeah, I guess that rules that theory out." Gregg's mind was still searching.

"What's on your mind partner?"

"Here's where I'm coming from. The Coast Guard and Japanese Search and Rescue knew within a kilometer where the plane disappeared from radar, confirmed by the Air Traffic Controller and the GPS reading."

"Come Gregg, get to the point."

"After three days sweeping in an 800-kilomter radius, they found...?"

"Yeah, no trace of any wreckage... Zilch... I got that."

"And then, almost a week later and in the same spot... *Bingo...* Wreckage! Shred in a million small pieces... *The conclusion...!* The plane was blown out of the sky by a bomb. It just doesn't make any sense Steve!"

"So, let's be stupid... stupid! The plane lands somewhere, wherever that is, dumps the loot kills the crew then flies the plane back again with two suicide bombers in the cockpit in the name of Allah!"

"Not so stupid Steve, remember Salibe and his brother are Muslims and they had pilot's licenses to fly passenger jets."

"Yeah, but why would Salibe kill the crew and the security guards then kill himself?"

"There's a third party involved… The Yakuza!"

"But one hundred billion Dollars? Even David Copperfield couldn't make that disappear! We'll be laughed out of court if we put that on Thomson's desk."

"Unless you have something better, Steve?"

"Gregg, I'm not saying you're wrong, it's just proving it!"

"Eh…" Gregg was at a loss leaning forward placing his hand below his chin resting on his elbow. "Well, what do *you* suggest?"

"How about some lunch…...?"

* * *

"Hanna…"

"You had better be nice to her Steve, you didn't exactly spray the compliments when we arrived."

"Yes?" Hanna looked from her desk.

"Hanna, I apologies for my rudeness this morning."

"Get to the point, what do you want?"

"Boy, can she read you." Gregg was laughing.

"Hanna, I tell you what, if you get on the blower and order our lunch from the Italian Deli, I'll throw in a fifty to cover yours and John's."

"Bribery, now is it? And from two CIA agents. This could be serious."

Gregg was doubling up watching Hanna 'pupating' Steve.

"Hanna, be a darling. I'm wounded." Steve held his hand over his heart in asilly gesture.

"Oh, all right then. I don't know why I fall for this sob story every time."

"It's your mother instinct Hanna."

"Don't get me started…! Now what do you want?"

"Bacon and egg on toasted rye and…Gregg?"

"Five grain bread with lettuce crushed avocado and fetta."

"Coffees?"

"Latte medium."

"Make that for two."

"If your including mine and John's, that fifty won't get you far."

"Okay." Steve sighed taking another bill from his fold. "Your torturing me Hanna, here's a fifty and a twenty, I mean were not buying from the 'Le Diplomate' where the Obamas dine!"

Hanna was laughing and as she was about to pick up the phone John appeared from his office.

"Lunch time Mr. Thomson?"

"You read my mind?"

"Guess what? The boys are buying today……"

* * *

"Now that we've satisfied our stomachs." Steve was sipping the last of his 'take away' coffee. "Let's get back to the loss of 'Global 10'."

"Okay, when Ken Daniels and his team checked out the security guard Giovani Quario with 'Black Hawk Securities' they had no such person on their staff. My conclusion and I'm sure you support me Steve, Quario was none other than Anbar Salibe."

"And the two Japanese security guards?"

"That's another joke! The two Suma's from the 'Kovan Chousacho' drew another blank. This whole security fiasco in my opinion was a set up by the Yakuza."

Steve put his hand to his chin. *Where the hell is this going?* He thought to himself.

"What a fucking shamble! Sure, I agree with you but this is all assumption and with not a thread of hard evidence. No bodies, no plane, no money, what a fuck up, and worse still, where do we go from here?"

"Let's look at the crew."

"If you say so." Steve was almost out of it.

"Collins, the Captain, is a straight shooter and the stewardess, a Sally Jenkins a nobody, but let's look closer at the First Officer… Chuck Stevens. A gambler and in debt up to his eyeballs with the wrong people. A womanizer and a part time acholic. Now let's say he was in on the heist. So, he wastes Collins and flies the plane with Anbar as the co-pilot."

"Maaan." Steve ran his fingers through his hair. "Gregg this is getting crazier by the minute. Look at it this way. If your assumption is correct, *where the hell did they fly the plane?"*

Now it was Gregg's turn to sigh.

"Yeah, I guess you are right, Steve."

Gregg had just finished his comment when Thomson appeared in a hurry, briefcase in his hand.

"I don't know about you guys but I'm calling it a night, I've had it for the day and I suggest you do the same. Hanna, if anything comes up you know where to get me……"

* * *

Steve closed of door of the BMW then turned the key.

"Safety belt buddy."

"Yeah… Yeah…" Gregg sighed.

"Lighten up partner its only 4:30 and we're on our way home."

"I know but I just feel so useless."

"Then do you fancy a beer?"

"Are you serious? *At this time of the day!*"

"We've done worse."

Steve, slipped the gear and drove slowly out the car park. The rain was still having its way and an early leave from the office was no bad thing. The Eastern Express Way would still be slow but arriving home early was a plus.

"I was thinking since we've gone down the street and back, on all of the scenarios, maybe we should request an interview with the three suspects in detention?"

"You mean, uncle Aziz and his to wing men… Dabar and Bishara? You gotta be serious Gregg! Thomson wouldn't have a bag of that. Besides Brennan would go ballistic.'

"Yeah, I guess your right but look what we're gonna end up with? *Another MH370!*"

"Lighten up Gregg, we'll crack a cold one when we arrive home and order some 'Chines' and get our feet up."

Gregg didn't reply he was still on 'Fantasy Island' looking for a 'plane a plane'.

"You're not on a guilt trip about LA, are you?"

"You mean with Marge?"

"And the beautiful Michelle?"

"Get out of it, you low life! Back on that tact again. Well if you must know I called Michelle and it's over."

"Your shittin me!"

"Hey, watch your driving… It seems that 'absence makes the heart grow fonder' is full of shit and a guy answered the phone a two in the morning."

Steve had to cover his mouth.

"Hey, watch you driving…..."

* * *

THE JOURNEY

Salibe had gone through the mill and at last finally entering the Business Class cabin on ANA 12 bound for Ben Gurion and his beloved Palestine.

"Good evening sir, can I see your boarding pass?" The pretty young stewardess in her light grey jacket with blue silk neck scarf and dark grey pencil skirt, asked.

Salibe obliged.

"Thank you… Eh, Mr. Sarraf. Seat 12a on you left, welcome aboard.

"My name is Akira and I'll be looking after you in our Business Class cabin this evening… 12a… Let me escort you to your seat."

The seats in business were 'semi bed' and Salibe was looking forward to finally relaxing on the 10hr flight, the lost Island of Shimaru Shima an experience he will never forget.

The intercom blared. "Cabin crew ensure safety belts are fastened as we are preparing for takeoff in fifteen minutes. Captain Kimiko and first officer Nao, will be ensuring your safe flight to Ben Gurion airport, Israel. Please be aware of the time difference between Narita and Tel Aviv is minus six hours.…..."

* * *

An hour into the flight and 11pm approaching, Anbar could hardly keep his eyes open and he pressed the mode button on the side of his chair to 'bed' then the other to raise the glass partition between the seats to provide unadulterated privacy, something he had almost forgotten.

"Brrrrr." He shivered, the aircon as in most flights becomes chilly and Anbar pulled the 'airways' blanket up to his chin then closed his eyes, food not on his agenda. His thoughts now drifting back to the unfortunate death of his brother Fadile and how he could break the shock news to his father

when they meet? Anbar's eyes glazed over at the thought. 'Peace came upon him and it leaves me weak… Sleep silent angel go to sleep……'

* * *

Brunch had come and gone and because of the time difference, 6 hours behind, it was afternoon and Salibe would touchdown at 4pm the same day. It felt strange but more to the point how he could contact his father to tell of his arrival. It was too dangerous to use his cell phone as Israel's Mossad and Shin Bet were ruthless in their pursuit to incarcerate the Commander of the armed wing and it was a real dilemma……

* * *

ANA 12 touched down with a text book landing and Salibe was glad that this leg of his long eventful journey was over. His next problem was Israel's Customs and Border Security, with a reputation of being one of the most stringent in the world. The Samsonite and Aluminum briefcase had gone through the security X Ray tunnels in Narita with a sticker showing a clean bill of health. But Immigration and passport checks at Ben Gurion were different. A yellow sticker is placed on the back of your passport with a 1 to 6 security rating… 1 safe… 6 high risk. And having a Palestine Passport was a risk …...

* * *

Ben Gurion airport is a modern well-equipped facility much as you would find in Chicago, London or Paris. The major difference is the security, with heavily armed police patrolling the gates and check points at immigration and with sniffer dogs at the luggage belts. Uniquely, everyone in Israel that has a Platinum Credit Card passing through the airport or as a Business Class passenger, can enter the famous 'Dan Lounge', free. The lounge is extremely comfortable with leather sofas and seating and TV entertainment. The main attraction is the first-class food and beverages, but as always, the down side is overcrowding, with even the staff taking advantage of the perks.

* * *

The que as usual at passport clearance seemed never ending with segregated lanes for Israelis, Palestinians and Others and Salibe had to maintain his calm to get at least a 3 or 4 rating on the yellow passport sticker. He had already completed the customs declaration form with 'nothing to declare', but the longer the que, the more impatient he became and he tried to select the least congested line, which as usual is 'Murphy's Law'.

The Immigration officer finally waved him forward pointing to the white line whilst staring at Anbar, his penetrating eyes making the Arab feel decidedly uncomfortable. Then he studied the passport picture before sifting through the pages, satisfied, he stared again, this time looking straight into Anbar's eyes.

(Speaking in Arabic)

"Ahmad Sarraf... ID nambir...?"

"WB50011987." He had memorized this number so many times, the Immigration officer was purposely putting him through the mill.

"Hmmm..." He checked the computer.

"And you stay in Gaza City?"

"That's correct."

"Why have you shaven your iahai, may I ask?" (beard)

"Studying in the US and with islamophobia after 9/11, it made safe sense to be clean shaven."

The officer half smiled, the reason was explainable.

"Shukraan." (thank you)

The officer nodded then placed the yellow sticker on the back of Andar's passport.

As Salibe walked to the baggage carrousel the last thing he wanted was to appear too anxious to look at his passport as the eyes and ears of the Airport Security Police were everywhere.

"Hmmm... A four." He pouted his lips relieved. Next, was his green Samsonite bag and he quickly walked to the Baggage Shute to gain the advantage of an early catch.

"At last!" He quickly grabbed the heavy green molded bag and wheeled it to the 'Green Lane' under the scrutiny of the Custom's Officers.

The tall officer in the crisp white shirt and the holstered Jericho 941 semi-automatic pistol looked at Anbar's passport then waived him through.

Relieved he was finally on his way but then suddenly the second officer called.

"Waqf w yrja aleawdat w fath kays al'akhdar." (stop, please return and open your luggage bag)

Anbar's heart was in his mouth… *it would be all over… a lost cause. Was this the end?* A long prison sentence in an Israeli jail? But panic was the last thing he needed.

The officer pointed to the large stainless-steel table signaling to place the Samsonite, his partner was more interested in the other passengers passing through.

Anbar did as he was ordered, his complexion now ashen grey, beads of sweat showing on his forehead and it didn't go unnoticed. His hands trembling, he rolled the combination barrel then keyed the locks.

"You seem unusually nervous Mr. Sarraf, do you have anything you to declare before I open the bag?"

Anbar was quiet on the grounds he may further incriminate himself. *Strange*, the key doesn't turn?

"I'm sorry officer the lock seems to be jammed." It wasn't getting any better.

The officer raised his eyebrows turning to his partner.

"Use the master key for Samsonite luggage."

The officer opened the bag exposing either side. Then he smiled calling for his partner.

"Ladayna eabr mudammad huna la wader anna' eabr." (we have a cross dresser here)

Both officers were laughing as they rummaged through the silk panties and bras and other ladies apparel.

Salibe was taken aback at the contents of his baggage, but also relieved.

"Albashari." (Pass) The officers were still laughing and shaking their heads, it's rare they come across a gay Arab crossdresser.

Salibe didn't need a second jolt and was on his way like a bat out of hell to the Taxi Rank.

"*What the fuck,* I've picked up the wrong bag!"

He had to move fast now before the other passenger reported the mistake to customs and expose the training manuals.

Taxi drivers are mostly Arab operating aged Mercedes and the last thing he needed was an Israeli and Salibe hastily searched for an Arab number plate. These are yellow and display the letter P in front of the numbers, whereas the Israeli plates are blue with the letter I. He had no local currency in his passion and he wasn't about to change his US dollars and que at the currency exchange counter. The distance by taxi to Erez, the border crossing to Gaza is approximately 73 kilometers or an hour's journey depending on the traffic and with an exchange of one US to three ILS (Israeli New Shekel) he had plenty of currency......

* * *

The cab driver with the checkered red and white head scarf gave a wry smile at seeing his young affluent looking fare. There could be a fat tip in the offering.

His orange peel wrinkled face throug constant sun exposure, most likely hid his real age looking much older than he really was. The spaced yellow teeth when he smiled were either tobacco stained from the overzealous use of the Hookah Shisha Pipe or too much chewing of the beetle nut. His Kaffia (the main clothing for Gulf men, with loose white trousers, Sirwal) had seen better days and was badly in need of some detergent, the dust laden feet and Jesus sandals added further to the carnage, but time was of the essence and beggars can't be choosers.

"Erez, Gaza?"

The taxi driver nodded then picked up Salibe's bag throwing it into the dusty trunk of the white 300SE Mercedes but not before spiting a stream of red beetle juice onto the dusty sidewalk raising a small volcano.

"Kam alththumun?" (how much)

"Two hundred and twenty ILS... I can speak English." He gave a toothy grin. "My name is Abel Bahar, at your service."

"Abel, how long does it take to drive to Erez?"

"It depends." The toothy grin again.

"If I make it two hundred US dollars that's over 600 ILS how quick can you get me there?"

Abel's pale blue eyes suddenly sparkled.

"In less than an hour if I take the back roads then slip off at the Ashdod and Gehu freeway sections."

"I don't give a shit, as long as you get me there in one piece!"

Salibe peeled off two one hundred-dollar bills.

"And there's another fifty in it to keep your mouth shut."

"I never seen you, I never met you." Abel grinned, pocketing the extra cash.

"Then let's get the hell outta here......!"

* * *

Abel was either an ex camel jockey or he was competing for a place in the 'Israel Cross Country Rally'. It was pedal to the metal through the back streets leaving a dust cloud like a sand storm.

Anbar smiled to himself whilst being thrown from side to side as the big Mercedes' rear-end protested. *'Thank God I didn't give him another fifty!'* the thought again making him smile.

Half an hour into the journey Abel turned to Anbar, his yellow toothy grin not the most attractive landscape.

"In another ten minutes, you will be more comfortable, boss. You can just see the Ashad 'slip off' to Highway 4 coming up on our left, then it's all the way to Border Security at Erez."

The Arab was no dummy paying attention to the smallest reaction from his mysterious passenger when he mentioned 'Israeli Border Security'. Maybe he was looking for another 'hear no evil see no evil' tip. It's the old saying, 'when it comes to money, you trust no one'.

Anbar didn't bat an eyelid. Could he trust one of his fellow countryman when push comes to shove? It was certainly a worry but he would cross that bridge when it comes. Once the bag 'mix up' had been reported and the contents exposed, all hell would break. His only ray of hope being the police wasting valuable time searching for him at the Airport and questioning anyone that could give them information regarding a passenger in western clothing in a desperate hurry, wheeling a green Samsonite luggage bag. On the other hand, a simple phone call to the security check points at both Erez on the Salah Al Din Road, the main arterial in Gaza vital to North south travel and the other 90 checkpoints when entering at the West Bank, manned by the IDF, would be a catastrophe……

* * *

Hamas chief, Khaled Meshall previously rejected any attempt to disarm the Palestinian Islamist movement in Gaza as demanded by Israel stating its weapons are sacred and not up for negotiations. Abdul Fattah, Anbar's father, has topped Israel's most wanted list for more than a decade having escaped five assassination attempts by Israel's 'Mossad Secret Service' and s the 'Sayerat Matakal'. Israel's Prime Minister, Benjamin Netanyahu stressed his determination to continue to disarm Hamas until the security of all Israelis is guaranteed.

In June 2007 Hamas seized Gaza, ousting the forces of Fatah, the faction led by the Palestinian Authority President, Mahmoud Abbas, effectively separating Gaza from the West bank in terms of administration. Israel intensified its security check points when Hamas began increasing its rocket fire into Israel fueled by neighboring extremists such as Iran and Egypt, feeding Hamas's arsenal with short range rockets......

* * *

Erez is the only border crossing to Gaza and is controlled by the IDF (Israel Defense Force). All nationalities must pass through this checkpoint which resembles a large concrete pill box and an electronic reinforced steel gate manned by armed Israeli soldiers. Taxis from Israel cannot proceed into Gaza although private and or commercial vehicles can, provided they have the necessary clearance documentation or Palestine registration number plates. Once approaching, your vehicle will be stopped by an Israeli soldier who may request you open your bags to search for weapons then check your passport and or permit to allow entry. You then wait outside the electronic gate for your turn to be called then enter the terminal and hand your passport to the guard on the other side to receive an exit stamp. From the Israeli perspective, the Israel Gaza Strip barrier is intended to control the movement of people between Gaza and Israel and stop the entry of arms into the territory. Palestine Taxis on the Gaza side are available for transportation to your destination......

* * *

The large fort like border crossing was now visible. It had just turned six in the evening and darkness in July falls at eight. It was important for Anbar to cross the Border before sunset to beat the eight hour 'on and off' electricity supply from Israel as the result of terrorist attacks on its power generation and distribution infrastructure. The que in three columns looked like a thirty-minute wait possibly not a bad thing as the Israeli guards get lackadaisical in the warm dry temperature of 30c after a long tedious day.

"I made the time boss just less, than an hour." Was Abel's proud reclamation.

The message loud and clear and Anbar crushed another fifty into the palm of Abel's grubby hand, better to be safe than sorry.

"Shukraan." The money quickly disappearing into his secret stash below his Kaffia.

"You can keep the luggage and give the contents to your daughter. The bag is unlocked."

Abel furrowed his forehead… *'Strange'* he thought, this was something different but what was the secret of the bag's contents? *Could it be a bomb?*

"Sorry boss, I must check." Abel was taking no chances.

Anbar was already walking to the check point it was a chance he had to take, the Arab taxi driver, a patriot or not?"

Abel quickly opened the trunk, then the bag. His reaction was like they say in the US, *'I'll be darned'* and he shook his head in disbelief as he rummaged through the female clothing. *At least the bag was worth something and with three hundred US in his pocket, it doesn't get any better!* He turned the Merc and joined the Taxi stand for a return fare, a grin crossing his face… 'who would have thought'……?

* * *

An hour seemed like an eternity when the officer finally waved Anbar forward. He studied the passport in minute detail glancing two and fro at Anbar's picture then his eyes. Then he reversed the passport to check the yellow sticker from immigration having determined by Anbar's passport that he had just arrived into the country from overseas.

"Why are you travelling with only a briefcase?" He asked intrigued.

"My bag was lost in transit from Tokyo and I can't afford financially to wait two or three days in Tel Aviv for its return. The airline has my contact number and when they call I will determine then how I can collect the bag."

Just then another officer called. "Ahron, I need your assistance I have a problem here." The officer was in a heated argument with an Arab.

"Okay you can go…. Asher open the gate."

The '4' on the yellow immigration sticker was the green light. All that was left was the exit stamp and he was on his way……

* * *

(Speaking in Arabic)

It was now approaching 7:30pm and darkness was falling fast as Anbar hailed a Palestine cab, the usual dusty Merc with a clear coat that has seen its best days.

The cab driver stared at Anbar with curiosity and caution, Salibe's western attire standing out from the locals. One can never tell when a passenger is beardless, if he is a Palestinian or undercover Jew.

"Madinat ghazzat Kam, Aimryka mal?"   (Gaza city American money)

He peered again at Salibe before deciding the fare.

"Miaya dular Aimryka." (100 American)

One hundred for 20k was bit over the top but then it had been three years since he had been home and the price of gas had escalated.

The middle-aged Arab stretched out his arm rubbing his forefinger and thumb together. He needed to see the hundred in the flesh. Anbar didn't like the cabbie's attitude but in hindsight who trusts anyone in Gaza when it comes to making a buck and he peeled off a big one from his bill fold.

The driver studied it for a moment then held it up to the fading light then finally nodded before the greenback disappeared into the large pocket of his Kaffia.

"Aism?" Anbar asked. (name)

"Raafid."

"Abdel Nasar Sharie, Rimal."

Raafid understood Anbar's destination, a man of few words and opened the rear door of the Merc pointing to the dust laden cracked leather seats.

"Shukraan……"

* * *

Gaza City is located north of the Mediterranean Sea and north of the Sinai Peninsula south west of Jerusalem. The city is of historical religious importance having been disputed since ancient times. Along with the rest of the Gaza strip, Gaza came under Israeli occupation in 1967 and in 1994, the city became the Headquarters of the New Palestine Authority which administers Palestine areas both in the Gaza Strip and the West Bank. The city is 42 square kilometers and has a population of 1.8 million and has three universities.

CODE RED

Steve, was in slumber land in the midst of a hot dream with the gorgeous Julie, when the phone rang.

"What the fuck!" He would never get back to that dream again and he glanced at the digital numbers on the bedside clock.

"I don't believe it! Six thirty, who the hell can this be?" He stretched over and switched on the bedside lamp uttering oaths that hadn't been invented yet.

"Yeah, Steve Nelson?" His voice slurred.

"Steve… Thomson here."

"Eh… Err… Yes John?"

"Something has come up, a 'Code Red' and I need you and Gregg in the office ASAP."

"Like now?"

"You heard me."

"Eh, sure john, I'll go waken Gregg give us 45."

The phone went dead.

"Hmmm…" Steve stared blankly at the receiver having been cut short then placed it back in its cradle, his mind still unclouding.

"I wonder… Well, there's no point in procrastinating, I had better get my ass outta here… *Gregg…….."*

* * *

"Hanna, *your here too?"*

"Yeah, and being the mother that I am to you two ungrateful louts, I've have a pot of fresh coffee on the perc."

"Now Hanna, don't be that way, you know we love you." Gregg was smiling as he hung his jacket on the back of his chair.

"More to the point Hanna, what's this all about?"

"*Steve*, you should know better by now."

"Okay, no more said, message received loud and clear. Gregg, can you fetch me a coffee while you're there?"

"*What*, are you paralyzed or something?"

"Who needs friends, huh?"

Suddenly Thomson appeared. "Take your coffees and come to the office."

Steve turned to Hanna and made a face.

"Don't even…" She gave that look

"Grab a seat. I've just received a 'Code Red' from Brennan, a top down from the 'Commander in Chief' himself."

"If you don't mind me asking John?" Steve as usual was mister motor mouth.

"*Yes, I do!* Now sit back and listen… A passenger arriving at Ben Gurion Airport yesterday on a flight from Japan, mistakenly collected the wrong luggage at customs. A green Samsonite bag. When the female passenger reported the mishap and after numerous calls over the Tannoy to other passengers on the same flight, there was no alternative but to open the case."

Steve and Gregg were now in suspended animation waiting for the kicker.

"Inside the case were instruction manuals in both English and Russian on the launching of a miniaturized version of the short-range Russian built missile, the Scarab SS21b."

There was a pregnant silence as Thomson's statement dropped out of the sky like the 'Hindenburg' 129.

"From your faces you may well ask, *what the hell is a Scarab SS21b* and I don't blame you? When the 'Code Red' landed om my desk I was in the same boat of ignorance. Here's the bottom line… The Scarab is a short range, road mobile, solid repellant, single warhead ballistic missile designed for battlefield deployment as a replacement for the FROG (free rocket over ground) missile series. The miniature version (b) entered military service in 1988 and confirmed reports is that it has been deployed in the Syrian conflict by the dictator Bashar Al- Assad with Putin's support.

The Scarab, has a 220kg high explosive conventional warhead and a range of 200 kilometers with anti-radar blast warhead capabilities. It has excellent maneuverability in flight to avoid ballistic missile defense systems, such as Israel's 'Scud' and 'The Iron Dome' using internal guidance combined with Global Positioning Satellite (GPS) and a radar TV optical correlation system, giving it an accuracy on target of 95 millimeters. In short, this thing can go up Camel's ass from 200 kilometers!"

Thomson's comment brought a stifled a laugh.

"Are you finished?" John was not to be messed with today.

"Okay, let's start again…The first version required a mobile transporter erector launcher (TEL) to make it a flexible battlefield system against military units and troop concentrations but these transporters were large and cumbersome and required a crew of three and easily spotted by surveillance drones, whereas the miniature (b) version can be discharged from the back of a 'Twin Cab' or Humvee or even a dug out 4x4 by 2 meters deep and computer programmed for remote firing. The new tubular heavy-duty frame system for launching can be assembled in under 15 minutes. At 650Kg and 3 meters long and 0.65 meters in diameter, the missile can easily be mounted manually by two operators. *But get this!* Intelligence sources identify that Russia has 1,200 of these missiles in their arsenal for sale in the open market to the highest bidder at 60 million US a piece!"

Serve and Gregg were dumfounded and didn't know where to start.

"Well, I'm waiting?" Thomson leaned forward resting his chin on both hands.

Steve was first as usual. "Let's start with the passenger that grabbed the wrong suitcase by mistake from the luggage carousel?"

"Good point Steve!"

Thomson placed two pictures on his desk then placed one in front of Steve and Gregg.

"This is a passport picture faxed to us from Shin Bet of the person that mistakenly took the wrong bag. He is a 27 years old Palestinian from the Gaza Strip. The name on the passport is Ahmad Saraaf. I want you to study his picture for few minutes. Now return the picture to me."

Steve turned to Gregg and sort of shrugged like, *'where is this going'?*

Thomson picked up a black felt tipped pen and shaded in part of the face.

"Now here's a picture of Anbar Salibe." He placed it in front of them. "And here's my artist's impression of the first picture only this time with a beard."

Gregg turned Steve in disbelief. *"I don't believe it!* Anbar Salibe and Ahmad Saraaf are one and the same… *But…"*

"I know what you're thinking… *How can that possibly be?* If you recollect you were both adamant that Salibe was one of the guards on the fateful Global 10. The only hole in that assumption was you couldn't prove it as McGill's computer was mysteriously hacked."

"John, I'm stuck for words." Steve was shaking his head.

"You're not the only one." Thomson was quick to reply.

It was Gregg's turn. "Im at the stage John, where I don't think we'll ever solve this one."

"I hate to admit it Gregg but unfortunately I'm of the same mind but let's just take a step back for a moment before I get down to the 'nitty gritty. We know that the brothers spent time in Russia and met with Sergi Shoigu himself at the MOD, then spent some serious time at The Department of Aeronautics and Rocket Science... *Is there a link?*"

"It ties up John but the puzzle is just getting worse. As an example, hypothetically, the brothers buy the Scarab. I mean Russia has no qualms who the hell they sell this stuff to, they are desperate for foreign currency."

"Your case has merit Steve, but at 60 million US Dollars it's not exactly a garage sale and that amount of cash is almost impossible to transfer through banks with the International Sanctions in place against the Kremlin. Then, there's shipping the hard ware to Gaza? *Man...*" Thomson was shaking his head. "There's just nothing that makes sense! Listen, I think we have thrashed that story enough so let's get down to the 'Code Red'."

Thomson leaned back in his chair, it was time to stitch this up.

"Taman Prado the Director of Shin Bet, has contacted Brennan for assistance and as usual it has landed on my doorstep. He is seriously concerned that should the threat of the Scarab be genuine it could be launched to destroy the Knesset, the Israeli parliament and its 120 members. The parliament is located at Giuat Ran in Jerusalem, approximately 80k from Gaza City, well within the range of the Scarab. Why am I telling you this? I'm looking for two volunteers for a secret undercover mission."

"Gregg?" Steve turned to his partner.

"I'm in."

"I guess I knew without a doubt you would both volunteer and you have my admiration. But before I accept your gallantry there's a few points I need to clarify. Having studied your records and your military service I noticed that you both speak fluent Hebrew and Arabic which makes you perfect candidates for this mission. So perhaps you can explain."

"John, you would have to be blind not conclude that we are both of the Jewish faith, hence our multilingualism, in fact Gregg and I have been friends since the age of thirteen when we celebrated our Bar Mitzvah. You may well ask why did we change our names? Unfortunately, in this crazy world we live in, there is still racial bigotry and that's the bottom line."

"Yeah, I can understand but now that's out of the way let's talk turkey about the mission. With American accents and fluent in Hebrew and Arabic, it could give a 'shoe in' to Hamas as they love American sympathizers. How you get their acceptance, that's a tough call but I'm sure you are both up to it having completed deployments in both Iran and Afghanistan. The mission… To search and destroy the Scarab S21b missile should the threat be real. You will be supplied with American Passports, new names and identities and the necessary visas, identifying that you are both naturalized Arab American citizens. You will attire yourselves in the traditional Arab dress. Upon reaching Ben Gurion you will clear Customs & Immigration without incident at counter 2, Shin Bet's officers will make this possible. From the airport, you will take a taxi to Erez and pass through the Israeli border check point. You will be given the number plates of both taxis, to Erez and to Gaza City. The second taxi will take you to a 'safe house' in Gaza City where you will receive your weaponry and stay at your discretion. You will each be given twenty thousand US dollars. It is recommended that you only change five thousand dollars to local currency at the airport as US dollars still talk the talk. You will be given a secret phone number to contact Shin Bet but only in a life or death situation or the location to 'take out' the Scarab missile. This information will be given to memorize before your departure. *Now, the serious stuff!* When you leave the US, you are on your own, in short Steven Nelson and Gregg Jonson never existed and no record of ever being CIA agents. Should something go wrong or you are captured as hostages of Hamas or worse still murdered or executed, I can't even inform your parents… The bottom line, *you are in 'no man's land'.* If the mission is successful you will return to the United States with no commendations or even the slightest mention of the CIA in the foiled Hamas terrorist plot and more so Russia's involvement. If you need time to reconsider your overzealous patriotism I can understand."

"That's a given John and I'm sure I speak for Gregg and myself, its affirmative. Now more importantly, when do we leave and do we fly Business Class?"

Steve's comment brought the house down……

* * *

The 20k drive on the Salah Al-Din Hwy, the main arterial road stretching from Erez to Rafa should only take 30 minutes in the evening traffic but one can never tell and Anbar settled down for the last leg of his monumental journey.

It had been over three years since he had seen his beloved family and he was concerned about their aging health and the stresses placed on the family as the result of his father's high profile and on Shin Bet's most wanted assassination list. 'Would Palestine ever be recognized as a state within itself?' He thought to himself. 'Would Hamas's plan to destroy the Knesset set them free from Israel's occupation or turn the world against them?' Whatever, there was no turning back and the plan had to succeed to the death, if for none other for his deceased brother, Fadile.

* * *

Abdel Nasar Street in the Rimal District is just behind and parallel to the square of the Unknown Soldier (Midan Al Jundi Al Majhool) in remembrance of the 1948 Arab Israeli war. Its monument set in a large fountain and public garden popular with unemployed Gazans during the day and families in the evening was a wealth of local information.

* * *

The headlights on the freeway were now becoming more and more prominent as darkness fell and Anbar could easily close his eyes but robberies are frequent in the impoverished Gaza State and the security of his briefcase was prominent. He had no weapon but most taxi drivers kept a handgun in the glove box and maybe just maybe he could catch a cap nap. That was the last he remembered......

* * *

The squeal of worn brake pads startled Anbar and he quickly came to his senses, his eyes now wide open.

"Nahn huna rayiysih." (we are here boss)

Anbar stared out of the rear window to see if he recognized anything of his old neighborhood. It was difficult as the street was only partially lit due to electricity rationing and he could hear the distinct hum of generators as he opened the Merc's door stepping into the dusty humid atmosphere. *For sure he was back to reality!*

"Shukraan."

The driver nodded then gunned the engine leaving a cloud of choking dust. Anbar's next challenge was to locate his father as he constantly changed his 'safe house' and he stared blankly for few seconds to gather his bearings.

"Now where's that baker's shop? It normally opens till at least eleven. If my memory serves me right it's on the left about 30 meters from here, in fact I think I can recognize it." Salibe spoke aloud.

The 'Taafeef Bakery' in Nasar Street is famous for its Pita, Lavash and Sangak traditional Arab breads and there was always a que no matter what time of day. But would Amir Taafeef, a close friend of his fathers recognizes him?

There was a que alright and Amir's son Aman was busy behind the counter. He was the same age as Anbar and had graduated at the local university 'Al Azhar' and was fluent in English, a plus when communicating as at least 90% of Arabs don't speak the language.

Anbar crushed by the que and stood at the side of the counter the smell of freshly baked bread enticing his taste buds and for a second Aman caught sight of the 'que jumper'.

Was it Anbar Salibe his friend, returned from the United States? No, it couldn't be!

"As-Salaam-Alaikum." Anbar broke the tension bringing a smile to his friend's face.

"Wa- Salaam-Alaikum." Amir's face lit up as he recognized his childhood friend and he immediately ceased what he was doing and grabbed Anbar's hand in both his, then touched his heart with his right hand, the traditional Muslim welcome of respect.

"Al Anbar… Gyri radar gala bile earned hu aquanaut leak?" (Anbar… I can't believe my eyes, is it really you?)

"Nm, li shyly aleaziz allicin naan sibayk fi iinlish?" (Yes, it's me my dear friend but can we speak in English?) Anbar sort of rolled his eyes toward the que who by now were gathering unwanted interest, in Gaza one can never tell.

The que was understandably getting annoyed at the delay in service some having waited for over fifteen minutes.

"Eindama item alhusul salaam hamartian?" (When are we getting served, a disgruntled customer yelled)

"Fi lazes lethally bialssabr." (In a moment, be patient)

"My father's is behind in the bakehouse. Come Anbar, I'll take you to him, he'll be so glad to so you."

Needless to say, the customers were none too happy and Amar turned to the now congested shop.

"Sa'aeud fi Lhasa." (I'll be back in a moment)

(Arabic to English)

"Father, look who we have here?" The old man stopped kneading the dough and looked up peering for a moment amidst the stifling heat from the ovens in the dimly lit bake room. Then a smile crossed his face.

"Anbar Fattah!... He quickly wiped his 'floured' hands on his heavily stained apron, then his forehead before warmly greeting Anbar in the Muslim tradition…....

* * *

"Hmmm… I see." Amar Taafeef in his late sixties pondered for a moment having listened to Anbar's brief explanation of his mission for the cause and the future of the Palestine State, the Taafeef family trustworthy beyond doubt.

'I'm finished now." Amar glanced at the flour coated wall clock then untied his apron hanging it up for another day. Amir had already returned to the counter, time is money.

"Come, I'll take you to your father." Amar pointed to the back door of the bakery and the ally where he kept his antique British Morris Minor. The old icon was built like a tank and Anbar hurriedly opened the heavy rattling door.

"It's around fifteen minutes from here in the winding back streets. You can never be careful enough these days, especially your father with a price on his head."

Amar turned the key the old lady protesting with a couple of stutters before bursting into life. With no aircon Amar opened the quarter windows, it was either suffocating in the humidity or choking in the dust cloud.

"I drive with only the parking lights as these streets are dangerous for robberies." Amar reached over and opened the glove compartment removing a Russian Makarov 9mm semi-automatic. "This is my insurance." He gave a wry smile before placing the loaded pistol in the side pocket.

"That bad?"

"And getting worse!"

Amar crunched the stick change into first then kangarooed for a couple of meters before 'Old Betsy' settled down……

* * *

Amar was right, it seemed to take longer than normal, the winding side streets a challenge to the best of drivers, the street lighting almost nonexistent, then suddenly he reduced speed.

"We are just about there."

Amar wiped the side window with the back of his hand his eyes straining in the semi darkness, his speed down to almost walking pace.

"Here we are…!"

The guard at the entrance to the doorway of the ancient white cement washed building was dressed in camouflage fatigues, a Kalashnikov slung over his shoulder, the red and white checkered head scarf wrapped tightly around his head and face exposing only his eyes, stepped forward blocking their car.

Amar hastily waved from the open window. *"Farid it's me,* Amar Taafeef, I need to see Syd Fattaah, its urgent."

Farid unshouldered his weapon and walked to the car, his Kalashnikov panting menacingly at Amar, he was taking no chances producing a flashlight and shining it directly into Amar's face then Salibe's. Satisfied he motioned to get out of the car.

"Who is this Amar?" Farid asked pointing his Kalashnikov at Anbar.

"Don't you recognize him Farid, its Anbar? Abdul's oldest son!" But it had been a long time and the guard was still unsure of this young man dressed in western clothes.

"Raise your arms." He ordered, then began a body frisk. Satisfied he bowed then clasped Anbar's hand. "My apologies Anbar but I have job to do."

"Shukraan."

"It's alright Farid we can find our own way. Come." Amir motioned to Anbar to follow him down the dark passageway.

The heavy wooden door with the half-moon top, an oil lamp shadowing the darkness, Amar knocked three times in succession then paused with another two, the code of entry.

Anbar's nerves were getting the better of him as the fortress like door slowly creaked open only to be faced with another armed guard.

"Klamath alssrr." He barked. (password)

"Jundi majhul." (unknown soldier)

"Albashari." (pass)

As Anbar entered the main sitting room he immediately recognized his father sitting cross-legged on the floor surrounded by his uncles and nephews having their evening family supper after prayers. The large brass engraved Dallah tea pot subjugated the glass topped table displaying a modest meal of Hummus, Manakeesh (the pizza of the Arab world) grilled Halloumi, Falafel, Tabbouleh and Pita bread.

The dimly lit room was full of shadows from the flickering oil lamps and Anbar's father stared for a moment at the newcomers before smilingly recognizing his old friend and compatriot Amar Taafeet, the 'bread maker'.

"*Amar*, come and join us and…?" Shocked Abdul raised his fingers to his mouth… "*Anbar, my son.*" Tears ebbing into his pale grey eyes as he rose to his feet spilling his tea in his haste.

Formalities aside they hugged one another as if it was their last supper, Abdul kissing his son on both cheeks. Then he stepped back.

"Let me look at you, you've grown into a fine young man but…" He looked around as if something or someone was amiss. "*Where's your brother?*"

It was Anbar's turn to tear up. "*Father*, how can I begin tell you… Fadile was mortally wounded in the line of duty…There was no way I could contact you and I'm deeply sorry…."

Abdul stood motionless in silence, his head bowed, tears streaming down both his cheeks. To lose a son before your own demise is a heartbreak no parent should ever experience in their life time.

"*Father*, he died a hero. He is with our savior now and in heaven, *Allah Ahmad.*"

Abdul was still in shock and just nodded his head, it was all too much. Then he composed himself kissing Anbar on the cheek once more.

"At least I still have one son but tragedies come in twos. I lost my beloved wife and your mother Aliya, six months ago." Abdul's eyes tearing once more.

"*Mother gone!* I can't believe my ears… *Mother gone…!*" Anbar couldn't control his emotions.

"Allah be with her that she didn't suffer, it was very fast."

"And Aesha my second mother?"

"She's good. She in the kitchen preparing food, she'll be so happy to see you… *Amar…*" Abdul turned to his friend. "I would be honored if you come and join my son and I to break bread."

"Shukraan, Abdul." Amar bowed it was an honor to join such a respected family for easha…… (supper)

* * *

The supper over the relatives departing for home it was always a special treat and an honor to break bread at their uncle's house after evening prayer and in true Arabic tradition their expressed their thanks.

"Aleum nashkirukum." (Uncle we thank you)

* * *

"Anbar, we must talk." The room now empty except for the 'bread maker'.

"I understand father but…" He turned and looked to Amar Taafeef begging the question.

"Don't worry, he one of us and a senior member of Hamas's military wing."

"I see father."

"Come, join me in more tea……"

* * *

"And the Japanese submarine with arrive off the cost in approximately 17 days, give or take?"

"That's correct father. And the money transfer?" Salibe asked.

"The Japanese are true to their word; 10 billion US Dollars was transferred to 12 Arab banks at different intervals in small deposits to avoid unreasonable scrutiny. The good news, Hamas now has sufficient funds to buy weapons and equipment.

"Anbar, your plan reflects your intellect, but now that I have lost my dear son and your brother…"

Amar suddenly interrupted. "Abdul, you have a new son and Anbar a brother." His comment met with confused looks.

"Amir, my oldest son… I pledge his loyalty to the Fattah family and to Hamas. Salibe can train him as the second man to replace Fadile for the launching of the Russian missile. This you have my word."

Abdul rose to his feet and hugged Amar, kissing him on both cheeks.

"I pray to Allah to thank him for your generosity knowing full well the danger involved in the mother of all attacks on the infidels. Allah be with you." Abdul bowed once more.

"When I return to the house I will speak to my son, but we have more pressing matters in that we must arrange a fishing vessel with a heavy 'jib crane'."

"I agree Amar." Abdul nodded his mind racing.

"Father I was thinking of……"

THE RIVER OF NO RETURN

"I suggest you grab yourselves a coffee. I'll tell Hanna to confirm your travel arrangements departing in three days' time as we need at least that gap to get your passports ready. It will also give you space to arrange your personal affairs." Thomson shrugged apologetically. "I wish I could give you more time but..." He shrugged again.

"If there's nothing else John? Gregg and I have a few matters to discuss so we'll take your advice and grab that coffee."

"Sure, unless there's anything else. *Eh...*" Thomson was about to lift the secretarial phone then changed his mind. "Steve, can you ask Hanna to come and see me when you pass her desk?"

"No sweat."

Steve and Gregg rose to leave. It had been a more than an eventful meeting but finally this was the mission they had trained for.

"Hanna, the boss wants to see you."

"So, how did your meeting go?"

"*Hanna*, you should know better." Steve couldn't help himself and with Gregg laughing in the background, it wasn't helping.

"*You two!*" Hanna picked up her pad and pen shaking her head as she knocked on Thomson's door then turned. "Im gonna miss you guys."

"*So, you do know?*" Gregg teased.

Hanna didn't answer, a cheeky smile crossing her face as she disappeared into Thomson's office.

"*Okay... Okay,* before you ask I'll go and fetch the coffees."

"Thanks partner, I owe you." Steve sat back in in his chair relaxing.

"*Well?*"

"Well what?"

"Coffee isn't free from the machine or hasn't someone told you?"

"Why you miserable…! You must've been a problem child."

"Cut the crap scrooge… *The two dollars."*

"God, this stuff is bad ass!" Steve screwed his face, complaining as usual.

"So, if I had paid, it would have tasted better, huh?"

"Gregg, I couldn't have put it better myself."

"Get out of it! Now let's get down to it we have a lot to do in two days."

"Yeah, I guess you're right, banking, our body corporate, direct debits, our cars… Stop shaving." The last comment making Gregg laugh.

Maaan…! I say we call it a day, I'm sure John won't mind. We can leave a note on Hanna's desk."

"Boy, will she be pleased?" Gregg laughed.

"Gimme that piece of paper… 'Mother' we had to leave early, see you in the morning, please make sure there's fresh coffee on the perc and some muffins'.

Gregg, couldn't stop laughing on reading the scribbled note.

"I'm outta here…..."

* * *

The Highway as usual was slow at lunch time and Steve and Gregg had a lot on their mind… *Who would have thought…?*

"This traffic is dead meat, are you feeling hungry?" Steve asked.

"Some… Listen, it's just after twelve and we are going nowhere fast so my suggestion is we kill two birds with one stone and have a 'Whopper' at Burger King, I'm sure there's an outlet just before the slip off to the Eastern Expressway."

"Sounds good to me."

"Just make sure Steve, you don't over shoot so my advice is that you stay in the right lane."

"Shit, here we are already!" Steve pushed the stock switch. "Thanks partner, we all most missed it!"

The car park was full, heavy rain had just started and many drivers it seemed had the same idea.

"Fucking car park just our luck." Steve was complaining as he slowly drove down each lane.

"Hold it Steve, there's one at the back."

"Yeah, I see it but we'll have to sprint through this fucking rain!"

"Come on man, it will keep you fit."

"Speak for yourself." Steve cut the engine. *"Well 'Michael Jonson'* what are you waiting for…?"

"Hmmm, it's been a while since I sunk my teeth into a Burger King whopper, and these hash browns… Far out."

"For once I gotta agree with you Steve but there's no Whoppers and French fries where we're going so we had better make the best of it." Gregg laughed, but there was a clouded tone of seriousness in his voice.

Steve took another mouthful of the charcoaled meat then washed it down with some diet coke to clear his throat.

"You know what's bothering me Gregg?"

Gregg stopped chewing. "I have a good idea."

"So, are we gonna phone when we get back to the apartment?"

"Yeah, it's better sooner than later. Let's finish up and get going the traffic should be lighter now……"

* * *

The girls were sipping sparkling chilled Prosecco whilst resting on the balcony catching up on their tan enjoying the afternoon sun.

"We haven't heard from Draper regarding our next flight." Marge commented as she poured another flute.

"Oh, he'll call soon enough but let's forget work today and just relax. The pool looks tempting but I'm just too lazy to make the effort."

"I thought we might have heard from the boys by now."

"Yeah, but I guess they are busy settling back into their routine after the Tokyo assignment. More to the point Marge what are we going to do tonight?"

"I'm lazy like you, so why don't we partake in some calorie indulgent Pizza and put our feet up and watch TV movies?"

"Why not!" Just then the phone rang. *"Now who could that be?"*

"I hope it's not that low life Draper cutting our R&R short… It's okay Marge I'll take it."

"Julie Rodgers here."

"Julie its Steve… *Steve Nelson.*"

Julie quickly covered the phone. *"Marge, its Steve!"*

"Julie, can you put me on speaker? Gregg and I have something to tell you both."

Julie pouted her lips and shrugged, this was different.

"Sure, just a sec Steve while I get Marge."

"Hi Marge, Gregg here. I'll let Steve talk the talk and I'll butt in when necessary but I just want to say I had a great weekend, it was something special and I hope that you feel the same?"

There was a pregnant pause then Marge replied.

"I don't want to hang my washing on the line. What can I say is that I also had a great time, it was very special?"

"Julie, I don't want to go down that path again as you already know how I feel but let's get to the bottom line and why the phone call? Gregg and I were planning to fly down to LA this weekend, unfortunately that's not to be. Our line of work is unpredictable just like yours, here today and gone tomorrow, so to speak. We are departing in two days' time on a special assignment in CIA terms a 'Code Red'. How long will we be away? Even we don't know and can't discuss it as a matter National Security. We shouldn't even be telling you, not even our parents or closest friends can be informed of our departure."

"My God Steve, is it an undercover assignment overseas?"

"Julie I'm sorry I can't answer that question."

"Is it dangerous?" Marge chimed in shocked.

"I'm sorry…"

"Let's put it this way." Marge wasn't going to give up. "On a scale of 1-10?"

Steve pondered for a moment, he was sworn to secrecy.

"Ten."

Julie's voice broke in shock. *"We have just lost two personal friends, Bill and Chuck, and I don't want to go through that again!"*

"I'm sorry honey but I can't say anything more."

Just then Gregg interrupted. "Marge, will you wait for me?"

"Of course, I will darling!"

"You've made my day. I promise you I'll return in one piece."

There was another pause as Steve waited in hope.

"Steve, I'm so screwed up, I couldn't bear losing someone that I have just fallen in love with. You are special but I've had enough tragedy in my life and all I can say is, I pray for your safe return."

"That's all I need to know… *Gregg*, is there anything else you wish to say…...?"

* * *

Friday had finally arrived and Steve and Gregg had spent the last three days memorizing their assignment and the series of points that Thomson had given them. To carry papers if exposed could cause an international incident but more so the 'crash and burn' of operation 'Golda Meir', code named after Israel's famous 'iron lady'.

Steve studied his new passport. "I don't know how they come up with these fucking names, Fadi Bishara, *you gotta be kiddin me…!*"

"But get your lips around this baby…! *Imad Halabi*, I've been reciting this one so much I'm even calling it in my sleep."

Gregg's comment made Steve laugh… *"Heh…Heh…* If it wasn't so serious it would be funny, and how about these 'get ups'?"

"I tell you man, I'm not wearing these Arab 'jump suits' to the airport we can change in the Business Class rest room when we arrive in Ben Gurion.'

"I'm with you on that one, its 'Ts' and blue jeans and decks for me but more serious, have you finished packing?"

"Yeah, I'm done… What time is our flight again?"

"12:30 from Dulles via Kennedy, United 06."

"Listen, we had better get our skates on, do you know the time is just on nine, and we haven't phoned a cab yet!"

"Christ Gregg, lighten up, besides we haven't even had breakfast yet!"

"Trust you, always thinking of your stomach. We can have breakfast at the airport lounge. *Now the phone.*"

"Yes, Dulles Airport international, United Airways… 'Chancellor Towers' on the Washington Circular in the West End… You got it… In fifteen minutes …Yes, two passengers…We'll be waiting on the sidewalk… Fifteen minutes then…..."

* * *

"Last check, passports, money, ticket print out…?"

"Yeah, everything." Steve replied shaking his head. "Christ Gregg, you're like an old woman and where's this fucking cab? We're standing on the sidewalk like two frigging refugees."

"Keep your shirt on, here it is now."

"About time!" Steve annoyingly glanced at his watch.

The cabbie pulled in and automatically opened the trunk of the yellow Ford Crown.

"Only two bags sir?"

"Yes, that's it." Steve replied as Gregg opened the rear door.

"How long will it take to the airport?" Steve asked, making himself comfortable in the rear seat next to Gregg.

"The traffic is not too bad this morning… *Say…*Twenty minutes."

"It's gonna be tight but business class should be okay." Gregg commented.

"So, what time is your flight?" The cabby enquired as he pulled out.

"12:30." Steve replied. "Eleven check in."

"Don't worry I'll get you there in plenty of time… So, where's it today guys? You can call me Jake."

"Err… Jake, its Tel Aviv, Israel." Steve replied not particularly amorous on continuing the conversation. Cabbies can be a pain of inquisition.

"That's different… Business?"

"You could call it that." Steve cut him short.

Jake must have got the message, silent for the rest of the journey…

"International Departures, United airways… Here we are Gentlemen." Jake read the meter. "Fifty straight, I'll go fetch your bags."

Steve passed him three twenties'. "Keep the change."

"A pleasure... Safe flight……"

* * *

The breakfast of Champagne and eggs Benedict over, Steve was relaxing in his over indulgence.

"*Man*, I don't know where you put that stuff! You know we are going to be eating on the plane again?"

"I know, but I couldn't resist it." Steve grinned as he relaxed on the leather sofa.

As for Gregg, he was looking forward to the sumptuous food in Business Class having just finished an egg sandwich followed by a sterile black coffee.

"You know I was dreading that call to Julie and Marge." Steve changed the subject.

"Yeah, it was an unknown as to how they would take it. I mean, it wasn't as if we had been dating for months. But for me Marge said it all."

"*Julie*... I was a bit disappointed but I can't blame her. It's bad enough losing your ex, but never knowing what happened and probably never will, I can just imagine how she felt when I gave her the bad news."

'This is the final call for all passengers on United 06 departing for Tel Aviv at gate 15. Please be reminded this is the final and last call.'

"I guess that's us Steve and maybe just as well as there's little point in continuing this morbid conversation."

Steve sighed as he rose. "Yeah, I guess your right Gregg, just let's just make sure we come back in one piece…..."

* * *

"Mr. Bishara and Halabi, welcome aboard United Flight 6 and the friendly skies. Your seats are 12A and 12B." The blonde beauty smiled. "I'm Tracy the senior flight attendant in Business Class. Please take your seats and as soon as the cabin is fully seated I or my assistant Nancy, will attend to your refreshments."

"Thank you, Tracy." Steve gave that phony smile almost matching that of Tracy's.

"My compatriot and I are looking forward to an enjoyable flight."

Gregg looked toward Tracy and gave an awkward smile. When it comes to blondes… As for Tracy, she had heard it all before.

"I just love these seats or should I say beds?" Steve commented as he crashed into the soft leather.

"Yeah, this *is* something and a new Dream Liner, it doesn't get any better. But I'm gonna miss the Champagne."

"I don't get you?"

"Remember… We are Muslims, *now do you get it?*"

"*Shit,* I forgot about that in the lounge."

"Don't worry no one would notice but on *this* flight, one can never tell who is watching."

"Refreshments sir…" It was Tracy. "Champagne, beer, apple juice or orange?"

'Eh… Err, orange please."

"Make that for two."

"A 13-hour flight and no booze this is torture!"

"We all have to make sacrifices for the Agency."

"Get out of it! Who are you, the last boy Scout?"

"Joking aside, it's a pity there's a stopover in Kennedy for an hour."

"But what gets me is the time difference. We depart at 12:30am from Dulles and arrive in Ben Gurion at 8:30am, the same day!"

Gregg laughed. "Imagine we arrive before we leave but just think, if it was your birthday you could celebrate it twice."

"Gregg, only you would think of that crap."

'Please fasten your safety belts and place your seats in the upright position…….'

* * *

The flight was uneventful except for the one hour 'temperance stop' at J F Kennedy.

"If I see another orange juice, I'll go ballistic." Steve, complained.

"It just shows you how the other half lives, huh?"

"Next, you'll be telling me it's good for my liver."

"Are you sure you want to skip dinner, we have lobster on the menu?" Tracy interrupted.

"How long before we touch down, Tracy?"

"We're only five hours into the flight, another eight to go."

"Gregg?" Steve turned.

"The lobster is tempting but I'm bushed and I just want to get my head down and save myself for breakfast."

"*What the hell!* I'm not calorie counting. Yeah, I'll go for the lobster."

"Would you like the chilled Vodka and Caviar as an entrée?"

"Your killing me Tracy…*The Vodka… Gregg?"* Steve turned looking for assurance much to Gregg's annoyance.

"*Don't look at me.* If you want to take a chance be my guest! I'm getting my head down, so keep it quiet."

"Okay Tracy, I go the whole nine."

"Dinner will be served in fifteen minutes. Can I get you a refreshment to start with?"

"Yeah, orange juice…." For Tracy, anything.

Tracy just smiled… Muslims… She had seen it so often, *so everyone's human,* what's the big deal……?

* * *

Breakfast had come and gone with both Steve and Gregg still in slumber land. It had been 'a long day's night' when suddenly the Tannoy annoyingly burst into life instructing the passengers to 'buckle up' for landing.

"*Gentlemen.*" Gregg felt the gentle push to his shoulder.

"*Hmmm… Eh… Err."*

"I'm sorry Mr. Halabi but we are about to land. Can you please waken your friend?"

"Eh… Sure." Gregg rubbed the sleep from his eyes.

"Im sorry you missed your breakfast but our rule is, if passengers are asleep we are not allowed to disturb them."

"Don't worry I'm trying to lose weight anyhow." Gregg flashed a sleepy smile.

"Mr. Halabi, thank you for your understanding."

"Halabi…? Eh… Of course, I'm still only half awake." Gregg almost blew it, with Tracy looking confused and he quickly sidetracked.

"Tracy, don't worry, I'll waken my colleague... *Steve… Steve."* Gregg shook him by the shoulder.

"Yeah… Yeah... What is it?"

"We're about to land… *Waken up…...*"

* * *

The Captain's usual boring communication over and the 'thank you' for 'flying the friendly skies' the 787 'Dream Liner' touched the tarmac with a pronounced jolt rattling the overhead bins, the noise compounded by the scream of the two Rolls Royce Trent's reverse thrust.

As the plane drew to a halt at the aero bridge, as usual the passengers were anxious to deplane standing in the isle trying to open the overhead bins much to the displeasure of the flight crew.

"Please keep your seats until the aircraft has come to a halt."

"Well partner we're finally here." Steve stretched both arms above his head. "Another day another challenge, huh?"

"If you put it that way. Say, can you remember the taxi number?"

"Of course, but we're not out of the woods just yet…"

"It was a pleasure gentleman and I hope to see you again in the friendly skies."

"Thanks Tracy, the pleasure was all mine."

"Maaan, you embarrass me at times." Gregg shook his head as they left the cabin. There was no point…

"And I thought Dulles was busy." Steve was crushing through the mad scramble to the passport and immigration counters.

"IImmmm, Foreigners to Counters 1 and 2." Gregg was studying the signs in both Hebrew and Arabic.

"Counter two, huh?"

"Yeah, I remember, but this fucking que is something else." Gregg was pissed.

"Finally." Gregg placed his passport in front of the Israeli officer who studied his picture almost in slow motion then motioned to place his thumb on the fingerprint camera.

"Vacation." He asked.

"Yes."

He stared at Gregg once more before placing the yellow sticker on the back of his passport.

"*Go… Next.*"

Steve went through the same rigorous check before catching up with Gregg who was patiently waiting at the baggage carousel.

"A one, huh, looks like we got the right guy." Steve was commenting on his yellow sticker.

"Yeah, but he had me going there… *Ah,* here's the bags now."

"You got yours…?

"Yeah I got it. Let's hit the green lane we still have to change yet……"

* * *

With the yellow sticker on the back of their passports being a 1 it was a breeze through customs. Steve and Gregg had versed themselves on the airport layout and their priority was to find the famous 'Dan Lounge' to use the Business Class facilities to change into their Arabic attire.

* * *

"*Now where the hell's this lounge?*" Steve bitched as he wheeled his luggage almost amputating a few sandaled toes.

"*Don't be so fucking impatient!* I'll go ask this security guard. Wait here, I'll be back in a sec…"

"So, what did he say?"

"It's about 30 meters to the right of that 'Welcome to Israel' sign.'

"Yeah, I see the sign now and not before time."

Steve must have rose on his wrong side or maybe he was just missing the attention of the lovely Tracy.

"This is some place." Gregg commented as they entered the packed lounge to the reception desk.

"Can I see your Platinum credit card or your Business Class ticket?" The young lady with the olive complexion, dark brown eyes and swept back jet-black hair enquired. The sand colored tunic and white collard open neck shirt didn't do her justice but her warm smile and perfect English made up for the deficiency.

"Sure." Steve replied returning the smile. "Gregg, do have your seat tab handy?"

"Yeah, I got it."

"Thank you?" Aida smiled glancing at the tab.

"Oh, and the restroom?"

"Just to the left of the bar counter."

"Shukraan." Steve replied, a flash of Arabic. Unimpressed as Aida went about her business.......

* * *

The restroom was uncannily busy, it seemed like the Camels were the only 'ships of the desert' when it comes holding their urine, fortunately there was a separate shower room with open lockers.

"Thank God. I didn't fancy bearing 'all' in front of the 'peeing fraternity', you can never tell with these Arabs."

"Cut the crap and let's get changed or our Cab driver will be deserting us!"

"I'm taking a shower first, I feel like shit."

"I think I'll join you."

"In the same shower! *Now you tell me!*"

Gregg shook his head as he started to undress. *"I give up..."*

"What do you call these baggy white linen trousers again?" Steve was laughing in the process of slipping into his Arab 'Pierre Cardines'.

"Sirwals... But I love these deep pockets, you can hide all sorts of stuff in them... *Now, before you ask,* this long loose white shirt is the Kaffia. Listen, I thought you were supposed to memories all this stuff?"

"Not when I have the 'Brains of America' as a partner! Now how do I look?"

Steve was fully dressed right down to the 'Jesus Sandals' all that was left was the cottoned red and white checkered head dress, the 'Ghutra' and the 'Igal' the black rope like cord to hold it in place.

Gregg couldn't stop laughing.

"So, what's so funny." Steve asked more than annoyed.

"You look like fucking 'Lawrence of Arabia'."

"Yeah, yeah… Now, who's the fucking joker?"

"I'll toss you for that later! Are we all set?"

"I feel like a fucking extra in a movie set."

"Well move your ass and don't keep the Camel waiting, we still have to change our Dollars…...."

* * *

The dust and the stale smoked air coming from the cab drivers sitting at their small road side tables energetically puffing their Shishas was lung congesting. while waiting for a fare.

"Hold it Steve, we gotta find this cab. Let's just look casual."

"Easier said than done, hell, there's at least thirty old heap Mercedes lined up."

*"Let's see…*Yellow number plates with the letter 'P' is our baby, but where do we start?" Gregg was scanning the column.

"Syarat ajruh?" (taxi) Came the repetitive call as the two stalked the rank.

"There it is Gregg… P 1376."

"Yeah, I see it but let's not be too hasty… "As-Salaam-Alaikum."

The cab driver stared for a second scrutinizing his potential fares from head to toe.

"Wa- Salaam-Alaikum." He offered his hand then touched his heart…. (Arabic to English)

"This airport should have been named after…?" Steve commented in anguish waiting for the password.

"Golda Meir." The cab driver answered.

Steve reciprocated. "Golda Meir." A broad smile crossed the Cabby's face.

"Aismak? Yunkin yu sabayik al'injlizia?" (Your name? Can you speak English?)

"Yes, and you can call me Abbad. That's my Arab name, enough said." He smiled touching his lips. Steve and Gregg understood as they had previously been informed their driver was a Mossad Agent and of course Jewish so they were in good hands.

Abbad opened the trunk of the antique Mercedes. "Your bags?"

"Sure." Steve and Gregg obliged.

"Now let's get on the first leg of our journey to Erez." Abbad opened the rear door.

"How much do we owe you." Steve asked.

Abbad smiled. "For the United States, this one's on Israel."

"Ntin" (Hebrew for thank you)

Abbad smiled again as he slipped the stock switch into drive. "It's good you can still speak our language…."

* * *

The three lane 'Highway 4' to Erez was in remarkably good condition although dusty with a few sand drifts. The heavy sixteen-wheel trucks weaving in and out of their slow-moving counterparts, as if competing in the 'Le Mans' their air drafts scary, almost blasting passenger cars out of their lanes.

"How far to the checkpoint, Abbad?" Steve asked.

"Around 73K, but with this old Merc, an hour and a half. She's still in good shape but at her age I don't want to push my luck. *We've no 'road side assist here!'* Abbad laughed with Steve and Gregg joining.

"You both look tired I suggest you take a nap. I'll call you around 15 minutes before we reach the check point."

"Yeah I think that's a good suggestion… Gregg? There was no answer, his eyes already closed…

"Fadi, we are almost here." Abbad called slowing down. *"Fadi, wake up."*

Steve stirred, it's never a good idea to have an afternoon nap as when you waken up you always feel the worse… *Fadi… Fadi…*He could hear the name echoing in his ears… *Who the hell is Fadi?"*

"Fadi…Fadi?" It was still not registering. *Then it struck him siting bolt upright.* "My apologies Abbad, for a moment there."

"Don't worry, new names, I can understand, I have the same problem. You had best waken your partner, we're here."

Abbad pulled into the carpark. "You should have no problem our agents are fully versed and waiting your arrival. I'll go fetch your bags" Abbad pressed the trunk release.

"Imad, for Christ sakes waken up!" Steve gave Gregg a solid nudge.

"Imad…? What the hell! Err… yeah, Fadi…" Fetching instant laughter at Gregg's de ja vu.

"Man, you're something else." Steve was still laughing.

"Thanks, Abbad for everything. If ever you come to the states, we owe you one."

"Don't shake hands it's too western but who knows I might just take you up on that." Abbad smiled. "I pray for your safety."

"Shukraan……"

* * *

The barrier open, it was now the last leg of their journey by cab to Gaza City. Taxis at the Erez cab rank on the Palestine side were lined up in a single row with easy visibility to their number palates all yellow with the prefix letter 'P'.

"There's our man he's signaling to us?" Steve pointed.

"Yeah but let's not be too hasty. In this environment, I wouldn't trust a llama."

"Sayarat 'arjuh?" (taxi) The driver signaled again.

"Shukraan." Steve replied trying to find a conversational line to the password which would be difficult and he had no alternative but to take the gamble. If it was a mistake, nothing lost.

"As-Salaam-Alaikum… Golda Meir."

The young driver gave a warm smile before replying. "Wa- Salaam-Alaikum… Golda Meir… I speak English, my name is Isam. Please give me your bags as I would like to depart as soon as possible. We are drawing unwanted attention from the other drivers as to why you selected my Taxi from the long que and I don't blame them after waiting so long for a fare."

"Makes sense." Gregg exclaimed anxious to be on his way.

Isam didn't spare the horses, his rear wheels raising a tornado of dust as he accelerated from the car park. The 12-kilometer journey would only take twenty minutes and another mountain to climb.

"How do I call you?" Isam asked.

"You can call me Fadi and my partner Imad."

"Fadi, once we reach Gaza Central I will drive you to the safe house in the Rimal district, Down Town. You can stay there as long as you wish but my suggestion would be to relocate to one of our few hotels where there is more opportunity to contact the Gaza community."

"I might just take your advice Isam once we settle in overnight and take the lay of the land."

As for Gregg, he was quietly staring out the rear window taking in the local scenery and severe poverty. Small shop lots and road side café's in dusty pot holed streets littered with throwaway garbage, the odd donkey and cart struggling on two flat tires, the old man in peasant clothes perched on top using a whip as an incentive for the stubborn mule carrying hay and sundries to the local shops as he uttered oaths trying to avoid young shoeless kids kicking a bamboo football, illiteracy high on their agenda. A big difference from "The Hill' but maybe they had something that was better than 'I' phones and TV dinners, that something called happiness!

The dust cloud dispersed as the Mercedes negotiated a tight corner of the narrow street slowing down to avoid the crisscross of the 150cc Suzuki motor cycles, the preferred mode of transport accommodating at least two adults and two children.

"Isam." Gregg broke the silence. "These houses decorated in alternate layers of red and white masonry are unusual, I've never seen this before?"

"Yes, these are a legacy from the Albac period originating from Romanian settlers who decorated their houses in this style."

"Hmmm... Interesting. You learn something every day."

"Another few minutes and we'll reach our destination."

The Mercedes came to dusty halt in front of a two-story dust laden white masonry building, its narrow open passageway leading to a back courtyard with several apartments situated in a square.

"Here we are gentleman... For your general information, the Rimal district is not far from the City Center and the Square of the Unknown Soldier. This is Abdel Nasser Street named after Egypt's President, Abdel Nasser Hussein who of course Nationalized the Suez Canal and formed the United Arab Republic with Syria, leading to Egypt's defeat by Israel in the infamous 'six-day war'. He was an ardent supporter of the Palestine cause, hence the street named in his honor. He died from a heart attack at 59 in 1970. Useless trivia but taught in our history class."

"No, it's interesting. In the United States, we are rather insular to the rest of the world and its geography." Gregg remarked.

Isam opened the trunk. "Grab your bags gentlemen and follow me through to the courtyard."

The heavy Moroccan Antique carved door, its doorframe in ornate wood and iron was a work of art and Isam paused for a moment to survey the open courtyard before knocking four times then pausing before another two.

"Kallamah alssrr?" Came the muffled voice. (password)

"Golda Meir."

(Arabic to English)

The heavy door creaked cautiously open only to be met by a middle aged greying haired man his smile saying it all as he hugged Isam.

"My son, I'm always happy to see you home safe and sound."

"Thank you, father. These are the gentlemen from the United States Central Intelligence Agency whom Shin Bet requested our help with temporary accommodation and the supply of weapons and ammunition."

"And you are?" He turned to Steve offering his hand.

"Fadi Bishara and…" Steve paused embarrassingly having problems getting his tongue around their new names.

"Imad Halabi." Gregg cut in.

"You are both welcome in my home." Then a thought crossed his mind. "But you must be tired after your long journey. I suggest you relax and join our family at the dinner table as we are about to have our evening meal… "Of course, you now know Isam is my son." He grinned. "But then you have still to meet my daughter and my lovely wife who are busy in the kitchen preparing the food… *Azra… Amini… We have guests from America…*"

"*Coming.*" The clatter of kitchen utensils suddenly silenced.

The two rather beautiful ladies dressed in colorful Abayas their olive skin and oil-black hair and those mystic brown olive shaped eyes painted a picture of the by gone days and the 'Magic Carpet', entered the lounge, their warm smiles contagious.

"My wife Amini and daughter Azra, Isam's younger sister."

"I's so nice to meet you and our sincere thanks for your generous hospitality." Steve was playing the gentleman.

"You must excuse us or you'll go hungry tonight." Ami smiled pulling Azra by the hand to break her hypnotized stare.

"You have a lovely family… *Eh?*"

"Anwar… Anwar Saraaf."

"Anwar."

"*Come,* take your seats at the table, the food will be served shortly, in the meantime we can enjoy traditional Arabic tea……."

* * *

The food was traditional 'Middle Eastern', a pleasant change from 'Starbucks's Coffee' and whoppers at 'Burger King'. Azra was the main distraction her natural beauty and intellect difficult to ignore.

"And you are both of the Jewish faith?" Anwar asked intrigued.

"Yes, and of course Imad and I are fluent in both Hebrew and Arabic."

"I *have* noticed." Anwar smiled.

"But like you we adopt Arab names. Jews are not the most popular in Palestine and Gaza."

"I *can* understand." Gregg replied. "But I'm intrigued… The 'safe house'… Israelis in Gaza…?"

"Let me explain. The 'safe house' is a misnomer, this was a directive from the top to provide support and assistance to the American CIA in a joint undercover operation to search and eliminate a potential terrorist attack by Hamas. We have confirmed information that Hamas's objective is to annihilate the Knesset with a Russian built short range ballistic missile, the Scarab SS21b. Shin Bet has already passed this information on to your superiors. You may well ask where do I and my family fit in? My son and my daughter and I are highly trained members of our special antiterrorist unit the Sayerat Matakal with which I am sure you are familiar. We operate under the cover of my taxi business to provide intelligence on rocket facilities and arms supply from Egypt and Iran. Although Gaza City has a population of 1.8 million it is really a big village where everyone knows your business and by the grace of God we have managed to stay under the radar and that is why I must ask you to relocate to a local hotel as soon as is reasonably possible as you can imagine two strangers arriving in Gaza, especially from the United States, is dangerous."

"Anwar your country should be proud of you and please understand Imad and I don't underestimate the risks you are taking. One night is sufficient and perhaps you can recommend on appropriate hotel?"

"Don't worry, Isam will drive you there tomorrow. I will provide you with a special phone number to keep in contact or if you need our immediate assistance."

"Thank you." Gregg interjected.

"What information do we have now? Azra perhaps you can bring Imad and Fadi up to speed?"

She smiled and began. "Anbar, Abdul Fattah's son arrived a few days ago. I know this because I have purposely become friendly with Amar Taafeef the son of the owner of the famous "Taafeef Bakery'. Anbar and Amir are the same age and boyhood friends having graduated at the same local university 'Al Azhar'. Now where does Taafeef's father fit in? Our intelligence sources have confirmed that Amar is a member of the council of the armed wing of Hamas and a close confidant of the man himself, Abdul Fattah. The plot thickens. Now here's the kicker… Amir his son has asked me to join him for coffee tomorrow evening accompanied with his friend Anbar and I want you to chaperon me as two old friends who have just arrived in Gaza on business and whom I became friends with while studying at the University of Michigan."

"That would be an excellent start." Steve turned to Gregg.

"Father, I think the Roots Hotel on the Strip in Al Rashad Street overlooking the beech would be a good choice to meet locals contacts. It has a good restaurant and coffee house."

"I agree, then that's it settled. Now that our stomachs are full Azra will show you to your room."

"Thank you but before we retire I wish to thank your lovely wife Amani for that excellent dinner……"

* * *

Being a guest in a stranger's house especially in a foreign country can be uncomfortable to say the least and for the two CIA agents it was no different.

"Sharing a room with you man is something else. Do you know you are a snorer?"

"If you say so." Gregg laughed. "Are you finished in that washroom yet?"

"Cold water from a tub with a ladle, *are you fucking kiddin me?"*

"Stop gripping, they're calling us for breakfast."

"Thank God I don't have to shave." Steve was chuckling to himself.

"It's about time." Gregg grabbed his towel and brushed past the streaker. "I don't wanna look, that grotesque sight would give me nightmares…."

* * *

"These Arab get ups are not too bad in this climate. Loose and airy." Steve commented finally slipping into his sandals

"Yeah, but we can't run around in one outfit for the rest of the duration or we'll be smelling like something other than the roses."

"Heh… Heh… Look on the bright side, maybe Azra can take us shopping?"

"Wishful thinking, huh?"

"Listen, I caught you staring at that beautiful creature."

"Was it *so* obvious?"

"What do you think I was doing?" Steve laughed.

"Enough of the wise cracks let's go down for breakfast."

"Hang on. How do I look and don't give me that Lawrence of Ariba shit!" Steve was admiring himself in the mirror.

"*Heh…Heh… Heh,* you took the words right out of my mouth…...."

* * *

"As-Salaam-Alaikum."

"Wa- Salaam-Alaikum." Anwar reciprocated. *"Please."* He pointed to the large cushions placed around the knee-high table. "Pour yourself some tea, my wife and daughter will join us in a few minutes. *"Amani… Azra,* come join us…"

"This food is excellent compliments to the chef."

"Thank you." Amani blushed. "It's very simple food."

"Anwar." Gregg changed the subject Steve's kowtowing becoming more than embarrassing. "I hate to further exploit your generous hospitality but Fadi and I have only one set of clothing and…"

A smile crossed Azra's face and before her father could answer. "Father may I suggest?"

Anwar nodded his approval for his daughter to speak. Israeli parent protocol is an essential part of the family culture.

"I can accompany Imad and Fadi to their hotel and once they have checked in take them to the local Souq and your favorite tailor."

"Azra… If it's not too much bother!" Steve interrupted.

"Imad." Anwar raised his hand. "The decision is made. Now let me refresh your tea." He leaned over with the large brass Dallah tea pot.

"Have you finished packing?" Isam asked.

"Yes, were done." Gregg replied.

"Then as soon as you finish I'll go fetch the car."

"In that case, I had better go and get changed father. Can I leave the table?" Azra requested.

Anwar nodded. "You may." Then he turned to Steve and Gregg. "I don't want to push but there is one other thing I must attend to, perhaps you can follow me to the other room?"

The room looked like any typical family room, TV, couches, scattered cushions and a finely knotted large Arabic rug.

"Imad, perhaps you can oblige me by rolling the rug, my back is not as youthful as it used to be."

Steve smiled. "I'm glad I can make myself useful sir."

And there it was! A two by four flush wooden trapdoor.

"Can you do the needful?" Anwar pointed to the steel rings and Steve and Gregg immediately obliged opening the heavy wooden lid only to expose an arsenal of automatic and semiautomatic weapons, including ammunition.

"My suggestion is the Glock 45 caliber double action with a 10-clip magazine." Anwar was holding the polymer grip. "Feels good though I say so myself. I'm sure you are familiar with this weapon in the CIA?"

"Yes, it's our weapon of choice." Gregg replied.

"Then please…" He pointed. "Unfortunately, I can only supply you with three clips each."

Steve smiled. "I think that should be enough Imad, don't you? Unless we are planning to start another 'six-day war'."

Even Anwar had to laugh at Steve's comment, a source of pride for the Israeli Military……

* * *

"Al Rashad Street is a bit of a drive from here say… Twenty minutes but it will give you a chance to see some of the city." Azra commented with a smile accompanying her brother in the front of cab. One would never read her as a trained assassin for the 'Sayerat Matakal'.

"I know you're not here on vacation." Azra continued. "But at this time of the year this hotel is very popular because of its spectacular location on the water front and the view overlooking Gaza Harbor to the Mediterranean. In US values, it would probably rank four-star but five stars in this part of the world."

"In our line of work Azra, we can't be choosers." Gregg was conversing.

"You Americans." She laughed.

Azra was on the money, narrow dusty streets then four lane avenues and high-rise buildings, undeniable poverty one the one hand and affluence on the other, but is it any different from Detroit?

"Here we are." Imad hung a right then climbed a steep gradient to a plateaued car park facing the facade of what resembled a hotel in the Swiss Alps with its peeked roof line and heavy dark wooden facings on a background of sand colored cement cladding. Low rise with only 60 rooms on three floors boutique style would certainly be a change from the Sheraton or sleazy 'Drive Inns'.

"I think I'm gonna like this place, it's certainly different." Steve opened the cab door to the dry 28-degree heat.

"I'm glad you like it, it's ranked as number two of the seven hotels in Gaza City *but wait till you see inside!*" Azra was energizingly leading the way to the hotel foyer, the Bell Hops already at the car collecting the luggage.

"I see what you mean Azra." Steve stopped in his tracks for a moment admiring the rich flecked grey marbled walls and the large oak stained wooden reception desk. On the back drop in two-foot beautifully carved brush script lettering Roots Hotel. To the left was a relaxation area with plush white leather seating and glass topped coffee tables pronounced on the mirror polished white marble flooring. It was certainly a piece of work!

"Checking in?" The bearded male receptionist enquired.

"Yes." Steve replied.

"Passports or ID's please."

"That's for… Misters Imad Halabi and Fadi Bishara?" He was studying the passports.

"Two rooms for what duration?"

"My colleague and I are here on business can we leave that open ended."

"I'm afraid not sir as the busy season is coming up and I need a departure date."

"*Hmmm…?*" Steve turned to Gregg. "Four weeks?"

Gregg nodded it was not up for open discussion.

"Two adjoining rooms… Let me see?" He was studying the computer screen. "22A and 23B. The room rate is 110US dollars per night or 398INS in including breakfast. Can I have your credit cards please to take a print?"

"We would rather pay in in full."

The receptionist was taken aback. *Cash in this day and age!*

"It's highly unusual sir, just bear with me for a moment to consult my manager."

Steve just shrugged.

The receptionist was back in a second. "Yes, that will be fine but you must pay in cash for any other services. Let me see 28 days… That will be 3,080 Us Dollars each."

Steve opened his brief case making sure the Glock was out of sight shelling six big ones and two one hundred bills. "Give the change to the Bell Hops."

"Certainly sir… These are your room keys… The lifts are to your right… floor 2."

"Shukraan."

"Azra… Imad I can't thank you enough.' Steve was at his best. "But tonight, you haven't mentioned the pickup time?"

Azra turned to her brother.

"Say around 7:30?"

"Is 7:30 then in the lobby." Azra gave that smile…...

* * *

Steve knocked on the adjoining room door. "Are you decent?"

"Yeah." Gregg yelled stretched out on the bed after taking a short nap and glancing at his watch…Hmmmm that time already… Come on through it's unlocked."

"There's no point in raiding the bar fridge." Steve grumbled grabbing a chair while Gregg flung his feet to the floor. *That's unless you want a coke!... Man,* you look like shit."

"Yeah, and I feel like it. I haven't showered yet." Gregg rubbed his eyes resting on the side of the bed.

"Well at least we have a change of clothing!"

"That's something… Man, your BO was operation 'Gaza city'."

Steve laughed. "Im getting worried about you with these wisecracks, your stealing my thunder."

That brought a smile to Gregg's face. "That wouldn't be difficult… Changing the subject, what do you think of Azra?"

"She's a looker alright and with the personality to match. But being a highly-trained operative of the Anti-Terrorist Unit the 'Sayerat Matakal' I wouldn't like to get on her wrong side."

"Now there's a thought. I tell you Steve I was taken aback by that market."

"You mean the Souq?"

"Whatever turns you on… *smart ass!*"

"I guess your gonna raise the gold merchant thing?"

"On the money! It's hard to believe that Gaza is reported to be unlivable by 2020 according to the UN Conference on Trade if the current economic trend continues as the result of the decade long Israeli blockade. Food shortages health problems and overcrowding… I mean, you gotta be kidding me! I've never seen so much gold not to mention the stacked fruit and meat stalls."

"Heh… Heh." Steve burst into laughter. "There's more gold there than Fort Knox."

"But joking aside… Our meeting this evening?"

"Like, how do we play it?"

"Firstly, it's gonna be strange meeting Anbar Salibe or more to the point Anbar Fattah in the flesh after 'catch me if you can,' half way around the world."

"So, we stick to our plan as wealthy sympathizers for the Palestine 'Two State solution' with East Jerusalem as their new capital and the recovery of the land lost by Jordan in the 1967 war."

"But what does that really mean Steve?"

"Good question… The sales pitch is we have contacts in Congress and the Senate and John Kerry to champion there cause in the UN. We also have access to the best legal brains and financial support from 'The Arab League of America'."

"It might wash…. Anyhow we must give it our best shot…" Gregg paused in thought. "If only we could get the 'loyalty ticket' to meet with Fattah and members of the armed wing."

"I'll let you do the talking or its boots were made for walkin. Remember anyone who isn't confused doesn't really understand the situation." Steve grinned waiting for the applause.

"Hell Steve, can't you be serious for one minute…! *Don't answer,* I'm off to shower… Enjoy your coke…..."

* * *

"Anbar, I'm sure we are on the same wave length. Am I correct in thinking Faraj Dahara?"

"He's got the boat father and he's a respected member of the council."

"But can his vessel accommodate these two containers."

"It's one of the biggest, if not the biggest in the fishing fleet. I'm not an expert father but from what I know Seiner fishing vessels are named after the Seiners trawling boom nets for shallow surface fishing for sardines and white bait. Their hulls are constructed with Aini and Teak and at least thirty meters in length and I believe they still use the Indian Ashok Leyland 12-cylinder 300 horse power diesel reaching 15 nots. It carries 800 liters of fuel to easily reach the six-mile limit and back. If my memory serves me right the hold capacity is around 140 cubic meters, more than plenty."

"Amar, I think my son just gave us a lesson on fishing vessels." Abdul sported a proud smile,

"Father, you are forgetting that when I was sixteen I worked on uncle Dahara's boat to earn money for my education."

"I almost forgot!"

"You have a good boy here, Abdul."

"And don't I know it!" Abdul's smile prolonged.

"Then that's settled. We'll bring Faraj from out of the cold when the security council meet next week but there's one other point we haven't covered and that's getting the containers ashore and transporting them to an improvised launch pad? There are number of air vents in the 'Terror Tunnel' network that we use for rocket fire into the West Bank settlements which *could* be utilized."

"That's a good point Abdul but I'm sure Anbar has left no stone unturned."

"Anbar?" Abdul turned to his son in anticipation.

"There's the old saying father, 'keep it simple, simple'." Abdul frowned turning to his baker friend who was also wrestling with Anbar's comment.

"Simple, you hit the button, father. We utilize the 'terror tunnels'… I'm sure you must have the latest diagrams on the tunnel network?"

"Makes sense." Abdul nodded. "But we've had a serious setback which has been well published in the Israel and International media…" Abdul paused a thought crossing his mind. "Of course, Anbar you weren't to know most likely being in Japan that we've had a disastrous few months as Shin Bet in a joint exercise with the IDF decommissioned over thirty tunnels after capturing that traitor Ibrahim Shaer who opened his big mouth and spilled the beans on our main tunnel system from Rafa to the Karem Shalom crossing on the Egyptian border."

"How bad?"

"It's not the end of the world so to speak. We've been working day and night and reopened the remainder of the shore tunnel running 5 kilometers from the water front and Gaza harbor below the old Aybaki Mosque and straight to the border crossing at Erez."

"Is there access to the tunnel from the mosque?" Anbar's mind was racing it seemed too good to be true.

"Yes, and well hidden. The IDF would think twice before searching our holy place of worship."

"This is perfect. We unload the containers onto a fish truck at the dock camouflaged with ice and the nights catch using the Seiner's deck crane. Then under darkness we manually unload the containers down the nearest air hatch of the shore tunnel then store them below the mosque."

"But the weight?" Amar asked.

"Each container is around 500Kg, four able bodied men could easily roll them off the truck then use the truck's winch to lower them down the air hatch… Father?"

"As the English say, 'the proof of the pudding is in the eating'."

"Heh… Heh… Heh." Amar laughed at Abdul's summation. "You're a cunning old dog."

"So, what *do you* think father?"

"I think we call it a night. Anbar, you must be beat after your long flight. Your room is still as it was, except for your brother… Allah be with him." For a moment Abdul's voice froze at the thought of his lost son Fadile and his eyes glazed over. "Eh… Err… Excuse me… *Amar.*" He turned to his friend. "Stay for a while and share some tea over the Hookah and reminisce old times, I have rare Al Fakher tobacco smuggled from Cairo."

"Good night father."

"Asha, can you fetch some fresh tea for Amar and me……?"

THE GAZA TUNNELS

The smuggling tunnels in the Gaza Strip are illegal Hamas dug tunnels connecting both sides of the Gaza Egypt border used to bypass the Rafa border crossing. In 1993 after Israel had withdrawn from the Sanai was the first discovery of the tunnels when the border was redrawn in 1982 after the Egypt Israel Peace Treaty divided Rafa and Egypt into an Egyptian and Gazan territory. The tunnels from the basements of houses in Rafa on the one side of the border and end in Erez on the other side. The Gaza Strip blockade resulted in a shortage of construction materials, agricultural necessities, food, medicines, clothes and car parts etc. and only eventually became a serious threat to Israel's security when Hamas began smuggling money and arms and in 2013 there were more than 1,300 tunnels running under the border to mitigate the effect of the blockade on Gaza and the hail of Iran supplied terror rockets upon the Israeli population and something had to be done……

THE MEETING

"You Took your time." Steve was grumping as usual.

"Did you enjoy your coke from the bar fridge?" Gregg was laughing as he slipped into his Sirwal before the pulling the Kaffia over his head. "Hmmm that feels better. I gotta hand it to these Arabs, natural air conditioning."

"Get out of it…" Steve stared at the empty bottle. "This shit that's meant to resemble coke, *I tell you!*" Chucking the empty into the garbage can.

Gregg checked the magazine clip and the safety on the Glock before pulling up his Kaffia and placing it in the deep pocket of his Sirwal.

"Beats the office suits huh?"

"Cut the shit… Do you know the time?" Steve was showing his colors.

"Keep your shirt on, *its only just turned seven twenty!"* Gregg slipped into his Jesus sandals. "Here gimme a hand with this miniature red and white table checkered table cloth."

"Man, your something else." Steve firmly placed the black rope cord Igal over the Ghutra to hold it in place.

Gregg smiled as he glanced in the wall mirror. "Pity we can't send a selfie to Hanna, now wouldn't that be something?"

Just then the phone rang.

"Don't answer it Steve we know who it is. Come on lets head to the elevator, we can't keep a lady waiting… God, I feel such an asshole dressed like this." Gregg commented.

The laughter was spontaneous as the 'born again' Arabs stepped it out to the elevator.…

* * *

"Amir, I think there's more to it than meets the eye with this Azra."

"So, you noticed, Anbar" Amir had that boyish grin.

Anbar, well… he just laughed. "How could I not, you have never stopped talking about her since we got into the car."

"Just wait till you see her, she is absolutely stunning."

"Do you have reservations Sir?" The Maître D' asked at the reception desk.

"Yes, for Amir Taafeef, a table overlooking the harbor."

"Hmmm…?" He ran his finger down the reservation list. *"Ah,* here we are." He raised his arm and snapped his fingers. "Abbad escort these gentlemen to table 16."

"How did you manage to reserve a table at The Lighthouse?" Anbar asked

"When you father makes the best bread in Gaza…?"

"Say no more." Anbar smiled taking his seat whilst glancing at his watch. "What time did you say? It's almost seven forty now!"

"Seven thirty, you know what they say about a 'woman's privilege' but joking aside she's most likely late due to the traffic."

"So, tell me a bit about the beautiful Azra, I'm intrigued."

"Not much really. She is a regular customer at my father's bakery hence where I met her. Comes from a prominent and respected Sunni family with the largest taxi company in Gaza."

"Drinks sir?" Abbad enquired breaking the third degree.

"Iced water to start, we are waiting for another guest." Amir replied.

"Shukraan, it will only take a few minutes." Abbad disappeared.

Anbar seemed to relax for a moment losing his inquisition whilst staring into the harbor and the sound of the Mediterranean Sea, the cool breeze on the roof top exhilarating.

"You know Amar, although I have been away from Gaza for a few years this restaurant still remains as I imagined it. I know it has been damaged in reprisal shelling's by the IDF but Mohammed Abu Mathkour the owner and a close friend of my father has done a remarkable job of restoration…."

THE LIGHTHOUSE RESTAURANT

In a territory plagued with chronic power shortages, poverty and scarcity of construction materials, this restaurant defies all the rules. The restaurant is well lit, the only negative the constant hum of the diesel generators. The tables are crowded and hard to come by and only for the few that can afford the luxury of restaurant food and one of the only places in Gaza to rebound and relax. The story of 'Level Up' is in many ways the story of Gaza. Its location on the top level of a high-rise complex is stunning and when nightfall descends upon the City the glittering lights of 'Level Up' seem to be the only bright spot in the darkened sky symbolizing the short-lived hopes for prosperity in this crowded seaside territory and providing a rare bright spot in a wrecked and darkened Gaza……

* * *

"Now, where was I?" Anbar was anxious to get back on track with the mysterious Azra.

"Sorry Anbar you'll have to save it for later, here she is now… *But who…?* She never told me she was bringing company."

"I gotta hand it to you Amar she *is* beautiful…."

* * *

At 5-8 Azar's slim figure was hidden in a sheer silk purple high necked Kebaya with gold threaded embroidery in traditional Arabic design to match her long-sleeved rimmed gold cuffs. Her dark brown olive eyes brushed in a pale matching eyeshade emphasized her long black lashes, her hair almost hidden by a lighter purple shade Hijab draping past her forehead and around

543

her shoulders. The gold leather high heeled sandals enveloped her dainty feet exposing her crimson painted toenails to match her manicured fingers. The Chenille black patterned hand bag and gold laced shoulder strap was the 'Fait Accompli' her beauty the envy of the other male diners, she could easily be the next face on 'Vouge' magazine….

* * *

"My apologies Amir but the traffic…"

"Apologies accepted."

"And this is?" Her eyes turned to Anbar.

"My boyhood friend from our university years at 'Al Azhar'. After graduation Anbar and his brother departed for further studies in the United States. In fact, he just returned to Gaza a few days ago after spending time in Japan."

"Anbar Fattah, it's my pleasure. "As-Salaam-Alaikum." Anbar touched his heart with his right hand.

"And…?" Amir turned to Steve and Gregg with a sliver of annoyance in his voice. "You never mentioned…?"

"Again, my apologies Amir, this was a last-minute decision on my behalf as my friends just arrived yesterday from the United States and what better to show them some Gaza hospitality over dinner at the best restaurant in town."

"Imad Halabi and Fadi Bishara." Steve broke the tension with the traditional greeting. "As-Salaam-Alaikum."

"Wa- Salaam-Alaikum." It's our pleasure. Please take your seats."

Abbad quickly obliged sliding back the lady's chair.

It was time for Amir to ask the obvious. "So, tell me Azra, where did you meet your friends?"

"We met while studying at the University of Chicago. It's not easy to find Sunnis and when you are in a strange country and more so Christian, we immediately hit it off and became good friends and have kept in touch ever since our graduation. Imad and Fadi always promised that one day they would visit my home country so you can imagine the surprise when they turned up unannounced on my doorstep?"

"Interesting." Anbar was quietly absorbing Azra's explanation. In Gaza, it pays to be cautious. Mossad's secret Service and the CIA often work together at the request of Taman Pardo the director of Shin Bet whose bed mate James Comey, the worst kept secret.

But Steve's intuition told him that Anbar was uncomfortable with the dinner crashers and was heading for the lie detector only without the hardware and he had to go on the offensive.

"Amir, mentioned you had just arrived from Japan, business I presume?"

"No, as a tourist taking a break on my way home. Japan has an interesting culture; the West should take a leaf from their book. No… It's a country I have always wanted to visit."

Amir was becoming obviously uncomfortable with the slight tension in the air and the last thing he wanted was to scare off the love of his life and a diversion was a necessity.

"Listen, why don't I order drinks to start with to cool our parched throats in this humid temperature, then we can relax over a nice dinner and carry on with our 'get to know'."

"Sounds good Amir." Gregg cut to the chase and Azra breathed a sigh of relief.

"Abbad can you fetch the menu, Shukraan?"

"*Hmmm…* These drinks bring back fond memories." Anbar commented studying the menu. "But so many new ones maybe Azra can help us decide?"

"I can only speak for myself… Let me see… I'll have a Karkadeh on ice."

"Good choice, I like Hibiscus… Now for me… I'll have red Sobia."

"Amir, you must have a sweet tooth." Azra was trying to lighten it up.

"I like the taste of the coconut milk and the powdered rice and sugar…" Amir laughed. "Kids love it, I guess I still haven't grown up."

"And for me… I'm a sucker for dates and grape molasses in iced rose water… Azra you should try it."

"Next time maybe."

Steve and Gregg were still struggling, nonalcoholic drinks were not their forty.

"I think I had better rescue my friends… Now my suggestion would be… *Ah,* here we are…The most popular drink during Ramadan… Karkade 3enab or better known as hibiscus tea, chilled, it's delicious."

"Then that's it settled, make that for two." Gregg was pleased Azra had come to the rescue.

"*Eh…Err…* I'll fetch these drinks immediately sir." Abbad looked wet behind the ears trying to memories the order. Maybe it was his first job, work for young people in Gaza is scarcer than 'hen's teeth'.

The tension eased Anbar was back in play.

"I must compliment your friends Azra as having lived in the US all their lives their lives their Arabic is excellent."

It was time and Steve interjected. "Our parents made it compulsory that we learn Arabic and when you are child I'm sure you agree its second nature to pick up two languages. Once a Palestinian always a Palestinian, our fathers taught us to never forget our roots."

"And your parents?"

"Both Palestinians of course… Immigrated to the United States during the British rule and Imad and I are both naturalized American citizens. But Amir mentioned that you and your brother studied in the United States?"

"Yes, at Cornell University."

"If you don't mind me asking?" Steve was purposely placing Anbar on the back foot."

"Excuse me your drinks." Abbad was standing like the 'Statue of Liberty'.

"You can serve them now." Amir instructed, a timely intervention. "While you're here Abbad it would be opportune to order our food. Have you any preferences? Anbar how about you?"

"You're the host, it's your call… I'm hopeless at ordering restaurant food."

"Hmmm… We'll start with some nice bread and dips."

"You're the expert in that field Amir." Azra was quick on her feet.

"Don't rub it in." Amir laughed… "Okay where was I…? Pita and Khabuz bread, most probably supplied by my father and with a Hummus dip… *Eh… Ah…* Let me see…The deep-fried chicken legs dressed in thinly sliced hot green peppers lemon and garlic look appetizing and… The clay pot baked lamb and finally Egyptian Koshari rice with macaroni."

"Amir, are you sure we can finish all this food?" Azra asked. "Im trying to watch my figure and you're wicked." Her comment fetching much needed laughter.

"Anbar getting back to our discussion. Cornell is one of best Universities in the United States next to Harvard and only the best is accepted, *that is if you are even lucky enough!* So, naturally I'm interested in your prospectus?"

Anbar was decidedly uncomfortable with Steve's line of questioning pausing for a moment to decide where to cut the ambilocal or weather the storm.

"If you must know, graduating with honors in Aeronautics and Rocket Science."

"*Wow*…I'm impressed, that's gotta be one of the most difficult courses."

"The secret, is if you enjoy it, it comes easy, just like when we gained our commercial pilots licenses to fly passenger jets…"

"You did!"

"Don't worry we weren't planning another 9/11." Anbar expressed an ugly grin as if he enjoyed it.

"And your brother…? Is he still in the United States?" Gregg cut in giving Steve a breather.

"Fadile…?" Anbar dejectedly shook his head. Unfortunately, he met with a fatal accident…*Eh."* He almost choked on his words, his Adam's apple protruding. "Fadi… I'd rather not elaborate further as you can imagine it's a sensitive matter."

"My sincere condolences. I can't imagine the sorrow of losing a brother."

"You were not to know. Now on a lighter note let's enjoy this lovely food…..."

* * *

"I suggest we finish this enjoyable evening with what better than the sweet aroma of good Egyptian tobacco and cool smoke from the Hookah?"

"You men, how about the lady in the company?" Azra joked.

"Heh…Heh…" Amir laughed. "But you're so right. Can I entice you with one of the restaurants famous desserts?"

"Oh there goes my figure… My favorite is Kanafeh Cheesecake with nut fillings and cheese and ice cream on the side."

"Boy, does that sound good!" Steve couldn't let it go.

"It's a specialty dessert originating from Turkey and Egypt. You should try it. It has a creamy pudding like filling baked in a noodle pastry shell made from shredded phyllo mixed with Ghee then fired and drenched in sugar syrup transformed it into sweet crunchy golden strands of heaven."

"God, my taste buds are reneging but I'll take a pass and settle for the Hookah."

"Wise choice Imad." Anbar seemed more relaxed.

"Then let's retire to the smoke room and I'll go and order Azra's figure destroying 'strands of heaven'." Amir's comment fetching instant laughter. Maybe this was going to be an enjoyable evening after all…....

* * *

"You seem to be struggling Fadi?"

Azra was quietly taking in the harbor lights enjoying her favorite dessert and half smiling at Fadi chocking intermittently whilst inhaling the scented smoke from his Hookah and she could tell Gregg was embarrassed.

"*Ah… Keh… Keh… Ah… Hmmm…*" Gregg cleared his throat. "This is new to us although but it's becoming more popular in the United States challenging the 'no smoking' brigade. You can't smoke here you can't smoke there… I tell you it's becoming a 'nanny state'."

"*Heh… Heh…*It's called democracy gone crazy." Anbar exhaled a cloud of smoke like a volcano waiting to erupt.

"But I must admit being a nonsmoker I'm beginning to enjoy this new experience."

Anbar had nothing to lose and went straight to the jugular. "So, tell me Fadi, why you are *really* here in Gaza?"

There was a moment's silence or was it shock and Azra almost dropped her spoon but Gregg knew it as inevitable, after all Anbar is the son of Abdul Fattah the commander of the armed wing of Hamas and if you don't like it…

Gregg shot back. "I had a feeling you would get around to that, it was just a matter of time. Firstly, we genuinely wanted to catch up with our dear friend Azra."

Gregg had to make sure Azra's summation of their visit avoided any suspicion.

"But you're on the money it's both business *and* pleasure!"

"Let me expand on Imad's comment." Steve was champing at the bit to mix it. "As I stressed before, although we are naturalized American Citizens our DNA is Palestinian and we feel for the oppressed people of this proud nation. "So, you may ask? Lots of Palestinians living overseas feel the same so what's new? And I agree, but the difference is we feverishly believe in the "Two State" solution with Jerusalem as our rightful capital. But how can we help the 'Palestinian Cause'…? *Money!* Our parents are billionaire entrepreneurs in manufacturing and finance. Secondly, they have contacts in high places on 'Capitol Hill' such as John Kerry, Hillary Clinton and Samantha Power on the UN Security Council and the list goes on. In short lots of fire power and of course we would like to discuss peaceful opportunities with your father and the Armed Wing of Hamas."

"*Hmmmm…*" Anbar rubbed his bristled chin. "I'm sure you are talking from the heart but we don't need American interference in our master plan. We have plenty of foreign currency and can purchase sophisticated weaponry from any country in the world, especially our friend, Russia. As you say in America 'Money makes the world go around'. I said before we are not planning another 9/11, too many innocent lives were lost and our cause is different from Osama bin Laden's. No, our plan is much bigger and with catastrophic consequences waging war on the Israeli Government, so much so it will shock the world with our weapons capability. This will be the mother of all attacks and the UN Security Council will have no option but to force Israel to agree or more attacks will follow. I've said more than enough. As far as a meeting with my father and the armed wing, I will pass it by him, that's the best I can offer."

"Its early days and our first meeting although not intended for business, I apologize to Azra." Steve was back to being the gentleman and 'what women want'......

$$* \quad * \quad *$$

The engine idling, Isam was patiently waiting outside the restaurant to drive his sister home and her new-found allies back to their hotel.

"That was a long dinner." He commented as he jumped from the passenger seat to open the rear door of the Mercedes. "I just saw Fattah and Taafeef leaving, how did it go?"

"I'll tell you on the way home." Azra replied, her normal glowing smile elusive. "The guys can take the back and I'll join you in the front that way we can better relax and talk."

"If you say so sis." Isam hit the gas pedal a dust cloud following the big car.

"Well, I'm waiting?" Isam was showing his impatience, the long wait getting to him.

"Who starts?" Steve cut in.

"The one thing that was good was the food." Azra opened the page.

"And?"

"Watch your driving… If you must know, the dinner got off on the wrong footing because I never informed Amir that Imad and Fadi would be joining us."

"Jealous, huh?"

"Something like that. I'll let Fadi take up the chase."

"This guy Fattah was on the offensive before we even had our first mouthful, bombarding us with questions."

"Fadi, that's how it is in Gaza with new faces. No one trusts anyone these days."

"I guess we found out what we really knew already. His brother is deceased supposedly in an accident but we know he was shot and killed in fire fight with an FBI agent in Tokyo. Then he bragged about how wealthy Hamas was with stacks of foreign currency and weapons. The CIA is 100% sure that this is US currency from the lost Boeing 777 freighter, Global 10 off the coast of Japan. The aircraft was eventually located in a million pieces from a bomb blast but get this, no bodies and no cargo. Now, we know Anbar Fattaah was on that flight but the jury is still out. He continued to run off at the mouth that something catastrophic was in the pipe line so big that the UN Security Council would force the 'Two State" solution in fear of further retaliation. We know what that is! Our offer…? He didn't buy one thread of it but I guess we had a good idea it would go down the toilet. The one positive thing, that is if we can take him at his word, he promised he would pass our offer by his father."

"Here we are at your hotel." The brakes of the vintage Mercedes protesting with a loud squeal like a cat had been run over.

"Thanks, Azra for all you have done." This time it was Gregg playing the gentleman. "How do we get in touch?"

"Don't worry we'll contact *you*. You have the password and you have the phone number but only in a life or death situation. By the way I really enjoyed your company." Azra gave her warm smile. *"Good night……"*

* * *

For a moment, there was silence as Amir drove the Morris Minor through the dusty streets of Gaza City, the old British icon blending in well with the ancient whitewashed buildings and Isam finally broke the silence.

"I must hand it to you brother that Azra…! She is special and beautiful with it."

Amir smiled proudly. "I think so. I would like to ask her to dinner again but this time by ourselves."

"Im don't blame you. Two's company but three's a crowd. The two American Palestinians, where did they come from out of the woodwork?"

"Like you Anbar, I got a shock when they appeared."

"Do you believe Azra's explanation and more so theirs?"

"Azra I can take but the born-again Palestinians…? I wouldn't trust them as far as I could throw them."

"It looks like Amir we are on the same wave length, they could be CIA."

"*I…* Don't know, but to be safe if they suddenly disappear who cares?"

"Im with you, I'll have a word with father and…" Anbar laughed. *"Heh … Heh… Heh…*It'll get them out of your hair with Azra."

"Two birds with one stone, huh?"

"If you put it that way… Ah, here we are! I'll catch up with you tomorrow once you finish at the shop... Tusbih ealaa khayr bather……" (good night brother)

THE ENCOUNTER

"I could get used to this hotel life." Steve was enjoying his breakfast.

"I agree, but these get ups! I can't wait to slip into a pair of blue jeans."

"You had better get used to it Gregg, the way things are going we're gonna be here for some time."

"Yeah, I guess so, we didn't get off to a good start last night, did we?"

"It's early days… I think I'll have another Turkish coffee I'm getting a taste for it." Steve raised his hand to attract the waiter when suddenly his cell rang and he turned to Gregg. *"Now who could this be?* It can't be from the States so it must be from Azra… Shall I answer it…? It could be a trap."

Gregg shrugged. "It's gotta be something really serious if it's from Azra or her father to take the risk… Don't hang around answer it."

"Nem fielaan?" (yes)

"Golda Meir… Be careful there's a contract on you." Before Steve could grab a conversation, the phone went dead.

"You look a bit pale, come on out with it."

"There's a contract on us."

"You mean like a hit man?"

"Is there any other."

"So, who was on the phone?"

"A man, he gave the password then the message and hung up."

"Hmmm, do you think it's Hamas that wants to take us out?"

"Most likely, so we had better be extra vigilant. Somehow I don't think I feel like that coffee now……"

* * *

"We've been here now for over a week and every contact we've made with the locals and greased palms have met with closed doors."

Gregg took a sip of the dark brew, deep in thought, digesting Steve's comment. *Another breakfast another blank!*

"Yeah, even Azra has drawn a cold case and the mother of all terrorist attacks has gone to ground. But who is the anonymous savior who alerted us our health and safety was at risk and so far, *a damp squib.*"

"Don't be so complacent Gregg, in this city anything can happen."

"But our mobile number and the password?"

"You heard Azra's explanation, we had to complete a request form for a new SIM card, it's necessary under Israel's security checks on foreigners."

"Yeah, but the password?"

"Azra recons it could be a Sayerat Matakal lone wolf undercover."

"I suppose it makes sense… *This country!*" Gregg sighed.

"We had a late night yesterday following up on the leads from Azra ad I think by now know every coffee shop in Gaza City!"

Steve exhaled pouting his lips. "You got that one right and if I ever see another Hookah, I'll go nuts."

"*Ha…Ha…*" Gregg laughed. I know what's on my cards, get out of this getup, have a refreshing shower then hit the cot until lunch time." He raised his hand to attract the waiter……

* * *

Gregg slipped the plastic into the key pad and opened the door. He had left the aircon running using his second card.

"*Nice…*" He quickly removed the black igal and the red and white ghutra. (the mini table cloth). "That feels better." He massaged the band mark on his forehead with his fingers. "Now to get rid of this tent, I can't believe men wear this shit 24/7." He pulled the Kaffia over his head and threw it carelessly in a heap onto the back of the chair leaving him standing in his Sirwal the long white baggy trousers. He turned catching a glimpse of himself in the wall mirror and burst into laughter. "*Now aint that a sight for sore eyes?* If Marge can see me now it would put her you off sex for life." He laughed whilst removing the Clock from the deep pocket and placed it on the bedside table but not before checking the safety, then his wallet beside it. "I had better go and run that shower I takes ages before that excuse for warm water comes through."

As Gregg walked to the bathroom something caught his eye, *but what was it?* Whenever he left his briefcase in the room it was purposely unlocked but with only one latch down. He quickly glanced at the case again… *That's it!* Both latches were down meaning someone has been in this room and more so may still be, having been disturbed. Gregg pretended to be uninterested and walked unassumingly to the shower box and turned on the facet, the loud spray clouding any noise. Then he noticed a movement in the vanity mirror an intruder whose face was covered with the ghutra except for his eyes flashed past the bathroom and as Gregg slowly walked toward the bedside table to retrieve his firearm he noticed a pair of dusty sandaled feet protruding from below the heavy blackout curtains. If he could just reach his gun in time the element of surprise was still on his side as the intruder had no vision. "Got it!" He quickly released the safety catch pulling back the slider.

"Come out from behind that curtain or so help me I'll put two bullets clean through you."

Too late… Gregg just heard the movement from behind and turned slightly as the second assassin crashed the heavy caliber hand gun complete with silencer down hard on Gregg's shoulder fortunately missing his skull and he staggered back half turning, the pain clouding his brain as he grabbed his assailant's wrist stopping him from putting a bullet through his head and in the struggle dropping his firearm to the floor, his accomplice now taking advantage putting a neck lock on Gregg. The adrenalin surge was off the scale as Gregg kneed the first guy in the groin with a scream that said it all whilst at the same time elbowing his partner in the ribs with all his strength the Arab's trigger finger uncontrollably firing two shots. One bullet spraying plaster fragments everywhere from the ceiling the second going clean through the adjoining door into Steve's room.

"What the fuck?" The splintered bullet hole meant only one thing and Steve grabbed the Glock and kicked open the door just in time. The first intruder now free pointing his gun at Gregg trying to get a head shot as he wrestled with his partner in a life and death bear hug, it would be all over in seconds. In a flash Steve grabbed a pillow from Gregg's bed and bagged it behind the back of startled gunman. "Splat… Splat…" The copper nosed 45's making a muffled sound as feathers and blood rained down like wedding confetti. The back of his skull disintegrating as bone and brain sprayed the wall like a red Niagara. But Gregg was still in trouble grappling with the other gunman who recklessly discharged another two shots into to the ceiling before Gregg head butted him, nose cartilage and bone going their separate ways followed by a scream of pain as the bridge of his nose collapsed like the 'Golden Gate' giving Gregg just enough time in the confusion to grab his gun from the floor and press it hard into the masked man's abdomen. There was

a sickening muffled explosion as the two heavy caliber slugs ripped open the assassin's stomach tearing through bowel and liver and splintering his spinal cord, even if he survived he would be a useless quadriplegic and he screamed in pain as he crashed helplessly to the floor, his body jerking mechanically before the final death croak.

"I'm okay… I'm okay Steve… It's not my blood!"

Steve stared at the smoking Glock. "That's the first time I've fired my weapon in anger!"

The assassin attempt was over, *but was it……?*

* * *

Gregg was panting like he had just finished a marathon his blood splattered Sirwal resembling a new design for the cat walk, Steve staring blankly at the two corpses lying in a crimson pool on the now heavily stained Arabic carpet.

"What the fuck do we do now? What a fucking mess!"

"We gotta get rid of these two cadavers that's for sure… We have to phone Azra, we have no option."

"You got that special number?" Gregg asked his face pale still in shock.

"Yeah…" Steve punched the numbers into the keypad. "Golda Meir… Help." He hung up. "It's a waiting game now. I think you had better shower and change Gregg you look like a butcher's apprentice."

"Trust you to pull that shit out of the bag…. And *I* suggest, you go back to your room and get cleaned up while I shower and change into another 'tent'……"

* * *

"The Americans are clean. So far, we have found nothing to link them with the CIA. Our men have gone through each of their hotel rooms with a fine-tooth comb and came up with a blank cheque." Anbar was just about to wrap up breakfast with his father when the subject was raised.

"Maybe they can help us, but it's a dilemma we really don't need… But on the other hand, let's not write them off."

"Then should we call off the hit? I purposely put it on hold as you pointed out before doing a thorough check on their backgrounds and motives."

"And?"

"It all ties up. To raise a point Father… Our Russian package arrives in a few days and the murder of two American's and the worldwide condemnation it would attract, we don't need, especially now, not to mention Shin Bet will be all over us like a pack of wolves."

"Then call it off!" Abdul paused for a moment rubbing his beard his penetrating eyes searching for a solution. "In hindsight Anbar, I've been thinking, maybe *we should* bring the Americans in from the cold… *Hmmm…* I'll raise it tomorrow at our next security meeting, of course you will attend."

"Then I had better get in touch with the hit men before it's too late… Excuse me father, while I go and contact Farid the guard, we gave the 'contract' to his two brothers."

Farid was standing guard his Kalashnikov slung over his shoulder. Anbar luckily caught him just in time as his shift finished at 10am

At the sound of footsteps Farid quickly turned pointing his loaded weapon toward the shadowed entrance.

"Password?"

"Farid it's me, Anbar."

"Password?"

"Okay…Okay… Jundin Majhul." Anbar stepped out of the shadow.

"I'm sorry Anbar but you can never tell."

"It's okay you were only doing your job. The reason I want to speak to you is to call off the attack dogs the contract is cancelled. Don't ask why, *just do it!"*

"I'll inform my brothers immediately… And the money?"

"Don't worry, they will still be paid the contact price each of 20k US."

"I only hope it's not too late…...."

* * *

Cleaned up Gregg was right it was a waiting game and he had retired to wait in Steve's room staring in silence at two corpses lying in pool of blood, one with half his skull missing exposing pulped brain, his stomach churning even though he had experienced much worse in Afghanistan. Worse still, *the fridge had only coke!*

Suddenly there was knock on Gregg's door.

"Stay put Steve, I'll go and check it out."

Gregg peered through the peephole. It was Azra accompanied by her brother, Isam.

"Thank God!" Gregg muttered under his breath.

"Password?"

"Golda Meir." Gregg quickly opened the door and checked the hall each way. *"Quick, come in…* Steve it's all clear it's Azra and her brother Isam."

Azra stopped dead in her tracks like a horse in an Equestrian deciding not to take the jump.

"This *is* something!" She commented settling down and showing little emotion, a hardened Sayerat Matakal special agent she had had her share experiencing death.

"Every picture tells a story and im not going ask you to explain the gory details. I'm only too glad it's not you two lying on the floor. *You did well…"*

"Sis, we gotta move fast and get rid of these bodies." Isam was panicking.

"You're right, I'll call the manager."

"You'll what!" Gregg, couldn't control himself.

"Call the manager! Don't worry he's one of us." Azra gave a wicked smile then lifted the phone hypnotic at the carnage.

"Saabar, Azra here, I need you to come up to room 22A, we have a problem."

"The Americans?"

"Something like that…*Oh,* and arrange another two rooms as they will have to vacate immediately."

"You're lucky it's off season." She heard the big sigh. "I'll bring the keys with me."

Steve had retrieved the assassin's semi-automatics and ejected the magazine clips before placing them on the coffee able.

"You should take these with you Azra."

"Hmmm… Makerof … Russian… Not bad, 9mill and a 12-round magazine not to mention the silencers. I've seen these before but now they are getting more common, looks like Anbar is right Hamas has plenty of cash and Russia…? *Well…*They'll sell their mother for the right price. I'll take ,e can always use more ordinance." She smiled.

There was a loud knock on the door. *"Ah,* that must be Saabar now." Azra looked though the peep hole, satisfied she opened the door.

Saabar stood for a moment before Zara dragged him in by the arm, who knows a guest may pass on the way to the elevator.

"Here's the plastic for 18a and 18b. I suggest you get your stuff and move out now."

"But how…?"

"*Don't ask!* We have our way of getting rid of corpses. *Hmmm…*" Saabar was weighing up the damage shaking his head. "Let's see… Plaster work… Door frame…Replace the carpet… Blood splatter everywhere and two corpses… I've got my work cut out but it could have been worse."

"*Worse?*" Steve couldn't hold his tongue.

Saabar grinned. "Yes, *it could've been you……!*

HAMAS SECURITY COUNCIL

(Arabic to English)

"Is everyone seated? *Good,* then let's get to it, time is not on our side." Abdul Fattah, the Commander of the armed wing of Hamas was chairing the meeting of the Security Council taking his seat at the head of the 10-man table. He shuffled a wad of A4's then settled down.

"To bring you up to speed… We now have sufficient foreign currency in 12 Arab banks in US Dollars from the hijack of a Boeing 777 freighter as the result of both my son's ingenious plan. Sadly, I must report that my son Fadile was fatally wounded in the operation, let us not forget the price he paid for the Palestine cause."

"Allah-Ahmad Saleem." Came the resounding support from each member of the council.

"Shukraan, 'Allah yakun meaak." (Thank you, Allah be with you.)

"Next on the agenda… The Russian Scarab short range missile will be delivered in around two to three days. Faraj Dahara has already agreed to collect the containers in his fishing boat and fetch them ashore. His boat has the capability to outsmart the Israeli Customs and Border patrol vessels. Faraj is well versed with the patrol times and has a good repour with the Custom's Officers if stopped. Once ashore the two containers will be transported by truck to a safe location where they will be stored for assembly and launch. Hadid that's where you come in with your heavy truck. For security purposes, you will receive further information nearer the time as to the delivery location. My son Anbar and his new-found brother Amir Taafeef will be in total charge of operation code named 'Knesset'. A name you are all familiar with… Are there any questions?"

Abdul stared in silence for a few seconds his penetrating eyes surveying each member for a reaction.

"*Good*, I gather your silence is affirmative… *Now,* to an extremely serious matter, the loss of the Scarab instruction manuals now in the hands of Shin Bet as the result of a baggage mix up at Ben Gurion. *Which means…*" Abdul gave a dejected sigh… "We can't afford even the slightest slip up and must be even *more* diligent as the Sayerat Matakal will be everywhere. Having the manuals, they now know it's something big but 'where and when' that's to our advantage. *But we have a further problem…* The Scarab 'A' was designed to be launched from a mobile Transporter Erector Launcher known as the (TEL) which were cumbersome and easily spotted by surveillance drones whereas the miniature version 'B" which Hamas purchased can be discharged from the back of a 'Twin Cab' or Humvee or even a dug out and computer programmed for remote firing. Unfortunately, we don't have the privilege of 'open air war fare' so there can only be one option and that is a below surface launch. Which brings me to the conclusion that without the instruction manuals we need technical expertise to construct the launch pad and assemble the rocket frame critical for detonation. Anbar my son agrees with my conclusion which brings me to the proposition I wish to pass by the Security Council. Anbar recently met with two Americans of Palestine decent at a dinner party arranged by Amar Taafeef's son Amir, and Azra Saraaf the daughter of the owner of the local taxi business. Azra had made friends with the Americans during her studies at the University of Chicago, being Sunnis, they had a lot in common. Their fathers were born in Palestine during the British rule and migrated to the United States to become naturalized citizens. They have been very successful in business and are multi- millionaires and now wish to help in any way possible be it finical or political to pursue the Two-State solution. Their names are Imad Halabi and Fadi Bishara and they speak almost perfect Arabic. The parents have contacts on the 'Hill' including the President himself, the Secretary of State and members of the United Nations Security Council. At first, we were convinced they were undercover agents for the CIA as Mossad's secret Service often work together at the request of Taman Pardo and his buddy Comey. There was only one solution to be safe and we placed a contract on them both which we have since aborted having confirmed they are clean and their reasons for being here check out. Now why the spiel? Halabi graduated in Mechanical and Electrical Engineering where as Bishara is a Structural Engineer, exactly the skills we need."

"So, what are you suggesting Abdul?

"We bring them into our confidence to design the launch pad."

"I understand where you are coming from but Americans, using the phrase are 'goody two shoes' when it comes to a terrorist attack resulting in loss of life. They don't understand we are at war with Israel. Furthermore, once we expose our plan and if they renege, *then what?*"

"Simple Abdi, *we reinstate the contract!*"

"Those in favor... Eight...." Anbar counted... *"Motion carried......"*

* * *

"The meeting went well father. I suggest we contact the Americans through a third party namely, Azra Taafeef. Amir, it appears has a crush on the woman and the message can be conveyed over a coffee is as simple as it gets."

"I agree Anbar, I'll leave it in your capable hands......"

* * *

Anbar punched in the secret number on his cell.
"Jundi Majul... Amir, the game has changed......"

* * *

"Halt...Password." Farid raised the Kalashnikov.

"Jundi Majul... It's me... *Anbar!* I came to see you to contact your brothers to come and collect their money."

"Anbar! At last..." Farid gave a nervous sigh. "I was hoping to see you today."

"Don't tell me the contract is...?"

"Not that I know of... I tried to contact them to pass on your message that the hit was off, *but they are nowhere to be found!"*

"Nowhere to be found...! Are you serious?"

"They have been missing for two days. Their wives and families are beyond themselves."

"Hmmm..." Anbar's mind was racing whilst rubbing his chin, this was an unexpected conundrum. *"Strange...*I will put the word on the street in the hope I can get some information as to their whereabouts. Farid, I'm sure there is a simple explanation. In the meantime, that's the best I can do. I have here half the payment for the hit, 10k in US dollars. Please pass this to the families. If they need any further financial assistance contact me as soon as possible for the rest of the money."

"Shakar."

As Anbar walked down the dark hallway his mind was deeply troubled at the news that two of Hamas's most efficient assassins had suddenly disappeared from the face of the earth. Could it be Shin Bet? It was not the first time that prominent figures from the 'Armed Wing' had disappeared never to be found. Held hostage and tortured was a common tactic of Mossad. Fortunately, Farid's brothers were not aware of Hamas's plans to annihilate the 'Knesset' and even if they did they would never divulge any information under torture. This was the last thing Anbar needed…...

* * *

"This fucking breakfast! I can just imagine, *hmmm."* Steve made those crazy eyes. "Beef bacon, scrambled eggs, French toast and freshly brewed coffee?... *Maaan!"*

"Steve, for Christ sakes stop gripping, we have more important things on our mind than an American breakfast! Eat your Pita and enjoy the Turkish coffee."

"Gee, thanks! I don't know how you can drink that shi…."

The musical ring of his cell cut the gripe with Steve turning to Gregg raising his eyebrows.

"Now who could this be…? *Hello?"*

"Golda Meir… Azra here. Something urgent has come up and I need to meet you and Fadi… It's nine now... Say 9:30 outside your hotel."

"Where to?"

"Don't worry, my brother will pick you both up but if you must know its Ghazat Afdal Alqahua, a popular coffee shop next to the Taafeef Bakery on Nasar Street. Amir will be joining us."

"Azra…?"

"Don't ask! One can never tell who may be listening to this call." The phone went dead.

"Did you get that Gregg?"

"I got the jest… We can discuss it in the taxi… Waiter…...."

Now… the big question is should we go armed?"

"Hmmm… If we get frisked from say, Hamas security or even stopped by the IDF we would have difficulty explaining where we got the firearms and why we are carrying loaded weapons on our person?"

"I agree… They are locked in the room safes so I suggest we leave them there. I guess it's a chance we have to take but with Azra there, I doubt if she would knowingly lead us into a trap."

"I still feel uneasy Gregg, but *if it is a trap* we would be out gunned anyways…...."

* * *

As predicted Isam was waiting engine running, the rear door of the Mercedes open.

"As-Salaam-Alaikum."

"Wa-Salaam-Alaikum."

A man of few words Isam promptly got under way the rear wheels of the antique Mercedes kicking up a cloud of dust searching for traction on the sand laden roadway.

"We should arrive in around twenty minutes so you can relax." Isam finally spoke.

"The plot thickens huh?" Steve turned to Gregg for his reaction, but 'Mr. Cool' was deep in thought. *"So…* What do you think this meeting is about, especially with Amir present?"

Gregg pondered for a few seconds, this could be the meeting they had been waiting for.

"Maybe we are going to meet Mr. Big himself, *huh?"* Gregg replied a half grin crossing his face.

"You mean Abdul Fattah!"

"I hope so, but then maybe I'm being over optimistic."

"Whatever we'll soon find out…...."

* * *

The coffee shop was typical Gazanian, clouds of scented smoke from the Hookahs choked the air, checkered head scarfs and pearly white Kaffias everywhere. Dusty toes protruding from their 'Jesus' sandals and some fingering their religious beads. As for Azra she was already seated in the company of Amir and in deep conversation.

"Ah, here they are now." Azra commented looking up.

"As-Salaam-Alaikum."

"Wa-Salaam-Alaikum."

The formalities over the agents took their seats.

"Coffees?" Azra was being polite with a conspicuous nervousness in her voice.

"No, we're good." Gregg replied.

There was a slight pause as if Amir and Azra were deciding who was to speak first.

"I'll not beat about the bush gentlemen." Amir took the lead. "Your sales pitch at The Lighthouse may have some merit and my newly 'found' brother Anbar Fattah would like you to meet with someone to explore the matter further… *That is of course if you agree…?* If you don't, then this meeting never took place… *Do I make myself clear?*"

"It couldn't be any clearer." Gregg was being slightly sarcastic.

"Azra, now that I have the American's agreement you can return to your office. I'll call you later and maybe we can repeat that dinner."

Azra just smiled. "If you can excuse me… Imad… Fadi… My father will be wondering where I've got to… Shukraan, my brother will drive me home……"

* * *

It seems old Mercedes E300's is in fashion. The large black dust laden car pulled up in front of the coffee shop, the driver's face covered in the traditional red and white checkered head cloth, his penetrating dark brown eyes only visible.

"Please." Amir pointed.

Steve turned to Gregg and made a face. Amir took the front seat next to the driver and Steve and Gregg, the back. Five minutes into the journey the car pulled over into a dark alleyway and stopped. *What now?* Steve thought more than concerned as they were unarmed. Suddenly Amir turned to face the unsuspecting duo pointing a mean looking Russian Makerov semi-automatic straight in their faces.

"Woah… Woah…!" Gregg raised his hands. "This is not part of the deal."

'Don't worry, I'll only shoot you if you refuse to put on these blindfolds." Amir grinned a sadistic sense of humor. "I'm sure you can appreciate our security requirements." He passed two 4-inch black strips of cloth. *"Please."*

"I suppose we have no option." Steve shrugged staring down the muzzle of the Makerof.

* * *

Fortunately, the CIA had prepared for such an emergency as kidnapping is rife in middle eastern countries, especially for Americans. Steve and Gregg had been supplied with modified cell phones with GPS secret tracking software. When the digit 2 on the key pad is pressed the phone will automatically track the route from start to finish and store it in the memory bank. The phone does not display the map on the screen unless 3 is pressed on the keypad hence the kidnappers have no idea they are being monitored.

* * *

There was little time and Steve stealthily placed his hand into the deep pocket of his Kaffias and pressed 2 but it didn't go unnoticed.

"Out of the car… the two of you." Amir waived the semi-automatic. "That had better not be a firearm you are concealing."

Steve and Gregg didn't hesitate and hit the dust laden sidewalk arms raised, the driver doing a body search.

"Cell phones." He held up Gregg's then passed it back to him. "They are clean."

"Abbas, before they get back into the car tie their blindfolds."

"Hasananaan." (okay)

The two 'blind mice' were guided into the rear of the Mercedes like a 'James Bond' movie only without the license to kill, their precious Glocks…...

* * *

The drive seemed longer than its 20 minutes, especially when you are in total darkness.

"We are here, you can remove your blind folds now."

Steve blinked his eyes as they adjusted to the brightness turning to Gregg who was also occupied doing the same.

"Password." Farid blocked their paths, Abbas remaining in the car.

"Jundi Majul."

"Pass." Farid motioned with his Kalashnikov.

The dark passageway negotiated by Amir led to a heavy dust coated Moroccan antique carved door, knocking three times.

"Password." Came the voice from the 'inner sanctum'.

"Jundi Majul."

The door slowly creaked open only to be met by Anbar.

"You took your time, my father has been a waiting patiently, he has a full schedule today. *Come…* This way." He motioned to Steve and Gregg.

Abdul Fattah was sitting at his desk sipping the usual Arabic drink, pale colored tea from a glass.

"As-Salaam-Alaikum." Starve and Gregg touch their hearts with their right hands, a mark of respect for elders.

"Wa-Salaam-Alaikum." Fattah pointed to the empty chairs, Anbar and Amir joining the meeting…...

* * *

Fattah was most likely in his late sixties, over weight and almost a twin of Yassar Arafat the deceased Chairman of the Palestine Liberation Organization. Strangely he wore a black and white checkered ghutra pulled down into a peak below his igal in the front of his brow. Maybe this was in recognition of his rank being the Commander of the armed wing of Hamas. His tanned wrinkled face was heavily creased with dark laugh lines almost hidden by his patchy grey beard and a nose that didn't do him any favors except providing shadow from the sun. The carnage continued with his repulsive yellow Hookah stained tobacco teeth and those hypnotic dark brown eyes that would scare lesser mortals. Eyes that have seen enough trauma and death to physiologically scar a man for life. This meeting would be anything but a walk in the park…...

* * *

"Anbar, my son, has brought to my attention the discussions you had over a dinner meeting. American Arabs especially of Palestine decent have noble intentions to assist our country against our adversary Israel and help achieve the 'Two State' solution and return Jerusalem to its rightful owners. Unfortunately, words are easy and diplomacy is a myth. Security checks with our contacts in the US confirm your backgrounds and your family's support to the Arab League, in short you are who you say you are and having given your case considerable thought I feel you have something to offer hence our meeting here today. But let me be clear, once you have agreed to enter that door there is no turning back. In short if you have second thoughts and don't want to continue you will end up on the missing persons list."

Fattah's statement brought deadly silence this, for Steve and Gregg this is really '*The River of no Return*'!

"Im waiting!" Fattah was drumming his fingers on his desk.

Steve turned to Gregg. *"You or me?"*

"We state our allegiance to the Palestinian cause and Hamas."

"Then place your hands on the Koran and repeat after me… I accept the rules of the Armed wing of Hamas and obey their orders in the war against Israel to the death."

"I… Imad Halabi promise to obey…..."

* * *

"The objective of Hamas is to launch an attack against Israel that will make 9/I1 look like child's play and force the EU Security Counsel to accept our demands knowing our capabilities in the war of attrition."

"So where do *we* come in?"

"I'll take it from here father." Anbar took the reins. "I suggest you come through to the board table."

Anbar quickly spread the blueprints on the table his father now appearing uninterested studying some papers.

"These are the technical details of the Russian built Scarab short range missile with a range of 200 kilometers and a 220kg payload, complete with anti-radar blast warheads. Are you familiar with this weapon?"

"No, we're not into military hardware but this baby is the real deal. Now, getting back to my question, *how can Fadi and me help?*"

"Due to a mix-up with my baggage…*Eh*… I'Il not go into that, it's a long ugly story… The bottom line is, we lost the instruction manuals which are now in the hands of Shin Bet."

"Not good." Gregg shrugged… *But…?"*

Anbar raised his hand as if to say, '*don't be so impatient'*.

"The Scarab 2 is designed to be launched from an in-ground platform from a specially designed heavy-duty frame. As you can see here." Anbar pointed. "The question now is how to design the launch pad and integrate the frame without the instruction manuals, and that's where your expertise comes in. Fadi you graduated in in Mechanical and Electrical Engineering and you Imad in Structural Engineer, exactly the skills I need."

"Hmmmm…" Steve rubbed his Chin… "I see… In my capacity, I would have to study the technical details in some depth and more to the point the launch sight."

"The missile will be launched from a vent hole located in one of our tunnels. Of course, it will require some modification. The underground platform specifications are clearly spelt here in section 'B'."

"When can we inspect the location?" Steve asked.

"When the time is right. In the meantime, I suggest you stay for lunch and the remainder of the afternoon. I'll leave you to it gentlemen."

"Oh, before you go Anbar, the time frame?"

"48 hours…...."

* * *

"What the hell have we got ourselves into?" Steve turned to Gregg who was peering over the blue prints.

"Don't get your knickers in a twist, I helped my father build the extension on our house when I was at college and I can remember the concrete we needed for the basement. Let me see…? Ah here we are… Weight 650kg and 3 meters long… *Hmmm,* not that heavy…And…? Platform minimum 4x4 and 3 meters plus deep and here's the pitch centers for the tie bolts. It's not that difficult. *Hey,* we have seen missiles launched in Afghanistan before!"

"If you say so!"

"What did you think of the man himself?" Gregg turned taking a breather.

"It's those eyes… Like a doctor enjoying giving you a colostomy on your birthday."

"Ha…Ha…Ha…" Gregg couldn't stop laughing. *"Man,* where do you get that stuff? At least Steve you still have a sense of humor… Now let's get down to it. Anbar has left stationary, pens and a ruler… "Let's go back again to B……"

* * *

Lunch over, Gregg had made some free hand sketches showing the form work for the concrete and specifying M25 compression strength concrete. The mix… 2 cement… 1.5 sand and 3 aggregate with 12 mill galvanized steel rod weld tacked in 4inch squares with 3-inch-high stirrups for a six-inch thick slab. Curing time 48 hours.

"Gregg, you never cease to amaze me."

"Thanks for the complement and I don't think!"

"Come man, I'm really mean it."

"Okay…Okay… I believe you thousands wouldn't. Now let's get down to the heat shield to prevent a tunnel cave in from the gas blast. Fortunately, the heat will also be dissipated into the tunnel on either side."

Gregg was busily sketching the ¾ steel plate with its dimensions and four right ang

le one-foot high mild steel brackets bolted into the concrete at one-meter intervals to support the heavy steel plate. Fastener will have to manufacture locally to the same specifications as shown on the prints and must positioned before the concrete can be poured.

"I think that's pretty clear, huh?"

"Nice job Mr. Structural Engineer." Steve was admiring the rough sketches and reading Gregg notes.

"Hmmm, just let me double check my writing again… *Hell,* do you know the time… Its 8:30!… *Anbar……"*

* * *

Anbar studied Gregg's drawings and write up, more than pleased.

"As you Americans say, 'Nice Job'." He smiled. "But you must be feeling hungry and fatigued it's getting late. I'll get the driver to take you back to your hotel unfortunately, blind folded once more. I can't take any chances as you are still new to our organization. I hope you understand?"

"Of course." Gregg replied. He had to play the game.

"It will take me at least a day to gather all the materials you need so stay low. You will be picked up… This is Sunday, *Eh…* Tuesday morning at nine. Your responsibility is to supervise the construction work and to make sure the deadline is met 48 hours from now."

"Your forgetting one thing." Gregg stopped the train. "Grade 22 concrete needs 48 hours to cure that means Wednesday at the earliest."

"As long as it's ready before Friday."

"Friday?" Steve interrupted.

"You'll soon find out! I'll go call the driver……"

* * *

Fifteen minutes into the journey Abbas reduced speed.

"You can remove the blind folds now we are only five minutes from your hotel."

Darkness had fallen so it was easy for Steve and Gregg to adjust their eyes. Abbas was on the money, taking only another five minutes before pulling op in the open hotel car park.

"Tuesday at nine outside your hotel. I can't park too long as Shin Bet is always watching from the 'eye in the sky."

Without another word, the big Merc spun its wheels and disappeared into the darkness.

"That's been one helluva day!" Steve turned to Gregg. "And *am I* glad that's over!"

"Yeah, but now we are in it up to our neck and naked as a 'jay bird' with only Azra as our contact. Let's get to our room and order room service, *I'm* starved……"

* * *

"Aircon at last! Those fans in Anbar's house… *I think it was his house…!* Looked like MiG-3 propellers from world war two and just as useless!"

Gregg just shook his head no comment, removing his ghutra and igal chucking them on to the bed.

"Am *I* glad to get that shit off and the next time I shave will be heaven, *whenever that will be?"*

"What I would do for Scotch on ice and a cool Michelob." Steve threw himself onto the large padded sofa, feet up.

"A suggestion."

"Im waiting." Gregg was studying the room service menu.

"We ask Azra to join us over supper. I wouldn't draw suspicion after all she is the 'third wheel' then we can bring her up to speed."

Gregg paused for second considering. "Yeah, that would work. You ring or I ring?"

Steve fumbled searching for his cell. *"These bloody pockets…*I'm being polite."

"Cut the fucking drama and get on with it." Gregg was not so accomodating.

"Golda Meir… Azra would you like to join Gregg and me over supper/" She got the jest of the message. "I would love to."

"Azra, can I ask you for a favor and if you think I'm outta line, just tell me." Gregg frowned listening in on the conversation. *What the hell was Steve up to now?*

"Do you think you can find a bottle of Scotch and some Israeli beer on the black market? I'll cover the cost?"

He could hear Azra laughing. *"You Americans... I'll see what I can do... Say... What time is it now... Nine... Nine thirty then."*

"Boy, *you've got some Gaul.*"

"Come on Gregg, lighten up......"

* * *

There was a loud knock on the door bringing Gregg promptly to his feet. *"That must be Azra now!"* He glanced at his watch. *"Who's there?"*

"Golda Meir."

"It's Azra." Gregg quickly opened the door checking the hallway both ways.

Azra was accompanied by her brother, Isam, both carrying cloth shopping bags as plastic is banned in Israel.

"Come in... Come in... Isam, nice to see you again. Here, let me help you with that bag Azra."

"Thanks, Fadi... I brought my brother along, I hope you don't mind, he's my chaperon." She smiled.

"Not at all... *Come...* Make yourselves comfortable. I hope you are hungry?"

"Not really Imad, it's the company that counts." Azra gave that special smile and Gregg almost saying, 'please don't encourage him'.

"Open the bag Fadi."

"I'll be darned... A bottle of 'Cutty Sark' and in the other, a six pack of Negev Israeli beer. *What can I say?* More to the point, what do we owe you?"

"It's a small thing, let's just say it's a present form my father."

"Fadi, the ice from the machine in the hallway."

Gregg's look sent the message.

"Eh... I'll get it don't worry." Steve picked up the ice bucket.

"Azra... Imad... I can only offer you a counterfeit Coke?" Gregg gestured.

"I'm good. We'll wait for the ice but that would be nice."

"Ah, here's the *ice man* now......"

* * *

"And you were both blindfolded there and back." Azra asked.

"Yes, but more importantly, *we're in! But get this!* We had to swear on the Koran our loyalty to the death to the armed wing of Hamas or we would be on the missing persons list."

"*Nice.*" Imad joked in rather bad taste to the annoyance of his sister.

"Imad, *it's not funny.*" Azra retaliated shaking her head at her brother's flippantness.

"Sorry sis, apologies guys."

"*No sweat.*" Gregg replied a smile on his face.

"But now we know the location of Hamas's HQ and the man himself, Abdul Fattah."

"*But you were both…?*"

Gregg grinned. "The CIA provided us with cells that have special soft wear to track a location in the case of kidnapping. It's not shown on the screen if the phone is checked by the captors and is stored in the memory to be reviewed later using a secret digit to recall the journey and the GPS coordinates."

"*That's unbelievable,* the Sayerat Matakal are way behind in this field, sis." Isam was amazed.

'*Ha…Ha…*" Azra laughed. "Isam, I'll let you complain to our boss."

Steve rattled a couple of fresh cubes into his empty glass before pouring another two fingers of the 'Cutty'.

"This is really a pleasure, not that we are alcoholics." Steve laughed." And this beer is not bad, a bit like Budweiser."

"It's brewed in Israel and very popular." Imad proudly replied.

"Now let's get down to business." Gregg interrupted the niceties. "The reason we really called you Azra is that we need your input."

"*Fire away.*"

"Here's the scoop… Fattah confirmed that Hamas is planning 'the mother of all attacks' on Israel making 9/11 look like kindergarten. We already knew from Shin Bet, Hamas has or will be shortly in possession of a Russian Scarab short range Ballistic Missile with a conventional warhead. Now *this is* confirmed as we were shown the technical details and the method of launching from a secret underground tunnel location by remote firing via a computer programme. Now you may ask, where do me and Fadi come in? We have been given the responsibility to supervise the construction of the concrete launch pad based on our phony expertise, to commence on Tuesday 24 hours from now. The location we don't know and once again we will be driven there blindfolded, but there again we have our phones." Gregg smiled. "Now the kicker is, when we stressed the concrete would take 48 hours to cure Anbar's through back was… 'Just make sure it's ready by Friday'."

"Friday… *Hmmm…?*" Azra was thinking. "Friday is prayer day but what's the connection? Come on Isan get your thinking cap on."

"I haven't a clue but if it's worth mentioning, the Knesset meets this Friday being the last day of this session before the summer holiday. There will be a full house of 120 MP's to pass through as many bills as possible."

"The Knesset…?" Steve asked.

"The Israeli parliament."

"That's it! What's the distance from Gaza city to Parliament House?"

"Around 90k." Isam replied.

"The Scarab has a range of 200k… *That's gotta be it!* Now the Million-dollar question where is the bloody missile?"

"Well, if all goes to plan you'll soon know by Thursday……"

THE DELIVERY

"Your late, we almost started dinner without you, come join me."

"It's been one of these days father, I underestimated the problem finding construction materials like simple sand and cement."

"You can blame Netanyahu for that, impounding all the available building and construction materials for the illegal Israeli settlements in the West Bank."

"*Whatever*, I managed to get enough to start for Wednesday except for the high tensile male bolts with metric thread and large rectangular base for concrete securing. They'll be delivered before midday. We'll just have to delay the pouring until then. *Hmmm…* This bread is good I gotta hand it to the 'Taafeef Bakery. Here, let me pour the tea."

"*As long as we meet our Friday dead line.*" Abdul stressed in no mean manner.

"Aesha, come and join us……"

* * *

It had just turned 7:30 in the evening with Aesha cleaning up after dinner… Anbar and his father relaxing with the Hookahs, the familiar scented tobacco filling the air.

"I hate to throw a spanner in the works father, but I'm worried about the delivery."

"*You said it would arrive today!* I have Faraj Dahara on standby?"

Suddenly there was a piercing noise like radio signals from outer space. *Could it be…?*

Anbar panicked dropping his mouthpiece desperately searching for his Motorola. "*Come on… Come on…!*" As normal with radio phones there is a few seconds delay before the crackle of a man's voice suddenly emerged.

"Fishtail."

"Eh... Ah... Fishtail." Anbar replied nervously. "Konbanwa Anbar san, Captain Katsuro Soto from RU18. Cargo delivered as per GPS coordinates must depart immediately to avoid ping detection by Israel Navy. Operation 'Fishtail'... Mission complete, Arigato..."

"Good news?" Abdul asked.

"The best! That was the Japanese submarine commander informing me that the stainless-steel containers have been released just inside the six-mile fishing limit. I have the GPS coordinates I just hope the tide is on our side."

Anbar glanced at his watch. "It's almost eight father, we don't have much time to beat the ten o'clock curfew." Anbar opened his cell and entered the numbers. *"Faraj,* the cargo has arrived, make way ready to sail in 30 minutes. I'll meet you at the peer. Now what's Hadid Rahal's number?" Anbar was feeling the pressure, time was against him. *"Here we are...* Hadid, get your fish truck down to pier 3 with at least two of your employees, ones you can trust. Stay out of sight but be ready to pick up the cargo by say... In one hour... *Have you got that?* Good... Be there at nine... The calls over Anbar turned to his father. "I'll go fetch the car... Father should anything go wrong you'll know if I don't return by 11:30."

* * *

"Password..."

"Farid, it's me Anbar...*Oh what's the use...* Jundi Majul... Now go call Abbas to fetch the car." Anbar was running out of patience.

"Anbar, I was hoping to catch you, it's about my brothers." Farid seemed nervous approaching his boss.

"Not now Anbar, it's not a good time."

"Abbas, the bosses' car......"

* * *

"Abbas don't spare the horses, drive to pier 3, I need be there in less than thirty minutes. You know Faraj Dahara's boat the Armelin?"

"Yes... I'll try my best boss as at this time of night the roads are in total darkness because of the electricity rationing."

"I forgot about that." Anbar jumped into the front passenger seat, Abbas was already accelerating.

The journey as usual when you have time constraints, seems forever.

"Can't you go any faster?"

"Not if you want to get there in one piece!"

Anbar didn't comment, hanging on to the handgrip above the door his knuckles white as the big Merc's tail had a mind of its own.

"I can see the lights on the pier now boss… Only another five minutes."

"You did well Abbas, it's just turned eight."

Anbar leapt from the Mercedes as it came to a screaming halt in a cloud of dust.

"Park the car out of sight until I return."

Faraj had already spotted the Mercedes. The Leyland 12-cylinder 300 horse diesel, *chug… chug… chugging,* ready to cast off, black smoke from the twin exhausts contaminating the air with diesel fumes.

Dahara was in the wheelhouse, his son on deck.

"Anbar, untie the mooring lines from the Bollard then jump aboard." Bakir called, the Armelin straining on its moorings.

Anbar hastily jumped the widening gap landing heavily on the deck.

"Not as fit as I used to be." He winced making Bakir laugh.

"My father requests you join him in the wheelhouse."

"And *you* Bakir?"

"I'll stay on deck and drop the Seiner nets whilst keeping a sharp eye for the Customs and Border Patrol."

Without hesitation, Anbar quickly climbed the stairs to the wheelhouse.

"Faraj, my dear friend. "As-Salaam-Alaikum."

"Wa-Salaam-Alaikum."

Dahara suddenly opened the throttle on the Amerlin, its twin props churning up the salt water like a cake mixer as the Skipper steered the wheel hard to starboard heading out to the six-mile limit. The antique Leyland 12-pot struggling to reach its maximum speed of 15 knots, the sudden change of course making Anbar almost lose his 'sea legs'.

"Are you alright?" Faraj asked, half smiling.

"It's been a while since I was at sea in this old tub." Anbar laughed.

"Yes, I can well remember. Now, *where to?"*

Anbar fished into the deep pocket of his Sirwal pulling out what looked like an ordinary Samsung cell phone and quickly pressed 'GPS Maps'.

"Anbar?" Faraj was scanning the darkness searching for the tell tail lights of the Israeli patrol boats as 9:30pm was normally their last run. *"We're not flush for time!"*

"I know… I know… Just bear with me… *Ah here it is."* Anbar could see the red dot flashing on the screen. "Set course hard to starboard GPS co-ordinates, North 38……"

* * *

"Why do we need the deck lights?" Anbar asked. "It's like signaling to the Israelis we're here."

"By law, if you are fishing at night, to avoid a collision with another vessel and a must for Customs and Border Security."

Anbar nervously glanced at his watch it was 8:45, getting dangerously near the curfew time and the possibility of being stopped by a patrol boat.

"Another four kilometers to rendezvous." Faraj was reading the information from the bright blue 'Kodon' marine radar screen.

"This is new! High tech, huh?"

"A lot has changed since you were last on the Armelin. During the high season, there's so many fishing boats at night accidents were common place, so the Israeli Fishing Commission made it law that all Palestine vessels operating within the controlled fishing zone must have radar detection."

"I thank Allah for it tonight." Anbar smiled.

At 15 knots, the Armelin was now approaching the pickup zone at speed.

"Throttle down Faraj the red dot on the GPS is flashing like crazy."

"What next?" Faraj was intrigued with Anbar's 'counterfeit' Samsung.

"I pray to Allah that this works." Anbar nervously pressed 3.

Suddenly there was huge muffled rumble followed by a mountain of bubbles resembling an atomic submarine about to surface, the stainless-steel torpedo shaped capsules jumping out of the water like two dolphins the compressed air blowing their tanks

"Get the grappling hook Bakir." Anbar yelled already on deck.

"Faraj, a little bit more to port… *A little more…* Hold it… Bakir, drop the anchor until we get the capsules on board. Can you operate the jib crane?"

Without another word Bakir started the diesel to drive the crane winch.

"To the left Bakir, gimme more slack to get the hooks into these lugs…..."

* * *

The cargo safely in the hold Faraj weighed anchor steering the Armelin to port then throttling up to full speed.

Anbar and Bakir quickly covered the secret cargo with heavy tarpaulin's then buckets of ice and finally the Seiner net catch of surface white bate.

"Israeli patrol vessel is approaching at speed on starboard, will arrive in ten minutes, get ready for the boarding party." Faraj yelled from the open window of the bridge. Anbar and Bakir were still frantically shoveling more and more ice to cover the catch.

Suddenly the loud speaker drowned the noise of the diesel.

"Amerlin 'heave to' and drop anchor... Israel Customs and Border Patrol."

Faraj immediately obeyed putting the Leyland into neutral. Bakir was already releasing the heavy chain.

"Give way Captain." The young officer commanded the crew securing the Amerlin with grappling hooks. The vessels stable the Custom Officers boarded the Amerlin, Faraj already on deck.

"*Captain Ezra*, it's been a while!"

"The feeling is mutual but there again you are never usually out fishing at this time in the evening."

"It's the best time for white bate."

"Sergeant Gutnick pull back the hatch cover."

The sergeant obeyed moving his gloved hand to and fro within the mixture of ice and bate the nauseating smell of fish expediting his conclusion.

"Everything is in order Captain."

"Can I give you a bucket of fresh bate Captain?"

"*Faraj*, you should know better... Boarding party return. You can now weigh anchor and head to port." Suddenly Ezra stopped in his tracks. "I know your son but who is this other crew member?"

"A friend of mine's boy who offered to help tonight."

"I haven't seen him around before."

"He just finished his studies in the States and arrived her a week ago. He's still looking for work so I offered him an opportunity to earn a few dollars to tide him over."

"*Hmmm...*" Ezra studied Anbar for a few seconds with Faraj preying that he wouldn't ask to see Fattah's ID.

"*Okay*, you had better get a move on or you'll breach the curfew and I'd hate to give you a citation."

"Thanks Captain, regards to your family. Don't worry I'll make it in time..." Bakir was already weighing anchor......

* * *

The Amerlin was making good time in the calm Mediterranean Sea and at 15 knots the three kilometers left would only take 12 minutes. Faraj had already instructed Anbar and his son to start unloading the cargo and ice into the large wicker fishing baskets to clear the hold ready for the transfer of the containers to Rahal's waiting truck.

Faraj throttled down to three knots turning the wheel to Port. Then thrust the props into reverse with the wheel hard to starboard bringing the stern into the dock. The sudden jolt almost knocking Anbar and Bakir off their feet.

"Are you boys alright?" Faraj cut the engine and switched off the deck lights, they would have to make do with the lights from Rahal's truck.

"Yeah, we're good."

Rahal was already waiting and quickly reversed his truck as near as possible to pier, switching on the cabin roof lights providing just enough light to avoid detection.

In record time, the containers were unloaded onto the truck's platform.

"We're running out of time Hadid, just cover them with a tarpaulin and any other junk you have around in case we are stopped. The white bate?"

"Store in the freezer hold until tomorrow's market. Thanks, Faraj we'll meet at the next council meeting, Hamas will be forever in your debt."

"Is it alright if I join you?" Bakir asked wanting a piece of the action.

"Yes, if you really want to? The more hands the better. You can join me in the Merc...Hadid follow us."

"Where to boss.......?"

* * *

"Abbas, you know the Aybaki Mosque in the al Tuffah neighborhood?

"Yes Boss."

"Take any route you want, *just get me there...* Hadid is following us, so don't lose him."

Abbas was quiet taking it all in concentrating on his driving, Bakir accompanying them in the back seat.

The big Merc was all over the place as Abbas peered into total darkness except for the few beams of light piercing the night from the uncurtained windows and the constant buzz of generators.

"Not long now boss!" Abbas was continually checking the rear mirror to make sure Hadid's truck was still in sight.

"I can see the lights of the Mosque now Abbas, slow down… *Good,* follow the road to the rear of the mosque. You'll see a dirt track on your left into the heavy bush reserve. Take that turn and at around 50 meters there will be a guard on duty, so slowly, slowly. I don't want a dead driver. Cut your lights to side only and signal to make sure Hadid follows… *Have you got that?"*

"Yes boss." Abbas was a man of few words. He either didn't like to be ordered around like a child or he was genuinely scared. Whatever, he was keeping quiet. *'You say it better when you say nothing at all'.*

The track, if you could call it that! Even farm tractors would have difficulty negotiating the large pot holes and the Mercedes shocks kept bottoming out thudding against its cone rubber stops.

Then, Abbas was suddenly blinded from the bright beam of a high-powered torch shining straight into his eyes and he hit the brakes throwing Anbar and Bakir around like rag dolls.

"What the hell Abbas?"

There were two guards on duty, their faces shrouded by their checkered red and white ghutras, only their eyes visible.

The guard with the torchlight walked briskly to the Merc and rapped on the widow with the muzzle of his Kalashnikov Abbas quickly obliged, the second guard locked and loaded was standing in front of Hadid's truck.

"Out…" The guard ordered. Without hesitation, the Merc emptied.

"What's your name." Anbar demanded.

"Raise your arms." He just ignored Anbar.

"Weren't you informed that we would be arriving here tonight with a special load?"

The guard just ignored him carrying on with the body search on both Abbas and Bakir. Over his shoulder Anbar could see the same procedure being carried out by the other guard on Hadid and his crew.

"Password."

"Jundi Majul… *Do you know who I am?"* Anbar was losing it. *"I am Anbar Fattah… Does that ring a bell!* Now move aside we have work to do and you can put down your weapon and help us."

The guard seemed unperturbed calling his compatriot over whispering intro his ear.

"We are sorry for the trouble boss but we were never informed."

Anbar had calmed down there was more important things.

"Hadid, fetch your men over and help us uncover the tunnel vent……"

* * *

"Jundi Majul… Farid, I'm in hurry." Anbar glanced at his watch, it read 11:15. He had made a promise to his father and if he didn't arrive home on time, Hamas would be out in force.

"But boss, I need to speak to you about my bothers. Three days have passed with no sign of them and worse still their car was found a burnt-out wreck on a secluded part of the Northern Beach."

That stopped Anbar, he was shocked. "I apologize Farid, it's just that I've been so… Oh it doesn't matter, there's no excuse. This *is* serious…*!* Listen tomorrow morning first thing I'll make sure you get the rest of the money for the families. Other than that, there's little I can do now but I'll mention it to my father. I'm sure he'll assign our best men on the case. I'm sorry Farid but I must go…"

Abdul was getting nervous, he didn't want to lose a second son should the worst happen. The IDS are trigger happy when it comes to Hamas, there's no love lost.

"Abdul can I refresh your tea."

"No Im good Aesha… *Where's that boy of mime?*"

"Don't worry Abdul, I'm sure he'll walk through that door any minute now."

"Father I'm home."

Abdul breathed a sigh of relief upon hearing his son's voice.

"What did I tell you?"

"Aesha I don't know what I would do without you." The commander of the armed wing of Hamas was human after all.

"Aesha, I think I'll take the offer of that tea……"

THE PLOT BEHIND THE PLOT

"Boy, am I looking forward to an American...."

"Steve, don't start that crap again, we're meeting Amir in...?" Gregg checked his watch. "In fifteen minutes, so get that coffee down you and let's get our butts outta here."

"So, you really like..."

"Cut the shit Steve, I'll go sign the room tab. I'll meet yo at the front door. *And make sure your phone is switched on!*"

"Hell Gregg, you're like an old woman."

"Yeah, but this old woman will keep you alive."

"Yah, this coffee..."

* * *

"I suppose it will be the old blindfold routine again?"

"Christ Gregg, you sound like Maxwell Smart!"

A smile crossed Gregg's face, he had to admit Steve could be funny at times.

"Here's Amir now." The dust laden black Merc pulled into the kerb, Abbas was driving.

"As-Salaam-Alaikum." Amir gave the traditional greeting, touching his heart with his right hand.

"Wa- Salaam-Alaikum."

"Shall we go gentlemen?"

Abbas was already standing with the rear door open and it was not difficult to make out the silhouette of the heavy Makarov Russian semi-automatic through his Kaffia, but then that was a have.

It was the same routine alright pulling into a side street, a body then finally the ultimate blindfold.

"Apologize gentlemen, but you are still on probation."

"That's comforting." Steve as usual was with the wisecracks…

* * *

The journey this time seemed to be shorter or maybe Steve and Gregg were just getting used to being in the dark. Then suddenly out of the blue they were thrown from side to side as the Merc drove down the dirt track behind the Mosque.

"This *is* something." Steve commented laughing. "Better than the rides on 'Coney Island' huh?"

Gregg squeezed Steve's arm. "Cut the jokes, your Arabic leaves a lot to be desired."

"*Imad…Fadi,* we have arrived but your blindfolds must remain until you enter the tunnel. Abbas and I will guide you. Now one step at a time then grab the top of the ladder and slowly turn placing one foot on the rung, the rest comes naturally."

The blindfolds removed Gregg and Steve quickly surveyed the territory. The tunnel was a fete of crude engineering around three meters by three with heavy wooden roof trusses and duck boards, even a narrow rail track for bogy transportation. The musty smell was overpowering but gradually disappearing through the large 12 feet diameter air vent. Lighting and electrical current was provided by diesel generator, the cables coming from deep in the tunnel to muffle the sound to a quiet hum. A petrol driven manual cement mixer was standing by next to a huge heap of sand, aggregate and bags of cement and even an oxyacetylene welding unit to cut and tack the 12-mill galvanized steel rod. Heavy wood planking for the 'form work' was stacked to the right of the tunnel. Anbar had thought of everything, for sure this guy was no dummy!

"Anbar will arrive in a few minutes to instruct the workmen to do as you request."

There were four Arabs stripped to the waist standing in there Sirwals but still wearing their ghutras. An array of building tools, shovels picks etc. lined the wall. These guys meant business.

"Amir." It was Anbar calling from outside. "I need help with this pile of bolts and brackets. They are packed in in a wooden crate that will need to be lowered by rope."

"You and you, climb the ladder and take that rope with you…"

Anbar descended the ladder to greet Steve and Gregg.

"As-Salaam-Alaikum. I see you are here ready to get started. I managed to find everything on your list, except for the heat shield which will arrive tomorrow. Abbas will return with your lunch before mid-day prayer. There are sufficient prayer matts Stacked over there." Anbar pointed to the left of the tunnel. "I want to talk to the workmen for a few minutes before I leave as something important has come up."

The conversation was brief instructing them to obey the Americans instructions and that they must stay until the concrete is poured.

"Just one point before you go. Where is the launch frame? We have the prints here with the bolt locations but it would good to check the actual hard ware."

"Fadi, tomorrow is Wednesday so there's sufficient time. Thursday is completion day just make sure the concrete is cured. When your finish tonight Abbas will drive you back to your hotel. I'll return tomorrow with the heat shield. Shukraan…Amir, I have something to discuss, I'll talk about it in the car.…..."

* * *

"Abbas, take us to the BonJoojx coffee shop in Buka Sekarang, its only 15 minutes from here and a nice view over the beach. I used to like that place. The Turkish coffee is good and we can relax over the Hookah."

"I know the place Boss, but not easy to park."

"Abbas that's your problem, besides we'll only be there for a little over an hour, I have other work to do…"

* * *

"Let's grab that table facing the shore, the breeze is refreshing…Two Turkish coffees… *Amir?*" Anbar passed the menu.

"Let me see… I'll have the Chebab pancake, and you?"

"I have a sweet tooth… The Baclava, it's a Turkish import. I just love the thin layers of phyllo dough encased in chopped nuts held together with honey… *Waiter…*"

"You *do* have a sweet tooth! Now you wanted to discuss something with me?"

"Yes… You were not aware that after our dinner at the Lighthouse I spoke to my father about the Americans and my distrust, suspecting they might be CIA agents. I can't explain it, I just had that feeling that they were just too good to be true."

"So…Ah, here's the coffee."

"Hmmm… It *is* good, what did I tell you? Now, where was I? Yes… We decided to place a contract on them as with operation 'Knesset' on the burner, we couldn't take any chances."

"You mean?"

"Exactly… But then after doing a thorough back-ground search we found they were clean and because of their technical expertise they could actually be an asset."

"And?"

"I called the hit off."

Amir shrugged, like why are you telling me this then?

"I know what you are thinking but at that time I didn't know if it was too late."

"Obviously it was cancelled in time as they are both still with us in the flesh."

"Or was it?"

"What are you trying to say?"

"Your food sirs, I apologize for interrupting."

Anbar brushed the waiter's comment aside with a wave of his hand, he was losing his train of thought.

"Shukraan… *Now…* Mysteriously the two hitmen suddenly disappeared. *But get this…* Their burnt-out car was found in a secluded part on the Norther beach and the latest… Two shallow graves were found not far from the car. Both men were identified as Farid the guard's two brothers. Of course, you can forget the Israeli police."

"I don't get it?"

"Just give me a minute to take a bite of these delicious Baklavas. Hmmm…"

"These hitmen are professionals, the best of the best and the only way they could be taken out is by someone that's better!"

"You don't think the Americans…!"

"I don't know… They certainly don't look the part but they could be highly trained CIA agents."

"But they're helping us with operation 'Knesset'!"

"I know, but it could be a front to infiltrate our organization… But there's one thing they don't know and that's the location of our HQ and the launch pad as they have always been blindfolded going to and fro from their hotel… *But…?"* Anbar winced.

"Anbar, it could be Shin Bet or even worse the dreaded Sayerat Matakal."

"Yes, that *had* crossed my mind… *I guess I'll sleep on it…* Now, I feel like a relaxing smoke, *what say you Amir……?"*

* * *

As promised Anbar returned on Wednesday with the heavy steel plate once again lowering it by rope into the large air vent. The concrete launch pad, you could say, looked professional, the bolts all in place embedded in the slab and the shuttering removed to assist the mix to cure.

Anbar studied the job for a moment both in surprise and admiration.

"This is exceptional! Well done… *Imad… Fadi…*You have surpassed my expectations. Now all that's left now is securing heat shield brackets to support the heavy plate. Can you install the heat shield today?"

"Afraid not, although the concrete is solid enough to walk on, it's too early to take the load. Tomorrow morning to be safe."

"Fadi your advice has been good so far, tomorrow morning it is. Then we can assemble the launch frame ready for Friday. I'll leave you to clean up. You will be picked up at your hotel tomorrow at the usual time. You can request Amir to take you back whenever you finish. Shukraan……."

* * *

"Boy, am I glad that's over!" Steve commented as the two men entered the hotel foyer. "I'm looking forward to a cold beer and the remainder of that 'Cutty Sark'."

"For once I agree with you but let's shower first and freshen up." Gregg pressed the elevator button, the doors opened.

"You know the giveaway?"

"No, *what?"*

"Our feet… Cement laden sandals!"

Gregg looked down then burst into laughter. "I wondered why the concierge was staring at us." The Elevator chimed…

"My room in thirty minutes." Gregg swiped the plastic.

"The first thing Im gonna do." Gregg closed the door behind him. *"Is turn on that fucking shower!"*

Within seconds the sandals, the Kaffia, the Sirwal and the Ghutra were lying in a heap on the bathroom floor.

"Man, is this good!" Gregg was conversing with himself as the tepid water streamed through his unkempt hair drenching his sweat laden face and body. "My hair's never been so long even on tour in Afghanistan." He frothed his face. "And this donkey beard stubble, I'll be glad when this assignment is over to get a haircut and a clean shave…"

The warm shower was relaxing and Gregg's mind drifted back to when their tour of duty in the Marcaine Corp was over and the "Soldiers of Fortune" decided to apply to join the CIA and save the world. A smile crossed his face. "Two 'Robin Hoods, huh?" Gregg had to laugh. But things were not as glamorous as the movies portrayed and after a couple of boring years with routine investigations into computer fraud and government leaks suddenly they were in the forefront of a major terrorist conspiracy that would take them half way round the world. But then there's always the good with the bad and the thought of Julie and Marge made him smile. *The future?* The next couple of days will tell. Suddenly Greggs thoughts were dowsed with the impatient knock… knock… knocking on the adjoining room door.

"Are you finished showering?"

"Just about!"

"Maaaaan… What are you doing in there, having swimming lessons?"

"Stop griping and can come and do something useful. Go fill the ice bucket, I'll only take another five."

Gregg quickly toweled slipping into his jocks and a freshly starched Kaffia.

"I gotta admit this *is* comfortable." Gregg brushed back his hair.

Steve was already making himself at home pouring two iced glasses of the famous 'Cutty Sark' accompanied with cold Negev beers.

"At least your good for something!" Gregg grabbed his Scotch and beer and settled down on the sofa in front of the coffee table.

"Cheers." Gregg raised his glass. "To a successful day."

"I'm with you on that." Steve took a slow sip of his Scotch. *"Mmmm…* You know Gregg these Kaffias are pretty comfortable without the baggie pants."

"God, I hope your wearing something below, I don't want to catch a glimpse of nakedness that will put me off sex for life?"

"Get out of it!" Steve was laughing at the thought. "Joking aside, I thought we were in trouble when Anbar mentioned prayer time."

Gregg had to laugh. "Yeah, but we did a good job following the workman. So good no one noticed we almost kneeled in the opposite direction from Mecca."

Gregg's comment made them both burst into laughter.

The laughter gone reality was coming home. Gregg took another mouthful of the amber liquid thinking quietly.

"Come on partner, *out with it.*"

"Tomorrow is Thursday the final day to install the heat shield and the launch frame and we have yet to come up with a plan to stop this devastation."

Steve raised his hand to his chin in thought. "You're not alone… But let's look at the positives… We have the GPS locations for the Hamas HQ and the location of the Launch sight for the Scarab. We don't know where the missile is hidden but I'm pretty sure you will agree it's somewhere in that tunnel. Now tomorrow we install the heat shield and assemble and bolt the frame in place then we will know for definite where the missile is hidden."

"I noticed the invertor for transferring the generator power from DC to AC for charging the lithium ion batterie's to ignite the solid fuel for the rocket motor. Remember Anbar spent time in Russia at the MOD and the 'Department of Aeronautics and Rocket Science' supposedly on a training exchange. Make no mistake, Anbar knows what he is doing. Now we know the Scarab is computer programmed for remote firing and my guess is the countdown will be celebrated at Hamas Headquarters, and it's now even more pertinent we meet with Azar tomorrow immediately after we finish for the day. I'll phone her now…"

"Golda Meir… Golda Meir…" Came the response. "Azra, Fadi here, listen, we need to meet tomorrow after we finish it's urgent… Good… Where do you suggest? Dinner at your home… Iman will pick us up… I'll call you when we arrive at our hotel… Shukraan."

"You heard?"

"Yeah, tomorrow at Azra's house…..."

* * *

The breakdown truck, its crane dangling the 3\4 by 4x4 heavy steel plate was slowly maneuvering the pot holed track behind the Mosque. Breakdown trucks are a common sight in Gaza with the number of antique cars and trucks on the streets.

Steve and Gregg had already arrived pacing impatiently. Amir could sense the tension and tried calm the situation.

"*Imad*, calm down, Anbar should be here any minute now." He glanced at his watch. "Besides its early days. You heard him say, 'as long as we finish by today'."

Just then the noise of a truck's engine reversing broke the silence.

"*Amir*… It's me… Get the men ready, we are about to lower the steel plate."

Gregg could hear the roar of the winch crane straining as the heavy heat shield was being lowered into the air vent.

"You two grab each side… *Steady*… Anbar reverse the truck slightly I need the plate to rest against the wall… *Gently*… A bit more… Okay steady as she goes… It's down… Now you two push it to the right… Anbar slowly raise the plate to line up the holes in the support brackets… *A little more…* *Hold it there…*You … You and you, slip these bolts through the holes and finger tight the nuts. Grab the wrench Fadi and start tightening."

"*Are you about finished?*" Anbar yelled.

"Yeah, were releasing the chains now from the lugs…You can winch the chain, we're good. Fadi put the maximum torque on these nuts, this plate is really heavy."

"Put up the ladder I'm coming down." Anbar's feet appeared on the rungs. Finally, with both feet on the concrete he stepped back to and admire the work, his voice almost drowned by the trucks engine revving, leaving a cloud of diesel fumes.

"Again, I'm really pleased. Now the frame… You three come with me." They disappeared into the north port of the tunnel.

There was a loud rattling noise of the bogey's steel wheels on the narrow rail track.

"Push harder, we're almost there."

A large Zeppelin shaped stainless steel container was resting on two bogies.

"Amir, get the men to unbolt the top and separate the container."

"Good, now the tubular steel struts should be numbered in the order of assembly and packed accordingly to match the diagram." Anbar was studying the large print sheet. "*Let me see… Yes,* here is number 1 marked in white paint."

"Imad…Fadi, its over to you." Anbar passed the print. "I must leave but I'll be back around three. I'm sure you'll be finished by then……"

* * *

Showered and freshly clothed Steve and Gregg were waiting in the hotel's coffee lounge for Isam to pick them up. They had phoned Azra when they had arrived back at 4:30 having finished earlier than anticipated.

"Tomorrow's the big day and I'm sure the Security Council will meet at their HQ for the 'countdown'." Gregg was pondering over his coffee. "The point is Steve, time is not on our side and what are we going to do to about it? *Ah,* here's Isam now." Gregg rose to greet him.

"I'm sorry to rush you but if we don't move soon we will be caught in the five o'clock traffic."

"And I thought Washington was unique." Steve laughed.

"Imad, it's the same the world over.

 "Come on Steve, you heard Isam… *Finish your coffee!*"

Within minutes they were seated in Britain's finest, the old Morris Minor bumping through the potholed streets of Gaza City avoiding all sorts of traffic on the way, from Camels to Donkeys even a large black Bear pulling a kart.

"This place is something." Steve commented taking in the scenery.

Isam suddenly hung a left down a narrow alleyway passing precariously close to food stalls selling a variety of homemade breads, oaths coming in plenty.

"Another few minutes."

"At least we're not blindfolded." Steve's comment made Isam smile. Then suddenly he swung another hard left through a narrow-pillared archway and finally into a dusty courtyard.

"You probably don't remember this place, it was dark when you arrived here last time."

The 'Morris' came to a grinding stop, the high-pitched squeal of its worn drum brakes made Steve cringe.

"Apologizes, I've been meaning to fix these brakes but I've been so busy."

Steve and Gregg got out of the car.

"Just follow me down the passageway." Isam pointed leading the way before finally stopping in front of the heavy oak door, knocking three times.

"*Password.*" Came the muffled reply.

"*Golda Meir.*" The door creaked open, its hinges protesting from the lack of precious lubricant.

Azra and her father were waiting anxiously to greet them as one can never trust Hamas.

"Eh…" Gregg began. "Imad and I thank you for inviting us to dinner these are dangerous times and we are putting you at great risk."

Anwar waved his hand. "It's our pleasure… Come, take your seats." He pointed to the scattered embordered cushions placed around the low dining table.

To sit crossed legged in a 'W' position was a challenge and Gregg and Steve bare footed uncomfortably lowered themselves to the floor.

"We can start with tea and pita bread, dips and olives." The large brass ornate tea pot in the middle of the table was a show stopper. "Of course, we have the best bread from Taafeef's Bakery." Anwar turned to is daughter and grinned.

Azra blushed… *Father!* Pay no attention to him, there's nothing between Amir Taafeef and me."

"That may be so but that's not what he thinks." Her father teased. "But at least we get the best bread." He laughed.

"Now don't you start Amir!" Azra caught her brother smirking.

"Azra, can you please pour the tea."

"Certainly father." Azra glad the subject change.

"Amani will be joining us in a few minutes, she is in the kitchen preparing the food."

As for Steve, he was quietly admiring Azra. Without her Hijab, she was stunning and as for that jet-black shoulder length hair… *No more said!*

"Imad your tea." Gregg gave Steve a nudge and that look to go with it.

"Eh…Err… Thanks, Azra." She just smiled, a woman's instinct.

"Azra can you come help me with this food?" The voice came from the kitchen.

"Yes mother." She quickly rose to her feet.

Amani and her daughter placed the dishes on the table.

"I hope you enjoy our humble food?" Amani smiled taking her place beside her husband. "There's, Lamb Kofta… Deep fried Sheri Fish, Allu Gobi and Kabsa rice."

"It looks delusions." Steve was playing the field.

"Then please……"

* * *

"Anwar." Gregg paused wiping his mouth with his napkin. "May I say, it's so enjoyable to join a family such as yours over dinner. It's been a long time since Imad and I have had a family dinner because of our work and I can't thank you enough for your generous hospitality and of course compliments to the chef."

Amani smiled, turning to her husband with a wicked smile.

"Anwar, it's nice to be appreciated."

"Do you see what you've started young man!" Anwar laughed. "But Amani my dear wife, we must talk business now that dinner is over and I don't want you to be alarmed with our conversation. Perhaps you can retire to the lounge and rest, you must be tired after preparing dinner. Azra will help you to clear the table after we are finished."

Amani knew that whatever it was, was serious and Israeli women know their place and she quickly rose from the table.

"Can I fetch you fresh tea, husband?"

"No, we're good and I also thank you for the lovely dinner."

"Compliments from my husband!" Amani laughed. *"Imad… Fadi…* You'll have to come back again, I could easily get used to this." Amani departed to another round of laughter…

"Okay, the floors yours Fadi." Anwar took another sip of his tea, with Gregg pondering for a moment for a shoe in.

"Let's recap on where we are and the reason Imad and I are here." Gregg began. "Firstly, we now know the location of Hamas's Headquarters and more importantly the Scarab launch site."

"But you were…" Anwar begged the question.

"Blindfolded…?" Gregg smiled. "Yes, but as we explained to Azra and Isam, the CIA, like a 'James Bond' movie, provided us with state of the art spy software incorporated on our ordinary cell phones in the event we are kidnapped. The phone has a secret number when pressed, automatically stores in the memory the route and the destination even though the screen appears blank."

"Amazing… The Sayerat Matakal should take a leaf from your book."

"Yes, but here's the problem… Sure, we have the GPS coordinates but when we try to study the route taken, we haven't a clue where the hell we are and that's where your local knowledge comes in." Steve had already opened the phones.

"Let me see." Azra was studying Steve's phone while Gregg passed Amir his.

"Im surprised studying this." Amir commented. "Hamas headquarters is just behind Jamal Abdel Nasser Street in Omar Mukhtar in western Gaza City. They constantly move their headquarters so they are always one step ahead of us. I know the building it's in the back streets of a dilapidated built up lower class area. A double story that was previously an office block now dormant. This phone is amazing…GPS-31degress-16N…It's all here."

"And yours Azra."

"This *is* interesting, the route leads us to a location just behind the old historic Aybaki Mosque in the Al-Tuffah neighborhood about thirty minutes from here. And you say this is a tunnel air vent?"

"Yes." Gregg replied.

"And you never saw the missile?"

"No, but they had a rail system for bogies that came from deep in the tunnel which based on facing Mecca, being North East, the tunnel continued North."

"That adds up, as according to the GPS it runs directly under the Mosque and most likely to the border town at Eres."

"Boy." Gregg shook his head. "I gotta to hand it to Hamas, their smart. Don't you see it? A plot within a plot!"

"Im not with you!" Steve interrupted.

"Okay let me explain… Shin Bet knows there's going to be a terrorist attack by Hamas with a Scarab Intercontinental Missile having found the training manuals. But they don't know from where, when, and how the Scarab missile will arrive in the country. Now supposing Shin Bet or the 'Eye" in the sky using heat seeking technology pin pointed the launch site… Of course, the location we now know, and launch a missile strike on Friday at prayer time. This would be devastating, not only destroying one of the most scared and historical Mosques and with the Scarab's 220kg of high explosives this would be another 9/11 killing over two thousand Palestine's at prayer time. Can you imagine the fallout and the condemnation of Israel worldwide playing right into the Palestine cause?"

Gregg's explanation was suddenly reality bringing a deathly silence.

"Now, we know the Scarab can be remotely launched via computer and the missile's GPS system. We already concluded that to inflict maxim casualties on the Knesset the strike time would be 11:30am. But if we provide the coordinates to Shin Bet to take out Hamas the collateral damage would most likely amount to…? What do you estimate Anwar knowing the location?"

Sarraf shrugged then sort of turned to Azra for input.

"I think father, knowing that district and considering prayer day, it would be light as most people are at prayers… Maybe fitty or sixty, mostly women and Avigdor Lieberman, the defense minister, could justify destroying the armed wing of Hamas, which is a terrorist group."

It was time for Steve. "Of course, Netanyahu would never expose the presence of the Russian Scarab Missile and how it slipped through Border Security, let alone the international fall out for Russia. Over to you Hadi."

"Here's the bottom line, there's only one solution…*We* take out Hamas on the proviso if we fail the 'Eye in the sky' is given the GPS coordinates of Hamas's HQ and if Shin Bet doesn't receive the 'mission complete' call by 11am, they take out Hamas by drone."

"You mean?"

"Yes Azra, if your father joins us that makes five."

"I think I'll have another cup of tea." Anwar's comment almost brought the house down.

"Azra, father…? Then that settles it we're in."

"Then let's plan the taking of Hamas……"

THE STING

"Azra, do you have a piece of paper and a pen handy?"

"Yes, I'll go fetch it."

"Fadi, I recommend we retire to my study, dining tables are not the most contusive to discuss 'sting' tactics as you Americans put it."

Sarraf's study was quite spacious the ideal size to manage his undercover activities and the taxi business front.

"Grab these chairs." Sarraf took the helm at his desk.

Within seconds Azra was back with a stack of A4's and a black marker pen.

"Okay…." Gregg began. "Amir, you say you know the location well having had many fares in that area?"

"Yes."

"Then I need you to draw a rough sketch of the streets and alleyways leading to the building. We need to know what we're up against in a surprise attack."

Amir began busily sketching. "It's pretty rough and it's to the best of my knowledge. I haven't been there for some time but I'm sure it hasn't changed."

"Hmmm." Steve was studying the sketch. "So, this is the entrance down this narrow close from the main street." Steve was pointing with his finger whilst screwing up his face, not too happy at what he saw. *"And you're sure the ground floor is unoccupied?"*

"Yes."

"There's obviously no elevator, so that means we have to use the stairway… Not good Hadi! The high ground always has the advantage."

"We've been in worse situations before, but Imad's right. Now the second problem, and this is only my assumption… The security council will be present for the 'moon launch'. Which means at least ten so called 'soldiers' which I assume are armed… Now guards… How many…? At least thrcc and that will be our first 'take out' before we storm the stairs. The one thing in our favor is that I know the password… *'Jundin Majhul'*. which we heard while being escorted blindfolded."

"How appropriate." Anwar grinned repeating the password. *"Unknown Soldier…* They've never gotten over the 'six-day war'."

"The timing?" Gregg picked up the chase. "Should we meet maximum resistance… Suggestions…?" He turned to the group.

Anwar threw his hat in… "If our deadline is eleven… Nine thirty, for operation 'Knesset'."

Gregg looked around the group for a reaction… *"Good,* then that's it settled… Nine thirty we storm Hamas."

"Now the reality check…We are outnumbered three to one, the odds are heavily against us but then we have the element of surprise in our favor… *Now ordinance…?"*

Anwar smiled. "Let's go through to the lounge, I'm sure you'll recognize this room."

"I can remember that rug and what's below." Steve grinned.

"Then perhaps Imad you can help Isam to roll it back and open the heavy wooden trap doors."

"My pleasure, sir." Steve was back in the picture.

"We've just had a new shipment and it couldn't have come at a better time."

"Wow!" Gregg was amazed there was enough ordinance here to start another 'six-day war'!

"I suggest the weapon of choice is our own manufactured 22 caliber Uzi sub machine gun used by the IDF. It's an excellent weapon for close quarter combat. Let me just walk through it. Amir pass me one… This is an open blow back operated sub machine gun with a fold in shoulder support. It has a rate of fire of 600 rounds per minute and weighs only 3.5 kg and is accurate up to 200meters. It has a magazine of 40 rounds and is fitted with a suppressor, better known as a silencer. Once you open the safety catch you must press this small leaver behind the magazine which is a second safety mechanism before the weapon will fire. It's simple and deadly. Now here we have the M26 fragmentation grenade made in the United States and deployed by the IDS. Im sure you are both familiar with this weapon having served in the US Military. And last, but not least, the M84 stun grenade made by the Picatinny Arsenal USA. I also have silencers for the Glocks which you'll be supplied with tomorrow… Any questions?"

"Any questions!" Steve burst into laughter… You gotta be kidding me."

Even Azra was laughing at Steve's remark.

"Joking aside, tomorrow Isam will pick you up at eight sharp to return here for a final briefing and ordinance supply. Dress as usual in your Kaffia and Ghutra to avoid attention but with whatever you feel comfortable below, jeans 'T" shirts sneakers etc. My son will drive you back to your hotel… *Tomorrow then…"* Anwar turned to his daughter. "Azra, now it's time to help your mother clear the table……"

* * *

"Are you good to go." Steve called knocking on the adjoining room door.

"In a few minutes, it's not locked." Gregg was busy checking the magazine of his Glock before squeezing the clip into the pistol grip then loading one round into the chamber.

"Getting prepared, huh?"

"That's what it's all about, I'm sure *you* remember."

"Yeah, it brings back memories. How did you sleep last night?"

"As well as could be expected." Gregg tucked the Glock below the belt in his jeans then slipped the Kaffia over his head.

"Have you got the time?"

Steve looked at his watch. "I make it 7:45."

"Hmmm…" Gregg synchronized his watch. "Gimme a sec to put on this head gear then we can go. *Okay…* Well, partner this is it. *Gimme a high five."*

Within minutes they were standing in the elevator. For a change Steve was quiet, their eyes staring into the unknown and the reality biting home at the possibility of leaving this troubled world forever.

The elevator chimed with Gregg giving a big sigh. "Sometimes I wonder Steve, how the hell we ever got ourselves into this."

"How many times have we said that…! There's Isam at the entrance, best not hang around."

"Morning Isam, have you been waiting long?" Steve asked.

"No, just arrived. We'll arrive at fathers in fifteen to twenty minutes. You came armed?"

"Yes." Gregg replied.

"Then let's be on our way."

Gregg glanced at his watch again… 8:10. Nine thirty would be here before they knew it and this twenty-minute journey will seem like an eternity……

* * *

"Good morning gentlemen." Anwar appeared relaxed sipping his morning tea. "Would you like a refreshment before we get prepared, it's good to calm the nerves."

"I think they would rather have a Scotch, father." Azra appeared from the kitchen dressed in Jeanes 'T' and sneakers, her hair swept back in a ponytail.

"I'm afraid I can't oblige gentleman, besides tea is better for you."

"I'm sure, but I think I'll take a rain check." Gregg smiled.

"You look so different Azra." Steve changed the subject.

"Is that good or bad, Imad?" She just smiled.

"I'll take the fifth." Steve jokingly replied his comment inviting some laughter but the tension was obvious.

Anwar finished the last of his tea then rose from the table walking toward the lounge.

"Let's get the weaponry and ammunition distributed......"

* * *

"Isam I need your help son. I'll pass the weapons to you… Uzi's five… Silencers and four clips each…That's 160 rounds… Make sure you use them sparingly… Remember, in automatic fire it's 600 round a minute and four magazines won't go far… Two magazines each for the Glocks and silencers… Grenades we're short with only two, so it's one each to Imad and Fadi… Stun grenades only one… Again, to Fadi… Ammunition belts… One each with pistol holster… And lastly, flack vests."

"I think we are back in the Marines again Fadi on Special operations. I gotta hand it to you Anwar"

Anwar grinned like a cunning old dog he could easily replace Jack Nicholson in a sequel to 'A Few Good Men'.

"Get kitted out we lave at nine for operation 'Knesset'." Anwar was back in command.

Unknowingly in the background out of sight was Azra's mother taking it all in. She knew when she was asked to leave the room last night that it was something more than serious.

"*Anwar.*" Her teared voice rang out as she rushed toward her husband throwing both arms around his neck. "Please, I beg of you, *don't go.*"

"Amani, my precious wife, I wish it was as easy as that. But this is matter of National Security which could wreak devastation to our Jewish Nation with the loss of life in the thousands."

"Anwar." She sobbed. "You have been a good husband to me and the children and now after all these years I feel I will lose you forever."

"Please excuse me." Anwar gently took his wife's hand and lead her into the dining room. Azra and Isam were visibly upset with Steve and Gregg looking for place to hide. It was a heart-breaking scene.

Anwar placed both hands on his wife's cheeks and gave her a gentle kiss on the lips. "Darling please stop crying." He wiped her eyes with his handkerchief. "You must be brave in front our children. "You have my word I will return safe and sound."

"Anwar, if something should happen to…"

He placed fingers over her lips. "Please darling, don't make it any more difficult than it is. Remember I love you and that's all that matters."

"I'll be waiting." She wiped her eyes with the back of her hand and gave her husband a departing kiss. "I love you…"

"Ah hmmm." Anwar returned his face flushed. "Are we ready to go? Good…Oh I forgot something…I have here our traditional skull cap the Kippah which I will ask each of you to wear, HaShem will protect us."

"And you forgot something else…*The number to call off the strike!*"

"888……"

* * *

"Cover your face with your red and white Ghutra leaving only your wyes exposed and stay undercover until Isam brings the car around."

Anwar may be old but no bones about it, he was in command.

A large black Mercedes five-liter V8 S Class appeared from nowhere coming to sliding halt in the courtyard in front of the 'valiant five', its windows heavily tinted.

Taken aback Steve was with the wisecracks as normal. "Looks like funeral car."

Anwar turned a grin on his face. "It is."

"Your shittin me! I'll be darned. Is this a good or bad omen?"

"At least it's not a Hearse… No wouldn't that be something." Gregg chimed.

"Leave the humor to me partner, but good try."

"Gentlemen it's not the time. I'll take the front seat with Iman there's plenty of room in the back for three."

"Anwar if you don't mind it might be better for your daughter to sit in the front as we are heavily armed."

"*Maaan…* Your something else." Steve muttered under his breath.

"Yes Hadi, on second thoughts that makes sense. But let's not waste any more time."

The big lumbering Merc fully loaded they were finally on their way for operation Knesset, as 'sting' that would change their lives forever……

* * *

"This reminds of sitting in a Bradly in Afghanistan.'"

"I wish it were a Bradly, that baby could take a hit from anything… Listen." Gregg changed the subject. This may not be the time but then there never is… Imad Halabi and Fadi Bishara are our aliases, our under-cover names. We are just plain Steve Nelson and Gregg Jonson. Of course, we are Jewish but we changed our names when we joined the military as there is still the race card against the Jews in the United States."

Azra interrupted. "I had a feeling when we addressed you that sometimes you were confused." She laughed.

"A woman's intuition, huh?" But before Steve could continue Anwar bruised in

"Locked and loaded, check your weapons, another five minutes."

"We're here Isam, slow down… Pull in just in front of that narrow entrance to the building, I can just make out the guard having a cigarette… Eh…Gregg… You approach him with the password, I'll take it from there." Anwar dropped the window on the passenger side the hammer on his Glock cocked.

The Uzi slung across his chest Gregg walked cautiously toward Farid hopefully confusing him."

"*Stop!*" Farid yelled, raising his Kalashnikov, the shadowed alleyway making it difficult for him to clearly see the masked man.

"*Jundin Majhul.*" Gregg didn't wait for the request.

Farid was taken aback but he wasn't going to take any chances, loading his weapon ready to take the shot…*To late*…Anwar's Glock kicked twice, splat… splat… The heavy caliber 45's drilling two neat holes in the guard's forehead, blood spatter bone and brain drenching the wall behind him like a house painter spilling his pot. Farid froze for a moment then in slow motion toppled to the ground like sack of potatoes in the process dropping his Kalashnikov with a loud clatter.

"Out… *Everyone out.*" Anwar screamed. "And keep your heads down."

"Fraod… Are you alright what was that noise?" The other guard came running down the passageway. *"What the…"* He froze then raised his Russian sub machine gun upon seeing Gregg and squeezed off a spray of automatic fire in a mad panic, bullets ricocheting off the walls and ceiling.

"Chit…Chit… Chit… Greggs Uzi cut him down like a corn stack, his finger locked on the trigger emptying the Kalashnikovs 40 round magazine, bullets sparking everywhere.

* * *

"Today is a day that will strike at the heart of Israel as at 11:30 am a Scarab intercontin …. *What was that?* It sounded like gun shots!"

The third guard had witnessed the demise of his comrades and was fleeing up the stairs two at a time.

"We gotta get that third guard before he raises the alarm. Steve take him." Gregg yelled reloading his Uzi.

But the guard was ready, crouching just in front of the door emptying his magazine, the sheer stream of lead making Steve retreat for cover.

"Shit, I've taken one in the shoulder… Gregg, hit him again before he reloads."

"Steve…Are you?"

"I'm okay man, *just do it…!"*

Gregg poured more lead in the direction of the stair well, but this bad guy wasn't going to go away easily.......

* * *

"Quick, turn the board table on its side facing the door and grab your weapons and ammunition."

Anbar opened the large wall cabinet exposing an arsenal of Kalashnikovs and a stack of magazines. Within seconds the rack was empty, each member of the council taking his position behind the heavy wooden table for a standoff. Anbar grabbed the computer from his father's desk and opening the adjoining door to the next room to store it out of sight locking the door on his return.

*"Pay attention everyone…*We must protect this laptop to the death, the timer has been set for remote firing at 11:30 and cannot be changed."

There was a loud, bang … bang… banging on the door as the guard fearing for his life was slamming the butt of his Kalashnikov against the wooden panels. He wanted sanctuary and in a hurry……

* * *

"What's this?" Gregg stared at his blood-soaked hand. *"A shoulder wound my ass!* You're out of it buddy, lye on your side to let the blood drain from your punctured lung or you'll drown in your own blood."

Azra, upon seeing Steve badly wounded, rushed to his side removing her jacket and placing it below his head.

"Don't worry, we'll get you out of here in no time." That was the last word she spoke as a second burst of fire cut her down.

Steve cringing in pain crawled over by her side grabbing her hand, blood seeping through her 'flak jacket' from a gaping chest wound.

"Gimme your hand honey, you're gonna be alright."

But Azra's hand suddenly went limp as her precious life drained from her body, her father now by her side tears streaming down his cheeks realizing the inevitable and he gently closed her eyes forever.

"It's too late Steve." His eyes said it all.

"Shit…Azra…!" Gregg shook his head in disbelief… *"First blood is never good!* We must take out that office and there's only one way left."

Gregg removed the M22 fragmentation grenade from his belt and pulled the pin.

"Here's looking at you kid." Gregg tossed the grenade landing it at the top of the stairwell the guard trying desperately to grab it.

"Fire in the hole."

The blast shook the building blowing the door from its hinges, the lung choking dust forming a haze with Gregg and Isam coughing their lungs out… As for the guard…? Lying in a blood-soaked heap, his body riddled with shrapnel.

"We take then now." Gregg gave the command leading the charge as the dust cleared. The five meters of stairway was a formable task carrying their weapons and ammunition and just as they reached the top they were met with a deadly hail of lead, bullets sparking everywhere

"Fuck it... Pull back...Pull back." Gregg yelled. "They've barricaded themselves behind a large table. This is worse than the fucking Alamo!"

Not knowing what damage, they had done with their blind fire Anbar gave the command to cease momentarily.

"Staffa, check it out."

Gregg, Isam and his father were now halfway down the stars, their backs pressed against the wall for cover and Staffa didn't hesitate. Taking no chances, he opened with his Kalashnikov spraying his 30 round magazine in all directions.

Gregg's Uzi now out of ammo he needed a kill shot with his Glock to take out this fucking trigger-happy maniac before her reloaded.

Splat... Splat... The 45's found their mark, one tearing a groove in Staffa's neck severing his jugular, blood spurting like a fountain with each beat of his heart, the second shattering his cheek bone and teeth as it met maximum resistance. In a few more minutes Staffa would meet the '72 celestial virgins'.

"Anwar..." Steve called. "Let's move before he's replaced with another crazy... *Anwar...*" Steve called again turning to find Isam cradling his father in his arms his Kafai like a crimson flag.

"He's gone Gregg...He's gone..."

"My God...!

There was one more option and Gregg unclipped the remaining grenade from his belt.

"Isam, you've gotta leave him. Pass me your father's Uzi." Gregg showed him the grenade. "When this baby explodes we rush the room no matter what."

The time? Gregg glanced at his watch it was 10:45, it was now or nothing and he pulled the safety pin still holding the release lever that activates the firing hammer before cautiously climbing another few steps. He had to make sure his aim was accurate.

"Are you ready... *I said are you ready Isam?"*

"Yes."

Gregg tossed the grenade through the open door the lever separating from the canister like a space shuttle releasing its booster rockets. The thud as it rolled into the room, the slow burning fuse about to ignite, was music to Greggs ears.

"Grenade...Grenade..." Anbar screamed diving for cover behind the heavy Kermes Oak table.

The blast of air from the explosion almost knocked Gregg on top of Isam who was following closely behind, the air clearing they could hear the groans and screams from inside the office.

"Come on Isam, let's use these baby's." Gregg checked his magazine before jumping over the bodies of the guard and Staffa, the unsung hero. The scene inside was absolute carnage with torsos and limbs scattered everywhere like a prosthetic limb replacement factory.

Anbar although wounded had rushed in front of the door to the adjoining room guarding it with his life, his Kalashnikov unsteady in his left hand pointing it straight at Gregg, his right arm severed above his elbow, veins and sinews dangling like demolition wiring on a construction site.

"I should never had trusted you Americans." He screamed. "The only way you'll get to that computer is over my dead body."

"Then I'll have to oblige." But before Gregg could squeeze the trigger a burst from Iman's Uzi ripped through Anbar's chest dropping him like a stone.

"That's for my father and my sister."

Gregg didn't waste any more time and sprayed the lock with automatic fire before kicking the door open.

"That must be it!" The military style laptop was sitting on its lonesome on the desk and Gregg didn't hesitate, blowing it into a million fragments with 22's from the Uzi.

"Now where's that fucking phone!" He fumbled nervously through his pockets. The horrendous explosion was the last he heard.

It had turned eleven and the Israeli Drone discharged two rockets destroying the Hamas headquarters and surrounding buildings for a radius of fifty meters… The taking of Hamas was over and operation Knesset would go down in history as the terrorist attack that never was……

* * *

Julie had risen early, it was their rest day but it was such a lovely morning and the sea breeze was so refreshing as she sat on the balcony.

"I thought I heard you up, why so early?"

"I don't know, I just couldn't find sleep."

"Coffee?"

"Yeah, that would be nice."

Marge ran her fingers through her unruly hair. "I gotta do something with this hair of mine. I'll put the perc on go and go fetch the paper."

Tomorrow would an early rise again for the LA to London flight the same old thing.

"Coffee and the paper." Marge place the cup on the glass table top. I'll go fetch mine and come and join you."

The noise of broken glass made marge jump.

"What the… Julie, are you okay?" Marge rushed to the balcony.

Julie was supporting her fore head with her left hand.

"I don't believe it."

"Calm down … Calm down honey."

Julie passed Marge the paper.

HAMAS TERRORIST ATTACK FOILED.

Israeli drones using heat seeking missiles destroyed the headquarters of Hamas in Gaza killing Abdul Fattah the number one commander of the armed wing and ten of the most wanted in a joint exercise involving Shin Bet and Israel's anti-terrorist organization the Sayerat Matakal. For reasons of national security, it has yet to be confirmed that an attack was immanent to destroy the Knesset, Israel's parliament building. The collateral damage to the surrounding property was minimal although five agents from the Sayerat Matakal lost their lives. Unconfirmed sources report that America's CIA was involved in the preliminary ground attack. The Prime Minister will address parliament today to…

"No, it can't be Julie… *It just can't!*" Marge was almost in tears.

Julie was shaking her head… *First Bill and Chuck and now Steve and Gregg!"*

"Julie, let's not jump to conclusions."

"I know what I'm gonna do." Julie opened her cell. "Let me see… The phone number of the CIA headhunters, Washington DC… Ah, here it is… 202…" Julie entered the numbers.

"I wonder if yu can help me… I urgently need to contact two of your agents it's a family matter… A Steve Nelson and a Gregg Jonson…"

"I'm sorry we can't give any information regarding our agents."

"Please… Please."

The receptionist could hear Julie sobbing and it touched a heart string.

"Give me a minute and I'll see what can do… Can you repeat these names again?"

The minute seemed like an eternity.

"Are you still there?"

"Yes." Julie answered praying for the good news.

"I'm sorry, I checked with personnel and we have no agents that bear these names… I am really sorry." The phone went dead……

* * *

"Good morning Hanna, can I trouble you for a cuppa?" Thomson had just entered the office. *"Hanna*, why the tears?"

She turned The Washington Post to face him showing the headlines.

Thomson stared at the bold print for a few seconds… "I had better make a call……"

THE END

Julie Rodgers is still flying the friendly skies…

Marge is happily married to a pilot Captain and has one daughter. Julie and Marge are still best friends and keep in touch whenever the occasion arises.

At a secret Ceremony attended by Obama and Benjamin Netanyahu, the parents of Steve Nelson and Gregg Jonson were presented with the highest award for valor given by the CIA, The Distinguished Intelligence Cross and Israel's Itur HaGvura for bravery above and beyond the call of duty.

The cargo of Global 10 was never found and the mystery of the missing crew was never solved.

Shimaru Shima is still an undiscovered island and the drug trade continues to this very day.

Okio Numero the 'Godfather' of the Yakuza is currently serving a ten-year prison sentence in a Tokyo prison for money laundering and tax evasion.

www.ingramcontent.com/pod-product-compliance
Lightning Source LLC
Chambersburg PA
CBHW071419190726
48292CB00001B/39